The Laughter of Carthage

M

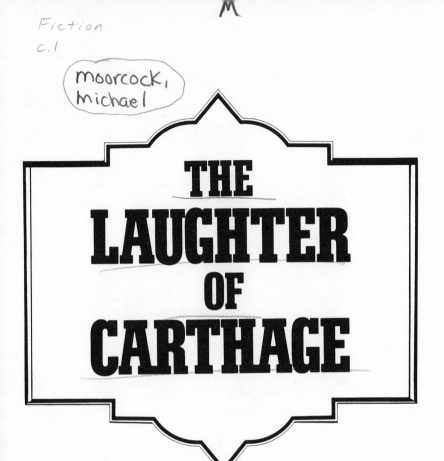

THE LAUGHTER OF CARTHAGE

Michael Moorcock

Random House   New York

First American Edition

Copyright © 1984 by Michael Moorcock

All rights reserved under International and Pan-American
Copyright Conventions. Published in the United States by
Random House, Inc., New York. Originally published in
Great Britain by Martin Secker & Warburg Limited,
London.

Library of Congress Cataloging in Publication Data
Moorcock, Michael, 1939-
The laughter of Carthage.
Sequel to: Byzantium endures.
I. Title.
PR6063.059L3 1984   823'.914   83-43179
ISBN 0-394-52997-9

98765432

Introduction

IN THE FOUR and a half years since I finished editing the first volume of Colonel Pyat's memoirs (*Byzantium Endures*) my own circumstances changed considerably. I became obsessed with discovering verification for some of Pyat's claims after I received several letters from people who had known him before the War and whose memories of him were radically different. As a result my travels took me in his tracks and at one time it seemed I had condemned myself to continue his wanderings where he had left off in 1940. A retired Turkish *bimbashi*, one of Kemal's revolutionary nationalists in 1920, assured me Pyat was an American renegade, a Zionist working for the British. Two vigorous octogenarians in Rome insisted he was a Polish Communist who planned to infiltrate the early fascist movement. In Paris it was generally agreed he was Russian, possibly a Jew, associated more with the criminal world than with the political underground. Not everyone knew him as Pyat (Piat or Pyate are variations). To several Berliners I met he was either Peterson or Pallenberg, but they readily confirmed that he was a scientist, an engineer. One German lady, presently living in Oxford, a Buchenwald survivor, was amused by my asking if she thought Pyat as successful as he claimed. She knew of at least one brilliantly successful invention, she said. Then she laughed and refused to continue. She had periods of mental instability.

In Kiev there are virtually no written records (since 1941 when the Nazis came) and even Babi Yar has no memorial (save the works of Yevtushenko and Antonov). It is part of a new autoroute. With its usual tact, the Ukrainian Soviet preferred not to recall an event which did not reflect well on Ukrainians in general (the Nazis were nowhere else offered the services of so many enthusiastic volunteers). America provided far more documentation, but this turned out to be as confusing as it was helpful. Some of the newspaper reports conflicted with Pyat's stories, yet there is every reason to believe he was in a position to experience directly what the papers could only surmise. (Mrs Mawgan, for instance, is scarcely mentioned in the New York World anti-Klan campaign of 1921–23, but Mrs Tyler, whom Pyat dismisses in a line or two, is presented by the paper as one of the chief villains.) Similarly, the greasy, creased news-cuttings in Pyat's own notebooks don't necessarily confirm his statements written on nearby pages and unfortunately the dates and origins are frequently obscured or missing. One headline (possibly from the New Orleans Times-Picayune, late 1921) reads BURNS TO INVESTIGATE KLAN (about the Department of Justice's Bureau of Investigation – pre-FBI – intending to take a thorough look at Klan affairs); the report verifies all Pyat says, except that the investigation began earlier than he claims. His accusations of bias and corruption are also frequently off-key. A case in point is that of The Memphis Commercial Appeal, which Pyat characterises as being 'in the pocket' of local politicians. In fact the Commercial Appeal won a Pulitzer Prize for its courageously relentless anti-Klan reporting and represents the considerable integrity of large numbers of Southerners who were outraged by and actively resisted Klan campaigns in, for instance, Mississippi, Tennessee, Alabama, even Georgia. (The Klan was far more successful in many Western States, including Texas and California, than ever it was in the Deep South).

Arkansas's Carthage Democrat Gazette certainly mentions Major Sinclair's airship in a piece headed LOCAL CITIZENS AID FLYERS (Feb. 27, 1922) whereas I could find no record in The Kansas City Star of Pyat's, by his own account, enormous reception there in 1923. Cuttings from The Toledo Blade, The Cleveland Plain Dealer, The Springfield Republican and The St Louis Globe Democrat all mention him as Peterson. The Indianapolis Times, The Dallas News and The New Orleans Times-Picayune are at best dismissive but frequently attack his 'vile distortions' of fact, his racial and religious bigotry. Sometimes Pyat seems to have failed to understand he was being condemned and proudly pasted the cutting into a position of prominence. The de Grion scandal of 1921 is mentioned in a Le Temps feature of the time and here M. Pyatnitski is described as a naturalised French subject. A piece headlined LOVE BLOSSOMS AS RED TERROR RAGES turns out to be a theatre review from a

ii

Northern Californian newspaper in the Grass Valley region: *Among the players in this moving musical drama were Mr Matthew Pallenberg, Miss Honoria Cornelius, Miss Ethel de Courcy and Miss Gloria Douglas.*

My travels were not entirely wasted. They were of use when at last I settled down in a remote part of the Yorkshire Dales to try to make sense of the collection of manuscript I described in the first volume. I used my tapes of Pyat's talks, a little of the other interview material from people I had met, but in the main again had to rely on the written work, discursive and repetitious as ever. While much of the earlier volume was written in Russian, a large proportion of this one was (except for sexual references, as always, in French) done in a peculiar semi-private language, predominantly English, Yiddish and German, with some Polish and Czech and a smattering of Turkish (as well as his 'own' largely untranslatable words) which characterises much of the material he himself identified as having been written between 1941 and 1947. There is nothing in Yiddish script. Again, without the help of M. G. Lobkowitz I could not have continued: Pyat, my friend believes, probably spoke all languages a little inexpertly, including Russian. Certainly his Yiddish, frequently mixed unconsciously with German and English, is a case in point. He claimed to have learned it when working for Jews in the Podol ghetto of Kiev.

Again I have retained a flavour of the original – spellings, grammar, polyglot ramblings and odd forms – together with a fraction (some might think too much) of his deranged outbursts. Where his opinions and interpretations changed radically, sometimes from page to page, as one bizarre rationalisation was replaced by another, I have let them stand, since they are the essential reflection of his personality. I have done my best not to make a specific choice or interpretation in the belief that another reader might easily understand something which I have failed to see.

It has not been easy to bring order to the work. Because of my own distaste for the majority of Pyat's opinions, and the time involved, friends have frequently suggested I turn my 'bequest' over to an academic institution which could remain perhaps more objective. However Quixotic it seems, I insist that I made a promise to Maxim Arturovitch Pyatnitski to see his reminiscences into print. I feel I must keep that promise, in spite of the difficulties.

Special thanks to all those who gave their help in the preparation of this volume: to Linda Steele, John Blackwell, Giles Gordon, Rob Cowley, Robert Lanier, Helen Mullens, Javus Selim, 'Petros', Jean-Luc Fromental, Lily Stains, Dave Dixon, Paul Gamble, Mike Butterworth, Geoffrey Dymond, Mr and Mrs Chaykin, Mr and Mrs Jacobs, 'Ma' Ellison, Christian von Baudissin, Francois Landon, Freda Krön, Natalie Zimmermann, Lorris Murrail, Larry Snider (of California State University, Long Beach, Library), Sister Maria Santucci, Martin Stone, John Clute, Isla Venables, Professor S. M. Rose, and those others who have expressed their desire to remain anonymous.

Michael Moorcock
London S.W.
October 1983

One

I AM ONE of the great inventors of my age. Rejected by its birthplace, my genius would otherwise be universally acknowledged; even by Turks. The *Rio Cruz*, loaded with snow and refugees, steamed from Odessa, heading for Sebastapol and the Caucasus. I was toasted by the British as a Russian Prometheus. How could I have guessed the irony? I was sublimely ignorant of my personal future. In those last days of 1919, having escaped an humiliating death, I became freshly inspired with my mission: I would bring scientific enlightenment to the world at large. (Now, chained, I still await my Hercules. *Es war nicht meine Schuld.*)

Within a day of my boarding, Mr Thompson, Chief Engineer of the *Rio Cruz* and by nature of his calling a cosmopolitan, a reader of learned journals, was my unqualified admirer. 'You must get to England as soon as you can,' he begged. 'So many have been killed. They need trained people more than ever.' Several other officers were equally encouraging. They were good-hearted fellows, spontaneous and sincere. The best type of Englishman; now extinct.

Until such time, as we were fond of saying, Russia came to her senses, England was the obvious country in which to further my career. Mr Green, my Uncle Semyon's business partner, had returned to London at the outbreak of the Revolution. He would have money for me. Moreover, the support I discovered abroad the *Rio Cruz* suggested I should rapidly secure an important government position once ashore in 'Blighty'.

By dint of these prospects, together with a little cocaine and wine, I was at least partially able to forget my earlier disappointments. Russia

1

was harder to put behind me than I had anticipated and it would be three weeks before we actually reached Constantinople. Immediately we were out of sight of land, high winds and seas attacked us. A good sailor, I nonetheless felt a moderate amount of nausea and periodically was infected with a terrible, debilitating gloom. At these times I would be forced to rush from whatever company I was in to return to my bunk where for half-an-hour or so my whole body would shake, as if in time to the vibrations of the ship. These bouts were quite as much a physical as a psychological reaction to events of the previous two years, but whenever they seized me I would be overwhelmed by an agonizing longing for a more innocent past, for my golden Odessa summer of 1914 when the whole world had appeared to open herself for me. In my quasi-delirium it seemed the noble city of Odysseus was lost forever to the Tartar, the Musselman, the Jew. In conquering Odessa they had captured something of my being and still held it. Trotski and Lenin leered gigantically and grinned: with bloody fingers they brandished that small, pulsing fragment of my soul. The elements wailed around the ship in massive chorus as I wept for Esmé, my little angel, whose blonde Slavic beauty represented everything true and honest in Russia. Dishonoured by anarchists, by Mongol riff-raff, my lost sweetheart could never be redeemed. She had mocked me for my horror at her stories of rape and abasement. Esmé, my greatest support after my mother, had been my muse, my hope. If she still lived she was nothing but a Bolshevik's whore. Esmé, as my body shuddered on its narrow bunk, I yearned to flee backwards in Time to rescue you. How different both our lives would have been if we had escaped together. I should have been loyal to you. *Kàbus göruyorum.* I am still, even in this decrepit body, loyal to you. For all that you betrayed me I bear you no ill will.

Before heading for Constantinople the *Rio Cruz* would call at several Black Sea ports, taking on passengers, disembarking troops and munitions. John Monier-Williams, her captain, was a grey, stocky Welshman with one side of his face badly scarred by an old fire. Though always polite to us, he plainly had some distaste for this commission, the last before he retired. Until now his experience had been with the Indonesian, Indian and Chinese colonies and to him our Civil War was an obscure local conflict unworthy of British involvement. A cargo-carrier converted to a troop-transport, the ship was not really suitable for passengers. Her cabins were mainly communal dormitories segregating men from women and children. Though Mrs Cornelius and myself had a private cabin, the necessary pretence of being husband and wife created unexpected discomforts for me, particularly at night, since she remained true to her Frenchman while I burned with lust in the bunk above. Mrs Cornelius was a wonderfully voluptuous woman. At that age (her early twenties) she was in her prime. It was impossible for me to put her soft pink flesh and erotic smell out of my thoughts. From time to time in her sleep she would interrupt her own delicious snores by murmuring and smacking those full, sensual lips, amplifying my desire and causing me to nurse both my homesickness and my poor, swollen penis for hours on end as the ship waded through dark, heavy seas, creaking, sighing and occasionally giving off mysterious coughing sounds, like an overburdened camel.

The other passengers were predominantly Ukrainians of the merchant class; *nouveaux riches* for whom I had little patience. When they were not merely dull the women were self-conscious snobs, the men complacent bores and their children and servants odious. Most pretended to noble birth; all constantly bemoaned the loss of 'everything' and all seemed to have carried at least two fur coats and three diamond necklaces aboard. They were war-profiteers fleeing the vengeance of the Bolsheviks, and a large percentage were Jews. I had vetted many such during my days in the Intelligence Corps and could smell them out. One or two must certainly have recognised me and initiated the malicious rumours which soon circulated: I was a Red spy, a German official or even, ironically, a Jew. I became aware of passengers who were either embarrassed in my presence or else obsequiously pleasant. My response was to avoid them. Happily, Mrs Cornelius and I did not have to mix with them much. We were invited from the start to eat at the small table set aside for Mr Thompson and most of the other ship's officers who, because of the crowded conditions, were no longer in possession of their own messroom. Starved of English, Mrs Cornelius gladly accepted. They in turn enjoyed her humour. Their company was far more intelligent and agreeable to me than that of my own countrymen so I too was pleased with the arrangement.

We steamed on through white ectoplasmic haze, through blizzards and troubled water and, because we had not yet left Russia behind us, I was still subject to painful extremes of mood. Sebastopol, Yalta and other ports lay ahead. I was of course free to disembark at any of them and I was troubled by this. It would have been healthier if my attachment had been severed at a stroke. However, I did not much look forward to

3

reaching Constantinople, which I understood was crammed with Russians unable to get exit visas to more hospitable countries. I consoled myself. After a few days at most in the Ottoman capital I would be on my way to London. Meanwhile I did all I could to drive the memories of Kiev and Odessa from my mind, to forget Esmé and my first flight over the Babi Gorge, the cheers of fellow-students at my matriculation speech, the delightful months spent with Kolya in St Petersburg's bohemian nightclubs. I made an effort to concentrate on the Future, on my practical visions for building a techniological Utopia. My thirst for knowledge and creative impulses were to some degree satisfied in the company of Mr Thompson, who helped me gain an intimate knowledge of the ship.

The *Rio Cruz's* old-fashioned reciprocating engines aroused in Mr Thompson, more used to modern turbines, a certain admiration as well as suspicion. He found it marvellous they worked at all. They had been operated for years by dagoes, he said. Dagoes were notorious for hammering a ship to death. Normal maintenance procedures were anathema to them. 'They treat their machinery the same as their horses, flogging them on until they die in their traces.' Moving through the dark, pounding innards of the ship, his red face and hair glowing and his sharp nose quivering with puritanical dismay, he would point out his repairs and improvements, gesture accusingly at stains and dents on the brasswork, at rust and patches on pistons and pipes. The engine-room was miasmic with hot oil. Coal-smoke drifted from the stokehold. In the writhing half-light I imagined rivets bouncing in loose plates and rods shaking free of their rotating arms. Mr Thompson had insisted, he said, on the whole area being washed from top to bottom, every cog cleaned and lubricated, before he had allowed this prize of war to put to sea again, yet one never left without a patina of grime. Mr Thompson thought it would always be a problem on any ship, no matter how sophisticated her ventilation systems, so I described my ideas for a ship needing neither coal nor oil, her engines powered by two gigantic wind-vanes standing like funnels above the vessel's superstructure and thus requiring merely an auxiliary motor and a small tank of diesel fuel. He was sceptical until I sketched the device for him, whereupon he became excited. He insisted gravely on my patenting these plans the moment I reached London. I assured him that this was my intention. At dinner that night he begged me to describe again the invention to his brother officers. They, too, were impressed. Captain Monier-Williams, who had served on sailing vessels, said he would appreciate my engine's silence. He missed the tranquillity which used to fall over a great clipper-ship, even when she was racing at considerable speed.

Mrs Cornelius grinned. 'I never 'ad no bloody sense o' tranquillity from wind,' she said and burst into laughter shared by all except myself and the captain. Later she would explain the pun to me. Then, however, she had succeeded in her object and destroyed the over-serious tone of the conversation. After pudding, most passengers left the saloon; when Captain Monier-Williams with one or two others went to attend to their normal duties Mrs Cornelius performed some of her turns. Her career had begun in the Stepney music-halls and she had a large popular repertoire. The sailors were visibly cheered by what were evidently familiar favourites although the songs were mostly new to me. Eventually I learned them all and on more than one occasion would escape trouble, proving myself British with a rendering of *Lily of Laguna* or *At Trinity Church I Met Me Doom*.

In the course of that particular evening Mrs Cornelius grew rather tipsy. Eventually I had to help her back to our cabin. She was always a slave to a weak stomach and the laughter, the singing, the movement of the sea caused her to lose control before we got to our door. I helped her to the side. After a while she murmured she was much better and was ready to continue. I, too, could not have been entirely sober, for once inside, in the dark, while she sang *The Boy I Love Is Up In The Gallery* I attempted to climb into her bunk. She broke off long enough to remind me sharply that we were both 'on our honour'. Ashamed of myself, I reluctantly ascended to my own berth.

When I woke the next morning there was pale light coming through the porthole. Mrs Cornelius, still in her pink and black silk dress, was sound asleep. Rather than disturb her (and somewhat unwilling to face her after coming so close to betraying her trust) I washed in our basin and went up on deck. This was to become my habit, partly because I was sleeping so badly below, partly because my lust intensified in the early hours of the morning and it was more than I could bear to lie above her while I desperately sought to maintain self-control. At dawn there were few people about. I could enjoy a solitary stroll and a smoke for an hour or two before breakfast. The only other passenger I encountered regularly was a thin, middle-aged woman never without very thick make-up, her face an arsenical green, her lips and hair bright scarlet. She would sit at a little deck-table playing Patience. The wind frequently disturbed her cards and sometimes blew them overboard, yet, apparently careless of this, she always continued with her game. I began to imagine her a creature from legend, an oracle, a captured Trojan seeress. There was certainly something of the gypsy about her black shawl decorated with large crimson roses, her vivid emerald dress and the red gloves to her elbows. Every morning, precisely at the same time, she took up her position. Concentrating on her cards, she never acknowledged my presence. Her husband, a crop-headed ex-soldier in a kind of civilian uniform of frockcoat and riding-trousers tucked into hunting-boots, would present himself to her the moment the first bell rang for breakfast; then she would gather up the cards, place them in a silver reticule, slip her long arm into his and go below. Although they never spoke they possessed a language of gesture and expression which suggested they were perpetually involved in the most intense intercourse.

During the first days of the voyage the ship's main deck was almost constantly flooded. Cold, grey water merged imperceptibly with the sky and sometimes it seemed we were consigned to Limbo; we might have sailed over the edge of the world, destined never to make landfall again. Sitting in the restaurant, which between meals substituted as our main saloon, I would watch the rise and fall of the waves outside. Mrs Cornelius usually joined me at about two or three when she had completed her toilet. We would order a drink and chat casually with the other passengers. They were not, as she said, much of a bunch; but she was tolerant where I found most of them impossible. Those who stood out somewhat from the merchants and their wives were two little neuraesthenic sisters, forever holding hands, whom I mistook at first for lesbian lovers. A portly grain-dealer from Alexandrovsk told Mrs Cornelius he had helped the Tsar escape to Roumania in early 1918. He was friendly with Monsieur Riminski, the ex-owner of Odessa's largest kinema, who liked to speak of his acquaintance with famous actors and plainly considered himself something of a film star. The signs of age on his handsome features were discreetly disguised with rouge and kohl. He planned, he informed us, to begin a new film studio in America and begged Mrs C. to become one of his first actresses. She giggled and said she would 'fink abart it'. Riminski introduced us to his closest companion on board, a most unlikely choice, the tall Moldavian Prince Stanislav, pink and delicate and spindle-legged, like a flamingo. The Prince's scatterbrained wife and their black-eyed twin sons smelled of eucalyptus and camphor and I avoided them, guessing them to be suffering from disease. Other

6

saloon regulars included a swarthy, thick-set Georgian coal-merchant with a dark, forked beard and nothing to wear, apparently, but the same suit of evening tails and wolfskin cloak, both of which grew steadily mustier by the day. A Mennonite farmer, his underfed, shivering wife and five daughters, all in grey, were the only people prepared to speak to a pale, pudgy young man in ill-fitting clothes of the sort a bumpkin buys for his first visit to the city (everyone suspected he was a Skoptsy, nicknaming him 'the eunuch' behind his back). Lastly a Major Volisharof, whose white Don Cossack uniform was similar to the one I had packed away in my trunk, told us he was accompanying his little son and daughter to Yalta where they would be joined by their aunt. In Yalta, too, he hoped to find his regiment. His wife had been killed by the Reds. Volisharof was full of his children, forever pointing out their virtues and their vices, their physical characteristics, frequently in their presence. 'Quick as a rat,' he said one evening, gesturing with his vodka glass to where his lad and daughter played in a corner of the saloon. 'Quick as a rat. But the girl's a mouse.' The chief feature of his nondescript military face was a moustache waxed in the German manner; clearly it rivalled his children for his attention. We talked about the Civil War. When he learned I had been fighting Reds around Kiev he remarked of campaigning difficulties in the Crimea. He was not leaving Russia, he declared, until either he or Trotski was dead. He had originally planned to disembark at Sebastopol but it had become impossible to know from day to day which side would control the city when we arrived. 'We can only hope,' he said.

Mrs Cornelius, as open-hearted as ever, gave a sympathetic ear to all. Sometimes, to relieve our routine, we sat on deck, huddling in our coats while other passengers attempted to take what they called exercise. 'Pore fings.' Mrs Cornelius was amused in a kindly way. 'Wat the bloody 'ell's gonna become of 'em?' Their exercise generally consisted of holding on to a rail with one hand, keeping clothing in place with the other, waiting for the ship to tilt in the direction they wished to go, then risking a few shaky, shuffling steps until the ship began her roll back, whereupon they lunged out and clung hard to the nearest fixture. 'They don't know 'oo they are any more, do they?'

Many of these refugees were permanently dazed, it seemed. Indeed I remained fairly disoriented myself. One never realises how closely one's personality is identified with one's past, or country, or even a certain street in a certain city, until one is forcibly cut off from them. For my part I grew increasingly attached to my black and silver Cossack pistols. They remained always in the deep pockets of my black bearskin coat. I would frequently reach in to grip their reassuring butts. They possessed no sentimental significance, having been the property, after all, of an uncouth bandit, and the episode in which I came by them remained a painful and humiliating memory, yet they nonetheless meant 'Russia' to me.

Bad weather delayed the ship for two days. Eventually snow gave way to sleet, the sky cleared a little, then the sea calmed enough to let us distinguish both an horizon and a coastline. Mr Thompson announced our approach to the Crimean peninsula, though we should not see Sebastopol until morning. We would lay off and await radio assurance that it was safe to continue in to harbour. Mrs Cornelius went aft to find Jack Bragg, one of the younger officers (who was almost comically enamoured of her). She returned with his binoculars. Through these we studied the cliffs. After about an hour I saw silhouetted mounted figures racing westward; I heard the firing of heavy guns, but found it impossible to identify the riders or which side cannonaded the other. When Mrs Cornelius grew alarmed, I told her we were well out of range of any artillery possessed by the Reds. The cavalry disappeared and with it the firing. The sea grew still, the weather milder. By nightfall we learned it would soon be safe to proceed.

After dinner Mrs Cornelius was persuaded to entertain us. Linking arms with Mr Thompson and Jack Bragg (his delicate girlish features characteristic of so many young Englishmen) she strode around the table singing *The Man Who Broke The Bank At Monte Carlo* until she fell down. Once more I helped her to her bunk before clambering into my own and lying awake full of melancholy and moral uncertainty. I had begun to wonder if I should go ashore with the Cossack major and fight the Reds. The idea was foolish and obviously my duty was to stay alive, to use my brains and skills in exile where I could most effectively bring about an end to the Bolsheviks. Nobody thought that decision cowardly. My own commander in Odessa had not for a moment criticised me. A White defeat, after all, was fairly inevitable. I would stay aboard. Yet the ghost of Esmé, of what Esmé had been and what she had represented, remained to haunt me. Her ghost questioned my reason, called me back to Russian soil. Why should I love my country, I told her, when the Tsar's self-indulgence, his stupid tolerance of the alien and the exotic, was almost as much to blame for my present plight

8

as the treachery of the Jews? Russia could have been great. All her resources could have been devoted to the establishment of a brilliant and exemplary new world. Instead my nation lay mortally wounded a mile or two from where I slept. She shuddered in her death-throes, torn by wolves and jackals squabbling over her remains. Raped, she could no longer scream; pillaged, she did not even bother to complain. I had written to them all and offered them a glorious alternative to this. That vision was a thin, bright outline behind the coiling black smoke and the unhealthy glare of the flames; a silver vision of clean, massive towers, of graceful airships, of peace and sanity, an absence of hunger and disease, an environment for wholesome, well-educated, upstanding people. A New St Petersburg might have risen, literally, above the old: a flying city of steel and glass. How easily they could have been made reality, those plans which had been abandoned with my trunks.

That night, as the *Rio Cruz* bounced at anchor in the choppy waters off Sebastopol harbour, seemingly a target for every mine lying across the mouth of the approach, I forced myself to abandon at least temporarily my dream of a wholly Slavic renaissance. With daylight, having had even less sleep than usual, I took a fortifying pinch of cocaine (making sure Mrs Cornelius should not wake and see me, for she disapproved) and went on deck. In a hazy glow, the green-skinned seeress was already spreading her cards. She did not look up as I passed. Everything was deathly still and silent, save for the slop of the water, the clack of pasteboard. Off the portside I saw low, snow-covered hills, a suggestion of buildings near the shore, all lying beneath a miserable grey sky. The ship still rocked a little, but her movements were no longer dramatic. Huddled in his donkey-jacket, hands in pockets and cap pulled tight over his ears, Jack Bragg joined me at the rail. 'That's Serich Point, I think.' He gestured. 'Thank God visibility's a bit better. I didn't fancy going through those mines completely blind. You couldn't see a ship's length in front of you earlier on.' Breath poured like exhaust from his mouth. 'Doesn't seem to be much activity. I suppose that's a good thing.'

A moment or two later, when the anchor began to lift, Bragg returned to his duties, but I remained forward. As we steamed towards Sebastopol I soon made out the entrance to the harbour where a sinister line of buoys indicated her mine defence. Beyond the buoys I could see a few low, modern buildings, apparently empty. There was not a single human figure visible anywhere; not a vehicle, not a whiff of smoke; not a sound. The greatest military harbour of the Black Sea seemed completely deserted.

Without a naval guard to warn us of potential danger or a pilot to guide us through the gate of the nets I felt the ship had little chance of getting in safely, but she continued to steam towards the buoys directly ahead. I gripped the rail, readying myself for the explosion which must certainly come, but somehow we passed into the harbour. A few minutes later we rounded the point to see the grey-hulled outline of a British man-o'-war at anchor: the only other ship in evidence. She did not acknowledge us and I began to believe she, too, had been abandoned. The same silence lay across the unpopulated hills and at the town below them. The sudden flap of a seagull's wing was startling and unwelcome. Nothing, save for a few birds, moved on water or land: a desolation of snow and ice, it was as if the Winter King had passed through, leaving no soul alive which might have witnessed his presence.

The *Rio Cruz* dropped anchor between the battleship and the huge main quay. By now a good many passengers were on deck, as affected as I by the silence. They spoke in low, puzzled voices. Jack Bragg passed me, grinning. 'Rather better reception than the last time the British came to the Crimea!'

The buildings of the main town rose as high as seven or eight storeys, mostly of the familiar neo-classical pattern, but here and there were signs of an older, more typically Slavic design, with the polished domes of churches and cathedrals, the baroque of ministerial offices, much of it in yellow limestone, reminding me of my own Kiev. Sebastopol's fortifications were sturdy and not evidently breached, but she flew no standards. Shaking his head, Major Volisharof came up beside me. He stared intently shoreward, as if into a mirror, and automatically squeezed a small pimple on his left cheek; then he began to brush at his moustache with his index finger. He reminded me of a gardener at work on a favourite piece of topiary.

'You know Sebastopol, major?'

'Oh, very well.' He pointed away to our left. 'All the planes have gone. That was the aerodrome. Not so much as a windsock. And the signal station's abandoned.' His hands returned to tease his moustache. 'I've seen this sort of thing before. Yet tomorrow both Reds and Whites could be back, fighting in the streets, and the quaysides choked with refugees.'

'Do you still hope to go ashore?'

'No, no. It's Yalta definitely now. Isn't that silence awful? When you get that, you can be sure there's a mound or two of corpses not far away.' He gave his moustache a pat. 'As if the place has been visited by the plague. It will be like this everywhere in a year or two. The whole of Russia wiped out.'

We listened to the light wind in the rigging, the flap of the bedraggled flags against their masts. Then the bell sounded for lunch.

At about one-thirty there was a noise off to port and several of us, including Mrs Cornelius, left the saloon to look. Coming away from the vast yellow quay was an old steam launch. She wheezed and spat like the boats I used to see in the summer taking Odessa's holidaymakers for trips, or the river-steamers I once serviced for the Armenian in Kiev. Her funnel panted out unhealthy black smoke and her machinery sounded as if it was held together only by ancient layers of congealed oil. In her stern was a middle-aged Russian officer wearing a green greatcoat and an astrakhan shako, his face pinched with cold, while in her bow a French infantry captain had on his regimental cap but was otherwise completely wrapped in fox fur. A British naval rating, in regular uniform, at the boat's little wheel displayed considerable skill in bringing her alongside. The officers reached up for the ropes our crewmen threw down. When the boat was secured they climbed up the waiting ladder to be greeted by our captain. I had gained the impression these might be the only three survivors of Sebastopol. Some of our hands shouted questions to the rating, but I could not understand his replies. At that moment the British battleship, now lying aft of us and to starboard, came to life. She was half-hidden by mist so the sharp sound of her bosun's whistle was all the more startling; this was followed by one single, deep note from her horn. The mood of desolation lifted just a little. People began to call out to the Russian officer, asking after relatives, for news of the Civil War, wanting to know what had happened to the port, but he merely shrugged and continued on to the captain's cabin.

A few minutes later the cook's boy passed us with a tray of steaming food and took it in. 'They ain't 'ad nuffin' ter eat fer a week,' he told Mrs Cornelius when on his return she seized him by the arm. 'I don't fink we'll be 'ere long, missus.' She and I went to sit and drink vodka in the saloon while around us a small army of merchants and ex-Princes discussed the significance of Sebastopol's silence. About an hour later

I saw Mr Thompson. He paused long enough to tell me that the Whites were trying to hold off the Reds at Perekop. We had arrived a day too late or a day too early. The battleship, H.M.S. *Marlborough*, was supposed to offer covering fire to the Whites in attacking the town. But Sebastopol had been taken before she could reach the harbour. Then, at the rumour of a large Red force coming through, the Whites and the majority of civilians had left. *Marlborough* had no orders and was sitting it out until she heard what she should do. Meanwhile suspected cases of mumps on board meant that she was in quarantine. There were a few refugees still in the town. The officers had come aboard to see how many more we could accommodate. 'We'll keep our steam handy so we can leave at an hour's notice. We'll probably be taking on wounded.'

Through Jack Bragg's glasses Mrs Cornelius and I again surveyed the town. Shops had plainly been looted of everything; on walls I saw familiar posters, both White and Bolshevik, and occasionally an old person would scuttle from one doorway into another. I saw two dogs engaged in sexual intercourse on the quay, as if they had realized that here was the largest audience they would ever have. Though several buildings showed signs of shelling they were not particularly badly damaged. I had witnessed many a town devastated by War, but none whose population had vanished so completely. It was very difficult to understand where everyone could have gone. Later three horse-drawn wagons, crude red crosses painted on their canvas awnings, stopped wearily at the quay and crippled men were helped into the old steam-launch which had to make several journeys, eventually bringing some thirty wounded soldiers aboard. In the meantime grey mist descended on the town. Another hour passed. Then a wealthy Russian family and their servants were brought out. They were taken to the last available private cabin. These tall, dignified people had their faces hidden in their collars but there was speculation they were members of the Royal Family. Neither Mr Thompson nor Jack Bragg could discover their identities and Captain Monier-Williams would not tell. They had their meals served in their quarters. By nightfall we were apparently ready to sail again. The Russian soldiers were all youths; those who could walk dined with the rest of the passengers and were treated as heroes. They had evidently not eaten decent food for months. They said they had been fighting with the British Military Mission. There was still a division of Black Watch somewhere between Sebastopol and Perekop.

Marlborough, in spite of her quarantine, would have to evacuate them if they ever reached the harbour.

Mrs Cornelius as usual began chatting almost at once to the White soldiers, noticing whose wounds were not properly bandaged, who needed a letter written and so on. She also learned a great deal about the state of the forces. It became clear to her that the Whites were being badly beaten. Before we went to sleep that night she laughed. 'I feel like Florence bleedin' Nightingale!'

By the time I got up next morning we were already lifting our anchor and preparing to leave. Sebastopol at dawn was still lost in mist and all I could see was the main quay. As the sun rose, figures began to appear in ones and twos. They moved out of the mist like the spectres of the dead, wrapped in rags. Then came horses drawing wagons loaded with potatoes and other winter vegetables, for all the world as if their owners were about to set up a market. Creatures with hand-carts containing carrots and cabbages beckoned to the ship. I heard voices calling. It all seemed sinister to me, though they may well have been innocent peasants trying to sell us what they had. At any moment, however, I expected them to push aside the food and reveal machine-guns. We turned, heading for the gateway, and the figures became increasingly agitated, jumping and waving. The ship sounded her horn, as if in reply and then we were passing the still silent *Marlborough*, negotiating the buoys and moving out to sea.

On the next stage of our voyage, we never lost sight of a coast seemingly as deserted as Sebastopol. By that afternoon we had reached Yalta, the Queen of the Black Sea, looking impressive in the thin sunlight, just as she had in her heyday. She was superficially unspoiled: a fashionable holiday resort out of season, backed by spectacular, wooded, snow-covered hills. She seemed to consist chiefly of solidly-built hotels and had something of the appearance of a small, more compact St Petersburg. Because we were only a short distance off I could easily see people of all classes, horses, motor-cars, soldiers. Yalta had not been shelled and remained able to feed her population. The hotels along her front presented themselves like a committee of dowagers, primly magnificent, perfectly groomed. Any poverty, anything untoward, was hidden in the back-streets and ignored.

Soon white launches flying the Imperial standard came out to meet us and smart sailors, polite and practical, helped some of our passengers to disembark. Major Volisharof temporarily put his children in

13

charge of a Ukrainian family and went ashore to find his sister-in-law and receive his orders. The wounded were taken off. My impression was that most of them were reluctant to leave the ship. The launches returned to the landing-stage and a while later, when the sun felt almost warm on our faces, began to bring out boxes, presumably of ammunition, which were loaded into our cargo holds. Next came the new passengers, mainly women of rank and their children, whose men had either been killed or had elected to remain to fight the Reds. Mrs Cornelius and I were especially impressed by a very tall couple who seemed unlikely companions – a Greek priest and a Roman Catholic nun. He was pale and haunted, but she was red-cheeked and full of smiles. 'Looks like she's gettin' a bit o' wot she fancies,' said Mrs Cornelius with a wink to me. I was still young enough to be embarrassed and turned my attention towards the shore.

Yalta had been visited by the Tsar and his family every summer. The idea that those wonderful villas, the tree-lined streets and parks, the palaces and gardens might eventually fall to Communist shells seemed impossible. Even Bolsheviks must respect such beauty, I thought. I was so sure they would not wish to destroy Yalta that I had the impulse again to take my baggage and leave the ship. Yalta had been under siege; she had known horror, yet she continued to look proudly insouciant; a great eighteenth-century aristocrat simply refusing to acknowledge the presence of Robespierre's sans-culottes on her premises. She was at once nostalgic past and hopeful present: a citadel of good taste and refinement. By her very spirit she must surely resist any attempt to conquer her. (In a few months, of course, Deniken and Wrangel would desert Yalta; the British and French would also abandon her to her fate, and Red Guards would urinate in her fountains, defecate on her flower-beds and vomit over her remaining furnishings. One might as easily have expected the Antichrist to acknowledge the sanctity of a village church.)

Those Bolsheviks had a genuine will to destruction, an honest hatred of everything beautiful, an almost sexual lust to wreck whatever was most delicate and cultured in Russia. Just as they had brought it to Sebastapol, they would bring silence to Yalta. In another year they would strike the whole great country mute. Then Stalin would freeze speech and movement entirely, forbid birdsong in the forest and the bleating of lambs in the field.

The Winter King would come. Stalin would breathe sleeping ignorance into the minds of his subjects and cool their hearts until feeling was impossible. The same men and women who had begun in 1917 by shouting in the streets at the tops of their lungs would, by 1930, be afraid even to whisper in the corners of their own rooms: the Winter King could bear no noise. Even the faintest creaking of an icicle startled him. Shivering in his ghastly isolation, terrified lest some vagrant murmur remind him of his crimes, suspecting all others of his own monumental ruthlessness, his rest could be disturbed by the breeze of a moth's wing fanning his ruined face. Then he would awake, stifling a gasp, dictating a memoir to his expectant executioners: all moths were State traitors and must perish by morning.

Major Volisharof returned to the ship with a dowdy woman of about forty; the aunt. She was introduced to us but I never heard her name and never again had occasion to ask it. He seemed to be paying even more attention to his moustache, as if anticipating the time when he need no longer feel his affections divided. He shook hands with me and begged me to continue pleading the White cause wherever I went in the world. I gave him my word.

'This is worse than 1453,' he said. 'If Christendom had believed the Emperor and sent enough help, Constantinople would never have fallen.' He looked back towards Yalta, seemingly impervious in her tranquillity. 'This business is the responsibility of every Christian. Tell them that.' I watched him kiss his children goodbye, give his moustache a couple of twirls, then follow the orderly, who had come with him to carry his kit, back to the launch.

The mysterious family of aristocrats disembarked and their cabin was taken by a woman, her little daughter and her servant. The woman was remarkably good looking and I was immediately attracted to her. Shortly after she had been installed, the ship was on her way again and an hour later it began to snow. Yalta, I thought, had let us go regretfully, but without complaint.

The Yalta refugees were altogether a better selection than those who had boarded in Odessa. Cheerfully, they made the most of their conditions, bringing with them a new atmosphere of camaraderie and good fellowship. The disappointed merchants and their complaining wives were soon shamed. After a day or so at sea the weather improved, the waves became less agitated and my own sadness at leaving beautiful Yalta to her fate was modified a little by the sound of children now able to play on deck; moreover, I at last had the opportunity to indulge in good conversation with people of my own intellectual capacity and there were women who, separated from their husbands, were only too pleased to enjoy a little mildly flirtatious badinage with a handsome young man. I began to entertain some hope that my appalling celibacy might soon be alleviated, if only briefly with one of their servants.

To this end I became a great and popular builder of paper aeroplanes and boats. I took innocent pleasure in the delight of the children whose admiration of my handiwork also helped me forget personal problems. My friendships with the little Boryas and Katyas led to contact with their nanyanas and their mothers, most of whom told me how wonderful I was with children and asked me about myself. I hinted, tastefully, at my aristocratic connections, Petersburg education, military service and my special mission. It was unwise, then, to be over-specific. The Bolsheviks were already planting spies amongst the refugees. I chose not to wear either of my uniforms but made it clear that once I arrived in London my business would be of significance to the White cause. Lastly I let it be understood that Mrs Cornelius and I were related, but not husband and wife. I was, in fact, a bachelor. The only thing which marred this general improvement in my life was an incident on the second night out from Yalta. I was taking my usual stroll, had just passed the wheelhouse, returning to the saloon, when I saw a pale figure, a handkerchief pressed to its mouth, retreat suddenly into one of the private cabins, as if startled. For a moment I had thought it was Brodmann, the Jew who had threatened to betray me in Odessa and who had witnessed my humiliation at the hands of the anarchist Cossack in Alexandrovsk. I felt faint. My stomach seemed to contract. I even uttered his name.

'Brodmann?'

The door closed and was immediately bolted on the inside.

Surely this treacherous coward had not followed me onto the boat. It was impossible. I had seen him arrested. Maybe I was experiencing a mild hallucination? I had dreamed once or twice about Brodmann. I had dreamed about most of the terrors of the past two years. Now, in my extreme tiredness, I might be imposing the dream onto my waking life. I reasoned that Brodmann could never have escaped in time to join the *Rio Cruz*. A kind of residual horror was getting the better of me. I went at once to my cabin and tried to sleep.

The following morning I adhered to my routine; later I did as I always did now, greeting the children, chatting with their mothers, devising new deck games, sympathising with young women who had left their sweethearts fighting in the Caucasus, bending an ear to widows whose husbands had died bravely for Tsar and Fatherland, and offering reassurances concerning movements afoot which must soon destroy the Bolsheviks forever and re-establish a legitimate government in Petrograd.

The image of Brodmann was forced thoroughly from my mind. I was lucky enough to meet one or two of those who had known Count Nicholai Feodorovitch Petroff, my Kolya. We spoke of mutually familiar acquaintances. We recalled the good old Tsarist days, spoke of the War and Kolya's relatives. I gained enormous stature in their eyes when they learned I had been with the Count's cousin, Alexei Leonovitch, in the Oertz which had crashed in the sea of Odessa, killing him and wounding me. Consequently this gave me the status of war-hero, a Knight of the Air, and thus I gained a little compensation for my sufferings.

The woman eventually showing the strongest interest in me was the good-looking creature of almost thirty who had taken the vacated cabin. Although Russian, she had a German married name: the Baroness von Ruckstühl. Her factory-owner husband, son of a 'colonist', had been shot by his Kharkov workers in 1918 after Skoropadskya fled to Berlin. The Baroness was not at all Germanic. She was a heavy, Slavic beauty with large blue-green eyes, a wide, smiling mouth and thick auburn hair which she generally wore bunched on top of her head. She favoured smart and simple clothes, chiefly travelling dresses and cloaks of conservative dark greens, reds and blues which suited her perfectly and added to her attraction; indeed, the only female on the *Rio Cruz* who outshone her was her own daughter (I must admit it was she who first attracted me). The daughter took after her mother in looks and complexion but had that air of vulnerability and courageous curiosity which has continued to fascinate me since childhood. Esmé had possessed it, and Zoyea, too. There is something wonderful about young girls with those qualities. They make one feel protective, lustful, happy and strong all at the same time. The little girl was about eleven and her name was Katerina, though we knew her as 'Kitty'. When they first appeared on deck, the Baroness seemed sad and abstracted, only arousing herself from her depression to smile at some antic of the child's. She never admonished her. This was left to the Caucasian nanny, Marusya Veranovna, a severe old hook-nosed woman with thick lips, very uncomfortable in the company of other passengers, who tended to glare defiantly at everyone except her charges, plainly hating all aspects of the voyage. For the first day or so she objected to Kitty's choice of myself as her chief playmate until the Baroness evidently told her not to interfere. I soon became close friends with Kitty, yet would say little more than 'Good morning' either to the mother or the servant. Meeting them on deck, I would raise my hat, as distantly polite as they. Of course nobody judged me perverse in my attachment to the child! In my desperate frustration I was grateful if occasionally I brushed her cheek with the back of my hand or held her by the shoulder for a second whilst steadying her against a wave. Indeed, my discomfort actually increased. I now burned for Kitty by day and for Mrs Cornelius by night! Without my company Mrs Cornelius spent much of her time with young Jack Bragg. Had I been of a jealous disposition I might have suspected a romantic interest, but I knew she would not betray her Frenchman's trust. Neither was there any question of my making sexual advances to the little girl. My feelings were entirely under control (and besides she was of good family; it would have been insane of me to have risked the scandal). At any rate, noticing the growing interest in me displayed by the Baroness, I began with controlled deliberation to transfer my feelings to the mother. It was not very difficult, since she was an extraordinarily handsome and self-contained woman. I know she felt at least a little of that competitive impulse so many mothers exhibit when a man takes an interest in their daughters. Ironically they are inclined to show particular favour to the man who courts their little offspring, until it becomes certain they have no chance of winning him; whereupon, of course, they become Furies, Tigers of Morality, Invokers of the Law. Thus, while I continued to 'court' young Kitty, joking with her, making her giggle, having her beg me for piggy-back rides and so on, the display was now chiefly designed to lure the Baroness. I am, I hope, a self-knowing and honest person and while not particularly proud of my technique in this matter, should remind you that I was not yet twenty. I was used to a full sex-life since I had spent the past months as a favoured guest in a whorehouse. What is more I had, in my heart of hearts, expected once at sea to enjoy the favours of Mrs Cornelius. The boy that I was needed warm, feminine company at night to help him forget his agony at leaving Holy Russia behind, for a Russian and his land are the same thing; to part them is to tear flesh from flesh: it is as if one's entire substance is stolen. Few Russians ever voluntarily go abroad; we are almost all unwilling exiles, and that is why we are so easily misunderstood. I am no molester of children! These stupid Londoners fail to appreciate the sadness of an old, childless man. Why should I heed their magistrates' warnings? I simply wish to give a little affection and receive some in return. I did not betray her trust. On the contrary, she betrayed mine. They always will.

Why do they avoid me, when I am so ready to give them everything they desire? Am I a rapist or a lecher? My powerful feelings are a noble force for good. What we did in Petersburg in 1916 the world now celebrates as new and 'liberated'. They tell us on television it is not a crime to love, irrespective of age or sex. That was how it was for us. Kolya taught me to love, without prejudice, every aspect of sexuality. It is not a love lacking in morality or without profound responsibility. How can those who have entrapped me even begin to understand? In their fear and their jealousy of my Promethean vitality they have bound me, gagged me and delivered me up to little birds which peck at my flesh. For thirty years I have been their prisoner, watched, checked, pursued by their idiot bureaucracies: and yet it was I who could have saved them! They put a piece of metal in my stomach. *Es tut mir hier weh.* They put iron into my womb and I refuse to forgive them. ('Yo're nuffink but an ol' 'ore at 'eart,' says Mrs Cornelius. She is affectionate. She means well. But who was it made me a whore? Who robbed me of everything, even my name?) When they confront me all they see is a miserable old stateless shopkeeper; but even in 1919 on the *Rio Cruz* Mrs Cornelius admired me. 'Y've got a way wiv ther ladies, I'll say that for ya, Ivan.' I could have had a dozen of the loveliest Russian gentlewomen. I chose the Baroness because she was older. I believed she would be more sophisticated and allow no unwelcome complications. Also I knew there had to be an element of self-interest in her attraction to me: from Constantinople she needed a transit visa to Berlin and she guessed I would be the man most likely to help her obtain it. Her husband had not been a German national. His father had taken Russian citizenship in 1885. She, of course, was Russian. She had some second cousins in Berlin who had already offered her a home and she spoke moderately good German. The child's security at least was assured there. All this I learned as at her suggestion we began to take coffee in the mornings and then tea in the afternoons. I still ate my meals at the officers' table in the far corner of the dining-saloon, but tended to leave earlier, to stroll for quarter-of-an-hour round the deck with the Baroness before she went to bed.

Brodmann, if Brodmann it had been, remained in hiding and I became sure I had invented him. However, I should feel much easier after the ship docked in Constantinople and I was on the last stages of my journey to England. Here there were too many malicious tongues, let alone Brodmann's; too many potential enemies prepared to lie about my past. To be fair there were also allies and the Baroness was one of these. She had an attractive, wistfully sad air, typically Russian and considerably comforting. Her voice was low and warm and musical; her sentences would tend to end on a falling, distant note. I understood such women and their romantic desires. I was able to make her smile with my little dry ironies, at once sympathetic and philosophical. It was not long before we were on closer terms. 'You are a disarming man, Maxim Arturovitch,' she said one evening, as we stood listening to the lapping water. She smiled. 'I suppose you also write poetry.'

'My poetry, Leda Nicolayevna, is to be found in specific configurations of steel and concrete,' I said. 'In what can be achieved with cogs, levers and pistons. I am a scientist first and foremost. I do not believe Man can reach for perfection until his environment is properly under his control. For me poetry is a giant aeroplane able to leap immediately into the air and fly infinite distances without a moment's danger, landing wherever its pilot pleases. Poetry is the freedom technology brings us.'

She was impressed. 'I cannot claim such vision, Maxim Arturovitch, but I do occasionally write verses. For my own consolation.'

'Will you show them to me?'

'Perhaps.' She squeezed my hand, flushed a little, then went quickly to the cabin she shared with her daughter and servant.

Involved with this gentle seduction, I scarcely noticed the ship reaching Theodossia, disembarking wounded and cargo and then taking on a group of Georgian officers who kept themselves apart from the rest of us, smoking monstrous meerschaums and talking in their own outlandish language. We were anchored amidst half-a-dozen other ships, well away from the shore. It was hard to make out details of the coast, let alone the port, yet every so often, when the wind blew towards us from land, there was a smell like new-mown grass, its origin impossible to identify. My Baroness was romantically inclined to ascribe it to 'the first scents of spring', but someone else said it was horse-fodder; another was convinced it was quick-lime. The Georgians, taciturn and impatient with all civilians, would not be drawn on the matter. In contrast to Sebastopol, here Russian and Allied ships came and went at a tremendous rate, reminding me of Odessa in her heyday. This was still one of the great centres of real resistance. Perhaps that was why the Georgians were so displeased to be leaving. They stood in a single surly rank at the starboard rail, leaning back and watching the smoke from a dozen great men-o'-war drifting low over the metallic water. I guessed they were unhappy with their orders. As we began to steam away, they all went aft to glare at the plumes of dark smoke which stretched into the sky like a barrier of birch trees which emerges suddenly from the Ukrainian steppe and which is at once a miracle of nature, a reassurance of human settlement. And when these were below the horizon, the Georgians moved about the ship in small groups, brushing at the spray which fell on their faded green uniforms, displaying resentment and downright rudeness when attempts were made to befriend them, as if we were responsible for their discomfort. Possibly they wanted to go to Batoum. To our relief, we learned they were to disembark, instead, at Novorossiske, our next port of call. In their uniforms, with their black astrakhan caps and their huge walrus moustaches they looked, as I said to the Baroness, like a converse of village postmasters. This made the Baroness laugh; she had no great liking for Georgians at the best of times, she said, but these seemed to have stepped straight out of the pages of an illustrated comic magazine. I wondered, years later, if this were not the secret of 'Uncle' Joe Stalin's success. It is often hard to hate a particular kind of stereotype. It became an important element of Hitler's astonishingly rapid rise, too. He looked so much like Charlie Chaplin many people could not take him seriously. The Georgians went off the next day in a lighter which came especially for them. They were glad to leave and the hands responsible for mopping their phlegm off the decks were no less regretful to see the back of them.

So many ships filled the Novorssisk sea-roads it was impossible for us to come anywhere near the port. Through Jack Bragg's glasses I observed an unremarkable but busy industrial and military harbour apparently getting ready to defend herself against a large-scale attack. For the first time since we had left Odessa I saw numbers of aircraft coming and going. It was a mixed bag of machines, some of them Russian, some Allied, a good many captured from the Germans and Austrians. In less than an hour I saw Sopwith Camels, Albatrosses, a Pfalz D II, a whole squadron of Friedrichshafen G III bombers, an Armstrong

Whitworth FK 8, a Breguet-Michelin IV, some cumbersome Sikorsky RBVZs, a couple of Caproni CA5s and many FBA Type H flying boats. These were a few of the planes I pointed out to my Baroness who was under the impression I had done most of my war service as a flyer. I saw no point in disillusioning her, since my work in aircraft research could have easily shortened the conflict and changed the course of Russia's history. This familiarity of mine with so many aircraft confirmed her guess (she was to tell me later) that I must be a well-known Ace removed from active service to deal with even more pressing tasks. She received no lies from me. From what little I had said she invented her own Romance. Sympathetically she slipped her arm into mine. 'Do you miss the freedom of the skies?'

'It is the most wonderful experience in the world.' I made a small, significant gesture with my hands. 'If that damned Oertz hand't crashed I might still be up there with those lads.'

'Perhaps they'll let you rejoin the Service.' She pressed her body against mine. She was trembling. The hare was ready for the hawk. 'When you've done what you have to do in London.'

'I shall certainly be flying again soon.' My senses grew keener, ready for the strike. 'But probably in an advanced machine of my own design.'

All around us in the pale morning half-light ships were sounding their sirens. A blue and white Hansa-Brandenburg FB patrol flying-boat came in low overhead, its engine making a sweet, steady drone as it circled over us. I felt my blood warm as she dropped closer. Her Austrian markings were painted out, but the new Russian insignia evidently had not been allowed to dry properly. Long streaks of paint could be seen on the bright undersides of her lower wings. 'She's beautiful.' The Baroness congratulated me as if I were the plane's creator. 'Like a huge gull. Would you take me up some day If the opportunity ever arose?'

I clasped her hand. I felt a rapid pulse. She was half-frightened, half-fascinated. 'Of course.'

At anchor off Novorossisk we awaited our next cargo. Mr Thompson said he thought it was artillery spares for Batoum and there was some confusion over the marking of the boxes. That night I took my usual turn around the deck with Leda Nicolayevna, then, just before she returned to her cabin, I kissed her. Now she was not at all flustered. 'I've been waiting for you to do that,' she murmured. She had at last made up her mind to have a love affair with me. We kissed again. We were both breathing heavily, our legs shaking so much I thought we must collapse, yet there was nowhere we could go. 'It will have to be tomorrow,' she said. I forced myself back from her. 'Tell the nanyana you have a headache and to keep Kitty out of the cabin until just before dinner,' I said. 'Will she suspect?'

The Baroness was amused. 'What if she does? I am her employer.'

I had forgotten how assured of their authority the Russian nobility still were. I returned to my cabin. Probably Mrs Cornelius was in the saloon, for her bunk was empty. I lit a cigarette and relaxed, still in my clothes, feeling full of the conquest and the pleasures to come. Then I disrobed and went almost immediately to sleep. I remember waking momentarily at dawn, hearing Mrs Cornelius stumbling and cursing to herself as she got undressed. Once she fell against the bunks and hissed 'Bugger,' saw me open my eyes and shrugged. 'Sorry, Ivan. Didn't wanna wake yer.' I grunted before I returned to my dreams; dreams far more settled and pleasant than any I had known in months.

By the next afternoon we were still at anchor, awaiting our cargo. A strong north-easterly blew, making us move in our moorings like a captive balloon. It did not matter to me where we were for I was stretched naked upon the body of a passionate baroness who stroked and scratched me while she whispered delicious, innocent obscenities into my ear. I discovered that she had all the astonishing passion of a virgin girl when to tell the truth I had expected to possess a cool, calculating and relatively experienced mistress: even a somewhat cautious lover.

The Baroness von Ruckstühl was neither cool nor cautious. Her experience had been limited, as was now obvious, but her will rapidly to learn all the arts of debauchery easily compensated for any awkwardness; indeed her awkwardness was itself attractive. I could not have asked for a more delightful understudy, as it were, for Mrs Cornelius. What was more, I reminded myself, as my greedy tongue licked her nipples and my fingers lightly touched her clitoris, she was well-connected; we could be of considerable use to one another. My depression vanished completely. As my first orgasm splashed across her thighs my future was suddenly golden again! For her part she was giddily amazed at my skills, if overly curious as to where I had acquired them. *Zolst mir antshuldigen,* as we say in Russia.

At the sound of the dinner bell we dressed hurriedly, grinning like happy dogs. I slipped from her cabin with my body singing, my brain full of tremendous new schemes, a thousand wonderful futures, a hundred fresh ideas for our love-making. And that night, during dinner, I was at my wittiest, so much so that Mrs Cornelius leaned over to wink at me and whisper, 'Wassa matter wiv you, Ivan? 'Ad a win on the 'orses?'

Later my Baroness and I met on deck to share a parting embrace before retiring to our respective cabins. In the deep blackness beyond the lines of waiting ships we saw the occasional flicker of fire and heard a distant explosion. 'Arsonists,' I told her, 'without a doubt. Red saboteurs. This is their idea of warfare.'

'What cowards they are.'

I agreed. 'The terrible truth, however, is that it is frequently the cowards who win the wars.'

She found this either too profound or too disturbing. After arranging to meet at exactly the same time in her cabin the next day, we went off in opposite directions.

I paused near the bridge to light a cigarette and watch the far-off flames as they subsided. When I looked up at the sky there was a figure suddenly on the narrow deck above me. It was pale and it plainly had no wish to be seen. A man, wrapped in a kind of shawl or short cloak, who coughed almost apologetically and nodded to me. I stared hard at him this time. Again the name came to my lips.

'Brodmann?'

If it was Brodmann, he was more frightened of me than I was of him. I laughed. 'What do you mean, up there, playing at ghosts?'

The man drew his shawl closer about his shoulders and disappeared out of sight. I walked swiftly round the deck, trying to reach the stairway down which he must climb if he was to return to his cabin. But he had been too quick for me. The door was shut and although this time I banged on it there was no light inside. Even when I pressed my ear to the louvred panel which, like mine, was stuffed with old newspapers, I could hear nothing.

I went to find Mr Thompson, to ask him when he thought we should arrive in Constantinople.

Two

NEXT AFTERNOON four coffins came aboard: four long wooden
boxes, probably of ammunition. We left Novorossisk with an additional
trio of elderly Russian women, a deaf old man, a wounded British captain and his Indian orderly, an Italian Red Cross nurse. We now had one
of the most curiously mixed groups of passengers any ship had ever carried. We would be continuously at sea for several days, heading into
warmer weather. Our last Russian port of call was to be Batoum. In my
new mood I began to look forward to Constantinople, to the prospect of
travelling in Europe and settling in London. I wanted so much to be free
of Brodmann (or rather the threat of what he represented). I wanted to
enjoy the Baroness without the sense that my idyll might be interrupted
at any moment. This, I now decided, might be achieved in Constantinople during the few days I would be there.

The delicious geometry of the Baroness blended in my imagination
with the more severe geometry of the ship. Both struck me as shuddering, powerful, uncertain beasts to be controlled with skill and delicacy.
On that second day I introduced her to the pleasures of cocaine-sniffing.
I heaped her with sensation upon sensation. She was greedy for everything I could offer. 'It has been so long. I have missed so much.' She was
a huge, arrogant cat which had elected to place herself absolutely in my
power. The more obedient she became in pursuit of her lust the more
my affection for her increased; yet she never seemed to lose her identity.
She remained the Baroness von Ruckstühl; almost an ally to equal Mrs
Cornelius. She called me her 'mysterious, dark stranger'. She had heard
the calumny, too. She said she would not care if I was a Jew and a char-

25

latan; but she believed in me, in my greatness, in my destiny. She thought, she said, that race was of no importance at all. *Ich verspreche Ihnen!* She was a woman of enormous, if specific, generosity.

I had some misgivings, of course. These were to do with my discovering the wealth of passion and sensuality I had unlocked in her; the considerable determination expressed in her feelings which, I feared, might at any moment go out of my control. It was not long, for instance, before her original intention of 'a brief, illicit love affair' began to transform into a desire for a longer, possibly more formal, liaison. Soon she suggested breathlessly it would be 'wonderful if we could be together for a whole night'.

I had already planned to spend more time with her, but I could not help fearing she would choose to interpret a mere inclination as a declaration of fidelity. I had already made it plain to her that my career took precedence over everything else. I looked directly into her great blue-green eyes and said as tenderly as I could, 'That's impossible.'

She responded wistfully. 'I suppose so.' Yet it was obvious she was already considering another approach. As the end of our voyage drew near, she hoped for some sort of reassurance from me. I was touched by the way she turned her massive head to one side and let her shoulder fall. She was like an enormous schoolgirl. I embraced her, stroking her cheek. 'Already there has to be considerable gossip,' I said. 'The more pernicious because Mrs Cornelius is still officially my wife. And you would suffer far worse from gossip than I.'

'I don't give a damn about their gossip, do you?'

It was true I did not much begrudge them their little crumb of scandal. It took their minds from their own troubles and within a fortnight I would be free of them. But it suited me to feign discomfort. 'I do care,' I told her. 'These are times when a little bit of malice can cost you your life.' Plainly it was up to me to keep a sense of proportion. Moreover, I was still thinking of Brodmann. He had the power to put me in front of a firing squad, should certain people believe him. Similarly, it was important to placate the Baroness. If she became vindictive she could embarrass me with the Allied authorities. Much better that the affair should be brought to a gradual, bitter-sweet conclusion, without anger or tears. Soon she and I would go our own ways. The entire voyage would be remembered as a passing interlude, a pleasant shipboard romance. The Baroness was bound to lose some of her infatuation for me when we disembarked. Nonetheless it was the first time I had enjoyed an affair with a woman denied pleasure for too many years and yet who was used to commanding authority. I was becoming fascinated by her. Even when she pretended to change the subject it was actually to amplify her theme. She stroked my head almost as if I were her child, or a favourite dog. 'There are people I expect to meet in Constantinople, Simka. You and they could work to your mutual benefit.' By which she revealed she now planned a future for us! She seemed to ignore my mission, my association with Mrs Cornelius, my own ambitions, and when I murmured something about them, she was dismissive. 'There's no harm in considering different options, surely?'

'You think of me too much.' I took her hand. I was gentle. Yet we duelled. 'You must first look to your own interests. I have protected myself pretty well for several years!'

'I see my interests as yours,' she said. It was the nearest she had come to a plain statement. In an effort to turn her mind from this course, I pressed my hand hard against her breasts and bit her ear-lobe.

Since I could not control her imagination I would have to resort to minor deception, using the 'secret orders' excuse which had served me excellently in the past. If I liked I could use it within a day of reaching Constantinople. I could even enjoy her company for a week after we disembarked and still leave with honour and little fear of her turning treacherous. At a pinch I would also recruit help from Mrs Cornelius. (Though currently I could not easily confide in her, since she spent most of her evenings with the English sailors. She was rarely in bed much before dawn.)

Satisfied I had evolved a good enough plan, I relaxed again, though the spectre of Brodmann remained a flaw to my overall peace of mind. At night I would spend an hour or more looking for him (or whoever it was who so resembled him) but without success. Twice I waited outside the closed cabin door, to be rewarded with nothing more than what might have been a faint groan, or a small, dry coughing noise which lasted a few seconds. I maintained my habit of rising early, often before Mrs Cornelius returned from her revels, and enjoying my own company on deck. A day or two out of Novorossisk the weather began to improve. Sometimes blue sky could be seen between clouds whose outlines resembled sleeping polar bears.

At length the ship appeared to be hemmed in by these massive white mountains. Perhaps she was adrift in one of those submarine caverns scientists say lie beneath our icecaps; caverns leading to undiscovered tropical continents where an explorer might find primitive nations inhabited by half-human races. The engines echoed loudly in my ears, filling the whole vast expanse. Had Russia drowned in the tears of the dying? Had we alone escaped? Were we sailing even now above the silent roofs of cities whose populations were corpses; corpses whose hair streamed like seaweed, whose damned eyes begged for release? It was impossible to stop. We could not help. We were searching for our Ararat. I began to fancy this was truly the end of civilization; ourselves the only survivors. Might it be my fate to lead these people towards a New Dawn. The best of them (especially the English) already believed in me as a prophet. Again I became fully inspired with the sense of my great destiny. Of course I did not really believe the world had ended, but the metaphor was accurate. Мне нездоровится! Уменя болит горло! У меня болит живот! I stood on the forward deck of the *Rio Cruz* in dignified fur. The black and silver Cossack pistols in my pockets continued to remind me of my heritage while I now believed as strongly as I ever had in the brilliant future which awaited me. Behind me was a beloved but thoroughly exhausted Russia; before me was Europe. She had learned the lesson of War and now must surely restore herself in a Golden Age of justice and human achievement where my engineering abilities would be immediately recognised and I would be called to play a major role in a great renaissance. The future was in the hands of the mighty Christian nations: Britain, France, Italy and America, even Germany. A future of skyscraper and undersea tunnel, of television, the matter transmitter and, greatest of all, the flying city. Let Russia with all her sins fall back into a Dark Age in which petty would-be tsars squabbled for dominance of an ever-diminishing territory. The West must become purified chrome and glass rising to the clouds, sophisticated machines and wonderful electronics, the true heritage of Byzantium: a Graeco–Christian Utopia!

Two thousand years ago we had lost the path. Now we had again been granted the chance to find it and follow it. The Turk was on his knees; the Jew scuttled for cover. Carthage was once more reduced and this time must never be allowed sufficient pause to regain her strength. I knew I could not be alone in this dream. All over the Christian world men and women were taking fresh breath, preparing themselves for the task. *Bu ne demektir?* People snigger at me now when I tell them what might have been. They do not realise how many of us there were; how easily (had it not been for the machinations of petty, greedy minds) we might have made the dream reality. Anyone who knows me will tell you

I have scarcely an ounce of suspicion in my nature; paranoia is foreign to me; yet only an idiot would deny the power of Zion. Theirs was a dark vision, opposed to mine and those like me. Mr Thompson was one such fellow soul. I sought him out. It was important to keep a reasonable distance between myself and the Baroness. I confided to Mr Thompson that I found it hard to imagine how I should survive in the non-Russian world. Again he assured me men like myself were needed everywhere, particularly in Britain. I was, he said, 'a wonder', an 'infant prodigy'. My talents would not be wasted. Sucking his pipe for hours on end he quietly contemplated my ideas, admitting that many were above his head. He was convinced, however, it was to be an engineer's future. 'I envy you, Mister Pyatnitski. Trotski's a fool to drive people like you away. I'm surprised you haven't thought of the USA. That's where I'd go, if I was young. They appreciate our sort in America.'

But the United States at that time had never captured my imagination, although the pictures of redskins, frontiersmen and buffalo (gleaned from my reading Karl May and Fenimore Cooper) were romantic enough. I believed there were no true cities in America and precious little civilization. It took time, in my view, to develop a true city. I shook my head. 'It's not my ambition to build farm-machinery or locomotives, or work out means of mass-producing cheap clocks. Let the miners keep their gold; I'll not part them from it in exchange for a few penny toys!'

Mr Thompson shrugged. 'You might find you're glad to be free of European squabbles. Yankees like to keep themselves to themselves. I know how they feel. The British are too fond of taking care of other people.'

'I'm a Russian and a Slav, Mr Thompson. I couldn't leave Europe in the lurch. Also I am a Christian. My loyalties are clear. But for the Bolsheviks and the Jews I should not be an exile at all. Everyone knows that Jews already control New York. I have nothing in common with the self-serving bourgeoisie aboard this ship. Let them go to America if they wish. They are all deserters.'

We were leaning against the funnel for warmth while this particular conversation took place, contemplating the black, featureless ocean. Our various lights, red, green and white, were reflected in the water and we might have been riding on dark clouds, through infinite space. Mr Thompson relit his pipe. 'You Russians seem a hopeless bunch of creatures, I must admit. I've seen the refugees in Constantinople, already. A man with your qualifications is welcome anywhere. But what do you think will become of the rest? The women and children? Will they be allowed back when the war is over?'

I could not answer. In those days no one believed what hideousness was yet to come. Many went back, during the so-called New Economic Policy period. Most were dead before 1930. I will not pretend that as the years passed I looked for hope of welcome, or at least recognition, in my homeland. I would not be alive today if I too had clutched at the straws offered by the Reds in the middle-twenties.

When Mr Thompson returned to his duties I was melancholy again. Against my usual habit, I sought the company of Mrs Cornelius. As usual she was enjoying herself in the dining-saloon with some of the officers. Jack Bragg was there, singing the choruses of *Knock 'Em In The Old Kent Road* and *Two Lovely Black Eyes*. I think he flushed when he saw me, confirming my suspicion of his amorous feelings towards my companion. He could not know how sympathetic I felt. Mrs Cornelius wore her yellow and black dress (she called it her 'tango frock') and was performing the traditional English dance known as the Knees Up. I took a glass of rum and sang along with the others, imitating every one of Mrs Cornelius's inflections and gestures. It was how my rather formal English, inherited from *Pearson's Magazine* and various novelists, began to gain that neat touch of colloquialism which would often confound native Britons and enable me to move gracefully in all walks of life.

Mrs Cornelius winked at me, as she usually did, and persuaded me to sing one of the songs she had taught me. I willingly displayed my mastery with a rendering of *Wot A Marf, Wot a Marf, Wot a Norf An' Sarf*. This has always remained one of my favourites. It was greeted with huge applause. Those Russians who had remained at the far end of the saloon, nearest the doors, were completely baffled. Mrs Cornelius gestured kindly for them to join us, but they displayed either embarrassment or downright surliness and disapproval. I too called they should 'let their hair down' and then, to my sudden horror, saw Brodmann, who had been huddled in a shawl and hidden by a fat dowager, rise from his seat. I could barely contain myself. It was a tribute to my iron will that I did not cry out. I forced myself to continue smiling and held my hand to the figure who hesitantly approached us. The smile turned to what was probably an inane grin of relief as I realised this creature was not, after all, my enemy. In response to me, he began to beam all over his red, greasy face, stumbling forward, singing some popular ditty familiar to me from my early days in Odessa. I would never normally have shown such welcome to a Jew, but now it was too late. 'I am so glad,' he said, when he had finished the first verse. 'I have been ill, you know. Afraid they would turn me off the ship. Measles or something, but I am completely recovered. I have seen you once or twice, have I not? At night when I was getting some air?' Before I could extricate myself, Mrs Cornelius put one plump, pink arm around his shoulders and the other around mine and was soon kicking up her legs in a kind of can-can. I had no choice but to make the best of it. By the time Mrs Cornelius broke away to dance with Jack Bragg I was left with the drunken, sickly Jew whose name, he said, was Hernikof. In his expensive, gaudy suit, with his gold watch-chain and huge diamond rings, he looked grotesque. He sweated a great deal, mopped his head and neck and insisted over and over again that he was 'perfectly recovered'. He began to tell me how terrible it had been for him in Odessa; how his family had died in a pogrom, how his mother had been crucified by White Cossacks: all the familiar exaggerations of his race. When a short time later he leered at me and asked me if I, too, were going on to Berlin 'with the attractive Baroness' it was all I could do to hold back my temper. Yet, of course, I remained relieved that the ghost had been laid. At last I managed to return to the table where Mrs Cornelius sat panting. I squeezed in between her and Bragg, refilled my glass and made a great show of concentrating on the words of *O, What A Happy Land Is England*. It was bad enough having to travel in close proximity to the likes of Hernikof, but it was far more hateful when they assumed an intimacy and similarity of ambition and character. True, I had left Odessa considerably richer than I had arrived, and with military promotion into the bargain, but these fat brokers, wailing for sympathy, had had nothing of the real experiences, had seen nothing of the true horror. They had neither been imprisoned by anarchists or Bolsheviks nor had they known what it was to give up any hope of living. They had not seen men and women kneeling in the snow beside the railway tracks waiting to be shot in the head. They had not been forced to keep company with corpses and crows, with louse-ridden Cossacks who might kill you casually from mere boredom. They had heard of a few arrests, the occasional execution, seen some

Jews being pursued through the streets, but their indignation was chiefly aroused by lost bills-of-lading, requisitioned houses, stock purchased with useless money.

That night I felt as if I had been driven back into my former mental condition; 'within the nightmare' as Russians say: that perpetual dreamlike state of frequently unadmitted terror I had known for over two years. My life and sanity had been attacked, my whole existence thrown upside-down by the cruel madness of Revolution and Civil War; my brain and body had throbbed, night and day, with fear. The terror becomes manifest. The dry mouth opens. Any words will come out of it. Anything which might save it. When the danger passes it is impossible to remember exactly what that frightened mouth has said. Neither does it matter, because you are still alive. Yet people look at you in contempt and call you a liar! They are lies, of course. I am not a fool. I will not deny it. My survival depends on self-knowledge. But are they like the lies Hernikof doubtless gave the British simply to gain sympathy and a passport to the rich pickings of Berlin Such slimy untruths would not work on me. While not proud of everything I have done, I scarcely feel guilty; because I survived. What did it matter if the Jews tried to ingratiate themselves with me? What if those jumped-up kulaks snubbed me? The condemnation of the privileged is meaningless. Besides, I was admired by the British. I was loved by a woman of noble blood. I was watched over by another who was both mother and sister to me. The Jew was somehow shaken off and I found myself swaying between Mrs Cornelius and Lt Bragg, singing one of the sad Cossack songs I had learned when a prisoner of the Reds. Jack Bragg was plainly moved. He would have remained to hear the rest of the verses but he had to go on duty. I was half way through and had reached the part where the second pony has died, giving up its life for the heroine, when Mrs Cornelius fell with a gargling noise backwards into my lap and looking up at me through her large, candid eyes said slowly, 'I fink ya'd better put me ter bed, Ive.'

I helped her back to our cabin. This time she controlled her stomach until we were both undressed and then, as I reached to pull the blankets over her, she was sick on my only nightshirt. By the time I had washed it out in the ship's toilet (the cabin had no running water or individual heating) she had gone to sleep. I stood supporting myself with a hand on the bunk looking at her in the yellow light from a hurricane lamp Jack Bragg had managed to find for us. The throbbing of the ship be-

32

came indistinguishable from the throbbing of my own loins. Once you become used to lust being satisfied it is much harder to control. I longed for her to want me, to open her arms to me. I leaned down to stroke her hair. She murmured gratefully and smiled. 'Thass loverly . . .' I touched her neck. 'Oo,' she said, 'you wicked fing,' and she wriggled in the bed. I sat down on the edge. I kissed her ear. Her eyes opened and her smile changed to an expression of shocked surprise. 'Ivan! Yer littel bleeder. I fort you woz . . .' It was evident she had forgotten the name of her Frenchman.

'François.' I began to stand up.

'Yeah.'

Aloft once more I fell into a troubled sleep, dreaming of Brodmann disguising himself as Hernikof and summoning vengeful Cossacks to torture and kill me. Waking from this I deliberately recalled the strong thighs, the red, eager lips of my Leda, her magnificent Slavic breasts, her hair, the sweep of her spine, the curve of her backside. Sex has always helped me to soothe away my fears. I became increasingly willing to risk a night or two in the Baroness's company. The consequences, after all, would not be considerable, even if she did turn against me. And would it be any more than I deserved? I was guilty of dreadful greed in my desire to possess Mrs Cornelius as well as Leda Nicolayevna. How could I forget the bargain I had made with my one friend in all the world; the person who had saved my life more than once: my Guardian Angel? Sometimes, even now, when Mrs Cornelius and I have known carnal love, I recall that incident with shame. I am not a monster. But I suppose it is in all of us to behave like a monster occasionally. Looking back, I blame Hernikof. When those about you are cynical and assume your motives to be as cynical as theirs, sometimes you behave as they do. We are all social creatures, unconsciously moved by the desires and expectations of our fellows. I am no different to anyone else. I have never claimed to be.

Now I understand my behaviour a little better. Unquestionably I was still within the nightmare. It takes more than a week or two at sea to dissipate the reaction to years of familiar terror. Terror truly becomes an old friend. One misses him. The sudden absence of threat can be almost as traumatic as the loss of security. For the same reasons, small wars frequently follow hard on the conclusion of larger wars. Any habit, no matter how self-destructive, is hard to lose, particularly when it is never fully acknowledged. Perhaps, too, something happens to the

33

body-chemistry when so much adrenalin is frequently summoned. We have all seen the small dog rescued from the fangs of the larger beast; frequently he will turn and fasten his teeth in the wrist of his benefactor. My love for Mrs Cornelius was far more spiritual than it was physical, though of course she was extraordinarily sensual. I was equally special to her, I know. She did not at that time wish to risk the destruction of our relationship by introducing common lust into it. She told me this many, many years later. I understand that perfectly now, of course. On the *Rio Cruz*, however, I found myself frequently baffled.

Next morning I got up as usual and went on deck. The air was considerably warmer and the light spray refreshed me. Two or three seamen were at work polishing our brass and scrubbing our decks almost as if they prepared for a special event. The sun shone through patchy, fast-moving cloud. I fancied I could smell the coasts of Asia, though I knew it would be some time before we sighted Batoum. The wounded English officer nodded to me as he limped past, leaning on his walking stick, his face pale with pain, his Indian batman a pace or two behind him, showing poorly-disguised concern for his master. The woman with the cards, my own personal Moira, played on, her black shawl rising and falling on her shoulders like the wings of a lazy scavenger. And the Jew Hernikof was there, offering a feeble grin, as if our contact of last night had made us boon friends. There was something about his features which still reminded me of the pathetic Brodmann. I did not want trouble. I nodded to him distantly and tried to walk on. But he followed. He was eager. 'I hope you weren't offended by anything I said last night. I can't remember too clearly. I suppose I'm not completely recovered. I'm normally not much of a drinker, anyway.'

'It's of no importance.' To escape, I began to climb the metal ladder to the forecastle. He clucked like a sick chicken and his feet moved involuntarily as if scratching gravel. Evidently he was frustrated at not being able to follow me.

'I think I might have lost my usual sense of decorum. The experiences were painful, you know.' His voice was hoarse, even desperate, as he craned his neck.

'We have all had them.' I reached the forecastle and peered down at him. There was nowhere else to go. At my back was the sea, parting in white foam before the bow.

'Oh, of course.' Again the hesitant grimace of a smile. 'They will never end, I suppose, for the likes of us.'

34

I was offended by his presumptive claim to be Russian. As I turned away I heard him say: '*Der Krieg ist endlos. Das Beste, was wir erhoffen können, sind gelegenliche Augenblicke der Ruhe inmitten des Kampfes.*'

I understood him perfectly but chose to tell him coldly and in Russian, 'I do not speak Yiddish.'

He protested. 'It is German. I gathered you're a linguist.' He blinked, too short-sighted to see me properly yet trying to read my expression.

I became furious. 'Is this a test, M. Hernikof? Do you think I am not what I say I am? Do you suspect I'm an *agent provocateur*? A Boche? A Red?'

He pretended innocence. 'Of course not!'

'Then please do not pursue me about this ship shouting at me in foreign languages.'

As he turned away his lips were trembling. Had I not guessed his intentions I might have felt pity for him. But he meant me no good. Also it was not in my interest to be seen hobnobbing with someone of his persuasion. Later it occurred to me that because of my dark hair and brown eyes he believed me a co-religionist; not the first time such a mistake had been made. The same looks were once likened to those of the Tsarevitch himself! Were the Tsar and his family Jewish? Friends have told me all my life I should not take such misunderstandings to heart. But it is a cruel thing, and sometimes dangerous, to be the victim of that particular error. On occasions it almost cost me my life. I was able to escape only by means of sharp wits, excellent credentials and a little good fortune.

After breakfast I joined Leda as usual. She was sitting outside the dining-saloon beneath the shadow of a lifeboat which swung gently in its davits. The sun was beginning to shine quite strongly and she held up her face as if a pale ray or two could warm her. She smiled at me. She pushed back her heavy hair so that the sun might touch as much of her flesh as possible. 'Good morning, Maxim Arturovitch.' We were always formal on such occasions. I lifted my hat and asked if I might bring a deckchair to sit next to her. I think she could see I was disturbed. 'Did you sleep badly?' Her strong hand moved a fraction towards me. She straightened herself a little. 'Only for want of you,' I whispered. Kitty came running up. She wore a maroon coat with matching hat and gloves. 'Will you play with me today, Maxim Arturovitch? I'm beginning to think you don't love me any more!' I was frequently struck, as now, by her remarkable resemblance to her mother. For a moment I was filled with enormous lust.

Leda laughed. 'You're a bad girl, Kitty. A flirt! What will become of you?' Yet I was forced to be her donkey, galloping round the deck two or three times with her warm little thighs pressed into my waist, before I feigned exhaustion. When I returned to my chair I found Hernikof balanced against the bulkhead. He was chatting to the Baroness who, well-mannered as always, seemed perfectly happy to give him the time of day. I seated myself without a word and pretended total concentration upon a paper aeroplane for the little girl, delighting in the sensation of her lovely, delicate flesh leaning against my own. I was so enraptured that I hardly noticed Hernikof leave.

'That poor man,' said Leda. 'You have heard his story I suppose.'

'I've heard a thousand like it. That poor man is, at best, an opportunist. I've been trying to shake him off since last night.'

'He's lonely.' She had that streak of philosemitism so familiar in romantic German women of the same generation and since I had no wish to upset her I remained silent. It was not impossible, I thought, that her own husband's origins had a touch or two of the Levant in them. 'He's a bore.' I finished the aeroplane and handed it to Kitty. The child immediately launched it into the wind. It disappeared on the other side of the bridge and she ran off in pursuit. Leda was laughing. 'You're certainly out of sorts today. Have I offended you?'

I was actually half-mad with a mixture of lust and rage. 'Not at all!' I reassured her enthusiastically. I drew in several salty breaths. 'If I seem in poor spirits it is because I've been separated from you for too long.'

Her face was glowing; she was at once amused and flattered. She controlled her own breathing. 'Well, I want you to try to be polite to M. Hernikof. Everyone on this ship snubs him. He's been very ill. And he lost his entire family, you know.'

I held my tongue.

'He was acquainted with my late husband. They occasionally had business in common. He was then very powerful. A financier. He still has considerable interests abroad. Perhaps he could be helpful, when your mission is over, in backing some of your inventions.' She arranged her plaid rug over her knees, her hand lingering in her lap.

I could not believe she did not know what Jewish money meant: it corrupted; the best of mankind's motives were twisted by it and always utilised to the benefit of Zion. How could she have witnessed the descent of Russia into Chaos and barbarism and still not understand the chief cause? Like many women she was moved too much by a personal liking for individuals. Probably the Hernikof who charmed her was in himself no villain. But he represented the forces which most threatened our Christian civilization. I saw no point in mindlessly attacking such a man. I never approved of concentration camps and pogroms; yet there were sound reasons for these things. And there were reasons for being suspicious of any smiling Jew who held out his bag of silver to you. Where did he acquire that silver? Ask Judas. Would the truth come cheerfully and spontaneously to his lips? Would it to any man's who had done what he had done?

'I have no desire,' I said to Leda, 'to be rude. All I meant to say was that I've little in common with him and have no intention of becoming his closest friend!'

'You're as much a snob as the rest,' she said. 'It's incredible.'

I refused to answer at first. Then it occurred to me to tell her how I had been betrayed by a Jew; how I had almost lost my life. I turned to speak.

She smiled at me. 'Well,' she said, ending the matter, 'he's a decent, kindly man. How lovely a little sunshine is after all that dreadful greyness.' She touched my arm, careless of the stares of the two little old monkey-sisters as they passed us. She put her face close to mine. 'I think sexual frustration is ruining your temper.'

I made an effort to seem cheerful. I smiled. The sun caught the waves for a second and turned them to silver. 'It's hard to live this ridiculous charade.'

'And your Mrs Cornelius? Has she complained?' The warmth of her voice was at odds with the nature of her question.

'She knows nothing.'

'I doubt that. Still, young Mr Bragg takes up most of her attention.'

A little offended, I bridled. 'She finds him amusing company, no more.' I had told her of the bargain between myself and Mrs Cornelius, how my companion intended to see her Frenchman as soon as we reached Constantinople. I suspected the Baroness of jealousy. She had somehow guessed, as women will, my feelings towards Mrs Cornelius and she was sounding me out, I knew. I remained on guard, even when she responded mysteriously: 'Then you have a wonderful means of avoiding certain evidence, my dear, for you are not a total innocent. I bow to the power of your imagination.'

This puzzled me. 'I fail to see the connection between my imagination, which many have praised, and my innocence, which few have remarked upon since I was sixteen.'

I could not understand why she was close to laughter, though I was relieved that she was not pursuing the matter of Mrs Cornelius. 'Oh, I know you have seen much more of life than I.' She made an exaggerated gesture of obeisance. 'And you are much better educated in almost every respect. Indeed, your only disadvantage in life, as far as I can see, is that you are male.'

That was my cue to dismiss her mysteries. Whenever a woman begins to speak cryptically of secret, female knowledge it is always best to ignore her. She is murmuring a spell which has meaning only to herself (if it has meaning at all). What a woman cannot verbalize she will classify, with superb pretence at authority, under the general heading of 'what a woman knows.' Thus, in argument, she baffles her male opponent, gaining the advantage while he wonders what it is his poor, insensitive masculine brain cannot comprehend. Frequently my confidence has been threatened by this trick. I have only recovered by virtue of my superior intelligence and perception. Why else would so many women have loved and admired me in my lifetime? They soon learn respect for someone who refuses to be drawn into their little traps. Life is in many ways an ongoing contest (which is possibly what Hernikof meant). We must forever be alert, particularly against those who claim they have our best interests at heart. None respects female intuition more than I, but sometimes women will read far too much into a simple situation. So it was with my Baroness. Infatuated with me, she presumed therefore that all women must be desperate to lure me to their beds. I was amused by her curiosity, but remained anxious lest it turn into that crazed feminine jealousy which is, at very least, inconvenient and often very dangerous. In the afternoon we made love as usual, drenched in our mutual fluids until we stank, as she put it, 'like cats on heat.' By now I was halfway to promising her a few days at least in Constantinople and she was growing excited in her anticipation. 'If only it could be sooner than that.' My hands were full of her flesh; of her breasts, her thighs and her buttocks and for a third time in succession I enjoyed the huge warmth of her magnificent cunt. She was like a Grecian goddess, and a welcome change from the young girls I usually chose. I felt I could disappear into her forever and remain safe from all the world's vicissitudes. In a woman like my Baroness it was possible to escape and explore simultaneously. As the dinner bell sounded I was still inside her. It was with considerable reluctance that we parted, washed as best we could, and emerged, reasonably well-groomed, to face the expressionless stare of Marusya Veranovna, the excited cries of young Kitty, full of the day's adventures.

Leda did not seem especially concerned, yet I had begun to resent the servant's unspoken criticism of us. And I hated the circumstances which made us end our love-making sharp at six o'clock, no matter what we were doing. Constantinople seemed a year away.

At dinner, Mrs Cornelius said to me across the table: 'Yore lookin' worn art, Ivan. Did I keep yer up larst night? Sorry abart bein' sick.'

I waved a careless hand. She appeared not to remember the rest of the encounter and I was grateful for that. Attacking her meat-pudding with panache, she smiled around at the officers as if to include them in her apology. Captain Monier-Williams joined us. He looked proudly down at his own piece of pudding before beginning to eat. He often remarked how well his ship was feeding everyone. 'A good bit of duff keeps your strength up a treat.' He had heard we should be able to approach Batoum without danger. 'And probably dock in the harbour, thank goodness. They've had very little trouble so far.' He uttered a small sigh of satisfaction. 'After Batoum, we'll be heading back in the right direction. I suppose you'll both be pleased to get to Constantinople.'

'As punch,' said Mrs Cornelius. 'Though I can't say this 'asn't bin a nice trip.'

The captain picked up his knife and fork, staring purposefully at his dinner. 'Only a few more days, then. After that, it's home and Blighty!' He ended this conversation by placing a large piece of grey meat into his mouth and chewing slowly. He dearly wished to be back in Dorset where he had lately bought a small house for his retirement, but had gone through the whole war as a volunteer troopship commander. All his male relatives had served either in the Royal Navy or the Merchant Marine and he spoke frequently of sons and nephews who had sailed with this ship or that. He was luckier than most, he told us, and had lost only two. He knew of whole family names which had been extinguished between 1914 and 1918.

As he ate I said to him, 'I agree with Mrs Cornelius. This has been, all things considered, a wonderful voyage. The Russian people will forever be grateful to you. There are some aboard who already think you little short of a saint.'

This brought a response. He swallowed his food and smiled. 'I'm doing my duty, Mr Pyatnitski. It's the British taxpayer they should canonise.'

'For my part, that debt shall be settled soon, sir. I suspect that when the Reds have reduced my country to total chaos a reasonable government will be called back. Only at that time shall I consider going home. By then I shall have passed on one or two ideas to your people which I'm sure they'll find useful. There's a strong chance I shall be a member of the future Russian government. In that case, England shall have a friend in me.'

He shook his head at this. 'If it happens I'll be the first to cheer. But my experience, old chap, is once a country embarks on a course of bloody uprising and counter-coups there's no restoring possible. Look how China is fragmenting. The pattern's already set.'

'Russia is not China, captain. Nor is she Indo-China, ruled over by a dozen contentious rajahs.' I was gentle but direct. 'She is a great imperial nation. Order must eventually prevail. The Russian people already cry out for a new Tsar.'

'Oh, I'm sure they'll get one,' he said. 'Of some sort.' And he remarked on the excellent suet in his mouth.

At that time I was upset by his apparent cynicism, but he was over sixty years old and I not yet twenty. His prediction proved, of course, to be completely accurate. I could not have afforded to believe it then, however, and retained my sanity.

Meanwhile, Mrs Cornelius took no interest in our conversation. She remained discreetly silent while Captain Monier-Williams discussed the characters of Trotski and Lenin as if he knew them personally. She had, of course, indeed known Trotski intimately and Lenin pretty well, and sometimes I detected amusement in her glance when the captain or one of his officers spoke authoritatively about Trotski's motives.

Jack Bragg, being something of a Red sympathiser, professed admiration for the Russian people. He admitted respect for Kerenski. At this I could not keep my peace. 'Lenin might be the chief villain now,' I said, 'but Kerenski's irresponsible and euphoric liberalism led to the present crisis. If Kerenski had been stronger he would have kept Russia in the War and we should have won. Constantinople would now be unequivocally Russian, as has always been agreed with the Allies. Rather than losing territory almost daily to our former subjects, we'd be reaping the benefits of victory. Kerenski sold us to Lenin and Lenin sold us to the Germans and the Jews. Soon Russia will have no more of a "homeland" than the Ottomans now possess. She will merely be Muscovy again. A shrunken Muscovy at that. As a result, every Western border will be overrun. Can't you see? We have held back the barbarian from Europe for a thousand years. Now Tatars will reclaim their old Empire. They will league with Turkey to establish the most powerful Moslem domain the world has seen! The Allies must remain firm and destroy Lenin. Russia must have more help, or civilisation itself will die. Christianity will be crushed.' I addressed this last remark directly to Captain Monier-Williams who shook his head. 'I can't see it, old man. I suppose you can hope a more moderate leader will emerge, but God knows what "moderate" means in this context.'

I could scarcely keep from weeping. His boyish features red with embarrassment, Jack Bragg put an understanding hand on my arm. 'You'll be back before you know it, Mr Pyatnitski. The Allies are bound to send more help. Then all this beastliness will be over.'

I made a small gesture of thanks. As he turned away I noticed a tear or two in his own honest blue eyes. He seemed so young, yet he was probably two or three years older than I. His was genuine sympathy, however, for he had known the horrors of sea-warfare and better than most was able to imagine my ordeal. A little in my cups by now, I spoke of all I had lost: the mellow glories of Kiev, the wide steppe, the rich mingling of cultures in old Odessa, the cool beauty of Petersburg, the comradeship of my fellow students, the charm of Kolya and his bohemian friends. Sometimes I could feel almost nostalgic for my months with the anarchist Makhno! I spoke of Yermeloff the Cossack who, in his way, had befriended me and had been killed as a result. But it was a mistake to resurrect such memories, for next I began to speak of Esmé. I checked myself and left the company as soon as dinner was over. Passing a small table near the door, where four passengers sat, I saw with some distaste that Hernikof had somehow managed to place himself opposite my Baroness and actually had his hand on Kitty's arm! In further confusion I went directly out on deck, into a cold wind, a curtain of drizzle.

Leda joined me almost at once. I said nothing about Hernikof, for I knew what her answer would be. 'Is something wrong?' she asked. She began to guide me into the darkness, avoiding the ship's lights and stopping at last in the shadow of the afterdeck. I listened to the screw turning through the water. I heard the movement of our pistons. I knew our machinery almost as well as Mr Thompson. I recovered myself and kissed her gently on the cheek. 'These English people mean well,' I said, 'but they occasionally revive memories which are best left to die.'

She understood. She stroked my face with her soft, loving hand. 'That is why we learn the habit of never asking questions,' she said. 'Of waiting until we are told.'

I looked at her a little sharply, wondering if there were anything more in what she said. But she seemed sincere. She did not have quite the same ability as Mrs Cornelius to make me relax, but she was calming me now. I sighed and from its case took one of my last papyrussa. Using a brass 'everlasting match' which someone had given me as part payment for passport work, I lit the cigarette with care. She leaned against me, chiefly to shelter herself from the cold wind which blew now from the North East. 'It is so hard to imagine the future,' she said.

'You mean in your personal life?'

She smiled. 'You, of course, have a very good idea of what the future should be like, even if your dream never comes true. That must give your life the momentum which mine, for instance, lacks. All I have is Kitty. She's my only reason for going to Berlin, where I may find some security, a good school. Yet I'm dependent on the kindness of distant relatives. My destiny is in their hands.'

'It was once the same for me.' I drew carefully on the papyrussa. The tobacco was too dry and the whole thing threatened to fall from its paper tube. 'It's terrible to be made a child again. And all for the sake of a real child, too. Is there no work you could do?'

She held out her hand to take the cigarette from me. She puffed at it once or twice, then gave it back. 'I was trained to be the wife of an eminent industrialist. Nothing else. The likes of me, my dear, are a glut on the market. There are thousands of us all over the world and only a handful of eminent industrialists! Some of us try to poach from those who have one; others become lost in a kind of mental haze. I even heard of one or two who took up with completely unsuitable young men.' Though she joked I became again suspicious. Did she now have it in mind to turn me into the creature she would best like to marry?

'You are intelligent and personable,' I told her. 'You have a little capital in Germany, eh? You should think of going into business. Become an eminent industrialist in your own right! Go to Paris. All the best Russians are in Paris. Found a Fashion Salon. Or a secretarial agency.' My imagination failed me.

'I would rather,' she teased, 'become an international adventuress and bring down kings and emperors.'

'But this is the age of republics and democracies. It is so much harder to seduce and ruin a committee.'

She laughed at this. 'Maxim Arturovitch, you are insufficiently romantic tonight. It's my function to be the realist, yours to be the dreamer. Would you rob me of my only portion?'

I forced myself to dismiss my suspicions. 'Very well, I shall continue to dream for you. And you may continue to be a sceptic. But I assure you the future I plan is very practical. A scientist makes it his business to know how things work, to be aware of the proper place of every nut and bolt.'

We parted at her cabin door. 'Until tomorrow,' she said, and then: 'We shall be able to be together in Constantinople at least for a while I hope.'

'I hope so.'

She said hastily, 'Batoum is safe. Couldn't we go ashore there?'

I agreed to consider the idea, which had not occurred to me. While I would be glad to break the journey I remained wary of our intimacy deepening, particularly at an earlier stage than I had planned. I returned to my cabin. As usual when Mrs Cornelius was absent, I indulged myself in a larger than usual sniff of cocaine for, by all accounts, Constantinople had become the capital of the drug world and I would be in no danger of running out of that particular means of moral support. I have never been addicted to anything in my life. I smoke and drink and take cocaine from choice; they give me pleasure. The mild effects of deprivation from cigarettes or from 'neige' are hardly noticeable when I am busy. Anyway, I would not buy what today's hairy children call 'cocaine'. It is no more than a mixture of household powders touched up with a taste or two of quinine or procaine to numb the lips and a dash of amphetamine to simulate the euphoric effect. One might as well mix ginger beer with dish-washing liquid and call it champagne!

They think they are so modern and daring with their 'narcotics.' They soften their brains with marijuana and sleeping pills to the point where they cannot tell one drug from another. I despise them, in their leather jackets; they look the same as those barbarians who swaggered through the Winter Palace in 1917, thinking they knew everything when all they had was a monumental arrogance born of stupidity. I see them every day, across the street, in Finch's pub. They whisper together and pass little paper packets back and forth and every so often the police come, bored and irritable, to perform some ritual search and take one or two of them away. They toady to negroes. The police merely restore the belief of these louts in their 'outlaw pride'. There is nothing different about them. No wonder the use of cocaine is frowned upon these days. In my youth it was the drug of the aristocrat, the artist, the scientist, the doctor. Ask anyone. Even Freud. And I have made no secret of my dislike for his views. (The Triumvirate which destroyed our civilisation is Marx, Freud, Einstein. It will be remembered in a million years as the greatest enemy of mankind. Marx attacked the basic foundations of Christian society. Freud attacked our minds so we doubted every opinion. Einstein attacked the very substance of the universe. And they say Goebbels was a Master of Lies! He was an *ingénu*. How that Triumvirate must laugh as it pushes down fragile walls and monuments, tramples the ikons, stands, with hands on hips, amongst the rubble of the world's greatness while rivers of blood wash its feet and Hope and Humanity are defeated, dying in flames whose light casts a monstrous shadow over the world; the shadow of the Beast, the three-headed symbol of Death.)

Freud himself helped ruin the reputation of cocaine. But they have no need to consider my arrest. I will not use that adulteration of talc and scouring powder they try to sell me.

Quietly enjoying my isolation, I lay down on my bunk to consider Leda's suggestion. It would be pleasant to go ashore in Batoum. By all accounts it was a handsome enough town, though full of Moslems. We would probably find a hotel without much difficulty and spend a night or two together. This would be both a holiday and an amiable way of easing our inevitable parting. Yet if she saw this as a sign of our enjoying a longer liaison it could cause embarrassment in the future. For all my caution lust once again triumphed and I decided to ask the captain what he thought of some of us going ashore. I would not, though, put the question at dinner for fear of hurting Mrs Cornelius's feelings, so I would seek the Old Man out next day and have a word with him alone.

I was asleep by the time Mrs Cornelius returned. I awoke to hear

44

whispering on the other side of the door and realised Jack Bragg was with her. I heard her giggle. There was a scuffle. It was obvious that he had also temporarily lost control of himself. In order to save them both embarrassment, I called, as if startled, 'Who's there?'

The whispering subsided. I believe she kissed him and murmured goodnight. When she closed the door behind her she asked if I would mind her turning up the lamp. I said it was all right. She was dishevelled and tipsy, but her usual happy self. She waved her fingers at me. 'Orl alone, Ive?'

She sat on the edge of her bunk to remove her shoes. She was wearing another frock, a pink and silver one. She had managed to bring a large, up-to-date wardrobe in several trunks. Mrs Cornelius always was fastidious about her clothes, at least when she could afford it. In later years poverty conquered both of us and we were forced to lower our standards considerably. 'Phew!' she said. 'It's a party ev'ry night aboard this bloody boat, innit!'

'Your energy is boundless.' I was admiring. 'It would exhaust me.'

'I'm sorta makin' up fer lorst time. That Leon was such a bleedin' pill. Fergot 'ow ter enjoy 'imself. They're orl ther bloody same.' Her view of the Bolshevik leaders was contemptuous and universally dismissive: they were a bunch of pious hypocrites, repressed middle-class intellectuals. If they had let their hair down a bit they might have been much happier and caused a lot less trouble. Not one of them, she would occasionally tell me in confidence, was any good as a lover. 'And some of 'em 're downright odd!' She had a soft spot for loonies. 'I'll prob'bly orlways end up wiv blokes 'oo're a bit potty. They're more int'restin', at least at first.'

With her usual skill she got into her nightclothes, smoked a cigarette, read a page or two of one of her 'books' – old popular magazines someone had found for her on the ship – and turned the lamp down. 'Night-night, Ivan.' Again I was left with only her snores which, in the darkness, could still be mistaken for the pantings and exhalations of lust. And as usual I sought consolation in masturbation and fantasy, recalling my lovely Slav only a hundred yards from where I lay. I was now determined to spend all the time I could with her in Batoum.

I was up early, having decided I might best consider my plans in the fresh air. Our cabin was always extremely stuffy by morning. We had the choice of taking the rags and newspapers from the louvres of the door and freezing, or being virtually unable to breathe. As I dressed,

45

Mrs Cornelius shifted in her bunk. Sleepily she said: 'You watch yer don' get in too deep, Ivan. Yore a clever littel bleeder, but yer got no sense . . .' Then her eyes closed and she was snoring. She had said nothing new. She believed me headstrong, my own worst enemy. She would tell me so through all the years to come, almost to her dying day (though I was kept from the deathbed by jealous relatives). I have been praised and condemned by great leaders, famous artists and intellectuals, but only her opinion was worth anything to me. Everyone remembers her; she became a legend. Novels were written about her, just as novels were written about Makhno. She could wrap politicians and generals around her fingers. She never lied to me.

'They should've given yer the Nobel Prize, Ivan,' she said one night in *The Elgin*. 'If only fer tryin'.' It was just before closing time on a Saturday night. The pub was a favourite with gypsies from the Westway camp; it was full of rowdy fiddles and accordions. They were the same seedy kind who had infested Odessa and Budapest and Paris fifty years before. It was almost impossible to stand up without being pushed over. Mrs Cornelius was rarely given to betraying strong feelings, but five pints of mild-and-bitter had relaxed her tongue. She felt sorry for me: it was not long after my last trouble with the Courts. I had also been insulted by a cloth-capped junk man, reeking of urine and motor-oil, when I tried to get to the bar. She was trying to show she at least still recognised my gifts. From Mrs Cornelius it was worth more than a knighthood. I am glad she was able to speak before she died, confirming her faith in me. That memory alone sustains me. I have suffered injustice for too long. Now there is no hope.

I helped her through the sweating singers in their collarless shirts and greasy coats, into the dark rain of Ladbroke Grove where the buses and lorries splashed and grumbled. I took her in my arms. She felt sick, she said. She bent over the gutter outside her flat in Blenheim Crescent, but nothing came up. Even then it was apparent she was very ill. She was dying. There was no need for her to lie. We were always honest with each other. She had a nose for genius, even if it were sometimes corrupt. Trotski, Mussolini, Goering: she had known them all. She shook her head. 'They never give ya yore due, Ivan.' It was true. She alone could testify that, but for the Bolsheviks, every Russian honour would today be mine. I would be a world name.

The Poles called the Tsarist Empire 'Byzantium' and use the same word today for the Soviet Union. The Polish talent for piety is almost as great as their talent for laziness. I did not become an émigré merely to own a little house in Putney and work for a record company. They are not martyrs. They are self-pitying *petit bourgeoisie*. They would complain under any regime. I wish people would stop introducing them to me. It is the same with the Czechs. We have nothing in common beside basic Slavonic. During the War it was all Poles. Now it is all Czechs. Mrs Cornelius told the neighbours how great I had been and how I had suffered. But I did not want their pity. I gambled, I said to her, and I lost. NONARAO, YTO STO TAK.

I go up to the canal near Harrow Road. It is so bleak there. Everything is rotting. Everything is grey. There is slime on the water. The tow-path is littered with filth. I look at the backs of derelict buildings where unhealthy children smash the remaining windows and piss on floorboards which are beds for tramps. They spray the bricks with their excrement and illiterate slogans. This is Sunday afternoon and this is my exercise! My day off, my stroll, my relaxation! I have seen the wonders of Constantinople, the glories of Rome, the masculine grandeur of Berlin before they bombed it, the elegance of Paris, the brutal magnificence of New York, the dreaming luxury of Los Angeles. I have worn silk from top to bottom. I have satisfied my lust with women of outstanding beauty and breeding. I have experienced at first hand all the world's noblest engineering miracles: the great liners, the skyscrapers, the planes and the airships. I have known the exhilaration of rapid, luxurious travel. But now I totter along a disgusting tow-path, staring at flotsam and smeared walls, terrified in my frailty for my worthless old life, praying I do not slip on a dog turd or attract the ruthless curiosity of some prepubescent footpad. Their noises echo over the water; the mysterious croaks and grunts of primitive amphibians heralding a return to bloody ignorance and unsentient savagery.

I have been here nearly half my life! Since 1940, in one part of London. *Dopoledne* . . . The first half was spent exploring and instructing the entire civilised world. Major Sinclair, the great American aviator and my mentor, warned me I was not doing the fashionable things. He too was ruined for his unpopular views. His friend Lindbergh was another great man brought low by petty, vicious enemies. Lindbergh once told me his closest-kept secret. He had never meant to fly to England at all. He had originally set out for Bolivia, but his instruments had deceived him. We had much in common, Lindbergh and myself. He knew why the Jews destroyed the *Hindenburg*.

47

Under the arches of the motorway (with which 'planners' bisected Notting Dale and Ladbroke Grove without a thought for those who have to live below) gypsies build shacks of old doors and corrugated iron, parking battered caravans amongst heaps of rubble and scrap. Their thin dogs run everywhere; their children are dirty and neglected. The wonderful modern road speeds traffic to and from the West, from Bristol and Bath and Oxford where people live in eighteenth-century elegance. It is a white, efficient road and has done much, they say, to remove traffic from residential streets. But to build it they had to knock our houses down. Unstable, featureless towers were erected in their place. On both sides of Ladbroke Grove, in the shadows of the Westway, stagger alcoholics of both sexes, young and old, begging for coins to buy methylated spirits, swearing at you if you dare to refuse. Or at night lounging boys accost you, their black faces snarling threats. From within the concrete caves butane gas sputters, just as the naphtha flared above the market-stalls in winter in old Kiev. They built a great white road to the West and thus created a warren for thieves and skinheads who cling to the surface of civilisation like detritus around a boat. Yet without civilisation they could not survive.

I do not say Portobello Road and Notting Dale were perfect. Taxi-drivers refused to take you to Golborne Road at night. We were famous for our prostitutes and half the population was on the borderline of crime. Policemen went in threes through our alleys. But the social workers and politicians told us this would be changed. The road, they said, would abolish injustice and squalor. The filthy lorries would go. There would be paradise in the city. And what do we have?

Rock and roll bands give free concerts in the motorway bays and exhort their audience to Revolution and the smoking of hashish. Whores give their customers a cheap time against the pillars and negro homosexuals squabble and shriek while the traffic moans above their heads, taking the Lords and Ladies to Bath and Oxford and Heathrow. Those planners dreamed of Utopia but denied all reality. Then Utopia was no longer financially possible. Perhaps it never had been. Nonetheless, they continued to build as if nothing had changed. They built their wonderful road, much as the natives of New Guinea build bamboo aeroplanes to coax back the marvellous cargoes which came from the sky during World War II.

They told us they would plant flower-gardens in the mud they had created. *It is bezhlavy.* They said they would build theatres and shops

48

and provide social services under the Westway: but they have even failed to deal with the gypsies who fight and drink beneath the arches from Shepherds Bush to Little Venice; murdering one another, beating their wives and children, refusing either education or work, while youth gangs menace old-age pensioners and wheezing mental-deficients display their diseased genitalia to little boys. And they had the temerity to laugh at me for my dreams! Is their Utopia any worse than mine? And where is the prosperity we were to see? The traders come from their suburbs to the Portobello Road on Fridays and Saturdays, wearing their bohemian finery, selling their high-priced junk. They make a tourist attraction of a slum. And they turn the tourist attraction even more into a slum when they leave. I see the bewildered Americans on a Thursday, wandering up and down the dirty streets looking for the glamour which, like a travelling fair, is only there at certain times, disguising the permanence of poverty and ignorance. Where are the Beatles and the bobbies on bicycles, two by two? Where are the great walls of Windsor and the bells of Old St Paul's? They have no wish for anything but the romance. On a Thursday, we are not capable of providing it.

Does any of that tourist money stay here? No. It is taken back to Surbiton and Twickenham and Purley; and at night the muggers and the alcoholics re-emerge as if nothing has occurred to interrupt their routines. The tourists return to Brown's and White's and the Inn On The Park. *Up the West End, that's the best end . . .* Disneyworld last year, Englandworld this. Each country a different theme-park, existing in isolation, cosmetically perfect. And the Westway carries the buses and the sports cars and the trucks over the grime, the unromantic desperate poverty, and nobody need ever know in what human degradation its great pillars are sunk. But it made a profit for Mr Marples and Mr Ridgeway; it made a profit for the speculators of the swinging sixties, the Feinsteins and the Goldblatts and the Greenburgs.

Mrs Cornelius hated the Westway. She said it destroyed the character of the neighbourhood. It attracted outsiders, too, who had no business coming. 'This woz orlways a friendly district. Everyone knew everyone else. Now 'arf ther people in ther noo flats 're from Tower 'Amlets an' Spitalfields. No bleedin' wonder there's more crime abart. They know their mums carn't spot 'em.' She firmly believed most thieves were young and did not properly understand the rules: you did not steal from your own. The old family gangs of Notting Dale used to fight amongst themselves. If you were not associated with the gangs you were left alone. The break-up of the family has had consequences even the Church could not anticipate. But we are watching civilization itself collapse, after all, throughout the Christian world. The Hun swarms again over our ruins and hucksters unpack their stalls in our holy places; travelling players perform lewd charades in our churches while the patrician hides in his villa outside the city, afraid to raise his voice against the very people who bought his birthright. So History repeats and Christ looks down on us and weeps. I thought to save the world from meanness and cruelty; instead I have survived to witness its degeneration. I might even live to see its final destruction.

I did my best. Mrs Cornelius alone appreciated the appalling irony of my life. I was a genius, but I lacked an appreciation of Evil. My Baroness called me 'charmingly amoral.' By this I think she meant the same thing.

Three

WE ARE THE shifting pastures on which the microbes graze, our dead skin is their sustenance and we are their universe. Perhaps we move in orbits as predictable to them as planets and that is why mosquitoes always know where to find us. It might only be delusion which makes us believe we travel at random or according to individual volition. Russian soil was to know my feet sooner than I might ever have guessed when I left Odessa. It was probably pre-ordained. I impressed the captain with a suggestion of business in Batoum important to the Government forces, so he willingly gave me leave to spend time ashore. The Baroness, too, would be allowed to go, though he made it clear he would not be responsible for any passengers who failed to board by the time the ship sailed again. 'We remain under orders to take off as many refugees as we can reasonably accommodate, Mr Pyatnitski. However, we are not a civilian vessel and there's some urgency about our commission, as I'm sure you understand.'

I gave him my word I would be on deck when the *Rio Cruz* cast off from Batoum. 'I hope to contact certain anti-Bolshevik elements while ashore,' I said. He said my reasons were my own affair. I immediately sought out Leda Nicolayevna who of course was delighted with my news and already planned to leave Kitty and the nanyana on board. Her excuse was that she planned to shop for a day or two. She thought we should stay just one night and return to the ship. If the *Rio Cruz* was still not ready to sail, we could then spend another night in Batoum, and so on. 'But how shall we find a hotel?'

'I will solve the problem easily,' I told her. 'I have lived by my wits all my life. I am extremely resourceful.'

Her love-making that afternoon was if anything more joyously zestful than ever and eagerly I began to look forward to our 'shore-leave' as she called it.

By breakfast-time next morning the air was much warmer but it had begun to rain with steady persistence. At the table, Captain Monier-Williams announced we should be docking in Batoum within two hours. 'It will be a relief to put in to a port where some sort of order survives.' This was his third visit in two months. The British had administered both town and harbour for almost a year. 'Though God knows what it's like now. The last time I spoke to Drake, the Captain of the Port, he was at his wit's end. Huge numbers flooding in from all over Russia.'

'The British should be flattered,' I said. 'It means they're trusted.'

'If you don't mind me saying so, Mr Pyatnitski, it's a terrible burden. What happens when we leave?'

'They'll pack up and move across the border into Turkey.' Jack Bragg cheerfully attempted to save my feelings. 'They can't be worse off.' Anatolia was only ten miles from Batoum. 'Perhaps we should go the whole hog and declare the place a British Protectorate?'

'I'm not sure the Russian Army would be pleased to hear that.' Captain Monier-Williams offered me a dry little smile. 'Anyway, at least here we'll get a fairly clear idea of what our job's supposed to be. Anyone wishing to go ashore had better get a chit from Mr Larkin.' The Second Officer was acting as purser and as liaison between the Russian passengers and the British crew. Mrs Cornelius was not yet up and I was grateful. I would have been embarrassed had she been there before I was able to tell her my plans. 'I'll warn you,' the captain went on, 'that Bolshevik agents are everywhere in town. A fair bit of sabotage and general mayhem, I gather. So be careful who you talk to.' This was addressed to us all. 'And we'll be checking papers and possessions pretty carefully when you come back. We don't want any bombs slipped into your suitcases.' He spoke sardonically, but it was evident his attitude towards his job was unchanged. He was as impatient as anyone to reach Constantinople.

As I rose to leave, the seedy Hernikof sidled up to the captain. He was dressed in dreadful tweed and smoking a German cigar. His unsteady eyes and weak mouth seemed to race through a dozen different configurations as if he sought the combination most agreeable to our commander. 'Sir,' he said thickly, in English, 'I would be grateful for a word.'

Monier-Williams, I am sure, liked him no better than I, but he was polite and patient with the Jew, as he was with all of us. Hernikof spoke softly and I could not understand him. I was anxious to withdraw, so made an excuse and went out on deck to join my Baroness forward. She was standing by the rail under her wide umbrella, dressed in dark blue. Kitty was playing nearby with two little wooden dolls, under the shelter of the bridge, while Marusya Veranovna sat stolidly beside her, at attention on a folding stool, eyeing the dolls as if they might be rabid. I lifted my hat to them both as the Baroness turned, smiling at me. We exchanged our usual fairly formal greeting, then I said quietly, 'In two hours we'll reach Batoum. But you must see Mr Larkin and obtain a pass. It will look best, I think, if we go separately.'

'Of course.' She had on new perfume. There were roses in it and it seemed to promise summer. For a few moments, while she went over to tell her servant that she would be gone for a while, I was reminded of my childhood, of the scent of lilac in Kiev at springtime, of cornfields and poppies and picking long-stemmed wild-flowers in the gorges with Esmé. I would have given anything to have returned for a little while to that relaxed state of innocence which had been completely destroyed in less than an hour, when I found Esmé in the anarchist's camp and she was laughing about what had become of her. She had been raped so many times, she said, she had callouses on her cunt. It would never again be possible to be sweetly, ordinarily, carelessly in love. I longed for that foolish happiness. I longed to re-experience it with my Leda, to believe our union unique, eternal. But it was impossible. With the exception of Mrs Cornelius, women were now a threat to my well-being. They betrayed one's finer feelings. I trusted men no better; but one did not as a rule put one's heart into the hands of a man. And children, as I was to learn again and again, can be the worst betrayers of all.

The Baroness returned in good spirits, with her pass. When I got to the saloon, however, I had to join a line of about ten people. I was immediately behind the odious Hernikof who turned and once again insisted on addressing me in tones of uncalled for intimacy. He would not be put off. He was telling me something about relatives he hoped to find in Batoum, the rumour that both Whites and Reds were ransoming Jews in order to finance their campaigns, that the Allies were discussing the idea of some Utopian Zionist State between Russia and Turkey to act as a kind of buffer against the Bolsheviks; so much nonsense I made myself deaf to it. Meanwhile Mr Larkin, long-faced and serious as always, with frowning concentration and glittering bald head, had seated himself at a little card table and busily checked papers or wrote short letters on sheets with the name of the ship stamped at the top. He spent far too long with Hernikof, but at last I received my own pass and he was quick enough, for of course he recognized me. A simple enough letter informing whomever it concerned that the undersigned, Maxim A. Pyatnitski, was travelling on His Majesty's Merchant Ship *Rio Cruz* from Odessa to Constantinople and had been granted permission to stay ashore in Batoum until five hours before the ship was due to leave port. I had to sign at the foot of the page and take my ordinary identity papers with me. 'The five hours bit is to be on the safe side,' said Mr Larkin. 'You shouldn't have any trouble if you're a little late.'

By the time I rejoined my Baroness, the coast was in sight, the rain had lifted and the horizon was beginning to brighten. 'Won't it be wonderful if there's sunshine?' She was animated. 'They say it's possible to have very warm days even at this time of year.'

I could not believe the British would abandon Batoum. 'Maybe we should think of settling there,' I said, phrasing as a joke my genuine distress at leaving Russian soil; distress which I knew she shared. She made a cheerful, fatalistic gesture. 'Let's enjoy the hours we have for what they are, not for what they might be.'

I decided to break the news to Mrs Cornelius. She was dressing when I knocked on the cabin door. 'Jes' give us arf a mo' ter get me knickers on.' She was looking extremely well, with her face flushed and her eyes bright, and she had on an orange dress. I told her I was going ashore to see Batoum for a day or so, hoping to look up one or two old friends.

'I'll prob'bly bump inter yer, then.' She grinned as she drew on her fox-fur wrap. 'I waz thinkin' o' poppin' over ther side fer a bit meself.' She laughed at my expression. 'Yer don' mind, do yer?'

It had not occurred to me she would want to leave the ship. I could do nothing but nod, shrug, smile, pack a change of clothes into my small folding bag and agree that we should think of having dinner somewhere together in Batoum. She was the last person I wanted to know of my liaison with the Baroness. I left the bag on my bunk and returned to the forward deck.

The water had grown suddenly blue and the clouds overhead had broken into white masses moving rapidly away to the North. As they rolled, the water became brighter, the ship's brass and woodwork glittered in the sun and we were like a golden barge afloat on a silver sea. Almost immediately everyone was out on deck, standing along the rails, removing clothing, chattering and laughing, like clerks and factory girls on a works outing. The wake of the ship broke behind us, cream foam on royal blue, and ahead were the snowy Caucasian peaks, the verdant slopes of the foothills, the contours of forests, even the faint suggestion of Batoum itself; hints of white and gold and grey, as the ship changed course and began to head directly for the shore.

The landscape was extraordinarily beautiful; a panorama of wooded hills and green valleys softened by the hazy sunshine. It seemed we had moved magically from the dead of winter into the simple fullness of spring. Flights of birds passed over dense forests. We saw pale smoke rising from pastel houses: a scene of astonishing peace for which we had been completely unprepared. People giggled and shook their heads like lunatics. More than one adult began to weep, perhaps in the belief we had been transported to Paradise. Gulls cackled in vulgar welcome and flung themselves into our rigging. The note of the engine grew brisker and merrier. Now we saw the ochre line of a long stone mole, the industrial buildings of an oil-harbour, the coaling-stations, the white quayside beyond, the sparkling domes of churches and mosques. British and Russian ships were tidily at rest alongside the landing-stages. Batoum was not a large town. She lacked the grandness of Yalta or the military solidity of Sebastopol, but in that haze, with her gilded roofs and her flags, she was infinitely more beautiful than any city we had ever seen. To us, used to uncertainty, destruction, death and danger, she looked at once fragile and permanent; a haven of security. She lay in a bay surrounded by densely wooded hills, with no major roads leading into her and only a railway connection with the rest of Russia. Her Oriental appearance made us feel that we had already reached our goal, that we were in legendary Constantinople, and we began to act as if this were indeed our ultimate destination. I was now genuinely tempted to have my trunks unloaded, to put down roots in soil which was, albeit Asian Russia, nonetheless still Russia. I have no idea what the result would have been had I followed my impulse. I nowadays sometimes wish I had chosen to leave the *Rio Cruz* there and then; but I was full of Mr Thompson's praise, of dreams of my great scientific career in London. I suppose I would have been frustrated in Batoum within a month. It was a beautiful oasis in a turbulent world; it would be years before its character was completely destroyed under Stalin. Yet it was not really the resting-place for a man who dreamed of gigantic aerial liners, of flying cities, and who carried in his wallet a new means of harnessing natural power.

Slowly the *Rio Cruz* eased her way into a space between a French frigate and a Russian merchantman, throwing her lines to waiting British sailors on the quay. Water slapped against warm stones smeared with bright green weed and rainbow oil. I smelled Batoum. I smelled damp foliage and roasting meat and mint and coffee. Palm-trees marched along her promenade; she had wide parks, public gardens full of feathery bamboo, eucalyptus, mimosa and orange trees; her streets were crowded with calm, dark buildings, the colour of vine-leaves, of rusty stone, brick or stucco. And flying high over what was obviously the public architecture near the centre of town, were the reassuring banners of two Empires, the Russian and the British. At dockside huts and customs houses smart Royal Navy bluejackets with carbines and bandoliers stood guard. The quayside was spotlessly clean. Polished brasswork and fresh paint was everywhere. I heard the hoot of motor-traffic, the clatter of trams, the familiar bustle of ordinary city streets. Through the lines of trees I made out hotels and shops, pavements populated with a mixture of races and classes. There were Russian, British and French uniforms, Moslem turbans and Greek fezzes, Parisian tailor-mades and Turkish tarbooshes. The Revolution had temporarily improved the life of Batoum, giving her an intellectual and fashionable element she had never previously possessed. I felt like a hound on a leash as I hurried to collect my little bag and wait impatiently at the side as the gang-plank was lowered. My pleasure was spoiled only by Hernikof's fat body sweating and eager (doubtless he had worked out a means of turning a profit while in Batoum) pressing against mine. He winked at me. 'A bit of a treat this, eh? Makes a change from stamping passports in Odessa, I shouldn't wonder.' Chilled by his casual intimacy with my past, I refused to be drawn and was hugely relieved when sailors and soldiers at last arranged themselves on the quay, barricades were drawn about the disembarking area, a desk was situated beside the gang-plank, officers checked one another's clipboards, shook hands, and finally the signal was given for passengers to come ashore. I was first down the bouncing causeway, well ahead of Hernikof, my coat flying, my collar open as I began to appreciate the heat. My gloves in my hand, my hat on the back of my head, I grinned like a chimpanzee at British officials who carefully inspected my papers, then handed them back to me. Abstractedly I nodded and mumbled at the Russian officer who searched through my bag and returned it. I almost sang to the Ukrainian NCO who again looked at my papers and checked my name and description in the large ledger he carried. He was a gigantic, fat man

56

with handle-bar moustaches and a kindly manner. 'Be careful, friend,' he murmured when I stepped at last through the final barricade and breathed the sweetly exotic air of Batoum. 'A good many people here don't accept there's a closed season for boorzhoos.' I turned to look at him sharply. He sounded like a Red. But he grinned. 'Just a well-intentioned word.'

When I saw that there were actually izvotchiks stationed beside the curb, underneath the palm-trees, I gasped with delight. The nags were almost as old as their drivers and the finery of the four-seaters was patched and faded, but one might have been in Petersburg before the War, or at least one of her suburbs. I approached the nearest. With his long whip, big coachman's coat, top-hat and thick, grey whiskers the cabby was an unchanged survivor from Tsarist days. I asked him what it would cost to take me to the best hotel in Batoum.

'The best, your honour?' A look of condescending good-humour came over his ruddy features. 'It's a matter of taste. And a matter of your politics, too, I'd say. Also a matter of there being enough room for you. What about the Oriental? It has a good view and reasonable food.' I think I actually gaped at him. He spoke pure Moscow Russian. 'How much? Well, it's a rouble, but nobody accepts roubles if they can help it. Have you any Turkish lira? Or British money would be best.'

'I've silver roubles. Real silver. No paper money.' In this respect the conversation was no different to any one might find elsewhere in Russia.

'Very well, your honour.' He scratched his cheek with the end of his long whip. 'Take your bag in with you. There's plenty of room.'

I was slow in doing as he suggested, for at last I saw the Baroness making her pre-arranged way along the pavement towards me. Then, to my horror, I realised her bag was being carried by the ubiquitous Hernikof. I did my best to ignore him as, according to plan, I raised my hat to her. 'Can I give you a lift, Baroness?' I had not, however, reckoned to have the company of a Jewish financier on our little idyll. He panted as he put the bag down, shifting his gaze from her to me and almost, I would swear, leering at us. She was polite. 'You are most kind, M. Hernikof. I think I will accept M. Pyatnitski's offer, however, since we were going in roughly the same direction.' She took her valise from his hand and placed it hesitantly on the ground. I placed my own bag in the coach and reached for hers. Hernikof smiled at me. 'Good morning again, M. Pyatnitski.'

'Good morning, Hernikof. I'm sorry I can't give you a lift.'

'It's of no consequence. I know my way about Batoum. Thank you.' I resented his insolent, mocking tone.

'You are too rude, Maxim.' She was embarrassed as she arranged herself in our carriage. 'You know poor Hernikof meant well. Are you jealous of him? He was not trying to impose.'

'I want to be alone with you.' I settled myself beside her. 'I'm determined we shall have an unspoiled holiday.' The cab started off at a smart Petersburg trot. With a petulant twist of her mouth she dismissed the subject of Hernikof. The sudden movement of the vehicle as it crossed the wide quayside towards the boulevard seemed to excite her and her lips opened as though she already gasped in the grip of a lust if anything greedier and hotter than my own. When we accidentally touched we could barely keep from embracing and in order to preserve decorum I moved to sit across from her in the four-wheeler. We pretended to be interested in the pleasant buildings, neatly kept flower beds, the shrubs, the tall palms. We attempted to make conversation, rehearsing our charade.

'What perfect sunshine.'

'The British officers were very pleasant, I thought.'

'And the Russians unusually courteous. Isn't it lovely to be in a proper cab?'

The ride was relatively short, through orderly streets, unspoiled by war, and we had soon arrived outside the Oriental, a tall and elegant building in Nabarezhnaya Street, looking out onto the harbour. The hotel's polished stone and carved Egyptianate pillars, decorated with gilt, filled me with an immense sense of comfort. While the Baroness waited in the cab I ran up the steps and entered the airy, peaceful lobby to enquire at the reception desk if they had rooms. A thin Armenian manager was elaborately upset, reporting there were no ordinary accommodations, only two suites left at three English pounds a day. He would be delighted to accept a cheque drawn on a European bank, at a pinch he would also accept francs, but desperately regretted he could not take any form of Russian funds unless they were gold. I pretended to dismiss this as perfectly normal and was a little disdainful, a little impatient. He became still more spasmodically apologetic, sending a Georgian porter to carry our baggage as I escorted the Baroness up a wide yellow marble staircase to the first floor. The carpets were of a pinkish-red and the wall-panels matched them, reminding me of the luxury of first-class train travel in pre-War days. Our suites were to be one above the other and when we reached her door I removed my hat, bowed, and loudly wished her a pleasant stay. 'I will be at your disposal the whole time.'

'I am more than grateful to you, M. Pyatnitski.'

'Perhaps you would care to dine with me this evening?'

'Thank you.'

'Shall I meet you here at six-thirty?'

'Six-thirty. Excellent.'

I signed for the porter to continue upwards. We parted. This little scene, of course, was for the benefit of the hotel staff. I took another flight on strawberry carpet, then followed my small bag through a doorway fit for a Calif into an elaborate sitting-room. Beyond this lay a bed chamber whose size and appearance resembled a small harem, with its large four-poster, gauze curtains, an ornamental ceiling in deep blue-and-gold arabesques. From the windows I looked out past tall palms at the blue sea. I had ascended to Paradise. I tipped the porter with a silver rouble, silently daring him to complain, and when he had gone I stood on the balcony, inhaling warm, spicey air. I had forgotten what comfort could be. This was a hint of everything I might expect in Europe. There would certainly be luxury in London to match this. Luxury in Paris. Luxury in Nice. In Berlin. There would be handsome motor-cars, the country-houses of aristocrats, servants, expensive restaurants, everything which, as little as two months earlier, I had never expected to know again. I began to realise that soon I could be living in cities which were not ruled by the moment; cities which could barely conceive of the possibility of sudden attack, which presumed an invulnerable culture and institutions; where Bolshevism was at worst a bad joke and where civil justice was taken for granted. I began to shake as I stripped off my overcoat and jacket and stretched on the blue velvet counterpane, drawing deep breaths, laughing to myself, feeling tears of relief stream down my face as it dawned on me exactly how fortunate I was, how dreadful had been the horror from which I had escaped. For me normality had become violence, suspicion, lies, sudden death, random denunciation, arbitrary imprisonment: but suddenly I saw it could so easily be secure and elegant surroundings and well-mannered companions of one's own choosing. My proper rewards were within my reach again. In an almost drunken mood I put on my jacket, let myself out of my door and walked with swift caution downstairs to be admitted, unobserved.

My delicious mistress, already stripped to her petticoats, threw herself, a soft, sweet-smelling, purring, voracious creature, into my arms. Still wearing most of our clothes, we fucked on the counterpane. Then we undressed, entered the wonderful linen sheets which were freshly washed and scented with lavender, and fucked again. How I wished I might have fallen in love with her, forgotten every element of sense, worshipped her, allowed myself to rise to heights of euphoria, planned marvellous weddings and promised to be faithful until death as boys of my age usually did. Common sense would not have mattered. Leda would have enjoyed the romance as much as I. Her body was so soft, so vibrant, so powerful and in the midst of love-making the expression of ecstasy on her face made her look like a goddess, in whose veins ran fiery copper. Nobody would have been harmed by my falling in love. Her lust was magnificent. My lust was her equal. We had boundless energy. We hardly made use of the cocaine at all. Later, while I hid in her bedroom, she ordered wine and food for lunch. We gorged on cheese and cold beef and salmon. We guzzled French champagne; and when six-thirty came we ignored our decorous dining plans and fucked standing up on the deep blue and orange Turkish carpet, then she ordered caviar and white Georgian wine served in her suite and we gobbled that as greedily as we gobbled one another's genitals. I was not in love. I could never love a woman, unless it was my mother or Mrs Cornelius. But she was in love and it pervaded everything; it made me gay. It almost made me forget Esmé and all I had lost. Leda said I must be the greatest lover in the world; we must never lose touch. I knew she dare not utter her real wish: that we should be together always. She only needed me to say the word. But I would not. I was already committed to my dream. With the Esmé I had known before the Revolution I might have fulfilled my destiny, for she had worshipped me uncritically from childhood. But Esmé was gone. She could not be replaced by this handsome, strong-willed aristocrat whose imagination and ambitions were equal to my own. Because she was used to power, Leda's wishes would always be in some ways opposed to mine. There was no woman like Esmé. Without her, I must achieve my dreams alone.

The next morning, somewhat shakily, we returned to see if the ship were due to sail. Mr Larkin said he guessed we should be in port for at least another two days. Like children released from school, we all but skipped along the palm-flanked Promenade to observe the little Moslem boys playing tag and knuckle-bones on the stony beach, then, at the Baroness's suggestion, we walked to the Alexander Nevski church, a building predominantly of blue marble, which had only been completed a few years earlier yet was the embodiment of Russian tradition, with its golden dome and spires. People entered and left the massive church at a surprising rate and it was my guess they prayed for lost relatives, even for the soul of Russia herself. We meant to stay only a few moments, merely to be able to describe where we had been when we returned, but the Baroness made us stay longer and I was grateful. In those days I had not discovered my Faith, yet I began to feel profoundly restful within those white marble chapels, beneath high, vaulted ceilings, amongst magnificent ikons. Here was evidence of the true spiritual quality of the Russian people, for each painted panel, set in alcoves throughout the church, was the work of a master. Coming to this tranquil shrine from the misery of Odessa and Yalta it was hard to believe that barbarism had so swiftly overtaken our country. (I heard later that after the British left Batoum, her Bolshevik masters argued amongst themselves about the function of the Cathedral. Some wanted it for stables, but there was noisy dissent from the Soviet's Greek Orthodox members. After a great deal of impassioned argument these dissenters finally compromised. 'We agree to your using the Cathedral as a stable. In turn, however, we must be allowed to use your synagogue as a lavatory!')

Near the High Altar we came upon a life-size portrait of Christ standing on the water. He stretched a helping hand towards Peter, who was sinking. It was a prophetic picture of Russia. Peter, our patron saint, was sinking. And Christ was his only hope. This mural made a deeper impression on me than I realized. At that time I must admit I was impatient to return to the Oriental and our bed, yet now I can still recall the elaborate carved marble framing the picture. Christ stands surrounded by golden light. Peter is up to his waist in the waves, his hands stretched towards our Saviour. I remember the flowers and the crosses cut from stone, the little electric bulbs set at intervals along the curved top. All of it was virtually brand new. Doubtless the Bolsheviks demolished it and sold whatever was valuable, knocking away Christ's helping hand.

Leda and I walked for a while in the Cathedral gardens and left by a side gate in time to see a detachment of Punjabis marching down the Boulevard. I am certain the British used these troops the way the French used the Senegalese: as a warning of what to expect if the Reds were victorious. Asia had not let go of Batoum, even during that moment of respite. The Punjabis went past at the double, in their khaki turbans with the rifles over their shoulders, making for the harbour. As usual the Baroness failed to see their significance. 'Don't they look splendid,' she said. That same remark might have been made by a woman in the eighth century as the Moors poured through the walls of Barcelona. (They doubtless felt they were returning home, for Barcelona takes her very name from a Carthaginian founder, Hamilcar Barca). When the Romans drove the Carthaginians from Europe as the Spanish, at great cost, eventually drove out the Moors, did they count that cost? In those days honour and religion meant everything. When Britain decided she could no longer afford her Indian mercenaries she marched them out of Russia, leaving her people prey to barbarian creeds, to the enemies of Christ. The West only waited a year or two before they began to sign Trade Agreements. The Trade Agreement is what destroyed the Chinese Empire. Genghis Khan knew its value. One might as well sign pacts directly with Satan and have done with it!

'Russia will be saved. Russia will be saved,' Leda murmured to me that night. But today I ask my Baroness, who probably died when Bolshevik bombs destroyed her flat in Brüderstrasse twenty-five years later, 'My dear woman, whom I almost loved, when will that be?' She lived over a Berlin antique shop, working for a Swiss specialist in ikons. I never knew if there was anything between them. The Swiss survived. He died of old age in Lausanne fairly recently, having become a millionaire from the profits on our ikons. She must have been fifty-seven. I bear her no ill will. I can still smell her. Indeed, I can smell us both. I feel the fine linen wrapping itself over our bodies, the depth and quality of the mattress; I taste the wine, hear noises in the street outside as soldiers keep the peace; the stars are clear and golden in a deep blue sky which outlines the palms; I see the lights of ships on the water, listen to the sirens and the nightbirds calling.

It took 20,000 British troops to maintain, in one small Russian city, an illusion that the past could be kept alive, or even rebuilt. Illusions cost their creators no small part of themselves. I am reminded of those familiar Arabian tales where magicians are drained of their soul's substance by the very phantasms they conjure. The reward is never great enough to justify the price. Look, says the sorcerer, there is a griffon and there a dragon! I do not see it, says his audience. Look again! Ah, yes, now we see! (But the energy has drained from the illusionist into the illusion. He is suddenly a corpse.) In the years of their dying all Empires are sustained in this way. And what has the Communist illusion cost the Russian people?

I shall not deny that in our ignorance we were pleased enough, my Baroness and I, to enjoy the fantasy while we could. We ate, we made love, we stared at the goods in the shops, we visited bazaars, I purchased a little poor-quality cocaine; we pretended we were in love. But that same night a shock ran through the Oriental, like an earthquake. Aroused from half-sleep we went to the window. Red flames poured upwards from the darkness of the water and huge clouds of black smoke obscured the stars. A ship was burning in the oil-harbour, on the other side of the mole, close to where our own ship was moored. I could see there was no immediate danger to the *Rio Cruz*. Nonetheless at Leda's suggestion I pulled on my clothes and went downstairs. A number of English officers were already in the lobby, some partially clad, some in dressing gowns. Their voices were loud and excited, though it presently emerged they were no better informed than I. Eventually, when a motorbike messenger arrived, one of the officers turned to another: 'Sabotage, of course. The Reds got a bomb aboard a tanker.' This was sufficient for me. I returned to the Baroness. 'Our ship might now decide to leave earlier. We'd best be prepared for it. But Kitty is safe.' The prospect of our idyll ending prematurely caused us to make love with increased passion.

We returned in the morning. On board ship Mr Larkin was completely confused. The *Rio Cruz* was covered in oily filth and her crew worked demonically to clean it off. A French frigate, at great risk to herself, Mr Larkin told us, had towed the tanker out to sea and beached her on a sand-bank where she now burned harmlessly. Foul smoke drifted over everything, settling like swarms of flies. Mr Larkin's face was half-mad. 'That's not the worst of it.' He lowered his voice. 'You knew that chap Hernikof, didn't you? His body was dumped by the gangplank last night. He was stabbed in at least six places. It was ghastly. He'd been stripped naked. There was a Star of David carved into his chest and someone had cut the word "Traitor" into the flesh of his back. I've never seen anything like it. God knows what madman did it. He had contacts in Batoum, I gather. It could have been one of them. Turned against him, perhaps. Reds? Whites? Zionists? I don't know. The military police aren't optimistic. They have so much on at the moment.'

The Baroness was leaning heavily against me, almost fainting. There was no blood in her face at all and her eyes were glazed. I supported her as she clutched my arm.

'What's more,' Larkin was oblivious to her reaction, 'Jack Bragg's missing. He went ashore yesterday afternoon and didn't return last night. There's a general search out for him. We still don't know if it's connected with the Hernikof business.'

'I must help the Baroness to her cabin.' I spoke gently. 'Mr Hernikof was a friend of her late husband.'

Larkin blushed. 'Leave your bags. I'll get a rating to bring them to you.'

Leda was almost in shock. After I had settled her in her bunk I told Kitty and the nanyana she had mild food poisoning and went to the saloon to find some brandy. On the way back I bumped into Mr Thompson, emerging from the engine-room. 'Morning, Pyatnitski.' He wiped grease from his hands. 'Sorry about the news.'

I indicated the cognac. 'The Baroness has taken it badly.'

'Well, at least you seem to be bearing up. It's probably nothing to worry about.'

The significance of his remark, which seemed a little offhand, escaped me until I left Marusya Veranovna with the Baroness and went down to my own cabin for a restoring sniff of cocaine. It was evident Mrs Cornelius had not spent the night in her bunk. I sought out Mr Thompson. He stood leaning on a bulkhead watching seamen swing the loading booms over the ship's forward hatch. They were taking off guns. 'Have you seen my wife, old man?'

The Scotsman was surprised. 'I thought you seemed very casual. You didn't know she hadn't returned? She was due back last night, for dinner. I gathered she'd met you somewhere in Batoum.' He glanced down at the deck, making a pattern in the film of oil with the toe of his boot. 'Well, it was the obvious assumption. Then, when you came aboard . . .'

'She wasn't staying ashore?'

'Not as far as we knew.' He was a bright red. 'Look here, I'd guess she got into some sort of minor trouble. And Jack Bragg became involved, perhaps tried to help her. We'll know soon. But it's early days yet to start worrying too much.'

I was interested in neither his speculation nor his reassurances. I ran back to the gangplank, down to the quay where the purser stood talking to one of the burly Marines. 'Are the police looking for my wife, Mr Larkin?'

Larkin tightened his thin lips and polished his spectacles with a grey handkerchief. 'Well, we've told them all we can, Mr Pyatnitski. I thought you must know where she was. She went off cheerfully enough yesterday to do a bit of shopping and sightseeing. I knew you had business in Batoum and thought perhaps you were meeting her. We weren't too worried.'

'But you're worried about Bragg?'

'Jack had his orders. He was supposed to be on duty last night.'

Presumably because he had made a fool of himself with the Baroness, Larkin was still embarrassed, very red about the neck. He cleared his throat. 'Why don't you try the MP Post at Number Eight dock. They might know something by now.'

I dashed along the quayside, my heart pounding from the double stimulus of cocaine and adrenalin. I was panic-stricken. If I had not realized it before I now knew that I cared for Mrs Cornelius more than anyone. Without her help my chances of reaching England would be alarmingly reduced.

The Military Police hut was a dark green building with red insignia. I banged on the door. A corporal in an ordinary uniform jacket but wearing a khaki kilt, opened up. He had the familiar white armband. He said something mysterious and when I cocked my head and asked him to repeat it, said slowly, as if to a moron, 'And what can I do for you, sir?' I told him my wife, an English woman, was missing in the town. He became friendlier and brightened. 'Mrs Pyatnitski, sir? She was last seen at the *Shaharazaad* cabaret around midnight. Our people are still trying to trace her, but you can't imagine what it's like. There are a thousand private wars going on here. Whites against Reds, Greek Orthodox against Turkish Muslims, Oofs against Lazis, Armenians against Georgians, Turks against Armenians, this bunch of anarchists against that bunch of anarchists, not to mention the family feuds.'

'My wife couldn't be involved in anything like that. She's never been to Batoum before. She has no political connections.'

'She's British, sir. That's enough for some of these wallahs. But we think she just went joyriding with a party of people from the nightclub. Some of the Russian officers are a bit wild, you know. Maybe they went up into the ruins.' He pointed towards the hills, assuring me I should have any news immediately he received it. I made my way back to the ship. A light drizzle had begun to fall. The illusion was thoroughly destroyed. I listened to the sound of raindrops striking the big leaves of the palms like machine-gun fire. My impulse was to rush to the old quarter and begin my own search, but that would mean leaving the ship. I dared not risk being absent if the Military Police had anything to report. I bemoaned my carnal selfishness which had led me from her side. What must these people think of me? In their eyes I had deserted my own wife and returned with another woman. Ashamed and depressed, I climbed back aboard. But I could not bring myself to leave the rail near the gangplank. When the old nanyana came up to inform me the Baroness wished to know where I was, I impatiently told her Mrs Cornelius was missing and I could not come. Eventually, after waiting two hours and seeing all the guns unloaded and borne away in a British army lorry, I went hastily to Leda's cabin. She was still in her bunk, with servant and child paying attendance. 'My poor friend,' she said. 'Your wife?'

'No news. How are you feeling?'

'Hernikof was a sweet, vulnerable man. So good to his people. Why should he have been murdered? He was like my husband. They did no harm. It's so horrible . . .' And she began to weep.

'One does not have to do harm to become a symbol of another's hatred,' I said.

'I think the Whites killed him,' she whispered. 'The Reds killed my husband and the Whites killed Hernikof. It's as senseless as that.'

'There's no evidence. Bolshevik friends could as easily have turned against him if, say, he refused them money. Or some extremist Zionists. Who knows what his business was in Batoum? Or Turks. In Russia you're no longer murdered for any particular reason. It could have been a simple mistake. Count yourself lucky you're still alive.' But I failed to comfort her. She remained agitated. 'What of Mr Bragg?' she asked. 'Still not back?'

'So I gather.' Formally I kissed her hand, feeling unjust resentment towards her for the time she was taking. 'You should try to sleep. Get some more brandy. I'll look in as soon as I can.' I returned to the quayside where Mr Larkin patiently checked his clipboard. The ship was thoroughly cleaned and new cargo was being loaded. 'It's a rum go, Mr Pyatnitski. There seems to have been a brawl at the *Shaharazaad* last night. Mrs Cornelius was insulted. Jack went to her aid. Then a general mêlée. A raid by the Russian gendarmes. Most of the customers got away. No bodies were found so that's one good sign. As for old Hernikof, it seems he was there for a while, too. Then he left with a couple of Cossacks, or they might have been local tribesmen.'

I was not interested in Hernikof. Why should I care if he had lost his life while engaging in some shady mercenary transaction? Doubtless he had considered me a useless *luftmentsh* of the kind which abounds in Odessa; I could guess from his eyes. Well, those eyes would never accuse me again. This is not to say that I approved of the manner in which he met his death. I might have cared about that more if I were not terrified for Mrs Cornelius. Had she survived the entire Revolution and Civil War only to be abducted by Caucasian tribesmen? Had she been raped and killed in some remote mountain village? I had heard such tales since I was a child. The Caucasian brigands notoriously owed allegiance to nothing save their own small community. They might claim to be Moslems or Christians, Reds or Whites, when whim or expediency directed, but they were at root nothing more than heartless thieves. I looked through the rain, beyond the town to the great peaks. If it proved she had been carried off, I would spend every kopek to raise an army of mounted men. I had ridden with Cossacks and anarchists and could prove myself as tough as any of them and infinitely more cunning. I was frequently underestimated in this sphere. People knew me as an artist, an intellectual, a man of words. But in my day I was also a man of deeds. I was determined not to lose Mrs Cornelius as I had lost Esmé. A woman of enormous natural goodness, she threw too much of herself away on feckless creatures who never appreciated her. I wondered if Jack Bragg was in trouble. Perhaps she was helping him. I went to the saloon for a drink. Mr Thompson followed me in. 'Let me buy you a whisky.' He sat me down near the portholes so I could look out at the quayside while he went to the makeshift bar. He returned with our drinks. He was at a loose end while the ship was in port. His stokers were cleaning boilers and engine-room. 'There's a dull enough explanation waiting for all this,' he said. 'You've a brilliant imagination and it's a wonderful thing. But at times like this I'd think it could be your worst enemy.'

I barely listened to him. While he droned on in this conventional frame I continued to sift through the few facts I had. Thompson was assuming, like the Baroness, that Jack Bragg and Mrs Cornelius were somehow romantically involved. I was no fool; I knew exactly what they were thinking. I saw no point in disputing this foolishness. Mrs Cornelius was always a woman of honour. She embodied the great English virtues. For me, when she died, England died. Nothing remains but mud and old stones over which the bastard races of a hundred petty nations squabble. The spirit of England flew away in 1945 when the Socialists broke apart the British Empire. I witnessed it all. I have more authority than bearded schoolteachers with insane eyes and red mouths screaming at me from pedestals, those *bezdušný*! I have seen their breed before. Civilisation is dying, nation by nation, piece by piece. The omens are everywhere: In the cracked pavingstones, the fallen railings, the graffiti-smeared walls. The omens are as loud as the voice of God. Who needs to tease out subtleties and nuances? That is where too many people go wrong. Mr Thompson detected an affair. I detected only jolly friendship and kindness. Is it better to see the obscure vice or the obvious virtue?

Those who belittle Mrs Cornelius's greatness merely betray the smallness of their own souls. But I am sure Thompson meant well. He said nothing outright as he tried to ease my anxiety. While ashore he had found a few copies of some English illustrated weeklies, *The Sphere, Illustrated London News, Pall Mall* and so on. In them were pictures of new gigantic flying boats and airships which planned transatlantic crossings. With the Great War's end, there seemed a fresh spirit of optimism in England. There were pages of smiling young pilots climbing onto the bright fuselages of monstrous aeroplanes, sketches of aerial cruisers with double-hulls and vast numbers of propellers and wings which in future might carry the mail across the Empire. Even in my anxiety for Mrs Cornelius I was captured by the excitement. 'There's people with money to spend on new inventions,' said Thompson. 'None of these things are cheap to build. You must remember to be cautious, like Mr Edison, and form a proper company. Too many innocent boys have been cheated in the past.' It was strange how he thought me a boy. I had not been that since Kerenski elected himself to power. Yet there were youths in England of my own age who had never slept with a woman, who had not even left school. In that respect at least I had an advantage, but none of my dreams could be realized without Mrs Cornelius. I looked to where, in the last of the

68

afternoon light, Mr Larkin was checking the documents of new arrivals. I became even more alarmed. The ship must soon be due to sail.

Mr Thompson confirmed this. 'In the morning. They're expecting more trouble here. That bomb on the tanker was just the opening incident, I gather.'

I decided, in spite of the danger, to take our luggage off the ship while I pursued my private investigation. The *Rio Cruz* would not leave until ten the next day. At dawn, if Mrs Cornelius had not been found, I would disembark. As I finished my drink the door of the saloon opened and the pale Baroness entered. 'Have you heard anything?' She sat down with a nod of thanks as Mr Thompson drew back the chair for her. Mr Thompson did not understand our Russian. 'Can I fetch you something to drink, Baroness? Or a cup of tea?'

'Some brandy, thank you.' While the engineer returned to the bar she leaned forward. 'I could not stay away. What can I do to help?' She would cheerfully have seen Mrs Cornelius dead, yet was trying her best to be humane. I appreciated her self-control. 'I shall have to go ashore if there's any prospect of the ship leaving without her.'

'Then I shall go, too.'

'That's impossible. There's Kitty. You have your duty. I have mine.'

'All our duties can surely be reconciled.'

I did not argue with her. If Mrs Cornelius had been taken away from Batoum and I had to organize an expedition, Leda would be an impediment. There would be no room for love-making. It would be a time for bullets and fast-firing carbines.

I lifted my head. Machine-guns sounded from the old quarter, near the bazaar. Two armoured-cars roared along the Boulevard, their sirens honking like geese. I heard one small explosion, then two larger ones. Smoke and flames began to rise behind the Cathedral. There were shouts. I rose to my feet, looking questioningly at Mr Thompson who said, 'It's just the usual trouble.'

Batoum was no longer a sanctuary. She had become a sinister trap; one of those beautiful gardens in medieval Romance designed by a sorceress to lure unwary knights. My instinctive terror of the East returned. It had been folly to believe the illusion. Where I had admired the domes of churches I now saw, in rainy twilight, the sinister outlines of Saracen mosques. Where I had been comforted by the smart discipline of British Tommies, I detected armed and turbaned figures hiding in every shadow. Shouts came from the quayside. A large covered navy truck began to pull up beside our little barricade. I thought it was the police. I left the saloon and was halfway down the gangplank when an electric torch flashed suddenly in my eyes. Blinded for a moment, I stumbled and almost fell through the ropes. As I recovered I saw figures standing near the truck. 'Is there any news?'

'Blimey,' said a familiar voice, 'it's Ivan.'

Mrs Cornelius seemed hurt. She was supported by two officers. I rushed up to her. 'Are you wounded? Was it the tribesmen?'

'Tribesmen? Do wot? Natives, yer mean?' She was baffled. I realised at last that she was drunk. 'Sorry, Ive. Lorst track o' ther time, didn't I. Jack woz good enough ter . . .'

A dishevelled Jack Bragg stood behind her staring glumly at me. 'Spot of bother, Mr Pyatnitski, with some Georgian irregulars who took a fancy to your missus. The upshot was they carried us off. I was drugged, I think. Mrs Pyatnitski was drugged, too, weren't you, Mrs Pyatnitski.'

'Drugged blind,' she agreed.

Jack Bragg's face was almost a parody of embarrassment and anxiety. 'We managed to escape this morning. But we got lost up-country.' He made a vague gesture towards the wooded hills. 'A patrol found us and brought us back. Luckily. We're a bit wet.'

'He has been frantic.' We all looked up at the ship. It was the Baroness. I had not known she spoke such clear English. She leaned forward on the rail, into the lamplight. She was a picture by Mucha, a Slavic angel. 'Poor Mr Pyatnitski has spent the entire day trying to trace you.'

'I think you'd better get aboard in a hurry, Bragg.' An invisible Captain Monier-Williams spoke from the bridge. He sounded more than a little angry.

'Aye, aye, sir.' Bragg turned to Mrs Cornelius. 'Will you be all right?'

'Right as rain,' she said. 'But could do wiv a dryin' orf!' Absently, she reached into her décolletage and removed a large black glove. 'Where the 'ell did that come from?'

Jack Bragg ran up the gangplank to make his peace with the captain. I felt sorry for him. He had suffered in a noble cause. Mrs Cornelius kissed the two young officers on their cheeks, wished them a cheerful goodnight, and leaning heavily on me began to climb the plank. 'Nick o' time as usual, eh, Ivan?'

I put her to bed where she fell immediately asleep. As I looked down at her breasts rising and falling in the glow of the hurricane lamp I thought her a true earth-spirit. I envied the unselfconscious spontaneity with which she lived each moment to the full. Sadly, it was impossible for me to emulate her. I myself must live for the future. I had to consider the next fifty years. My life, as a result, was hardly my own.

I went forward to placate Leda. The tanker was still burning in the distance, aground on the sand-bar; flames sent a shudder of shadows across the fo'c'sle. She stood looking at the town and her expression was sad. I guessed she was thinking of her husband. Then I realised she was mourning the worthless Hernikof. 'You should not grieve so much.' I put my hand on hers where it gripped the samson post. 'You hardly knew him.' She glanced down at the water. 'He was so miserable without his family.' Her huge blue eyes were full of tears. I took her in my arms, careless if we were seen. 'At least he is with them now.' I could not approve of the manner in which Hernikof had met his end, yet it was a relief no longer to be pursued by him. I sometimes think back to my time in the *shtetl*, when I had been in a fever. Had I said something so terrible to the Jews there that they had placed a curse upon me? Would I forever be followed by some snivelling, mealy-mouthed nemesis? It is foolish to be so superstitious. It is ridiculous to assume that they slip pieces of metal in a person's womb. I hold with none of that rubbish. Hernikof had not been popular on the ship. It was even possible he had brought about his own death if he had gone deliberately where he should not have gone, or seen those he had no business seeing. It is a form of suicide we have all witnessed at one time or another. I said nothing of this, of course. I was sensitive to her grief. I let her weep a little. I cared for her.

When eventually I made my way back to our cabin, Mrs Cornelius had recovered consciousness and had undressed herself. She was tying her hair in pieces of paper. 'I 'ope I didn't put yer art, Ivan. 'Course the story we tol' woz a bit of a fib, but I didn't wanna git Jack inter trouble.'

'You lied!' I was momentarily hurt; I knew a flash of suspicion.

'There wasn't no Georgians, really. We got put in clink by ther Russian coppers. Drunk.' She looked back at me. 'An' more'n a bit disorderly, ho, ho. It woz Jack got us art, wiv a bribe. An' give false names.'

My suspicion vanished. She had all my sympathy. I know what it is to live in prison. It is humiliating. Those who pointed the finger at me in Kiev never knew what I suffered. One's whole identity is stolen.

71

They can blame me, but I do not blame myself. To name a few names is nothing if they are already on a list. It was a formality when the Varta released me. I betrayed nothing. The Reds call me a profiteer and trump up charges. They always will. It is jealousy. There is no such thing as friendship between them. 'It must have been dreadful,' I said.

'It could've bin worse. We still 'ad their bleedin' vodka!' She laughed. I admired her courage. It was as great as my own. 'But not a word ter nobody else.' She put a finger to her delicious lips. 'Jack'd get ther sack.'

'Nonetheless, I will thank him for what he did,' I said.

'If yer like.'

I left her to finish her toilet and returned to the saloon to buy Mr Thompson a nightcap. He could see I was greatly relieved. We stood by the bar listening to the strains of the *Kamarinskaya* played by one of the loyalist soldiers on his accordion. A few children still made attempts to dance while their mournful parents murmured of death and torture, of injustice, destruction of their hopes for the future. 'Will Jack Bragg be all right?' I asked.

'The old man's pretty peeved with him. But no great harm's been done. The captain's hated this run since we began. He's more sympathetic if a chap steps over the line a bit. A tongue-lashing and double-duty for a night or two won't do Jack any harm.'

We wandered out onto the deck. The rain had stopped and the sky was clearing. The distant flames had died down. 'The weather should improve on our way back to Varna,' said Mr Thompson. He saluted me. 'Well, goodnight, old man.'

I was left alone. I walked once round the deck, then returned to the cabin, got into my bunk, smoked a cigarette and listened to Mrs Cornelius as she sighed and twisted. I knew she was dreaming what she liked to call her 'nice dreams.' For once I was not much disturbed by her and was soon asleep.

I met Jack Bragg on deck next morning as I took my usual exercise. The *hadacka* with the green face was dealing her cards. She had evidently found a new pack. She was laying out the full deck as I passed. The Russian ship had left in the night and there was a two-masted schooner in her place. The sun was bright. Batoum seemed cheerful again. I moved to the rail and looked down at the schooner. Her raga-muffin crew were still asleep on deck. Armenians, Turks, Russians, Greeks, Georgians, they looked like pirates from a nineteenth-century storybook. They had pistols and knives all over their bodies and were dressed in a crazy mixture of uniforms, of Western and Asian clothing. They reminded me a little of Makhno's anarchists. Jack and I paused on the poop. He had been on his watch duty since midnight. His eyes were red, his chin slightly unshaven. 'Mrs Pyatnitski told me the truth last night,' I said. He showed some alarm until he saw I was not angry. 'About your getting them out of prison,' I said.

'Oh.' His voice was hoarse. 'It was nothing. A few English sovereigns work wonders these days.' Even as he spoke he began to look more ghastly than ever. 'You must think me an awful blighter, leading your wife astray like that.'

I was able to smile. 'Nonsense. If I know her, she did the leading! How did the captain take it?'

'Not too badly, really. I say, do you think those chaps are smugglers?' He indicated the schooner.

'Very likely. They're from all over the place, aren't they? Doubtless they're taking advantage of the present situation while they can.'

'These waters are still supposed to have corsairs in them, you know.' Jack Bragg swayed at the rail. The sun caught his bloodshot eyes and dirty fair hair, made his skin look even greyer. 'What about it, Mr Pyatnitski? Fancy walking the plank?'

'You'd better get to bed.' I was jovial. 'I promise to warn you if I see the skull-and-crossbones on the horizon.'

He stumbled sleepily down the deck and almost fell into the seeress as she reshuffled her pack. I continued to study the schooner. She was a filthy vessel. Her furled canvas was tattered and patched. I had no idea where she came from but made out a Russian word on her side: *Phoenix*. Probably she had begun life as a fishing vessel. Some of the sleeping men wore bits and pieces of Tsarist Navy uniforms. Others had on army coats, expensive cavalry boots, artillery caps. They were doubtless moving regularly between the Turkish Black Sea ports and what remained of free Russia. Very likely, too, they would take passengers for a high price. I could not blame them. They had no future at all if the Reds won. In the distant streets I heard the noise of a window breaking and turned to look. The bell in the Cathedral began to toll. An old horse hauled a creaking, overladen cart along the road beyond the quay. Then two big army lorries pulled up outside the barrier to unload more passengers: wounded White Army soldiers in dirty English greatcoats; peasant women with babies; old men who might have come straight from the most backward and remote regions of Georgia; grandmothers in black shawls and skirts. They flocked, bemused, towards us. I was horrified, certain the ship must sink under their weight. I watched Mr Larkin run down to meet them. The other officials, Russian and English, began to assemble at their posts. I could look no longer. The smugglers (or pirates) were waking as if, hearing the refugee babble, they scented sustenance. I made my way into breakfast. This might be my last peaceful meal before we reached Constantinople. An hour or so later the ship's engines turned and I cheered up at the prospect of being at sea again.

We were pulled from Batoum by a little tug. When she released her lines they twanged and glittered in the crisp air. The sun was hot on my face; Batoum was apparently at peace, though smoke from the burning tanker still occasionally drifted over the harbour. With a more knowing eye I looked back at the palms and bamboos, the malachite houses and shady streets, bitter that my hoped-for idyll on Russian territory had been so savagely interrupted, hating Hernikof for his vulgarity and the horrible manner of his dying. Into smooth water, her old machinery complaining, the *Rio Cruz* turned towards the farther shores of the Black Sea. Her last port of call before Constantinople was to be Varna in Bulgaria, a country which would show considerable hospitality to its Slavic brothers. The peasants sat in groups near the forward hatches. They had spread carpets and bundles everywhere and were eating food they had brought with them. We were loaded almost beyond safety point, but Captain Monier-Williams had his instructions. All we could do, he said, was pray for good weather. Whatever I thought of the poor creatures on deck I was deeply moved when one of the bearded peasants rose to look back at Batoum, removed his cap and began to sing in a high, pure voice *Boje Tzaria Krani* — *God Save The Tsar*. Almost unconsciously I found myself joining in our National Anthem. Soon it seemed the entire ship was singing.

First Batoum disappeared and then eventually the white tips of the mountains. The *Rio Cruz* was again alone on a grey sea under an overcast sky. Fortunately for the refugees on deck it did not rain, but the waves grew gradually more agitated. I became afraid we would never lift above the steep watery walls as the ship, groaning and wheezing, trembled in the water, moving ungracefully through cold Limbo.

It was almost a relief to resume my strict daily routine with the Baroness, though perhaps I fucked with a little less enthusiasm as I detected in my sweetheart a certain frantic desperation, the consequence, I suspected, of Hernikof's murder. She no longer made a pretty pretence of refusing my cocaine. Now she would nag at me until I prepared it. If her lovemaking became more experimental, it was also less joyous. I was sympathetic. I held her tightly for long moments. More than once that first day out from Batoum we cried softly together, listening to the random bumps and thuds on all sides of us, wondering if we would ever be as happy as we had been during our time when Russian passion had bloomed unchecked on Russian soil.

Mrs Cornelius also seemed particularly happy to return to her habitual pattern. That night she sang and danced her way through a score of favourite songs. Jack Bragg was on duty again, but Captain Monier-Williams remained to sing a chorus of *My Old Dutch*. Mrs Cornelius said he was a great sport. She sat on his knee, coaxing a chuckle and a smile from his stern Welsh features. In the far corner of the saloon a group of Russians gathered around an accordion and we shouted at them to give us something cheerful. The player, a young, fair-haired one-legged soldier from Nizhny Novgorod, began the *Kalinka*. Soon Mrs Cornelius crossed to join a dozen middle-class dowagers in a boisterous dance while we men clapped and stamped our feet. Again the captain was persuaded to join in for a while before murmuring to me: 'If there's much more stamping, I'm afraid we'll all go through the bilges.' He straightened his cap, leaving the room with almost a jaunty swagger. When Mrs Cornelius pulled me into the circle to dance I found I had become rather mournful, as if Hernikof's memory haunted me. I had nothing to be ashamed of. A Jew was a Jew. I had not been cruel to him; but now I recalled his drunken eagerness for friendship. Had it been in quest of friendship that he had disappeared into the streets of Batoum to be knifed and robbed and branded?

Claiming a need for fresh air, I returned to the deck. It was stupid of me to react so and my resentment towards Hernikof increased. I climbed rapidly to the top of the ship to stand beside the funnel overlooking the engine-room hatch. The deck-passengers had wrapped themselves up in their carpets for the night, though some were still smoking and talking. Candle-lamps burned here and there, together with the ship's own lights. It was a strange, fascinating scene, but it had become impossible now for me to be alone there. I retreated to my cabin and by means of almost half my remaining cocaine fled into fantasies of the future, of my own success, and put Hernikof out of my mind.

Next morning I took my usual stroll but was intensely irritated by the people on the forward deck. For the first time the green woman had left her post. I saw her sitting under one of our swaying lifeboats, slowly arranging her pack. I decided it was time I attempted to address her directly, since we were both so discommoded, and was making my way towards her when our signals suddenly began to clang and the engine-note changed. The whole ship shuddered. She slewed sickeningly round. My first thought was that we had struck a rock, or another ship. The deck-passengers jumped to their feet yelling and pointing off the portside. I ran to the rail. In the choppy water, not more than a few yards from us, was the vessel we had almost hit. It was a long barge of the sort normally only seen on canals. She had no engine, no passengers, but was piled high with all kinds of trunks, suitcases, bundles and bags over which tarpaulins flapped. It was a strange and disturbing sight, for the barge had no business being at sea. We passed her and slowly she dropped behind us, rising and falling in the thickening mist. Her cargo might have been Bolshevik loot or the effects of a single aristocratic family. It could have been valuable, but with our decks so crowded it would have been madness to try to get alongside her. The water became choppier and the barometer was falling by the minute. Our breath steamed and joined with the mist. Gradually the wind increased and for a while the air was clear, but later the wind again dropped, the night became very foggy, and Jack Bragg was positioned forward with a searchlight to keep a look-out for ice.

After dinner that evening I joined Bragg at his post. He was smoking his pipe and humming a tune to himself as he pointed the little beam this way and that across the black, unpleasant water. The ship's gloomy foghorn sounded every few minutes. The Baroness had gone to bed early, claiming to have caught a slight chill. I raised my coat collar, for some reason unwilling to return to my cabin. Instead I offered to take a turn at the light, but Bragg refused. 'I can't afford to get in the captain's bad books again!' Although the yellow beam did not pierce the fog very deeply, we were moving at half-speed in a heavy sea so there was not much danger of us running hard into another vessel or the pack ice which in the past two hours had begun to appear here and there. The inky waves made a horrible hollow sound on our hull. For a while Jack and I smoked and chatted about nothing in particular; then, suddenly, he frowned, his eyes following the beam. 'Hello! What was that?'

I had seen nothing. He moved the beam back a few feet to reveal a dark outline not a hundred yards away from us. 'You'd best take the blasted light after all,' he said, 'I'll warn the captain.'

My hands were shaking as I did my best to keep the beam on what was obviously a fairly large vessel. We were passing very close. It seemed our course must inevitably bring us into direct contact with her. Now, as Jack went off to the bridge, I saw little white blotches everywhere and realised to my astonishment that these were human faces, apparently scores of them. When their thin cries gradually became audible across the water, I shouted back in response. They could hear nothing, of course. There were no engine-sounds and it seemed they were stranded. A moment later from the bridge the captain's amplified voice called out our name, telling them we would try to come in closer. But the sea was beginning to rise even as we approached. I could see the vessel fairly clearly now. She was a little harbour-tug. There must have been two hundred people crammed on every surface of her. I thought I could read her name at one point, the *Anastasia* out of Akermann, but that might have been my imagination. Whoever commanded her was now shouting back, begging for help. They had lost their engines. Their propeller had been tangled in a hawser. Jack joined me again at the searchlight. We were by now both soaked in spray. 'Poor bastards. They seem to be taking on a lot of water. They're sinking for certain. She must have been hauling that lighter we saw. When the cable snapped it wrapped itself round their screw. Listen to the wailing! Isn't it pathetic' He told me there was nothing the captain could do. He dare not risk his own people's lives. He could only radio the nearest British warship and ask them to go to the tug's assistance. 'God help them,' said Jack. 'They can't last another hour in these seas.'

Soon the tug with two hundred terrified faces had disappeared in the wild darkness. Our own deck-passengers had scarcely stirred. The sea grew heavier and colder. It was to remain bad for all the time it took us to reach Varna. We never learned if the tug was rescued, but Captain Monier-Williams asked me not to mention her likely fate. He did not want to distress anyone. In our hearts, we knew she had gone down.

At Varna we lay off near the harbour entrance while, to my great pleasure, boats removed over half our passengers. The ship seemed at peace again, though pack-ice still bumped our sides occasionally and there was snow in the air. To me the snow was almost welcome. I was not sure if I would ever be completely happy without it. My Baroness, her daughter and nanyana, stood next to me as the peasants, many of them shivering and blue, apparently seasick, were loaded into the boats. 'At least the Bulgarians are Slavs.' Leda was wrapped in her own thick, black fur. We must have resembled a pair of Siberian bears, for we both had black 'three-eared' caps pulled down over our heads. 'But what's to become of us in Berlin and London, Simka?' She had taken to using this diminutive quite openly sometimes. 'Won't we seem strange, exotic creatures to them?' She glared miserably at the leaden sea.

I told her I thought she was being a trifle melodramatic. Other nations read our literature as thoroughly as we read theirs. We had music and painting in common. The sciences. 'We can rise above the differences, Leda, because we are educated. You'll see. It would be worse for the likes of them,' I indicated the frightened peasants clambering into the boats. 'They have only Russia.'

She would not be comforted. 'Certainly it's pointless to worry. After all, there's every chance I'll be stuck in Constantinople for the rest of my life.'

I refused to be drawn. A wind had grown from the East to obliterate the Westerly. I fancied it still carried imploring voices from the tug. I had been unable to rid my mind of them, just as Hernikof still insisted on haunting me. I sympathised with the captain who had been forced to an unwelcome decision; the only decision possible. For all that, I had a dim sense that I had myself betrayed those little white human faces. In comparison, Leda's concerns were rather feeble and I found them irritating. 'I'm sure you'll survive,' I said.

'You'll help me if you can, Simka?' It was almost an order.

I sighed, forcing myself to smile. 'Yes, Leda Nicolayevna. I'll help if I can.'

The fog was too thick for us to see anything much of Varna. I have heard it is an unremarkable town. I was surprised so many disembarked there. I said as much to Mr Thompson shortly after we had left the harbour's sea-roads and were heading with some speed towards the mouth of the Bosphorus. He frowned. 'Can't you guess, Mr Pyatnitski? We've put every suspected case ashore. And that's two-thirds of the people we had on board. We've been lucky, I think. Larkin's guess is that Hernikof was suffering from it, though of course it's unlikely he gave it to anyone since he'd recovered by the time we reached Batoum. It's impossible to say now. We can just hope we're all right. It's typhus, old man.'

So Hernikof had managed to infect a large number of honest Christians before he had been killed. I was thankful my suspicions about him had been accurate.

'But none of the crew has it?' I asked.

'Not so far. Of course, the pity is we'll probably be under quarantine when we get to Constantinople.'

At that moment I believed I would never be free of the *Rio Cruz*. It was January 13th, 1920. The next day was my birthday.

Four

THAT NIGHT WHILE overhead the Russians celebrated with thread-bare conviviality the eve of their New Year I made love to my Baroness, privately praying she was still healthy. Her servant and daughter had been permitted to stay in the saloon until twelve. She had claimed a headache; I had said I had papers to put in order. Of the passengers, only Mrs Cornelius and I were party to the truth; the others had rumours which, in the manner of desperate people, they ignored or turned into jokes. There was fog in the Bosphorus, Jack Bragg had said, but tomorrow, sooner or later, we should see Byzantium. We steamed past the coast of Bulgaria, holding a slow but steady course, and I plunged in and out of my paramour like a mad rabbit, to squeal my pleasure in the certain knowledge my voice was drowned by a chorus of exiles and the boom of our engines.

At midnight, our exhausted legs took us back to the saloon. All the officers had returned, but Mrs Cornelius was still there. She had linked arms with two drunken Ukrainian matrons in *Stenka Razin* (which she insisted on pronouncing *Stinker Raison* – I believe it was the only Russian song she knew). Kitty, sleepy and clutching a toy dog purchased by her mother in Batoum, kissed us both goodnight before her heavy little body was borne off by her nanyana; then we went outside. It had grown warmer. The ship quivered on calm water and I wondered if we had yet entered the mouth of the Strait. We had again sailed into that huge black cavern; there were no stars or moon. There even appeared to be an echo.

Mrs Cornelius, full of rum and good will, joined us. An army cap on the side of her head, she leaned gasping on the rail. "Appy Birfday, Ivan.'

I was touched by her consideration. She swayed forward to kiss me on the cheek, then looked about in surprise. 'Cor! It's like bleedin' pitch art there!'

The Baroness frowned uneasily; she could not understand the Cockney accent. For me Mrs Cornelius's English was often easier than the purer language of the officers. I had, as it were, cut my teeth on Cockney. Leda made no attempt to speak English. She said in Russian, 'I had best see how Kitty is. Marusya Veranovna seemed to have drunk more vodka than usual. Goodnight to you both.' With some coolness she bowed and made her way back to her cabin. Mrs Cornelius spat into the water. 'Carn't seem ter clear me fuckin' marf. It's ther rum. Picks yer up mentally but lets yer darn socially, as they say. Woz I bein' a gooseberry?'

I reassured her. I was glad to have this time alone with her. 'Have you heard anything more? About the sickness?'

There was no news. But the officers, she said, were not over-worried. With an arm around my shoulder she let me get her back to our cabin. My brain was full of history. I saw the trappings of the Hun ponies, the banners and the spears and armour of hungry Ottoman Turks as they turned hot ebony eyes towards Europe and readied their primitive nomad philosophy for war against Greece. Why must they now claim originality and superiority? If they had been so proud of their culture Turks would not have called their own land Rum or Rome. Such deep hypocrisy. It was passed from generation to generation, strengthened in every century. They were trapped in their own perverse mythology. This is a planet of lies and shadows. Civilized men are ever the prey of envious shepherds. Even so, the truth occasionally glints through, yet I fear my generation was the last to recognize it.

As for these innocent-seeming outriders for the Hun hordes, these Turkish 'guest-workers,' I know their game. I surprised a group of them a few days ago in the *Paddington Arms* near the station. They were standing around a shrieking one-armed bandit and arguing. After I ordered my vodka from the bar I said casually, to no one in particular: *Rüzgâr kuzey doğudan esiyor.* I was amused by their consternation as I walked back to my table. Some of us still understand why such an arrogant people are prepared to do menial tasks in a foreign land. They are all, of course, Fifth Column spies: the saboteurs, the advance-guard. I have given up trying to alert this country. The British will be crushed beneath the weight of their own complacency, an illusory belief in their innate superiority. They will go down, in the words of their Poet Laureate, with

Nineveh and Tyre. I have done far more than honour and duty normally demands. I can do no more. *Elle serait tombée.* Mrs Cornelius told me they would never understand. 'Yore wastin' yer breaf, Ivan. Ya orta be lookin' arter number one.' But I was always an idealist. It is my Achilles heel. I had so much to give. I sit beside the cash-register in the deep end of my shop, looking out on the Portobello Road. It is like a film. Year by year the white faces grow fewer. The loping West Indians and arrogant Pakistanis, the swaggering Turks and Arabs multiply. It was all white when I first came here. The shops were ordinary and decent: newsagents, grocers, tobacconists, cobblers. Now it is imitation gold bracelets and cheap cotton prints like the poorer bazaars of Constantinople in 1920. And Kensington Market, crammed with kangaroo-skin boots and diamanté silks, begins to resemble the Grand Bazaar. People continue to ask why this has happened! They can have no knowledge of the past. No wonder young women grow bored with feeble English loungers who live only to smoke keef and claim the State's baksheesh. No wonder white girls seek out the spurious vivacity of the grinning Negro, the secure wealth of a fat Asian patriarch. Here again is Byzantium in decline; the last years of a senile civilisation.

I have seen the same effects in a dozen great cities during their ultimate decline. When Christian girls decide to desert the ways of virtue to fornicate with the Pagan, then chivalry is lost forever. It is the same in New York and Paris, in Munich, in Amsterdam. Oriental Africa has once again married brutality to cunning and given birth to Carthage. *Burada görülecek ne var?* The self-mocking West, dismissing the moral convictions of three thousand years, is ripe for conquest. And of course the one to benefit most will ever be that sly desert herdsman, your Jew.

Constantinople was our greatest single prize of the War. Had we kept her all our sacrifices would have been worthwhile. We should have experienced a tremendous revival of idealistic Christianity; a fresh awakening of the Russian spirit would have swept Bolshevism away. Throughout the War the Allies promised us the return of Tsargrad, our Emperor City, our Byzantium, seat of the Orthodox Church. The British were too weak. Rather than reclaim Constantinople for Christ and risk offending Catholic Europe they meekly returned the city to Mohamet. The Turks themselves were astonished. And in the end, of course, the Jew benefited most. The best possible climate for the speculator is a climate of uncertainty. To produce that climate you attack old, honest ideas, accepted habits of morality and scientific examination. Marx,

Freud and Einstein did that much better: they invented new languages and prepared the way for their merchant co-religionists just as British missionaries in China prepared the way for opium-traders. By promiscuous questioning of the eternal verities they make our children seek bewilderedly for fresh intellectual and moral security. While we are confused, their legions fall upon our harvest. I know these Jews. I speak their tongue. They put a piece of metal in my stomach. They robbed me of everything. I blame my father. My mother was too kind. I will have nothing to do with old harpies who pick over my stock like carrion flapping on the body of the lamb. They receive short shrift from me. I would rather give my time to the wandering descendants of those Egyptians who refused shelter to the Virgin and Child. At least the gypsies are Christians now. As for the Turks, I say the same thing: *Çok ufak* or *Çok büyüt* and make them go away. I do not want their cash. I am not a Jew. It is a matter of *derkenen*. I am not a fool. I have made my mistakes. I do not deny it. *O wieku, tys wiosna, czlowieka! Na tobie ziarno przyszlosei on sieje, Twoim on ogniem reszte wieku zyje!* as the Poles say. I am not afraid of the *fremder* or the *frestl*. I live with them. I have lived with them for years. To be familiar with something is not to be the same as it. That is why I get so angry if mistaken for a Jew. Is a health inspector the bacteria he examines? The city-builders must be forever vigilant against the greedy nomad. It is not always wise to build convenient roads through the walls.

From the first I was suspicious. The Westway could bring no benefits to us. I had my own ideas for our district: a marvellous North Kensington; a model for the rest of London. Most West Indians and Asians were to be moved to Brixton or back to countries where they would be more comfortable. A greatly reduced population would have assisted the creation of a garden suburb more beautiful than Hampstead. It would have raised the value of property and attracted a better class of person. I sent a detailed plan to the Council. I received a letter back from a Knight of the Realm. My ideas were stimulating and he would bring them to the attention of his colleagues. But the socialists silenced him, for I heard no more. He was not re-elected, which speaks for itself. Mrs Cornelius thought my ideas 'bloody marvellous' but she was nervous about an increase in the local taxes. One had to pay for perfection, I said. That was my last attempt to help my adopted country. Throughout the War I made all kinds of offers to the authorities. I described my gigantic bombing aeroplanes, my rocket-propelled bombs, my Violet Ray. In the meantime I saw some of my ideas taken up. But I received no credit. Barnes Wallace, that appalling charlatan, my antagonist from the thirties, claimed my ideas as his own. Anyone who spoke to me in 1940 and later saw *The Dambusters* will know what I mean. This stealing is taken for granted in scientific circles. No wonder Mr Thompson warned me to patent my ideas. Look at that thief Sikorski's reputation since he left Russia! My plans are all secure at last. Whoever inherits them will benefit and so my memory will eventually be honoured. The British Government is the loser. The Patent Office cannot be trusted. The last letter I had was from someone called Yudkin. I learned my lesson a little too late. I did not learn it in Russia. I had not learned it by the time I reached Constantinople. God knows how many millions of my rightful pounds have gone into other pockets. Then, however, I was not thinking of my own interest. I was still too impressed by the epic nature of my journey. A Russian who visits Constantinople and the great cathedral of Hagia Sophia as a matter of course makes a pilgrimage. Hagia Sophia is at once the greatest symbol of our slavery and our ultimate redemption. Though not very religious in those days I was still a patriot.

The Russians fully appreciated how bravely Britons had fought the Turk. You lost enormous numbers at Gallipoli. You died in Mesopotamian deserts. You rode against Mecca itself under Lawrence of Arabia. We thought you felt as strongly as we did. We thought Constantinople would be safe in your hands until we were ready to take it over. We knew what bonds of brotherhood existed between Greece and England. But that which was powerful idealism in us was, it emerged, only sentimentality in a nation of shopkeepers. We put too much faith in British determination to resist Italian and French ambitions. These Roman Catholics had no wish to see the true centre of Christianity liberated. British blood had won the Dardanelles, the Sea of Marmara, the Bosphorus. The British had conquered half Asia, swept back the descendants of the Mongol and the Hun, brought Christianity to the unenlightened, raised up churches in the Himalayas and the jungles of Burma, enforced the Reign of Justice, contained the barbaric spread of the yellow races. Who better to entrust with our birthright? I can understand and forgive them their betrayal. But can God? He only forgives them that confess their sins. With their Empire gone, their economy collapsing, their culture in ruins, they drown in a sea of rotting flotsam, the detritus of Colonial glory. And as their self-satisfied little island sinks do they at last shout '*Mea Culpa*'? No! They sing *Rule, Britannia*. It is a horrifying spectacle.

At dawn next morning I went on deck to discover the ship completely fog-bound. I could not see as far as the forecastle. As I drew my scarf to my face I noticed an indistinct figure staring over the side. Hearing my footsteps, she turned to reveal a green, rouged face. It was my card-player. She looked more than ever like a bizarre character from a Guignol puppet theatre. I was about to ask her if she needed help when she said in poorly-accented German: '*Mir ist schlecht. Bitte, bringen Sie mir ein Becken.*' I was shocked. She was unquestionably a Russian but she had all this time taken me for a German, or even a Jew. I went to fetch the basin she wanted but when I returned she was already being helped below by her husband in his usual riding coat and jodhpurs. My impulse was to run after them and let them know I was as Russian as themselves. Instead I contented myself with a feeble: 'Хеlаn вам s opoвb !' which I do not believe they even heard. It was a sign to me, of course, though I could not understand it then. I have been set apart. I am taken for an alien even by my own people. No one will claim me. At least in London I can be nothing but a foreigner. It does not matter how much I worship at the Orthodox Church or how frequently I preach the word of Christ. I will always be an outcast. I am a British citizen. I have lived here for half my life. I gave this country better service than many who were born here. What does it mean? Still *fremder*, still *frestl*. Something happened in that awful Ukrainian *shtetl* when I was a captive of the Jews. What Judas saw my mind was weak and injected me with the metallic fragment of inescapable despair? I shall never be able to find out. My father betrayed me. He took a knife to me, his baby son. What demonic command was he obeying? Surely it was not the word of God. I am freezing and I cannot afford their paraffin.

These days I am made to live on scraps; their chips, their pieces of cold fish. The borscht comes in a bottle and is more than I can pay. It is kosher; there is no ham bone in it. The soup is in tins. Good food is no longer within my means. I have dined exquisitely off gold and drunk from crystal. Yet I secretly knew I would some day be here. There is thin carpet beneath my broken chair. I wear gloves on my hands, one to hold the paper, the other to grasp the pen. There is no one to listen, no one to read what I write. It is private. I trusted only Mrs Cornelius and she is dead. I have been made to pay too dearly for my dreams.

Drunken black men come into my shop and spit on my jackets. When I complain they bring the Race Relations police. I am too old for arguments. I am without power. The British protect no one. It suits them to believe me a complaining old Jew. And I am the one who tried to warn them! It is like a terrible nightmare. I speak but I am not heard. I am not seen. It is an irony only a Russian truly appreciates. I was recognized before the War. By France, by Italy, Germany, America, Spain. But for that dreadful misunderstanding in Berlin, brought about by the jealousy and malice of small people, I should even now have my place in History.

'It don't do to think of the past,' said the man in the Post Office the other day. Five years ago it cost a mere 3p to send a letter! It seems impossible. They meddled with our currency. At a stroke they robbed us of half its value. What is that but International Finance? And is not International Finance simply a euphemism for World Jewry? They say 'the past is the past' as if that somehow excuses everything. But the past might also be the present and the future. In the twenties we believed Time had substance and could be measured, analysed, manipulated like Space. We were more confident then. We spoke of Time 'repeating' and 'feeding back on itself,' of having 'cycles.' We read John Donne's *Experiments with Time* and went to see the plays of Sir Jack B. Presley. Time became a small, comfortable mystery for a while, an old friend. Not the grinning, bony horseman of the Middle Ages. Then came Nuclear Energy and the Expanding Universe. Time was reclaimed by Einstein's gloomy moralists, his finger-wagging Jews. We fell again into the power of those pinched-lipped nomad shepherds.

The Jew brings dark confusion to the city. Here he can divide and rule. But he does not understand what he conquers. His rules are at odds with our rules: nomads cannot conceive of individuals with many functions and forms. They think a man who is more than one man is somehow evil, that a God who is Three cannot be. They demand consistency of an environment which to survive must constantly change. Christ was the Prophet of the City. He preached optimism and practical control. In the cities He was heard and accepted. The city is History, for the city is Man: He has created His own environment and rules. He built Sumer. Sumer was only destroyed when it became impossible for her to live by that blind obedience which means survival in the desert and which is suicide in the city.

86

I know these hippies. They go to the country to look for God as soon as it is Summer. But God is the City. The City is Time. The City is our true Salvation. We adapt it and are adapted by it. Science alone can help us return to God. I have lost the battle, but surely somewhere the War continues. The nomad cannot have won everything. *There shall be War in Heaven*, as the great Henry Williams said. They must listen. The English are conservative and condescending. They acknowledge only those of their own blood. If they had listened to me they could have had the laser, the jet engine and nuclear reactors long before the Americans. Arrogant in the twenties, Lloyd George planned further Imperial expansion. He should have consolidated, held the line. Others would have come to help. They decided to proceed alone, as deluded as the very Turks they had defeated, and followed in their complacency the crumbling road of Abdul Hamit, last true Ottoman Sultan. Mrs Cornelius listened to me with real attention. She had vision. In 1920 I thought her a typical representative of a generation of keen-eyed British people. I was wrong. She represented the past. 'Ther British are ther most open-minded people in ther world,' she would say. 'Look at orl ther fuckin' foreigners we let in.'

Time after time I tried to warn you. You were being destroyed from within. Even your scientific journals ignored me. *The New Scientist* is controlled by Communists. It has yet to print one of my letters. Party-line science is not true science; it is no better than magic; it is worse than alchemy. If the scientific ideal is perverted for political expediency you soon find yourself controlled by a Lysenko or Hoyle: dancing bears who will caper to any tune. They provide whatever their masters need. Mrs Cornelius was my comfort. Only she appreciated how profound my dedication was, but she feared neither for my sanity nor my soul. She knew the world's praise would come, perhaps after we were both dead. All I wanted was knowledge. I stood the brunt of every insult, spiritual, moral, physical. I am a little steppe-rooted tree which bends in the wind and is never blown over. Put me in the Portobello Road, surround me with blacks and Asians, feed me Jewish Wimpys and Cornish Pasties, and still I survive. Some of the older people in Finch's and *The Princess Alexandra* listen to me. I am too miserable to go to *The Elgin* now Mrs Cornelius is dead. Her friends understood suffering. They remembered the thirties and two Wars. But only the old Greek knows what 1453 really means. He sells fish and chips across the road from my shop. He stinks of grease and vinegar. His clothes are stained and his flesh splashed with patches of brown. They show him no more respect than they show me.

When the last Emperor of Byzantium died on his own battlements, his sword in his hand, the Turk wore chain mail and gilded helmets. He bore the banners of Islam and he cried the name of Allah. He came with his scimitars and his slaves, his eunuchs and his seraglios, his mosques and his imams, and he established himself in Constantinople. But now the Turk disguises himself. He laughs at Buster Keaton in the National Film Theatre, he attends lectures at the London School of Economics, he drinks beer in pubs and sleeps with Surrey virgins. He becomes a stage-star or a dentist. He smiles agreeably and his voice is soft. Yet behind the façade it is always 1453. His ambitions have not changed in a thousand years. They are the same as when his Hun ancestors first rode towards the West, when Bayezid the Strangler led his troops upon Constantinople and was repulsed. His is the spawn of Attila and brother to Tamburlane. From Jews he learned how to bribe the corrupt, to buy the desperate, to assassinate the strong. Arabs believe themselves free of his Empire, yet continue unconsciously to do his work. The old Greek knows the Turk ('he has a sword behind his back, a begging bowl stretching towards you') but because he is a Greek does nothing about the problem. He only talks. He smiles and offers me his day's leavings, his limp haddocks, his cooling scraps of cod. 'You are a good Christian,' I tell him. He and I both know kindness and meekness are self-destructive. But what is the alternative It is the paradox we must all live with. It is the core of the Christian mystery.

I have frequently been asked this question:

FOR HOW MANY MORE MILLENNIA MUST WE OF THE GENEROUS, GENTLE WEST SUFFER THE AVARICE OF THE CUNNING EAST?

The answer is simple. I wish I had known it in 1920 as the *Rio Cruz* steered into the Bosphorus. I reply now:

UNTIL A CHRISTIAN EMPEROR TAKES MASS IN HAGIA SOPHIA!

With his Cross and his Sword of Light he will come out of the West to redeem us! He will trample the dark descendants of Carthage beneath the silver hoofs of a pure white horse! Carthage knows no ideal save conquest, no joy save cruelty, no comradeship save that of the sword. Hers are the children of Cain, infected by an ancient evil. They must perish. The Lamb must stand astride Constantinople, two feet in Europe, two in Asia!

Fleeing to Australia is not the solution.

The Hun is in Vienna; he is in Brussels and Paris; he is in Berne and Baden-Baden. He has reached the gates of Stockholm and Oslo! Did our Christian knights die in their thousands for nothing? Has nobody heard of the standard Communist strategy? When direct attack is blocked, infiltrate. Was Senator McCarthy crying in the wilderness?

They say Adolf Hitler had a dark brain. If that is true then I too have a dark brain. I know the enemy and I am aware of his tactics. For this, they put me in the madhouse? Only last Sunday some English general wrote in the paper that he could not understand why so many Cossacks, Ukrainians and White Russians joined the German Army. I sent a letter. They enlisted to take vengeance on everyone who had betrayed them. Stalin was afraid of patriot and traitor alike. He killed all survivors. A Georgian, we used to say, is only a Turk who has put on a clean coat. My voice is weary from crying out warnings; my body is weak. I am lost in this wilderness of filth and decadence. I am attacked on all sides. I am slandered. MOTHER OF GOD! WHAT MORE MUST I GIVE? *Is there no one to whom I can pass my knowledge? Where are my sons and daughters? One child is all I want. Is it too much? The white light purifies my brain and mercury flows from my eyes. There are angels in the snow and their swords are silver. Little girls in cotton dresses run to me with scraps of paper and I cannot read them. They dazzle me. Carthage is on the horizon. Byzantium blazes like a mirror. It is to be the Final War. And the Knights of Christ are sleeping. Oh, how I envy those confident Jews!*

The fog was in my mouth.

The fog was in my mouth. The ship crawled through noisy, invisible water. Every so often she would let out a mournful moan almost immediately muffled and distorted. I shivered in my coat, my hands tight upon my pistols. The deck made fussy little movements beneath my feet. I saw dark shadows come and go on the bridge, but nobody spoke. It seemed the foghorn was sometimes answered, but it could have been an echo. Philosophically I wondered if I might be about to make a symmetrical ending to my life and die on the same day I was born, before I ever caught sight of Constantinople. This amused me. I was fatigued, I suppose, from lust and over-use of cocaine, but I was suddenly certain that I had the symptoms of Hernikof's typhus. I felt tranquil, however, and reconciled. Again the horn, like the Last Trump, made the whole ship vibrate. I moistened my lips with a damp glove. The fog clung like the hands of the dead to our oak and brass. Failing to see anything of either shore, I decided to use more cocaine. I had great faith in the drug's restorative powers and it would at least sustain me until I had a glimpse of Byzantium. I could not bear to miss what I had often been told was one of the world's most wondrous sights. If I were to die, I promised myself, it would be looking upon Heaven. I went down the companionway to our deck, opened the door of the cabin, and found Mrs Cornelius unexpectedly awake. 'Cor,' she said, 'wot a night, eh? Believe it or not, I fink I'll 'ave some brekker this morning.' I was re-assured by her cheerful normality. 'Eaten yet, Ive?'

'Not yet.'

While she rose to wash and dress, I sat down weakly on her bunk. Keeping my back to her as had become our custom I was able to draw a little cocaine into my nostrils. Almost immediately I felt better. She was now wearing her green silk dress with a mink coat thrown over it. 'Good enough,' she said of herself.

In the dining saloon she ordered a large breakfast. 'Bloody fog,' she said. 'I was 'opin' fer a view. Never seen it from this side, really.' She noticed with dismay some stains on her frock. 'Where'd they come from?' She brushed. 'We 'ad a few larst night, didn't we?' As if express-ing a sense of achievement she crossed her plump silken legs. The boy brought her bacon and eggs which looked revolting. All around us Rus-sians were taking black bread, omelettes and tea. She smacked her lips and shook sugar onto her fried bread, her usual custom. 'Yer never know when yer gonna get yer next proper breakfast,' she said. 'It was six bloody years, larst time, fer me.' She ate rapidly, ordering more bacon and eggs even before she had finished the first plate. 'An' yer better bring some toast an' marmalade,' she instructed the boy. My own stomach was too weak for this. I told her I needed some air. 'I'll see yer on deck,' she promised.

The fog was thinning, but it was not yet possible to see a shore. The wake of the ship became visible, however. I smoked a papyrussa and rested against the sterncastle rail. The Baroness found me as I began vi-olently to cough. I did my best to stop, but merely shook and spluttered more. 'You look ill, Simka. Could you have caught whatever it was poor Hernikof had?'

This alarmed me so much that the coughing continued afresh. I could tell her nothing of my fears. It was in nobody's interest to start a panic on board ship.

'Have you and your wife found somewhere to stay in Constantinople?' she asked.

I shook my head.

'We must be sure not to lose touch.'

I nodded in agreement. Another fit of coughing consumed me. The Baroness was distant and cool. Perhaps she deliberately prepared herself for separation. To me, however, she seemed offended. I frowned at her. I could not speak.

She took my frown for a question and apologised. 'I'm not myself today. The anxiety, I suppose. It will be the first time I have been to a country where Russian is not generally spoken.'

My fears for myself were rather more immediate. I determined I would seek out a nurse or a doctor as soon as was discreetly possible.

Jack Bragg strolled up. He pushed pale hair back from a pink face framed in navy blue. 'Not much of a view, I'm afraid. Frequently you can see both banks by now. But the fog's clearing nicely.' Then half to himself, 'With any luck the whole bloody place has been swallowed up.' His brother had been a prisoner in Scutari during the War and he had no love for the Turks. 'Where will you be staying? The Pera?'

I said my wife had made the arrangements. He warned me. 'Can't you ask someone you know to put you up? Even the best Turks will rob you if they can. And as for the Armenians . . .' In the Turkish capital Armenians were regarded much as Jews were in Odessa. A little sun now filtered through the fog. Bragg looked up like a hound catching the wind. 'Ah!' He peered forward, then pointed with his pipe. Both the Baroness and myself turned to look. The fog was pouring back now, like a stage curtain, and the ship emerged suddenly into clearer water. I saw a dim grey strip that was a shoreline with what seemed rather ordinary square buildings, a stand or two of trees; certainly nothing of the spectacle I had been promised.

'Constantinople seems rather drab.' The Baroness uttered a nervous laugh. 'Like everywhere else, I suppose. The reality's always disappointing.' A few distant horns sounded from hidden ships. A caïque with a triangular sail went by to starboard, leaning hard into the freshening breeze. I began to hear many more small, mysterious noises, as if of vigorous activity just out of sight. The ship took a turn or two to port. Then the rest of the fog broke away from our bow to stream like torn clothing off the rigging. We were immediately in open sea. Ahead the coast became more sharply defined. On the water's edge I distinguished large buildings apparently rising directly out of the sea. They seemed to be made of a greyish limestone. A light drizzle fell from clouds like discoloured pearl. Tugs, two or three small steamers, a sternwheel paddle-boat, a scattering of sailing vessels moved busily in the distance. The shipping seemed to span the entire millennium. On my right lay the European shore, on my left the Asian. I glanced from one to the other. I had expected far too much, it seemed, but the mist was heavy on both coasts. We passed little clusters of white houses and flimsy trees, tiny wharves against which single-masted fishing caïques were tied, where dark-faced men in shirt-sleeves rolled barrels, shifted bales and mended nets, like waterfront workers the world over. Most of these, however, wore the red tarboosh of Islam. Still more ships began to crowd around us, rushing this way and that across the water, puffing, creaking, hooting, apparently without any predetermined direction. The caïques sped crazily back and forth like dodgems at a fairground. I felt a sense of excitement at the ordinary commercial bustle around us. It had none of the hushed, nervous, doom-laden quality of recent Russian ports. Yet still I was disappointed. Constantinople was an ordinary, busy seaport, larger than Odessa had been before the War, but not much different. Still, it was cheering to see so much ordinary activity and not have to listen to gunfire.

The *Rio Cruz* slowed to quarter-speed, slipping gradually to starboard, urgently sounding her siren as she was narrowly missed by a side-paddle steamer full of impassive Levantines which drove directly across her bow. Thirty swarthy heads turned without much interest to watch us: a collection of greasy turbans, fezzes, burnooses and cloth-caps. The paddle-boat was painted bright streaky red. She carried a silver Islamic crescent on her smoke-stained funnel and clattered like a sewing-machine as she made her painful way towards the Asian shore while our own ship grumbled, an ill-tempered old lady discommoded by rowdies.

Human voices now emerged amidst the noises of the harbour traffic. I smelled smoke, burnt oil and sweet spices. My suspected typhus forgotten, I grew more animated as the Baroness for some reason became increasingly withdrawn. Polyglot shouts rose and fell with the movement and slap of the waves. As the drizzle was dissipated by the sunshine Jack Bragg returned to supervise his sailors making themselves busy with ropes and rigging; then the ship's engines changed to a violent, slow thud, shaking our entire hull every few seconds. On the bridge the captain's clear, commanding English was absorbed in a general babble from the port as we drew steadily closer to the European shore. I could distinguish individuals now, little cafés with balconies stuck out over the water, full of arguing, coffee-drinking Turks who ignored us completely. There were dense rows of evergreens, innumerable tracks leading inland from the clustered buildings, the boxes, barrels and bales heaped upon the wharves.

Then at last the sun broke through with full force so that the misty barrier was completely scattered and revealed the view. I was startled by it, for I had been unaware that so much had remained unseen.

Suddenly Constantinople was dramatically illuminated. Speech became impossible. I believe even the Baroness gaped. My senses ceased to register ships, voices or any ordinary details of dockside life.

Through massive, darkling clouds the sun sent a mile-wide golden fan of rays directly above the twin cities of Stamboul and Pera which lay upon hilly banks on both sides of the Golden Horn. In moments the mist vanished utterly and buildings glared and shimmered in a cool, delicate light. Old Byzantium was on my left with her crenellated turrets and fortresses, and commercial Galata on my right, a mass of newer buildings seeming to lean one against the other all around her harbour. Like Rome the old city was built on seven hills and each hill was rich with languid poplars, green parks and geometrical gardens, slender towers, massive domes. Directly from the waterfront Constantinople ascended tier upon breathtaking tier, a unique alchemy of history and geography; the accumulated architecture of two thousand years. Winter sun gleamed on marble roofs and gilded minarets, warmed the soft green cypresses. Everywhere were mosques, churches and palaces. Our ship, the harbour itself, was dwarfed by the enormous weight and variety of monumental stone. Merchantmen, destroyers, frigates, tugs, swarmed at her feet like midges on a pond. I had expected nothing so huge, so much like an Oriental fantasy. Even the industrial smoke rising in thin pillars from a dozen different points could as easily have poured from an exotic Arabian pyre. I half expected the smoke to form itself into the shape of gigantic genii or flying horses. At that moment I might have been Haroun-al-Raschid himself or wandering Odysseus first glimpsing the grandeur of Troy. This was a vision almost painful in its variety and beauty: our Emperor City.

The *Rio Cruz* began to steam in close to the low bridge stretching between Stamboul and Galata, its structure almost completely hidden by a multitude of ships and boats moored to it. Near either end of the bridge stood a huge domed mosque flanked by tall, delicate towers of the purest marble. The last of the clouds fell back towards the horizon and remained there, white and huge beneath glittering blue, and still more of the two cities was revealed: minaret upon minaret, dome upon dome, palace upon palace, into the distance above our heads. Here was the glory of Byzantium repeated a thousand times by the envious successors of Suleiman who believed themselves custodians of Constantine's tradition, even though they imposed their alien religion upon his city. Their mosques had all been built in imitation of Hagia Sophia, itself now a mosque, the noblest cathedral ever raised to the glory of Christ. Glowing green, gold and white in the soft sunlight the city was so much larger and more complex, so much older than anything I had previously known that I was momentarily overcome by a sense of terror. How easily one might be swallowed by Constantinople; to be lost, forgotten, unnoticed in the warrens of her complicated bazaars.

In comparison Odessa seemed no more than a small provincial town. When Jack Bragg rejoined us for a moment he was sardonic. 'It's impressive, but wait till you smell it. We'll dock near the European Customs House on the quay there. First we have to cross to Haidur Pasba to be cleared.' He guestured towards Asia. 'On the Scutari side. At most points this bit of water's no wider than the Thames. Astonishing what it separates.'

I resented his matter-of-fact voice; it interrupted my reverie, almost amounting to prayer. I had tried to cram, as it were, all the city into my eyes at once. The ship now turned her back on Byzantium and began her approach of the Eastern shore where the tall, official buildings were newer and built further apart, although there were still domes and minarets visible amongst the trees. We sailed towards a row of foreign warships flying the flags of Italy, America, Greece, France and England: the crosses of Christ, the tricolors of Liberty. All that was missing was our Russian flag. We had been pledged for centuries to restore Constantinople to Christ and at the moment of success we turned and destroyed one another in a bloody Civil War.

I believe I was weeping a little when Mrs Cornelius, holding to her face a handkerchief soaked in eau-de-cologne, came to stand unsteadily between me and the Baroness. She peered vaguely at the view, her from this side, dunnit?' She had passed through Constantinople with her Persian lover in 1914. 'So near and yet so bleedin' far, eh, Ivan?'

In twos and threes the Russian passengers began to come up on deck. They shared a sense of awe and, I suspect, trepidation. Constantinople was central to our deepest mythology, meaning far more to us than Rome to a Catholic. *Mimari Kimdir!* Millions had died in recent years profoundly certain their sacrifice would see our Tsar in person ultimately raising the Russian eagle above the Sublime Porte. The posters had clearly told us that a victorious Tsar, sword lifted in triumph, would set his heel upon the neck of a fallen Sultan. Then he would lead his knights to the doors of St Sophia to claim our oldest church, after five hundred years of humiliating thraldom, for Christ again. That was the worst the Bolsheviks stole from the Russian people when they told us to stop killing Turks and destroy one another. My only consolation was a glimpse of the Greek's blue-cross flag flying close to the Union Jack. When Lenin's Jewish masters withdrew our forces from the Crusade the Greeks had heroically picked up our Saviour's banner. But soon the Greeks would be cheated, too.

The *Rio Cruz* now sounded her whistle, a greeting to the other ships. I wished then that I could step ashore in Don Cossack uniform as a true representative of my nation. But it would have been madness to follow the impulse. I contented myself with a small, private prayer. Three old Russians were already on their knees. Many more sobbed and clasped their hands upon the rail. Hagia Sophia was released from Islam! We thought Christ redeemed. How could we predict his next betrayal? Even as the *Rio Cruz* stopped engines beside the stone quays of Scutari, Europe's Jews, secure in their financial fortresses, manipulated the assets of Allied capital. Soon one nation would be pitted against another. A Jew calling himself a Greek and bearing an aristocratic British title would become chief architect of the treachery to follow: Zaharoff the Armaments King already sold weapons to Greeks, Turks and Armenians alike. He ate the bread of Prime Minister Venizelos and accepted scented coffee from that unregenerate Champion of Islam, Mustafa Kemal. He lied to each in turn. He boasted his veins flowed with the blood of St Paul, then delivered up the city of his birth to Mahomet. The betrayal of Constantinople became just another page in the account books of Vickers-Armstrong.

The ship was finally at her moorings. Tall British naval officers stood on the dock chatting easily to khaki-clad Turks in red tarbooshes. They hardly glanced at us. The high shuttered windows of the Customs buildings provided perches for fluttering, eager gulls who seemed far happier to see us. A Crossley staff-car drew up at the gates. From it emerged a Medical Officer and his nurse. Either from excitement, terror or physical weakness I began to tremble. Perhaps I realized for the first time that I was free of Russia. The umbilical was being cut. The Baroness scarcely noticed my condition. She went to attend to her daughter. Amidships Jack Bragg held a megaphone to his lips and told our passengers there would be a delay until necessary checks were made. The Greek priest interpreting for Jack had a face as calm as an ikon; his black arms flapped as he made placatory movements with his hands.

I looked back across the water to shimmering Byzantium. It was from here I supposed the first Hun hordes rested on their pommels, shielded their eyes and licked their lips in greedy anticipation at their prospective prize. The mercantile pivot of the world, Byzantium had been in a state of decadence, even then, for over a thousand years. I could still make out her far off palaces, her green and golden hills. At this distance she seemed unchanged, just as she might have looked in the time of Theodosius or Justinian the Great. For those thousand years moralists had called her decadent and predicted her end, yet no city, even Rome, retained her original character as thoroughly as Constantinople.

Mrs Cornelius glanced at me. 'You orl right, Ive?'

Still trembling, I shrugged off her concern. I tried to speak, but could not. My throat was too dry. I think my legs gave out, though I did not faint. I remember her saying, 'Oh, shit. Wot bleedin' orful luck.' Through the rail I could see the first officials beginning to come aboard. I tried to stand, but failed. I fell heavily against her legs. Having been granted my vision of Heaven, I felt now I must surely die.

Five

ON WEDNESDAY, JANUARY 1st 1920 I died a Russian and on January 14th (by the Western calendar) I was born a Cosmopolitan. I had suffered a mild attack of typhus. For his own convenience the British doctor diagnosed nervous exhaustion. *Ich Kann nicht so lange warten.* According to Mrs Cornelius and the Baroness I babbled in half-a-dozen different languages. I had visions. I spoke of my loved ones, of my mother, of Esmé, Captain Brown, Kolya, Shura and the rest. I relived the glories and horrors of my past. They told me I had most frequently believed myself a boy in Odessa. This did not surprise me. I lost my youth in Odessa (but I was to discover my humanity in Constantinople).

By the time I recovered my senses it had grown dark. I was cradled in a wide, high-sided bunk. Shadowy lamplight revealed the Baroness seated beside me, her hair unruly, wearing a brown velvet dress and yellow apron. She was holding my hand but was half asleep. Weakly I tried to rise, only to discover I had lost the use of my legs. Believing as always in the power of mind over matter, I refused to panic. I knew I must eventually walk again; it required only an effort of will. When I squeezed her hand her eyes popped open mechanically, as if she were a trick toy. 'Where am I, Leda Nicolayevna?'

'This is Captain Monier-Williams's own cabin, Simka. The doctor thinks you are in some sort of shock. You don't have typhus, though everyone's been tested. There doesn't seem to be sickness aboard, after all.'

I held my tongue, letting her think whatever most comforted her. 'Mrs Pyatnitski?'

97

She had helped nurse me. Currently she was enjoying a late dinner. 'She said she'd look in before she goes to bed. And Jack Bragg and Mr Thompson will be visiting you. We're all, of course, in quarantine. But it won't be for long.'

At that time I believed as firmly as now that a miracle had occurred. I had been saved in order to fulfil my proper destiny. 'My cocaine is still in my luggage, I hope.' I trusted more in the drug's powers than in the quack's.

'It's impossible for me to get. I said nothing, naturally, to the doctor.'

I slipped back into sleep. I had no dependence on the drug, but its healing properties would help me recover. Even then cocaine was beginning to receive a bad name. Artists painted men collapsing in their wives' laps and labelled the pictures 'Cocaine!' The Coca-Cola Company was forced to remove the drug from its recipe. This persecution anticipated prohibition. While cocaine remained freely available it was something International Pharmaceutical Companies could not control. These companies wanted it all to themselves, so they could put their own name on it and trumpet it as a 'wonder cure.' They conspired therefore to lie about its bad effects and campaigned to characterise the ordinary user as a degenerate. Ironically of course my sparing use of cocaine probably saved me from full scale typhus.

I awoke only half-an-hour or so later. Leda was still there. 'You must forgive me if I acted strangely this morning.' She was tender. 'I thought you were unnaturally cool towards me. I now realize you were feeling ill. Do you still wish to arrange a meeting in Constantinople' She reached forward with a damp cloth to wipe my forehead. 'There's a restaurant where Russians go. If we're separated, we should look for each other at Tokatlian's.'

'I'll remember.' I spoke feebly, still more than a little surprised to be alive.

She moistened my lips. 'Poor little Ancient Mariner.' The reference was as obscure to me then as it is now. I had never seen an albatross, let alone killed one with a crossbow. People fond of literary references always disturbed me. The poems and stories they read mean something only to them and possess virtually no relation to reality. But she was romantic, my Baroness, and I suppose I was fond of her for it. Perhaps I am too much a man of science. I have known many great poets. Few of them ever struck me as being very stable. As for the modern T. S. Eliot school and its attempts to glorify the language and manners of the gutter,

I am repulsed by it. I heard such rubbish in its birthplace when the likes of Mandelstam and Mayakovski used it to cheer on their Red patrons. I see no virtue in elevating the football hooligan and the petty spiv to the status of demigods.

She turned the lamp down when I explained it hurt my eyes. Did I wish her to read to me? I asked if it was possible to find a newspaper, preferably an English one, on the ship. She had seen a *Times of Cairo* somewhere and left to look for it. Whoever had undressed me had put me in a pair of pyjamas not my own. I searched for my clothes to see if I had left any cocaine in the pockets. But they were presumably being disinfected. I wondered why our quarantine was to be so short. Now it is obvious they were afraid of starting a typhus scare. For that reason they chose to diagnose my attack as 'nervous exhaustion.' I was too naive then to realize how frequently authorities acted from motives of straightforward expediency.

Leda returned with the paper. It was all news of Peace Conferences and temporary solutions. There were a few references to Russia, how Mr So-and-So sought negotiation with 'Mr Lenin' or 'Mr Trotski.' More informative were ordinary reports from London: the King opening a new airship works, a rabid speech from Lloyd George, propagating that intemperate radicalism which eventually destroyed him and his Party. Many were warning of Socialism in England. Already Germany was threatened by a Red take-over, as were France and Italy (where the Vatican was in league with the communists). Few had learned from Russia's present agony. Did people actually envy us our death-struggles? I told Leda I wanted to hear of human achievement, not human folly. She could find little enough to read after that.

For two more days I remained in the captain's bunk, drinking tasteless soup, sipping vile medicine, until a pasty-faced, fastidious Medical Officer, who could barely bring himself to touch me, pronounced me well. Mrs Cornelius had by then gone ahead to Pera and was staying at the *Palas*. The ship had crossed from Scutari to the European side, my documents and trunks had been cleared. I could leave the ship whenever I chose. Jack Bragg had helped the Baroness find temporary lodging with a German family near the Artillery Barracks. My own destination was closer, in the main part of Pera. There were no cabs easily available at this particular part of the Galata docks (Galata and Pera lay on the Bosphorus shore of the pontoon bridge) and I was advised to use public transport. Captain Monier-Williams shook hands and promised my luggage would be sent on to the hotel. I asked to be remembered to Thompson and Bragg, who had already gone ashore. I packed the small bag, still feeling a little weak, and made my way along the decks of the deserted *Rio Cruz*, down the gangplank and onto the stone flags of the quayside. On solid ground after so long it took time to regain my land-legs. Handing me a little coin, a Marine sergeant escorted me through the barriers, past the grey respectability of the Customs offices and up the steps to the busy street where the buildings were immediately far more disreputable-looking, with peeling whitewash, layers of posters, flaking paint, broken windows. The sergeant pointed to the hand which held the coin. 'You can get the tram here,' he said. He indicated a filthy green sign. 'You'll want the Number One.' He did an about face and swung off. In the hills overhead there was a little sunshine, but down here were only the remnants of mist.

For a moment I felt deserted by everyone. Bitterly, I thought the captain could have had the grace at least to instruct a rating to take me to the hotel. Later, however, I was grateful. It is always best to be thrown into the middle of a new city; then one quickly learns how to get about, which languages are understood best, and so on. French was the weakest of my tongues, but I found it appropriate to remember as much as possible when I noticed the signs and advertisements everywhere. Half were in French. The Number One, I had been told, went to the Grand Champs des Morts, the Foreign Cemetery. I must get off at the Petit Champs. I waited on the narrow, dirty pavement, hemmed in by dozens of ramshackle buildings, trying to get my bearings. The dockside offices obscured my view of the harbour, but I could see some masts and funnels and glimpsed the nearby Galata Bridge. This was perpetually full of human traffic streaming back and forth between Stamboul and Galata. Near the tram-stop were a few shops with unwashed windows, selling shoddy household furnishings, bric-à-brac, lamps and inlaid tables. On all sides the crowds moved slowly yet were marvellously animated; a spectrum of the Levant: Turks, Armenians, Caucasians, Jews, Russians, as well as sailors from all the great European nations. Not a white man on the street, however, could go more than a few yards without some Jewish beggar accosting him. No matter how hard the Jews were beaten down, they still continued to lift crooked, imploring fingers.

The gloomy streets leading steeply up to Pera were mysterious canyons. Many were broken by crazy flights of steps to ease their sudden ascent. They sheltered mendicants of every description, sellers of carpets, oil-jars, sweets. In some of them boys on bicycles with car-horns attached to their handlebars tried to clear a way through the press of automobiles, donkeys, bullock carts, elegant carriages and even an occasional sedan chair. These alleys stank of horse-droppings, dogs, human urine, coffee, roasting mutton, tobacco, spices and perfumes. Veiled women with swift eyes like pebbles on a tide were almost as numerous as men. Since I knew it was unwise for foreigners to show interest in Turkish ladies I avoided looking at them. I already risked having my throat cut for my gold; I did not want it cut for a misplaced glance.

At long last, crackling and sputtering, the dirty green Number One drew up at the stop. Its brass and wooden sides were so battered it might itself have served at the Front. As I made to mount the footboard I was engulfed. From everywhere suddenly came Turks in fezzes, Greeks in bowlers, Armenians in astrakhan caps. I was swept upward, having time only to offer my silver piastre piece in exchange for a first-class ticket printed in French. The conductor carelessly accepted my money, took me by the arm and pushed me towards the back of the tram where there were fewer people. As I began to sit on one of the wooden benches, there came a great wave of hissing from behind me. Black eyes glared over veils. I realized with horror that I was in the Ladies Only section. The conductor had seen me. He shouted in Turkish, pointing a severe finger at the sign so faded it was unreadable. Blushing, I eventually settled beside a dignified Circassian, in bandoliers, long-skirted coat, soft riding boots, who held a brief-case in his lap and stroked at grey moustaches, which lay against his nose like suckling rodents, and stared out into the teeming street. I said 'Good morning' to him in Russian, but he made no response. It began to drizzle. The tram juddered, whimpered, then continued its painful journey up steep, winding streets. On all sides of the vehicle men and women, youths and girls, swarmed apparently at random. Most wore some form of Western clothing, frequently blended with Oriental dress, and none was particularly clean. But at least I was witnessing ordinary life; life as I had known it in, say, the backstreets of St Petersburg and in my native Kiev before the War. Conquered though they were, the Turks continued about their ordinary business. They had not been forced to creep cautiously, looking over their shoulders in terror for their lives and liberty, as was the case in so many Russian cities now. Indeed the contrast was increased for me since Pera was also Constantinople's main Russian quarter. Many of my countrymen still wore their uniforms. Others wore suits of typical Moscow and Petersburg cut. Aristocrats and peasants were equal here as they would never be in Russia, all desperate for passports or work, for someone to buy what remained of their treasures. I would have recognised them as easily from their dazed expressions, their haunted eyes, their uncertain movements, as by their clothes. I put one hand into my coat pocket to grasp the butt of a pistol. I had looked at such faces for too long and was determined my own should never again resemble them.

Leaving the water behind, the tram approached another, coming from downhill. I thought they must certainly crash head-on. The two vehicles passed so close, swaying wildly in the narrow street, that their sides almost touched. There was a general clanking and whining and ringing of bells. Our tram swung round a corner to the left then almost immediately took another to the right. I was shaken, disoriented, uncomfortable, but happy to be in a city again, no matter how strange. Everywhere I looked the unstable wooden buildings, several storeys high, often unpainted, their foundations shaken by half-a-dozen earthquakes at least, seemed about to collapse into the street, yet from time to time appeared a magnificent Islamic dome, a mosque which had stood like a rock for centuries; elsewhere were marble towers, a little green park; and everywhere, suddenly, were clumps of poplars, cypresses and pines. We passed ragged, blackened gaps where houses had been razed by fire; there were piles of rubble, as if from shelling, new buildings half-constructed then apparently abandoned; elsewhere grandiose modern façades were already cracking and crumbling. Pera might have been the back lot of a run-down cinema company. What was substantial was in poor repair, what looked imposing was a sham, what looked most theatrical was probably the best piece of architecture in the town. This 'new' ghetto, where successive Sultans had confined their foreign visitors since the treaty with Genoese traders in the sixteenth century, had been allowed to exist in deliberate contrast to the Moslem city on the Golden Horn's opposite bank. I glimpsed Stamboul occasionally through gaps in the buildings as the tram swerved this way and that. From Pera the view of ancient Constantinople was unspoiled and magnificent. I was reminded of some dreaming, elegant Caliph swaddled in sensuous luxury, carelessly unaware of the noise and poverty, the common stink from which he was separated only by a short expanse of water, a couple of narrow bridges.

The tram now began to move up a wider street containing better proportioned, more evidently European stone buildings. There were well-ordered trees, shops selling better-quality goods, yet still thoroughfares were crowded, smelly, full of vagrant noise. The conductor yelled at me from the far side of a dozen greasy fezzes. 'Arrivé,' he shouted. 'Arrivé, monsieur!' He gestured towards the wall of a small park which I could just see through the windows. I pushed through hard, unhelping flesh towards the exit, climbed down the tram's wooden steps, checked my possessions were still about me, and as the vehicle moved on, stood upon a broken flagstone looking up and down the street. I was in the Grande Rue de Pera, the avenue of embassies, hotels, and popular legend. My childhood thrillers had not properly prepared me for the reality. I had expected something closer to the Nevski Prospect or the Nicholas Boulevard, something wide, imposing, secluded. But I had forgotten the cleverness of Turks, who put all foreigners together where they might fight amongst themselves, where they could be subjected to daily inconvenience. I wandered back and forth across the street, dodging bicycles, horsemen, dogs, a kind of rickshaw, and at last recognized the wrought-iron balconies of the *Pera Palas*, said to be the best hotel in the city. (And also, I was soon to discover, a notorious haunt of Kemalists and foreign agents.)

Lack of serious trouble in finding my hotel, however, dispersed the remains of my poor temper. I had become almost jaunty as I walked into the cool lobby, going straight to the reception desk. The place was relatively peaceful after the noise outside, and fairly clean. The cacophonous streets were somehow muffled, giving the place that proper sense of untroubled tranquillity and security, the mark of any first-class hotel. In common, too, with many other hotels of its day, the *Palas* had a tendency towards plush, black rococo cast-iron and gilt. Uniformed porters, in frockcoats, tarbooshes, and wearing white gloves, were in abundance. Even the Greek manager, waxed and fat, contrived to look French. I announced myself. He consulted his register. At length he nodded. 'So pleased you were able to find us, m'sieu.' He handed my key to an Armenian porter and the man, looking like some janissary from the Sultan's guard, strode to the lift with an air of quiet dignity. We ascended smoothly to the third floor. My room was displayed with a touch of ceremony by the porter who appreciated my mumble of approval. The room was small, looking out over the Grande Rue, and was opulently comfortable for what it was, with its own wash-stand and toilet facilities. Again I used a silver rouble to tip the porter. Silver of any currency was perfectly acceptable to Turks, though I learned French Napoleons and British sovereigns were (perhaps since Lawrence) the common coin of larger dealings. I ordered some hot water. The bed, with its carved and gilded headboard, its red velvet coverlet, was luxurious. I had an armchair, a little writing-desk, a box-room for my trunks and a large wardrobe. The little dressing-room had solid, if old-fashioned, facilities, including a full-length mirror. While I waited for the water, I took from my toilet case my razor, hand-mirror and a packet of cocaine. For the first time in a month I could enjoy my drug in relaxed and pleasant surroundings. A good-looking youth brought my water, some fresh towels, and soon I felt completely myself again. I had on a clean shirt, a smart dark brown three-piece suit, and I had oiled my hair. Now I was myself again: Colonel M. A. Pyat, late of the 13th Don Cossack Regiment, scientist and man-of-the-world.

I was arranging my brushes and boxes in the dressing-room, when there came a knock on the door. Adjusting my tie I went to answer. It was only the bellboy with a note on a salver from Mrs Cornelius. *Welcome ashore, Ivan. Sorry I'm not here to show you around but I know you'll do all right by yourself. Back in couple of days. Love, H.C.* I was disappointed. Doubtless she was visiting her Frenchman. But I refused to become depressed. I would have time now to see something of the city before we continued on to England via the Orient Express (or by another ship). I had of course looked forward to having my first meal with her, but consoled myself: Soon I would be dining with Mrs Cornelius as often as I liked in London. All that really mattered was that I was at last in a true metropolis. There was no immediate threat from an invading enemy for the police of five Allied nations kept the peace. In Constantinople, too, one might enjoy every conceivable form of pleasure. I remembered the old saying that here the Moslem lost his virtues and the European added to his vices. There is nowhere quite as thrilling as a city recently emerged from War. Men and women develop eager habits of living to the full. From my window alone I could see dozens of restaurants, little theatres, cabarets. It was not yet lunch-time and already music came from the cafés. Fair-skinned, uniformed young men walked up and down the Grande Rue with unveiled, laughing Turkish girls on their arms. Everyone seemed so carefree. It would never be possible to capture the joy of my youth in Odessa, but Constantinople promised at least a taste of that old exhilaration. In fact it would be here I really discovered my ability to become quickly at home in any great metropolis. It would take me a few hours to learn the chief streets, a few days to discover the best restaurants and bars. A cosmopolitan city has a common language frequently making speech unnecessary. People come to be entertained, to buy and sell, to exchange ideas, to be artistically replenished, to embark upon sexual adventures. The complexity of trade is in itself the central stimulus. This is true of the poorest citizens as it is of the well-to-do. Only the very rich seem to know the kind of boredom which comes upon me, for instance, in the countryside; but such people would be bored anywhere; they have nothing to buy, nothing to sell, no nemesis save the ennui itself. To my joy I could hear Russian being spoken in the Grande Rue de Pera; I could hear French and English, Italian, even Yiddish, Greek and German. My blood quickened as it recognized its natural environment and I began to experience the rush of pleasure which accompanied the almost immediate revival of my complete old self. For too long I had experienced a half-life. Now I was about to set elegant patent leather upon real streets again.

In those days I had not discovered the consolations and demands of religion. For me my soul and my senses were the same and God's work could only properly be accomplished by means of the investigations and applications of Science. Perhaps this was the form of *hubris* Prometheus suffered. Perhaps that was why I, too, came to be punished. I wished to enlighten a world I believed had a positive will towards peace and knowledge but, as a young man, I was also full of unexplored emotional and physical desires. I wanted to discover the limits of my appetites. In 1920 the political fate of Constantinople did not at all concern me. I naturally assumed the Turk was conquered forever; Britain or Greece would run the city until Russia was sane again and ready for the task. In the meantime, I hoped to taste as many of her pleasures as I could. I had been starved for too long. In Kiev, after the Revolution, I had frequently managed to entertain myself, but my enjoyment had been coloured by the pervading uncertainty of the times. This had also been true in Odessa just before I left. But in Constantinople there were no Bolsheviks or Anarchists threatening my peace of mind. I had never heard of the so-called Committee of Union and Progress. I knew certain Young Turk officers and soldiers had refused to lay down their arms and disappeared into the Anatolian hinterland, but I assumed they would soon be rounded up. My overriding thought was that I was free. I had been resurrected as a citizen of the world. Russia's tragedy was no longer mine. I unclipped my plan-case to look afresh at my drawings and equations, my neatly written notes. Here was my fortune and my future. My nose would be against the grindstone soon enough. In the meanwhile I deserved a small vacation. Dressed and groomed to perfection, I locked my door behind me, took the lift to the ground floor, handed in my key, said I would be back before dinner, and joined the life of the city outside. I had no real fear that anyone I had known in Odessa might casually recognize me out of uniform (or, if they did, I knew they would be wary of me) and could not really believe there was any immediate chance of meeting enemies from my Kiev or Petersburg days; most of those, after all, must have been killed by now. In fact I was perhaps a shade over-confident, certain I could easily overcome any danger, drunk on the freedom of the captured Turkish capital. Yet I cannot say I was a fool. My eye, from habit, was forever cautious. In the steppe villages I had been afraid because I could not interpret most of the gestures, signals and subtleties of their environment; but here, though the place was new to me, I could read most signs very readily and those not immediately recognisable could be rapidly learned.

Instinctively I took a side street here, a main thoroughfare there. Crossing a little park I entered a shadowy café, ordering a cup of coffee while looking at everything and everyone, absorbing information swiftly and steadily: the little ways people had of using their hands, inflexions of speech, when they adopted passive mannerisms, when they felt able to seem aggressive. I knew I too was the object of their interest, because I was dressed so well, but I did not worry about that. Good spirits are one's best protection anywhere. An open heart frequently saves you in the most appalling confrontations. In that sense it is always better for a city-dweller to be an innocent rather than to carry a gun. And one must be a good, natural actor: every day in a large metropolis we are called upon to play a variety of subtly different roles. It is nonsense, all this modern talk of what is a 'real' identity and what is not. We are the sum of our backgrounds, our experience and our environments; the self we present to the greengrocer is merely a different aspect of the self we present to the police inspector. The more conscious one is of this necessity of city life, the less one is confused, the easier it is to take action when action is called for.

I studied the traffic. I stood in the cemetery of the Petit Champs, beneath poplars and plantains, and looked across the glinting Golden Horn at old Stamboul on her seven, misty hills. I turned to my left and saw the Bosphorus lying between me and Asian Scutari. I marvelled at the volume of shipping. It crowded the waters as densely as any city-street. Yet it was nothing compared to the unguessable vastness of the ancient city. I had never realised any metropolis could sprawl so far in so many directions and in this case on three distinct shores. Russian cities, even St Petersburg, were tiny in comparison, virtually embryonic. Constantinople had no visible limits. She seemed spaceless as well as timeless, inhabiting a universe of her own devising: an infinite island existing outside the planet's ordinary dimensions, where all races, all ages coincided at once. So strong was this impression that I found myself trembling with pleasure at the notion and became reluctant to leave the gardens until, somewhere beyond a wall, a donkey (or perhaps an imam) began to bray, destroying my mood. I continued up a narrow, shady street cleaner than most, its terraces of apartments apparently occupied entirely by European families. At the end of this street was a parade of shops selling stationery, books, perfume, flowers, sweets and tobacco, reminding me of any decent middle-class part of Kiev. The titles of the books were in every European language, including Russian. I bought a packet of papyrussa and thus changed one of my Imperial roubles, knowing I was cheated on the rate but not caring. I turned back, eventually, into the Grande Rue. From a little boy who squeaked at me in an unidentifiable language I purchased a button-hole; he made strange smacking sounds with his lips. I bought Russian-language newspapers at a kiosk. Sitting at an outside table of a coffee-shop, I drank sherbert and read the papers, amused by their grandiloquent Tsarisms and empty pomposities. I smiled at girls with heavily painted faces and cheap finery who winked at me as they passed by. Every other woman appeared to be a whore and every whore looked beautiful to me. There were also dozens of upper-class ladies in expensively cut Parisian clothes and elaborate hats and even some of these spared me a glance. I loved such an ambience. It is gone completely from modern life.

Tolerantly I waved away street-sellers offering me everything from their brothers' buttocks to their sisters' second-hand dolls. I bought some candy for a few *kuruş*, tried a little and handed it to the first child who begged a coin from me. Soon I had a reasonable sense of my location. The high part of town, Pera, was predominantly European, full of embassies and the mansions of the rich, offices of banking houses and shipping companies, better-quality shops. Sprawled below this, its border marked by the Galata Tower built by the original Genoese traders, were the mean, twisting alleys and jerry-built warrens of the poor. Further up the hill, beyond Pera, were suburban villas in spacious gardens, a predominance of lawns and parks. From the waterfront Galata Bridge led across the Horn to Stamboul, dominated here by Yeni Cami, the so-called New Mosque, with its unbelievably slender towers and clustered domes of different sizes. Stamboul was the Turkish city, though it also possessed a Greek quarter whose occupants traced their ancestors to before the time of Christ. Here were most of the older Orthodox Churches; the ancient, vaulted cisterns which were still in use, and the original walls of Byzantium, all productions of a superior culture the Turks might frequently imitate but never better. The most magnificent building of Stamboul remained Hagia Sophia, visible from Pera and distinguished easily by her bright yellow dome. This most beautiful of Christian churches the Ottomans continued to use as a model for their mosques. Although the majority of famous monuments were in Stamboul, making her the true site of Byzantium, perhaps Pera was the real Constantinople. Pera was where the Byzantines had buried their dead (it was still full of vast cemeteries for most races and religions), where the Osmanlis had hidden foreigners necessary to their trade; a city which flourished between dusk and dawn, given over to subtle diplomacy, exotic pleasures, obscure crimes and even more obscure vices, yet during the day the outward appearance of dignity and moral respectability, one of the marks of a typical European capital, was preserved. I was curious, of course, to visit Stamboul, but the pleasures of Pera took priority. I made no effort to restrain myself. I was a child given limitless credit in a sweetshop. I considered some sort of programme. It would not be wise to break immediately with the Baroness, unless her clinging proved inconvenient, neither must I lose contact with Mrs Cornelius. However, there would be no harm in my making fresh acquaintances. The more people I knew the more possibilities for self-improvement could present themselves. I reminded myself of every habit I had developed during the War and the Revolution. I remained wary of acquaintances from my former life, whether they displayed friendship or not. So many refugees filled up Pera I must inevitably run into some who might embarrass me. They would know me under a former name or might have met me when I posed as a Red or a Green. People were untrusting and might easily refuse to believe I had been forced from necessity to play these roles. It did not suit me to become again an object of suspicion. Thus I gave particular attention to Russians, surreptitiously inspecting every face. It would have been difficult if I had bumped into the young women I had known in Petersburg, for instance, or some radical bohemian who believed me a Bolshevik pederast because I had kept company with my dear friend Kolya. I could still see Brodmann, pointing his finger at me, screaming 'Traitor'. This had been the direct cause of my precipitous flight from Odessa. Nevertheless, I remained confident that in most cases I could bluff out any such confrontation.

It was important to preserve the reputation of a man of breeding and education and continue to move amongst the better classes. The British were prepared to take me on my own terms. I was a brilliant engineer with a good War record, forced out of Russia by the Reds. If broadcast, the unimportant details, while they did not touch on the essential truth, could conceivably make life difficult for me. So anyone who called me 'Dimka' would be ignored (unless I had known them really well). I would grow a moustache at the earliest opportunity. Strolling on downhill, into the little, miserable back streets of the Galata quarter, I deliberately absorbed impressions of poverty as well as wealth. I had not expected to find so many tall wooden buildings. Little remained of the original Genoan architecture. Here and there was an old house mounted on pilasters but the most substantial building was now Galata Tower raised to commemorate Italian soldiers who had fallen in battle, called originally the Tower of Christ. The rickety wooden apartments rose five or six storeys high, leaning at all angles, like a German expressionist film set. If a single one of these were demolished, I thought, a thousand more might collapse as a result. Perhaps such bizarre structural tensions (makeshift, workable, incapable of logical analysis) closely reflected the city's social tensions. Constantinople survived then as Calcutta is said to survive today: superficially in conflict, everyone depended crucially upon everyone else.

Fez, turban, top-hat, military pith, panama bobbed in those agitated human currents. I walked back towards Pera. The short side streets running between Rue des Petits Champs and Grande Rue de Pera were full of little bars and brothels crammed, in turn, with men and women of every racial type and class. Hybrid girls and youths touted for trade in doorways not a stone's throw from great foreign embassies, dominated in turn by the monstrous stone palace of our Russian Consulate. From basements and upper windows jazz poured into alleys. Whores hung over baroque balconies, gossiping with friends on the other side of the street, occasionally pausing to yell at a potential customer. It was like a city of Classical antiquity. Had Constantinople remained unchanged since the Greek colonists founded her six hundred years before Christ? Had Tyre been like this? Or Carthage herself? I was entranced. Here was the heady lure of Oriental fantasy. I daydreamed of beautiful houris, the languorous seraglios, unbelievable luxury, fantastic delights. Constantinople offered still richer variety than she had presented under the most decadent of Sultans, for now her inhabitants experienced unusual freedom as well as uncertain thraldom. No longer did the Lords of Islam administer absolute power from the Yildiz Kiosk but even in Pera the muezzin still called thousands to prayer. The tyranny of Islam could not be abolished overnight. To clear Byzantium of such alien authority might take years, or never be wholly accomplished, but today such authority was held in question by people who previously had never dared allow themselves such thoughts. The fierce, mad puritanical Faith, therefore, had suddenly lost much of its sway. As a consequence those freed from it were presently possessed of a lust to sample all that had previously been forbidden. To this was added a fresh element of corruption – desperate refugees eager for the slightest opportunity to make a few lira. In some of those wooden tenements aristocratic Russian families lived ten to a tiny room. Greeks and Jews had taken advantage of the Ottoman defeat to turn the tables on old Turkish rivals; Armenians occupied the palaces of Abdul Hamid's disgraced officials or the villas of Arab merchants who had been ruined by their support for the Sultan's cause. The Turks, so far as it can ever be said of Turks, were momentarily demoralized. In two years they had seen their vast Empire, built through centuries of conquest, reduced to that pathetic 'Anatolian homeland' from which, in the thirteenth century, Osman their founder had sprung in all his ambitious ferocity, to sink his teeth into the throat of Europe. Now few believed Constantinople would remain even nominally Turkish for much longer. Already into this uncertain ambience the greedy carpetbaggers of Western Jewry had arrived to pick at unearned spoils. For me and millions like me the war against Turkey had been a Crusade. But as with so many other

Crusades this one had rapidly degenerated to a mere squabble over treasure and power. I realized none of this at first, I must admit. I saw only a superabundance of potential experience, an exotic blend of human types, infinite possibilities of fulfilling not only my wildest desires but of discovering tastes as yet uncultivated. That afternoon, at a bar serving only the best class of Europeans, I sipped cognac presented to me on a silver salver by a Russian Tatar in Moldavian shirt and White Army breeches. I could not possibly guess how radically my destiny would be influenced by this city.

(I had passed through ruins, slums, festering heaps of offal, yet I saw a new Byzantium rising on both sides of the Golden Horn. She would be the capital of a World Government, founding city of a future Utopian State. Peace would surely follow the crisis. The only question remaining was how this peace must be maintained, who should most fairly rule. What I did not know was that already Kemalists, financiers, Bolsheviks, schemed division and destruction. The formulae for Utopia in my document-case were available to everyone. Is it my fault the world refused its redemption?)

Slowly and extremely cheerfully I made my way back to the hotel. I bought a map and changed a little more money into Turkish lira. I hoped to make it last until I left Constantinople, for this was not the best time or place to sell the jewellery I had brought from Russia. In London I could get the proper market price. On the other hand I thought I might give a bracelet or a necklace to the Baroness. She was, when all was said and done, a decent enough woman. I would not want her or Kitty to suffer the fate of other refugees.

In my room I was delighted to discover that my luggage had arrived. I changed immediately into Don Cossack uniform. Now a veteran Colonel, not yet twenty-one, looked out of the full-length mirror, bearing himself with dignity impossible in even the best-cut civilian clothes. The uniform had been earned by my suffering. It redeemed my father, honoured my mother, celebrated my country. However, I knew it was still unwise to wear it in public. Regretfully I removed it, folded it and put on ordinary evening clothes before going downstairs for an apéritif. A number of high-ranking British and French officers were in the bar, mingling with well-to-do men and women of the finest type. I was glad Mrs Cornelius had been able to get us the rooms. Seating myself on a stool beside the stiff but slender back of a British army major I ordered in English a whisky-and-soda. He turned at the sound of my voice and nodded to me. 'Good evening,' I said. 'I am Pyatnitski.' He seemed surprised at my command of his language. 'Good evening. I'm Nye.' He had washed-out blue eyes, abstracted but kindly. His tanned skin was stretched tight on near fleshless features and he had a neat, greying moustache. After a glance around the bar he half reluctantly agreed to take a large gin-and-tonic. When I explained I was a flyer shot down over Odessa while observing Bolshevik positions it obviously eased his mind. As if in apology he said he had just recently arrived from India. 'In their wisdom, our top brass seem to think my experience of Pathans on the Frontier will be of use in Constantinople!' He was otherwise vague about his commission. Learning I had only that day stepped ashore and planned to travel on to London, he warmed further. I did not resent his caution. As he said himself, later, one had to be frightfully careful of the people one talked to at the *Pera Palas*. I knew little of the campaign in Anatolia against Turkish nationalists. Mustafa Kemal's name meant nothing. Although I gathered a Greek army currently advanced into the Anatolian mainland I was ignorant of the detailed issues. It simply seemed just that Greece should be claiming her due. Major Nye willingly offered to sketch the background but would say nothing, of course, about British policy. He had every admiration for the heroism of our White Army he told me. Russia should be given charge of Constantinople as soon as possible. 'She knows the Turk best. You must understand, I'm no supporter of Russia's territorial ambitions elsewhere, not in Afghanistan or the Punjab at any rate.' He smiled as he sipped his gin. He thought the British should meanwhile administer the city in the name of the Tsar and King Constantine. 'Until things calm down a bit. The East has to be contained. I have every respect for the Asian mind and naturally I love India. There's much we can learn. But if Asia ever really adopts the manners and ambitions of the West, masquerading in English pinstripe and spouting German metaphysics, she'll become a danger to herself and to us.' He pointed in the general direction of Scutari. 'The Turks can have Smyrna for their capital, by all means. Let them take the whole of Anatolia. In other words they should stay in Asia. The Greeks can then take Thrace, while the Russian exiles shall have Constantinople, which I agree is theirs by tradition. With British support the Greeks and Russians will then form our strongest barrier against Eastern and Bolshevik expansion. It will mean a proper balance between East and West. Everyone will see the benefit almost immediately. Credit where it's due, Johnny Turk's a damned brave little chap. But he shouldn't be allowed to pretend he's an Occidental.'

I was tremendously impressed by his grasp of politics, his positive vision, his fair-mindedness. Major Nye was that excellent type of Englishman who wore neither his heart nor his religion on his sleeve, yet who held profound and well-considered moral convictions. I told him how much I agreed with him. Russia had been ruined by her Eastern expansion. Everyone knew Chinese, Moslems and Jews now supplied Lenin's main initiative. At this the major became enthusiastic. 'Exactly!' He was about to elaborate when, noticing a waiter's signal, he looked at his watch. 'I'm committed to dining with a chap. We'll talk more about this, though. What d'you say to later this evening? I owe you a drink anyway.' With a wave that was almost a formal salute, he disappeared into the adjoining restaurant. He had contributed to my already excellent good spirits. I was soon chatting with a Russian captain attached to British H.Q. at Haidur Pasha. He had overheard some of our conversation. His name was Rakhmatoff. A nephew of the old general. 'I gather you're a flyer?'

'I've flown,' I admitted modestly, 'in the service of my Emperor. And you?'

'Just an ordinary infantryman. Major Nye's one of the few British who properly understands our position. We must all pray that his influence will prevail. I believe he's here as an advisor of some sort, isn't he? To do with the uprising in Anatolia?'

I could honestly answer that I did not know. I became a little cautious of Rakhmatoff. With his world-weary, decadent droop of eye and mouth, he was too drunk for so early in the evening. Refusing his invitation to dine I asked the waiter for a table overlooking the courtyard, where I would not be disturbed. I ate sparingly, sampling several Turkish dishes, especially the skewered meats. Much Turkish food is similar to Ukrainian, so it was a relief to be free, for a while at least, from the endless duffs and dumplings of the British. I enjoyed a bottle of St Emilion, the first I had tasted in more than two years, and as I finished my coffee considered the idea of rejoining Major Nye as he had suggested. For the moment, however, the pleasures of Pera remained my most pressing interest. Starved for too long of the excitement of bustling metropolitan streets I was curious to discover what commonplace adventures awaited me at night in the Grande Rue de Pera. I returned to my room, changed my clothes, put on an ordinary top-coat, and sallied forth.

Dance music issued from almost every doorway. Electric signs advertised cabarets and bars. Trams squealed and rattled, sending sparks into the upper air; women of every age, race and colour smiled at me. Girls in sequinned frocks swung their hips along the narrow, cracked pavements; Italian policemen in tri-cornered hats and capes aimlessly blew their whistles and turned their eyes towards invisible stars, unwilling to involve themselves in anything likely to distress them. Kurds, Albanians, Tatars rushed here and there under the weight of huge loads, or stood on corners to scream ritualistically at each other. Shop windows were filled with silk and gold. Mumbling Jews staggered with bales of bright printed cotton into the open air, begging passersby to test the texture between their fingers. The flickering lights of Stamboul were in the distance and a white sea-mist gave the whole city the appearance of a dream, for only her cupolas and minarets were clearly visible above the banks of cypresses and sycamores; everything else was either jet-black silhouette or invisible. While here in Pera one might feel oneself in a jabbering, jostling, desperate Hell, Stamboul remained as tranquil and as remote as Nirvana. Great hooting ships came and went in her harbours; ferries with oil-lamps dancing under their canopies pushed towards a yellow haze that was Scutari. The sea resembled a series of dark mirrors placed at random upon an indistinguishable surface. Dissonant Arabian music wailed and barked then gave way to equally cacophonous jazz. I heard the tango and the fox-trot. I heard balalaika and saxophone and the wild din of a gypsy orchestra. Further along, men in tasselled caps and the white ruffles of Greek soldiers ran suddenly from a Turkish bath-house. They looked both embarrassed and satiated. A dozen cinemas advertised their films in as many languages. It had been so long since I had visited a cinema I hesitated for a moment between *Birth of a Nation* and *Cabiria* before deciding that while London had films, she could not offer Constantinople's other entertainments. Hoping my Baroness did not wait for me inside, I passed Tokatlian's, the restaurant she had mentioned as a favourite meeting-place of Russians. Tonight I was in search of younger company. The *Café Rotonde*, with its blue electric sign and eerie green windows, attracted me. I pushed through a rabble of harlots whose heads barely reached my chest, giving my hat and coat to a red-haired

114

witch at the door before following a jaunty dwarfish Syrian waiter to a table. Within seconds I was besieged by half-a-dozen deliciously sleazy girls in cheap satin and bedraggled feathers who begged me to drink and dance with them. I selected two, as had always been my habit, and dismissed the rest. They were both Turkish. They gave their names as Betty and Mercy but spoke scarcely a word of English, had some Russian and slightly more French (chiefly sailor's argot). Betty was fourteen, Mercy was a little older. That evening and part of the night I spent in their lascivious company, chiefly on the couches of the *Café Rotonde's* back room when the garish lights began to hurt my eyes, the jazz music grew too loud for my ears, and their lewd language became too arousing for my loins to bear the lust any longer. My little girls might have come straight from the Sultan's training-schools. I was not disappointed in them. They reminded me of Katya, the child-whore, cause of so much trouble between me and my cousin Shura in Odessa, but their skins were darker, their liquid eyes larger, and their arts far more sophisticated. It was no crime to enjoy their flesh. It was fairly paid for, as others had paid. I know these girls. They are naturally depraved. There is a myth about female innocence I have never understood. True, some are also naturally innocent, but others are born with an animal desire to explore all the wanton secrets of their own senses. Nobody forces them to live as they do. I did not invent the games we played that first marvellous night. They are games as old as civilization, as subtle or as crude as the players themselves. It is a way of life for them, as often a passport into Heaven as it is into Hell. People should not condemn what is alien simply because it frightens them.

Next morning, profoundly relaxed, I decided to breakfast in my room, congratulating myself that my luck had turned at last. My cocaine protected me from most venereal dangers and Mercy had told me where I might obtain fresh supplies. Neither child was a stranger to the drug. They had, moreover, information where to sell gold at top prices, where to buy a cripple if I should ever desire one, what the best private lodgings were. A friendly whore is one's best source of knowledge in any large town. She moves in a wide social sphere and hears everything. True she has a penchant for sensational gossip, mystery, conspiracy and romantic mysticism, but that can be discounted. In a single night I learned of bordellos staffed entirely by young Circassian boys, of women who made and sold absinthe, of 'dealers' from Trieste and Marseilles who continued an age-old white slave trade to markets in Syria,

Egypt and Anatolia. I now knew of an Athenian who would sell me a modern revolver and ammunition. If I left the hotel and walked for three minutes towards Galata I should find someone to prepare me a fresh passport in another name. Had I needed to live on my wits, as in Kiev and Odessa, it would have taken me two days to make all the appropriate contacts. The Pera bohemians prided themselves on their city's reputation, just as my old Moldavanka friends spoke warmly of local gang leaders and madames as others spoke of film stars. In refusing to judge such people I was quite unconsciously following the edicts of Nietzsche and formulating my own morality which, in time, would be stronger than anything I could have learned in a comfortable and conventional life. Without that background, it is unlikely I should have survived at all.

Lifting myself on my sweet-smelling pillows, I pressed the bell beside my bed. A waiter answered almost at once and I ordered the small breakfast, an English newspaper, some hot water. He returned with my tray and a note from Leda Nicolayevna. Jack Bragg had told her where I was staying. She suggested lunch at Tokatlian's. She would arrive at twelve-thirty and would wait until two. Sentimentally, full of languid love for the world at large, I decided to keep the appointment. My evening was already planned (I would spend it with Mercy and two of her friends. Betty had a previous engagement), but it would be unwise to snub the Baroness altogether. There was nothing to be gained by hurting her feelings. Moreover I was now in a position to help her get to Venice, should she wish to go. Betty had told me of a man who earned his living illegally ferrying refugees to Italy. The fare was very high, of course. I would offer to pay it.

Dressed in my dark green Irish twill I arrived at Tokatlian's by one. The restaurant occupied the lower part of a private hotel (Mercy had spoke of its doubtful reputation) and had recently been modernized in the Persian style, with a preponderance of green, yellow and red mosaics. I never discovered if an Armenian called Tokatlian still owned the place. The manager was Dutch. Mr Olmejer had committed some crime, or offended some institution, in the East Indies and could not return to Holland. The restaurant's huge plate-glass windows revealed a crowd of Levantine businessmen, Allied service officers, diplomats, journalists, many apparently well-to-do Russian émigrés. A tango orchestra played softly on the far side behind potted palms. I would be reminded later of those elaborate cinema foyers we used to have, when films were worth watching, told the truth and were therefore still popular. A tail-coated head waiter bowed and asked if I had made a reservation. I was meeting the Baroness von Ruckstühl I murmured, peering through the ferns and palms to glimpse her at a table in the second gallery, overhead. The waiter bowed again, offered to lead me to her, but I thanked him and made my own way through the restaurant. Her magnificent head tilted back as she talked to the tall man dressed formally in frock-coat and dark trousers who stood smiling beside her chair. He had conventional good looks and was obviously army-trained. I was almost glad to feel a pang of jealousy. It made me realize I retained feeling for her. The meeting would not therefore be as difficult as I had feared. Her brown velvet luncheon frock and a toque of pheasant feathers gave her a pleasantly pastoral look; an eighteenth-century aristocratic shepherdess. As I mounted the half-spiral of the stairs she saw me and waved a gloved, animated hand. She introduced me to her companion. Count Siniutkin seemed a shade embarrassed. I suspected he had wanted to leave before I arrived. 'But perhaps you already know each other' she said. 'From Moscow.' I said I had never visited Moscow, but he seemed slightly familiar, and I, he said, to him. His expression was pleasant and open, unspoiled by a scar running from the right-hand corner of his lip to his jawbone. Indeed, the scar enhanced what would otherwise have been unremarkable good looks. His manner was self-effacing, his voice soft and a little sad. I found him attractive. My jealousy disappeared. I apologized to the Baroness for failing to contact her the previous evening. ('A meeting with some British military people.') I invited the Count to join us. He hesitated. 'Oh, for a few minutes, you must!' The Baroness spoke from generous good manners. Plainly she preferred to be alone with me.

So the three of us sat in a semi-circle round the marble table and ordered complicated American cocktails. We were all very mystified by the odd names and bizarre combinations. Then the young Count suddenly smiled, then said hesitantly, 'I believe we met at *Agnia's* once. In Petrograd.' This placed him as one of Kerenski's young liberal supporters. He had doubtless been acquainted with my friend Kolya. 'Of course you knew Petroff?' I was always happy to speak of Kolya.

'Very well indeed. We served together in the same department.' He became animated. 'When Lenin started taking over, Kolya advised me to leave Petrograd. He could read the signs so well.'

117

'He and I shared an interest in the future,' I said. 'Did you by any chance hear how he died?'

Siniutkin was surprised. 'Who on earth told you he was dead?'

'His cousin Alexei. We flew together. He was very bitter about it.'

'After the October counter-coup, Kolya went to ground. He hid with me in Stryelna for a couple of months. Then his sisters joined him and they all got to Sweden by boat. I had a letter from him not much more than a month ago. He's alive, Mr Pyatnitski.'

For an instant I honestly believed this whole episode, the city, its pleasures, my Baroness, was part of an elaborate fever-fantasy, surely I was actually still aboard the *Rio Cruz*! Then I became almost hysterical with joyful disbelief. I had mourned Prince Nicholai Feodorovitch Petroff since his cousin had drunkenly crashed us in the sea off Arcadia. Had I not been in a state of shock at the news of Kolya's death, I should probably never have boarded the plane at all. Slowly the reality impinged on me. My beloved friend was safe. Somewhere he still made his usual ironic jokes and enjoyed life as he had always done. 'That's wonderful! Do you know where he is now?'

'He was in Berlin, but he talked about going to Paris or perhaps New York. The idea of a "government in exile" was an over-familiar farce. He wrote that he had played in one too many such farces. Perhaps it was a joke, but he said he planned to emigrate. To teach Russian to Jewish radicals in America.'

The Baroness laughed heartily. She put her hand on mine. 'I've never seen you so cheerful, Maxim Arturovitch. Aren't you pleased I introduced you?'

'I'm eternally grateful!' To celebrate, I ordered three more cocktails. 'You can't possibly know, my dear Count, how much your news means to me.'

'I'm so pleased. Kolya's a splendid chap. Tremendously amusing no matter what happens to him. You could probably get in touch through an expatriate society, you know. But I'll gladly find that last address for you.'

'You're very kind.' I remembered my manners. 'And what brings you to Constantinople, sir?'

'A little of this and a little of that. Intelligence work, of sorts. Some interpreting. Luckily the Turkish I learned as a cadet has proven useful. My own escape was eventually made through Anatolia, after I had been drafted by the Reds, who were short of officers.'

'You plan to move on again?'

'I must see how things go. There's pressure, of course, to join the Volunteers, but sadly I've no faith in our present leaders or their politics. I backed Kerenski. I remain a republican. Maybe I'll go back when Lenin and Trotski calm down.' He shrugged and pretended to study his fruit-filled glass as the waiter set it carefully before him. I think Siniutkin had been embarrassed by my question.

The Baroness broke the silence. 'Well, one of you gentlemen must find me new accommodation. The family I'm living with is extremely German. Not at all pro-Russian. They spent the last twenty-four hours complaining bitterly about the new Sultan. Apparently Abdul Hamid was a saint in comparison, even if he did throw the odd houri into the Bosphorus. Germans have an uncanny ability to distinguish fine differences in tyrants. A sixth-sense not permitted the rest of us. They are boring me, Maxim Arturovitch. I must be rescued as soon as possible.' She was ill-practiced as a coquette. She had chosen an unlikely mask for her anxiety and despair. Obviously Count Siniutkin was as little deceived as I. 'I'm sure one of us can find you a decent hotel.' He blushed, as if he had let slip an obscenity, and brought a genuine smile to her lips. She said, 'As soon as possible, my dear.'

Finishing his drink quickly the Count said he looked forward to seeing us again, then went downstairs to join two French officers at the long black and gold bar. Leda touched her knee to mine under the table. I was a little repelled by the urgency of her passion. 'I have not forgotten you,' I said. 'I'm doing everything possible.'

'Can't we meet tonight?' She flushed in mixed lust and humiliation. 'I'm longing to make love. I can invent an excuse to the family. I'll agree to any plan.'

'I share your desire, my darling. But there's so much to be arranged here.'

'You won't abandon me?'

I found myself automatically reassuring her, insisting my duties presently took up most of my time. 'The military people keep irregular hours, you see. I must work on their terms. They have the power.'

' She straightened her shoulders as she plucked up a menu. 'And Mrs Cornelius? How is she?'

'I haven't seen her. I understand she left the city. I've no idea when she'll return. Leda Nicolayevna, there's a chance I can get you and Kitty to Venice. From Italy it will be much easier to reach Berlin. I

119

didn't want to say too much about this until I had concrete information.'

'That isn't the immediate worry, my dear.' With a gloved hand she fingered her lips. 'Apparently the British authorities are herding Russians of all classes onto some desert island. Is it true?'

The infamous Lemnos camp was at the other end of the Dardanelles. I sympathised with her fear. There were dreadful rumours of overcrowding and near-starvation. People apparently paid hundreds of thousands of roubles for a passage back to Constantinople rather than stay there. Visas were impossible to obtain. There was disease, insufficient medicine, needless death. Again I reassured her as best I could. I explained I only stayed on in the city for her sake. She said I must be resentful. I denied it. 'I'm worried and rather overworked.' She melted and asked me to forgive her. 'You understand I'm so terrified for Kitty. And I couldn't bear to lose you. I'm not asking for all your time.'

'Of course. Give me your address. I'll drop you a note in a day or so. There's a chance I'll have good news.'

We ate a light meal. My mind was largely taken up with the wonderful news of Kolya's 'reincarnation.' His inspiration, his love had meant so much to me. Leda thought it was her company which made me so happy so she relaxed marvellously. We parted at the table. Again I spoke of my affection. I kissed her hand. It trembled. Count Siniutkin was still deep in conversation with the Frenchmen. I nodded to him on my way out. He looked a trifle startled, as if I had surprised him in some dishonourable transaction. From Tokatlian's I went immediately to *La Rotonde* to forget the embarrassments of lunch and to celebrate Kolya's return to my world. My celebration, as it happened, went on for longer than I had planned. Thanks to some unusual sexual invention, the extraordinarily high quality of the cocaine, the simple ambience of the city itself, Time began to pass at an accelerated rate. During the next three days I experienced one long, steady rise to increasing, undreamed of heights of pleasure: passion I had thought lost forever. When I remembered, I would check occasionally at the *Pera Palas* to see if Mrs Cornelius were back and would write a hasty, regretful note in reply to one of the many sent by my desperate Baroness. Twice I crossed the Golden Horn by the Galata Bridge, an excited whore on either arm, to taste the magic of Stamboul and her massive mosques. The old city still reeked of enormous power. Here the Sultanate seemed strong as ever. The power was of all kinds, spiritual and temporal, and not all benign. I had been unprepared for the scale of Stamboul's palaces and monuments, her public squares and gardens. When I ventured, with Mercy and a little giggling thing called Fatima, into the Grand Bazaar it felt infinite: cavern after magical cavern twisting away into further mysterious labyrinths, selling the exotic bric-à-brac of two or three millennia. This astonishing market was the meeting place of the centuries. Timeless, it offered the impression of all human history somehow consolidating in this one gigantic warren whose shadowy roofs echoed to the cries of traders speaking every civilised tongue, ancient and modern: echoes of voices which had advertised these same wares a thousand years before. Unexpectedly, as you rounded a corner, a ray of golden light would break through some high, domed glass roof and pierce the antique dust; another window would materialise where no window should logically be and you knew if you looked through it you might see anything: a squadron of Roman gladiators, marching at double-time to the Circus, a Byzantine Court procession, the triumphant cavalry of Europe's Crusading knights, an Osmanli harem's scented opulence. Once within the Grand Bazaar I became afraid I should never leave, that it was a place without boundaries or familiar geometry. We bought drugs (opium, hashish, cocaine), confectionary and coffee; we sat on soft carpets and talked to merchants whose eyes were as old as creation, who smiled and offered us arcane blessings. We stared at brightly-coloured captive birds, monkeys, peculiar, hybrid cats. Our senses were enraptured by the most delicate and powerful fragrances. And then, somehow, we were in Stamboul's evening streets again, with the sun setting, the moon and early stars beginning to appear in a sky of dark blue crêpe-de-chine. Even here, the magnificent kiosks and mosques, with their marble and gold and mosaics, frequently stood only a short distance from tottering wooden tenements. As in Galata there were whole blocks desolated by fire; other parts had received heavy shell-attack and remained unrepaired. Nevertheless the pageant of our whole Western civilisation, as well as that of the parvenu East, was apparent in each broken stone and blackened timber. This filled me with a sense of purpose.

After the Turks were gone it would be upon these ruins we would build. Equally elegant modern architecture would rival the old. The sky would fill with the shimmering wings of silent aircraft. Bearing the polished steel of gently murmuring motor-vehicles, silvery overhead roads would curve and sweep between spires and domes no longer mosques but churches dedicated to our own, Greek Christ. Here exemplary human aspiration and dignity would expand. Constantinople would be a synonym for enlightened moderation. Before the benevolent power of electricity, steam and oil poverty would vanish. To her courts would come Arab spice-sellers, Christian tycoons, great poets, engineers, musicians. All would live in marvellous harmony, each knowing his place in the scheme of things. And ruling our Emperor City, if my dreams were to be fully realised, would be a noble, tolerant, far-sighted Tsar. A Tsar of a united world: a Tsar with the joyous vision of a positive Future. In his justice and wisdom he would reign justly over all men. This wonderful place, half-metropolis, half-garden, would exist in eternal summer. By science her light and temperature would be controlled beneath a glowing, transparent dome radiating the rainbow colours of the sun; a dome as beautiful as the dome of Hagia Sophia herself. That great Cathedral, symbol of our endurance and our Faith, would continue to dominate the city's seven hills. All religions would be tolerated, but the Christian religion would flourish supreme, exemplified by our Greek liturgy. This creation of a better world on Earth would be a sign of the world to come. She would serve as a model to which other cities and cultures might aspire. Finally, thanks to the construction of enormously powerful machinery below the foundations, she might herself ascend one day to the heavens.

At first I tried to explain these visions to my companions, but they were inarticulate, even in their native tongues, and their schooling non-existent. Sometimes I felt more like a village schoolmaster than a rakehell. Eventually I contented myself with making the notes I am using now. In 1920 it seemed easily possible to manufacture reality from my dreams. I could not possibly know that, while I imagined this best of all futures, Turks, Jews, the dregs of Oriental Africa, schemed its abortion. They dare not let Paradise flourish on Earth, because all they have to offer is a modest reward in the world to come. They divided us and now they rule. Compromise was to be the order of the day; the very name of our century. Those who refused to compromise were, one by one, broken and destroyed.

I had been less than a week at the *Pera Palas* and was returning up the Grande Rue one morning, pushing my way through touts and hucksters, European officials in top hats and frock-coats, soldiers and sailors and women of quality, and feeling more than a little exhausted, when I heard my name called. Peering across the street I saw Major Nye, in khaki, standing on the corner waving to me with his swagger-stick. Behind him, in a leopard-skin coat and matching hat, stood Mrs Cornelius. An omnibus moved between us, a Turkish boy with a long cane clearing the way ahead, and I almost ran into it, my weariness forgotten, as I rushed over to them, shook the major's hand and kissed Mrs Cornelius on both cheeks. The major was smiling. 'We were wondering what had happened to you, old boy.' But Mrs Cornelius was in poor humour. Her usual genial manner was strained. She wore more cosmetics than normal. 'Have you been ill?' I asked her. 'Well, I'm not me usual chipper self, I must admit, Ivan.' She spoke in what she called her 'posh' voice, which she affected sometimes in the company of certain types of Briton. 'How have yer bin?'

'I've managed to hold back the anxiety,' I said. 'I've been so worried about you.'

She did not soften. Major Nye explained they were about to have a drink before lunch and with his stick indicated the doors of a little bar. 'This suits you, old man' We strolled into the semi-darkness as happily I told her of my discovery that Kolya was still alive. I was longing to get to London. From there I would locate him easily and let him know my whereabouts. She grew a little gloomier at this last remark of mine. 'It's not gonna be that simple, Ivan, I'm afraid. A couple of days ago I found art I'm a rotten Russian subject. Officially, any'ow. On account o' that bleedin' – dashed – certificate. I'm your wife. 'Cause that's 'ow we registered on the ship.'

'But we were never really married. What does it mean?'

She fell silent and made an effort to smile at the major. He was ordering our drinks. Her voice lowered for my benefit, she glared. 'I'm bloody well stuck 'ere, that's wot!' Then she added in a peeved tone, 'I've been fuckin' lookin' fer ya orl over! Wot the 'ell ya bin up ter? I'm now dependent on *you* gettin' a visa for both of us. Fat bloody chance, eh?'

Major Nye turned back to us. 'Mrs Pyatnitski has explained your difficulties. It's a vile position. I'm trying to contact the appropriate authorities and clear the matter up. But everyone's so overworked.'

I told him I understood. I had after all been an Intelligence Officer in Odessa, with similar duties and identical problems. One did one's best to retain one's humanity, but there were so many needy cases.

'Perhaps we could get you an exit visa if a high-ranking Russian officer vouched for you?' he suggested. We sat in a row on the bar stools and looked out into the turbulent street.

'My superiors are all dead,' I explained. 'Had it not been for Mrs Cornelius – Pyatnitski – I should have shared their fate. There's Captain Wallace, an Australian Tank Commander I worked with last year. My C.O. was Major Perezharoff when I acted as a liaison officer between the Volunteers and the Allied Expeditionary Forces.'

Major Nye sighed. 'There's too few records and too much confusion. I'll do what I can. Perhaps a wire to Perezharoff, wherever he might be. But the powers above have to contend with French, Italian, American and Greek opposite numbers. The Russian Army chaps also want their say. The paperwork alone is wretched. Nonetheless, sometimes these things go far smoother than you expect.'

Now there was the faintest hope of a solution, Mrs Cornelius soon recovered her usual spirits. 'Marry hin 'aste an' repent at leasure, eh, major? Chin, chin.' And she finished her drink. 'By the by, Ivan. Thet Baroness's bin eskin' orfter yer.'

'I offered her my help, as a Russian gentleman. It appears now that I need help myself.' I smiled wistfully.

'Certainly looks like it. You bin up orl night' She placed demure lips upon the rim of her glass.

The major insisted we take another drink. I could not count much on his assistance. I was merely an acquaintance, one of half-a-million voices lifted in the desperate babble filling the entire embassy district. Privately I pinned my hopes on Mrs Cornelius's ingenuity. The boat to Venice had also become worth our consideration. Still speaking in an undertone, she told me to calm down. 'Ya look a bleedin' wreck. Yer inter the snuff agin?' I assured her my consumption remained moderate. She would do what she could, she said, but I would have to stay in touch. We might need to move rapidly and at short notice. I said how sorry I was I had become a burden to her, yet she was my only certain means of reaching London and my money. I could not act on my own, much as I felt I should. Our lunch became a rather forced affair. The major did his best to lift the mood. He told amusing anecdotes of Turkish duplicity, Greek recklessness, French pigheadedness, American naïveté and British disquiet. He mentioned Mustafa Kemal and problems with the nationalists. He had also heard the Reds were making solid gains now in Ukraine. These stories served to decrease my hopes of making an early departure, particularly since I had tasted most of Constantinople's pleasures and was quite ready to move on to England. A deep weariness began to return, even as I did my best to respond with interest to the major's stories. That afternoon I would visit my Baroness, to spend at least one night with her. After my recent exertions it would seem sedate and restful. As lunch ended, Mrs Cornelius adjusted her leopard pillbox with its miniature veil and said she had arrangements to make. She told me to be ready to leave at a moment's notice.

I returned to the hotel desk where the quasi-Frenchman handed me notes from Mrs Cornelius and Leda. There and then, on the hotel's stationery, I wrote a short letter to the Baroness, telling her to meet me at Tokatlian's that evening, whereupon I went straight up to bed for two hours, to sleep off the worst of my worries. On awakening, my improved mental state was consolidated with the help of the good new cocaine I had obtained through Mercy. It was six o'clock by the time I had bathed and dressed, so I decided to go for a drink at *La Rotonde* and say farewell to my agreeable little girls. With the exception of Betty and Mercy I had been seeing rather too much of them for my own good. It was time to take stock of myself, to pull back, to arrange, at very least, a change of companion for the next few days. It might even be wiser to employ only the Baroness as the object of my lust. Entering the green haze of the café I sought out my chief friends. Betty and Mercy always sat at the same table during this slow part of the day, but at present they were gone. I assumed they had found an early customer. However, when I asked the grotesque Syrian when they would be back he seemed deliberately vague, scratching at his warts and frowning. They were probably working in Stamboul, he said. They had not been around for a couple of days. He scuttled off to his quarters. One of Mercy's closest friends, a slender blonde Armenian known as Sonia, had overheard us. As soon as the Syrian was out of earshot she came, with a rustle of muslin, to sit at my table. 'He's lying,' she said in Russian (she was a Christian) and she glared into the smoke which clung to the ceiling. 'I knew Betty and Mercy hadn't seen you recently. You were with Fatima and that lot, weren't you' I agreed. Sonia went on: 'The Syrian told us they'd gone abroad with you. He didn't want a fuss. But why should he say that?' She pursed flamingo-pink lips. 'I think they probably did go over to Stamboul for a night. There's an old woman there, a rich widow, who likes to play games with them. Nothing much. But they were always back at the house by morning. Simka, dear, my guess is they've been kidnapped.'

I knew the average whore's delight in sensationalism, so I smiled indulgently. Certainly kidnappings were common enough in Constantinople. 'But who would pay a ransom?' I asked reasonably.

'Nobody,' said Sonia. 'Their parents died in prison. I'd guess they've been sold by now. The Macedonian buyer came in a couple of days ago. They were almost certainly on his shopping-list. I saw him make a note. I warned Mercy at the time, but she thought I was joking. The Syrian had something to do with it. He must have.'

'But where would they be sold? Not in Stamboul?'

Sonia glanced down at her glowing nails. It was now obvious that she was close to tears. Her breasts rose and fell rapidly. 'Egypt? Somewhere like that. Jedah? There's lots of places. There's brothels in Europe, too. Berlin, in particular. But if they made too much of a stink, they might even have taken the Sultan's Road.' She meant they had been thrown, weighted, alive into the Bosphorus. I was upset. I was in no position to try to find them. I knew the Turkish authorities were not in the least interested in such commonplace problems, while the British were in the main powerless. I told Sonia to get in touch with me if she heard anything else, good or bad, and I gave her a couple of American dollars to buy herself a drink. Then I went out of the café and crossed the street to Tokatlian's.

I was cheered by the dark, glowing colours of the place. The obvious wealth of the clients, the Persian décor, helped ease my anxieties. On the little stage, lit by amber and emerald-green, a negro trumpeter was squawking some Mississippi slave lament. Weakly the rest of the orchestra attempted to accompany him. They were all Jewish and would have been far happier playing Hungarian polkas or Austrian waltzes. The long bar was crowded with a group of Italian soldiers celebrating a comrade's birthday. One of these was trying to sing a lugubrious aria against the caterwauling from the stage. I glimpsed Count Siniutkin, seemingly a permanent resident, as he got up from his table and disappeared into a back room. Private apartments, behind and above the restaurant, were frequently used for assignations. A tap on my shoulder announced the Baroness. She wore a new red evening dress which did not much suit her, though it emphasized her heavy, well-proportioned figure. I still found her attractive, particularly as a substitute for Mrs Cornelius. Both were of the old-fashioned kind of beauty which I appreciated as much as the boyish flappers who were then beginning to emerge. I pride myself I have catholic sexual tastes. Kolya always insisted this was the mark of a humane personality. I kissed my Leda's hand. I was almost passionate. I felt her stiffen with hope. With some difficulty we passed through the crowd to our table. A word with Mijneer Olmejer and we were assured of a room overhead when we were ready. The Baroness regarded me through sleepy, passionate eyes as I deliberately forced myself to relax and concentrate on this luscious epitome of Slavic womanhood. The little whores were just two amongst thousands, after all. It would be stupidly sentimental to feel overly anxious about Betty and Mercy. They could easily be enjoying a life of unheard-of luxury. Such girls took certain risks. I should be worrying about how Mrs Cornelius and I were to escape this increasingly sinister city. But even that was put to the back of my mind as I used all my charm to prepare the Baroness von Ruckstühl for the ravishment she so clearly craved. Both she and I ate sparingly, drank fairly heavily, and then discreetly, by means of the stairs leading from the toilet vestibule, repaired to the black plush and mirrored panels of a Tokatlian guestroom. Even as I stripped off her dress she seized my penis and began to press it with her fingers, forcing me to calm her down with the offer of some cocaine. She had been starved of both my cock and my drugs for so long, she said, that she had gone half-mad. She had quarrelled with her child's nurse and generally behaved very badly. I was not interested in her domestic confessions and silenced her by drawing her head down to my unbuttoned fly while I prepared the cocaine on the surface of a little marble table. I had become used to my responsive whores and she was a little surprised by my unromantic gesture, but she did not resist the budding, circumcised instrument of pleasure which was both my own joy and my shame, for in his insane revolutionary embracing of modernism, my father had unwittingly given apparent substance to the ghastly rumours of Jewishness which have so frequently led me into social embarrassment and even, on occasions, grave danger. By offering me up to that foolishly enlightened surgeon, he had placed upon me the mark of Abraham. Now, when almost every boy is divested of his foreskin at birth, it means nothing; but in my day it was a badge of race and religion, calculated to horrify unsuspecting women and to determine certain men in their decision whether one should live or die. Not that this was true of the Baroness von Ruckstühl as she applied her greedy teeth, tongue and lips to the object of her near-mindless lust and so allowed me to escape from the worries of the day, for her very inexperience was in itself relaxing. There is much to be said in favour of the forceful love-making of a mature, determined woman when one has problems to avoid. I gave myself up to it. At the *Pera Palas* a bribed waiter would relay any news from Mrs Cornelius so I did not need to feel uneasy on that score. Through a long, unhurried night I enjoyed the intensity of Leda's lust, satisfying her desire while at the same time restoring her confidence in my affection for her (if not in my fidelity, which she questioned several times, though without rancour). I revelled, too, I must admit, in the knowledge that this beautiful Russian aristocrat was absolutely in my power, and I began to consider the possibility of introducing her to my 'harem' of little whores.

By morning, when we parted, there was no message for me at the hotel. Neither Major Nye nor Mrs Cornelius was anywhere to be found. My messenger had not seen them since they had dined together the previous evening. I was glad she continued to cultivate the British officer. She knew exactly whom to seek out when an emergency arose. She had an unerring nose for power, even when it was in the least obvious guise. I was confident we must soon be on our way to London.

I slept until noon, then went to *La Rotonde* for lunch. I was curious to see if Sonia's speculations had proven groundless and I planned to meet one of my new friends, a Bulgarian engraver specializing in visas. At that moment I felt wonderfully content, in perfect control of myself and my world. I remember whistling *Marching through Georgia* (Jack Bragg's sole contribution to my repertoire) as I swung my cane and moved on light feet down the Grande Rue towards *La Rotonde*. Mind and emotions were thoroughly balanced; my sense of proportion had never been better, and my perspective on life was excellent. I was a man at one with himself and knew no hint of care.

It remains, therefore, a source of profound puzzlement to me how it was possible, only a few hours later, to find myself inescapably in the power of an all-consuming obsession; an obsession which would dominate the rest of my life and determine almost every aspect of my destiny. I do not regret what happened; I simply do not understand how I could become the victim of such an impossible coincidence. I sometimes look to ancient Greek mythology and see myself as some doomed hero upon whom Zeus has placed a curse and thus began a remorseless chain of consequences which must decide the ultimate fate of gods and mortals alike.

Wheldrake, greatest and most neglected of Victoria's poets, speaks for me in English far more eloquent than mine (but then he also knew the dreadful suffering and humiliation which compulsion can bring to a man):

O, Prometheus, by what subtle glamour
Was thy power constrain'd?

Six

I AM A RATIONALIST. I have always been a rationalist. I believe in the power of the human imagination, in scientific investigation, analysis and description, in the Christian philosophy of humane tolerance and self-discipline. Other more obscure forms of mysticism are to me at once foolish and deeply misanthropic. It is true I have always had a greater capacity to love the world than to love most of the individuals in it; but I am not like these hippies who worship gods from Space and tell you they were Sir William Scott in a previous life; neither will I listen to silly girls who talk of poltergeists, hauntings and psychic perception. Yet I probably possess a greater accumulation of evidence for the belief in reincarnation (or even less likely phenomena) than anyone alive. My experience in Constantinople might have shaken a man with less character and unbalanced him for the rest of his days. Only an overriding, saving sanity, an improving understanding of the meaning and power of prayer, has helped me maintain my reason. It would be self-deceptive, at very least, for me to claim I was always so stable. The shock of a new country and culture, my youth, my realisation that I was both an exile and an unwelcome guest, must all have contributed to my state of mind. I was well-educated. I knew many languages. I had mastered the power of flight; but I was also something of a hothouse plant. I received a diploma from the St Petersburg Institute by the time I was sixteen. I was, at twenty, both a Master of Science and a Colonel in the Volunteer Army. My brain, as we used to say, had grown faster than my soul. They took you, Esmé, in your youth and in your innocence. They took you away from me. They transformed you into a whore and gave you a hard, grinning mask. You became a bandit's camp-follower, an anarchist, you who had lived only to serve the sick and needy; you became a cynic who saw love as the arch-folly and the past as a stupid illusion. Yet did we not smell the lilacs together in the old parks above Kirilovskaya, as the sonorous bells of St Andrew's pealed the Easter jubilation? Can you deny we ran bare-legged, hand in hand, through the grassy gorges of Kiev while the sun made all her buildings soft and golden? We sat under autumn oaks, did we not, and let the red leaves cover us? Was all that an illusion, Esmé? Or must it be called one now, because it cannot be reclaimed? *Wann werde ich sie wieder sehen?* You were fucked so much you had callouses on your cunt. But you came back to me. Perhaps God sent you. You came back disguised as a harlot and were transformed into the tender, loving child who had admired and supported me in my youthful idealism. You were restored, purified, made whole; and it was granted to me that I should be the medium of your salvation. Esmé, my aspiration, my angel! My muse! God grants few of us the opportunity to relive the past, redeem our mistakes, take advantage of a happiness we usually only value when we have lost it. I am not ungrateful, God. I thank You and am repentant that I thought in those days You played a trick on me. I thought You unjust to bestow such a gift, then take it away again, dooming me to a lifetime of miserable disappointment, a hopeless Quest, to change my whole perspective of life. Is it my punishment, to suffer for all of them? Is that my punishment, God? I have wandered the Earth praying for an answer. *Wie lange müssen wir warten?* They accused me of so many crimes. They whipped me with their Cossack quirts. They humiliated and tortured me. They imprisoned me. They mocked me. They called me such terrible names. They cannot understand.

I saw her in *La Rotonde*, sitting on a bar-stool, swinging her little legs and sipping lemonade, for all the world like a lively schoolgirl on holiday at Arcadia. She wore an old-fashioned pinafore and skirts and her golden hair fell in ringlets around her wide, fair face. Her blue eyes were large and unutterably innocent, merrily curious, and she was Esmé Loukianoff, my angel come back to life: in every perfect detail the same girl who had been my constant childhood companion. It was Esmé, the true Esmé, returned to me. I was a boy again, crying out my delighted surprise in that seedy café, making heads turn, not caring. 'Esmé! Melushka! My darling!'

The stupid Syrian got in the way. Perhaps he did it deliberately, the shrunken devil. Drinks flew, glass smashed. I went down. I had not seen him there. I straightened up and began to rise to my feet. She was leaving with an American sailor, a thickset redheaded brute with tattooed arms, all in white. She could not hear me. 'Esmé!'

They were in the street before I had reached the lobby. 'Esmé! Esmé!'

I did not bother to collect my coat. It was cold. The day was grey and threatened rain. All the electric lights were coming on. There was mist in the streets, rising from the harbour. They stood in the little green shelter by the tram-stop apparently reading advertisements pasted over the inside. They were laughing. They were gesticulating to one another. The sailor was obviously drunk. My stomach turned over. There was a piece of metal in it. 'Esmé!' (He saved my life, she said. It was not much of a rape.)

I reached them as the tram sighed and squealed to a stop. Esmé, my darling, my sweet virgin, smiling at the sailor. I could read his depraved mind. I knew his filthy plans. I was disgusted. 'Esmé!' I recovered myself. I was panting. There was sweat on my face. People were staring. 'Excuse me, young lady, I believe we're acquainted.' I caught my breath, trying to smile, to bow. I was shaking. She frowned. 'From Kiev,' I said, still forcing a grin, trying to seem casual. 'Do you remember Kiev, Esmé?'

She had amnesia, I thought. Neither she nor the sailor understood my Russian. The tram drew up with a groan beside the stop. My English would not come to me. I was ten years old again. 'Esmé!' They made to board. Its destination was Galata Bridge. I followed them on. I rubbed at my head, trying to recall just a few ordinary English words. The sailor was shorter than me, but more muscular. He had huge forearms, like Popeye. He glared into my face. 'Piss off, buddy.'

I was desperate, panting at him like a placatory dog. The English returned. 'You don't understand, sir. I know this girl. She's from my home-town in Ukraine. An old family friend.'

He laughed sharply. 'Sure. And she's my sister. OK?'

I was shocked. *Moja siostra! Moja rozy! Sl??once juz gaslo! Po dwadziéscia! Cieniu! O Jezu Chryste! My sister and my rose. My darling! Twenty lice-ridden soldiers stood outside your hut making coarse jokes among themselves then went in one by one to relieve their animal lusts upon your body.* 'She is the daughter of my mother's –' I failed. 'My mother's –' I reached for her. 'Esmé! It is I, Maxim from Kiev!'

She shrank back. (I have a boy. He wants to marry me.) The sailor must have hit me. My face was against rattling boards, there were people treading on my arms and back. The side of my head was numb. Brown hands tried to grab me. I wriggled free. I hated the stink of those Turks. 'Esmé!' The tram had reached Galata Bridge and I could see nothing. My eye hurt. It was growing dark. The conductor yelled at me, driving me off his tram, pointing to his own skull and making ludicrous faces. He thought I was crazy.

I found myself on the pavement, near where I had first come ashore. The water was grey, a repeated, unrhythmical slap against the pontoons. Ships cried out. A million people swarmed across the bridge and then vanished. The mist grew thicker. There was a rushing noise. The bridge was suddenly deserted, empty. I moved down the steps and made to cross, thinking my Esmé had gone that way. A Turkish policeman at the barrier put his long rod against my chest. He shook his head and wagged his finger. I pressed on, trying to brush him aside. He became firmer, pointing to a sign in Arabic and beginning to hector me in the way only Turks can. There were Roman letters below the sign but I could not read them. Behind me was a ululation of street-sellers, the sound of motor-horns, of reined-in, impatient hooves. I looked back the way I had come. She was not visible in any direction. I screamed at the policeman. I offered him money. I pleaded with him to let me pass. He shrugged and pointed, relaxing as I understood what he was showing me. I could not cross now. The middle section of the bridge was parting to admit the big ships into the Horn. There was a line of them, flying a dozen different national flags: battle-cruisers, tramp-steamers, oil-tankers, grain-carriers; and flitting around them, like parasites around the whales, were the little red- and yellow-sailed caïques. The policeman refused to understand my French. '*Ma soeur! Ma soeur!*' He poked me with the tip of his stick, shaking his head again, with more impatience. '*Sorella! Sorella!*' I shouted. '*Schwester. Shvester! Shvester! Hermana!*' I racked my brains. I was angry with myself for learning too little Turkish. By now I should have known more. I was paying the price of laziness. '*Kiz kardesh!*' He shrugged and relaxed. The steamers were moving through the gap, confident and graceful, into Galata Harbour. Why should an American sailor take her to Stamboul? Or had they gone off in another direction altogether? I was quivering with frustration as I sat against the barrier while a great crowd of Turks, Albanians, Arabs, Persians, Montenegrins, Greeks and Jews began to form behind me.

It had grown dark by the time I was allowed to pay the toll and cross. I walked all the way to the other side, the boards bouncing under my feet, up the tree-lined streets where Moslems kneeled and made noises in the backs of their throats, into a sudden silence. Men were on their faces, sprawled in front of the Blue Mosque. The sky had lost almost all its colour and the outline of the mosque was massive ebony. It frightened me, that citadel of heresy and superstition. I passed hastily between the faithful, crossing a square to Hagia Sophia, almost a twin to that other monstrous building, but still a Christian church in her vast tranquillity. Down steps, along alleys, through the reeking fish-market, past the main entrance to the Grand Bazaar, up streets filled with the glare and flicker of lamps and candles and tiny braziers, where coppersmiths and armourers still worked, between rows of dimly lit tobacconists where the shags and flakes were heaped in piles, each pile topped by a lemon. I went by restaurants, peering in every one but seeing no white women or even American sailors; mosques and fountains, black and white arches, tiny streets with walls covered in vines, columns, pilasters, corridors, and eager voices shouting, little hands plucking. 'Capitano! Caballero! Kyrie! Eccellenza!' Rugs and silks and cushions. Horses, camels and hawks. White-robed Arabians; dervishes in conical hats and hair-coats; Hebrews in yellow cloaks; Albanians with pistols in their belts; Tatars in sheepskins; negresses in Cairo motley; bearded Circassians in black and silver; Syrians in Byzantine dolmans, their style unaltered for two thousand years. I stumbled without bearings through this confusion of centuries, hunting for that tiny fragment of my own past which had so briefly been within my grasp. I sat on worn marble and wept for my stolen optimism, my sister, my bride. We were to marry. My mother wanted it so badly. I had walked too far. There was no evidence even that they had crossed the bridge. I suppose I assumed she was leaving the vice of Pera for the virtue of Stamboul; but there was no virtue in Stamboul, merely an illusion of godliness, a tenuous cloud over the accumulated miseries and evils of Oriental ignorance, cruelty and greed. She had looked so respectable. Was she the daughter of one of those old Greek families who lived in the Kondoskala quarter, near the Cistern of the thousand and one arches An escaped slave, taking advantage of the Allied occupation She had not understood Russian, yet had looked pure Ukrainian. I realized I had temporarily been insane. The girl could not really be Esmé. I had seen Esmé with the anarchists only a few months earlier. She was much older. This child could not be more than thirteen. How had she appeared amongst these dark-skinned people? Perhaps she was Circassian. The daughter of Russian exiles who had come years before to Constantinople? Or could Loukianoff have fathered a child here? The likeness was so striking I was certain she must be a relative. A cousin at very least. If I could find her, I would learn of some obvious connection. In the gloomy archways nearby I heard scuffling, muttering, and remembered how everyone said it was unsafe, even these days, for a European to go alone in Stamboul at night. I made for a lighted thoroughfare as quickly as I could and was lucky enough to find a cab returning to the Pera side. I took it across the Horn to *La Rotonde* and pushed my way inside to grab at the horrible Syrian gargoyle, that dwarfish trader in tender little bodies, and growl at him, threatening him with the Law, the vengeance of the whole Cossack nation, the curse of the world's deities, unless he told me the truth.

'Where is she? Who was that sailor? Where does she live? What does she call herself? What was she doing here?'

'She's a Greek kid, I think.' He wriggled under my hands like a dogfish, looking wildly about for help, knowing few would bother themselves even if I squeezed him to death on the spot, yet so automatically devious he still answered questions with other questions. 'M'sieu Pyatnitski, I'm not her father! She's new – calls herself – what is it? – Helena? What are you accusing me of? The old lady doesn't ask for birth-certificates. How many times has she been in? Once or twice, maybe? Aren't you a man of the world? Do you say I had something to do with what happened to Betty and Mercy? Am I that kind of monster?'

I dropped him and told him to get me some absinthe. I was shaking in every bone. Sonia tugged at my sleeve. 'You're bleeding. Sit down. Tell me what's wrong.'

I swallowed the drink the Syrian brought. He shrugged at me. 'You don't have to pay. But I'm not to blame for any of this.'

When he had gone I put my head in my hands. I was sobbing. Sonia tried to comfort me, touching my face, dabbing at the cuts. 'I must save her!' I repeated this over and over. 'She cannot be allowed to sink into the quagmire. Do you know her, Sonia?' I looked up at last. 'Do you know a Greek girl. A blonde who calls herself Helena?'

'I've seen her. She's pretty. One of the ladies from Mrs Unal's sent her across a couple of days ago. God knows why she was looking for work there. Just as well she came over. You talk as if you know her.'

'I do know her. Sonia, if you can get her address, I'll pay. But let me have it at once.'

'She might live down near the Roman Catholic Cathedral, towards the old bridge. She mentioned it once. Would that make her Italian?'

'Perhaps Polish.' I grew calmer. 'Or Ukrainian.'

'You must fancy her a lot, Max.' Sonia was sympathetically amused. She dabbed again at my face.

'I love her.'

I could see the Armenian girl was impressed by my sincerity. Her eyes grew tender and she smiled. Like many an older whore, she had a huge reservoir of sentimentality. 'I'll do what I can,' she promised. 'But don't break your heart, Max. Not over one of us.'

It was on the tip of my tongue to tell her that my Esmé was not to be compared with the likes of her, but that would have been ungracious of me. I got to my feet. I was unsteady. 'I can't help myself.'

I tried hard to remember what I had arranged to do at this time. With some effort I recalled Mrs Cornelius and the Baroness von Ruckstühl. At that moment neither woman had any real substance. I attempted to recall what they had said to me, but my mind was empty. I should have returned to the hotel, but when I left the café I found myself standing by the tram-stop. Then I wandered off the Grande Rue, down towards Galata, into the little, horrible sidestreets where rows of Islamic washing clung to my face and the strange odour of perfumed tobacco came from grills set at the base of the houses. Dogs ran everywhere carrying shapeless pieces of offal in their mouths; babies wailed their grief at having been born into such misery, men and women exchanged loud insults; the dogs looked up from their disgusting meals, growling and barking at nothing in particular. I tripped on some cobbles and bruised my knee. There was very little light except that which filtered from latticed windows or from behind threadbare curtains; the occasional yellow naphtha flare from a confectioner's shop where veiled women gathered to purchase pastries, their only pleasure, while their men disobeyed the edicts of Islam and sought consolation in the grogshops or played backgammon on the greasy tables of the coffeehouses. I crossed at least two different cemeteries, for this was the city of cemeteries, and almost by accident, with the lights of Pera and Stamboul distant and unattainable, I reached the Roman Catholic church. It was an unremarkable, mock-gothic building, built in the English style and might as easily have been found in Worthing or Fulham. It was impossible for me to identify the streets and the church was deserted. There was nobody I cared to ask. Only a few cafés and bars were still open in the area and these were crowded with the usual riffraff. I knew it would be unwise to approach them.

I fell in behind a group of very old men in greasy European clothes who wore Turkish slippers on their feet. Each one carried a huge, mysterious bundle on his head. The procession turned a corner and began to ascend the steep lanes. A family group passed by, the women totally covered in black cloth, the men in fezzes and shapeless dresses. The leading boy raised a rush torch to light their way. I might have been in Jerusalem at the time of Christ. Rain was falling now and across the water Stamboul disappeared as if behind a discreet curtain. I hobbled back to the Grande Rue, understanding with perfect clarity that I was quite insane, yet incapable of freeing myself from the obsession. The single-mindedness which had allowed my genius to flourish at an early age, which had driven me safely through every danger, was abused in pursuit of a mere delusion. Did she really exist at all? Had she been a figment of my imagination, her face distorted by the café lights and my exhausted eyes into the likeness of Esmé? I had to find out. If I saw her again in different circumstances and she was not really Esmé, I would be satisfied. I told myself it would not be Esmé. The other possibility, that she was Esmé's twin, was too fantastic.

Having calmed myself down, I returned home. There was a message from the Baroness. She was at Tokatlian's. I would spend the evening with her. If only for a few hours, my Leda would surely help me forget this madness. I changed my clothes, groomed myself, and went directly to Tokatlian's. She was seated at her favourite table on the second floor. She was plainly in some distress, but she became alarmed when she saw my wounded face. 'What's happened to you, Simka?'

'Part of the job. I'll be all right.' I refused to discuss my cuts and bruises. There are few varieties of discretion which impress a woman more, yet almost invariably the simple cause of such secrecy is a man not wishing to admit being bested in a fight or otherwise made a fool of. To change the subject I asked after Kitty. The Baroness shrugged. Her daughter was bored. There were no suitable schools for the child and she could not speak the language well enough to take lessons with the German children's governess. 'She reads the few suitable Russian books we find. In the afternoons we walk in the park. Today we went up to the Russian embassy.'

I had heard it was bedlam there. She agreed. 'People sleeping shoulder to shoulder in the old ballroom. No space left for the smallest baby. And fed like paupers from big soup tureens. It's very sad, Simka. Those people are from the best families.'

'They are alive.' I had little sympathy for them. After all, I had issued many of them with their passports. This was better than anything they might have faced if they had stayed. 'Unlike their Tsar,' I added.

'It depressed me terribly. And so many orphans. What would become of Kitty if something happened to me? There are thousands of human predators in this city. The police are useless. I was insulted twice, you know, on the way here. By Europeans! Nobody will accept authority. The British do their best, but one can't always find the redcaps. And Marusya Veranovna's taken to drink.'

I was tired. I suggested we go at once to our room above the apartment. She rose with alacrity, all her morbid, petty little concerns forgotten at the prospect of satisfying her lust. I used her with gusto. She offered herself up to any game I suggested. Women, as I well knew, only become downhearted when they do not receive enough attention; and I gave my Baroness the best attention possible. That night, lying beside her, I dreamed Hernikof the Jew and I were together on the ship. It was a steamship, but it carried the triangular sails of an old Greek warboat. Hernikof was in rags. Blood poured from a dozen wounds. I think the Baroness and Mrs Cornelius were present. Hernikof was accusing me of his murder and I did not know if I were guilty or innocent. I asked the others there what they thought, but they were concerned with the ship's course and had no time for me. Hernikof pointed at himself. He smiled and said he forgave me. I tried to push him overboard, shouting that I had no need of his forgiveness, but at least I should earn it if he died now. I wanted him to be quiet, but he gripped the rail like an owl with its prey and stayed where he was, smiling that terrible religious smile. Then Kitty ran up and held out her hand to him. He took it and gently she led him off. I was jealous. I wanted to drown him and Kitty of all people had rescued him. The Baroness woke me. 'You're sweating dreadfully, Simka.' I was shivering. She rearranged the bedclothes over me. Her naked body aroused me. It was huge and solid, yet soft, and I loved its smell. We made love until dawn and so once again drove the image of Hernikof entirely from my head, while keeping the ghost of Esmé, too, at bay. Leda knew how to be reassuringly silent; a quality younger women do not have. But by morning, after we had revived ourselves with cocaine, the obsession gradually returned with full force. Rather hastily, telling her I had business with another military person, I arranged to meet her for lunch at our usual table. Then, when I was sure she was on her way home, I returned to *La Rotonde.*

In the café a few wretched Kurds were cleaning the floors and tables. The Syrian sat at the top of a stepladder, smoking a meerschaum and ostensibly supervising the Kurds. When I appeared he put the pipe carefully between his few black teeth and began to climb down. Without acknowledging me, he carried the ladder into the kitchens. One of the Kurds told me that no girls were expected for at least another hour. I asked him, in a dreadful mixture of languages, if they knew a little girl called Helena. She might be Polish, I said. To please me, they made a pretence of thinking. It was obvious they had no information and were embarrassed by my questions. Outside in the Grande Rue heavy rain poured down the gutters, rushed off roofs and filled the holes in the pavements. The streets became a mass of black umbrellas and oilskins. I sheltered under the striped, sodden canopy of the *Café Luxembourg,* then moved first to look in the window of Wick and Weiss's well-stocked bookshop, then to stare at ornamental brass lamps and tables, poor copies of French Empire originals. Some of the cinemas and music halls had already opened. The occupying armies kept many such places going round the clock. The rain freshened Pera's air, momentarily driving away the more unpleasant smells from Galata. Posters started to peel from the wooden sides of newsstands, from tobacco kiosks, pissoirs and tram shelters, as if the city were being magically prepared for a new layer of advertisements. A troup of Punjabis went up the steep hill at a trot, arms sloping. As in Batoum, the British had stationed great numbers of nigger soldiers in Constantinople, presumably because Moslems might be less likely to offend the Turks. It was a mistaken notion. Turks are more arrogant towards people they regard as their inferiors, particularly former citizens of the Ottoman Empire. I think they viewed the occupation of their city by blacks as a planned insult. It was bad enough for them to be bested by Greeks, but to be ordered about by Africans like the French Senegalese was inconceivably appalling to them. For all that they had fully earned every possible humiliation (their cruelty to subject races, particularly Armenians, was legendary) they still did not understand why they were being punished. In 1915, while the world was concerned with other things, they had marched some million Christian Armenians into the desert to die.

139

Many still insist it was the logical thing to do ('People forget those Armenians were very rich'). Your Turks remain the true descendant of bloody-handed Carthage. They never change. They join the United Nations to protect them when they invade Cyprus; they imprison innocent Christians; they bully and steal as thoughtlessly as any of their Hun forebears might have. History is not a book of rules, but its examples are too often ignored. By showing continued respect to Turks we are like that woman who believes repeatedly her brutal husband will reform. It is an indication of her optimism, but never a reflection of the man's true character.

The rain eased enough to let me return to the *Pera Palas* where I bathed and changed. Then, with no word from Mrs Cornelius to make me alter my plans, it was time to go again to Tokatlian's. I stopped at *La Rotonde* first. A few girls were there, and the redheaded Italian madame, but none of them had seen my Esmé. I said they would be rewarded if they discovered her for me, or could get her address. I believe they had the idea I wished to buy her and seemed very agreeable.

At the restaurant I found the Baroness again enjoying the attentions of Count Siniutkin. They might have been lovers. He lifted his handsome, scarred face to smile pleasantly at me. It would have helped me at that time if the Baroness had transferred her affections, or at least shared them with another, but I think she was still faithful. Count Siniutkin, in very good form, greeted me warmly. We discussed the campaign in Anatolia. The Greeks were finding some resistance, he said, mainly from irregular units similar to those I had described in South Russia. I told him I had known Makhno personally; I had observed Hrihorieff at close quarters and Petlyura himself had tried to enroll me. Siniutkin named a couple of bandit leaders. He called them '*condottieri.*' The most famous and most worshipped was someone called Çerkes Ethem. He was to Anatolia what Pancho Villa had been to Mexico. 'Similar circumstances seem to throw up similar types, eh? Meanwhile the French are being hit very badly in Northern Syria.' I was not interested in Turkey's internal squabbles and listened only from politeness. 'They're fighting old-fashioned issues with old-fashioned means,' I suggested. 'A bandit on a big horse can't achieve a thing. Can it really matter who wins Every single one is an atavist.'

'Some are more progressive than others,' Siniutkin insisted mildly. His blue eyes studied me. 'Modern weapons, after all, demand modern bank accounts.'

'Not necessarily, Count. In Kiev some seven or eight years ago I designed and built an excellent cheap aeroplane. Thousands of them could have been made for the cost of a hundred conventional machines. An entire army could be made airborne with my plane.' I was not one to boast but I had my point to make. Siniutkin was genuinely interested. 'This plane was a success?'

'Very much so. My maiden flight was witnessed by all Kiev. You must have read about it, even in Moscow.' I smiled ironically.

'I have a vague memory, yes. But surely your machine could have been used in the War?'

'I shall not list my frustrations now, Count Siniutkin. Enough to say the plans were submitted to the War Department in St Petersburg, together with several other inventions of mine, and the Tsar's moribund bureaucrats did what they knew best. They ignored them. Of course I received no acknowledgement. But others were not so slow in seeking my help. One of my machines helped in the last defence of Kiev. Were it not for the cowardice of the nationalists, it would have turned the day. Petlyura thought so.'

Count Siniutkin had become enthusiastic. His features, in spite of the scar, were full of boyish excitement, 'By God, Pyatnitski, you could make a fortune!'

'That would be incidental. If I can in some way improve the condition of the ordinary man, I shall be happy. One must live, but first and foremost I am dedicated to the creation of a better future.'

'I can see why you and Kolya were such friends.' He was admiring. 'Sometimes you sound just like him.'

'We had much in common.'

'I should have thought the Bolsheviks would have wanted you to stay in Russia. Even they understand the value of innovative engineers.'

'I would never help Lenin or Trotski take the blood of innocents. Any reasonable government would be welcome to my inventions. But I refuse to serve tyrants.'

Siniutkin leaned towards me. His face had become earnest. 'I wish you the very best of luck, Pyatnitski.' He began to frown, then, and become abstracted. I think he had seen someone he knew downstairs. With a bow to us both, he stood up. 'I hope to talk again.'

'Little genius!' The Baroness patted my cheek. She had disguised the bags under her eyes with powder. She wore a tiny hat with a fashionable half-veil and rather more perfume than usual. Perhaps through indirect association she was losing the appearance of a beautiful young matron and taking on the appearance of an upper-class woman of the world. 'I think you have impressed our Count. I love to hear you talk your machine talk, though I understand hardly a word. But think how much better you would do in Berlin!' I had caught, as usual, her drift and patted her hand. She sighed. 'It is very difficult with Kitty. The Germans resent my absence. I tell them I'm nursing an old friend, but they suspect the truth. We must leave Constant as soon as possible, Simka.'

'I am due to meet a man this afternoon,' I assured her. 'I might have some news, in fact, by tonight.'

'You won't abandon us, my dear?' This was overly dramatic. She had no easy means of expressing her real fears. 'Of course not.' I stroked her arm and handed her the menu. As we ate an inferior borscht and some stuffed cabbage leaves, my eye went rather too frequently to the street outside. Rain rushed down the plateglass windows distorting the appearance of the pedestrians, most of whom began to resemble those varieties of half-men who populate Classical mythology; then, once or twice, I was half convinced I had glimpsed Esmé. I knew I was behaving ridiculously, pursuing the phantom of what was almost certainly a creature of my own invention. I concentrated on my food, but the Baroness, noticing my agitation, asked casually after Mrs Cornelius. I made some conventional reply and tried to think clearly. I knew I was suffering from mild concussion and lack of sleep. I would be a fool to become the slave of such a ridiculous delusion and obviously I had made a mistake in *La Rotonde*. If I found Helena she would prove to have dyed hair, a swarthy skin, green eyes and be about twenty. But, for all this reasoning, my willpower was inadequate to act upon it and again I left Tokatlian's hastily, having made some vague promise to meet Leda soon, and crossed the street to take up my familiar position at the *Rotonde* bar. Girls came in, shaking umbrellas and wet cloaks. Some greeted me. Some tried to sit with me. I dismissed them. The Syrian gargoyle emerged from his sleeping-quarters and scowled to himself when he saw me. I ordered a drink from him and won him over with a large tip. His wizened features relaxed; he looked up at me and offered me a smile of astonishing, almost convincing, sweetness. We were once more part of the same alliance, if not exactly friends. I sipped absinthe and watched the crowd. The band played a bizarre mixture of Turkish accordion music and American jazz; men and women stepped onto the tiny wooden dance-floor and moved like marionettes, jerking back and forth to inexpert syncopation, imitating some dance they had seen demonstrated only in a poor quality cinema-film. Sonia arrived, shook her head at me as a sign she had no information, then left on the arm of an elderly Italian officer. I dozed over my drink. I considered writing a letter to Kolya. I knew I should at least leave a message at the *Palas*, but convinced myself the boy would know where I was if he could not find me at Tokatlian's. I walked into the little back room where the Syrian changed money at a disgusting rate and bought a few English sovereigns. To remain alert I sniffed up a large quantity of his overpriced cocaine before returning to the absinthe and boredom of cheap fragrance, soft shoulders, bobbed hair and shiny frocks. What I sought now was blonde curls and petticoats, pink skin and honest blue eyes.

The rain had stopped. I walked down the sloping streets to the coffee shop opposite the gate of the Galata Bridge and ordered a medium sweet demi-tas while I watched the nations of the Earth come and go. On this side, the vicinity was full of street-sellers instilling impossible virtues to their pathetic wares; fat Turkish businessmen in fezzes and dark European clothes standing in groups, gesticulating as they occupied their time discussing unlikely bargains. Against my better judgment I bought some *ekmek-kadaif*, the 'bread-and-velvet' Turkish women found irresistible, a combination of flour and cream. There were probably at that moment in Constantinople more minds turned to the invention of new confectionery than ever considered the profound problems facing the future of their city. But perhaps Turks were best employed in this way. Another favourite of mine was called 'the iman fainted.' *Iman-bagildi* was the most delicious dish I had ever tasted, and remains for me finer than any of the great concoctions of Vienna or Paris. I had eaten two of these by the time twilight came. It was at twilight that I had last seen my Esmé and I sat there in the superstitious hope she would re-emerge at the same time tonight. As ships assembled on both sides of the bridge, waiting for the pontoons to part as they did twice a day, mornings and evenings, I wondered how I might stow away, preferably on a British or American vessel. Every so often the regular ferries to Venice were subject to rigorous police checks; it was impossible either to go aboard or disembark without all kinds of paper authority. The time might come when I had to make urgent efforts to find my Bulgarian forger and commission appropriate sets of papers.

Though I wanted to help the Baroness von Ruckstühl, it might be necessary, as she feared, to leave her here. She would quickly find another protector. Her circumstances were not as bad as most. The best of Moscow and Petersburg society was to be seen every morning crowded outside the embassy buildings of France, Germany, Britain, Italy, even Belgium. The French had a joke. They said you could tell how desperate a Russian was when he found himself having to choose between suicide and Belgium.

The flower of Russian blood was left to dry and dissipate on the bleak Lemnos shores. Professors of great academies, scientists, lawyers, artists of every kind, musicians and philosophers, were squeezed into the island camps to die of typhus or pneumonia. Royal princes crawled cap in hand before petty officials of a Germany they had meant to crush. One could not help be reminded of the ancient pagan conquests of great Christian cities, of Rome and Kiev and elsewhere, whose occupants had been forced to endure similar humiliations. Decent, devout Christians were exploited and misused, allowed to rot and perish. And the world pretended to sympathize while showing every sign of satisfaction. Tsar Nicholas and his government had been committed to outmoded institutions. Even Russian monarchists agreed on that. Now Russia's surviving nobility paid a terrible price for their autocrat's shortsightedness and folly, for their Tsarina's lusting after a self-styled holy man whose advice produced some of the greatest strategic blunders of the War.

When it grew darker I left the waterfront to walk back through rubble, up stone steps and between buildings which jutted overhead at drunken angles, leaning in an insane geometry of impossible curves and corners. Somewhere a blaze started and from the Galata Tower, built for the purpose, came the frantic ringing of a huge bell. One of the city's many private, self-appointed fire brigades (usually incendiaries themselves) rushed by, a confusion of bare feet, fezzes, turbans, old donkeys, hoses and copper drums of water; a loutish group of cutthroats who looted as much as they saved.

I had just turned into the electric familiarity of the Grande Rue when I saw Mrs Cornelius's head emerge from a motor-cab. She waved at me, shouting something I could not catch. I tried to run after her. She was angry, glaring back at me. 'Unless yer pull yer bleedin' socks up, Ivan, we're never gonna git arta 'ere!' Then the cab turned down towards Tephane and disappeared. I did not know whether to follow her further, go to Tokatlian's and the comforting bosom of my Leda, or try once more to see if Esmé had visited *La Rotonde*. Almost before I realised it I had passed through the doors of the café and was surrounded by warm commercial flesh and brutal serge. Always, since my Odessa days, I felt at ease in such environments. Perhaps it is because very little is ever expected of you in those places. You are tolerated in drinking clubs, working-class pubs and bordellos as long as you can keep your mouth shut and pay your way. You are at once amongst friendly company and anonymous at the same time.

Because the tables were all occupied, I made an effort to reach the bar and order absinthe as usual. I saw neither Sonia, the Syrian, nor 'Helena'. I felt ridiculous, believing everyone there must be secretly laughing at me. I was wasting far too much time, as Mrs Cornelius had said. I should be laying out escape routes, preparing documents, checking tables of boats and trains. Nonetheless, I did not leave. I still hoped to see the girl just once more, to confirm that I had invented her likeness to Esmé, and besides I was already an expert at sitting still. In recent years, as cities fell and were recaptured, changed governments, revised their laws, I had learned to bide my time and wait for the right opportunity. I fancied myself a reptile, sometimes, a patient old lizard able to lie on his rock for days until his prey moved into range. If necessary I can abolish impatience, almost abolish Time itself, drifting into a kind of semi-conscious hibernation. This utterly inappropriate response to my situation's present urgency began to possess me at *La Rotonde*. Finding the girl became of paramount importance. Rationalizing, I told myself I could easily live and work in Constantinople. There were plenty of recently arrived entrepreneurs who would finance my prototypes and moreover I could always get work as a mechanic. In a villa overlooking the Sweet Waters of Europe I could live like a pasha. I should have fellow countrymen for conversation, hundreds of books and magazines published in Russian. I could not imagine cold, stern, dignified London being anything like this. I should not have my pick of so many young girls in England, either. By remaining here I could live a very quiet, aesthetic working life and when relaxing could taste all Constantinople's many delights whenever I pleased. Such a routine suited my temperament; I was not merely a man of thought; I was moved by enormous physical passions and enthusiasms. I should become the principal architect for the new, gleaming, Christian city.

When I look back I can never logically see why I did not choose to stay and become one of Constantinople's institutions. The severity of Ataturk's first years hardly touched her. He said she was a Western harlot. He turned his back on her, refusing to let her be associated with his régime. He let her mosques fade with poverty or become museums for tourists, he refused to allow her educated men permission to work there, so they were forced to move to Ankara. But he did not actively trouble the city which brought all Turkey's wealth to her. He never disdained the gold which continued to flow through his 'Istanbul'. In spite of him, Constantinople remained the centre of the world. Ataturk raised his flag over the collection of mud huts that was Ankara, his new capital, imposing on his people all the puritanical severity he rejected for himself while he drank and whored his way to early death and so imitated, with ironic completeness, the hypocritical Sultans he had swept aside. Constantinople scarcely noticed and she did not much care; she was used to despots and their high pomposities; she had existed under them for at least three thousand years. I began to tell myself it might be sensible to live closer to Russia. It would be much easier to return home when the time came. I saw myself as the successful, triumphant prodigal of Odessa, stepping off a ship, greeted by a brass band and a cheering crowd, and bringing home Esmé, my childhood sweetheart, my bride.

She came in alone, and at first I had become so accustomed to discounting the inventions of my wishful eye I almost ignored her. Tonight she wore faded blue velvet, at least two sizes too large, and had bundled her hair beneath a peacock aigrette. All her cosmetics and tawdry wardrobe could not disguise her. Barely able to contain myself, I felt my head begin to beat sickeningly as my glass went down on the counter with a crack. My heart was painful against my ribs, but I held myself in rein, watching her out of the corner of my eye. Uncertainly, clutching a little sequinned evening bag to her chest, she picked her delicate way between the customers. I was trembling violently as I rose slowly to my feet; then step by wary step I moved towards her, as a dying man might approach an oasis he fears must be a mirage. I was now directly in front of her. She stopped. I bowed. My mouth was bone dry, but I mustered all my charm and appeared, I am sure, outwardly calm, even a little distant. 'Would you care for a drink, young lady?' I said to her in English.

She frowned, puzzled: 'I am a Catholic.' She spoke halting French with an accent I could not place. She thought she was answering my

146

question. This brought a gentle smile to my lips, whereupon she smiled back. It was Esmé's same, flashing parting of the mouth and widening of the eyes; her whole face coming alive at once. She realised she had misunderstood me and said something in Turkish. I shrugged and made a pantomime of apologetic obtuseness. I knew such unbelievable joy. I had not been mistaken. This was Esmé's twin. She laughed. It was Esmé's unselfconscious laughter, full and musical. 'You call yourself Helena, do you not?'

'Helena, yes, m'sieu.' She nodded rapidly as if I had displayed unusual perceptiveness and she wished to encourage me.

I took her gently by the arm and led her to the quietest corner of the café. 'You will have absinthe? Or lemonade, perhaps?'

She understood my French and chose lemonade, proving to me that she was by no means a hardened whore, but a wholesome schoolgirl who had, by some dreadful mischance, become mixed up in this life. There was still time to save her.

Disdainfully ignoring the Syrian's leering, conspiratorial wink, I ordered the drinks. 'Do you recognize me?' I asked her.

She frowned, then quickly put an embarrassed hand to her mouth. 'Oh! The man on the tram!'

'I alarmed you and I'm sorry. But you are the image of my dead sister. You can imagine my own shock. You seemed a ghost.'

I had not frightened her. She relaxed again, her curiosity, if nothing else, encouraging her to stay. She put her little head to one side, just as Esmé did, and said sympathetically, 'You are Russian, m'sieu? Your sister was . . .' She could not find the word. 'Bolsheviks?'

'Just so.'

'I am sorry for you.' She spoke softly, yet in that same vibrant voice Esmé had always used when moved to emotion. Even her tiny, nervous gesture of concern was the same.

'You understand why I searched for you? Do they really call you Helena?'

She hesitated, as if she wanted to give me her real name. Then caution returned. She inclined her head. 'Helena.'

'You're Greek?'

She shrugged, attempting to resume a mask which was still unfamiliar to her. 'We're all something, m'sieu.'

I felt enormous tenderness for her. She was Esmé, my darling rose. I wanted to reach out there and then to scrape the coloured powder

147

from her cheeks, revealing the lovely skin beneath. I wanted to touch her in kindness as I touched Esmé, whose love I took for granted, whose confidence I never doubted. Esmé worshipped me. They tore her from her destiny as they tried to tear me from mine. They perverted her soul. They made her commonplace: a child of revolution with a twisted grimace where once there had been a natural smile.

'Your parents are still alive?'

'Of course.' She waved an arm outwards, towards the door. A copper snake flashed, green enamel eyes glittered. 'Over there.'

'What nationality?'

I think the question began to make her nervous. Sighing, she spread her awkward hands, covered in penny rings, on the table. 'Roumanian,' she said. Within the mask her blue eyes were candid. 'They came before the War.'

'Would you keep me company tonight?'

She lifted fingers to her inexpert coiffure. 'It's what I'm here for, m'sieu.'

I shook my head, then decided not to explain. I was terrified, still, that I would startle her, send her running to where I should never find her again. So I contented myself with, 'So you've no special friend?'

There was a hint of assumed world-weariness, the suggestion of a play-acted sigh which reminded me of Leda's similar responses. 'Not yet, m'sieu.'

I ignored her pose and touched her hand for a moment. 'My name is Maxim. I wish to protect you. Can I call you Esmé rather than Helena?'

She was puzzled by this, and not unamused. 'If you like.' Her expression was transformed to one of genuine sympathy. 'But do not be sad, M'sieu Maxim. We are here for pleasure, no?' She fell silent, peacefully content to drink and watch the other couples dance. She had the poise of Esmé, the same unstudied movements of head and shoulders, an identical air of self-contained amusement at the world's antics. I wanted her in a wholesome dress, hair properly brushed and rearranged, but I was still too cautious to suggest anything of the sort, frightened she would take to her heels if I moved too hastily. At that age girls can be singularly whimsical. She seemed perfectly glad to be in my company, yet at any moment might resolve to leave with someone else or decide she hated the shape of my nose. She had not been a whore for long or she would by now be taking a merely professional interest in men.

'What did you do before you started coming to *La Rotonde?*' I asked her casually.

'At –' She pursed her lips. She was trying to be discreet. 'I worked.'

'And your parents?'

'Father's a carpenter. Mother used to go to the big houses.' She pointed up towards Pera's well-to-do suburb. 'Now she can't. So I come here.'

All this confirmed my growing knowledge that I had been selected by Fate to rescue her. She could not have had many men before the American sailor, if any. 'Well,' I said, 'I might be able to offer you a job. I'm considering employing a companion. It isn't a trick. Ask anyone here. Any of the girls. Even the Syrian will vouch for my honesty. If you, for instance, were interested, I would see your parents and ensure everything was properly arranged.'

She did not completely understand. She nodded vaguely. From her bag she lifted a packet of bad-quality cigarettes, inexpertly fitting one into a cheap wooden holder stained to mock ebony. I stretched out a hand with a lighted match, glad she was evidently unused to smoking. I continued to be careful not to introduce the slightest note of criticism or morality. Young girls carry a weight of guilt as it is. Anyone who reminds them of it is likely to be regarded with hatred. I proceeded delicately. I joked with her. Laughter always takes women's minds from their inhibitions and in that respect is both better and cheaper than champagne. She grew steadily more at ease and tried to translate a joke from Turkish into French and failed prettily, but caused us both to double up with laughter. I suggested she might enjoy a certain cabaret in the Petite Rue and enthusiastically she got up to come with me. The theatre was a long, low building, full of smoke, sweat and naphtha lamps, where gross, chuckling Turkish merchants watched the cavortings of third-rate French music-hall entertainers pretending to be belly-dancers and dandies. But she loved the comic dances and clung helplessly to my arm in a spontaneous frenzy of laughter at the antics of a pair of moth-eaten trained seals. Esmé and I were at the circus in Kiev. It was Spring. Captain Loukianoff had given us a little money; my mother had made us a packet of bread and sausage. It was the first time we had been out alone together in an evening. The great white tent was garnished with coloured lamps. Limelight blazed on the rich-smelling ring where bounding tigers disturbed the sawdust and half-dressed nymphs performed a golden ballet in the shadows overhead. Esmé wept for the melancholy elephant and was afraid the clown had really been hurt after his friend hit him with a bucket. When we left, the air bore the scent of fresh, damp grass and May blossoms. This circus was huge. It covered the entire bottom of the Babi gorge where later I should fly. I was looking for Zoyea, my gypsy girl, and hardly hearing Esmé's excited voice. I was a fool not to acknowledge her love. I should have protected her better. She was too good. She wanted to be a nurse and help the soldiers to live again. The soldiers recovered and made her a whore.

We walked for a little in a nearby graveyard and she seemed thoroughly at peace, willing to act on any suggestion I made. I took her to Tokatlian's, entering through the side-door. I did not want to be seen from the restaurant. There I arranged with Olmejer for my usual room while Esmé waited in the narrow, dimly-lit lobby. She was still laughing in recollection of the comedians and tried to restrain herself as she mounted the stairs. I told her to be natural. At this she snorted through her nose. I laughed, too. She was making me so happy. I opened the door of the room and showed her everything that was there. She gasped. Evidently, she had never seen such luxury. 'First,' I said, 'we'll walk a little more. The fresh air will be good for us.' I took her away from the rowdy dazzle of the Grande Rue, towards the embassies and the little squares, the smaller, quieter cafés.

The worst of the bustle fell behind us. We were in a little park, almost a zone of silence, some monument to a dead pasha, and could clearly see the million tiny lights of Stamboul from where we stood. At length I paused and drew her into the shadow of a gnarled, sweet-scented cypress. 'Are you hungry, Esmé?'

She looked directly up into my eyes. She seemed startled, as if all at once she realised how profound my feelings were, how significant to both our destinies this encounter was. Gravely, she composed her little face. Her expression was candid and serious.

'Oui.'

Seven

TO CONSECRATE MY resurrected ideal, the birth of my Muse whole, as it were, from the head of Poseidon, I required a parental blessing. Next day found myself and my girl descending to Galata's wretched slums, that world of crippled dogs and myriad degenerate humanity, to visit her mother and father.

Esmé's name had been Elizaveta Bolascu. After some political trouble, her parents moved to Constantinople in 1909, from Husch near the Bessarabian border. He had been a master carpenter until, Esmé said, ill luck had lost him his trade. Their one-room apartment was at the top, as she proudly told me, of seventy-five unstable stairs. He was, I realized at once, a drunkard, in appearance indistinguishable from the miserable Armenians and Sephardim who infested most of the building. Every vein on his face was broken and inflamed. The smell of cheap alcohol was, however, a blessing, since it disguised the general stink of the place. Esmé's mother, half mad and apparently without will, wore a black shawl around her head like any peasant woman; her skin was as yellow as her husband's was red. She said she would make us tea, but Esmé stopped her. 'My mother is sickly.'

M. Bolascu spoke only his native language and some Turkish. His wife knew a smattering of Russian, but I could barely understand the dialect, and some French. Esmé was thirteen. As they laboured through their miniature vocabularies I wondered where Captain Loukianoff had been in 1907. Had Madame Bolascu ever heard the name? She said it was possibly familiar, but I suspect she thought I was searching for a distant relative's next of kin. (Esmé was two when they moved from Husch.

151

It was perfectly possible therefore that the girls were half-sisters. To this day I am convinced of it. Loukianoff's wife had deserted him after only a year of marriage, after Esmé was born. Why should he not have sought consolation, later, in the arms of a Roumanian carpenter's robust wife?) Madame Bolascu asked if he was a policeman. She spoke in a hesitant, reedy voice, anxious to please. No, I said, he was a Russian officer. A gentleman. Her eyes became blank, as if someone had switched them off. I wondered if this were an indication of guilt. These two had reached the very bottom, although it was evident they had once been respectable. The Turkish capital could have that effect. Something in the air rotted the honest Christian soul. They had been slowly starving to death but now, thanks to Esmé, they were gorged on the cans and preserves she had bought with her body. Strangely, both mother and father were swarthy. I knew Esmé could hardly be the drunken Roumanian's daughter. Loukianoff had doubtless passed through Husch on his travels to and from Ukraine. I could not remember exactly when he had come to settle in Kiev, but it was after 1907. 'Loukianoff,' I whispered to the crone (she was not more than fifty in actuality). Her husband moaned like a sheep and complained it had grown cold. She went to rearrange the sacking at the window, pinning the fabric on rusty nails stuck into bare wood. Esmé lit a candle. Bolascu coughed and brushed at his grimy forehead. He did not want us there.

'Très bon. Très bon,' insisted the mother. Even her French had plainly seen better days. She patted her lovely daughter's head. She tried to grin, but her few yellow teeth plainly hurt her mouth. Neither she nor Esmé was entirely certain why I was there. I tried to explain again. The child reminded me of my murdered sister. I wanted to provide for Esmé's wellbeing and theirs. Husband and wife nodded at last and became thoughtful. We had reached the bargaining stage.

In the end I paid two English sovereigns for her. Having fairly purchased their blessing, I was now, in their eyes, the sole owner of their child. Her mother assured me she was a good girl, a virgin, a pious Catholic. She kissed her daughter farewell. The father snarled over his money. She said she would come to see them soon. We went back down the swaying stairs to where a nervous cabman waited, feeding his horse from a nosebag. I ordered him to return us to the little sidestreet behind Tokatlian's. There I had already taken one of Olmejer's private apartments, rented on a monthly basis. This suite was a red cavern with low, curved ceilings and deep carpets all of the same colour. It was their best. It must be a secret, I told Olmejer, to everyone. I had paid him in advance. The rest of our day was spent with the couturiers who came to dress her in decent clothes, befitting her age. I had her thoroughly washed. Her hair was brushed and tied back with ribbon. At length she resembled an ordinary thirteen-year-old girl again. I left her with her dresses and her mirrors and returned for a while to the *Pera Palas*. There were no messages for me. I began to believe myself forgotten by Mrs Cornelius. I hoped to see Major Nye in the bar, but he, too, was gone. I was sure the Baroness, on the other hand, would continue patiently to wait a while longer.

A week went by. I ignored Leda's increasingly imploring notes. Then I let it be known I had been ordered to Scutari. I did not want my idyll interrupted. I was at last in love. It was a rapture of nostalgia, of dreams come true. We visited cinemas, fairgrounds and theatres. We did everything I had always intended to do with Esmé. And now Esmé did not hold back, primly examining the cost or warning me not to lose my head, as she had in Kiev. I was able to enjoy everything to the full and never think once of the future. Love-making was sweet and delicate, unlike anything I had known before, almost in the nature of a happy, childish game, though not without passion. Esmé was greedy for life, reaching for it urgently as one does when one has believed it permanently lost. She was in fact more eager for sexual pleasure than I. I was frequently content merely to lie with her cradled in my arms while I told her little stories, made jokes, fed her with sweets. My whole world had a rosy warmth; I knew the joy of a father reunited with his daughter, brother with sister, husband with wife. She accepted my romantic tenderness as prettily as she accepted all my gifts. I asked for nothing; merely that she be herself, the object of my affection, my little perfect goddess, rescued from vice as I had not been able to rescue her geminus. I remembered to write a few hasty notes to Mrs Cornelius. I told her I was in contact with people who could help us. I informed the Baroness von Ruckstühl I had encountered unexpected difficulties. The official who promised to arrange her visa was now being unhelpful; moreover, relatives of mine had arrived in Constantinople and required some of my time. Day after ecstatic day I put off meeting both women. While I lived in heaven, whole armies were routed, new countries were established, others were completely destroyed or rechristened with unlikely names. The empires of old Europe fell to bits like rotten wood. Esmé proved an excellent linguist. She rapidly expanded her French and soon learned Russian, as well as a little Italian. With her help I was able to speak slightly better Turkish. The skill for languages was one we shared and increased my belief that we actually were twin souls.

The maintenance of this secret apartment over Tokatlian's meant selling jewellery intended for London. The Pera cocaine was good, cheap and plentiful. Nonetheless Esmé proved a voracious user. Once they have overcome their prejudice and sampled it, most women develop an authentic passion for the drug. Some would even claim it is above all a woman's drug. The deterioration of my finances was rapid and did not take long to become obvious. I had not paid my bill at the *Palas* and quite rightly Mrs Cornelius had refused responsibility. She had left Russia with much less than I. Accordingly I began to consider selling either my knowledge or my abilities. During the Civil War I had learned to survive very well in Kiev, and had become a successful businessman. Now I must attempt to do the same thing in Constantinople. It was Esmé's habit to sleep most of the day, so I would go down to the docks where under the old arches I found dozens of motor repair shops. I became friendly with several people specialising in boat engines. I helped them out whenever they needed me and in a short time became not only assured of work, but had several important contacts amongst small ship owners who plied the Bosphorus, Aegean and nearer shores of the Black Sea. The majority of these owners were either Greek or Armenian. I eventually met cousins of my old mentor Sarkis Mihailovitch and was treated thereafter as a family friend. They, too, were mechanics. Few Turks ran such repair shops. Turks tended to feel they lost face if they let their hands get oily or even attempted to understand the mysteries of the internal combustion engine. They had lived on the backs of others for centuries. Up to now they had employed German and Britons to build their machines for them while the lesser races of the Ottoman Empire were ordered to maintain them. The British had built the underground funicular which ran between Pera and the Galata docks. The Germans had built the tram system. No Ottoman was responsible for a single innovation. Even the designs of the mosques were copied from the Byzantines. When a class or nation is reduced to a reliance on pride and slaves, it gives up the right to rule. They had no claim on Constantinople. Byzantium's true inheritors could construct the machines needed to run a city which Roman engineers had given fresh foundations. The ancient warrens of two thousand five hundred years were a tribute to the simple fact that to survive was to embrace and understand new technology as it emerged. Working in the harbours of the Golden Horn, where galleons of Venice and Chinese junks had met regularly in the course of trade, I could watch flying boats land and take off: Macchis and Porte-Felixstowes flying from Italy and Gibraltar, taking important military personnel back and forth. I longed to pilot one of those machines, at least until I built my own. They were a reminder of what the West meant to me. They revived my imagination. They made Europe real again. Even the most magnificent ships could not convey this ambience. The planes flew to their home bases within hours, coming and going so casually. I dreamed of flying Esmé and myself to freedom, to Genoa or Le Havre. I would build a more sophisticated version of my first machine and escape with her on my back, a flying prince and princess, those staples of Oriental legend.

I was touched when Esmé told me she dreamed one day of keeping house for me, of becoming my wife. I was only seven years her senior. When I reached thirty she would be twenty-three. There was nothing wrong with a man of twenty-five marrying a girl of eighteen. We planned like children, knowing little of normal domestic life. Esmé was admiringly curious of my designs, sitting silently as with set-square and slide rule I worked on a plan for a new steam engine which would use rapid heating chemicals, suitable for powering a motor car. Naturally, she could not follow the mathematical formulae but the symbols themselves fascinated her. For hours she would stare at them like a cat, her eyes following my pen as it formed them on the paper.

We continued to dine in obscure backstreet cafés. She wanted to cook for me, she said. She named Turkish and Roumanian dishes. Contemptuously she said the restaurants could not prepare them properly. She had been educated at a charitable convent school until she was ten. For a time she thought of becoming a nun. Then her father's fortunes worsened. The Turks had grown unwilling to employ Christians in their War Effort. So Esmé herself had looked for work. During the War there had been few jobs. She tried to be a domestic servant like her mother, but most of the usual employers, the well-to-do Greeks, or people attached to foreign embassies had left the capital. Now, with so many refugees, the competition was impossible. Two friends of hers had gone to work at Mrs Unal's. They told her money was good in the brothel once you were used to the hours. I guessed Esmé had been so obviously innocent Mrs Unal had sent her away. Even in Pera and

Galata there were laws of sorts. The British did their best to maintain them, though much of their time was taken up settling disputes between different groups of Allied servicemen and attempting to discourage Turkish police from demanding bribes. Esmé said she even thought of returning to Roumania and finding cousins, but she had been her parents' only support. They would die soon. In the meantime she had to care for them. To ease her conscience, I had already promised them a few shillings a week.

The von Ruckstühl correspondence grew hysterical. Those intolerable Germans wanted her to leave. Marusya Veranovna had disappeared. Kitty was heartbroken. There was no money. Had I 'dropped' her? Reluctantly, I arranged to see her. In my room at the *Pera Palas* I actually enjoyed myself with her. I felt a return of spontaneity which had vanished during my time with Esmé, for it is hard not to treat a little girl as a delicate toy. Leda had become inventively lascivious. All her fantasies and frustrations had given her time to explore her range of lust. With genuine emotion I told her how much I had missed her. 'But you are always in Scutari,' she said. 'Have you a woman there?' I reassured her. 'It's because the influential Turks live in Scutari.'

'Are you a spy, Simka? When I told Count Siniutkin you were a flyer who served with Intelligence, he said you must be a secret agent.'

'All you need to know, darling Leda, is that I am a Russian patriot. I hate Trotski and his gang. I really should not say more.'

'Then your work is dangerous I am so selfish. It's the anxiety. I feel it more for Kitty than myself. But I shall have to find a job.'

When she left I offered myself the luxury of an hour in the bath alone and tried to collect my thoughts. I was indeed living fairly dangerously, though not as the Baroness guessed. In spite of my work, my savings were almost exhausted. Somehow I had put myself in the position of deceiving three women and, worse, I had diverted from my 'life plan'. I had to find a way to resolve all these difficulties. Changing into fresh linen, I went downstairs to the bar and to my delight saw Mrs Cornelius. She had on a new soft silk frock of pale blue and sported a navy blue 'picture' hat. She was not in the least surprised to see me, but I believe I must have blushed under her searching eye.

'Afternoon, Ivan,' she said. She was distant and disapproving. 'Ya got me note, then.'

I shook my head. 'I'm this moment returned from Scutari.' I was anxious to win back her good opinion. 'I'm working. Trying to earn some money by doing mechanical repairs for the Turks.'

'Where the 'ell've yer reelly bin? Silly little bleeder. Unless ya pull yer socks up, yore gonna be in an 'orrible mess. I carn't 'elp yer.'

'You've already done more for me, dear Mrs Cornelius, than anyone.' I spoke feelingly and with dignity. 'If I am keeping you here, then you must travel on alone. I will join you as soon as I can.'

'Oo's bin torkin ter yer? I don't fink you *want* ter git ter London!'

'I assure you I do.'

'Then why ain't yer doin' somefink abart it?' She was so pretty, even when her eyes narrowed with impatience.

'We need documents. Divorce papers, if necessary . . .'

'Divorce!' She was exasperated. 'I tol' you abart that in ther larst note. It turns art there's no bloody record of our marriage. I've orlready 'ad that sorted art. Wot yer fink I've been doin' wiv meself? It's not me should be worrying. I don't need nuffink 'cept a birf certiff ter prove I'm British. An' that's on its way. Are ya delib'rately tryin ter do yerself darn? 'Oo is it? That bloody Baroness?'

'I've been earning money. I assure you it's true. At the docks. You forget I'm a first class mechanic.'

'First clars wanker more like.' She sighed. "Ave a drink.'

I asked for anis.

'I'm doin' me best fer ya, Ivan.' She was superficially more calm. 'But yore not 'elpin' yoreself.'

'My personal life is complicated,' I admitted. I was yearning to tell her everything, but she gave me no time.

'Personal life! Ivan, ya carn't start ter bloody 'ave a personal life until yer git ter bleedin' London! Not unless it's direc'ly connected wiv a passage on a ship. 'Ave an affair wiv an admiral. It's orl ya kin afford!'

'Someone else is now involved. A relative I found here. An orphan. I want to save her, too.'

'Come orf it, Ive. Ya've orlready tol' me yore an only child!'

'You've heard of Esmé This is her half-sister.'

Mrs Cornelius stiffened. 'Git rid of 'er.' She spoke urgently and firmly. 'An' double quick. Yore talkin' bad news, Ivan. Dump 'er. Do wot yer 'ave ter do. But do it nar.'

I was offended. 'This is not a passing affair, Mrs Cornelius. The girl in question has been of considerable help to me in a dozen ways. I am prepared to say, quite frankly –'

Mrs Cornelius lifted an imperious hand. 'I've 'eard it.' With the other hand she signalled for the waiter to bring us more drinks. 'Yore a babe-in-ther-wood, Ivan. I fought some bint woz takin' yer. An if they ain't, then it's even worse. Yore takin' yerself!'

This was to me the most appalling blasphemy. 'You must hear me out, Mrs Cornelius!'

'Let ya make even more've a fool o yersel'? Do me a favour.'

I was enraged. I thanked her for the anis and got to my feet.

'Pull yoreself tergevver.' She spoke in a fierce hiss. I knew she meant well. She cared for me greatly. If she had met Esmé she would not have said what she did. And she compounded the error with every statement. 'Git art o' it, Ivan. Every bloody man fer 'isself!'

'She's my responsibility. Only a child. Thirteen years old, Mrs Cornelius!'

She sat back, pursing her brilliant lips. 'Don't involve me, Ivan.'

'We could say she was adopted.'

Mrs Cornelius told the waiter to leave both drinks. She opened her navy blue handbag and paid him. By then I was insulted as well as furious. Without speaking further, I left the bar.

I realize now she had my best interests at heart, but my mind was clouded by my desires. I could not be separated from Esmé. I began to think Mrs Cornelius must be jealous of my little girl. I walked up the Grande Rue in a wild rage, careless of wind and rain. I felt severely let down and misunderstood. Since I could no longer trust Mrs Cornelius, I would seek my own way out. I needed only Esmé. I paused, finding myself in a Turkish cemetery. This one was the oddest I had seen, for almost every stone bore a life-size sculpture, some of them mundane, some of them utterly bizarre. Here a shoemaker worked on his last, there a baker prepared bread, while elsewhere a man seemed to be hanging from a gibbet, his body twisted and his face in agony. Scarcely a stone in the place did not have one of these realistic monuments and I came to realize they represented not only the occupants, but their trades and the manner in which they had died. The cemetery was surrounded by an old yellow sandstone wall. The rain fell relentlessly but without much force. Crowds of rooks flew screeching across a miserable sky. Gulls sailed on the colder currents, complaining. The old garden breathed like a dying man. I stumbled over cracked slabs to the shelter of a wall and found myself staring down beyond it at Italianate slate roofs, groves of bare trees which bent in the wind, a clear view of the Bosphorus. A gnarled Turk in lopsided fez and sodden woollen overcoat reaching almost to his feet, passed by on the path. He stopped and, careless of me, began to urinate against the wall. Upon consideration I could not bear the prospect of losing Mrs Cornelius. I was fully aware I had let myself drift away from my original course. There was a possibility I might never find it again. But must I be forced to choose between Esmé and my destiny? Many men were asked to make the same dreadful decision at some stage in their lives. Yet surely Esmé was as much part of my destiny as my engineering ambitions. She was my imagination and inspiration. Mrs Cornelius would not be angry with me for long; she was incapable of holding a grudge. If necessary I would get to England by my own route. Then I would look her up in Whitechapel as soon as I arrived. My commonsense restored, I left the cemetery and walked towards the lights of the Grande Rue.

Returning with relief to the admiring comfort of Esmé, everything else was put from my mind. My plans for the steam car progressed. I let it be known around the docks and workshops that I had an invention worth millions to an investor. In less than two weeks I made several contacts and almost concluded an arrangement with Mr Sharian, an Armenian financier. He offered to fund me for the prototype and intended to sell the first cars in Paris. Then Mr Sharian was murdered in broad daylight on the Galata Bridge and I was dragged to the police station as a suspect. I gave my address as the *Pera Palas*. There were people who could vouch for me. I mentioned, among others, Major Nye and Count Siniutkin. The Turkish police were already in the process of ignoring everything I said and turning me into the murderer but happily the British redcaps were more cautious. I said my wife, Mrs Cornelius, would be able to speak on my behalf. I began to feel as if I were within the nightmare once again; this was overly familiar to me. A British MP sergeant interviewed me and I had to repeat everything. My unlit cell had iron manacles stapled into mildewed stone and had probably been built in the middle ages. After some delay the sergeant returned. He told me Major Nye had been recalled to London and Mrs Cornelius had already left the *Pera Palas*, taking a train to Paris. At this I became frantic and I am not sure what I said, though I remember begging the sergeant to help me, swearing I was not capable of killing anyone. He told me he could only do so much. I could not think properly. How long would Esmé wait before she panicked? If she spoke for me, it would betray our secret and cause me dreadful embarrassment. I

159

could imagine what the gossips would make of my pure, wholesome love for her. I felt I was going mad.

Six hours later the authorities released me. The murderer had been caught. A Circassian identified by all witnesses, a man with an old grudge against Mr Sharian. The Turkish police told me none of this. It was the British MP who apologised. 'Were you supposed to travel with your wife? Well, send her a telegram and tell her you'll be on the next available train.' Fearing the worst, I rushed back to Tokatlian's where I found Esmé weeping. She had been convinced I must be dead. In a short while she was comforted and cheerful again and I was able to spare the time to go over to the *Pera Palas*. The manager came to me while I waited in the lobby. Mrs Cornelius had indeed left a forwarding address. It was c/o Whitechapel High Street Post Office, London E., England. Major Nye could be reached through the War Office in Whitehall. In the meantime, said the Greek with hypocritical apologies, my baggage had been removed from my room. They would be pleased to return it on receipt of a month's rent. Most of my plans, my clothes and half a kilo of cocaine were in the trunks. After I had fetched the money from Tokatlian's I was almost completely out of funds. The trunks were transferred to my rooms by two huge Somalis who normally acted as commissionaires in the evenings. I did not tip them.

That night I sold almost the last piece of jewellery and took Esmé to the music hall. I was desperate to get a grip again on reality. When I was in her company nothing seemed of particular gravity. Mrs Cornelius would soon be in London and I could write to her there. She was in a much better position to get permission for me to enter the country. If I looked at it from certain angles, things could even seem as if they had improved for me.

On the other hand my Baroness, whom I saw the next afternoon, was growing increasingly distraught. Her anxiety made her less attractive. Rather than make love, she preferred to discuss her dilemma. She had still heard nothing from her husband's family in Berlin. Her German hosts felt she had overstayed her welcome. Kitty needed far more attention, now that Marusya was gone. Was there some way she could earn money?

I could think of very little that was respectable. There were few openings for someone of her class. I myself was forced to disguise the way in which I earned what was after all a meagre living as a jobbing mechanic. I assured her, of course, I would continue my efforts to help her get to Italy or France. She had heard rumours that a full scale Civil War was imminent in Turkey. The nationalists grew steadily more vociferous. The Sultan's rule was seriously threatened because he too willingly dealt with the British. The British, for their part, had made many political arrests and so increased the tension. Haidur Pasha was being reinforced. Count Siniutkin, she said, predicted more trouble soon. A large proportion of the Turkish army had refused to disband. Bashi-bazouki bandits in the hinterland terrorised villages, killing Turks, Greeks and Armenians indiscriminately. Constantinople herself might soon be attacked.

This last seemed highly unlikely. I told her the Allies could easily defend the city. The whole civilized world would lend aid, if necessary. A few brigands were no threat. Down the centuries she had held firm against entire nations of enemies. But Leda refused to be calmed. 'It's getting exactly like Russia. Can't you see that, Simka? The whole horrible world's going the same way! That's why I worry about you. I don't want to lose you.'

I laughed heartily. I was indestructible, I told her. Like Leonardo, I moved from city to city, always able to gauge the wind in time. Someone could be relied upon, no matter what my circumstances, to find my genius of value to them.

She was sceptical. 'Then why are you still here?'

I had, I reminded her, my loyalties. Moreover she should take into account the murdering tendencies of the Turk. My Steam Car Company had been a mere day or two from reality when Mr Sharian was killed. 'But I shall find another Mr Sharian.'

'Oh, Simka, it is such a shame. You deserve better. You should not have to go cap in hand to Armenians. If I had the money you would never have to know this awful frustration. Somewhere I'll get a job and keep us both. I am good at arithmetic. My husband always admired my accounts.'

'You must think of yourself and Kitty first. I can always find honest employment.'

'I have become a miserable burden to you. No wonder you see so little of me.'

'I have distant relatives, don't forget, in the city. One of them is thought to be dying. And my vocation, darling Leda, I have always said to be my first mistress.'

'Mrs Cornelius went to Paris, I hear. I would not have left my own husband in such a predicament.'

I refused to listen to this petty criticism. 'You always knew it was a marriage in name only. Mrs Cornelius had already spoken of her plans and I had insisted she go.'

She began to weep very discreetly. 'I doubted you. I'm sorry. I will not be a check on your freedom, Simka. I'm not jealous, though I could not bear never to see you.' Her expectations, I thought, were now even lower than the last time. She had become a realist. I felt renewed sympathy for her. 'Actually, my darling, Mrs Cornelius begged me to go with her.' I hoped this would make her feel better. 'She was angry when I refused. I told her it would mean leaving you.'

The Baroness laughed and shook her head as she wiped the tears from her cheeks. 'If only it were true.'

I was offended, but she did not seem to notice. I rose and dressed. The cheap room, which offered a special rate if you took it for a whole night, had no carpet on the wooden floor. I felt a splinter drive itself into my foot and I cursed. I pushed back one of the shutters to see while I eased the little shard free. Outside a mob was demonstrating. It was impossible to know, from the Arabic on their banners, what their grudge was. Leda pulled a dirty sheet to her shoulders. 'Don't be upset. You must look after yourself. I haven't any illusions. I'm almost ten years older than you.'

I lowered my foot to the floor. Affection and understanding suddenly returned. Crossing to the bed and kissing her, I promised I would see her very soon.

By the following day, however, Esmé had become ill. A cold had become something more serious, perhaps influenza, and the doctor's prescriptions were costly. Obsessively, I nursed my child, brought her nourishing food from the restaurant, did extra work at the docks and continued my quest for another backer. Her tiny face, in a frame of sweat-drenched blonde hair, smiled bravely back at me whenever she was awake. Again I had no time for the Baroness. The cards I had ordered were delivered: *The European and Oriental Steam Automobile Company Ltd.* I distributed these widely. I saw no point at that stage in alienating Turkish interests. The steam cars were for the world. Did it matter, in the long run, if the finance for their development came from the Orient or the Occident? The money was better spent on cars than on guns! I had many false hopes in that period.

Esmé grew well and was gay again. I began seeing Leda occasionally. The spring came. I took Esmé into the hills. We ate *Iman-begildi* under fragrant mulberry trees while we watched goats and sheep graze. The sun was silver in a pale grey sky and the walls of the villages were washed with faint lilac, pink or yellow. Shrubs were starting to bloom. The distant sea was tranquil. Constantinople's dignified seaside suburbs were nothing like the yellow houses of Kiev's outskirts. The scenery was more exotic, more evidently Islamic. Yet my childhood was completely revived: that confident, egocentric childhood when I was beginning to realise my unusual capacities and give proper detail to my dreams. Esmé listened to me as Esmé always listened, and I described the glorious promise of the future. She would gasp. She would grow round-eyed. She would remark on my cleverness and anticipate a marvellous career for me, with herself as my loyal companion. Then she would indulge her own fantasies, of the kind of house we would own, when we were rich, how many servants we should have and so on. She supplied everything I had taken for granted from the first Esmé. But this Esmé I did not take for granted. I had lost one and could never bear to lose another. She had my daily attention. I made certain she was entertained, was healthy, had the food, the clothes, the toys she most desired, that our lovemaking was to her taste even when it was not to mine. I knew the dangers of being over-solicitous and tried to avoid them. Esmé realised how much I loved her, what she meant to me. She accepted my concern as her right, the care of a real father.

Constantinople became gradually more familiar to me while, with the changing of the seasons, she also grew more magical. By now I had friends around the docks, acquaintances who were engineers on the vessels sailing regularly to and from the city. I was of service to many émigrés still inhabiting Pera. These continued to increase, for the Red Army pushed our Volunteers further back. Some Russians presently fought beside the Greeks in Anatolia. Others had been recruited into the brigand gangs taking advantage of the War. Everywhere groups of renegades joined the service of petty chieftains. There was an entire unit of 'Wolfshead' Cossacks helping to establish the régime of a Chinese warlord. Others had gone to Africa to join the Foreign Legions of Spain and France. Some white officers were even lending their expertise to the pirate khans of Indonesia. They had thoroughly turned their backs on our cause. So many Russian mercenaries were little more than children; as a trade they knew only battle and would rather sell their swords to Islam than live on Christian charity. The Allies, caught up in their own political machinations, had no time left to help our Russian Army consolidate. Generals departed for America daily, apparently to lecture on the Terrors of Bolshevism, but actually to join relatives in Toronto and Miami. The Baroness von Ruckstühl was lucky. In April she became a receptionist at the *Byzance*. We met twice a week in her little room at the very top of the old hotel. Kitty received private lessons on those evenings, from a Madame Krön, attached to the American school. We still spoke of leaving. She continued to apply for a visa to Berlin, but both of us considered ourselves fortunate compared to the thousands of wretches reduced to hanging around the Galata Bridge or the harbours, selling ikons and furs to grinning soldiers and sailors.

The cabarets had taken on a distinctly Russian air in parts of the Grande Rue. Noble princes and princesses who before the War had learned a few tasteful folk dances and little else, now performed them for drunks to the sound of out-of-tune balalaikas, while disinherited Cossacks nightly displayed their skill with pistol and whip. Counts gave riding lessons. Countesses taught drawing and music. The Tsarist upper crust had become a troupe of beggars and third-rate circus performers half a million strong. To be Russian in Constantinople was to be a laughing stock. One preferred when possible to claim another nationality. On occasions I was Polish or Czech. Sometimes I let people think I was British, French, even American. Similarly, the Baroness carefully retained her German style, though sometimes she dropped the 'baroness' (since every other Russian had a title) and became Frau von Ruckstühl. Because of my dark looks, I was frequently taken for an Armenian, and it was not always practical to deny it. I knew a few phrases from Sarkis Mihailovitch, chiefly technical terms, and these proved useful to me. Armenians are not Jews, whatever people say. They were very friendly to me and some even called me 'the nephew of Kouyoumdjian'. They began to ask me to take on the more complicated jobs, almost always ensuring I had the entire fee for myself. Five or six steam engines belonging to the ferry boat owners soon became familiar exasperating acquaintances. I learned a great deal about marine machinery and steam engines in particular. Whenever I could I experimented, making little improvements to my automobile designs.

In the evenings Esmé and I would hire a carriage and a driver. We would tour Stamboul or take the little white coastal roads winding beside the pure turquoise of the Bosphorus and the Sea of Marmara. The sky was equally blue, a colour I had once believed the fanciful invention of painters. We ate well, in restaurants overlooking wooded bays and tiny fishing ports. Listen to languorous Turkish music we watched the sun set on impossible landscapes. Spring mists diffused the light, especially at dawn and dusk, and we saw the hills of Scutari and Stamboul quiver in copper-coloured haze. Constantinople was a jewelled treacherous beast. She could fascinate you with her beauty, then strike you down suddenly, to suck out your blood and your soul. Her attractions were potentially fatal. I earned good money as a mechanic, had a worshipping child-bride, a mistress who was equally devoted, but must always remember that my true vocation was to be found in the more vigorous West.

The Allies grew increasingly uncertain of their rôle. Peace talks continued. Europe was divided up, her future settled by her victors. The Byzantine city became an embarrassment to them. We heard more of Mustafa Kemal and his henchmen, of nationalists active in the capital. Many French and Italian military people thought Constantinople should remain Turkish rather than Greek. The Greeks, they argued, were just Englishmen in white skirts. The British alone gave genuine support to the Greek cause, supplying them with munitions and ships. Britons considered themselves the true inheritors of an Homeric tradition, thus in helping Greece, they reinforced their own self image. But could it be wrong to want control of the Straits while Islam and Bolshevism threatened to join hands in the Caucasus and Anatolia. Together they would form a Red Horde more ruthlessly effective than any Tamburlane or Attila directed against Christendom. It was not madness to predict the Antichrist's army one day massing against us. Having fought and won a great battle, the Allies were exhausted but tomorrow that battle would seem as nothing. The mountains were bursting; from scarlet fire galloped the very armies of Hell. Into the fray came swaggering Carthage. The citadels of civilization were attacked on every front. The West must entrench herself, restore her energies! The real enemy was still alive and on the march!

These condescending young men, with their beards and tartan shirts, come into the shop trying to put Labour Party posters in my window. They have no idea what they were rescued from. The Communist and the Oriental remain serious threats to everything held dear by the West. Those decent men and women voting for Adolf Hitler did not believe they voted for tyranny. They were hoping to contain the spread of evil. Hitler's greatest mistake was to make a pact with Stalin. His ordinary followers felt a wavering of their faith in him. The Third Reich truly began to crumble when it lost its internal morale and its supporters abroad. Some innocent people were caught up in the great struggle and did indeed suffer an unjust fate, but most who exaggerate the evils of Hitlerism and speak melodramatically of a 'Holocaust' are the very ones who thought they had a right to enrich themselves by exploiting their host nations. I am not a political person. Even in my present circumstances I believe in decency and the Fellowship of Man, in good will and tolerance. As a youth, my idealism was even more pronounced. I believed that Turks were open to reason, that they would be grateful to be left alone in Anatolia. I even sympathised with aspects of their struggle. My trust, as was to happen frequently in my life, was abused.

On Friday, 1st May 1920, I kept the usual evening appointment with my Baroness. If it lacked passion, at least our loveplay was comfortable. When it was over she poured me a glass of Polish vodka, the kind we used to call 'Bison-water.' The musky and dimly lit room was crammed with her possessions, including many framed photographs of herself, Kitty and her dead husband. She seemed unusually excited and full of secrets as she fetched a box of candied figs and offered me one where I lay in bed. 'I am growing fat in Turkey,' she said. 'It's better than living off German dumplings, I suppose.' I wondered if she had at last found another lover. She had that air women often display in such circumstances, of possessing private power, of being inwardly amused, of having easily appeased a slightly troubled conscience. I stroked her face. 'You grow more beautiful every day.'

'I've something to tell you, Simka.'

'That's obvious. Is it Count Siniutkin?'

She was puzzled; then she laughed. 'Oh, you expect everyone to be as bad as you!' I had taught myself to forgive her these little insults. If it suited her to see me as a rake and a charlatan and so preserve some sense of identity for herself I did not mind. 'I believe I have some good news for you.'

I became alarmed. She was pregnant! Yet I had been careful. I racked my memory for the likely date of conception.

'I said "good news", Simka.' She sat back on her heels, rubbing cream into pink breasts and belly, massaging neck and shoulders. 'I think I have found a financier for your inventions.'

I was delighted and considerably relieved. What did I care if the financier was her lover? All I wanted from him was the chance of bringing to physical reality just one of my ideas. From that, my reputation would automatically grow. 'Who is it? Another of your wealthy Jewish friends?'

'I wasn't given his name. But your guess in one respect was right. He is an acquaintance of Count Siniutkin.'

I had not seen the Count for several weeks. After being a fixture at Tokatlian's, he had disappeared completely. There had been talk recently of Tsarist officers leaving to fight in Paraguay or in the Argentine where there were already large numbers of Russian soldiers. I had assumed him en route to South America. Leda wiped the corners of her mouth. 'I don't know a great deal about it, but the Count thinks it's an excellent opportunity.' In two weeks Siniutkin would return to Constantinople, she said. He would then be ready to negotiate on behalf of the backer. 'He's interested in your one-man aeroplane. Could you prepare something on paper? An estimate of production costs?' She frowned, trying to remember what Siniutkin had told her. 'The factory space and tools needed, what raw materials are required, and so on. He'll understand that you won't want to reveal details, but needs as much as possible. He's absolutely serious. The Count assures me that he's above all a man of his word.'

I was content with this, reflecting how in finding Esmé I had somehow rediscovered my luck. For me, she would always be associated with my one-man plane. 'Everything's ready. I can easily work out costs. I know people in local factories. The engine is the main outlay. It could be made cheaply in large quantities. Did the Count mention money?'

'He said his backer was not a spendthrift but would pay fairly.'

'It's all I ask.' I kissed her. 'My darling, you have won your passport to Berlin!'

We celebrated with the remains of the vodka and with the cocaine I had brought. When I returned to Tokatlian's rather later than normal Esmé was asleep in front of the English primer I had bought her. Her exercises, written in a surprisingly clear, rounded hand (one of the benefits of her convent) had scattered across the floor. Tenderly I picked up the pages and stacked them together. She murmured in her sleep as I lifted her and put her gently to bed. If I left Constantinople soon, I had determined I would also take the Baroness and Kitty. My chances of entering another country unnoticed in the company of an under-age girl were poor. The schools of Constantinople already supplied the brothels of Europe. Officials would make the obvious assumption. A man and woman travelling together, a little Turkish girl as the daughter's companion, would seem perfectly respectable. Moreover I now owed the Baroness that much at least. In bed, while Esmé settled to sleep in my arms, I considered the problem.

The Baroness had complained recently that Kitty was alone for too long; the girl knew no children of her own age. Leda feared Kitty would grow bored and begin to wander the streets. I had already thought of introducing Esmé to Kitty, since my girl also needed a respectable friend. I would refer to Esmé as one of the distant relatives I had already mentioned. I would say I had promised her dying father to care for her. Would the Baroness, out of the kindness of her heart, agree to look after Esmé? I would pay all expenses. As long as Esmé agreed to the deception, the plan could not go wrong. Esmé was used to lying as the necessary consequence of poverty. I would explain how this little deception offered her a passport to the West and, eventually, marriage to me. More to the immediate point, if Esmé had a friend to amuse her it would ease my mind. Once my aeroplanes began production I could be away for days at a time. There were two weeks in which to lay the foundations of my charade. It meant the Baroness would be seeing far more of me. I was sure she would not be displeased.

From the following day on, my schemes went forward without a hint of resistance. Believing she had won back my heart, Leda became extraordinarily happy and affectionate and within a week was discussing elaborate arrangements for our journey West. She would go first to Berlin and join me later in London. She was confident, now, of finding employment. Her main concern was Kitty. It was the moment to mention my recent meeting with my cousin from Bessarabia who had been here for some time now. He was dying of TB and was at his wit's end, with five daughters and a niece to care for. The niece was called Esmé, a good-hearted child. She had nothing to do all day, however, and my cousin feared she could easily go to the bad. Further elaboration and the Baroness was close to tears. 'The poor child. Have you met her? What's she like?' Esmé was a sweet, shy creature, a little young for her age, but without a hint of vice in her character. She was too innocent for Pera. 'I will write to your cousin,' said Leda. 'Give me his address.' The house where he boarded was unreliable, I said, so she should let me have the note and I would deliver it.

Next morning I told Esmé what she must do. The Baroness was an old friend, a kind woman, very fond of me. She had once been my paramour. Nowadays she was useful to me and I in turn wished to be of service to her. If Esmé befriended Kitty we should all benefit. Esmé thought the deception a wonderful, harmless game. She agreed at once. That evening I went back to the Baroness bearing a note exquisitely written by one of my destitute waterfront acquaintances. With dignified, old-world elegance my cousin said he would happily allow his ward to visit the Baroness; he was more than grateful for her thoughtfulness.

From then on I began to enjoy a kind of life I had never previously experienced. The child I had lusted after on the ship and the girl who was now my mistress became great friends, playing together, sharing toys, being taken to parks, museums and the more suitable cinemas by their loving guardians. Reliably, the Baroness made no displays of passion in the presence of children. Esmé and Kitty found they had much in common and the language barrier was soon crossed. All was rather comfortingly bourgeois and for me was an attractive change. Leda von Ruckstühl even met my cousin once or twice. A broken-down cavalry officer, Blagovestchenski would do anything for a rouble or two. I justified all this play-acting in the knowledge that the Baroness already characterised me as a rogue and I was not therefore doing anything she should not expect. Besides, no harm was coming of it. The arrangement was helpful to everyone. All that was necessary for me was to rent a room near the Galata Tower while continuing to keep Tokatlian's a secret. I was pleasantly surprised at how smoothly everything settled into a pattern for us; how relaxing it was to be a conventional patriarch.

It was almost a month before Count Siniutkin contacted us. The Baroness and I arranged to meet him at a restaurant called *The Olympus* in the Petite Rue. A Greek bazouki orchestra was playing so loudly when we arrived that we found it impossible to talk properly until the musicians retired. The food was greasy, unremarkable, but the Count explained there were certain people he did not want to meet at present. Otherwise, with us he was warmly enthusiastic. I asked him if he had travelled far, for he had a kind of weather-beaten look to him. He said that his business had taken him a fair distance, but explained no more. He was anxious to discuss my work. 'I will be so happy if this opportunity leads to something. From the first I've been amazed at the imaginative simplicity of your idea.'

I said he was kind to flatter me. 'Wait until you see the first machine take to the air!'

His handsome features were eager. 'That will not be long now.' His principal was currently unable to visit Constantinople but would be in Scutari in a matter of weeks. If I supplied the estimates they would be passed on at once. If all went well, as he was sure it would, I could expect to meet my potential backers and arrange a contract. I assumed he represented a group of international businessmen and for this reason needed to keep his association with them secret. We spent the rest of the evening together. The Count showed considerable familiarity with South Russian problems. He knew both Kiev and Odessa. He had also, it emerged, met Petlyura who was still, he thought, active in some corner of Ukraine. 'A brave man,' he said, 'and a strong nationalist.'

I was tactful. I agreed Petlyura was fighting for what he believed in. I saw no point in airing my own opinions. Count Siniutkin had been a radical in St Petersburg. He had witnessed the consequences of Revolution. Yet he still believed in such causes if they were far enough divorced from his own direct experience. We spoke instead of Kolya, of the people we had known at *The Harlequin's Retreat* and *The Scarlet Tango*. He was sorry the likes of Mandelstam, Mayakovski and Lunarcharsky continued to support Lenin. 'But some will always cling to a political ideology as firmly as a woman clings to her faith in a worthless man. It is what they wish were true, not what is.'

I agreed. One might almost say he described the tragedy of the whole Russian people. 'We seem to require religion as a necessity of life,' said the Count. 'As others need bread or sex. Apparently it doesn't matter what form it takes.'

We grew a little drunk. The Baroness began to speak of life at their dacha in Byelorussia and the little country church where she had been married. She described the priest who had run her school, and might have been speaking of God Himself. 'I am sad Kitty will never know a proper Russian childhood. We were all so fortunate. We thought it would be the same forever.'

'The Tsar's sentiments exactly.' Count Siniutkin darted a sardonic look at me. 'It's what led to our present circumstances, isn't it?'

The Baroness as usual refused to discuss politics. All she knew was they had destroyed her life and taken everything she treasured. 'I have only Kitty now. And, of course, Simka.' Sober, she would not have made this sentimental display. Politely the Count ignored her. I was grateful to him. Leda's emotional state next led her to telling him how she now had 'two daughters' to look after and how she enjoyed the responsibility. At this, Siniutkin stood up, making his excuse. He would be in touch soon, he said. He kissed the Baroness's hand. 'In the meantime –' He placed a small chamois bag on the table. '– from my client.' He bowed and saluted. 'Good evening, M. Pyatnitski.' He walked out into the evening crowd.

The Baroness lifted the leather purse. 'It's gold!' In my little room near the Tower we counted ten sovereigns. I gave her five. 'Your commission.'

'Marvellous,' she said as she loosened the ribbon on her drawers. 'We can arrange for the children to buy new dresses on Monday.'

This wonderful family charade took root so successfully I considered making it permanent. If the Baroness came to know of and tolerate my carnal affection for Esmé, or at least turned a blind eye, there would be no reason for our ménage not to survive intact forever. Once or twice I came close to hinting at the truth, but held off, for fear of losing the status quo which had been achieved. My nights, as always, were spent side by side with Esmé at Tokatlian's, but evenings were devoted to the woman Esmé now called 'aunt'. I decided, moreover, that it was unwise to inform Esmé of my continuing intimacy with Leda. Female jealousy has ruined many of the world's greatest schemes. While Esmé enjoyed deceiving Leda, I doubted that at her age she would appreciate the irony of her own deception.

A few days later a message from the Count informed me his clients were impressed. We would soon be discussing details. Was I willing to travel a short distance? I replied I would travel across the world if necessary. I met him alone at a bar near the Tephane Fountain. He said his backer's group could not be certain when they would next be in Scutari, so I must be prepared to leave at short notice for the Asian Shore.

'If they genuinely want my plane, I'll drop everything and come at any hour of the night or day.'

'They think they can be here in about two weeks.'

'You'll accompany me to the meeting, Count?'

'Of course. But rest assured my friend is a man of honour.'

Suspecting his client to be a Jew, I made it clear I was not at all radically prejudiced; neither was I disapproving of another's religion. In this way I connived unconsciously in my own delusion. Mrs Cornelius often remarked I was my worst enemy. My faith in my fellows, my happiness to live and let live, to offer a helping hand, expecting to get one in return when needed, all proved my undoing. For years I was too ready to explain my ideas to anyone who showed interest. And today who hears of old Pyatnitski? Yet everyone has heard of Lear. People show surprise at my profundity. My remarks are drawn from experience, I tell them. This hatred of Bolshevism is not notional. It is hard-won by a man who understands what it means to suffer under the Reds. I know now I should not have quarrelled in Odessa with my cousin Shura. That, too, was the fault of a girl. My worldly education was thus interrupted at the wrong time. If as a boy I had remained in the city I should have learned realistic caution. Odessa's catacombs still echo to the murmur of an unfulfilled future; ghosts still tread the Robespierre Steps. Somewhere in the sky over the Nicholas Church flies a solo aeroplane, a graceful thing bearing a young man. His outline black against a yellow sun, he sweeps over the city of sleeping goats, the city of Odysseus. He looks down on streets which are falling to pieces, at houses nobody can repair, at grey wretches standing in the rain for bread which never comes. He weeps for them and his tears are silver. They rush forward. They try to catch the glittering drops. They quarrel amongst themselves; they kill one another for a silver illusion. The youth ceases to weep. Now his laughter is insane as he rises higher into the sky to where it grows black; and then he is gone beyond the horizon. Odessa, city of greed, city of reality. City of what might have been. There was a Jew in Arcadia who held my hand. He knew why his people put a piece of metal in my stomach. They made me cry. Hernikof bleeds and his eyes contract with disbelieving pain. *Es tut sehr weh.* They made us kneel in the snow. They scourged us with their whips. Brodmann told them. They pushed us into barbed-wire nets and lifted us over their fires like squirming fish, while red-tongued dogs sat on haunches, eager for the flesh to be cooked. I trusted them to release me. I trusted them with my life. I told them the truth. But in those days perhaps I did not know what the truth was. How does one prove one is worthy of keeping one's own life? In that night, in those deserts, I prayed to stars because I thought they might be angels who would save me. I have done no harm, unless to love is harmful. I have betrayed no one. They betrayed themselves. It is not a crime. I said to them: 'It is not a crime!' Still they turned their backs on me. Let them find out what suffering can be. Let them wander as I have wandered. Let them long for dignified death. Brodmann was a wretch. Life is useless for its own sake. In the end dignity is the best one hopes for. But even that is usually denied. They must reinforce their rationale for doing what they do to you; and this means stealing your self-respect if they can. The planet turns. We are too small. I love the universe and all its wonders. I asked for no reward. I only desired to enjoy the gifts God bestowed on me. I am no better, no worse, than Hernikof, surely? The other men? I could have become that respectable husband, with a handsome wife and two fine daughters, taking the air of the Grande Champs on a Sunday afternoon. I could have been that stockbroker in frock-coat and top-hat, watching his children whirl their hoops beside the Round Pond in Kensington Gardens, or strolling with his wife on his arm in Central Park. I could have had a name, reputation, family, every honour. But to earn them I had to forget my trust in my fellow men. The price, I think, would have been too high.

A couple of weeks after my first meeting with the Count, I received word through the Baroness to board a three o'clock ferry for Scutari. Count Siniutkin would meet me there. I hastily went to Esmé and taking her by the shoulders told her to be good. I would be back next morning at the latest. I left her some money. She stood on tip-toe, put her slim arms around my neck and kissed me. 'You will be a great man,' she said in Russian.

My confidence reinforced by her love and faith, I set off on light feet, stopping only to say goodbye to the Baroness. I assured her I would be careful. She had, she said, great trust in the Count himself, but I must be certain of his friends before I committed myself. I promised her I would be properly circumspect.

I went down to the Galata Bridge and at two forty-five boarded the first available ferry to Scutari. Treating myself to a padded seat for a few extra coppers, I leaned back to enjoy from the sea the wonderful panoramic views of Constantinople's three great cities. The sun was high in the sky. The domes of mosques were awash with light. Everywhere I looked I saw a different shade of green or soft blue, shimmering white. The smell of brine and spices, flowers and coffee mingled. It was possible, I thought, that I would return to Pera a wealthy man. The world would very shortly hear of my achievements. I would not need to slip away from the city like a felon. I would march into London or Paris a celebrated lion: Pyatnitski, the creator of the flying infantryman. Pyatnitski, the inventor of the patent steam car; Pyatnitski of the aerial liner and the domestic robot. The fame of Edison would fade. Where he had created toys, I was about to create an entire civilisation!

How proud Mrs Cornelius would be of me, I thought, when she heard of my fame. I could imagine her reading the news in the *Daily Mail* and boasting to her neighbours how we had once been married. I would move about the world with all my lovely women; a great patriarch in the old Russian tradition, yet also a modern man and a man of the future. And it would all have started here.

Thus the centre of the old world would be transformed, becoming the hub of the new.

Eight

BLINDED FROM TIME to time by the reflected sunlight on the water, deafened by the babble of some score of dervishes wearing mud-coloured conical hats and robes all crowded together at the front of the boat, sweating in my European suit and doing my best not to breathe too much of the stink of the donkey traders and silk merchants who filled up the rest of the steamer, I fixed my attention on the Asian shore. In Scutari Carthage had re-established herself far more thoroughly than in Stamboul. In Scutari virtually nothing of Greece or Rome remained. Here were the cemeteries of Turks, who would rather have their corpses interred on Oriental soil, some of whom had built themselves tombs so grandiose they rivalled the massive mosques, also erected as memorials by Sultans and Sultanas to dead relatives. Lacking much of the commercial squalor of the rest of Constantinople, Scutari seemed tranquil and graceful in comparison, and far larger than she appeared either from the Golden Horn or the Sea of Marmara, with her vast barracks and warehouses in unusually good repair. She had been conquered long before the European city fell and thus the Turks held her in special esteem. Not far from here Hannibal, disgraced and defeated, exiled from his own ruthless homeland, had sought the protection of that good-hearted Greek, Prusius, King of Bithynia; and here Hannibal, in terror at being captured by Scipio Africanus, had sipped coward's hemlock and died. Like Rome and Stamboul, Scutari too was built on seven hills, but she lacked their density. Large areas were still given over to foliage, from which her domes, turrets, minarets and roofs emerged, adding to her sedate beauty. Here were the villas of Ottoman dignitaries and aristocrats, with their pools and fountains and cool arcades. Once they had been secure in the knowledge that here, too, most of Turkey's armed forces were garrisoned. Even now, from fortresses and blockhouses, came the distant sounds of bugles, of marching feet and shouted orders, as the little ferry pulled into the quay beside a wide, busy square where horses, carriages, motor vehicles and carts moved apparently at random, under the tolerant eye of Italian policemen. Ahead of me the dervishes went ashore in single file and crossed the square where they were soon hidden behind market stalls. Eventually I took a few steps over the wooden gangplank and looked about me in the hope of seeing Count Siniutkin.

The square itself contained the usual whitewashed Turkish cafés, the offices of various shipping agencies, a couple of banks and official buildings, and from it narrow cobbled streets led upwards between yellow and red houses covered with vines and creepers. Tall plane trees shaded the roofs and everywhere were trellises over which trailing, sweet-smelling plants had been grown. It seemed warmer here. I removed my hat, took out my handkerchief and wiped my forehead, wondering if the Count had, after all, misled me, when, from out of the mass of donkeys, horses and push-barrows, an old De Dion Bouton saloon car emerged. At first I thought it was an army vehicle, since the chauffeur at its wheel wore a red fez and a smart, grey uniform, then I saw my friend's scarred face peering from the back. He waved to me, jumped out of the car and ran towards me, effusively shaking my hand and apologizing for not being there to meet me. Everywhere around us men and women carried huge bundles up into the shadowy streets or moved similar loads onto the ferries. The sky was a pale shade of blue behind the steeply banked houses and the air felt hushed in spite of the considerable commotion in the square. The Count handed my bag in to the driver and politely stood to one side as I climbed aboard. It was a large, well-sprung, comfortable interior. The car, said the Count, had been lent by his colleague. Sitting side by side, we moved off and were soon passing between latticed walls and wrought-iron fences behind which I could glimpse the great, low mansions of the rich. The road rose and fell, twisting through great clumps of trees, fields of tombs and white marble monuments, the awnings of restaurants where well-to-do Turks lounged and smoked in the bright sun, as if there had never been a war, an uprising, a palace revolution, to disturb their enduring tranquillity. Later the white roads grew dustier and the walls lower, revealing lawns and gardens, the glittering mosaics of magnificent villas. The air was scented by brilliantly coloured

176

shrubs and flowers, filled by the sound of splashing, tinkling water from courtyard fountains. It was to Scutari that the rich retired and they were anxious to be as far removed from the dirtier, noisier aspects of their fortunes as possible. It was not long before the villas grew further apart and I saw what I took to be a farmhouse, with a herd of goats nearby. I remarked that I had assumed we should find Siniutkin's principal in Scutari itself. He shook his head. 'We Europeans are particularly noticeable in Scutari. He thought it best we meet where it is more private.'

I asked if we were bound for a country estate. With some amusement Count Siniutkin told me to relax and enjoy the journey. 'This could be your best opportunity of seeing the real Turkey. It has broadened my understanding of their attitudes and made me more sympathetic to what is presently going on in Turkish politics.'

I was having my usual difficulty with my nervousness at entering a singularly rural environment, with no image of our ultimate destination to reassure me. The road had become poor, causing the car to bump and bounce. I did not wish to be rude, but it was on the tip of my tongue to tell the Count that I had not the slightest interest in broadening my sympathies for any worshipper of Islam. 'How long before we return to Constantinople?' I asked him.

'Not too long. A day or so. Perhaps a little more.'

Now I was forced to suppress distinct panic. 'I had not expected to be away even one night,' I said. 'I trust it's possible to send a telegram back to Pera. People there will worry about me, you see.' I did not want either the Baroness or Esmé to become so worried they would disturb my careful plans. There was no telling what could go wrong if I was gone more than twenty-four hours. 'Of course.' Siniutkin patted my arm. 'Write the message. I'll see it's sent.'

The thickly wooded hills gave off a heavy, damp scent I found relaxing. Bit by bit I recovered myself. 'Is your backer a cripple, perhaps?' I wondered why he could not travel to Scutari. 'This is an expensive car. An Armenian, eh? Or a wealthy Greek?'

Siniutkin laughed, as if I had made a deliberate joke. The car emerged from the wood, turned a corner and began to ascend an even steeper hill. We reached the crest. A beautiful valley stretched below, with small lakes, rivers, vineyards and groves of fruit-trees. On the far side of the valley was a great mountain, its tallest peak still covered in snow. The valley might have been from Greek antiquity, a lost land, untouched by time, unspoiled by modern industry. 'There's Mount Olympus,' said the

Count, as if to reinforce my fantasy. 'Or so the first Greek colonists thought. Your new business partners live on one of its lower slopes. As I know you've guessed, they're Turkish. But not the old kind of Turk. You'll get on with them. They're more progressive than most Russians.' This, I was sure, was more a tribute to the Count's optimism than his good judgement, but I kept my own counsel. I did not care for the contradiction of a 'progressive' Turk, but any backer in those days was better than none. As long as the Turks refused to use my ideas to support Bolsheviks, I would deal with them. I could not readily see how the Turks would wish to war on anyone at present, unless it was those they traditionally persecuted.

The air became hotter as the day went on. We lost sight of the valley more than once during our descent. Eventually I could no longer tell exactly where we were. The road wound through little canyons and woods, passing tiny farms and plantations and drawing ever closer to Olympus, which Turks, the Count explained, called Mount Boulgourlou. Here and there were remains of grim Crusader fortresses, Moorish castles, Greek and Roman columns. The region's whole history seemed represented by a magnificent junk pile. I was lulled into unsuspicious ease by this landscape. It was without doubt the most delightful I had ever experienced. The sun set behind us; the car took another steep, winding road then turned suddenly into a wooded driveway, rattling its gears to negotiate a final sharply ascending gravel rise and bring us to the forecourt of an impressively large old villa. The place looked as if it had not been lived in for some while. I had become so used, however, to the carelessness of even upper class Turks towards repairs and maintenance that I could no longer be sure my impression was right. The villa's style was more Neapolitan than Turkish, but its windows had the usual intricately carved geometrical lattices. There were long, white balconies with wrought-iron railings, mosaic terraces, a blue-tiled fountain, slender pillars. I half expected a salaaming, exotically turbanned Nubian to open the car's door for us. Actually the chauffeur did this, saluting as we got out, then an ordinary, barefooted house servant in fez, baggy white trousers and sleeveless jacket, ran quickly down the main steps and spoke in Turkish to Count Siniutkin, who understood him. He indicated we should climb to the first terrace where, under a silk awning, we found a table laid with glasses and plates. Looking at me the servant asked a question in thick, impassive French. 'Will you take some *masticha*?' said the

Count. 'This is an Islamic house, I'm afraid. The other choices are tea, coffee, lemonade.' I accepted the *masticha* and we sat down.

The house was surrounded by thick woods but here and there it was possible to see the slope of the mountain above, the glint of distant ocean. 'This is where the Byzantine Emperors built their hunting lodges,' said Count Siniutkin. 'It is supposed to have the loveliest of all views.'

On a tray the servant brought the drink: a jug, with ice and water. Count Siniutkin poured a little *masticha* into a glass, then topped it to the brim with water. I held the drink to the light to enjoy its opalescent colours, then sniffed its sweet aroma. The heavy air carried a scent of roses, jasmine and fuchsia. As the sky darkened to a greenish blue I was filled with a wonderful sense of well-being. Almost to counter this, I pulled myself together and reminded the Count of his promise to send a telegram. 'Give me the message,' he said, rising at once. I took my writing case, addressing a sheet of paper to Mademoiselle Esmé Loukianoff at our suite in Tokatlian's. I told her not to worry about me, to seek out the Baroness if she needed company but to remain discreet. All was well. I should see her in a matter of days. I remembered how she had wept when in the past I had been gone only a few hours. Yet the telegram was the best I could do, though it upset me that Siniutkin was now more intimate with my private life.

'A lady?' He lifted an eyebrow.

I had to explain she was my ward. (My fear was that somehow Leda would find Esmé at Tokatlian's and thus doubt the rest of my story.) But I had done all I could. I waved my hand. 'Family matters. I would be obliged if you mentioned nothing of this telegram when you next meet the Baroness.'

'My dear chap! Of course!' Count Siniutkin was playfully sober. 'I'll get this off immediately. A servant will take the message into Shamlaya before supper.'

'I thought for a moment there was a private wireless. The owner of this villa is evidently wealthy.'

'He comes from a very old family.' Count Siniutkin bowed then before ascending a short flight of steps leading through an archway into the house. 'I'll deal with this now.'

I leaned back on my divan, enjoying the delicious tranquillity of that magical garden. Birds began a dusk chorus, the fountains sang, the air grew richer by the second. Soon I hoped to buy a similar villa as a reward for all my anguish. While certain I was unobserved, I took a quick pinch of cocaine from my little silver box and added a final touch to my exquisite mood. All I needed was a *tchibouk* to smoke, a couple of lovely little *haremliks* to worship me and I would be happy as any Sultan. It was my first real experience of the way Orientals lull their guests, making them drunk on exotic sensations, using nothing as crude as wine. Yet I had no reason to doubt Siniutkin. He was Kolya's friend. A man of impeccable background and Christian. He would never betray me to a Moslem.

When the Count came back it was with a grey-bearded little fellow in the uniform of a Turkish *bimbashi* whose grave, light blue eyes stared from a face scarcely darker than my own, though his was tanned by the sun. He shook hands, greeting me formally in good, clear Russian. 'I am Major Hakir, Monsieur Pyat.' The Count said: 'Major Hakir represents a friend who cannot be here.'

I have had occasion, in my life, to accuse myself of many things, but stupidity is not one of them; although I would agree I have sometimes been over-trusting or naïve. It was dawning on me very rapidly that the Count's radicalism had not ended with Kerenski's overthrow. He had merely transferred his loyalties to the Kemalist cause. Now, of course, the nature of his earlier questions became clear. And my replies, meant only as tact, had reassured him I shared his politics. Naturally, I became deeply perturbed, but dare not show it. I had escaped one terrible Civil War. I had emerged with my life after being the prisoner of Ukrainian bandits. I had survived torture, prison, attempts to assassinate me. I certainly had no desire to risk exposing myself to such dangers again, particularly in Turkey where I did not even speak the language. My first duty to myself, therefore, was to humour these people; my second was to escape as soon as possible. How I loathe radicalism and the manipulative tricks, the despicable cunning of those who will descend to any level in the name of a cause in which they always invest the highest virtue. Yet once again if I was to save my life I must curb any expression of anger, nod and smile at the Turkish major, make a pretence at relaxation.

Bimbashi Hakir said slowly, with that distant, pseudo-courtesy typical of the Osmanli, 'Count Siniutkin says you have agreed to help us. We are very grateful.' He gestured at the servant who poured him some *masticha*. 'Certain hotheads in our movement wish to seek Bolshevik support. But our struggle is different here. We have no intention of putting a torch to history and religion. We merely believe that certain practical reforms are necessary. A cleaning of the stables, as it were. You can be of enormous help to us, M'sieu Pyatnitski. We must convince the pro-Bolshevik faction that we can have progress without absolute destruction of our heritage. You, I understand, are of the same thought.' Fixing his pale eyes on me, he lifted his glass and sipped. I was reminded of Sultan Abdul Hamid pictured in middle years. Hakir had the same intense, unblinking, almost birdlike stare which he turned directly on whomever he addressed. I babbled silly catch-phrases to satisfy him and he smiled. These egocentric revolutionaries demand only confirmation of their solipsistic delusions. 'I hope you will be my guest tonight. We shall travel together in the morning. As you can imagine,' he made a gesture which was meaningless to me but which evidently gratified him, 'I am taking something of a risk in occupying my own house!'

What choice had I? I was furious! The victim of deceit, I had been lured into a nest of snakes and must now hiss and writhe and seem equally venomous lest they turn and strike at me in unison. I would take as much of the Turk's gold as I could, giving him an inferior design for his trouble and reporting all I knew to the authorities as soon as I had the opportunity to get clear. Presently, however, it was of paramount importance to bide my time, let them think me a willing volunteer. Another might have lost self-control upon finding himself unexpectedly in the power of his hereditary enemies, but I managed to suppress emotion, presenting an almost enthusiastic face to the bimbashi. Neither he nor Siniutkin, whom I now perceived as a traitor to his race, his religion and his class, for a moment guessed my deepest feelings. Let them hang themselves, I thought. With important information about the Kemalists, I could easily approach the British and thus win myself and Esmé a passage to England, where, moreover, I should be safe from the Osmanli's vengeance. It was my duty to learn everything. While Siniutkin and Hakir talked of 'corruption' in the Sultanate and Allied 'machinations,' I pretended smiling enthusiasm. Soon after sunset we entered a wide, low room, hung with expensive silks and tapestries, furnished with low divans and richly carved tables. We ate what I must admit was an excellent, if simple, meal. The bimbashi was one of those Turks who prided himself on the elegance and near asceticism in his lifestyle (frequently the mark of an Islamic fanatic) and spared not a second's thought for the miserable subject peoples who provided it.

We retired early, with further expressions of friendship and mutual idealism. In a room full of Moorish arches and screens, with the breeze moving my four-poster's mosquito curtains, I lay looking up at the rounded ceiling whose delicate colours were illuminated by brass lamps suspended on chains, and I carefully considered my situation. I might be able to get up later and steal the motor car, but with no proper driving experience, possessing only a rough idea of where we were, not even knowing how much petrol was in the tank, I set that plan aside as being only good for an emergency. Again I found myself having to cope with my anxieties about Esmé and the Baroness and pointlessly brooded on Siniutkin's treachery. He had to be insane to betray so thoroughly his own ancient blood. He was one of those who supported indiscriminately any revolutionary cause: a latter-day Bakunin, hiding a corrupt and murderous soul behind a charming, aristocratic exterior. I should take particular pleasure in denouncing him as soon as I returned to Constantinople. It had become increasingly clear that the post-revolutionary world threw up huge numbers of subtle opportunists like him, but outside Russia this was my first direct experience of the breed. I would become far more cautious in later years. Men like Siniutkin take a perverse pleasure in betraying the people who trust them most; they are the willing agents of every tyranny. This kind would later lure friends back to Stalin's Russia to be killed, become journalists on émigré newspapers, discover the secrets of poor souls trying to help friends or relatives still trapped in that 'Union of Soviets,' then slyly pass the information over to the Cheka. They willingly practised the most despicable forms of hypocrisy to achieve Trotski's maniacal dream of World Revolution. Inevitably, of course, most were themselves betrayed. Fittingly Siniutkin would be assassinated very probably by direct order of the NKVD. His kind did more damage to the cause of peace than any number of warring armies. The motives of Turkish mutineers were at least understandable, if scarcely reasonable. Men of Siniutkin's stamp however remain to this day a baffling mystery to me.

Next morning, to my dismay, the traitor had gone. He left the excuse of needing to keep contact with French arms dealers in Scutari. I suspected that actually he could not bear to face me. All I could hope was that he had sent my telegram as promised. I was now entirely in the hands of the little grey-bearded bimbashi. Hakir was as superficially polite as ever. I think he never quite realized how Siniutkin had tricked me. He treated me without suspicion as a fellow conspirator, although he remained reserved. As a Christian and a Russian, I was still his ancient blood enemy. I determined to give him friendly responses for as long as necessary. I knew their radical cant. I was capable of making as much hot air about self-determination and universal justice as Lenin himself. We ate a small breakfast, then left Hakir's villa, climbing back into the De Dion Bouton again. The chauffeur took a different road down the mountain, I received tantalising glimpses of distant Constantinople, her towers and roofs bright above the morning sea fog, then we were moving inland, leaving the lush, dreaming beauty of the hills behind and progressing relentlessly towards the barren, blood-soaked plateaus on which the primitive Osmanli hordes had first gathered themselves to launch, with ferocious jealousy, their attempted conquest of Christ, civilization and the gentle humanitarian virtues of the Greeks.

Hourly the earth grew poorer. The forests disappeared until the only shade came from occasional clumps of plantains or a poplar grove beside a small riverlet. Sometimes the road ran beside a railway track; at other times it would pass through a collection of dusty houses built around a miserable square, with the inevitable mosque, an occasional fountain and sometimes a police post. We passed poor farmers with heavily laden donkeys (or more frequently wives), two or three British army lorries, a car flying the flags of France, Italy and Britain, from which white, hard faces stared. I hoped we might be stopped by Allied police, but the deeper into Anatolia we went, the fewer Europeans we saw. At first the police posts had both Italian and Turkish officers; later only Turks could be seen. Once a detachment of Turkish cavalry went by, flying the standard of the Sultan. My companion scowled at this. 'They believe they are patriots. In fact they support Turkey's most vicious enemy.' I wondered if this bimbashi had taken part in recent attempts to assassinate the ruling Sultan who, in my view, was more realistic than most of his predecessors. Now and then Hakir was saluted by a policeman who seemed to recognize him and I realized I must maintain caution everywhere. Superficially there was no telling who was a Kemalist and who was not.

We stopped only once, at a farmhouse, to buy some bread and olives and to relieve ourselves. By afternoon we were climbing again into cool hills while the road became steadily worse and more than once we had to stop or swerved to avoid a hole. The bimbashi would sometimes admonish the chauffeur, sometimes apologize to me. He sat upright throughout the journey, occasionally lighting a cigarette, or reaching out to hold the silk cord near the window. Twice he pronounced the name of a town which I did not recognize. He pointed out the ruins of a Classical temple, a Crusader tower, the more modern remnants of a recently demolished village. Towards evening we descended into a narrow rocky valley containing a river and some stunted oaks. The car was forced to halt at a narrow track. Through clouds of gnats, the bimbashi led me down beside a stream, then across a shuddering, creaking bridge to a wooden house resembling a rundown Russian dacha. Originally it had been white, but most of the paint had peeled. The boards of the veranda were as unstable as the bridge and I thought the whole thing must fall as we went inside. The dusty rooms were sparsely furnished; they had not been lived in for years. As we progressed we heard murmuring voices towards the back, then we came into a low covered courtyard surrounding a brick well. Beyond it were quarters occupied by several horses and close to the well itself sat or squatted three of the bimbashi's henchmen. They were not unfamiliar to me. With slight variations of features and dress they might have been Hrihorieff's bandits, the sort now calling themselves Cossacks. They had the same wolfish, aggressively challenging, appearance. They did not bother to stand as the bimbashi and I came into the courtyard, though they showed respect for a man who now crossed from the stables, grinning at Hakir, lifting an eyebrow at me as if we were old friends. From the way he held himself, this leader had obviously been a soldier; now he was almost as ragged as the others, who had never been anything more than third-rate brigands, self-styled 'irregulars': bazhi-bazouks. They wore sheepskin caps, bandoliers criss-crossed their bodies, cartridge pouches bulged at chest and hip, and their belts were crowded with knives, swords, pistols, most of which were rusty. Crouching like apes beside the well they tried to light a fire under a cooking pot. The leader grunted something, offering to share the congealed contents of the pot with us, but we shook our heads. Eventually we accepted some pieces of bread torn off a grey, communal loaf. Outside, the stream rushed over rocks with such a din, I thought it must flood and wash the house away, but this amplified sound was merely a feature of the courtyard. As soon as Major Hakir and the chief bazhi-bazouk led me into another room, there was relative silence. Hakir and the bandit talked for a while in their own language. I could only understand a few words, mainly to do with military matters. At last Hakir turned to me. 'We shall rest for an hour or two, then press on, although there's very little daylight left. Can you ride a horse, M'sieu Pyatnitski?'

Reluctantly, I told him I could, though my experience was limited. The car, said Hakir, must return to Scutari. It was too conspicuous now. Besides, it was not really capable of crossing this sort of terrain. An intense depression slowly crept through me as I realized I was severing yet another important connection with the civilized world. Now, as I had been in Ukraine, I was reduced to a pony. I consoled myself with remembered reports of Greek gains in Anatolia. There was a good chance Kemal and his bandits would be overrun in another day or so. I might soon be rescued. My main consideration therefore must be to avoid becoming mixed up in the shooting and accidentally killed. I forced myself to forget my worries and attain that sort of trance, almost a coma, which had served me well in the past. I was virtually able to anaesthetize my brain, becoming hardly conscious of what I said or did. Meanwhile I retained at all times the will and capacity to escape as soon as an opportunity arose. Soon I was like an automaton, mounting with the others, riding slowly up the valley floor, through a narrow defile and out again into that awful, barren landscape.

Under a desert moon, astride an ill-fed, badly smelling pony, I trotted across terrain so ugly, so unkempt and worthless, I could not believe anyone would wish to fight for it, let alone die for it. Perhaps, I thought, they were so deluded they could see lush fields where there was only lifeless dust.

In answer to my casual questions Bimbashi Hakir told me we were 'some distance from Karagamous,' which was absolutely meaningless to me. In any case, my attention was soon divided for I recognized the bite of my first louse. I began to re-experience all the familiar miseries of bandit life. It remained ironic, I thought, that once again I had aimed for an enlightened future and landed in the ignorant past. In my document case my plans for a marvellous new flying machine could change the nature of twentieth-century life. Yet, here I was riding with men whose habits and attitudes had not progressed in a thousand years, who, in every detail save for more sophisticated weapons, resembled their savage ancestors. Plainly, Kemal had fallen into the same trap as Lenin, summoning up atavistic forces, peasants and bandits, to turn the battle in his favour. Consequently exaggerated power now belonged to the people most likely to resist change. I was reconciled a little by the observation that Bimbashi Hakir fared little better on horseback than I. He was horribly uncomfortable, attempting to keep up-wind of his 'irregulars', avoiding as much as possible direct contact with their unbelievably filthy bodies. They in turn were plainly amused by our discomfort, stroking their greasy moustaches, staring at us from beneath thick, black brows, mumbling and grinning. Once we stopped amongst gnarled dwarf pines and watched a big locomotive shriek through the night, lights blazing, only about a hundred yards below. I noticed they did not look directly at the train but slightly away from it, as if they felt it would only attack if they made eye contact.

By the small hours of the morning, when we rested the horses, I was reduced to hoping the promise of rebel gold meant more to these cutthroats than their curiosity about what I carried in my bag. We travelled a few more miles until dawn, when we came upon a small, mephitic village. Here we breakfasted off bread and kid's meat, under the eyes of residents scarcely distinguishable from their dung-coloured houses and their straw-coloured streets. All, including dogs and goats, seemed designed to blend with the surrounding countryside. I was able to sleep in relative peace as the Osmanlis attended to their prayers, but we were soon on our way again. Now yellow grass and sticky mud clung to our ponies' feet, sometimes making it almost impossible for them to walk. It drizzled for a while, then grew humid under a grey sky. Once or twice we passed an ancient ruin, weather-worn, its origins lost. The plain seemed infinite. We came upon lone herdsmen with flocks of black and white sheep. Big tawny dogs ran at us, barking and baring fangs, until they were called off. For a few hours that night we camped in the open, with nothing to eat but figs and olives. Then we were on our way again. Without a map or compass I could not understand how anyone could not get lost in this wilderness. Every so often we crossed the railway track, but the bandits were not using it to find direction. Rather, it seemed an inconvenience to them. The sight of the railway, however, always cheered me. It meant there was a link with civilization after all, though the rebels evidently preferred to travel more discreetly. On the third day, as we watered our horses beside a small lake, a De Havilland with grubby markings, either French or American, flew low overhead, plainly interested in us. The bimbashi was barely able to stop his bandit companions from dragging out their rifles and firing at it. This, more than anything, reminded me we were in a country still at war.

Later that same afternoon the ground began to rise sharply, then a high ridge appeared in the distance and behind it a range of tall mountains. Major Hakir seemed relieved and smiled at me (I believe now he had feared himself lost). He pointed ahead. 'Ankara,' he said.

The town came into sight on the crest of the ridge; a broken outline of weather-beaten roofs with a few minarets lifting above them. The outline ended abruptly at the southern edge where a huge, square featureless fortress stood. On the steep face of the ridge I saw fire-blackened ruins and took these as indication of recent attack. When I voiced my guess, Hakir was amused. He shook his head. 'Oh, no,' he said. 'It was the damned Armenians. They wouldn't leave.'

Behind the ridge the peaks of jagged volcanic mountains formed a backdrop of intense blue for the brown and ochre of the pathetic town. Ankara was as timeless as any of the other settlements I had seen on the way. Here and there on the outskirts were ruins plainly Roman; elsewhere the remains of Anatolia's ancient Greek conquerors. Below the original town modern buildings had been erected, but they were little more than two-storey shacks. Over the largest flew a red and yellow flag, standard of that modern Hannibal who even now gathered another horde from the plains and mountains of Asia Minor, to ride once more against Rome and all she stood for. I made out artillery emplacements, trenches, sandbags. Obviously the town was well defended. Half the weapons guarding Kemal's New Carthage were of recent Christian manufacture. I saw neat rows of army tents, then makeshift shelters, large marquees, pavilions of silk and cotton which might have come straight from some Arabian desert. There were lorries, motor cars, at least two dismantled aeroplanes, yet horses still predominated.

The camp was chaotic, evidently in preparation for battle. Large mounted bands of brightly clad bazhi-bazouks raced in every direction, whooping and yelling; over this were the ululations of the imams and an occasional shot, fired into the air. For all its immediate confusion the camp was well run. It had the air of discipline I only once witnessed before, in the anarchist stronghold of Nestor Makhno. The odour of woodsmoke was pervasive, mingling with the stink of oil and cordite, issuing from hundreds of small fires burning in dugouts on the outskirts of Ankara. Bimbashi Hakir was awkwardly proud of his citadel but the force still looked far too small to withstand the Greeks. Again I consoled myself that perhaps all I had to do was sit tight and wait to be captured. Guards allowed us through the first ring of defences and into the town until, on the northern side, we arrived at the large nondescript wooden villa flying Kemal's standard. It stood on its own, some distance from a cluster of barrack-houses, had evidently been painted recently and was in considerably better condition than most. We dismounted. With his hand on my elbow, Hakir led me inside.

We were not stopped by the uniformed guards at the first archway. Coming to attention, they saluted Bimbashi Hakir, staring curiously at me. They looked like men who had been fighting for too long yet were neurotically impatient to begin again. My dark overcoat was layered with dust and mud. My Homburg hat was wrecked. It was impossible to see anything of my patent-leather spats. I had set off dressed carefully, to meet a great financier, but would have been more suitably costumed in the rags and Phrygian cap of the Mob. I was not happy with the condition of my clothing, though I continued to curb my temper, smiling enthusiastically at whoever was introduced to me, nodding here, bowing there. We must have shaken hands with half the bimbashis in the Kemalist army before we got to a little anteroom and closed the door. A large, yellow-bladed fan cooled the air overhead. At first I was surprised, assuming it to be electric. Then I realised it was worked by a hidden slave: an apt image of their new 'modern' Turkey. The room was whitewashed and had lattices at the windows, but no glass. On the wall furthest from the door was a large map of Anatolia, one corner of which flapped in the draft of the erratically turning blades. It was almost twilight, but still miserably hot. In front of the map several tables had been arranged, like school desks, and at the nearest of these, his chair turned to face us, sat a tall, slender individual smoking a cigarette in a holder. He had discarded his fez in favour of a French-style képi, but otherwise his uniform, though stylishly cut, was Turkish. He apologized in Parisian accents that he had never learned Russian and smiled ironically to acknowledge his people's ancient feud with mine. Then he got up quickly, shook hands, and offered me a chair. I was impressed by his manners, if not his attitude, and in other circumstances might have found him charming. His green eyes betrayed far more intelligence than those of Bimbashi Hakir who saluted, murmured something in Turkish, then bowing to me said he was at my service but in the meantime would leave me with this gentleman. He closed the door carefully behind him as he went out and I was alone with the elegant Turk.

'Are you hungry or thirsty, sir?' he asked.

I shook my head. 'Not particularly. But you have the advantage of me. Am I in the presence of Kemal Pasha?'

This amused him. 'Unfortunately the great general is still on his way to Ankara. His time is increasingly taken up with civilian politics rather than military matters. I am Orkhan Pasha. You know my friend Count Siniutkin, I believe?'

I agreed I was acquainted with the Count. 'I am very flattered by your interest in my designs.'

'I must apologize for having to ask you to travel all this way, and in such rough company. But we are in the middle of a war, m'sieu. As I'm sure you understand, it is not as easy for me to come and go in Constantinople as I would wish. Our friends in the city have not yet achieved the necessary power. However, like our President and Commander-in-Chief, I am dedicated to modernizing my backward country. When Turkey is restored to her proper dignity, we shall be able to invite men of science from all over the world, to help us fulfil our great dream.'

In honesty, I was able to tell him it was a dream I shared. I did not add that I was sceptical of Kemal or any of his other lieutenants, however well cut their uniforms, ever making reality of their dream. (As it happened, I was quite correct. Giving the vote to women is not necessarily a mark of progress.) 'Do you wish me to show my plans to your Commander?' I asked.

'The interest in your invention, M. Pyatnitski, comes directly from myself and from a certain Çerkes Ethem, who commands our largest force of irregulars. I think you might actually find us more representative of the nationalist cause than Kemal himself.' Swinging his legs over a bench he moved towards the window, almost as if he expected someone to be listening there. His boots were as brightly polished as the rest of his accoutrements. I recognized a dandy, just as I was quick to scent internal politics, jealousies and plots within the camp. These I might exploit to my advantage.

'You are plainly a far-sighted man, Orkhan Pasha.' I hesitated. 'I'm surprised a peasant irregular like Çerkes Ethem should support your ideas, however.'

The Turkish officer shrugged, lighting a fresh cigarette. 'It's probably accurate to say he supports me rather than my ideas, m'sieu. He is primarily a soldier. He wants to see this business accomplished as swiftly and efficiently as possible. What is more –' he hesitated in some embarrassment, clearing his throat – 'his gold will finance your planes. I suppose we should discuss such things. I have no head at all for business, I fear. Are you a practical man? I have never had to deal with the commercial aspects of soldiering.'

I recognized this typical Turkish attitude. To him the very idea of bargaining and discussing money was distasteful. Coming as I did from noble Cossack stock, I shared a little of his attitude. 'There is no need for immediate discussion, Orkhan Pasha. I would prefer to bathe, as my first priority, if that is possible. I should also like my clothes cleaned. There was a misunderstanding earlier. As a result I brought no changes with me.'

Much relieved, he became solicitous. 'Excellent. And then we shall dine.' He clapped his hands. When an orderly appeared he gave rapid instructions in Turkish. 'Very well, m'sieu. We shall look forward to enjoying your company in a little while!'

I was escorted to a decently equipped bathroom, with huge fixtures all in marble and gilt, where the orderly took my clothes away. I spent some time in the bath, collecting my thoughts and reviewing what I had learned. In these days, amongst most bandits and rebels, a good engineer or mechanic was regarded as a valuable asset, not to be too easily disposed of. I had become a commodity again, as I had been amongst Hrihorieff's rabble, and at least knew I would not be quite so vulnerable to the arbitrary decisions of a petty warlord. I finished bathing as the orderly returned with my suit and fresh European linen in my sizes. Feeling considerably refreshed, I allowed myself to be led down a passage, up a short flight of stairs, to a long room on the second storey where hot food was being served from large dishes on a kind of massive sideboard. This appeared to be the officers' mess. There was only one other present and he was already helping himself to aromatic sausages, stews and sauces which, if properly prepared, can be amongst the tastiest in the world. My mouth was watering as I greeted this stranger. He was evidently the bandit leader, Çerkes Ethem, whom Siniutkin had called the Zapata of Turkey: one of those charismatic 'Robin Hood' figures produced by almost every national revolution. His swarthy Mongolian features, his glittering narrow eyes, black beard and rough, brutish manners identified him. That such a creature should consider using any kind of aeroplane was astonishing. Orkhan Pasha appeared behind me soon after I had entered, leading me towards the brigand chief and introducing us. Next he removed the plate gently from Çerkes Ethem's hand and waved us both towards a table, which had been laid for three in the European fashion. He clapped and signalled to servants standing ready against the far wall, speaking in rapid, humorous tones to Çerkes Ethem and then, turning to me, said in French: 'The stewards feel very hurt if we did not require their services.'

Çerkes Ethem shrugged and put himself in his chair rather as if he were mounting a half-trained pony, but he was smiling, too. His Turkish was slower and easier to understand. He thought these men should be out fighting, not waiting on tables. It soon emerged that his hatred of Mustafa Kemal was greater than any dislike he had of Greeks, Armenians, Bulgarians, Georgians, British or Albanians. Evidently Kemal had tried to enforce discipline on the bandit, who resented it. His men lived off booty. Part of their prize was the privilege of taking any captured village's women, Turkish or otherwise. Kemal was being stupid about that tradition. What was more, he demanded large shares of any treasure they found. As I listened to these criticisms, I began to suspect Ethem of being the likeliest man responsible for the recent burning of Ankara's Armenian quarter. His wholehearted contempt for that persecuted race was almost admirable in its dedication, like a Cossack's fierce, purified hatred of the Jew. As the meal progressed I found myself quite enjoying the bandit's company, perhaps more than that of the sophisticated dandy seated next to him. Orkhan Pasha leaned back in his chair, eating little, smoking a great deal, listening with amused relish to his ally's ravings. In other circumstances I might have grown to like Ethem, notwithstanding his dedication to Allah and his unselfconscious anti-Christian bias. He was then, I later learned, a much greater hero in Nationalist circles than Kemal himself. If he had succeeded in his bid for power, Çerkes Ethem would have withdrawn entirely from Constantinople. He told me he had no use for the place and was willing to trade her for an Allied pledge to recall the Greeks. He knew of Lord Curzon's plan to expel all Turks from Stamboul, Galata and Pera, an idea supported by Winston Churchill and a handful of other visionaries in the English cabinet. He had nothing against the scheme, he said. 'Then those people would have to bring all their wealth and knowledge to Ankara. It seems the only way you would get them out of their harems, eh?' He revealed a knowledge of German, a little French, and a smattering of Russian from his pre-war 'private expeditions' across the border, so I had no trouble in following him. Orkhan Pasha, on the other hand, sometimes used such convoluted sentences, with such an affected Parisian accent, I frequently failed to grasp his meaning. However, the situation itself was clear enough to me. While Kemal busily prepared for a big campaign against the Greeks, these two intended to build my planes. At a critical moment they intended to unleash the machines upon the enemy, proving themselves not only 'better Turks' than Kemal (who was disliked for his Westernizing notions) but also men with a practical command of modern technology. They needed to impress the politicians as well as their troops. By building the planes, I saw immediately, I would actually be driving a wedge between two parties of Nationalists and so rendering the whole force weaker. I could, in clear conscience, help Çerkes Ethem, if I so desired. I should be able to see my machines tested in the air while at the same time striking a blow at the Kemalist cause.

Orkhan Pasha asked when I could begin. I said I could start at once, given proper materials. I had unrolled my sheets of linen paper and was explaining likely unit costs and potential problems, when we were interrupted by a distant booming from the western perimeter. Strolling to the shutters, Orkhan Pasha opened them and peered through the lattice. Flashes of fire turned his face red and made his eyes as animated as a devil's. 'A Greek air attack,' he said. 'They've had wind of our mobilization and are trying to slow us down. Now you can see how urgently we need your aircraft, M. Pyatnitski.'

'They're damned cowards.' Çerkes Ethem wiped soft bread over his empty plate. 'Like all Greeks. They hate to fight man-to-man. But what can you expect of British lapdogs' He grinned. 'Not that it's Greeks attacking us now. Do you think those flyers were born in Athens?' He stuffed the bread in his mouth, chewed for a moment, then swallowed. He shook with amusement at his own wit. 'The only way to get a Greek into the air is in a vulture's beak!'

The guns of Ankara were firing back, but it was field artillery, useless as anti-aircraft defence. I heard the whistle of bombs. I had hoped never to be so close to another battle in my life and for a moment felt sick. I made myself go to the window. This attack was nearer than most I had experienced in Russia. In the flashes from bombs and shells, from flares which seemed to cut across the sky at random, I saw horsemen galloping hell-for-leather through the roiling smoke. I never discovered what they hoped to achieve, unless they simply dared the planes to hit them. Turks love to die. Death must be so much preferable to most of them, I suppose.

Orkhan Pasha turned away from the window with a shrug. He closed the shutters. 'We have some planes,' he told me, 'but nowhere suitable for them to land and take off. That was why your idea appealed so much to us.' He made an elegant lifting motion with both hands. 'A man who carries his own machine on his back, who can rise into the air and come down again at will, like a bird, is exactly what we need. Certainly he can drop bombs and observe troop movements, but he can do much more. He can invade garrisons, occupy whole towns from within.' His eyes became dreamy. I suspected he rolled hashish into his tobacco.

Çerkes Ethem had no scruples about financial questions. 'How much would it cost to equip, say, a thousand men in this way?'

'If you had your own factory?'

'They could be made in secret. In parts. Let's say in the workshops of Scutari.'

'You'll see from this note here. I'd guess, if we placed a bulk order for the engines, that we'd get them for about fifteen sovereigns apiece. Then there are the propellers, the wings. All must be made by skilled engineers and from specific kinds of wood. Another fifteen pounds, if produced in quantity. Say thirty sovereigns each.'

Çerkes Ethem began to scowl to himself. Orkhan Pasha let his chair drop forward. He dabbed at his eyebrow, removing a droplet of sweat. He looked almost desperately at his comrade, virtually willing him to speak and was then hugely relieved when the bandit said, 'Thirty thousand in gold. Cheaper than a conventional plane. They cost about a thousand each.' He pulled back his kaftan and drew a little, tasselled bag from his cummerbund. 'There's enough for four planes already!' He shook with amusement. 'The Greeks will give us more. And if they won't, surely the Armenians will take pity on us.' He winked at me. 'This will get your factories going. We'll let you have the rest shortly and we'll make sure, incidentally, that you don't betray us, Christian. The supply line will be easy enough. We'll take the planes in boats up to Eregli, then bring them overland on mules. But first I suppose we'll have to see one of your machines demonstrated.'

'Naturally a prototype will have to be developed.' I picked up the money. 'But I would guess we could do that fairly quickly.'

Orkhan Pasha placed a hand on my shoulder. He was smiling. 'And we shall want to see you fly it. Yourself.' He uttered a soft, well-bred laugh which acted as a suitable complement to Ethem's snorts and roars and which, on another level, was infinitely more threatening. 'Then we'll know how much faith you have in yourself.'

I resented their mistrust. 'Enough to fly my first machine. I'm sure I've enough to test the next. Where can I begin? Have you machine shops here?'

Orkhan touched the tips of his fingers to his forehead. 'My friend, I believe you. There are a few repair sheds. But it would not be good to work in Ankara. Çerkes Ethem will take you to a better place.'

I subsided, realizing this plot was to be kept secret from their so-called President. My anger had clouded my judgment. Now I was to be dragged even deeper into the Anatolian interior.

Çerkes Ethem put his unshaven face next to mine. 'You can even help us raise the money. That is as it should be, eh, Christian?'

He was to play variations on this moral irony (or what he perceived as one) for at least a further week. Three miserable days later, as my pony limped over a rocky mountain track, I was convinced I had become lost forever. The trousers of my suit had worn through, my overcoat had holes in three places, my hat was virtually useless, my shirt and underwear were crawling with vermin. My shoes had fallen apart and had been wrapped with rags and strips of leather so I probably resembled a very unsuccessful bandit, a leper or a wretched Hassidic rabbi. I was plunged in gloom. The gold Ethem had initially given me was tucked into my belt. When the bazhi-bazouk rode back to the end of the column from time to time he continued to remain, in his own way, extremely friendly. I was mounted on their oldest beast, behind the supply waggon. Ethem clearly enjoyed my misery. 'Christian, this will give you all the more incentive to build yourself a flying machine!'

No one else called me 'Christian' (or occasionally 'Infidel'). I think he had a romantic notion of himself, like so many bandits, as a hero of popular fiction. His men, of course, loved him for it, probably quite as much as they would have loved Douglas Fairbanks or Rudolph Valentino had they ever had the opportunity to visit the cinema. Ethem had all the grand gestures, the flowery language, the bravado, the way of pulling at his white stallion's reins to make it come to a swift, sliding stop. I do not believe he could read, but I was certain someone had once entertained him with the same boys' adventure tales I had enjoyed in my childhood. His larger-than-life manner, however, almost certainly kept up the morale of his men, who were prepared to suffer any hardship or peril for him. It was easy to see why so many preferred him to the rather dour Kemal Pasha, with his notoriously long-winded sermons, his strict morality and his tendency to consider obscure political consequences. I believe Ethem was conscious of the impression he had made on his men and played it up, courting them with displays of humour and daring as another might court a woman.

For this purpose, too, I was an ideal butt for his wit. His frequent calling upon Allah to save the poor infidel, his characterizing me as the very symbol of decadent city life, gave his simple-minded brutes hours of amusement. For my own part I was glad to be presently useful to his ambitions. While I remained so, I did not have to fear for my safety. He continued, nonetheless, to keep me mystified about our destination and even became reluctant to let me know which day of the week it was. I began to suspect that he had no set plan at all, but was wandering the countryside in the hope of discovering something he needed. Twice he left me in the company of the women and carts, taking his men off towards a nearby village. He returned exhilarated while behind him the object of his destruction gave off tremendous volumes of black smoke. 'I have just financed five new flying machines!' he announced the first time and, the second: 'Three more planes, Christian.'

The villages were described by him either as 'pro-Greek' or merely 'Armenian'. This was sufficient justification for his attacks. I suspected they were neither. Again I found myself wondering if it was to be my fate always to be the slave of some brigand. Attila was said to have kept philosophers about him for his own entertainment. But I used the time to advantage. My day-to-day knowledge of Turkish improved slightly, though most of Ethem's men were to say the least laconic. But it had become possible for me to utter more than a simple *Agim* or *Susadim* when I was hungry or thirsty, and stand a fair chance of my more complicated notions being understood. And I began to make it clear to Ethem that time was running out. It was not cost-effective to drag me around with him on his raids like this.

When for the third time the bandit rode off towards a town he was away longer than usual. I could hear shots and what seemed to be artillery fire: a full-scale battle, in fact. Once or twice, men returned in a hurry to drag boxes of fresh ammunition up onto their horses and gallop back over the hill. Ethem had evidently grown ambitious and was attacking a more difficult position. Then, some two hours after the firing subsided, several bandits came riding back to the carts hell-for-leather. One of them dismounted and ran to bring a horse to me, ordering me into the saddle. Rather reluctantly I complied, clinging to the bridle and the mane as the horse galloped off with the others over swampy, yellow ground. I felt sick, certain I must fall, but it was not long before we reached a good-sized town, with several well defined streets, tall buildings, a railway station and a telegraph. Half its buildings were already in ruins, presumably from previous battles, and many more were just beginning to burn. There were corpses everywhere. This time I barely held back my urge to vomit.

In the main square groups of terrified citizens had fallen to their knees: they were arranged in ranks about an ornamental fountain, still placidly playing. Soaked through and grinning, Çerkes Ethem stood on the pedestal in the middle of the fountain, striking one of his more melodramatic poses. From out of a large Greek Orthodox church in the middle of a group of burning houses a line of men and women carried boxes and bundles. These people were either Greek, Armenian or both. Submissively, and to Ethem's evident pleasure, they arranged their treasure along the edge of the fountain. His men still came and went through the smoke and the ruins, firing as they ran into buildings, whooping as they ran out. Even as I dismounted from my horse I saw one screaming young girl raped in the street by a fat bazhi-bazouk who had more trouble pulling down his breeches than controlling his prize. I averted my eyes.

Çerkes Ethem noticed my discomfort. 'See how gladly your co-religionists pay for your machines, Christian!' He was in his element. He shouted something in dialect to one grinning lieutenant, then splashed back through the fountain to put his arm around my shoulders. 'These people are ignorant. You mustn't worry about them. Now I'll show you why we fought so hard for this town.' He guided me out of the square and down a dusty sidestreet, pausing with a benevolent gesture to display what was left of some kind of garage. On a bench just inside lay a small petrol engine, very similar to the one I had drawn in my designs. 'Here's your chance. You'll stay for a day or two and build a plane in peace. They'll be too scared to bother you. I'll leave a couple of men.'

Behind us the screams and firing began again. I was terrified, nodding dumbly by way of agreement and thanks. I wished desperately, with all my being, that I was not where I was, that I might never suffer such terror. How could I have escaped it in Russia merely to find myself plunged into it again in Turkey, where I had even less chance of survival? How I hated the Orient and all it meant!

Ethem patted me on the back. 'Tell Hassan what you need.' He beckoned a boy of about fourteen from the shadows of the workshop. Hassan smirked at me. 'I'll be back in three or four days. Some Greek soldiers need killing.' With a strange, avuncular gesture, he returned to the square.

To shut out the awful sounds, which grew in variety and intensity as the day progressed, I made Hassan help me close the flimsy doors of the machine shop. I told him to bring lamps, to find people to clean the place. There were oily wood shavings on the floor, a few antiquated tools in a rack on the far wall. The place had probably been the only one in miles where people could find the services of a mechanic. Whoever had owned it had either been killed or had run away. There were very few spare parts, but a small crucible and bellows remained alive in one corner and here and there were the implements of the blacksmith's craft, a clue to the workshop's origins.

Thankfully, I was able to do what I had done more than once in recent years, and make myself blind and deaf to anything but the immediate job in hand. I concentrated my attention first on the engine, to see how it could be properly adapted to turn the propeller. I now knew a great deal more about aerodynamics than when I built my prototype. By that evening, when Çerkes Ethem returned, I was beginning to get some idea of my problems and how they might be solved.

'Work well, Christian,' he said. He placed a large, embroidered bag on the bench. 'This will keep you going until I'm back.' The bag was full of dead fowls, part of a lamb, a leg of a goat, all just slaughtered. I was revolted. Hassan, on the other hand, was ecstatically grateful.

The bandit left, displaying amusement as always, and a few moments later I heard him yelling to his men. There was that disturbingly familiar sound of rapid hoofbeats, followed by an equally familiar pall of silence; whereupon the wailing began.

Not much later, my spirits improved considerably, for it had struck me suddenly and with some irony, that for all his cunning Çerkes Ethem had not allowed for a simple fact: Once I built my plane I could fly clear of his disgusting horsemen and their rifles, rise as magically as any Thief of Baghdad into the clouds, mocking all below, and be in Constantinople within a matter of hours! This cheerful notion set me to working with much greater confidence and enthusiasm; no longer

197

was I building a war-machine for Islam: I was constructing the means of my own salvation.

Over the next two days, supplied by what was left of the cocaine, I worked virtually without sleep. Hassan proved himself a conscientious if rather clumsy assistant. Trembling wood-carvers and carpenters were brought to me by the guards Ethem had left behind. I had seamstresses. The whole town (or at least its survivors) was at my disposal and as a result it was not long before almost every piece of equipment was assembled. Parts which could not be found or adapted were forged in the crucible. The propeller, of some local hardwood, was turned and polished to perfection, exactly as I had specified; the wings would have made Daedalus himself envious. It was remarkable how those townspeople lent themselves to the work (especially the Greeks and Armenians); it was as if some dim racial memory drove them to their task of aiding me in my escape from that modern equivalent of the Cretan monster. I became impressed by the correspondences as I worked, thinking that whereas Daedalus had built Minos a labyrinth, the maze I built my captors was one of illusion and abstraction in which they themselves might with chance become lost.

I now realized I might easily be ready to escape before the bandit chief returned. The machine, almost the cause of my destruction, was to become my salvation. I would certainly demonstrate its efficiency! With Ethem's gold in my pockets, I would not only soar away from this desolate place but would arrive back to amaze Constantinople's entire population! I would glide between the minarets of Hagia Sophia and the Blue Mosque; I would alight on the Galata Tower, on Leander's Tower, on all the towers of Byzantium and the air would be filled with the murmur of their wondering voices, the hum of my glittering screw. I would receive so much publicity I would never need more. When I offered my valuable information to the British I should have an open visa to any country in Europe. It would give me intense personal satisfaction to denounce Count Siniutkin for the traitor and spy he was.

By the morning of the third day there was no news of Ethem's return. The hush of hopelessness which had fallen over the town was gradually changing to the ordinary sounds of domestic life, though the faces of the population remained utterly expressionless, reminding me of masks in some old Attic tragedy. Carefully, I tested each part of the machine. Then I assembled it on the bench and had Hassan pour in a little fuel. The engine turned sweetly; the propeller whirled as smooth as steel through oil. I had the wings strapped on to me, as well as the frame which would take engine and blade. I ensured I would be able to direct myself wherever I wished to go. I had made some important modifications. What had happened to me in Babi Yar would not happen in Turkey. When I was satisfied, I ordered a party of local men to carry my equipment carefully to the nearby wool exchange overlooking the fountain and the Greek church, this being the tallest and most substantial building still in one piece.

I could not believe my good fortune! As we reached the wide, flat roof which looked out over the rest of the town towards the featureless Anatolian plain, I barely stopped myself from revealing my glee to Hassan and the other bandits. The boy and the men helped strap the engine onto my shoulders. The propeller of this machine was mounted higher than on my previous design so I could be confident I should suffer no concussion this time. The wings of this model were a little larger; but essentially it was the same plane I had tested in Kiev. It was, of course, fifty years ahead of its time. Today the powered hang-glider is only a slight modification of my original specifications (but predictably I receive no credit, the conspiracy of silence is complete). I thought how privileged this little group of bandits and Turkish townspeople were. They were witnessing the first flight of its kind outside Russia. I steadied myself beneath the weight of the machine. This weight would effectively decrease, of course, once I was airborne, but it was fairly difficult to stand up on the ground. Now I was prepared to take to the skies and show my enemies what foolish, ignorant men they truly were!

I had not allowed, of course, for the profound cunning of the Turkish mind. When I had taken up my position, ready to run the length of the roof before I launched myself into the air, I told Hassan to spin the propeller. There came nothing but a coughing sound from the engine overhead. I ordered him to spin it again. I was beginning to run with sweat as the sun climbed higher.

'Hassan, you little fool! What's wrong?'

He shook his head and put all his power into another pull on the propeller, nearly overbalancing me altogether. The remaining men muttered amongst themselves and chuckled. I ordered them dismissed. Reluctantly they climbed back down through the door in the roof. Now I was alone with Hassan who stood mutely by, his brown eyes round and blank.

'Again!'

This time the propeller turned twice. I started to run, but had hardly moved a yard or so before the engine died once more.

I was baffled. Everything had tested perfectly. I asked Hassan if he had put more petrol in the tank.

At this the boy let his jaw fall and he shrugged, as if I had said something amazing to him. 'Of course not, master!'

I swore at him. 'You're a cretin. Get the can.'

He shook his head rapidly, wringing his hands, his eyes shifting in every direction. 'I cannot.'

'It's back in the shop. You know where!' I was exasperated. 'Hurry, boy!'

'It's all gone, effendi.' He turned his eyes away. He looked towards the railway line. There was smoke on the horizon. He frowned.

The sun was burning my head and the engine, which should by now have lifted me into the air, was making my back ache horribly. I almost fainted as I stumbled towards the boy, begging him to fetch the petrol, threatening him with a thousand punishments, screaming at him that he would roast in Hell. But nothing moved him. All he did was stay just out of my reach, shake his head and say occasionally, 'It is all gone!'

Eventually, of course, it dawned on me. Ethem was by no means the fool I had assumed him to be. He had left Hassan specific instructions to let me get as far as this but no further. The petrol would not be forthcoming until he could be certain of trusting me.

'Benzin!' I croaked imploringly. 'A sovereign for just one can! Nobody will know.'

Staggering under the weight of the engine, waddling and bent like a hunchbacked penguin, I moved away from the edge of the roof. Below in the square a crowd had gathered and was looking up. Some of the faces had become almost animated, like spectators at a circus. A few voices shouted at me to begin. They were growing impatient. I half expected them to applaud. No matter how much I yelled at Hassan he would not change his single response. 'It is all gone, effendi.'

I had not designed the equipment so that I could easily unstrap myself. My legs began to buckle. I was shaking in every part of me, was close to tears as my voice grew hoarse from imploring the boy's help. More frequently now Hassan's eyes went to the horizon. The smoke grew fuller. There was a locomotive somewhere up the track, still out of sight. It was then I thought I heard the rattle of machine-gun fire in the distance. With considerable difficulty and not a little pain, I turned in the direction of the sound. Just detectable on the ridge above the swampy plain was what could only be a squadron of tanks. They had the blue and white flag of Greece emblazoned on their sides, but they were British Mark IIIs in all their glory. And running behind them on two sides, with their bayonets fixed, I could see some three hundred Greek soldiers, firing as they charged.

From the town, the remaining bandits were trying to set up some sort of barricade. Clearly they had not expected such an attack. They moved hastily, in panic, cursing each other and shaking their fists at the Greeks. Two or three were already on their horses and fleeing in the opposite direction.

I panted now, the pain increasing with every breath. I felt as if I were being crucified: crucified on the cross of my own imagination. Hassan stared at me uncertainly. Then, with a look almost of pitying apology, he turned away. He ran towards the steps, pausing for a moment to watch me. I begged him to come back, if only to undo a couple of straps. I fell on my face, struggling to free myself from the constricting harness of the flying machine but becoming more entangled at every spasm. I was doubly desperate. I had no guarantee the Greeks or the British would not take me for a traitor, deliberately selling arms to the Turks.

Hassan disappeared below.

I let out a howl of terror which something pragmatic in my unconscious almost immediately turned into a song. When the Greeks finally found me on the roof I was beginning again on the second verse of Blake's *Jerusalem*.

Nine

HAVING PROVIDED POPULAR amusement for Turks, I was now a source of cheap comedy to the Greeks. The soldiers were dressed in British khaki tunics and tin helmets but had on white trousers and green puttees. When they saw me, they grinned, lowering their rifles. I stopped singing and, still struggling, glared back at them. They made no effort to help. I was close to weeping, trying weakly to get to my feet. In English and French, I implored their assistance. They refused to understand, rubbing unshaven chins, making jokes about me as if I were no more than a hamstrung calf. When I began to cry out my few words of Greek they found this still more hilarious, only subsiding when their officer emerged onto the roof. He was about thirty-five, with large black eyes and a dark Imperial. Unlike his men, he wore a complete Greek olive-coloured uniform. He carried a long, curved sword, a holstered pistol at his belt. Wrist on hip, he stared down at me, his legs spread, brows furrowed. When he spoke it was in Greek to silence his men, then in Turkish, to me. I shook my head, anxious to rid him of that impression immediately. 'M'sieu, if you will allow me –'

Half-smiling, he said in French: 'Aha! It is not a bandit at all, but a pigeon. A pigeon too fat to fly!'

Summoning all possible dignity, I craned my neck to look directly into his face. 'M'sieu, I am an officer of the Russian Volunteer Army. Would you be good enough to release me from this harness?'

'A Bolshevik pigeon, is it? Even better. Trying to carry a message back to General Trotski?'

'You misunderstand me, m'sieu. I am a loyal supporter of the monarchy. My wife is English. I live in Constantinople. I have been a captive of those Turkish brigands for some time and was attempting to escape when, thank God, you attacked. I am also a scientist. I have credentials. The highest. From St Petersburg.'

'I'd heard the Nationalists had Russian officers with them,' said the captain, ignoring most of what I had said. 'Are you sure you're not lying, m'sieu?'

'On my oath as a Christian and a gentleman, I'm telling you the truth!'

'But how did you join these Nationalists?' Though I doubted they could understand him, his men continued grinning broadly. He did nothing to admonish them. He signed for two of them to help me to my feet. I was sweating horribly; my back was in agony. 'I did not join them,' I said patiently. 'I was lured here by means of a trick. I have plans they want.'

Slowly, with studied curiosity, the captain strutted round me. He tested the wing on my right arm. He looked at the tailplane sticking out from behind. Squatting down he pulled at one of the wires leading from my ankles to the rudder. 'Then why on earth didn't you fly away?'

'I had no petrol,' I said.

The officer could not resist translating this to his men, whereupon they became almost helpless with laughter. He chose to think I had simply forgotten to put petrol in the tank. 'M'sieu,' I said to him desperately, 'I am in some considerable pain. Would you oblige me by unstrapping these wings so I may relieve myself of the engine?'

He gestured at me, giving an order. With surprising gentleness his men began unfastening the little straps. Future planes, I decided, must be made lighter. I had learned from this experience. Certain features must be redesigned. I must invent a quick-release mechanism, to avoid similar dilemmas. Soon the Greeks had stripped off the various pieces, piling them carefully in the middle of the roof. I rubbed my bruised and chafed body, accepting a sip of brandy from the captain's flask. I saluted. 'My name is Major Maxim Arturovitch Pyatnitski (it was impolitic to claim my rank of Colonel) of the White Russian Army. I have served as a flyer and with Intelligence. I was recently evacuated from Odessa on the British vessel *Rio Cruz*. All these things can be verified, m'sieu.'

The captain seemed abstracted, nodding vaguely in reply as he looked over the plane. 'Does this fly?'

203

I felt somewhat impatient with the question. 'I was about to find out, m'sieu!'

He wheeled suddenly to face me. He shook my hand warmly. Apparently I had passed some kind of test. 'Good afternoon to you, sir. I am Captain Paparighopoulos. You are a brave man. Let's have a drink together.'

Hobbling beside him as we descended into the street, I became aware of sounds similar to those I had heard only three days earlier. Here almost an identical scene was being re-enacted, only now it was Turks kneeling in the square by the fountain while other Turks carried treasures from their mosques. Elsewhere, Greek soldiers shot at every bobbing fez they caught sight of, or dragged threshing women from their houses. I could not find it in my heart to criticise this savagery. Greeks had been persecuted for hundreds of years by the Turks and were taking vengeance at last. Since the fall of Byzantium they had longed for this. More buildings began to roar. The heat was terrible. The thick smoke made my eyes water. As we crossed the square, two soldiers appeared. They had found my miserable Hassan. He cowered between them, looking pleadingly at me. 'He says he's your assistant. A mechanic.' Captain Paparighopoulos told me after questioning the boy in rapid Turkish. 'Is that true? We need mechanics.'

'He's a bandit,' I said.

Hassan became passive as they led him away. On the tower of the mosque they were raising a Greek flag. It was a deeply moving sight, the white cross on its blue background waving in the Turkish breeze. Captain Paparighopoulos had set up his headquarters in a carpet shop looking onto the square. Here we drank strong, clear liquid which he said was local vodka. It made my head swim. He offered me a little bread and sausage. 'The Turks took most of the food with them.' I realised I had eaten virtually nothing in two days, so obsessed had I been with building my machine. Hassan, I knew, had sold the meat left us by Çerkes Ethem. 'The rebels passed us to the North,' said the captain. 'Looking for our position, I think. We in turn were hiding in the hills, trying to find their base.' He gave a shrug of sardonic disappointment. 'I was certain this was it.'

They had been pushing up from Smyrna all spring. By the end of the year he predicted the whole of Anatolia would be under Greek control. 'Kemal's a good soldier, but he has poor human material. The bandits are out for themselves. They serve with us when it suits them. These people don't care who rules them. They probably think Greeks are a reasonable change from Turks.' He regarded without expression the scene in the square. His men were executing Moslems. Three soldiers, evidently drunk, herded a group of naked girls from one wrecked emporium into another. 'They're used to cruelty here.' He spoke as if I had criticized him, then he yawned and began to roll himself a cigarette. 'We'll get you back to civilization, M. Pyatnitski, don't worry.'

The French and the Italians betrayed them. Greece had only recently rediscovered her pride. She brought the banner of Christ into the heart of Islam. She carried the sword of vengeance. Byzantium was in Christian hands! The Turkish nation had all but ceased to exist. It would have vanished, absorbed by a nobler Greek Empire, a wonder of the world. But the French and Italians, fearing that shining alliance of Greek and Briton, put their heads together to find a way of blocking this marriage of Old and New Hellenism. They used the easiest means. They gave guns to Kemal; they encouraged Zaharoff and his Jews to sell the Turks cannon and tanks, even as Zaharoff himself shook hands in Athens with Venizelos, swearing eternal brotherhood. In Marseilles brokers who had never heard of Ankara sent arms there and made enormous profits while New York stockmarket men spoke softly into telephones and killed a thousand Greek warriors. Merchants in Rome and Berlin, serving neither Cross nor Crescent, grew rich because in Anatolia the two were locked in a death struggle. And Lloyd George, and Lord Curzon, Winston Churchill, Venizelos, Woodrow Wilson, all the politicians, full of fine intentions, full of ideals and willing to cheer every Greek victory, themselves became confounded, were turned from their purpose.

They were too long over the maps, debating new boundaries, worrying about Pakistanis and Arabs whose feelings might be wounded if Islam were routed in Thrace. Concerned for their own Egyptian and Palestinian possessions, they wavered in their enthusiasm. The children of Athens and Sparta marched into Asia Minor's barren vastness naked and defenceless behind the flag of Christ. Innocently they had believed the sentimental assurances of old, empty men. They had no weapons. Lloyd George sent them no cannon and Winston Churchill gave them no ships. Lord Curzon next feared that by 'giving' Turkey to the Greeks he might 'lose' India. And so the greatest opportunity of the World War was lost: the one real advantage that would have provided us with universal peace was let slip while Crusader conquerors, as they had done so frequently before, quarrelled and connived.

Those noble Greeks lay dying in Anatolian deserts and Armenian swamps. Their blood ripened Islamic corn to feed Islamic soldiers. Meanwhile the King of England cried 'Kneel Zaharoff' and 'Rise Sir Basil', touching the great sword, which for centuries defended Christ's honour, to the shoulders of that Satanic Jew. In the Houses of Parliament, wearing ermine robes and golden crowns, new-minted barons laze on benches, lifting jewelled cups in mock homage to the Union Jack, the three crosses which are One. Swaggering lords of the East have insinuated themselves and their families into the very heart of England, as once they inhabited the Court of Byzantium. They control the destinies of Christian millions. They even pretend to worship in Christian churches. They have made this island retreat a base for international crime. They are worse than common pirates, for they take no personal risks and steal the lifeblood of nations. Does their booty contribute to the glory of England? No! It sits in Switzerland where every day little pink women come to the vaults with buckets of soap and disinfectant to scrub the gold bars until they gleam like mirrors. Where were the gentlemen of Blighty? What happened to an Empire which sent Lords Byron and Shelley to drown fighting in the Hellespont, leading their brave little armies against the might of Osman?

What insanity corrupted the British after the Great War? It was commercial greed and debilitating socialism, united by the mortar of false pride. I have seen Empires collapse across the world, and it is always at the hand of the Red and the Jew. 'Look,' cries Harold Wilson, 'you are rich. You can swing. You can join the Common Market. You can give up your homes to Pakistanis.' I have heard him on the television. 'You must compete,' he says, 'like the Americans. You must borrow more money. You must be better than your neighbour.' And when the worker refuses to work, because his job is threatened by a black, this great Socialist, Champion of the Mob, turns on the worker. He is unpatriotic if he asks for more money. He is reminded of the Spirit of Dunkirk, of his national honour and pride. But Harold Wilson has said that honour and pride are old-hat. Money is of paramount importance. And they come into my shop with their posters to tell me the Labour Party looks after my interests! It looks after nobody save financiers and party members. It is no different to Moscow. Stalin destroyed a nation, then called on the ghosts of great nationalists, on those he had himself murdered, to rally the people against Hitler. Honour means nothing to them. It is only a bell to which people salivate; but when it rings, nobody answers. The people yearn desperately for the restoration of their pride and their religion. It returned briefly to Greece, then the Reds, the Jews, the Mapmakers arrived to steal it away again, purchasing it for forged currency, grinning at it, mocking it as if at Christ Himself. It was Socialists, not Tories, who celebrated Pragmatism over Honour. National pride was sold as a job lot during the Swinging Sixties. It was sold in Carnaby Street and Brussels, on Union Jack underpants and Lord Kitchener carrier-bags. It left the country on umbrellas, baskets, ashtrays and plaster guardsmen carried back to America and Japan. When they came to call upon it, in their need, there was nothing left. National Pride was a melted ice cream on the steps of the Tate Gallery, a broken trinket on the floor of an Air Singapore jumbo, a comic bowler hat sported by a Saudi schoolboy. The Silver Jubilee will be a miserable remnant sale. Scraps of honour will be hawked by Asian ragamuffins, like false holy relics, to drunken foreign mobs along Pall Mall. For if Britain betrayed her past when she betrayed the Greeks, she also betrayed her future, the greatest folly of all. They sent Greeks naked into battle. The British watched Russians run from Ukraine and Georgia and did nothing. They watched Polish cavalry flood into Galicia and Moldavia, grabbing lands coveted for centuries. They watched Socialists march through the streets of Munich and Hamburg. Helplessly they threw up their hands as Gandhi hurled his dissident armies against the Crown, as Irish Republican gangsters blew up police barracks and bombed post offices. And fastidious America drew away from the chaos she had helped create. She said she was disgusted with Europe and elected a President who turned his back on his own heritage, driving his nation towards the dream which almost destroyed it.

They gave women the vote, listened to Nellie Melba on their radios and thought they saw the road to Utopia. Here and there pockets of far-sighted men tried to stem the tide. Admiral Horthy fought against Communism. Hungarians knew what it was to fear the Turk. Still the Great Powers laughed in putrid complacency while signing papers sentencing whole countries of Christians to tyranny and death. But the single, most powerful symbol of this betrayal remained their refusal to support Greek against Turk. Christ was stripped naked. He was flogged. He was recrucified. Not by the Pharisees, however. It was the Romans, the very people He sought to save, who betrayed Him. Jehovah was a Jew, but Christ was a Greek. Let the Jews have their drooling Jehovah, their Judah Ben Hur, their Jonah, Jeremiah, Joshua and their Judas. We shall keep Jesus. We shall defend Him. Kyrios, the Lord! The Cross is Greek. Byzantium is our capital. *Wann werden wir Zurück sein?* We shall take up our spears to drive forth the red-eyed wolf, the hot-tempered jackal and the gibbering ape! Our honour shall shine golden as the sun. We shall be radiant with our zeal and our courage; we shall be like Angels come to Earth, reclaiming the pride of Christendom, erecting the Cross at the centre of the world. Let no man try to injure me, for my shield is strong. It deflects all lies. I cannot be confused by their calumnies. They would turn me from my true path; they whisper about my blood. Mine is the blood of the Christian Cossack! No metal can pollute it. No metal shall pour its rust into my veins! I am mercury. I am silver. My stomach is strong. They tried to weaken me, praying over me when I was too small to resist. That quasi-Abraham! What did he mean by it? My father took his knife and cut me. In the name of Progress he branded me with the mark of Judas. But I have laughed at all my enemies. On clashing, silver wings I fly over their heads and resist the bodies of their whores. I escape their arrows as easily as their threats! My honour is whole. They shall not condemn me as they condemned the Greek.

I sat drinking with Captain Paparighopoulos and was soon unable to feel the pain in my back. From time to time one of his staff would run up to the carpet shop requiring orders. He would give them airily after a while, quite as drunk as I was. But a certain order seemed to have reference to me and towards evening, he gripped my shoulder, pointing towards the roof of the wool exchange. He chuckled, handing me his fieldglasses so I could see better.

They had strapped my prototype onto the wretched Hassan. Helplessly I watched them pour petrol into the engine, spin the propeller and send the boy screaming and wailing from the roof to his death. Captain Paparighopoulos was highly amused. 'I wished to help you test the machine.' I tried to tell him it needed expert handling, but he refused to listen. It had been Hassan's chance, he said, to fly either to freedom or to Paradise.

The machine was smashed to pieces. Through the glasses I saw the boy's twisted, bloody body twitching in the wreckage. He deserved no more, I suppose, for his part in tricking me, yet it was an unpleasant sight and has remained imprinted in my memory. A thoroughly wasted opportunity.

A day later I was borne back to Scutari, first in the armoured train, then in a Crossley car, with all honours. On the train a Greek colonel acted as my host, taking notes as I gave him my information. Count Siniutkin would be arrested, he promised; also those who worked with him, Turkish and foreigners both. The colonel had a bronzed genial face and a walrus moustache. He looked like a good-natured Georgian patriarch. He told me I should go to Athens. Greeks respected courage and learning. I wish I had listened more carefully. When the Greeks had conquered Turkey, he said, they would secure the Balkans and the Caucasus until they could easily challenge Trotski himself. My mother, he promised heavily, would be saved. I believed him. How was I to know that secret treaties in Whitehall and Washington already sealed the doom of Greece, supplying them with unkept promises with which to go against Zaharoff's eighty-pounders Hellenic youth was to be crucified on Turkish bayonets stamped 'Made in France,' torn on barbed-wire twisted by Roman Catholic women in the factories of Turin. It was once said of Lord Palmerston that if an individual behaved as he made his nation behave, he would immediately be ostracised by Society. Palmerston reduced English politics to their crudest, most self-serving, short-sighted level, then compounded it all by making a Jew his successor! His shadow fell across the conference tables and condemned half of modern Europe to death. They thought it more important to squeeze a few more marks from Germany than to preserve the ideals for which their kinsmen had died.

The Crossley took me directly to Haidur Pasha where again I was cleared by the British authorities. I attempted to give them my information, but they said they already had the Greek colonel's report. I was to return home with very little to show for my adventures. I had discarded my ruined business clothes for a Greek army shirt and breeches, British shoes and puttees, a French great-coat. I resembled any of those Russians presently falling back in growing numbers from Bolshevik ferocity. As I went down to the Scutari square, to the quays to board a ferry, I found myself in the company of several poor devils just evacuated from Yalta. They asked whom I had fought under and in what part of the country. I told them I was from Kiev, a liaison officer with the Allied Forces, though I had been a prisoner of Reds and Greens. They were half dead with fatigue, completely confused. They hoped to get to South America and join the Argentines, since there was obviously no hope for them in Constantinople. They knew this from relatives in the city. Their next step was to sign on a banana boat as soon as possible.

Letters from comrades reported rich pickings and an easy life for trained soldiers in South America. As we stepped off the ferry I wished them luck, then, in trepidation, made my way on foot up the steep Galata streets until at last I reached the Grande Rue which, for no specific reason, I had expected to be changed. Incredibly, I had been away for no more than ten days. It seemed like months and I was frightened something had happened to Esmé. Without my protection she could have fallen victim to any one of the entrepreneurs prowling Tokatlian's. Had not Count Siniutkin used the place as his headquarters I was sure some white slaver had already priced her beauty. I therefore had a sense of gloomy expectation of disaster as, from the alley, I slipped through Tokatlian's back entrance and up to our suite. I was convinced the Count had never sent my telegram.

Somewhere between Scutari and Ankara I had lost my keys. I knocked on the door of our suite, expecting no answer. My heart thumped. I was drenched in nervous sweat. From below in the restaurant, even though it was only four in the afternoon, came the sound of music, the hum of conversation. All I had to show for my adventure were a few sovereigns and a bruised back. My prototype was destroyed, my plans burned.

The door opened. Esmé was there. She gasped, began to cry, then smiled. After a second's hesitation (doubtless because of my strange costume) she threw her little soft arms around my neck and enthusiastically kissed me all over my unshaven face. I shook with sudden relief. My fears had been groundless and all was well. Had she received a telegram? She said she had not. She had believed herself deserted. Then she guessed I must be dead. I should never have crossed to the Asian Shore, she said. The Turks were animals over there.

As I bathed and changed I told her something of my experiences. Although still unusually nervous, she was open-mouthed, reacting dramatically to every new piece of my tale. This attention, displaying her evident pleasure at my return, helped refresh me. Flinging myself onto our cushions, I asked her to bring us some cocaine and I sent downstairs for coffee and food. She prepared the drug in the way I had taught her. I saw our supply was extremely low; far lower than I liked it to get. I smiled tolerantly. 'You've been a greedy little monkey!' She flushed. Wearing only her white lace petticoats she looked as pretty and ordinarily wholesome as any well-bred Russian girl. Filled with love, I took her in my arms and kissed her. I was sorry I had not brought her a present, I said. She began to stammer a reply, then I pulled out the purse containing Ethem's gold and threw it into the air for her to catch. 'But we can leave whenever we choose.' I was amused by her delighted response.

'In that case we should go very soon.' She was gravely urgent. 'It's getting worse by the day in Constantinople. There are more and more murders. People of all kinds are disappearing. Not just girls. The Baroness told me for instance her friend Count Siniutkin has vanished. Swallowed by the Earth, she said.'

'You've seen the Baroness? That's good.'

Esmé paused while she concentrated on chopping the cocaine crystals. She nodded. She studied the white lines with unusual intensity.

'Is she well?'

'I think so.' Her tone was offhand.

'And Kitty?'

'Yes, she's well.' This almost in a whisper.

'You've been playing together?'

'Not recently.'

'I'll see her for a few minutes later on. As soon as we've had something to eat.'

Esmé handed me the ornamental mirror with the exactly-made lines of cocaine on it. She was as usual extremely neat in this respect. I took the silver tube and placed it to my right nostril, sniffing hard. It was wonderful to be reunited with my drug in this way. At once I felt a fresh surge of enthusiasm and pleasure. The food was delivered, but we ate only a little. Esmé wanted to make love.

It was almost midnight by the time I climbed the staff staircase of the *Hotel de Byzance* to tap softly on the Baroness's door. She opened it immediately, but was startled when she saw me. She did not look well. Her face was drawn, her skin coarser than usual. There were bags under her eyes. Her hair was brushed back, ready for bed. 'Are you alone?' I whispered. Kitty normally slept on the couch by the window. I made to enter, but Leda blocked me. She was beginning to sway. 'Are you ill? Surely you haven't caught typhus?' My own guess was that she felt faint with the profound emotion of finding me alive. 'Did you think I was hurt, Leda?'

I was amazed by her reply. 'I had prayed that you were.' She spoke in a violent, almost hysterical whisper. She made a dismissive motion with her hand. I could see over her shoulder into the room. Kitty was turning in her mother's bed. I thought Leda did not want the child disturbed. 'I tried to send a telegram, but I was a prisoner.' Even as I spoke I felt my tone was overly apologetic. 'Shall I see you tomorrow?'

She said in a small but far clearer voice, 'I shall send you a letter.'

A little puzzled, I nonetheless made to kiss her on the cheek, whereupon she pulled back hastily, glaring. The whisper was vicious steel now. 'They warned me you were a monster of deceit, but I would not believe them. I have never even heard of any action so vile!'

I was flabbergasted. 'Has Count Siniutkin been speaking to you? If so, I must warn you he has already tricked me —'

'I have not seen Count Siniutkin. He may have been arrested by the Turks.' She was closing the door. 'Please leave me alone. I do not wish to lose self-control over someone as worthless as you.'

'Leda!' I insisted on remaining. She came out into the passage now, wearing the blue silk kimono I had bought her in the Grand Bazaar. 'You look beautiful,' I said. She pulled the door shut behind her. She had grown impressively red. I had never seen such fury in a woman. She hissed: 'Maxim Arturovitch, I wish never to see you again. I did not intend to warn you of this, but I am seriously of a mind to inform the authorities against you. Even in this degenerate city there must still be left some decent people. That you deceived me so horribly, that you encouraged Kitty to play with your child-whore, is bad enough, but to have seduced the creature in the first place — and under my nose — to have invented such a despicable fantasy — is unforgivable!'

I was enlightened at last and my heart sank. I heard myself responding feebly. 'I did not seduce her. She was a whore when I found her. I rescued her. You contradict yourself, Leda!'

'And you manipulated Kitty and me into becoming part of that horrible pantomime of family life! What took place in your disgusting dreams? What did you plan for us?'

This was too near my true fantasies. I backed away. What I regarded as joyous and beautiful, this demented, puritanical, jealous Fury was determined to depict in the worst possible light.

'I hoped at very least you had paid a high price for your infamy.' She was advancing towards me now. I retreated as far as I could before I was stopped by the bannister. 'I thought you still worthy of suicide. I hoped you had been tortured and murdered. I was relishing the prospect of the police finding your body in the Bosphorus and asking me to identify it.

I intended to refuse, or tell them it was not your body, to make sure you were put in a communal grave with all the other scum of this filthy city. But here you are, a nightmare come true. You kissed me with lips that had touched her. You confirm people's worst prejudices against you. I have not dared ask Kitty what went on between you when I was absent! That poor, innocent girl!'

'I love Kitty like a father.' I was whispering too, now. 'Leda, you must realize I meant no harm. I did it for you. How did you find out?'

'Hasn't your little whore told you? She was convinced you had been killed. You had become a drug to her. She didn't know what would happen to her. She had drunk too much when she found me. I said I would help her home. That was how I discovered your horrible love-nest. You were living with her in our special hotel! Oh, how you must have laughed at me! You're not a human being. You're the vilest of devils. It all came out, bit by bit, that night. She at least was repentant. But you – you show no remorse at all! Merely anguish at my discovering the truth, to the frustration of your plans. You are a discredit to your race!'

'The appearance is far worse than the actuality.' I spoke as calmly as I could. 'It is all the result of a series of accidents.'

'You have put my daughter at risk. You deny you've been making carnal love to a child no older than Kitty? That you betrayed all my finest feelings, cynically used my love and my best sentiments for your own perverse ends! How can you lie, even now? Oh, how I prayed your death was slow and painful!'

'This is extremely unfortunate. Be assured, Leda Nicolayevna, my feelings, too, were of the finest. My darling, I am a father to Esmé, as I am to Kitty. My emotions are platonic, I swear. Anything else she told you is a child's misunderstanding or a wild fantasy of her own invention.'

'Maxim Arturovitch, you prove yourself still more despicable with every utterance. I have seen your clothes! Your bed! Your notes to her!'

'It is not, however, what you think. You have condemned me hastily. I believe you will regret that.' After my dreadful ordeal, I could stand no more. I drew myself up. 'I shall not argue with you on this public landing. I intend to leave. If, when your senses are restored, you wish to speak to me, I would ask you to be good enough to send a note first.' I raised my hat. 'Adieu, Leda Nicolayevna.'

I believe the woman went so far as to spit at me while, with an appearance of calm, I descended her stairs. It is never pleasant to see a lady of good breeding driven to the manners and language of the gutter.

Considerably glad to be removed from the harridan's nonsensical accusations, I returned to the relative tranquillity of my suite at Tokatlian's where I found a frightened, guilty Esmé. She knew she had done wrong, but how could I be angry? Still dazed by my encounter, I sat down in my chair, stroking Esmé's weeping head and trying very hard to make sense of my thoughts, for fresh plans were urgently required. The prospect of the Baroness out of malice reporting me to the authorities was alarming. I could probably prove I was not the one to have had initial carnal knowledge of the child. I hoped she might admit she had known at least one man before me. I could insist I was merely her guardian, that I had saved her from sin, but the scandal would certainly hinder me in obtaining a visa for England. I became decidedly anxious as the time went on. I did not sleep that night while I considered my few options. It seemed the whole world again conspired against me. Must I be punished simply because I had given my being in all generosity to two women, had in fact made both happy? I had anticipated the dangers of arousing the Baroness's jealousy. Now I was proven wise in my judgment. She pretended to be a woman of the world, but I had always known better. If she acted in haste, she could cause me immense inconvenience. My liberty could be at stake. There was no threat of mine which might silence her, no offer she would not in her present mood reject. I knew deep despair. Beside me in the bed, little Esmé, the cause of all this, snored gently in girlish slumber.

In spite of my desolation I forced myself next morning to hurry directly to the British Embassy. I somehow managed to drive my way through the crowd outside and from sheer panic was able to reach the front hall. I had been of great help to the British. They had been able to arrest a master spy on my information. I had a wife in England. I had served with the Australians. All this was explained to those soft-faced boy-policemen who blocked my path. Yelling over the imploring din outside I outlined my predicament: I had been involved in valuable espionage in Anatolia. I had more names to link with Siniutkin. But now my life was in danger. I was carrying plans, I said, of great importance to the British Government. By the time I stopped, my brown suit was drenched with sweat and impassively they told me to submit my request in writing. I began to demand to see someone in greater authority. It was at this stage that one of the soldiers said I should piss off back to whatever rathole I came from. Now I was not only insulted by officials, but was being set upon from behind by desperate Russians and foreigners close to hysteria. In their efforts to secure some privilege they made revolting beasts of themselves. There was nothing for it but to go down to the docks and look for my Armenian friends. I was seeking a person whom I had already met. They directed me to a certain grubby coffee house near the Quarantine Harbour.

After I had trudged up and down hundreds of alley steps, passed under scores of lines bowed with threadbare washing, avoided the droppings of dogs, donkeys and Turks, I eventually reached a shop in the half-basement below a great tottering wreck of wood and brick which had once been painted green. In French its faded lettering boasted housing Alfasian's Famous Tropical Bird Emporium. From within, the occasional squawk or mutter of a parakeet echoed in an emptiness suggesting Alfasian's was not a thriving concern. The broken planks of the steps down to the coffee house were slippery and rotten. In my haste, I almost fell into the basement area. The interior was packed with Armenians and Albanians smoking their long meerschaums and staring up at me from dreamy, suddenly cautious eyes. At the oilcloth-covered counter I asked for Captain Kazakian. A large, thickset man wearing a filthy American navy cap rose in the shadow of a cubicle and motioned with his cigarette. I recognized him and went to join him at his table. 'You're the Greek who fixed my boat so well,' he said in Russian. 'Well, friend, what can I do for you?'

I told him I remembered his mentioning how he frequently took tourists back and forth to Venice; that he would sometimes carry the odd passenger who perhaps did not have all his proper documents for entering Italy. Noncommitally, he nodded. 'You have a friend in trouble, Mr Papanatki?'

'Myself and my sister. We must leave at once. When do you next plan to sail?'

He sighed. 'The competition has been terrible this season. And before that was the damned War. The bigger people are taking all the tourist trade from me. I'll only be able to return from Venice with, say, half-a-dozen passengers. They will scarcely pay for the running costs.' He looked miserably at me. 'Therefore, it would have to cost, for the two together, a hundred.' By the figure he meant gold. I had that in sovereigns. 'You can take our trunks and so on?' I asked him. 'Of

215

course,' he made a generous gesture with his hand. 'Trunks. Suitcases. Cats and dogs. No extra charge.' He laughed as he saw my relief. 'I'm not short of space on board. At the moment I'm half empty.' We agreed where we should meet and what procedure I should follow. It was to be at the 'Little Quay' near the Tephane Docks. I left the coffee house beginning to feel I had accomplished the most important part of my escape. The streets stank of damp and decomposing spices. I was oddly intoxicated by the time I reached my next destination, a grog shop near the Tower, behind which my Bulgarian forger had his office. Another fifty pounds bought me crude exit visas as well as reasonably made British passports for myself and Esmé. The documents would be of no use for entering England itself, but would prove helpful in countries less familiar with originals. I gave my name as Cornelius and supplied him with the necessary particulars, including photographs which I had prepared some time before. While I waited he made up the passports, peering through a gigantic magnifying glass as, in the light of a naphtha lamp and muttering admiringly at his own handiwork, he bent over an old, chemical-stained mahogany table.

By the time I returned it was late afternoon. Esmé, evidently miserable, was utterly dishevelled. She was even more frightened than when I had left her. The Baroness had called quite early. Finding me gone, she had left a note. Esmé's hand shook violently as she presented me with the envelope. Putting on a brave face, I comforted her. Everything was ready and all she was required to do was pack whatever she wished to take. At this, Esmé burst into floods of tears and the whole scene emerged. 'She said I would be arrested. My parents will be arrested. You they will shoot!'

Although privately furious with the woman for her cowardly terrorising of an innocent girl, I contained myself and merely shrugged. 'She's insane. Jealous.' I opened the note. It proved without doubt her unstable mind. She wrote that she could have jumped too early to conclusions. She had thought over what I had said last night. Now she believed I had been led astray 'by a little Turkish harlot.' Esmé was probably connected to the gang which had kidnapped me. If I got rid of the child at once it would probably save me and the Baroness would consider forgiving me, perhaps even go with me to Berlin, so simultaneously avoiding scandal and retribution. I must meet her in the restaurant at ten that evening when we could discuss what had to be done. I found this *volte-face* baffling, but decided it would do no harm to see

216

her once more. By placating her for twenty-four hours I should certainly be able to make my escape without trouble from the authorities. I showed Esmé the note. She could not read the Russian. 'It's blackmail, of course. But I'll go to see her and buy us time.'

Esmé had made an effort to calm herself. 'What shall I be doing, Maxim?'

'As I said, you must get our things into trunks and cases. Tomorrow a car will pick us up. It's all arranged.' I hugged her. 'You mustn't worry. Be a brave little monkey. We are on our way to Venice. You've always wanted to go. From there we can reach Paris, if we like. And England. You'll be quite safe, my darling. Those countries are truly civilized. Not like Turkey.'

She was by no means convinced. Now our escape offered to become a reality, I think she grew nervous. She had known only Constantinople. In one way or another she could survive here. How would she fare abroad? I appreciated her anxieties. I had originally felt much the same about leaving Odessa. 'It will be all right. We'll be happy.' I tried to cheer her up.

'The Baroness has friends in those countries.' She remained wary. 'They will arrest us, Maxim.'

'She has no power. That's nonsense. Only here is she a little troublesome. She thinks she has more to threaten me with than is true. Someone like that is never much of a problem. We'll be travelling as Maxim and Esmé Cornelius, British subjects. She won't know that.'

Again, Esmé attempted to pull herself together, though her mind was clearly not at ease. I laughed and kissed her. 'Within a week we shall be strolling down the Champs Elysée together. You'll have a new Parisian dress.'

She said, 'Perhaps it would be better to go to Athens first. Or Alexandria?'

This amused me. 'You really are a child of the ancient world. Is it so hard for you to relinquish it? We must think in terms of London and New York, my little one. You mustn't be afraid. I shall always protect you.'

She shook her pretty head, again close to tears. 'You have already been captured once. If it were to happen in Venice . . .'

'It cannot happen in Venice. These are genuinely civilized countries. You can't know what that means yet, but you must have faith in me.'

217

I spent the rest of the evening calming her. Eventually she began carefully to take clothes out of cupboards and drawers and inspect them, like a sensible little Hausfrau. Then slowly she folded her silk dresses. Just before ten I kissed her and was off downstairs to keep the appointment with my volatile Baroness.

Tokatlian's was impossibly crowded. The uniforms of a dozen nations squeezed together at the tables, frequently sandwiching soft, naked shoulders. As usual the band played its hideous jazz while waiters were scarcely able to push through the mass to find their customers. Arabs in burnooses and Turks in fezzes, Albanians in sheepskin, Montenegrans in felt, Circassians in leather, argued together and sang together or separately collapsed in corners. Russians in magnificent Tsarist uniforms, all of them looking the image of the late Emperor, picked their way from place to place, looking for friends, asking after lost relatives, producing rings, necklaces, small ikons from their pockets to sell to haughty Levantines. These aristocrats had learned to beg. For generations their ancestors, disdaining all forms of commerce, had looked down on influential financiers and great merchants. Now, reduced to the level of bazaar boys, they carried their pathetic goods wherever they went, unable even to afford the rent of a market cubicle. At first, in the dim light, I did not see the Baroness who was already seated at a window table. Then a tram went by outside and its glaring lights revealed her. She was wearing her best red and black dress and what remained of her jewellery. Her back was unnaturally stiff, a sign of deep nervousness. She saw me and waved. When I eventually reached her and sat down I noted how heavily painted she was. She had been weeping. 'You should not cry,' I said. 'Your fears clouded your mind. You made hasty decisions.'

'I don't think I missed the essentials,' she said firmly. 'You must not lie to me any more, Maxim. If we are to save you, you'll have to swear from now on to tell me the whole truth.'

I sat back, making a display of offended pride. 'My dear Leda, I do not intend to be questioned by anyone about my decisions! I should have thought my word would do. I have had my fill of interrogation during these last days!'

'But you must tell me the truth.' She was emphatic. 'Do you swear?'

I inclined my head. 'If you like. Very well, I swear.'

'I need to know exactly what hold she has over you. You're so utterly impressionable. She could lead you into any trap, you know. Are you afraid of her?'

'Of course not.'

'You said you would tell me the truth.'

Reluctantly, I was forced to say what she wanted to hear. Frequently that is what people are actually demanding. 'I am a little scared,' I admitted. 'She has relatives in Constantinople. They might be criminals.'

'She hinted at some of this. Doubtless they in turn have contacts with the Turkish rebels. Did they threaten to expose you?'

She knew nothing of Siniutkin's part in my kidnapping. I thought it best not to confuse her. 'I went to meet the Count in Scutari.' The waiter came over so I dropped my voice. Leda ordered us a light meal. 'When I got there I was bundled into a car. Next thing, I was being driven inland!'

'And you still did not suspect her?'

'At the time, it did not even occur to me.'

Leda now wore an expression which was new to me, a mixture of moral urgency and depravity suggesting I was right to believe her mad. Thus, I became willing, more than ever, to humour her. 'Then that was how they knew where to find me,' I said wonderingly.

'Exactly! She's a second-rate juvenile Mata Hari. She's probably been working as an agent for years. She pretends to innocent vulnerability. It's her best disguise. I'll admit she hoodwinked me at first. But when I saw last night how shocked you were, I put two and two together.'

I was not convinced the Baroness completely believed this rationale herself. But a Russian who finds a rationale is, as we say, already well on the way to action. She could now explain everything within the context of my having been deceived. She had named an appropriate villain. Since Leda did not want to part from me, Esmé must become the monster which, only yesterday, I had been.

'I shall have to be careful,' I murmured, 'if I am to escape from her.'

'You must go immediately to the British. They will want to know about the rebels. I doubt they trust the Sultan for accurate information. And half the present government are Young Turks already favouring the Nationalists. Still others are in French and Italian pay. I have all this on good authority. You should get down to the harbour tomorrow, see if the *Rio Cruz* has left, or when she is due back. Captain Monier-Williams will put you in touch with the right people.'

Leda had forgotten our ship had been on her last voyage in these waters. The *Rio Cruz* was gone for good. But again I said nothing. The poor creature was half crazy, largely I suspect from lack of sleep and cocaine withdrawal, since I had not been supplying her. The Baroness frowned to herself. She had eaten hardly any of her food. 'Did Mrs Cornelius know what was going on with that girl?' She seemed to have a list of questions already prepared in her head.

'A little. She, too, tried to warn me.'

The Baroness uttered a superior sigh. 'Oh, Simka. You're only a boy. You've been led astray so terribly. How could you allow her to do it?'

'She reminds me of Esmé Loukianoff, the girl I was due to marry.'

From her beaded handbag Leda took a scented handkerchief and placed the tip of it against her eyes. 'You are too romantic for your own good, my dear. But look where it has led you. She asked for your "protection" I suppose, wanted to be introduced to influential people?'

'She had nothing, you see.'

'Nothing!' The Baroness laughed. 'She probably earns more than the Sultan himself, selling our secrets to her masters in Ankara. That was why she tried to trick me, when she thought you trapped and gone for good. She needed to get to Count Siniutkin. She might even have succeeded. The poor man has disappeared completely.'

'So I gather.' Mention of the Count's name made me turn suddenly, as if he might be standing behind me. Instead, near the bar, deep in conversation with a French officer, I observed the slight, dapper figure of Bimbashi Hakir. The Turk stared distantly back at me for a moment, then resumed talking. I became genuinely anxious, realising that not all the gang had been rounded up. They would know who had accused them and were bound to be vengeful. 'It doesn't feel safe here,' I told Leda. 'Let's go to my little apartment for a while. We can say more where there's less chance of being overheard.'

Without hesitation, she agreed. I paid our bill and we inched our way clear of the restaurant into the relatively cool air of the Grande Rue. A procession of closed horsedrawn carriages was going by. It filled the street. On both sides of it were Turkish soldiers in ceremonial dress. This mysterious caravan disappeared down near the Galata Tower and, as if they had been held by an invisible dam, the ordinary trams, donkey carts, motor cars and horses suddenly flooded back. The glare of gas and electricity, the wailing, horrible music, the lurid signs and the constant whining of beggars made me feel suddenly nostalgic. I could understand Esmé's reluctance to leave this city of her upbringing. I should have been glad to stay here at my own convenience and was determined to return one day, when the Turks were gone and Greeks or Russians ruled. A restored Orthodox Church would bring pilgrims from all over the world. But would the new order diminish Constantinople's oriental excitement?

As the Baroness and I turned up towards the little cemetery, a couple of pistol shots sounded close behind us. I heard a police whistle. They were the normal sounds of the Pera night and neither of us ever paid them much attention, but I had responded rather more nervously than usual. I found I was glancing into doorways. In one, Major Hakir's fierce little face peered down the sights of a revolver. Elsewhere I saw bazhi-bazouks jumping from alleys. There was potential danger on all sides. The night was humid, but the sweat on the back of my neck was cold. I was unusually glad to get up to the apartment. Here Leda virtually threw me onto the couch with the violence of her sudden, greedy passion. 'I love you,' she declared. 'I could not bear to see you hurt, Simka.'

As we undressed, I decided this was a reasonable price to pay for my twenty-four hours of grace. What if, I wondered, I acted out the rôle she had prepared, would she again have changed her tune? The problems of living in this city had overtaxed her mind. It was fortunate for me that I had found this out before offering her the opportunity of travelling with Esmé and myself. She might have threatened far worse harm had she decided to denounce me in a Western country. With rather less enthusiasm than usual I gave her my body, explaining away my obvious uninterest with the claim that I had become fearful of Esmé and her Nationalist friends. Tokatlian's was evidently a hotbed of revolutionaries, ruthless adventurers and desperate men and women of all kinds. I could not stay there any longer. I would move, I said, to this apartment. Then I would inform the authorities of our suspicions about Esmé.

'But how will you stop her realizing?'

For my own amusement, I let the Baroness discuss a variety of notions involving the betrayal of my darling. If I had been a cynical man, I might have thought the whole female race treacherous and without conscience. So many women spoke of morality only to maintain their own position when it suited them, to gain power, or, as in this case, to threaten. In Constantinople everyone scrambled to get tiny pinches of power for themselves, and consequently everything was for sale. The women, the slaves, the subject races, all schemed and squabbled in the shadow of the Sultan's palace. A few years earlier, Abdul Hamid, last true Emperor of the Osmanlis, possessed unlimited power, yet carried a pistol with him at all times. If someone disturbed, displeased or frightened him, he frequently shot them with impunity. Millions of souls had been at his disposal. Such absolute tyranny makes its subjects greedy for mastery over some small aspect of the world, whether it be animal or child. Thus Constantinople was a city famous for its dogs. People with the least power keep the most dogs.

That night when I returned to Esmé, I had been shocked by the levels of duplicity a woman was capable of reaching in her jealous desire to hold a man. Equally I was somewhat admiring of her, even though she began to cut a ludicrous figure of a person whose deceits and subterfuges are transparent and therefore harmless. I found Esmé almost catatonic. There were clothes tumbled everywhere and nothing packed. She sat in the middle of a pile of frocks looking pale and frightened. Her pretty hair was tangled, her eyes red. 'I do not know what to do,' she said. She was paralysed by the prospect of leaving. Patiently I began to fold the cloaks and dresses and put them down in the trunks. She watched me helplessly as if I were abandoning her.

'I'm not sure it's wise to go,' she said.

I explained the Baroness intended to expose her as a spy. I laughed about it. 'We'll be gone before she can do anything.'

At this Esmé began silently to weep again. I almost lost my temper. She was behaving like a whimsical child. 'After tomorrow,' I promised, 'you'll be Esmé Cornelius. They'll be searching for a Roumanian girl called Bolascu. Even your parents won't know where to find you.'

'But they must! We have to send them money.'

'I have already made the arrangements. They'll get even more from now on.' I was prepared to say or do anything to reassure her.

'Can I see them before we go?'

I hesitated. I could not risk being again separated from Esmé. 'Very well. We'll visit them tomorrow morning.'

'I would rather go alone.'

'It's too dangerous.'

She appeared to accept this and raised enough energy to help me do a little of the packing. By the small hours we were ready to leave at a moment's notice. We slept until eight, then prepared to visit her parents' tenement. It was a clear, misty morning. Constantinople shone with those wonderful, faded pastels for which she is famous. There was a cheerful mood to the streets. We carried two suitcases of clothes Esmé had discarded. She wished to take them to her mother. Though fearing we should run out of money before we ever reached Venice, I had agreed to give her parents another two sovereigns. The decrepit couple received us with their usual lack of emotion. Monsieur Bolascu had already bought himself a new suit which he had promptly ruined in some local gutter. Madame Bolascu was filletting a large fish at the table. Esmé kissed her. 'We are going on holiday,' she said in Turkish. 'I wanted you to have these clothes.' The woman nodded and wiped her mouth on her sleeve. Suddenly she looked at me and grinned. It was shocking to see that stony face break into such unlikely mobility. The fangs were revealed, yellow and black, and a kind of birdlike gargle issued from the throat. 'Bon voyage, m'sieu,' she said. Esmé wanted to stay. She pretended to talk to her father, who now dozed in a corner and could not hear a word. She hugged her mother. Madame Bolascu patted her on the back while continuing to grin at me. 'She is a good girl.'

'She's a very good girl. She'll get an education in Paris.'

This the grotesque creature found even more amusing. I was evidently a wag. In French she told Esmé to enjoy herself. Life was short. She must not waste it. We made a very pretty couple. She must be sure to be obedient for she would find few gentlemen as kind as Monsieur. She added an afterthought in Turkish. Esmé nodded and bowed, sucked in her upper lip and became sentimentally animated for a moment. Then, passively, she put her arm into mine, just as if we were about to have our photograph taken, and we stood there stock still while the woman, without pausing in her skilful gutting of the fish, looked us up and down. The sun streamed into the room, onto the dusty, unpainted boards, the bloody, stinking table. The eyes of the fish winked like jewels.

On the way back we stopped to buy Esmé pistachio nuts and almond cakes. She was behaving as if I were taking her to prison. The vendor shrugged his shoulders, pretending to search for change, banging on his bin for his boy to come over, and I looked across at a little shaded square where plantains grew like huge fungus around a green copper fountain. There on a wooden bench sat a swarthy Turk. He wore a for-

223

mal European suit and a fez. He was staring at me intently. I reached towards my hip. I had brought a revolver with me today. I should have been a fool to go unarmed with Count Siniutkin's friends everywhere in the area. Since I had never fired one in my life, I doubt if I could have aimed the weapon accurately. I let the sweet-vendor keep his few pennies and hurried Esmé on. She looked up at me in alarm, I told her we were being followed.

Once back at Tokatlian's she began to tremble alarmingly. She pleaded to be allowed to take the train. Every time she got on the ferryboat she felt sick. Was there no other way to leave Constantinople?

'Oh, yes,' I replied savagely, 'there are several other ways. But one must be dead before they become available! Do you want to join the Brides of the Bosphorus?' Only a few days earlier divers had been sent down by the British, searching for the wreck of a ship. They had reported finding a forest of bodies waving on the bottom, each of them tied in a sack and weighted with chains. These were chiefly girls who had ceased to please Abdul Hamid, but a few more bodies, similarly weighted, would scarcely have been noticed in that crowd.

Begging me not to raise my voice, she said I was scaring her all the more. I relented. I took her on my knee. I told her of the glories of Italy, the pleasures of France, the monumental certainties of Great Britain. 'And these countries are all Christian,' I said. 'They are all Catholic. You will never have to risk persecution again. There is no one to threaten you or sell you into a harem or force you to work at Mrs Unal's.'

She dried her tears, looking up with a half amused sniff. 'It sounds boring.'

'You are a bad, bad girl!' I kissed her. 'Your mother told you the truth. You'll find few as kind as me. You must be obedient!'

This seemed to have an effect. She grew apparently much more cheerful and began to pack up her cosmetics (of which she had hundreds) putting the different little pots and jars carefully into their places in a vast wicker hamper I had bought her from Simsamian's in the Grande Rue.

By the evening we were completely ready. I ran across to the *Byzance* where the Baroness was at her reception desk. 'It's all arranged,' I said. 'I'll meet a British Intelligence Officer tonight.'

She was full of triumph. 'Do you want me to come with you?'

'I'm to go alone.'

'When shall I see you?'

'In your room, late tonight or tomorrow morning.'

As I left she blew me an excited, conspiratorial kiss, that inexpert Lady Macbeth. I winked back.

Not knowing if there was to be a curfew I had ordered the car for immediately after twilight. Two hired Albanians carried our trunks down to the waiting Mercedes while Esmé, pale and hesitant, dressed inappropriately in a shot silk teagown and fur-trimmed winter overcoat, stood with her hands in her ermine muff. She also wore one of her largest and gaudiest hats. At least, I thought with relief, she looked twice her age. I carried my own plan-case. In it lay my future and my fortune. The car was hardly able to squeeze through the little cobbled alley, yet had already been surrounded by a score of street Arabs, some of whom were evidently not native to the city, but spoke fluent, trilling Russian. I was becoming used to the sight of this new breed of blond-haired mendicants. Even as Esmé bowed her over-weighted head to get into the car I looked across the alley, thinking I saw the movement of a potential assassin. But it was only a little Turkish girl of about six. She had been relieving herself in the doorway and was concentrating on straightening her clothing. She looked up with a smile of recognition, as if hearing a familiar voice, then she saw me and her expression changed to one of alarm. She began silently to weep.

I joined Esmé in the car. It could be a few hours before we left for Venice, but I thought it prudent to be on our way. The chauffeur started the car, scattering the children in all directions. As we turned into the Grande Rue I looked back. We were not being followed. Pulling down the blinds of the car I noticed that beside me on the big leather seat Esmé had begun to shiver. I worried in case she was actually ill. She seemed to have a slight temperature. As soon as we arrived in Venice, I promised myself, I would get her a good doctor, even if it took our last penny.

By the time we reached the Little Quay and made the car stop as close to the barrier as was sensible, my girl had turned decidedly pale. I patted her hand while the driver at my request fetched her some sherbert from a nearby café. Behind the barrier the Customs people were still at their posts, but were beginning to pack up for the evening. They stood in relaxed groups, chatting and smoking, sharing jokes. Bored British and French military police wandered here and there, the reason for their presence mysterious even to them. The dark water was

225

smeared with oil reflecting the light of naphtha lamps and gas-flares, and from a nearby bar came the flat slap of Turkish drums. A number of sailors approached, showing a passing interest in the limousine. I replaced the blinds. Esmé continued to shiver beside me, sipping her sherbert, her eyes on the neck of the impassive chauffeur in front. One of the sailors casually tested a door, but I had locked it. When I next looked out the bulk of several large ships blocked most of my view beyond the harbour. Esmé and I would have to pass between two large iron gates to get to the wharf. There was one guard on duty, an Italian, and he had been primed by Captain Kazakian not to look too closely at our papers. A while later I saw the lights of a launch flicker on a few yards out from the wharf. The Italian army guard put his rifle against the gate post and turned a key in a padlock. Within a few minutes a large horse-drawn charabanc appeared at the other end of the street. It moved like a hearse over the cobbled pavement, drawing up directly in front of the gates. These were Kazakian's other passengers. Ostensibly in order to compete with larger shipping concerns, he was running a night service to Venice. It was time for us to leave the car. I told the driver to wait where he was until the luggage could be brought aboard and crossed the street with Esmé clinging to my arm. She virtually fainted as the Italian made a charade of inspecting our documents, stamping them and finally letting us through. When he spoke a few words of English to Esmé she did not understand him and looked utterly panic stricken. I hurried her towards the launch. By now my own stomach was churning. I had never known quite that sort of fear. I still half expected a motorcar to roar out of the darkness at any moment and a tommy-gun to spray us with bullets. Such assassinations were then commonplace in Constantinople. Al Capone was by no means an innovator. I relaxed a little once we joined the line of passengers walking towards the launch. Her engines turning slowly, she had pulled in beside the wharf and lowered her gangplank. She was a nineteenth-century sidewheel paddlesteamer equipped with wooden benches under a rather tattered awning on her upper deck. Her lower deck had a few slightly more elaborate sleeping berths. She was capable of little more than three or four knots and scarcely seemed seaworthy. But she was a better boat than she looked. This, at least, I knew from my own work on her. Captain Kazakian was nowhere in evidence. As soon as we had boarded and taken our places on the upper deck I sought him out. Sitting against the wheel post on his bridge, he was eating sausage and drinking wine. He winked at me as I handed over the hundred sovereigns and became almost languorous at the feel of gold in his hands. Yawning, he looked up at the sky. 'It should be a good trip, Mr Papandakis. This is the best time of year.' I asked him to make sure our baggage was brought on board and cleared through Customs. 'It is being done,' he said. 'I saw you arrive. Your trunks have been portioned out between fifteen of the other passengers!' He laughed heartily. 'Are you a gun-runner, using my poor boat as transport? Or do you own a dress-shop? Don't worry, they won't be checked. This is all a ritual. The Customs people don't care who leaves. They only worry about who comes in. And everyone makes a decent profit this way.'

I heard a motor revving in the street, then whistles and revolver shots. Electric torches flashed in the alley. Someone shouted in Turkish. There was a shriek and the sound of running. 'What was that?'

Kazakian dismissed it. 'Someone who couldn't find his fare to Venice, maybe. There.' He straightened himself and pointed. 'Your trunks are coming.' To my relief I saw half a dozen Greek and Albanian sailors crossing the gangplank with our trunks on their backs. 'Is there a chance we could take one of the cabins?' I asked him. 'My sister is unwell. Nothing catching.' He was regretful. They had all been sold long since. But it was a warm time of year, a calm sea. I should enjoy the journey. It was easy to sleep on the benches.

I was more cheerful when I returned to Esmé. But she had sunk into her clothes and stared desperately back at the wharf. 'I don't think we should go,' she whispered. 'I have a premonition.'

I scoffed at her. 'You're upset at leaving, that's all. You'll feel better when we reach Venice.'

'The ship makes me so sick.' She got up. 'Really, Maxim, I must get off!'

I restrained her, conscious of the curiosity of the other passengers, frightened lest we draw the attention of the police still on the quay. In panic, I hissed at her. 'Sit down, you little fool!'

'You're bruising my arm.' Her eyes came to angry life.

'Then sit down!'

The launch was rocking. Very loudly the engines exploded to full throttle. Wind caught at the canopy. It flapped like an applauding seal. The paddles churned and spray hit us suddenly from the starboard side. I heard rods connecting, pistons turning. Almost losing her footing, Esmé cried out, half falling heavily onto the bench. The other passengers, muffled in coats, were noisy and cheerful, pointing out exotic aspects of Stamboul's rich skyline. Her palaces and mosques had turned to pale grey against the blue-black night. I forced Esmé to sit where she was. She began to struggle, to moan. She was hysterical. While the other people on deck turned to admire the massive outline of the Suleiman Mosque coming up on our port, I gathered my strength and dealt my child a controlled but powerful blow to the jaw. Instantly she collapsed in my arms and started to breathe deeply like a tired dog. We pulled clear of the wharves. By the time we entered the Sea of Marmara the steam launch was vibrating dramatically. A few night gulls squawked curiously overhead, a variety of inhuman voices called from the harbours and the dark, surrounding water. Hidden ships hooted and shrilled. The air grew thick with the heavy, heated perfumes of Byzantium; with brine, with a hint of sweet fruits, palm trees and exotic gardens; the stink of the stirring beast that was Asia.

More shots and explosions sounded from the Pera side of the Galata Bridge: a rising cacophony of police whistles and sirens. Motor horns hooted. There was a confusion of shouts that rose and fell only once. The launch rattled like a cheap mechanical toy as she adjusted her course for the Hellespont. I believe I probably saved Esmé's life, as well as mine, by silencing her. If she had begun to scream we could well have been arrested.

The boat's vibrations were now less violent and water was a reassuring rush in the paddle blades. The shore fell away from us on all sides as we headed for Gallipoli and the narrow straits for which so many men of the British Empire had died in vain. Beyond Gallipoli lay the Aegean, that most hallowed of seas, where civilisation had been born, where the philosophy of Christ was created. From the Aegean grew the Mediterranean and Italy, from which Law and Justice were carved out of the Chaos of pagan barbarism. I was sorry Esmé was not awake to share my joy. The boat grumbled and clanked. She wheezed and squealed, but I did not care. I knew that Odysseus was going home!

Esmé stirred once or twice, then fell into a deep, natural slumber. Only later, when we were actually in the Hellespont and the water was growing choppier, did she wake up. I was dozing myself by then. I heard her gagging and spluttering and hardly realised what was happening before I recognised the smell and felt dampness on my chest. She had vomited all over me. This was one of the few things she had in common with Mrs Cornelius. I accepted the discomfort as fitting revenge for the blow, cleaned myself as best I could, then, putting her head back on my shoulder, stroked her to sleep. It seemed my destiny to fall in love with women who had weak stomachs. The sounds and scents of the sea altered subtly as we slipped into the Aegean, passing close to Lemnos and its big Russian refugee camp. With a certain amount of malice I thought that sooner or later the Baroness and Kitty must arrive here. It would be a shame if the child suffered, but Leda deserved a short spell in such conditions. Only then, I thought, would she come to realise from what I had saved her, how much she had lost because of her hysterical folly and her unreasonable jealousy. I had been more than careful to consider her feelings. Now she, in my absence, could consider mine!

By midmorning of the following day it became apparent that Captain Kazakian was not the mariner he had claimed to be. By the afternoon it was also obvious neither he nor his boat was fitted for the voyage. The paddlesteamer was mechanically sound, in the sense that most of her parts functioned properly, but she was hardly a seagoing boat at all, being more suitable for ferrying work on inland waters. I caught the captain twice puzzling over maps and staring through an old telescope at the coast. We had never gone out of sight of shore. The launch now stank of burning oil and several times I had awakened from my doze in alarm, thinking we were on fire.

I did everything I could to keep my knowledge and my fears from the almost comatose Esmé. Mostly she lay full length on the bench, very occasionally taking faltering steps to make dry, retching noises over the rail. She had eaten nothing since Constantinople. For that I was selfishly grateful, though increasingly I was concerned about her. I could not believe anyone would react so badly to mere anxiety. Sometimes she looked up at me to ask in a tiny voice if we had arrived yet. I was forced to shake my head. All I could reply was 'Soon.' Then I would go to the wheelhouse and discover the bulky Armenian struggling with charts, frowning at instruments and scratching his head with the peak of his filthy cap. His reply to my question was usually a grunt and always the unreassuring information that we were 'not far from Greece'. I admit my own geography had also been at fault, for I had believed Captain Kazakian when he said Venice was little more than a day's voyage. At length, when I forced a more specific answer from him, he admitted our position was 'somewhere near Smyrna', which was almost the last place I wished to be. He tried to ease my mind by pointing at his obviously malfunctioning compass. 'But we are on our way to My-konos.' He explained Mykonos was Greek; an island 'not far from Ath-ens'. By that evening, as the sun went down below a mysterious range of bleak cliffs and while Kazakian muttered in tempo with his engine, still puzzling over his sea-maps, Esmé was asleep and I was starving. It had not occurred to me to bring food.

Later, one of the passengers offered me a piece of thin sausage and some pitta which I gratefully accepted. He was more outgoing, more confident than most of the others (who now seemed like fellow refugees rather than tourists); a big man in a black overcoat and black astrakhan hat. He introduced himself as Mr Kiatos and was reassuringly content with the progress of the voyage. He had travelled on the launch several times, he said. She always managed to survive the trip in one piece. He was a businessman, dealing mainly in dried fruits, and he had cousins in Constantinople. He lived at Rythemo, he said. A regular steamer never took this route. If he travelled by more conventional means he would have to transfer boats once or twice and thus lose a great deal of time. I asked him where Rythemo was. It was on Crete. Captain Ka-zakian, I said, had given me the impression we were going straight to Venice. At this Mr Kiatos smiled without rancour in the folds of his smooth, well tempered face. 'I think the Captain goes wherever we pay him to go, sir. And he tells each passenger he is sailing direct to that place!' He chewed with pleasure on his sausage, returning his attention to the placid surface of the sea, while I stretched out on one of the empty benches and managed to sleep.

I was awakened by the night's chill. We were moving slowly beneath a magnificent yellow moon. To our port the craggy cliffs ran with foam. The sea was still relatively calm but I could hear breakers rushing on a beach. The lights of our launch swung back and forth and human silhouettes stood leaning against the rails. Esmé was sitting upright, clinging with outstretched arms to the back of the bench, like a cruci-fied doll. I asked if she were better. She wanted some water. I went be-low to where their tongueless Bulgarian cook sat playing cards with one of the other unwholesome-looking crewmen. I signed to him. I needed water from the barrel. He made an expansive, hospitable gesture. Cleaning out a mug, I carried it back for Esmé, who swallowed, splut-tered, then asked if we were sinking. I pretended to laugh. 'They're put-ting a passenger ashore, that's all. A minor delay. It won't be much longer before we're in Venice.'

She rolled her eyes upwards like some Godforsaken martyr, then again subsided into sleep. She seemed feverish so I dabbed the rest of the water on her forehead. I noticed my own hand was shaking. I forced myself to be calmer.

With a good deal of yelling and cursing from Captain Kazakian, his men brought the launch closer to shore. They started to unship one of the boats. A large Gladstone bag at his feet, Mr Kiatos stood over me, wanting to shake hands. I had become so abstracted, I had not at first noticed him. 'This is where I leave you, sir.' He smiled with sympathetic humour. 'I hope it isn't too long before you arrive in Venice.' He bent down and placed the rest of his food and a little packet of dried figs on the bench beside me.

I watched him clamber gracefully over the side, then came to my senses enough to move to the rail. A seaman rowed him through choppy water towards the beach. I waved at him, but he did not see me. For a moment I wondered why they had not docked at the town's wharf. Then it occurred to me we were probably closer to Mr Kiatos's home and Kazakian was avoiding port fees. It might also be that Mr Kiatos was a smuggler.

By morning the boat was shaking and squealing across a calm sea beneath pure blue skies and I was trying to get Esmé to take some crumbled biscuits and milk, which an Italian woman had given me. The land was almost out of sight and Captain Kazakian therefore was making frantic efforts to get closer in to what he guessed might be Hydra. He was inclined to panic if, even for a few minutes, the horizon consisted only of ocean. For my part I had sunk into that peculiar stupor which over the years has helped me stand many kinds of boredom and several sorts of terror. I sat with Esmé's poor little burning head in my lap, staring forward, watching for clouds and praying a storm did not come. By now I was perfectly convinced the launch could not possibly ride anything more than a squall. Captain Kazakian's need for reassurance no longer seemed unreasonable. Further passengers were put off, usually in obscure coves of nameless islands. Sometimes a person would object, claiming he did not recognise the coastline or that it was not the exact place to which he had paid passage. At this, Captain Kazakian would shrug. He would argue. He would stab his filthy stubs of fingers at the charts. He would offer to take them on to his next port of call or carry them back to Constantinople. Then eventually, resentful and suspicious, they would disembark. It had, of course, become absolutely clear we should not be sailing into Venice via the Grand Canal. We should be lucky if he landed us on a stretch of pebbles less than ten miles from the city. Not that this likelihood disturbed me very much, since it was important to avoid the authorities if at all possible. I was actually comforted by the knowledge that almost every other person on board was also anxious to remain inconspicuous. Now no embarrassment existed between us; nonetheless very few fellow passengers attempted to communicate. It seemed we shared a similar reaction to our plight. Nothing we could say would improve our situation; so we said nothing.

The worst problem I could imagine for Esmé and myself, as we got a little closer to Italy, was the transporting of our trunks to the city. There would not be porters at one of Captain Kazakian's landing stages. I refused to voice my fears to my little girl, whose fever subsided after I had managed to get her to take some cocaine. The drug's restorative properties rarely failed and in this case helped to bring her to her senses. I could now force her to nibble on Mr Kiatos's figs and sausage. We were sustaining ourselves entirely on borrowed food. Without the silent kindness of those other people we might have starved to death. Kazakian and his crew had certain supplies, but had no intention of sharing them with what they plainly regarded as a troublesome cargo. They would have treated cattle better.

By the next afternoon Esmé had recovered still further. She looked fragile; her eyes had a bleak, wounded quality, but she was better able to move and to talk.

'Where are we now, Maxim?'

'Nearing Venice,' I said.

The sky had a few strands of cloud but was otherwise perfect; the sea might have been an ornamental lake. The engine steadily turned the paddlewheels which, with light glinting on their green metal covers, sent refreshing spray into our faces. The gods, it seemed, were favouring this Odyssey, at least for the moment. I sat with my darling beneath the stained canopy and held her hand, murmuring of half-remembered Greek legends, the glamours and treasures of the Venetians, the engineering marvels we should find in Europe. Meanwhile Captain Kazakian came up onto this deck and, with a nod to us, stretched himself full length on the planking beyond the awning. Stripped to the waist and smoking a cheroot, he was enjoying the sun. Occasionally he would turn his massive head towards us and call out encouragement. 'Everything's under control. Just a few more hours.' They were meaningless words. He was relaxing because he had actually recognised the coast of Cephalonia and had recently passed a number of large ships. Every time Captain Kazakian had seen one of these he had given a cheerful greeting on his whistle. The nearer we were to land, the more vessels there were in the immediate vicinity, the happier he was. We had flown the Turkish flag when we left Constantinople but were now carrying Greek colours. That evening, just after dark, we let off three passengers and took several more on board.

The newcomers were all middle-aged men walking with that swaggering gait I identified with well-to-do bandits or comfortably corrupt police officers. Until dawn, they remained standing around the wheelhouse, chatting to the Captain and later to the bosun who relieved him. They offered no recognition of the other passengers and never looked at anyone else directly; they were of the type for whom eye-contact is a weapon, a means of threat or persuasion. They did not waste it on casual socialising. Eventually a small sailing vessel drew alongside and took them in the direction of Corfu (according to Kazakian, who seemed greatly relieved when they had left). He reassured me we would be in Venice 'tomorrow'. He nodded at me, as if I were a mute baby. 'Yes,' he said smiling. 'Yes.'

By noon the next day the engine suddenly stopped. I at first assumed we were making another rendezvous. The boat drifted under a copper sky, away from the hazy outline of land to starboard. Esmé lay in my lap breathing deeply and the world was filled with an enormous silence. I was enjoying the sensation until, from the wheelhouse, Captain Kazakian began to yell fiercely in all the languages of the Levant and Mediterranean.

I saw the engineer come running along the deck. He was waving his arms and screaming. I sat upright. Thick black smoke gouted from the little engine-room and drifted towards us. It was menacing. Like a sentient, supernatural creature which might devour us if we moved.

A few moments later Kazakian left his post and with one eye on the cloud, as if he shared my impression of it, walked slowly up to where we stood. He was grinning and shaking his head, his hands going through their entire vocabulary of gestures, a sure sign of his utter terror. 'I thank God you are with us, Mr Papadakis, for you are the only one who can help us with our problem. You are a genius of a mechanic. Everyone in Galata says so. I know it.' This litany of praise was merely a preliminary and I suffered through it, waiting for him to reach his point.

'Will you please look at our engine?' he said.

Esmé had become frightened again. In spite of the sun's warmth, she pulled her coat about her and withdrew to the bench.

Reluctantly I followed Kazakian into the tiny engine-room, having taken the precaution of placing a handkerchief over my mouth and nostrils. I staggered before what was almost a tangible wall of heat. I gave instructions to shut everything down and tried to look for the trouble. The engine was typical of its kind, of no specific manufacture and operated by people who treated it with more superstition than mechanical skill, repaired so many times that scarcely an original part remained. I had become used to understanding the individual logic which went into these pieces of machinery; one had to guess the quirks of another's mind. There was no manual which would have been of the slightest possible use to me. After a while it emerged there was a blockage in one of the pistons. I set about dismantling the whole primitive system, having them clean each part as we went. The launch was burning any fuel she could find and the engine was patched with rags, bits of metal, even the remains of a corned beef can, while the boiler was a nightmare of welded scrap iron. Carefully I reassembled everything and gave orders to make steam again. To my enormous relief she ran more smoothly than before. I had not looked forward to being some minor Daedalus to that seedy Minos.

Delighted, Captain Kazakian insisted we go to his cabin. It was little more than a cubbyhole behind the wheelhouse and smelled worse than any other part of the boat. He wanted to drink some *arak*. But by now I was firm. First, I told him, I must see if my sister was all right. It was growing dark. I found her shivering on the bench where I had left her. I was worn out and inclined to greater anxiety. I was determined to get us to Venice before anything else went wrong with the boat. I returned to Kazakian's cabin. I thought Esmé had typhus, I said. This impressed him. He looked grotesquely startled, as if he suspected himself of giving her the disease. Then he insisted vigorously that she was merely seasick. I had lost patience with him.

'You had better understand, I think, that it is not only possible to lift a curse placed on an engine. I can also make a curse. Without moving from here, I could immobilise you completely.'

He sneered at me but I had obviously impressed him. My guess was that he was too superstitious to risk very much. Also I had proved so useful to him he was willing to placate me. He called his bosun in and gave orders that Esmé be taken below to one of the recently-vacated cabins. 'At no extra charge,' he told me with the air of a man who knew he was being stupidly generous. The stuffy cabin had a bed with a single dirty sheet on it, but it was better than the bench. Lifting her fragile little body onto the bunk, I made the others leave; then I undressed her and washed her. She awoke for this and did not resist me, showing no interest when I told her the engine was working well and we were on the last lap of our journey. 'We should be sighting the Italian coast tomorrow. I have taken charge here.'

As soon as we landed, I said, I would find her a doctor. She became calmer as the night progressed. Her fever had dropped radically by morning. I left her alone long enough to demand a cup of coffee from the boat's galley and remind Captain Kazakian of my threat. He flapped his hands and shrugged. 'It is where we are going!' he said, as if I were an unreasonable and demanding child. 'Where we are going. Of course!'

I stayed with Esmé until evening, keeping myself awake with cocaine. At about nine o'clock there was a knock on the door and Captain Kazakian entered. He was smiling broadly. His attitude was completely changed. This suggested he was now more certain of his position. 'Tonight,' he said. 'Yes. Actually tonight. In Venice. Will your sister be well enough to go ashore?'

'Where will you land us?'

'Not far from Venice. A village. You can get a train. A matter of half an hour.'

'I am almost out of money, Captain Kazakian. I can't afford any further travelling expenses. You promised to take me all the way to Venice, remember?'

He scratched the back of his neck and became embarrassed, placing the tips of his fingers into the pocket of his greasy, embroidered waistcoat. After some hesitation he produced three sovereigns. 'I will give you these back. Your fee for helping us with the engine. They will pay your fare to Venice.'

It was a mixture of peace offering and sacrifice to the gods; a reluctant libation to the little spirit who watched over steam launches. I accepted his gold. It was my right.

'My men will take you to this village,' he said expansively. 'You'll find a good doctor there. The Italians are excellent doctors. They have many of them.' He looked with shifty alarm at Esmé's tiny, pale face. 'You're sure it's typhus?'

'We shall ask the doctor.'

At about three in the morning the Turks and Albanians began to unload our trunks and bags into a boat until it sat so low in the water I thought it must sink. I followed with Esmé in the other boat. The sea grew more boisterous as we rowed towards land. Captain Kazakian stood outside his wheelhouse watching us impassively. He did not wave. The ship carried no lights but the moon was full. We had little difficulty reaching the beach and dragging both boats above the water-line. I was so delighted to be ashore I felt I had to suppress a cheer. The night was warm. I could smell fresh-mown grass and trees and hear insects calling. Somewhere, far away, a donkey brayed.

One of the Turks left us suddenly. He set off up the beach at a run, disappearing behind the dunes. Unconcerned, the others unloaded and stacked our trunks. They were pleased with their work. I smiled at them in thanks. With a few words of farewell they refloated their boat. They rowed back to the launch which we could just make out near the tip of the headland. She looked incongruous in these waters, as if she had lost her moorings at a holiday resort.

Eventually the Turk who had run off returned. He seemed proud of himself. Everything was being done as if they were new to it. Was Kazakian again playing things by ear With the Turk was a tiny old man in a black jacket and trousers, a dirty collarless shirt and bare feet. The old man seemed bemused, but cheerful enough. 'Buon giorno, signore, signora.' He nodded with hesitant politeness.

I almost embraced the poor man. I was close to tears. For a little while I had suspected Captain Kazakian of putting us off on some convenient Greek island, but now I knew this was Italy! We were safe. Nearer now, a donkey brayed again. The old man turned and clucked into the darkness.

The Turkish seamen and the venerable Italian carried our luggage up the beach. Eventually I followed, supporting a tottering Esmé. We reached a narrow track and there stood a little cart, the donkey between its shafts. The cart had nets in it and a sack evidently containing fish. The old man moved the sack to the seat and began loading the trunks. When he had finished there was only room for Esmé on the board in front. We helped her up. She seemed to respond well to the little fellow's murmuring voice. There is nothing more soothing to the nerves than the sound of soft, kindly Italian. The old man and myself stood together, watching the Turk return to his boat and shove off into the deeper darkness. Then, giving the donkey a sharp tap on its flanks, the old man led it up the track. I walked beside him.

He spoke nothing but his own language of which I knew only a few words. I told him I was grateful for his help and hoped we were not inconveniencing him. He did not understand but smiled and said: '*Son contento che Lei sia venuto.*' As if in reassurance.

I pointed ahead to where I could see a few lighted windows, wondering if perhaps we were closer to our destination than the Captain had told me. '*Venezia?*' I asked.

He seemed surprised, but shrugged. I repeated myself a couple of times and he frowned. '*Si. Venezia?*' He added several sentences which I could not understand. Then I said: '*Dottore?*'

He was agreeable to this. '*Dottore? Si, si. Dottore!*' He motioned with his stick towards the lights.

'In Venetia?' I asked him.

This caused an unexpected reaction. He stopped in his tracks, looked up at me, waved his arms and began to cackle uncontrollably, bending over in his mirth. '*Ah! Ah! Venezia! Ah!*'

He became almost inarticulate with merriment as he tried to point towards the lights again. '*No! La capisco! La città!*' He pointed with his stick as soon as he regained control of himself. '*Otranto,*' he said.

I had never heard of Otranto and found the old man's response to my mistake excessively humorous. The place was far smaller than I had hoped, with some winding streets, a ruined castle and several taverns. When we reached it a faint line of light had appeared over the horizon and an early cock was crowing from a red rooftop. Old and dusty, the town might have been Greek, judging by the Byzantine appearance of its main church, but from the look of its castle could also be Moorish. It was not what I had expected to find in Italy, this clearly defined mixture of architectural styles. It was almost as if Otranto had been invented by someone wishing to describe the national and historical influences of the past twenty centuries. Yet the whole was in fact not incongruous. I found it attractive. I would have thought it wonderful if I were not so disappointed at not finding Venice. It was, in fact, a small town, and could not have supported more than two thousand inhabitants.

We soon had a room, however, in a little medieval inn where a thin, cheerful woman took care of Esmé. I paid the old man with some of the silver left in my pockets. He seemed delighted. He and the landlord attended to our trunks. There were so many they half filled the tiny, low-ceilinged room. By the time they left, Esmé was in bed, enjoying the luxury of freshly laundered linen and I had gone downstairs to breakfast with the couple who addressed me in friendly, eager voices and made no sense to me at all. In the end we merely smiled and made various signs of goodwill. I returned to the room where Esmé now slept peacefully, her sweet face as pure as an angel's, and drew the curtains. I undressed, got into bed, took my girl into my arms and did not wake up until afternoon.

To me Otranto seemed a haven of tranquillity. I could have stayed much longer and even today have an urge to return. Then, however, I was anxious to get to a large city, where we should be unnoticed in the cosmopolitan throng. Esmé was still sleeping. I washed in cold water, dressed and went to seek the landlord and his wife. I found them on a bench together at the back of the inn. They were plucking chickens. When they saw me they called out. I could still understand nothing of their Italian but enquired again about a doctor, explaining with gestures and a few Latin words that my sister was sick. The skinny wife was the first to understand. She babbled at her husband who carefully set aside his chicken and rose to leave. The heads of the dead birds stared at me in ghastly amusement as if they saw something about me which others did not. To the wife I asked the distance to Venice. She shrugged and said 'Treno?' which I took to mean 'train.' I nodded. I did not mind how I got there. Kazakian had said it would take half an hour, but I did not trust him. The woman uttered another string of sentences in which the names Roma, Napoli, Brindisi, Foggia and half a dozen more were mentioned. It was then it began to come clear to me we might be much further from Venice than even I supposed. Captain Kazakian had been so anxious to get us off his boat that I suppose we were lucky to be in Italy at all. It seemed it would cost at least the three sovereigns he had given me back just to get to Venice. I wished that it were possible for me to lay a curse on his engine. As it was, I closed my eyes and tried to visualise the machinery. There was certainly no harm in trying.

When the gangling doctor arrived, seeming far too young for the fringe of beard around his face, I was relieved to discover he spoke

French. Dr Castaggagli informed me Esmé had nothing more worrying than neurotic tension which would almost certainly disappear with rest. 'Have you been travelling for long?' He was aquiline and prematurely bald. He reminded me of a Jesuit eagle. I told him she had never left home before. Our trip had been rather tiring. He nodded. 'She needs to be somewhere peaceful,' he said. If possible I should engage a professional nurse. He frowned to himself, adding, 'But not here.'

I was delighted she had nothing seriously wrong. I offered Castaggagli one of my remaining sovereigns. He refused the coin with some amusement. He was a country doctor, not used to large fees. If I had no small sums, he would take payment in kind. So, since he was about the same across the shoulders as me, I gave him one of my overcoats. It had a good fur trim and was rather too warm for the climate, moreover it would have to be lengthened in the arms, but he was delighted. He offered to let me have a hat and scarf as 'change.' I said that I would rather have a timetable of the trains from Otranto. He smiled. He would do what he could. It would probably be best if I went to the station myself. He asked where I would go. I told him.

He shook his head at this. He thought Venice might be an unhealthy place for a sick child, even though there was nothing seriously wrong. It was smelly in Venice and extremely noisy at this time of year. However, he would make some enquiries about the best connections. Probably it would mean a change in Foggia, at least.

To forestall his curiosity (and possibly his reporting us to the local carabinieri) I told him I was English. My sister and I were on our way to Corfu by steamer from Genoa when Esmé became ill. At my insistence the captain had put us off here. Perhaps there was a large city closer to Otranto than Venice?

Doctor Castaggagli said it would be far easier to head for Rome or Naples, particularly with all our luggage, and presuming us to be returning to London. He did not think Esmé should travel for several days or for very far. She must be installed in a good hotel room where she could have tranquillity and rest. Then she would soon recover. If I needed a specialist opinion (which he admitted was unlikely) I should certainly make for Rome where it was 'very modern.'

Although regretting I should not see the beauties of that famous old city, I was already thinking it would be better to travel to Rome and thence to Paris. From Paris I could obtain legitimate papers and then proceed to London. I still had enough to pay our fares and a few more

239

weeks at moderately priced hotels. Even if our money ran out we were in a law-abiding country. I could earn what we needed.

In Paris, if he had not yet gone to America I would find Kolya. He would help me. And there would be other friends: St Petersburg alive again on the banks of the Seine! In a mounting mood of optimism I made my decision. In spite of the doctor's advice, I was certain that familiar comforts, streets, traffic, crowded cafés, would revive Esmé more thoroughly than any rural retreat. However, I thanked Doctor Castaggagli warmly; I knew that he meant well. He asked if he could be of further help. I needed to change money and buy tickets. He took me in his pony and trap to the town's bank and there my sovereigns became lira: huge, magnificent, flamboyant notes. Next we went to his house. He insisted I wait in the trap while he dashed inside to return with the promised hat and scarf. They were both of good quality and, in spite of having several suits, coats and other accessories (though the bulk of our luggage was Esmé's) I was grateful to him. At the little station, which looked as if it had been in Otranto since the time of Christ, I bought two first-class tickets for Rome.

The doctor insisted upon purchasing a bottle of wine, to enjoy a farewell drink. Reassuring myself that Esmé still rested and was content, I joined him in the courtyard of the little inn. We sat down together. The old marble bench might have come originally from a Roman villa. In the little garden beyond the courtyard the landlord's wife clipped her evening roses. Doctor Castaggagli stretched his long legs out before him, his heels describing cryptograms in the dusty earth whenever he shifted position, and spoke of his love for this little town, his birthplace. In some ways I was envious of him. Over the years I have longed so for simplicity: the one gift God refused to grant me. However I enjoyed a certain contentment that evening, looking up at the crenellated Moorish castle and its monument to slaughtered victims of the Turks. The Osmanlis had raided Otranto in 1480, killing everyone they could find. I was reassured. No longer need I fear immediate threat from Islam, Israel or, indeed, Bolshevism. I was securely on Western European soil, and everywhere saw confirmation of progress; a civilisation I had always yearned to know. Here, such things were taken as casually as the weather, as the ubiquitous old monuments to an enduring history.

My own past thoroughly behind me, I felt I had entered the future. I was, amongst these ancient hills and vineyards, truly about to take part in the twentieth-century adventure. For this civilisation was not decadent as was Turkey's. It had continued to grow; it marched confidently on, paying decent respect to the past but never yearning for its return. I felt a distinct contrast between this world and the crumbling monuments of Islam, the noisy, stinking, degenerate streets of Pera, whose denizens clung desperately to scraps of wreckage so rotten they turned to dust almost at once. Italy herself was reviving, as she always revived! She was a new, flourishing nation, ecstatically welcoming, as perhaps nowhere else, the Age of the Machine! Her greatest hero was her finest symbol: the poetaviator d'Annunzio! Here was a figure one could unconditionally admire. Magnificent in his manly dignity he showed the Bolshevik demagogues up for the petty, unwholesome creatures they were. D'Annunzio had taken up the sword in his nation's cause. He had refused to allow the Mapmakers and financiers their shallow compromises. Personally, he had marched at the head of his soldiers into Fiume, claiming the city in the name of Italy. The city was Italy's by every honourable right; it had been promised her, as Constantinople had been promised to the Tsar. Oh, for another ten d'Annunzios to take the conquered cities, the betrayed cities, the noble, forgotten cities of the world and give them back to Christ!

Doctor Castaggagli talked a great deal of d'Annunzio, whom he admired, and it was the inspiration I needed at that moment. 'He epitomises the new Renaissance. He is a man of science, yet a great poet; a nobleman who embraces the future. He is a man of action.'

Here was someone with whom I could thoroughly identify. I saw much of myself in d'Annunzio. One day I intended to meet him. Together we could do so much. As the simple country doctor said, there was a Renaissance about to dawn all over the West. Greece was flourishing. France was restoring herself. England was extending the Reign of Law. And Germany, too, must soon recover from the trauma of defeat, putting an end to the sickness of socialism which currently infected her wounded body politic. America was resting, yet she would rally, I knew. A great brotherhood of Christian nations would emerge, united in its common purpose, to drive the Bolshevik wolf to its death and send the Islamic jackal scurrying into the desert from whence it had come. A little drunk on the rough young wine, I spoke of these dreams to my Italian friend. He toasted me enthusiastically and spoke of his country's renewed friendship with mine (which he thought was

England). He had a dream: the future would show us a world balanced between two great Empires, the British and the Roman, each mutually admiring, each complementary, each with its own distinct character.

'It will exemplify the Renaissance ideal,' he told me. 'The ideal of Harmony and Moderation. Science will flourish in all forms, but it will be humane, tempered by the wisdom of the Church.'

As if to confirm this statement, there came a high-pitched drone from above. The sun was setting bloody and huge behind Otranto's castle, and out of it flew the distinctive silhouette of an SVA5 biplane. It lifted its nose above the fortress battlements and then, turning lazily to circle the red tiles of the old town, began to bank down towards a dark green line which was the sea. It was seemingly swallowed back into a magical realm where the ordinary rules of nature did not apply, flying as easily through water as it had through air. Then it disappeared.

Drunkenly, the doctor and I applauded it. We toasted d'Annunzio once more. We toasted Otranto. After some debate, we rose to our feet and toasted the Pope.

Later it occurred to me the plane was probably a Customs spotter, hunting out illegal shipping. I wondered if it had seen Captain Kazakian's steam launch off the nearby coast and was searching for smugglers or secret immigrants. As soon as we could we should be on our way to Rome. (I learned soon afterwards I had been far luckier than I realised. Italian coastal patrols had been doubled in recent months. There was an influx of stateless refugees desperately fleeing the ruined countries of Eastern Europe and Asia Minor.)

That night I told Esmé we were going to Rome, to the seat of her religion, to a city older than Byzantium. The wholesome food and the inkeeper's wife's loving attention had restored her considerably. My news made her almost gay. She began to apologise for her behaviour. I told her how I understood. It is a terrible thing to be torn up by the roots, even if those roots are buried in poisoned soil.

Soon afterwards we took the train to Rome. A little group of our Otranto friends saw us on our way. The journey proved extremely comfortable, if mainly dull. It was good, however, to know the luxury of true first-class travel again. The seats and the general appearance of the train impressed Esmé. She grew animated; her wonderful, girlish self; her eyes as bright as ever by the time our final train pulled in to great Central Station.

It was Sunday, July 4th 1920. Esmé and I had arrived at last in

Rome, that city of lush gardens and timeworn stone; that city of the automobile where every second citizen seemed a priest or a policeman and where, consequently, Church and State were neither remote nor frightening institutions but familiar, ordinary and reassuring. A helpful cab driver recommended the *Hotel Ambrosiana* at 14, Vicolo dei Serpenti. We took a suite there. Warm sunlight poured through the French doors leading to our own little balcony. Esmé danced with pleasure. She was rapidly putting even a hint of her old terrors behind her, becoming ebullient, eager to go onto the streets, to visit the cafés, the shops. 'And there must be circuses,' she said. 'I've heard of them. Cabarets, too. And the cinema, of course!'

It was a wonderful new world. It smelled free in a way Galata never had. Esmé marvelled at the straightness of the streets, their cleanliness, the relative absence of dogs and beggars. This, she said, was very much as she had thought of Heaven, when she was younger. And she had identified Rome, of course, with Heaven.

I asked her what she wanted to do most urgently. She skipped beside me, her hand in mine, her eyes smiling up at me.

'Oh, the cinema!' she said. 'It has to be the cinema!'

After a light lunch at a pleasant little café near the Barberini Palace we went to look for a picture-house. We rushed straight in to the first one we found. They were showing *Gli ultimi giorni di Pompeii* and we were entranced, almost overwhelmed by the film's epic reality. There could have been no better choice, no better place to watch it. Esmé hugged me and held my hand all the way through. Occasionally, in her delight, she would kiss me. I could not imagine happiness more perfect.

My rebirth was consolidated at last.

Ten

THE ETERNAL CITY had seduced us both. Hand in hand we walked everywhere, entranced. Amidst the casual accumulation of three millennia, the conventional symbols of an antique greatness, her ruins, her churches and her modern monuments, Rome's citizens conducted a routine life reminiscent of my own salad days in Odessa. Romans struck matches against Caligula's columns and strung washing from balconies where Michelangelo or Raphael might have leaned to improve their view of St Peter's. Motor-cars, trams, buses and trains buzzed and crashed around the Colosseum and the Circus Maximus, cheerfully unimpressed by this weighty glory. The natives were if anything amused by foreign pilgrims who piously gasped at their pagan and their papal shrines. Rome herself was looking forward, was more consciously a modern city than ever before.

In the little bars, dance halls and night clubs around the Via Catalana we would soon find convivial company. Here intellectuals and bohemians gathered; futurists clashed swords with socialists, d'Annunzio was toasted and Giolitti, the Prime Minister, slandered. Plans were made to build a new Empire whose legions would advance by rail and in tanks, pausing to establish factories rather than forts wherever they went. Yellow sandstone and pink marble walls were covered with every persuasion of political poster, indiscriminately mixed with advertisements for sports cars, air races, cinema films; all these equally of consuming interest to the Romans. They were attracted to the romance of technology, by the thrill of the great, simple deed. They were simply entertained or irritated by the petty bickerings of corrupt liberals and apoplectic anarchists. In

244

this tolerant humanity they were again like Odessans. They lived in warm, friendly sunshine, in their cafés; in their restaurants they ate and drank with gusto; in the streets they laughed and danced to the music of little brass bands and accordions; they even dressed with the gay flamboyance of pre-war Odessa. If they expressed admiration for Bolsheviks it was both dismissive and ironic, acknowledging the Reds as successful criminals, not with a pursing of the lips but with a sardonic laugh. Lenin was 'that noble successor to Ivan the Terrible' or 'the greatest Byzantine monarch since Julian the Apostate', while Trotski was either Joshua or Attila. Artists of Mayakovski's bent were 'the glorious children of Marinetti' whose canvases were whole cities, whose materials were dynamite, gunpowder and ruptured flesh: Poets of a New Apocalypse opposed to all that was old, devoted to everything that was new, born into a world where electricity, the internal combustion engine and powered flight were commonplace, 'to use, not to examine'.

We had arrived on the morning of a mass march through central Rome. Traffic crawled. Men in overalls waved mysterious banners and women in red shawls shook their fists and shouted, stepping in time to the music of rough-and-ready bands which played loudly and in conflict. When I came to ring the service bell in our room I found that it was the manager's wife who answered it. She apologised. The restaurant waiters had gone on strike and the hotel staff had joined them. She said she could bring us sandwiches and mineral water, that she was hoping to prepare a meal of some kind in the evening. She advised us, however, to look for family-owned restaurants which would still, with luck, be open. Strikes were so frequent that people took them for granted. Normally I would have been furious at the inconvenience, but I was deeply glad to be in a Western city. I found myself shrugging and smiling, whereupon she began to cackle and made several jokes in Italian which I could not follow but at which I laughed anyway.

Thus Esmé and I spent our first day in Rome looking for somewhere to eat. That was how we discovered Via Catalana where many restaurants did, in fact, remain open. We were delighted with the novelty of everything and would probably not have noticed if we were starving. We marvelled at the sights and sounds of that civilised, ancient city; even the political rhetoric, so alarming in Russia, was here merely part of the vibrant air. Esmé breathed it in and became more wonderfully alive than ever. Rome in the summer of her most chaotic year, with workers occupying factories and ultimately D'Annunzio being expelled from

Fiume, was a haven of sanity and order compared to what we had put behind us. For this was, if nothing else, the capital of a free nation. The debate was not whether one should live to see the next morning, or how one might escape the brutality of self-appointed militiamen, or what movements had arisen overnight radically to change our fate, but what kind of elected government could best rule. The old artistic and intellectual vitality of St Petersburg, before Kerenski ruined everything, was here reproduced in even more vivid colours. People discussed ideas with an easy gaiety which suggested all politics was fantasy, worthless unless it was outrageous enough to entertain the population for at least one Roman evening.

Esmé, when we went to bed that night, was astonishingly passionate, making sexual demands on me which I found at first surprising, for I had no idea she harboured such secret desires. Nonetheless I flung myself into this new experience with a will and all but exhausted our remaining cocaine in the process. Next morning, aching but utterly relaxed, having slept hardly at all, I told her we would start having to make friends rapidly, if I was to discover fresh supplies of our drug. She pinched my cheeks and told me that I was too prone to 'stewing': everything was bound to turn out for the best. She lived for the moment, my Esmé. She was the eternal present and that was possibly the reason I loved her so much.

I have always been a man of many worlds, able to move easily from one social ambience to another. Remembering the bohemian character of the district near the Tiber's left bank more or less between the Capitol and Isola Tiberina, a stone's throw from the Orsini Palace, I returned there with Esmé that same afternoon. We were in such a pleasant state of euphoria we soon selected a café, sitting outside under its red and white awning, swatting at mosquitoes, and drinking *citrons pressés* from trumpet-shaped glasses. Half an hour later we were in conversation with a dark and attractively ugly little man who mistook us at first for English. Learning we were Russians, he became extravagantly delighted. He hardly needed to tell us he was an artist, with his wide-brimmed slouch hat and his scarlet silky cloak. He introduced himself as Fiorello da Bazzanno, painter. His monstrously wide mouth, full of yellow uneven teeth, made him grotesque; half-man half-horse in the head alone. His puny, underfed body, which twitched perpetually, completely contradicted the animalistic, pagan quality of his face. Yet the combination was magnetic. Moreover he revealed a facility for language which

246

matched my own. To us he spoke a bizarre patois of Russian, German, Italian, French and English. He had been born in Trieste where most of those cultures meet. He insisted we drink a bottle of Tuscan wine with him. After an hour or so he had revealed he had been a petty thief, a street arab. Then in the trenches he had met his hero, the Futurist Umberto Boccioni, and discovered broader horizons. I told him of my own life in Petersburg, my engineering achievements, my flying exploits. He was quick to see similarities in our lives. Drawing a great gold watch from within his rather dirty white shirt he told us we were to be his guests for supper. He paid the bill at the café and led us down the street towards Mendoza's Café in the Via Catalana, which was distinguished by its black and yellow striped umbrellas, and thus known locally as 'The Wasp.'

"You'll have the fried artichoke to begin." Fiorello was grave for a moment. 'It's Mendoza's speciality and creates more spiritual uplift than a dozen Papal audiences.'

A woman was waiting for him at one of the outside tables. She was dressed entirely in black and was almost twice his size. She had dark bobbed hair, a black smock, black stockings, black shoes. The only contrast was in her rather pale skin and the scarlet cord tied around her waist. This was Laura Fischetti. She wrote, said Fiorello almost apologetically, for the socialist press. We shook hands. A plump, motherly, good-humoured woman, she was forever picking and patting at her tiny lover. While he talked she leaned back from him, her hand on his chair, and smiled at us, the proud parent of a spoiled but clever child. Occasionally she would bend her head towards Esmé and ask her a question. My Esmé opened up to Laura, telling her the version of her life story I had said would be most acceptable in Europe; how she had been orphaned, raised by Turks, was about to be sold to a Syrian merchant when I found her, recognising her as my long-lost cousin. If Laura found the story fantastic, she was too well mannered to pursue it. Instead she confined herself to enquiring about life in Constantinople where her father had been attached to the consulate before the war, but which she had never visited.

The artichoke was as delicious as Fiorello had promised but the various pastas and meats which followed were better still. During the course of this wonderful meal, various friends arrived and seated themselves around us. When the table proved too small, they drew up another and placed it at an angle to the first until half the area belonged to one large group, all of them talking, drinking, eating and gesticulating with such energy and pleasure I should not have cared a second if I understood a word of what they said. Two or three of them had visited Russia before the war. They said they were poets. I suspected them of anarchist affiliations. It was Italians who so affected Petersburg's bohemians on every political and artistic level. I did not mind. They were not the savage, primitive anarchists I knew. To them anarchism was the logical persuasion for an artist, any artist, and particularly Italian artists. The Italians are the great individualists of Europe and anarchy is merely a formal description of the country's fundamental attitudes. (That was why so few people properly understood Benito Mussolini, his philosophy and his specific problems.) Meanwhile a tone-deaf guitarist wandered in and out of the restaurant singing popular sentimental songs for an indulgent lira or two while Fiorello remembered another item on the menu we must try and ordered innumerable bottles of wine. It was heavenly for me, to sit there eating grilled fish and macaroni and enjoying the fabulous luxury of unchecked conversation. It was Laura, that night, who found us good cocaine ('the drug of all true Futurists') and Fiorello who insisted on paying for it ('pay me when your first aerial liner sails for Buenos Aires').

Their friends were equally generous. For the first week of our stay in Rome virtually our only expense was the hotel. We went every day to the Via Catalana and from there would be taken on to restaurants, night clubs, private parties. The Roman bohemians were eager to hear my tales of the Civil War, of the Turkish nationalists and life in Constantinople. With these stories, sometimes just a little embroidered, I paid for our suppers and wine. If I had too much to drink, I might also draw on Mrs Cornelius's first-hand knowledge of the leading Bolsheviks. I continued to borrow her name, since it was on our forged British passports. I did not wish to risk confusing the authorities and I still could not be sure, in that company, who might be a police spy. There was always bound to be at least one in any group.

Our new companions, for all their apparent carelessness, did not take the fate of their country lightly; they could become furious, near hysterical, aggressive, violent with one another over the most obscure points. Every shade of anarchism, monarchism, socialism and nationalism was represented. Few Romans were fascists. *Fascisti* in those days meant merely 'a bundle' or 'a bunch of flowers'; that is to say it was slang for a group. It was left to the Bolshevik press to give the word its sinister connotation. Many of Fiorello da Bazzanno's friends, like Kolya, possessed

248

an obsession with the future which mirrored my own; they gave words and pictures to my ideas. My scientific rationalism and their poetry formed a perfectly balanced combination.

Fiorello insisted, one warm evening beneath burning strings of coloured electric bulbs on Mendoza's terrace, that the old warring families, the Borgia and the Orsini, had their contemporary equivalents in the makers of motor-cars. 'Soon it might be necessary to declare one's loyalties, my dear Max, and if necessary fight for them.' He jumped up, pushing his hat away from his thin, dark hair, striking a pose with his cane. 'Avanti! I am Count Fiorello da Bazzanno, henchman to the Ferrari!' This amused him so much that, his lips curling back over his yellow teeth as he laughed helplessly, he had to sit down again.

'And who will be the next Pope?' Laura patted his back. She spoke in her usual quietly sardonic tone. 'A Lancia? A Fiat?'

Fiorello gasped at this, shaking his head violently, controlling himself long enough to get to his feet and put his hand on my shoulder. 'He could be a foreigner. There's already a movement in the Vatican to elect a Ford. But the French support the Peugeot Cardinal.' He leaned forward in mock-seriousness. 'For my part I'm behind the dark horse. The Infant Cardinal.'

'Who's that?' We all bent our heads towards him.

'Why? None other than the Baby Rolls-Royce, my friends. Mark my words, you'll hear more of him in a year or two. He has stolen your plans, Max. He means to lift St Peter's closer to heaven. The whole papal city is to be seated on a massive dirigible, floating free of the Earth, no longer bound by temporal ties, removed from all petty politics. And when the Pope flushes his toilet, his piss will fall on Catholic and Protestant alike!'

'And Turks,' I begged. 'Let it fall on Turks as well.'

He was generous. 'They shall have the entire Vatican sewer. And with their land covered in such holy shit, they'll perforce grow nothing but Christian food. Thus they'll be converted, as our own ancestors were converted, through their bellies.'

When she was drunk, Laura was inclined to become a little sombre. 'I think Ford and Austin are already sufficiently powerful to do as they please.' She also tended, in this condition, to take a disapproving view of Fiorello's flights of fancy. 'It's cash in the end which impresses people. Buy their oil and so give them enough money to buy our cars.'

'The triumph of trade!' I, too, responded perhaps more earnestly than was necessary. 'Trade makes all men friends. A wealthy world is a peaceful world.'

Laura began to scowl. 'But who'll have the greatest share?'

'That issue's being decided in Russia at the moment.' The little man did not want to be brought down to earth. 'When the result is announced, we'll all know how to proceed. What a sublime clarifier is Lenin. Perhaps we should ask him to be Pope? Then everyone will feel much easier about him.'

I, too, became anxious to counter Laura's socialistic pieties. 'We'll simply move the flying Vatican City to Moscow!'

'But what about the Patriarch of Constantinople?' asked one of their friends from over Fiorello's shoulder. 'Where will the poor old fellow go?'

Fiorello raised his cane. 'I have the answer. A triumvirate: Pope Henry Ford, Patriarch of the Greeks and Romans Vladimir Lenin, and Dictator D'Annunzio. *Ist es gut so?* All shades of authoritarianism represented. A holy compromise.'

Esmé was utterly fascinated by his strange little face, his animated movements. From time to time she would burst into giggles at completely inappropriate moments; or she would sit staring at him, her face a combination of uncertain expressions, her eyes wide, like a child at the play. She loved his comic poses, his melodramatic gestures, his trilling eloquence; applauding his braggadocio for its own sake. I felt no jealousy. He was a natural clown and I wanted nothing more than for Esmé to be happy. This company and its attendant ambience had consolidated her good health, I knew, and I was grateful. I prayed we would find similar friends in Paris and London, for this was my natural habitat and, ideally, Esmé's as well. Here ideas and money, politics and art, science and poetry all mingled. Amongst such people I must inevitably find those who would appreciate my inventions and help me make them reality, just as Kolya would have done if he had been allowed more time in government. (This is why I am convinced Lenin was personally responsible for my frustration and misery, because Kolya fell when Kerenski was overthrown.) Now, however, in Rome and elsewhere I foresaw a future where these young men could truly build Utopia. They would plead with me to be its architect. Fiorello's rhetoric further inspired me. He spoke of 'the violence which powers the engine.' Society would have to accept violence if it wanted progress. 'Can a train run without the flaming energy in the boiler of the locomotive? Can steel be forged without a furnace? Can the aeroplane fly without consuming oil? *Ich glaube es nicht!* And, by the same reasoning, a nation cannot be hammered into perfection without blood and bayonets. Out of violence comes forth order! That wonderful tranquillity which falls on us after the battle. My Russian friends, I give you "Peace Through War!" and "Order Through Struggle!"'

As we cheered his histrionics we could not know he was the genuine herald of a vigorous and realistic new age. That glorious reawakening of Italy's pride would be marked only two years later by Mussolini's March on Rome. 'You must stay with us, my dear Cornelius!' With one hand Fiorello lifted his wine bottle, with the other his hat. 'Stay with us and help us create –' He fell back again, giggling. '*Excusez-moi, Der Motor ist uberhitz!*' And he put his head into Laura's tolerant lap, falling into sleep with a series of immense snores. Delighted as I was, I did not really take him seriously, yet his poetic vision was to prove splendidly accurate. Under the guiding hand of her remarkable Duce Italy began her glorious celebration of all that was vital, noble and modern. Mussolini's only failing was his willingness to believe in the worth of turncoat friends. I would eventually identify with him even more than with D'Annunzio. The engineer of a brilliantly reborn nation, his dream was uncannily close to mine. I am the first to criticise the excesses of Hitlerism. The tragic injustice was that Benito Mussolini came to be tarred with the same brush. Sometimes the blackjack and the bottle of castor oil must be displayed, as a dog is shown the stick. He was martyred because he could not see the evil in his allies, in men who called him Master while plotting his downfall. It heartens me in England today when many people at last begin to realise the virtues of those leaders. Even the thankless defender of his nation's pride, Sir Oswald Mosley, is finally accepted for the honourable patriot he always was: a man whose intellectual powers and imaginative instincts rivalled my own. But he must feel horribly bitter, sitting out his lonely exile in that rural French château, seeing all he warned against coming to pass. I was able to shake his hand only once, at a dinner given for Pan-Europeans in the late forties. It struck me then that a simple physical factor might have turned his destiny. As he thanked me for my support there were tears in his eyes; but what I noticed most, to my eternal discredit, was his hideously bad breath. I wondered if anyone had ever pointed it out to him. I spoke to his loyal lieutenant, Jeffrey Hamm, suggesting that an ordinary commercial mouthwash, if used daily, might seriously enhance his leader's fortunes. I was misinterpreted. Hamm ordered me thrown from the room. He told me if I ever returned he would see me beaten black and blue. So much for good intentions. Together, Mosley and myself might have saved Britain from her steady slide into socialistic fantasy. Mussolini did not have a breath problem, or if he did I did not notice it, since the heavy use of garlic and olive oil in the Italian cuisine (not to mention tomato paste and so forth) makes everyone smell the same. Hamm's anger did not stop me voting for Mosley in 1959 when he stood for this district as Member of Parliament, but by then the rot had set in. The negro vote won the day.

The twentieth century is a graveyard of well-intentioned heroes and unrealised dreams. When they talk about their mythical Six Million they never consider the real victims of Socialistic Reductionism: the magnificent, golden visionaries, the clear-eyed fighters for Order and Justice, the tireless, selfless Knights of Christendom who, from Denikin to Rockwell, took up the sword against Bolshevism only to be cut down by cowards, deceived by traitors, betrayed by followers who lost their nerve at the crucial moment. They dragged poor Mussolini to a black tree and hanged him. The mob, the very men and women who had worshipped him, tore at his body, ripped him to pieces, and years later they sold scraps of his clothing to tourists in the Via Veneto and St Peter's Square. Mussolini should not have trusted the Pope and his Cardinals. They pretended to support him, then as soon as the British and Americans began to win the War, they turned against him. Mussolini's nation was ironically the ultimate Roman Catholic state, more a product of its Church than any passing political fad.

If it had not been for Hitler, who took everything too far, Italy would now be the world's most advanced nation. But Hitler went mad. He turned against the Church. His hatred of Bolshevism, worthy of itself, clouded his judgment. His attempts to compromise with Stalin lost him those of us who had up to then supported his policies. The forces which conspired against him also conspired against me. Benito Mussolini was one of the many who recognised me for what I was. It was little, jealous, creeping people, whispering together, laying despicable petty traps, making miserable plots, who undermined the very rock on which our visions were founded. Those are Bolshevism's heroes: pale, mean faces with squinting eyes which never saw the light of the sun. I hear them whining outside the shop on Saturday mornings and I drive them off. They scatter and squeal like the cowardly vermin they are. I

hear them sniffing round my windows at dead of night, scuffling behind my doors, scratching on my walls. They melt away when I challenge them to display themselves. Would Mussolini or Horthy, Mosley
or Hitler melt at my challenge?

It was important to leave Rome and get to Paris as soon as possible,
before Kolya went on his way to America or Berlin, but the city was like
a possessive mother. Every time I gathered up the willpower to go, she
found something new to astonish me, to distract me from my purpose.
One morning, for instance, after we had spent half the night discussing
how best to reach Paris, we were making our way from the *Hotel Ambrosiana* to the *Café Montenero* just across the river in the Trastevere
quarter where we had arranged to meet Laura, who lived there. Along
the main street and heading for the bridge came a great double-decker
tram of the old 'Imperiale' class, with two more single-deckers connected behind her, rolling smoothly and very slowly in the direction of
the eastern suburbs. A triple-coach tram was not a particularly unusual
sight in Rome, though the double-deckers were more characteristic, I
was to learn, of Milan and London, but these were painted a jet, shining black, the only colour on them being their brasswork which was
polished to gleam like gold. The sides and the rims of the following cars
were rich with multicoloured flowers, forming wreaths, vines, loops,
while inside, dimly seen behind half-open black curtains, were the
weeping mourners, also in black. I had never seen anything like it, but
I realised it was a modern funeral procession, with the coffin, also covered in great masses of flowers, clearly seen on the upper deck of the
leading vehicle. The trolley pole hummed and crackled in a rather
light-hearted way, considering the gravity of the occasion. The driver
sat, in a special black uniform, stiff and sombre at the front (the 'Im-
periales' had only one driving seat and one set of stairs, at the back). I
was virtually mesmerized by the sight, removing my hat and paying
homage rather to the miracle of up to date technology than to the poor
corpse within. How readily, with so little fuss, did Italians adapt themselves to and advance the course of twentieth-century thinking! When
I told Laura and her friends about the procession they were amused by
my excitement. Apparently the funeral trams were a regular service in
many parts of Italy and elsewhere. I was realising how drastically cut off
from genuine culture I had been during the Civil War and my sojourn
in Turkey. In my enthusiasm for Rome's forward-thinking transport
system I did not this time forget to mention our urgent need to reach

Paris. I asked Laura if there was work I could do. I still had some money, but I should feel happier if I had earned what I needed for our first-class train fares. She told me she would consider the problem. That little square in Trastevere, just off the Piazza di Santa Maria, was an oddly quiet corner of the city, away from the crash and clamour filling Rome's main streets. The houses were like those one found in the country. Their walls were painted a faded, peeling pink or blue or green. The awnings of the cafés were like ancient parchment; they might have been there since the reign of Caesar Augustus. On many roofs were gardens so unkempt they appeared totally wild, while the faces of the inhabitants were faun-like. One felt one had been removed in time to a pagan past. Almost the whole of Rome had something of that same mellowed, sun-bleached quality, particularly in the early morning sunshine, or at twilight. When one was able to see the surrounding hills one could easily imagine oneself protected forever from all mundane problems obsessing the rest of Europe. From Trastevere it was possible to wander across a crumbling bridge to the Tiberina Island. On that tiny strip of land in the green-brown waters of the river stood a building (I think it was a monastery) apparently built up over the centuries. It contained fragments of the architecture of the past thousand years. Here Romans fished, tied up their boats and simply lounged on weedy slabs of stone, smoking and regarding those rooftops, like the dome of St Peter's, which could be seen beyond the trees. A few wild cats lived here, and presumably the monks (though I never saw them). Even the cats had a subtly different appearance to those which stretched their muscular little bodies in the sun falling on the ruins of the Circus Maximus. If Constantinople were a city of dogs, then Rome was a city of cats. You might easily have expected to find a Temple to Bubastes somewhere nearby. One rarely saw a building without a cat on a step or window. Orange, black, grey, brown, white, marmalade and ginger, they washed themselves, slept, made love, utterly uninterested in the swarming human beings, merely watching with neutral eyes those which came close, displaying wary curiosity if there was a chance of someone feeding them. They prowled over marble which had been flooded with the blood of martyred Christians; they defecated on granite carved to the satisfaction of the Imperial ego; they copulated beneath columns erected to the glory of Gods and Goddesses, and in some ways they symbolised the enduring spirit of the city and her population. Esmé found them fascinating. There were days when she would spend most of her time watching them with much the same expression as they watched others. Her eyes fixed, her little chin in her perfect hands, she breathed slowly, languorously, with unfathomable contentment. It was not only I who noticed. Laura would often look at her and frown, at once understanding and mystified. Even Fiorello the Futurist, full of his own eloquence and self-absorption, would sometimes spare her a curious glance and smile at me in bafflement at the ways of femininity. Yet I was not myself baffled; I felt I knew what she experienced. Perhaps I merely imposed my own imagination onto her, believing her capable of profundity of feeling which was in fact non-existent. She was, I admit now (though I would have denied it vehemently then) at least in part my creation: the apparent fulfilment of my deepest desires. A little of this occurred to me then, when she would look up suddenly and brighten with a smile as if in response to my unspoken command. But I refused to consider such implications. They were extremely distasteful to me. They remain distasteful, but I am not one to avoid the truth for long.

Through Fiorello we met the young man who was to prove a great benefactor in the years to come. Bazzanno's cousin, he lived and worked primarily in Milan but travelled frequently to all parts of Italy and many European cities. He was as handsome and as well-formed as his cousin was misshapen. Fond of severe tailored suits, he liked to show, as we used to say, a lot of cuff. His shirts were always apparently brand new and his silk ties impeccably knotted. His manicured hands were heavy with gold and his white teeth were also occasionally punctuated with gold. His name was Annibale Santucci. This flamboyant dandy was three or four years older than me. He had what in Kiev we called a 'Black Sea taste' for white suits, black and white shoes and lavender ties; though he could also dress more conventionally when the mood or the occasion demanded. Walking past the fountain in the Piazza di Santa Maria one misty morning we first saw him: or rather we saw his car. It roared into the square, a huge blue and red Lancia booming and yelling, filling the whole quarter with shocking echoes. Fiorello was with us. He turned to snarl at the car until with a cry of glee he recognised the driver.

'Balo! Balo!' he shouted, and was rewarded with a dove-grey salute before the car changed gear and went bellowing down an alley scarcely wide enough to accommodate it. Fiorello capered with pleasure, twirling his stick and throwing up his hat, but Laura did not seem so delighted. Esmé was merely puzzled. She returned immediately to telling Laura about a dress one of her friends had been given soon after she went to work for Mrs Unal. I had tried to check her, but it was useless. She was oblivious; so I shrugged and let things take their course. It was not particularly important what Laura Fischetti believed about us. We arrived at the *Café Montenero* and took our usual places. The little old man, who was the only waiter, emerged to wipe an already clean table for us and bring coffee and rolls. Fiorello was babbling on about his cousin. 'He'll have presents. He always has presents. You must meet him, Max. He loves the English. He did a lot of business with them during the war. And the Russians, too.' (He had made up his own version of our origins, which he retailed to everyone, and it suited me to humour him in this.) 'I wonder where he was off to.' His face dropped, then brightened swiftly. 'He's bound to look us up before he leaves Rome. He's an utter bastard. A complete crook. A monster. Laura disapproves of him. He is the epitome of the capitalist disease, she thinks. But she can't resist him either, can you, Laura?'

Laura shrugged. 'He's got a coarse sort of charm, if that's what you're saying.' She smiled then, mocking herself. At that moment the whole square seemed to vibrate and the howling, the vital whine, the blustering, joyful roar approached from somewhere within the maze, as if a pack of drunken baboons had invaded a Trappist retreat. The red and blue Lancia sprang clear of an alley, skidded in a turn which threatened to bring the rear of the monster crashing into our little enclosure, and stopped. Out of the huge front seat rose Santucci, peeling off his kids and his calf-hides, smoothing back his hair and replacing his helmet with a grey fedora. He pulled his camel-hair overcoat over his shoulders. He dragged his wide brim down over one eye. He touched his lips with a silver cigarette holder, kissed the silver head of his perfect stick and sprang like a demigod to the pavement. He was splendidly unashamedly, vulgarly romantic; enjoying his own antics as much as he knew we must enjoy them. He was the perfect foil to the equally grandiose but tiny Bazzanno who, with monkey-like agility, leapt to balance on the rail, then bounded to the street to embrace his cousin. Almost six feet tall, Annibale Santucci possessed the rather crude good looks of a music-hall juvenile. He would have been a perfect film star. He shook hands with me, kissed the tips of Esmé's fingers, made a number of general compliments which came automatically to his tongue and immediately ordered us wine and more food against our insistence that we had already eaten enough and it was too early for alcohol.

'Never say "too early",' he cautioned dramatically. 'For you will quickly find it has become "too late" if you do.' This, too, had the sound of an aphorism he had frequently found convenient, likely to impress the cautious. Indeed, it impressed Esmé. She laughed loudly and received, for a moment, his lordly attention. Then he drew up a chair and proceeded to tell us about Naples. He had had business on Ischia, the island beyond Capri in the Bay, where his mother and father now lived. There had been a boatmen's strike and it had cost him a fortune to find some means of reaching Ischia: 'A sailing boat. A prototype for the Ark!' Then coming back he had been unable to get benzine for his car because of the strike at filling stations. He laughed. 'This is the prelude to a true anarchism, when every individual is forced to fend for himself. We'll have our own petrol pumps, our individual water supply, our own cow, repair shop. Unless we check this trend, we shall soon know utter boredom, with time only to maintain ourselves and our machines. Fiorello! Laura!' An elaborate flourish and he produced from the inner pocket of the camel-hair coat two black velvet cases, handing one to each. Within were matching diamond-studded wrist watches, a man's and a woman's. 'My friend from Marseilles was grateful. He said to give these to my mother and father!'

'You are a dutiful son,' said Laura sardonically, putting the watch upon her muscular wrist and admiring it.

'What use would they have for these? To tick away their autumn hours? Pointless!' He turned, all contriteness, to us. 'Please, please forgive my rudeness!'

Esmé and I would have forgiven him anything. His smile was calculated to disarm, and did not fail him. Fiorello told him we were planning to head for Paris but were a little short of money for the ticket. Did his cousin know of any engineering work available?

Santucci became matter of fact. He presented his open palm to the sky. He spoke casually. 'But you will come with me. Keep me company, eh? I can be there in not much more than a day.'

I mentioned our large amount of luggage, but I was greedy for the Lancia. I began to feel the tiny shivers of pleasure with which I always anticipated the Escape of Motoring.

Santucci shrugged this off. 'My car is of infinite volume. She has been designed by my kinsman Bazzanno to conquer the ordinary limitations of space. Did he not tell you?'

I looked towards the car, almost believing him. Fiorello smiled and was unable to answer.

'He is too modest!' Annibale clapped his cousin on the back. 'This ugly little dwarf is the greatest metaphysical inventor in Italy.'

Laura kissed him on the cheek. You are addressing a real scientist, Balo. Signor Cornelius has designed and flown his own planes. He invented the Death Ray used against the Whites at Kiev! You read about it, surely, in the newspapers.'

Annibale bowed from his chair. 'Then you must certainly come with me to Paris. I'll milk your brains on the way!'

I accepted. A perfect opportunity, it solved several problems for us at once and meant we should probably have far less trouble at the border. I recognised a man who was used to living on his wits, who was familiar with the situations we were likely to face. Expecting only a vague reply, I asked him what his business was. I said he seemed very successful.

'I buy and sell. I travel. I am in the right place at the right time. Just like now! I buy cheap ewes in Tuscany and sell them dear in Sicily where with my profits I buy wine and sell it for a fortune in Berlin. But it is all on paper, Signor Cornelius. I scarcely ever see the commodities themselves.' He extended his manicured hands for my inspection. 'Not a spec of grime, eh? Not a callous. I am an entrepreneur. I learned, in the War, the secret of being a good general. Never get to know the troops. Keep everything as abstract as possible. I, myself, was a driver. I drove trucks and armoured cars. There were, of course, business opportunities attached to my trade. After the War I simply kept on driving. Wherever I stopped I did some buying and selling. Now I have no money to speak of, but I have good suits, a wonderful car, and plenty of girls. I am not respectable – but I am respected. Better, I am needed. I have a flat in Milan I hardly ever see. Otherwise I do not even have to pay rent on a permanent office. There is my office!' And he pointed to his Lancia. Lines of heat rose from her bonnet; her scintillating enamel glowed from under a coating of fine dust.

Laura said with a small twist of her lips, a kind of smile, 'He's telling you he's a gangster. In Ischia he was probably selling his mother and father.'

'What can you get for an old man and an old woman these days?

258

They're out of fashion. I am a common gangster, if you like. But as an artist I am unique. Vouch for me, Fiorello!'

Laura nodded vigorously. 'You're certainly unique, my darling.'

Fiorello insisted his cousin was the finest artist to emerge from the War. 'Art is action. Action is Art. The logic's simple.'

'And like most simple logic it's ridiculous.' But Laura was laughing now.

'I wish I could come to Paris with you.' Fiorello looked disgustedly about him. 'Rome's a stale cake. Bite her and she'll break your teeth. Too little's happening. She needs to be softened up. With dynamite. I blame the government.'

'The government,' Santucci winked at a passing tom, 'is doing its best.'

'Too tolerant! We need bloodshed in the streets!' And Fiorello was off on his favourite horse, galloping and whooping. 'Where are the Cossacks! Signor Cornelius has fought in Russia. He's half Russian. Or is it half Jewish? He's half something. He knows the wonderful sport true tyranny provides. Where are our own tyrants, this country which once provided the world with its finest despots? Are they too timid to come out of hiding? I'll accompany you to Paris and discover a genuine Napoleon. *Nicht wahr?*'

'Then be ready by next Wednesday. That's when I leave.' Santucci threw some bank notes on the table. He said he would pick us up at our hotel. We would travel via Milan and through Switzerland. Did we know the Alps? It would be a wonderful experience. 'There is a truly stale cake. But the frosting is magnificent.' The weather was perfect for motoring.

I was already relishing the prospect of travelling again, especially with Santucci. I have always loved large, expensive cars; to enter one is to forget every care. The few problems I still had would be left behind once the Lancia was moving. Even if I had not originally planned to go to Paris I would probably have accepted the lift, just for the experience of being in the car. Esmé, too, was excited, although she had grown attached to Rome, her cats and her coffee shops. 'Will Paris be as wonderful?' she asked. I promised her it would be. Fiorello bent over us, neighing with pleasure. 'Ah, my dears. Tonight, by way of celebration, I shall take us all to the *Caffè Greco* in Via Condotti. You shall meet new friends. Everyone at the *Greco* is both foreign and an artist, so you will feel at home. Then we shall go to the cinema. Are you familiar with Fairbanks? A marvellous comedian. And Chaplin? And *Fantomas*? They're all together tonight! Then tomorrow we'll borrow a car, or a horse and trap, and spend the day at Tivoli. I intend to make sure that you see everything so that you'll want to come back to us as soon as possible!'

'But you're going with us, Fiorello,' said Esmé.

He bared his yellow teeth in a grin. 'My dear little girl. My cousin knows me. I cannot live without the air of Rome. She and I are of the same stuff. We are symbiotic. Beyond Tivoli I begin to dissipate. If I went as far as Milan, now, I should fade to nothing. But you will go to Paris for me. I shall think of you there. And you must write, so that I can enjoy the experience through you.'

He was a bizarre little creature. I was almost inclined to believe he spoke the truth.

That evening at the cinema I got up between films to visit the lavatory. As I came back to my seat in the semi-darkness I saw a squat, familiar-looking figure sitting in the *secondi posti* section near the front. I was convinced it was Brodmann. I spent the rest of the programme glancing in his direction, hoping he would turn so that I could see his face. I became afraid. Next I thought I saw Bimbashi Hakir, and Yermeloff. I knew for certain that Yermeloff was dead. I felt the agony of the Cossack whip. I was pursued by vengeful Jews. Carthage schemed against me. I was glad when we all rose and shuffled out into the warm, brilliant air of the Roman night. Soon we were sweating with the effort of eating huge plates of fettucine and fritters at the *Pastarellaro* in Via San Grisogono, not far from the Piazza di Santa Maria.

I think we remained drunk the whole of the rest of our time in Rome. On our last night, Fiorello embraced me with regretful affection. 'You must return to us next year, Max. Italy needs you. Laura and I need you. In Rome you will find exactly the resources you require. Believe me. Come back to us!'

'As soon as my affairs are settled in England,' I promised.

We parted sadly and more than a little unsteadily.

In the morning Esmé was up before me. I was yawning and groaning alternately. She parted the curtains, leaning over the little wrought-iron balcony, waving into the street. 'Look, Maxim, darling. He's here!'

Santucci had kept his promise and had come in a huge, glistening new car to meet us; only it was not the Lancia. From somewhere he had provided himself with an American Cunningham almost the size of a truck. It was an outrageous green with brass trim. Its horn was loud enough to herald the Day of Judgment and its throbbing engine was of the very latest design, producing over 100 hp. Santucci sat at the wheel smoking his cigarette, chatting amiably to a horde of ecstatic little boys. Other vehicles in the street slowed down to look at the Cunningham. He was in danger of creating a traffic jam. When he saw us on our balcony he beckoned for us to join him. Our luggage was ready, and we dressed rapidly while porters took our trunks, loading them in the back of the car. We discovered the bill had been paid, presumably by our flamboyant benefactor. All I had to do was tip the porters. We both climbed into the front seat, with Esmé in the middle, as Santucci opened the car's throttle, let go the clutch and steered his vast machine between the gaping drivers, almost comically pleased with the attention he received. Since he gave no explanation for his change of cars, I felt it tactless to press him for one. We were soon passing through Tivoli again, where he stopped for a few minutes outside a little brown house and went inside, then re-emerged with an expression of satisfaction. (Tivoli was the scene of an important moment for me when I returned to Italy at the Duce's own request. I had originally been so naïve I had thought it a beer-garden, like the ones I had known as a boy in Arcadia.)

After Tivoli the roads were frequently bumpy and often very dusty, but some were the best I had ever known. It was Italy, after all, which was the first country to build a specific *autostrada*. We made astonishing time. The Cunningham could touch over eighty miles an hour and Santucci pushed it to the limit whenever the chance arose. He talked constantly for the first two or three hours, as warm, yellow villages and vast tawny fields went by; then he cocked his head, listening to me with an expression of grave concentration as I replied. We were talking mostly about cars and transport in general, a subject of abiding interest to both. Esmé did not seem to mind. She stared ahead, tranquil and happy, enjoying the sights of the countryside, the sensation of movement. At around noon Santucci asked us to get the basket which sat on the seats behind us. From it we dragged chickens, sausages, bread, wine, sliced meats and bottles of Zucco from Palermo, a wine to match that of the best French vineyards. The warm Italian wind in our faces acted with the alcohol to relax us further. Our silk scarves kept most of the dust from our mouths and the goggles Santucci had given us protected our eyes. 'These are the ultimate cars!' said our host, peering forward because he thought he had seen a policeman (the speed limit in Italy was then 30 mph). 'The best the War produced, eh?' He shared some of Bazzanno's notions. He too had been a friend of Boccioni. He had been at the painter's side when he was wounded. 'Boccioni needn't have died. It was a stupid business.' He would not elaborate. Although he appeared to dramatise everything in his life and make some kind of verbal capital from it, he in fact had a strong sense of discretion which I would call 'gentlemanly.' Later I came to recognize this trait in people of his type, but then it was fairly new to me. I am still uncertain why he chose to take us to Paris with him. No matter how often I think of it I usually conclude he was moved by amiable generosity, by altruism and by a simple wish to enjoy our company on a long journey. I grew to like him very much, though I was still not used to people who saw virtue in War.

Perhaps because Italy had experienced comparatively little fighting on her own soil, her ex-soldiers looked at things differently. Certainly Bazzanno and Santucci were not the only Italians to return from the front invigorated, anxious to find fresh worlds to conquer, fresh stimuli for their creative impulses. Italy gained impetus while other nations sank into exhaustion. Something in the Italian blood will make the most of any grim situation. They kept their idealism; they deserved to press on, to conquer Africa and destroy the threat of Carthage, which they, better than any, knew so much about. Their Achilles heel would be the Roman Catholic church. Without it, they could have owned an Empire from the Atlantic to the Red Sea. The Son is the Son of Light, but the Father is the Father of Ignorance, wiping spittle from his chin with an ornamental crook, his mitre falling over his eyes to blind him, while his limbs tremble with senile palsy. This is the way the old suck life from the young. They deny us our power; and they are jealous of our vigorous movement, the quickness of our brains, the joy of our bodies. The Curse of the Latin countries is unreasoning loyalty to outmoded papal institutions and a marked willingness to compromise with Judaism. You do not hear of such compromises from the Patriarch of Constantinople.

The country was a thousand shades of gold, amber, old ivory, sprawling like a lazy lion beneath the sun; our nostrils were filled with the scent of petrol and wild poppies, of lemons, mustard and honey, our hearts with an innocent relish for simple freedom. Nobody pursued us. Brodmann was a ghost invented by my over-tired brain, as was Hakir. Turks and Reds could be a million miles away, fighting in a different universe. Europe's complacency in those days seemed more like genuine optimism, an apparent willingness to reject past vices and favour modern virtues. I was even heartened when, just outside Milan, I saw the decorated caravans of a Gypsy tribe beside the road and was reminded of Zoyea, my first love. These gypsies symbolised the continuation of Romance, an element of the past which did not threaten, which spoke to me of permanence without decay. They were camped beneath a wall of thick hedges, their horses cropping the grass of the verge and their thin dogs running back and forth looking for scraps. This nomad people had survived a thousand European wars. They spoke a language older than Sanskrit and had come from the East not as conquerors, or as merchants craving power, not as a proselytisers for a dark religion, but as natural wanderers full of ancient, simple wisdom. I have never understood the prejudice expressed towards this people. The so-called gypsies, the travellers of the motorway camps, are merely a shiftless, thieving riff-raff, too lazy to work, too slovenly to seek the responsibility of permanent housing. These degenerates have merely failed to meet the ordinary challenges of urban living. The true Romany, with his dark curls and his gold earring, his violin and his sixth sense, has always attracted me. The women, with their bold eyes and aggressive stance, are amongst the most beautiful on Earth. I was glad to see them. I waved at them as we raced by and wished they had waved back. In my view Hitler went too far when he extended his War against nomad invaders to the harmless gypsy.

Santucci had already apologised for Milan, which he said had nothing to match Rome, but to me the city, when we arrived, was a revelation: factories and massive office-buildings, a sprawl of general industry which took my breath away. Vast numbers of trams running smoothly on intricate track. We had nothing so huge in Russia, not even Kharkov. Milan stank of chemicals and hot steel, of smouldering rubber and blazing coal; her streets were a jangle of metal, of roaring machines, of gloriously energetic people. So much of the architecture was modern, Milan might have sprung up overnight. I had been told the city was ugly; instead I found it magical in its dirty, productive splendour. Here an engineer could work and create, taking his materials from close at hand, drawing on abundant expertise. To me Milan represented a twentieth-century land of plenty, a Garden of Eden with infinite possibilities. It is no wonder this city was the true birthplace of Mussolini's dynamic new movement. It was the pulsing core of a splendidly impatient nation; a dynamo to power a mighty dream which would become the concrete expression of a true Industrial Revolution. As in Rome, I could have remained longer, breathing in smoke as another breathed ozone, filling my lungs with the essence of metal and oil. But Esmé hated it. She said it left dirt on her skin. It was frightening and too grey. It was noisy. I laughed at her: 'You must get used to it, little beauty. It's your future as much as mine.' She sank back into her trance until the evening, when Santucci took the road again. We spent the night at a tiny pension just short of the Swiss border. We could see the Alps rising before us. Santucci said they were the battlements of a fortress: a fortress of bland certainty, of neutrality, of bourgeois safety. 'The most magnificent mountains in the world protect the world's dullest human beings. It is a paradox which captures my imagination. If it's cleanliness and peace you prize, Signorina Esmé, you should not have to look anywhere else. In Switzerland people complain if a cowbell clanks above the legal level or the tulips grow an inch too tall. It is the very essence of bovine egalitarianism, of the middle-class desire for comfort at any cost. And it is the death knell to Art. In no other country is boredom so thoroughly identified with virtue!'

We crossed the border next morning and were treated to disapproving civility. With innocent efficiency they studied our papers not for clues to our criminality or radicalism but for evidence of penury. Presumably they found us rich enough to be admitted for a day or so to their mountain fastness. To be poor in Switzerland is regarded as the gravest breach of taste. We drove along smooth, well kept roads. Esmé admired the neatness of the flowerbeds, the spotless lack of character in each of the orderly towns, the freshness of the paint on chalets and precisely thatched farmsteads. I half expected to see men outside their barns with brushes in their hands, washing their cows as today the suburb-dweller washes his car. It was strange how in Switzerland three dominant and vital cultures could come together to form, as it were, a vacuum. Possessing neither tension nor vision, Switzerland was the symbol of one particular future; the future desired by those same small minds who eventually sought to diminish my own achievements and thus preserve the status quo. When, that evening at sunset, we crossed into France at a little town called Sainte-Croix, Esmé yearningly looked behind her; Lot's wife expelled from some sanitary Sodom.

Santucci seemed as relieved as I to leave the oppressive orderliness of Switzerland. He began to sing some popular song in a loud, unmelodic voice. Like most Italians he believed he was naturally musical, just as negroes labour under the delusion they are all naturally rhythmic. The wind was cool in our faces now and the white lamps of the car outlined massive oaks on both sides of the road. There were no obvious signs of the recent War, but since my geography was so vague I was unsure if the conflict had reached this part of France or not. The sweet air and the silent little towns contradicted the impression I had of Ypres or Verdun: here things looked unchanged and unchallenged for centuries. The smoked goggles we all three wore had the effect of mellowing the landscape further.

With the confidence of familiarity, Santucci swung the car along narrow roads and round sudden bends, singing all the while. As we swept through the villages he would call out names dimly familiar from the newspapers. He knew France well, he said. 'This is where I received my business education.' He had been attached to an aerodrome while on duty here in 1916 and had made himself an indispensable supplier of whisky and gin to Allies and Axis alike. 'I'm no narrow nationalist but a practising international anarchist!' He laughed and passed Esmé the wine bottle from which he was drinking. She seemed to have forgotten her regret at leaving Switzerland and drank deeply, wiping her mouth on the back of a lovely little hand. Santucci winked at her. She attempted to wink back. She squeezed my arm. He asked me to put a cigarette into his holder for him. I did so and lit the fresh 'Hareem Lady,' the brand he favoured. 'Why are you going to England, Signor Cornelius? You seem to prefer, like me, to travel. Are you visiting your family?'

'I have a wife there. And business, too. I wish to register a number of patents. Everyone has told me it is best to do that in England.'

'You should go to America instead. Most of my brothers and cousins are there. But it's much harder now, I suppose. You can't get in officially. Not if you're Italian. They think we're all arsonists!'

I smiled. 'I'd heard you were.'

'By nature, certainly. But by training we are very law-abiding. Our loyalties are to the church and to our families. People frequently don't understand.'

We stopped that evening in Dijon where he insisted on buying us a dozen different pots of mustard. He was dressing a shade more conservatively now, perhaps out of respect for the French. 'One should always buy mustard in Dijon and sausage in Lyon.' He was evidently well-known to the little woman who ran the pension. She welcomed us through her low doorway into a hall of white plaster and black beams; Villon himself might have sprawled, pen in one hand, grog-pot in the other, upon her polished wooden floor. When we were seated at a carved elm table near the inglenook she brought us our first real taste of French food. Even France's worst critics forgive her arrogance and un-called-for attitude of superiority when they taste her cuisine. Esmé smacked red lips and filled her tiny stomach until it was round and hard. Her eyes became dreamy. She was in heaven again. Our hostess smiled like a benign conqueror as she cleaned away the dishes. Santucci exchanged a few polite sentences with her and then we all went slowly up the narrow stairs to our chambers.

In the secure confines of our timbered room Esmé prepared herself for bed. I laughed at her. With her papers and creams she was like a child playing at being a woman. 'This magic goes on forever,' she said as she climbed into the four-poster, 'but isn't there a price, Simka?'

It was unlike her to indulge in such considerations and I was unrea-soningly surprised, almost angry. Her remark seemed like ingratitude, though I was by no means sure why, and I found that I was disturbed, impatient with her. Surely this was misplaced pessimism I curbed my bad temper, however. 'I think the price has already been paid. By you. By me.' The bed was white and soft in the warm darkness of the little, low-ceilinged apartment. I enjoyed an infantile sense of safety. 'All of it is my reward for my sufferings. And you are sharing in it. You, too, have suffered.' I fell back on my pillows with a grunt of pleasure. They were edged in intricate lace. She grinned and leaned against me, her mood untroubled again. I appeared to have reassured her easily enough and consequently reassured myself. Esmé had no business voicing un-comfortable notions. With her firmly in my arms, I went to sleep.

Santucci at breakfast was eager to get on the road. He had a friend to meet in Paris. 'An eminent soldier with a small army for sale. I shall need a larger car on the way back.' It was a joke, we realised. He was wearing his formal suit of wheat-coloured silk. I envied him his ele-gance, for my own clothes were rather inappropriate to this part of the world. I decided to equip myself and Esmé with a new wardrobe as soon as we settled in England. I had grown self-conscious about my Russian clothing which had seemed so modish in Odessa and rather ahead of the fashion in Constantinople. Here, however, it felt heavy, shapeless and dowdy. Again I was tempted to put on a uniform, but realised it might look inappropriate worn by a man travelling with a British passport. Some of my existing luggage could be sold and what it fetched invested in one decent suit. Such details I would decide in Paris. I planned to return to my Russian identity and acquire papers for Esmé establishing her as my sister from Kiev.

When I considered the difficulties, the amount of work I should have to do, I became almost reluctant to reach Paris. I consoled myself that I should be in London within a week or two. I still found it almost impossible to believe only a couple of hundred miles separated me from Mrs Cornelius and her beloved Whitechapel. London, of all those great cities, had seemed remote, legendary: as abstract as my unrealised dreams. Now Rome and Paris took substance, but Odessa and Constantinople became merely a hazy fantasy from which I had emerged into reality. I had conserved our cocaine as we travelled, not wishing to risk famine in Paris. I had used no more than a pinch or two in the morning after waking. Cocaine has always had the effect of bringing me down to earth, forcing me to examine the realities of life. I determined to apply myself to these problems as soon as we were established in the city. I would seek out Kolya, in the hope he had not yet left. Kolya would help solve everything. I also tried to imagine what life would be like in Whitechapel. I knew a quick thrill of excitement mixed with some trepidation. I remembered my last unfortunate meeting with Mrs Cornelius, her expressed disapproval of my liaison with Esmé. My friend was bound to change her mind when she met my little girl.

As we went out into a beautiful, soft morning of pine-filtered sunlight, driving through Dijon's picturesque streets, a cheerful Santucci described the new car he meant to buy as soon as it came on the market. An electric racer, he said. Citroën were developing it. We drove now through thinly forested hills, vivid yellow crops of mustard. Occasionally we passed an old château, a distant brown stone village, a farm. Passive livestock grazed in the fields, adding to that sense of timeless permanence so characteristic of rural Ukraine before the Revolution. Might my Ukraine one day return to her former perfection? Surely, I thought, the corpses and the broken gun carriages must soon sink into the cornfields and be forgotten. How could I know? How could I anticipate Stalin's capacity for cruelty and hatred? He placed a sentence of death upon an entire country. The Bolsheviks starved the granary of Russia! They mined meadows, forests, whole villages to blow up the population, together with any invader. As I have observed many times, people grow so used to conflict and terror and death they cling to them as certainties, in the way the more fortunate cling to old, peaceful rituals. Why do most human beings resist any change, when change usually means their continuing survival? Santucci asked me my opinion of the Citroën Electric. I told him some of my own ideas for cars. These, too, would not be dependent upon benzine. They might be powered by rockets or beam wireless. I even had plans in my case for a car driven by tiny charges of dynamite.

Naturally, he liked this notion best. 'Dynamite! There's your answer, Signor Cornelius. From dynamite our New Europe will arise like a phoenix. All this' – He waved a magnificently gauntleted hand at the little hills and streams – 'must be blown away. The job was only half done when they called it off to arrange that miserable Armistice.'

I could see little reason for such destruction. 'There's room for everything in my future.' I was somewhat pious.

'To produce a genuinely different world one must wipe out every memory, every sign, every clue to the past. History must go!' He was laughing. We took a humpbacked bridge and flew for a few seconds before returning to the road. The long bonnet of the Cunningham glittered in the sun like the barrel of a Krupps cannon. He even pointed the machine as if it were a gun. He took joy from his control.

'You're a Bolshevik, then!' I shouted over the engine. 'You should visit Russia. Go soon. They're already putting your theories into action!'

He took this in good part, shaking his head and grinning. 'But with so little style, my friend. If a thing is to be done properly, it must be done with grace! Any Frenchman would tell you that much.'

I had met such dandified nihilists in Peter. Most of them had died or been imprisoned in the first days of Lenin's triumph. Not only did I refuse to take Santucci seriously, I felt a certain pity for him. If he ever experienced real revolution he must surely become an early victim. He was far more a bad poet than a bad politician, however, and one can always forgive bad poets. Power is the last thing they want. They are usually too frightened by the responsibility involved. Sometimes this does not happen: then a ferocious combination is achieved. Our good-humoured driver however was in every way amusing and entertaining.

His charm remained as potent as ever. I wished he would decide to go on to London or Berlin. While one moves one does not 'stew.' The Escape of Motoring is best when one has no true idea of one's destination.

Yet when Paris eventually appeared, my uncertainty vanished. We approached through suburbs, sometimes on a slight hill, sometimes in a shallow valley. I had never expected to see the Eiffel Tower so soon. It dominated the city: a wonderful pyramid of steel and cast-iron: the nineteenth century's salute to us, the inhabitants of her future. Here was the city of Jules Verne, who had been chiefly responsible for my decision to express myself through the medium of science and technology. Here the engravings from my *Pearson's Magazines* came to life, while elsewhere the monumental tributes to Napoleon, his arches, tombs and museums, and the glorious palaces of the great French kings, almost unearthly cathedrals and churches, were ordered like the model of a pure, eighteenth-century mind: a little too rational, perhaps, a little cool, but with a superb and almost simple tidiness. We drove through suburban streets in the evening mist, with the sun red and huge above, this sense of orderliness countered to a degree by slums, buildings in poor repair, featureless apartment blocks, narrow alleys and busy, chaotic traffic quite different to Rome's, yet moving at the terrifying pace common to old Petersburg's. Paris at twilight began to bloom with electricity. She was a city of light. A city of delicate glass and fine traceries of stone. Her gas lamps were a vibrant yellow. Flaring charcoal from her street stoves glowed the deepest possible red. I thought I could hear music, hear her heart pounding as Santucci drove his monstrous Cunningham deeper and deeper towards the centre. Paris smelled of rosewater, coffee and fresh bread. She smelled of motor exhausts and garlic, of chocolate and wine. I looked towards Esmé and saw there were tears in her eyes. She was now truly looking upon Heaven.

Faithless creatures, we forgot Rome at once. Paris instantly became our new love. Santucci's letting forth with a piece of Rossini did not disturb us. Bells pealed from Notre Dame. Boats hooted on the Seine as we negotiated the bridges of the Isle de la Cité. Paris was herself a symphony of ordered movement and colour. The scarlet and gold sails of the *Moulin Rouge* were the spokes of a cosmic wheel. The Cunningham boomed along Rue Pigalle and turned back along Boulevard Magenta towards Place de la République, with Santucci swearing he could never get to grips with the streets of Paris, until we pulled up suddenly just beyond the green, gold and purple doors of Cirque d'Hiver, the little amphitheatre housing the Winter Circus in Boulevard du Temple. Children playing on the pavement around the plane-trees gathered as always to Santucci, staring at the huge car. It might have been a vision of the Madonna. Their silence was broken by his salute, a squeeze of his horn, then all let forth with their questions. He sent one boy into the little hotel, whose sign was illuminated by a single purple bulb. Out came the plump porter. He wiped his lips on the back of his hand which could easily have been a penguin's wing. Waddling up to us, nodding, swaying, he was delighted to see Santucci. Our friend called him 'sergeant,' shook hands and spoke of the trenches. Santucci seemed to exist in a network of relationships, some business, some personal, some filial. He never dealt with a stranger. Even the man who filled his petrol tank knew him as M'sieu Santucci, mentioning a common back complaint and the new cure he had read about in *Le Figaro*. Now I listened while the porter asked after his cousins in America and the weather in Naples. He was introduced to Esmé and myself and we might have been Santucci's blood relatives, judging by the ceremony with which he presented us. We, too, shook hands. He said he was at our service. Would we require supper? Santucci said we had an appointment to dine elsewhere. The porter blew a whistle. Out came another boy to guard the car while we were shown to our accommodation. Our room contained an old double bed, a washstand, a couple of chairs and little else, but it was perfectly adequate. After the luggage arrived we washed and changed, but soon Annibale Santucci knocked on our door to beg us to hurry. Back we went to the limousine. With horn blaring we drove faster than ever through the glamorous streets, back towards Notre Dame where the massive cathedral shone in golden glory over the black water. Across the bridge again and along Saint-Michel, into a narrow backstreet near Saint-Germain. Parking the Cunningham half on the pavement, half in the road, Santucci told us we had arrived. Disembarking, we entered a discreetly illuminated restaurant whose windows were curtained from the street, whose interior, lit by gas, was warm as yellow ivory. White linen and silver, potted palms, hushed air, revealed this place to be a temple of food, one of thousands, I was to discover, in the city. From the far end, in a curtained alcove, a thin, elderly man rose to hold out a hand, delicate as a dying orchid. The hair of his head and his moustache had the appearance of a fine mould. He smelled like a flower past its prime. His small, sad smile made me think him more priest than soldier. Feebly he gestured for us to sit with him, though he seemed upset at our presence. We were cousins, Santucci told him, from England. We would eat with them, but the business could be discussed later. The old man accepted this gracefully enough, though plainly the arrangement was not much to his taste. Folding his fingers before him in a gesture of disciplined patience he bowed again to us. His skin was probably painted here and there; it had a parched brown quality to it where it was not unnaturally pink. His hair was sparse. Only his English tweed suit, his excellent tie, did not look worn out. Indeed they seemed unnaturally new. He wore them like a borrowed carapace. He was never introduced by name, though I had the impression he was an aristocrat, a high ranking general. Any curiosity I had about him was dispelled by the quality of the meal. It was superb. We had oeuf en meruerte to begin, a cassoulet as our main course, some Neufchatael cheese and crême brulée. While Esmé and I sat drunkenly at the table, too full to speak, capable only of grinning stupidly. Santucci and his client moved away to the bar where they ordered their cognac. The business took hardly any time at all. When it was over the soldier did not rejoin us at the table, but slipped away. Santucci returned, insisting we have some Armagnac 'to celebrate.' 'All settled,' he said. 'And, as you see, I did not have to inspect the army personally. No money changed hands. Yet everyone is satisfied. That is the essence of international finance.'

'Where's the army going?' It was rare for Esmé to ask a direct question.

'Going?' Santucci pretended astonishment. 'Why, to a war, of course, pretty dove! The details aren't important, I assure you. They are soldiers. They know only fighting. One provides a service – in this case a war – which will satisfy their blood lust and keep them from doing much harm to honest civilians. But it is all a question of telegrams and the telephone. By now I have a good commission waiting for me in Benghazi. The secret is to have pockets of credit all over the world, then travel towards them. Spread the money as far as you can. Have people pay it into banks in London or Lahore. It gives you an incentive to visit places you might otherwise never go to. Once there, why a fresh opportunity usually presents itself. If someone is looking for a stockbroker, I am a stockbroker. If they want to buy corn, I become a corn merchant. It's easy enough to be a middleman. One relies on the impatience, the greed, the uncertainty of one's fellows. People would rather deal with a jack-of-all-trades who is personally attractive and willing to talk the dirty business of money and transportation, than with an expert who is aloof. Since the goods rarely pass through my hands, I remain innocent of any misuse or minor breach of the law. I'll never have the massive fortune of a real entrepreneur, but I live well and, most important,' he winked at Esmé, 'I have girls in every port.'

'I can't think why more people don't do what you do.' She was honestly puzzled. His matter-of-fact tone had convinced her. She had missed his irony.

He stroked his perfect waistcoat then broke wind behind his hand. 'Because they are not Annibale Santucci, little dove.' He expressed sober regret. He was profoundly sympathetic of everyone else in the world. 'I'll take you back to the hotel. I have some personal business now. You'll forgive me if I don't invite you.'

The bill was paid in banknotes of intricate beauty.

We saw our friend briefly the following morning, when he kissed us both farewell and whispered to Esmé that the hotel bill was settled for the next two weeks. 'By then you'll be on your way to London.' He turned to me. 'I wish you luck with your inventions, professor. Write me a postcard. Invite me to stay with you when you have a place. There must be business I can do in London. It is after all a city of thieves – a nation of thieves, by God!'

Laughing, I told him I did not have his address in Milan. Where could I write to him?

'To Mendoza's in Rome. He'll always find me. To *The Wasp*. Any of those regular cafés.' He paused by the door to draw a piece of hotel notepaper from his inside pocket. 'I have written down the address of some friends. Wonderful people. You'll fall in love with them. They're exiles here. I've written a note. Visit them if you can.'

We watched the gigantic green automobile move into the traffic of the Boulevard du Temple. She was like a ceremonial barge negotiating a fast flowing river. Her horn sounded. Her engine began to rage like a million demons as Santucci accelerated towards the animated statuary of the Place de la République. It was a beautiful morning. We did not go back into the hotel but, hand in hand as always, we turned down the Rue de Turenne in the general direction of the Hotel de Ville. A light rain was falling through the early autumn sunshine. Everyone had umbrellas except us and we did not want one; we welcomed this gorgeous rain as enthusiastically as we welcomed everything Paris offered. Most leaves were still green, but here and there they were golden or brown. There was a strange atmosphere, a mixture of sweet melancholy and a hectic, celebratory air. In Paris, since November 1918, a huge party had been taking place, twenty-four hours a day.

Before long we should be invited to join that party. We would unhesitatingly accept. For us at least the Jazz Age had its beginnings in Paris.

Eleven

PARIS IS NO COMMON HARLOT. She is still a queen-whore, disdaining pimps, dismissing suitors with careless flattery, knowing that if her beauty fades a little year by year, she still remains elegantly attractive, for what nature takes away, cosmetics can easily replace. Paris of course has no heart of gold. She is a cold, mercenary goddess, pricing sexuality as precisely as she weighs confectionery; and she can be surprisingly prim, because fundamentally she remains a provincial matron. She sets high store by appearances. She knows the exact value of every pretty sentiment and she retails Romance by the gram. She is lace starched into stone. She is a corset braced with bone. She is a lure, a fly, a scent; a whiff of delight designed to part you from your cash with a girlish wink. The wink alone is worth a hundred francs. Charm has its commodity price; it would be quoted on the Bourse if someone ever dared reveal the truth. But no one ever will, or will ever be listened to, at any rate: for Paris, more than any other city, is dedicated to obfuscation, disguise, misleading decoration, since where there is ambiguity, as everyone knows, there is always money to be made. Few Parisians would ever accept the truism that the more one finds talk of love, flirtation, declarations of undying sentiment, the more one will discover rapacity, venality and hard cruelty. Soft words often exist in direct ratio to the greed they disguise.

Paris has been a grand courtesan for hundreds of years. She has suffered indignities (what harlot has not?) and even known periods of enforced virtue, domestic dullness, of half-hearted remorse; but she has recovered herself soon enough, flashed her scarlet petticoats, put on her most ravishing hat, displayed herself in all her well cut coquetry with its tiny betraying touch of vulgarity, the suggestion of a bawdy pout; but how outraged she is when her virtue is questioned! How she shrieks and threatens the Law. Moreover, if she fails to receive satisfaction by this means, she will forget her ladylike pretensions altogether. She will rush to attack. Yet possibly the person she threatens refuses to be frightened by her: whereupon she becomes her soft-voiced, placatory, eyelash-fluttering, melting professional self, full of crooned apologies and endearments, offering comforting luxury in her arms. Later, if she feels she can succeed without detection, she will murder her supposed conqueror while he sleeps, strip him naked and toss his body from her carriage into the river.

Paris is a wistful, acquisitive lullaby. She is able to pretend to good manners with all the skill of the truly arrogant. She preserves her looks at any cost, whether to friend or foe. When she has fallen to an enemy it has been with a glance over her shoulder, to make a virtue of surrender: it is hard, but what else can I do? I am helpless to defend myself. This harlot is a screen upon which men project their supreme fantasies, invest her with qualities she does not actually possess, which no city could ever possess, but which their imagination demands *should* exist. And women are defeated by her, too. She takes them by the arm, she shows them the secrets of her beauty, she pretends to make them confidantes while plotting their profound destruction. Occasionally, if her plans all fail, she will let herself go. Her hair falls prettily out of place. She slumps. Her little dress speaks of impoverished courage, she sings with hopeless, sardonic determination of betrayal, death and the end of romance. And so again, with this affectation of vulnerability, she wins sentimental allies, makes new conquests, until it is safe to be her old, jaunty, grasping self again. She knows how much to drink and exactly what she should eat. She is dedicated to appearances above principle, graciously applauding the appropriate lie while impatiently frowning upon inexpert honesty. And how she loves to entertain soldiers; preferably her own, but any soldier will do. She has a relish for gold braid and silver medals; the sniff of wounds and gunpowder from a safe distance is sufficient to excite her without alarming her; the brave sound of a marching band, the curl of an unblooded banner, the prance of the parade-ground stallion are as good as cash in hand, for she knows the weakness of soldiers and can price them out to the last sou. She loves fame. She pursues lions. And if no lions exist, she will manufacture some out of whole cloth. Where there are inflated egos, there are wallets to maintain them. And equally she worships intrigue; the more secrets there are, the more golden louis there are to buy silence. So her politics are conducted in hidden chambers, in bedrooms, in alleys and well guarded houses, while the rhetoric of her deputies is excessive in its glorious idealism, its talk of honour, glory and morality. Paris does not possess the shallow cynicism of the wounded young; frequently she will feign a horror of cynicism, make a huge protest in favour of the virtues of sentiment and humanity, but by her actions, like any very successful harlot, she is actually cynical to the core, and the only value she places on affection is what she can store in her private safe. Paris will rob the stranger more prettily, if she has to, than any other city. She begins by taking your money and then, if she finds it is worth something to her, your heart, your talent, finally your life. In contrast to Paris, all other cities are peopled with amateurs. She looks upon rivals with contempt or loathing. If they are brash or obvious or crude, she is offended, fearing their bad name might attach itself to her. She does not wish the game to be given away. She has been called an aristocrat, a madonna, an angel. She believes one day she will wake to discover she no longer need maintain a pose and will overnight have become a genuine gentlewoman, a dignified dowager like Vienna or Prague, able at long last to age gracefully, her power gained not by means of blackmail and flattery, but from the world's respect. It is impossible. She knows it is impossible, but she clings to the hope as another might cling to her religion.

In Paris rather than in Rome one discovers the final expression of refined Catholicism. The Italians are notoriously careless of their history; they once ruled the world and know they could do so again if they cared enough; but are too easily bored with power. Even Mussolini began handing over the reins of his nation almost as soon as he gained them. His death was a tragedy. He had already shrugged and walked away. He might have wound up living a happy life, running a shop next door to mine, perhaps a little restaurant or a dry cleaner's. And Rome is a fierce mother. When she tries to sell her favours she stands on a broken monument lifting her skirts and shouting for customers, just as if she were hawking hot chestnuts or ice cream. She has neither the patience nor the ambition for suggestive pouts or coy glances. She would rather get it over with and have something approaching a good time while she did it. She is and always has been more pagan than Catholic. To her, religion is worthless unless full-blooded and passionate. French priests, famous for their intellects, their cunning manipulations, their calculating and controlled ferocity, are symbolised best by Cardinal Richelieu who foreshadowed Lenin, a fanatic willing to destroy any individual who, by his very individuality, threatened the abstract idea of the State, his actual religion: himself. By definition a dedicated Catholic seeks power: every law his Church maintains speaks of it. The demand of women to multiply has the twofold effect of subjugating wives and increasing the numbers of children over whom power can be exercised. How beautifully the French have shaped their religion to their needs. It is a religion which makes no real demands upon its followers, save that they maintain appearances. There are certain prices to pay for the continuation of the proper façade: the occasional discreet penance. But God, to them, is an eighteenth-century Grand Seigneur, turning a blind eye to any crime so long as His own convenience is undisturbed. He possesses the practical rationality of the merchant, like so many French philosophers, and keeps neat accounts. And He would rather cathedrals be restored and decorated and organs not play out of tune, than have vulgar people throw themselves upon the floors of His houses in a flurry of unseemly hysteria. The French have refined their religion to its highest possible point. The Italians have left theirs alone in all its half-pagan incongruity, while the Spanish, who never quite lost the habit of human sacrifice, are barely restrained from soaking His altars in the blood of bulls and goats.

With what chill and lofty dedication did Richelieu destroy the Huguenots! Probably not a single expression of emotion ever passed his lips. He understood their point of view. But the Spanish Inquisition pursued its butchery with genuine lust, with hatred and hot cruelty, glad of the opportunity to fulfil its love for ritual murder; honouring its dark God with the screams of a million souls in the extremes of anguish; sending the stench of burning flesh to grace His quivering, bovine nostrils, for it is Moloch Himself who hides behind the mask of the Spanish Jehovah. Here lurks Carthage and all the sons of Shem, the descendants of Babylon, Assyria, Canaan, Aramea, Arabia, Ethiopia and Israel. The bull-gods grumble and prowl through the streets of Barcelona still.

The knives of the French are needles to prick a man's life out of him, inch by tiny inch. They pretend friendship. They made me the toast of the town. I was one of their lions for a while. But Parisians only pretend to accept the manifestations of progress; to them these things are toys. One has to make bright, noisy, colourful things to impress them. Paris has a whore's taste in trinkets. Santos-Dumont became their idol because his balloons and airships were gaudy and buzzed and because his attempts at powered flight were spectacular, highly publicised, conducted in machines of multicoloured silk! Much the same can be said of all their flyers, who had dash and filigree and well cut uniforms, but were rather poor at application, like the show cavalry of the nineteenth century. They were interested, as always, in appearances rather than pure science. To prove myself to them I was forced to become something of a Barnum (one of their favourite Americans). I was very quickly a darling of the Left Bank. I met every artist and intellectual worthy of the name. I was courted and proposed to by both men and women. I smoked opium in the houses of fashionable hostesses and sniffed 'coco' in Lesbian garrets. They took me up. I was their Monsieur 'P', their 'Professeur Russe,' their 'Petit Colonel.' Esmé and I were Hansel and Gretel wandering into the Palace of Versailles. We were overwhelmed. From Santucci's friends, the exiled anarchists called Peronini, both of whom sported dyed red hair and masculine evening dress at all hours of the day, we moved into the company of criminals and radicals. I shook hands with Lamont himself. I shared a table with Antoinette Ferraud and Wanda Sylvano at Laperousse. The great astronomer Lalande would lunch regularly with us at the Café Royal and there I met his cousin Apollinaire, just returned from four years in the Foreign Legion. But for all they protested undying friendship and admiration of my creative genius, not one could help us in our efforts to reach England.

By the end of two weeks my optimism was waning. The British Embassy refused me the most ordinary kinds of information; the Russian émigré organisations could promise me nothing and had no concrete news of Kolya. Paris was awash with Russians, many of whom had credentials even better than my own, and the authorities were sick of us. Esmé, I could tell, began to have doubts about me, particularly when we were forced to move from our pension and take two miserable rooms in a street little better than an alley in Montparnasse. Rue de la Huchette consisted of a number of seedy bars and so-called 'dancings'; there were cheap fishmongers, butchers and sellers of mouldy fruit and vegetables. Whores infested it. The alley was a rendezvous for every clochard on the Left Bank; at least one of the buildings was completely derelict, taken over by tramps and beggars of the worst sort. Our rooms were nearby, at the top of a crumbling house, scarcely any better than the squalor from which I had, in Galata, removed my Esmé. I was conscious she must be thinking this. The only advantage to our quarters was that they were high above the noise of the street. Esmé at first made the best she could of it, even sweeping and tidying and cleaning, but she quickly became depressed and lassitude set in. She implored me to spend more and more time outside, in the lively company of our new friends, inhabitants of the Montparnasse and Montmartre cafés, who at least were always generous with their wine. I think they meant well, those who swore they could provide Esmé with proper papers. They took photographs; they examined my own Russian documents. They claimed friendships with the highest and lowest: a master forger in St Germain, the secretary to the British Ambassador. But they were useless. I hated to be so dependent on them. There were no easy engineering jobs for me in Paris as there had been in Kiev or Pera. The French Army had disbursed thousands of half-trained jobbing mechanics upon the nation and most of those could find no work. My only hope lay in finding a backer for one of my designs. I knew it had to be an invention to impress the light-minded Parisians, something which would seem sensational to them. So I said I intended to build a great airliner able to fly to America with a hundred passengers in record time.

Esmé begged me to be cautious. 'You have no plans for such a ship, Maxim! We must not attract the police.'

I reassured her. I laughed loudly. 'What can the police do? Prove I am not a legitimate inventor? My little dove, if I get a bite – then it will be the work of a few hours to draw up the plans. In fact, if it will improve your state of mind, I'll start at once.'

I began to mention my invention around the cafés. I spoke of the enterprise's automatic success, how huge fortunes would be made from it. 'Indeed, it must be considered as a sound commercial venture and nothing else,' I would say.

American tourists had virtually taken over Montmartre and the Champs Elysées. The faster they could be brought in, and in the greatest numbers, the better for everyone, I said. Tourism would from now on become one of the main sources of any great city's revenue.

By pawning my fur coat I paid for new visiting cards advertising *The Franco–American Aerial Navigation Company* and these I judiciously handed out at every sensible opportunity. My reputation slowly infected the Parisian consciousness. Many said they already knew of Professor Pyatnitski, the Russian aircraft expert, the same boy genius who had built Kiev's Purple Ray and single-handedly held off the Red Cavalry. One of Lalande's journalist friends interviewed me for his newspaper and in due course a large piece appeared about me. It exaggerated, but in my favour. I was described as 'Le Quichotte Cossack,' a man of science and a man of action combined, an adventurer to rival Munchausen. I still have the cutting. It is from *Le Review Coucou* for 15th September 1920. This was by no means the only publicity I received. Everywhere toasted me in print.

My chief fear at the time was not that I should fail to survive but that Esmé would become bored and disenchanted. I had, after all, failed miserably to keep my wonderful promises. We were overly dependent on others for our entertainment. Since Rome, she had developed a profound craving for the cinema and the money was not always available to pay for the latest Pickford or Sennett. As my anxieties increased I paradoxically grew plump on the free dinners supplied by bohemian friends. What was worse, Esmé felt ashamed of her clothes. Even Paris's artists had a certain style and their women looked elegant no matter how eccentric their frocks, and try as she might Esmé could not emulate them. I assured her she looked wonderfully attractive to me, but women never trust their lovers in these matters.

Meanwhile I persisted in my enquiries about Kolya. I was discovering Paris to be a city of people who cannot bear to say they do not know something. So many pretended to have heard of him; a dozen Russian exiles claimed to have met him in some nearby thoroughfare or to have dined with him only a night or two earlier, but most of these turned out to be rogues, only interested in getting money from me. Possibly because our Russian nobility had always looked to France for its manners and its language, Paris seemed to have almost as many émigrés as Constantinople. Russian restaurants were in vogue. Russian artists gave exhibitions of their garish paintings. Russian dancers shocked a sophisticated world with bizarre choreography and costumes, with hideous music. Those very elements of decadence which ushered the triumph of Lenin were now, like dangerous spoors, infecting France. As a result – and who could blame them – Parisians became wary of us. I had made an initial mistake in admitting my nationality. I should have been better off if I had claimed to be a Jew or an Egyptian! Either

I was besieged by bluestockings telling me soberly how much they 'sympathised with your country's terrible plight' or I and my fellows were regarded as members of some gigantic circus come to town merely for the purpose of entertaining bored sensation-seekers.

Paris will seize on any passing fashion. I heard only recently that her latest craze is American comic-strips. The Minister of Culture awards prizes to the illustrator of *Little Orphan Annie* while Paris's municipal authorities renamed the Avenue Roosevelt. Now it is Boulevard du Batman. So thoroughly do these modern French make nonsense of any claim to cultural superiority! They imitate the worst American and English pop music, the worst cheap fiction, the worst films. They presumably identify this trash with a vitality they themselves lost over half a century ago. I had hoped De Gaulle would pull his country together (though he seemed a pompous dullard when I met him in 1943). His reign is marked by student riots and an increase in violent pornography. He failed to subdue Algeria as he failed to put his harlot capital in her place. (More sinister rumours concerning his race and real loyalties I discount for lack of evidence. It is significant, however, that he proved inept at reducing Moslem power abroad yet thinks nothing of welcoming the Arab and the Turk to his capital! As a rational man I refuse credence to the conspiracy theories so prevalent these days amongst Western Reds. The truth is that the real conspiracy has been hatching for centuries, so perverting the Christian world it is nowadays barely recognised!)

Our material circumstances grew worse and worse. Esmé wept at the grey sheets, the filthy windows. She said we should never have left Rome. Italians were certainly more generous than the French. The news from Russia was appalling. Our loyalist armies, pushed back at every turn, received scant help from the Allies, now involved with the Turkish question. Newcomers from Southern Russia, questioned by me for news of my mother, my friends, had nothing to offer. The poor souls were still dazed, still 'within the nightmare.' It seemed as dangerous to try suddenly to wake them as it was to wake a somnambulist. There were plenty of Russian language newspapers of all political colours, from rabidly monarchist to violently nihilist, reporting opinion rather than fact. Russian publishing companies and Russian information centres, together with certain cafés operated and patronised entirely by Russians, dealt chiefly in gossip and blind hope. These exiles and their Berlin counterparts were the lucky refugees. Elsewhere, hundreds of thousands were crushed into civilian concentration camps, dying of disease or sheer despair. Even amongst these pathetic refugees Lenin and Trotski had their supporters. Though the appalling consequences were visible everywhere, French socialists plotted a similar fate for their own nation! Perhaps resistance to all this would have been stronger if our newspapers had not published true stories of atrocities so ghastly the average Parisian could not accept them, dismissing them as partisan lies. I insisted they were true, for I had seen such things with my own eyes. I had suffered at the hands of Red irregulars, barely escaping with my life! But I soon learned to say nothing. During that everlasting, frenetic post-War party, people hated you if you spoke of death and terror (or even less dramatic realities). All they wanted was the latest American jazz, the newest dances, the most outrageous fashions. The heroes of the War were already forgotten. Sweating Negro banjo players were hailed in their place. And when the cost of these fresh sensations proved too high, they demanded money from an exhausted Germany! (In due course Germans grew tired of such demands. They marched back into the city, whereupon Parisians merely shrugged, doubled the price of drinks to German soldiers, and danced on.)

And Esmé was as eager as anyone to join the party. Her relish for the good life became alarming. Being young, she needed to go out and about, but of course I could not find the necessary cash. Soon I was forced to sell a valuable patent for a few hundred francs. My 'agent' was an Odessan Jew called Rosenblum. It was all I could do to force myself to be civil to him, stop myself automatically drawing back from his slimy hand when he put it, with an assumption of fraternity, upon my arm. He told me where I must go to meet his client.

It was in Montmartre, in a tourist Bal du Danse, one seedy afternoon while the Angelus bell clanked in the Savoyarde towers of Sacré Coeur. I was fond of this church. It seemed transported from somewhere further East. The usual press of visitors had dispersed. The bandstand was empty, the chairs stacked, the bar closed, yet the place still stank of the cheapest perfume, the youngest wine. I stepped inside. The door was closed and barred by the man I had agreed to meet. He was also Ukrainian, but from Marseilles, where he had lived since 1913. M'sieu Svirsky wore a loud pin-striped suit, a white trilby; his hands were covered in heavy gold rings crudely set with semi-precious stones, mostly crimson. He said he was a broker for important Southern industrial interests with branches in Paris. He was no more than ten years older than me but his face hung with loose skin, like a bloodhound's, as if the flesh within had wasted away suddenly. This gave him a sad-eyed look. His eyes in actuality were hard brown stones. He asked me about the invention I had for sale. He stared as he listened, his face wrinkling, mouth smiling, as if he felt obliged to pretend intelligent interest in my description. This peculiar, agitated little fellow relaxed immediately when I indicated I had finished. Then he glanced nervously about the bar. Plainly he was uneasy, perhaps wishing to behave correctly but unsure what was expected of him. He reminded me of a half-trained spaniel. Yet he had money in his wallet, together with a piece of paper I must sign: a contract bearing the name of a Marseilles engineering firm. It promised royalties when my safety brake was commercially sold. (This device was attached to the accelerator of a car. It automatically operated when one lifted a foot completely off the pedal.)

We chatted about Odessa and the good times we had known there. He was familiar with some of my favourite cafés. He recalled 'Esau the Hairy,' remembering the name of the accordion player who had been a regular for so long. When I mentioned my Uncle Semya he was impressed. Everyone knew Semyon Josefovitch. 'So you're his nephew. It's a small world.' He grinned. 'I'd better have another look at this contract. You signed it too readily. Why didn't you go into the family business?'

'He sent me to technical college instead. He wanted me to be a lawyer, but I had no vocation for it.'

Svirsky accepted this soberly. 'Your family doesn't gravitate naturally to Law.'

I asked if he knew my cousin. Svirsky said he thought Shura might be in Marseilles. 'No,' I said. 'He was killed. I heard.'

But Svirsky was certain Shura was alive. 'He turned up a couple of years ago, asking for a job. I suppose he'd deserted. It would have suited him to let people think he was dead, eh? He switched papers probably, and got on a ship. It's commonly done.'

Was all the world being resurrected? I was amused by this thought. It sounded like Shura. I asked Svirsky to tell my cousin to get in touch with me if he felt like it. We had quarrelled over a girl. I regretted falling out. I was sure he did, too. Relatives should stick together in these times. 'Oh, indeed,' said Svirsky. 'The Ukrainians are still very thick in Marseilles. Since the War, of course, the old trade with Odessa has dwindled almost to nothing. It was a great shame. Everyone did well out of it.' He yawned, far more comfortable now he had my measure. We agreed things could never return to normal in Odessa. The Golden Age had passed. Against a volume of evidence, only Paris attempted the maintenance of her first optimistic flush of 1918. Apocalyptic political ideas threatened every aspect of European life, promising new wars, new régimes. Svirsky still hoped the Bolsheviks 'would relax a bit' as soon as they had definitively won the Civil War. 'They're bound to open the ports for trade. They'd be mad not to.' But he had almost no direct experience of that particular form of insanity. I told him I was less optimistic. Those people would destroy whole nations who threatened to give the lie to their lunatic myths. Svirsky insisted 'things will settle down.' I thanked him for his money and left the Bal du Danse after shaking hands. It would be several years before I should see him again. Then he would freely admit my foresight.

My automatic brake kept us for more than two weeks. We bought splendid new clothes. We saw *Das Kabinett des Dr Caligari* and were horrified at its madness. This modernistic 'expressionism' provided every evidence that in defeat Germany had grown deeply neurotic, almost psychopathic. Even more ordinary, less irrational, films reflected an identically morbid obsession with death and mental sickness. Esmé enjoyed *Halbblut*. One would never have guessed it to be the work of someone who later gave us the magnificent *Metropolis*, *Die Nibelungen* and *Die Frau im Mond*. My preference at the time was for *Die Spinnen* which was altogether more wholesome. We shared a taste for Charlie Chaplin, however, and visited *Easy Street* and *The Immigrant* several times. My own favourite was Mary Pickford, who reminded me in so many ways of Esmé. We saw *The Little American*, *Rebecca of Sunnybrook Farm* and *M'Liss*, which whetted my appetite for the stories of Bret Harte, in turn making California an imaginative reality for me. I think my favourite Mary Pickford film was *Daddy Long Legs*. I told Esmé if I were not already in love, Mary Pickford would claim my heart. Esmé said she thought Mary was far too 'good and sweet.' I laughed. 'Then she's an ideal rival for you!'

In Paris America came to mean far more to me than ever before, thanks to D. W. Griffith, who brought his country vividly to life for me in the greatest film ever made. For a while we were both obsessed with *Birth of a Nation*. We saw it at least twenty times. As a direct consequence I began to realise what potential for social and scientific progress there was in the United States. If I had made a film, it should have been that one. Griffith alone showed the world that his country was not comprised merely of pilgrims, savages and gangsters. His ideals were uncannily close to mine! I promised myself that as soon as my airship company was successful, I should go at once to the USA and personally thank him. I would suggest he turn his attention to the problems of Russia. One film, showing the horrors of Bolshevism as graphically as Griffith had shown the evils of the scallawags and carpetbaggers, who incited the negro as cynically as Lenin incited the Mongol, and the whole world would rush to my country's rescue. (Ironically, the Bolsheviks themselves realised this. With almost admirable cunning they employed the plagiarist Eisenstein to present their own distorted case. With the clever imitative skills of the Jew he looted Griffith's work, fashioning a paean of praise to his bloodthirsty masters, presenting them in a ludicrously heroic light: a fanfare of histrionics which made the mob, so loathed by Griffith, seem somehow noble! This revealed that techniques are never good just for their own sake. It depends who manipulates them. That is why an inventor, too, must always be careful. These days I keep my inventions to myself. Too many people, over the past fifty years, have abused them.)

Paris continued to dance. Every street maintained its nightclubs, whorehouses, bars. Jaded people poured in from all over the world, eager to join the party. Americans could be found everywhere. They had money to spend, though typically they always claimed poverty. In my favourite Left Bank cafés I began to meet international journalists, painters, poets. I asked those from the USA if they knew Mary Pickford or Lillian Gish, but they could give me less information than I could find for myself in the film magazines. Some of them (mostly New Yorkers) did not even know who Douglas Fairbanks was! It would be like a Russian not having heard of Stenka Razin or Tsar Saltan. I pitied them their deep ignorance. They had come to Paris frantically anxious to prove themselves 'high-brows', reading impossible French novels by Gide, Ouida and Mauriac, salivating over the filth Willy-Colette issued in the guise of literature. At the same time they spoke grandly of the 'popular taste' and flung their limbs about in imitation of black cottonpickers experiencing the last throes of some lethal palsy. They laughed at me, I knew; yet I was far more in touch with the pulse of the age than ever they could be. They did not know it, but they actually represented the past. I was a true Man of my Time. They were merely trying to relive a nostalgic, nonexistent *fin-de-siècle* fantasy. Nonetheless some of them condescendingly bought the shares I issued for my Aerial Navigation Company. It was on this money, carefully accounted for in a notebook, that we lived. Esmé again began developing headaches; a lassitude similar to the condition which had overwhelmed her on Kazakian's boat. At first I would stay with her, working at our only table, drawing up my plans, writing to anyone who could help us get to England. Gradually it became necessary to go out more, to leave her with an oil lamp and the second-hand novels I bought for her on the nearby quays. Money had to be gathered somehow and it was not always easy to pay for our necessities. The price of cocaine alone in Paris was exorbitant. It was suddenly a fashionable drug amongst the demi-mondaine; waiters openly sold it in nightclubs and restaurants. I became panic-stricken, certain Esmé must soon decide to leave me, for she was not meant for poverty or drudgery. London was set aside. I had no choice but to spend more time than I liked seeking a main financier for my great airship. People were increasingly wary of anyone wanting their money, no matter how sound the scheme. Parisians were concentrating on taking it from others. I grew at once horribly obsessed and miserably over-tired, following one wild goose after another. All the while Esmé withdrew deeper into herself until even the cocaine was of no help.

I prayed I should find Kolya. I left messages everywhere. I pinned them on notice-boards in émigré hostels; I left scraps of paper with strangers. I took advertisements in the Russian langauge press. Meanwhile I wrote to Mrs Cornelius, to Major Nye, to Mr Green, begging them to send us the fare to England and to use their influence with the English authorities both there and in Paris. I was making myself a laughing-stock with the Russians. They would mockingly ask me 'Has your Prince come yet?' or 'Is the airship flying today?' It was hideous. At last, just to avoid this sort of cruelty, I began to deny I was Russian.

One day I was standing outside the Cirque d'Hiver, near the hotel in Rue du Temple where we had originally stayed, waiting for the artistes to emerge from their afternoon rehearsals (for I had heard that many Russians were now performing as equestrians), when I definitely saw Brodmann, dressed to the nines in black homburg and overcoat, striding rapidly towards Place de la République. He hailed a cab with his umbrella and got in, waving to another man to join him. The man was more casually clothed, in brown cords, evidently a French intellectual.

He carried a bundle of newspapers under his arm. It was obvious to me he was a radical. Smiling and laughing Brodmann gave no attention to the outside world. He was plainly doing well for himself, as that sort will. Doubtless he had made himself out to be a revolutionary hero. Almost certainly he was a Chekist bent on infiltrating some non-Bolshevik organisation. Shivering, I immediately hurried home. Esmé was pale, eating little, mouthing her way through something by Gautier. I could say nothing to her. I was terrified of distressing her further. But I stayed in for the rest of the evening. Next morning I left my face unshaven with the intention of growing a beard.

I caught a tram for the Montparnasse Cemetery. There was a theatre near it and a café, called something like the *Pepe Napa*, which had once been a favourite of Italian actors but was now the haunt of Russian anarchists. I had sunk so low I now rubbed shoulders with scum. It was for Esmé's sake. I would do anything to escape our present squalor. Descending from the footplate of the tram I crossed the street to the café, the railings of the cemetery at my back. Sunshine was pale in the cool autumn air. The café had only just opened for business. Inside waiters were still taking chairs off tables. The only customers were grouped at the bar drinking little cups of coffee and sharing out their cigarettes. Some spoke a dialect familiar to me – the country speech, part Russian, part Ukrainian, of the Katerynoslav *gubernia*. I knew enough of this dialect – at least its inflections – to greet them. Nonetheless they regarded me with surly suspicion. They had probably been in Paris for several months and they still had something of the wolfish look I associated with their kind. Most wore ordinary cheap working-class clothes, though a few still had the vestiges of uniforms – a cap, a pair of trousers or boots. They were unimpressed when I told them I was from Kiev. They warmed a little upon learning that I had ridden with Nestor Makhno. The little *batko* was still their greatest hero. A tall, thin faced man with a pronounced limp, his left arm hanging uselessly at his side, asked a couple of questions plainly designed to test me. He was satisfied by my answers. 'What were you?' he asked. 'A Green? Or one of those city anarchists who tried to tell us how to fight the Reds?'

Instinctively I decided to tell them the truth. 'Neither,' I told him. 'My sister was a nurse with Makhno's army. Maybe you knew her? Esmé Loukianoff?'

'The name's familiar,' said the tall man. 'Pretty little blonde?'

'That's her.'

'So what were you doing?'

'I'm a teacher. And an engineer. I was with the education train until the Whites captured me. They locked us up in a synagogue to die. Then some Australians came through and took us to Odessa. Hearing that the Whites had overrun the whole place and that Reds were shooting anarchists, I got on a refugee ship.'

They did not wish to hear tales of heroism, these men. Many were themselves the defeated remnants of so-called Hulyai-Polye Cossacks. They had no call to point the finger at another escapee.

The wounded one was called Chelanak, evidently a German 'colonist' in origin, with a Jewish tinge to him which made me mistrust him. He said he had been left for dead after a Bolshevik ambush at Holta in September 1919. 'We were winning, too, then.' He paused and stepped back from me a pace of two, as if inspecting a painting. Then he continued. 'I crawled to some woods where a troop of Greek infantry mistook me for a White officer on account of what was left of my jacket. I was sent to Odessa, put on a hospital ship. For Bulgaria, I think. But I got off in some little fishing village which we stopped at for no good reason. I tried to get back – it was near the border. I was captured by renegades who were overcome by Reds before I could be shot. I got away again, first into Poland, then down into Vienna and eventually into France.' He frowned, his voice trailing off. 'But I know you, I'm sure.'

I had never seen him before.

The café was beginning to fill with veterans. He leaned against the bar and sipped his coffee. His next statement had no particular relevance to what he had just said. He spoke significantly, however. 'I was with Makhno when we executed Hrihorieff in full view of his own army. Remember that? Chubenko fired the first shot, Makhno the second, I the last. We did it because of the pogroms, I think. I do know you! You were one of the Barotbist liaison people we found with Hrihorieff. Brodmann!'

This was the most dreadful thing he could have said. I felt instantly sick. I tried to smile. He put down the journal he held and snapped his fingers. 'Brodmann. Someone said you were in Paris.' He looked about him.

I was near screaming. 'I am not Brodmann! For God's sake, man!

My name is Cornelius! It's true I was captured by Yermeloff, but I got away. I was Hrihorieff's prisoner for a few days, that's all! Then I rejoined my sister in Hulyai-Polye. I swear it's true.' I was appalled. I had seen Brodmann only a day before. That in itself had been nerve-racking. But to be mistaken for the dreadful, treacherous Jew by ex-bandits was worse. 'I met someone of that name. He was a Bolshevik, though he posed as a Barotbist for a while.' I regretted even this admission as soon as it came out of me.

'Brodmann's comrade, then? I know your face. I know it.' He was not particularly unfriendly. It was as if he did not personally carry any hatred for his old enemies.

It was unlikely his tolerance would be shared by the others. I know I was sweating, almost pleading with him not to pursue this line of association. My hands implored him. I had never seen this half-dead creature before and could scarcely believe the accident which led him to associate me with one of the people I most feared and despised in the world. I tried to shake my head. 'Which Brodmann? Red beard? Alexandrovsk?'

Chelanak began to laugh. 'No! No! I saw you at the meeting! Day before yesterday. Near Rue St Denis. I thought you were Brodmann, then.'

'I wasn't at a meeting, comrade. Please don't go on with this!' Was Brodmann, after all, to be the death of me?

'Brodmann claims now he helped kill Hrihorieff, did you know? You didn't kill Hrihorieff, did you?'

'Of course not.'

'I apologise. We get Chekists in here quite frequently. You must have a doppelgänger, comrade. Unpleasant, eh? A doppelgänger who's a Chekist!'

The chief danger seemed over, but I remained nervous. I had only come to this place in the hope of getting news of Kolya, who had had some anarchist associates in the old days. More and more exiles were crowding through the door, speaking every Russian dialect, as well as French, Polish, German. They carried their rolled newspapers casually, as they had once borne swords and rifles. I began pushing through them on my way out. Chelanak plucked at my coat. 'But you are Brodmann's friend, surely? Still a Barotbist, maybe At least tell me what you're here for!'

'Prince Petroff,' I said.

'Why the hell are you looking for a Prince here?' He was beside me again. 'We're a bit nervous of spies, Brodmann's friend.'

'I'm no friend of Brodmann. The only Brodmann I knew was caught and shot by the Whites in Odessa last year. As for Petroff, he's done as much for the cause as anyone – and suffered as much. Is there now a class qualification for the Movement? If so you had better make plans to expel Kropotkin!' I hated all the eyes now on me. I willed myself to speak levelly. 'You're a fool, Chelanak.' I pushed at him, striking his dead arm which began to sway like a pendulum. 'I can't understand why you're picking on me. I've done you no harm. We were part of the same group not so long ago.'

He took hold of his wounded arm with his good hand and stopped its swaying. He looked at the ground. 'I apologise, comrade. We've no Petroff here, unless he's changed his name and his caste. I'm not sure what got me going. Just something in you.'

Both of us were panting slightly. We stood outside the café now, staring towards the cemetery through the iron railings on the other side of the road.

'You look a bit like Brodmann to me,' he said, compounding the insult. 'But I can see you're not him. You haven't the clothes or the complexion of a Chekist. It's obvious in the daylight. I apologise again. What can I do for you?'

'I'd hoped to find Prince Petroff, that's all.'

'Only exhausted and defeated anarchists come here. We share a common bond of bitterness and self-pity.' He smiled, straightening his cap. 'Maybe that's why I mistook you for a Chekist. You don't look crushed enough. Go in peace, comrade. But be careful. Your face is wrong for this kind of place.' His mouth softened. 'Your eyes have too much future in them. These cafés are citadels of a lost past. We don't have the energy to take another step forward.'

I do not remember saying goodbye to him. I ran up the Rue Froidevaux, past the theatre. I was running not from Chelanak but from Brodmann. I was sure the anarchist was right. Brodmann was a natural candidate for the Cheka. He would delight in destroying me. At that moment I could have run all the way back to Rome. I had to be a fool so passively to have accepted Santucci's lift. I had thought it would be easy to get to London from here. It would have been better to have remained in Constantinople. It was imperative, I thought, at least to get out of Paris, possibly to the South or to Belgium. From there we could choose Holland or Germany. I would sell all my clothes. Every treasure I had retained. I found myself in the Luxembourg Gardens with their thin, unfriendly trees. The place was far too exposed for me. I dashed into the Boulevard St Michel and its crowds, was almost hit by a tram and at last reached our alley. It had become a sanctuary. I was seriously out of breath by the time I got to the top of the stairs. Within, it was as gloomy as ever. Esmé, sitting up in our grey bed, read an old *La Vie Parisienne* and merely nodded as I entered. I went immediately to our little store of cocaine to pull myself together. She still had last night's papers in her hair. She was turning into a slattern and it was my fault. Could Brodmann, I wondered, have come specifically to Paris to seek me out? The Bolsheviks had assassins in every major city. Their job was simply to wipe out those who had escaped them in Russia.

For once I was glad Esmé gave her entire attention to her magazine and did not see, thank God, my anxiety. How was I to tell her we must flee? She could only grow worse and it would be impossible to travel at any kind of speed with her an invalid and Brodmann in pursuit. He must surely be aware of my presence in Paris and since I had left my address everywhere in the hope Kolya would eventually be given it, Brodmann or one of his Chekist agents might discover it at any moment. I prayed they would spare Esmé. My first decision was to take my Georgian pistols to the expensive shops on the Quai Voltaire where tourists bought their old Louis XV chairs and Napoleonic medals, their carved saints looted from churches destroyed during the Siege. It was a short walk for me, along the Seine. I was bound to get enough for our rail fares out of France. However, I moved slowly. I felt I was renouncing the last vestiges of my heritage, selling my birthright, betraying a friend. But I had no choice. Refugees all over Paris were making exactly the same decision.

I believe I was singularly blessed in those days by a somewhat flamboyant and depraved Guardian Angel, the same who had started me into the bohemian Petersburg world and introduced me to Kolya. He now appeared, shrieking and waving his long, limp arms, on the Pont Neuf where it joined Quai de Conti. It was as if he had sprung from one of the grotesque buttresses of Notre Dame itself, dressed in a bright yellow cloak, green cravat, blue velvet jacket and white Oxford Bags. From habit, my first impulse was to avoid him; then I shrugged as he leapt across the roadway, cloak and trousers billowing like the silk of a deflated balloon, and seized me. He hugged me to his monstrous chest and breathed peppermint vodka into my face. He still had his exaggerated good looks, his theatrical speech and gesture. It was also obvious that his lust for me (first felt on the train when I was a boy travelling from Kiev to St Petersburg and the Polytechnic) was utterly undiminished. It was the ballet-dancer Sergei Andreyovitch Tsipliakov. 'Your own Seryozha, my darling Dimka!' He kissed me passionately on both cheeks and then again on my forehead. 'Oh, Dimka! You are not dead! I am not dead! Isn't it wonderful? How long have you been in Paris? You don't look well.' He held me firmly in his huge hands and inspected me. 'I told you Paris was the place to be and you remembered! Wasn't I a good judge? I came here in '16 with some of the other Foline members. To entertain the troops. And I've been here ever since. Lucky, too, don't you think?'

I seemed to remember he had once been absolutely firm that I should stay in Petersburg. I wanted to know how he had managed to reach Paris when it had been almost impossible for Russian civilians to travel. 'My dear, Foline is a genius. Heartless, selfish, thoughtless, but a genius. He talked someone into believing our performances would improve the morale of the troops fighting in Flanders. And they let us go. About half of us, anyway. They wouldn't have me, dear, in the army. And I didn't pout about it. A tremendous piece of good fortune. We're loved by everyone in Paris. I've had offers from Diaghilev and from that plagiarist Fokine. Not only did he steal Foline's name, he's stolen almost all our repertoire. But it doesn't matter. There are hundreds of marvellous composers here, as you know. Where are you off to, Dimka dear?'

Having gathered that Seryozha was doing well, I had begun to consider my ideas. Perhaps I could borrow the money I needed, or at least sell him some shares in my Airship Company. I told him I was merely out for a stroll, whereupon he insisted we must go to a nearby café, L'Epéron. 'I was on my way to it anyway. It's marvellous there. Everyone's so handsome and beautiful. Do you feel like an omelette? They have wonderful omelettes.'

We strolled past box after box of secondhand books lining the embankment then back up to Boulevard St-Michel, as crowded as always. Seryozha seemed to know half the people in the street. L'Epéron was one of those huge, modern places which had become so fashionable since the war. A glass enclosure filled the best part of a block and inside it was crowded with dirty, long-haired, bawdy self-styled painters, writers and musicians. I was only grateful the stage inside was presently unoccupied by the inevitable jazz band. We had to share a table with two obvious homosexuals who to my chagrin immediately assumed I was Seryozha's catamite. But I was prepared to suffer even this if it meant escape for me and Esmé. Seryozha, for my benefit and for that of half the vast café, began to boast of his achievements on the dance stage, what the Parisian critics had said of him, how Diaghilev himself had tried to lure him away from Foline. This, too, I endured patiently, nodding and smiling; the price I paid for the omelette, which was large but mediocre. My acquaintance ordered a whole bottle of *anis* which he insisted we drink. I had forgotten his taste for alcohol. By the time we rose to leave I was fairly drunk and had agreed to go back with Tsipliakov to his rooms in Rue Dauphine. As we walked unsteadily over the cobbles I asked if he had seen anything of Kolya in Paris. 'Oh, yes,' he said. 'I was seeing him fairly frequently about six months ago. He always dines at Lipp's in Boulevard St-Germain. Do you know it? Not to my taste. Country food, mainly. But he has a sentimental attachment to peasants, as you know.' He stopped, took out his key, opened a huge courtyard gate and ushered me ahead of him. On the other side of the courtyard a flight of steps led to the door of his flat. It was spacious and light, but he had the taste of a kulak. Little nick-nacks were perched on every surface: china pigs, china roses, candlesticks, gold vases full of garish flowers. It was heavy with stale perfume. 'Take those Japanese cushions,' he said. 'You'll be most comfortable.'

I hoped I would not have to stay long. I removed my coat and lowered myself into the cushions, reaching up for the glass of yellow Pernod Seryozha handed me. 'I take it you're still partial to snuff?' he said. I wonder if he ever knew I stole his cocaine box on the train. I nodded. 'The chief necessity of my life,' I told him.

I watched him as he sat down at a black and gold lacquered table and began to prepare the 'snuff'. 'I should explain,' he said abstractedly, 'that Kolya and I are no longer on speaking terms. I regard his life-style as miserable and his choice of companions – well, Dimka, dear, unconventional for him. He had the nerve to cut me the last time he saw me. He's become massively respectable. Wants none of his old pals.' The thick lips, the huge eyes, the flaring nostrils, turned to offer me a look of deep, but mysterious, significance. He brought me the cocaine in a little marble dish and I sniffed it through a long, gold tube. It was better quality than we had been getting. I would at least discover Seryozha's supplier before I left.

Then suddenly he had taken a leap – a balletic jump – to land beside me in the cushions. What remained of my drink spilled and I tried to find somewhere to stand it, but he wrenched it from my hand with a loud laugh and flung it behind him. 'Ah, Dimka, dear. It's been so frustrating! Has it been the same for you? I dream of those days on the train. You were so young and sweet. Sometimes, before I go to sleep, I can still smell you. There's nothing like that odour. No chemist could ever reproduce it. You still have a little of it now. How old are you?'

'I'm twenty-one.' I rolled awkwardly in the cushions.

'A major at last. Ho, ho!' He touched his lips to my shoulder and looked up at me with his brown eyes; a swooning cow.

'And what are you doing in Paris?'

'Looking for work. For money. The Cheka is after me. Because of my activities in Odessa.'

'You have no money?' I admired the way he sprang so easily to his feet. A desk drawer was opened. Several large-denomination notes were taken out. He was down again beside me, pressing the money into my shirt. 'That will keep you for a while. Buy a suit. You could do with a good suit.'

I did not wish to offend him, so I said, 'I'll pay you back, Seryozha. This will help with the doctor's bill, thank God!'

'You're ill? Consumption?'

'Sadly, no. It's crab lice. I got them in Montmartre, I think.'

Again he was on his feet, unconsciously scratching at his thigh. 'You still have them?'

'I must tell you the truth. I was on my way to find out whether I'm cured or not.'

'Oh, but I should not keep you!'

I was surprised at the effectiveness of my ruse.

'I'd love to see you again,' I said, clambering to my feet and staggering from cushions to floor. I was scarcely able to stand upright, though the cocaine had partially cleared my head. Probably I could thank the cocaine for the alacrity with which I had invented my unpleasant affliction.

'You shall, Dimka, darling. Tomorrow. Let's pray to all the saints this awful ordeal is at an end for you.'

I think I saw him give the cushions a sidelong inspection as he showed me to the door. He blew a kiss. 'Until tomorrow, Dimka, my dear.'

I was not sure whether I would be able to tolerate another encounter with the huge dancer, but he was my only real link with Kolya and a source of money, which in turn meant I could return to our pension with bon-bons for Esmé and some flowers to cheer her up. She almost wept when she saw my presents. 'Are we rich again, Maxim?'

'We are on the road to riches, my little dove. I think I know where to find Kolya.'

She was not much impressed by this. To her my Kolya was a myth, a symbol of hope rather than a reality. She tended to become depressed when his name was mentioned. She needed something more concrete. 'I promise you, Esmé, that we shall soon be free of all this.' I sat on the bed and squeezed her hands while she chewed her chocolates. 'Kolya will be able to help me get my Airship Company going.' It was all I could tell her. Presently, I should have been grateful for somewhere else to live, where Brodmann and his Chekists would not be able to find us. Even Esmé noticed the caution with which I locked up that afternoon. I went out again at 6 pm. I told her to be careful, to answer only my knock.

It was raining by the time I got to Lipp's. In contrast to the street the restaurant's ornamental brasswork and plate glass was cheerful. It was an old-fashioned family restaurant on two floors, catering to a wide clientèle, many of them Jewish. Somewhat nervously I pushed through the revolving door and presented myself to the head-waiter. The place was already crowded. He asked if I had made a reservation and when I admitted that I had not, he shook his head. I could tell he might have allowed someone else in but he did not much like my looks. Depressed, I walked out into St Germain. I remained in a succession of shop doorways for an hour or two, watching Lipp's entrance in the hope of seeing Kolya. Eventually I went home. My clothes were becoming too shabby but if I were to wear either of my uniforms I should become a sitting target for the Chekist assassins. I decided I must have a new suit.

Next morning, just before noon, I went to visit Seryozha again. By now I had a clearer idea of how to resist his advances. When he opened the door he was still bleary, but he brightened when he saw me. He wore a multi-coloured silk kimono which he did not bother to tie at the waist. Doubtless he hoped the occasional glimpse of naked thigh or genitals would increase my desire for him. I was already familiar with both. I remembered them vividly from the train, when he had the top bunk and I the lower. I had no means, however, of guarding against him when he kissed my lips (his own stank of stale alcohol) and squeezed my waist before padding over to the bureau to find his cocaine, offering it as another might offer coffee. Naturally, I accepted. Now, gradually, he remembered our last encounter. 'How was your visit to the doctor, Dimka? Are you completely cleared up now?'

'Almost. The best treatment is some kind of lotion, but he says it's expensive. The other treatment's slower.'

'You've been sleeping around too much, Dimka. I always knew you had the makings of a little whore.' Reaching back into his desk, he opened a drawer. He took out some more money. 'Will this pay for the lotion?'

I controlled my rage at the insult, but the rage itself helped me accept the money without conscience. Let the pervert think what he liked! I would never sleep with him. There is such a thing as love between men. I do not deny I have experienced it. But whereas any reasonably good-looking woman is worth making love to, if only for an hour or so, a man has to be outstanding in every way and there has only, really, been one such man in my life, just as there have only been two true loves amongst women. I spent a little time with Seryozha, learning about the Foline and its plans for touring, his quarrels with the management ('They say I drink too much. I say who would not drink too much with those leaden-footed ballerinas to heave about the stage!') He asked where I was living. There was nothing to be gained from lying. I told him Rue de la Huchette. 'But that's a squalid place! Those awful little restaurants. You have to take your own bread and your own knife and fork into them! Oh, my dear Dimka, that's dreadful!'

It was not politic to mention Esmé. 'I was on my way to England,' I said. 'Travelling with a friend. The friend decided to go on without me, taking virtually everything I owned, including most of my documents.'

He was suitably horrified and sympathetic. This gained me an extra line of cocaine, since he now remembered not to touch me. 'Oh, my dear. As soon as your trouble is cleared up, you must move in with me. I've tremendous amounts of room, as you can see. You could have your own bedroom. Your own dressing-room. Honestly, you'd be so welcome. You know how much I've always liked you, Dimka.'

I pretended to be delighted at the prospect. 'That's wonderful, Seryozha. I'll go round to the doctor now and see if he has the lotion. It must only be a matter of a couple of days.'

'You poor thing! I had no idea you were suffering so dreadfully. What happened? Were you picking up women? Or Belgians? They never know if they have lice or not, in my experience. That's my rule in life, Dimka dear. Never have anything to do with women or Belgians – and be careful about American transvestites, too. They don't change their underwear. But then you know Pigalle, down there, do you?'

'Don't worry. I'd have no part of them. In this case, however, I think a Turk was the culprit.'

'Oh, well, *Turks!*' And Seryozha shuddered. I had mentioned the almost inconceivable knowing that to him a Turkish louse must somehow be even more disgusting than any other kind. 'You poor, poor thing. Were you raped?'

'One day I'll tell you of my adventures in Constantinople, Seryozha. Is it all right to come back at the same time tomorrow?'

'Of course, my darling. Or later tonight, when I get home. No. Not tonight. Yes, the morning. Just after twelve. Wonderful.'

I went straight to the outfitter in Rue de Turenne. Happily my figure, except when it inclines to plumpness, has always been good: the ideal 'standard' for a man. I had no difficulty in selecting a three-piece suit, a fresh shirt, some collars, a tie and some shoes. Seryozha's money – including that which remained from the previous day – covered the bill. I wore the clothes when I left, my others wrapped in a neat parcel.

Back at Rue de la Huchette I drew a few stares from the local clochards as I entered our miserable doorway and climbed the stairs. Esmé was no longer in bed. She sat in her dressing-gown at the table, slowly writing on a form torn from a magazine. 'It's a competition,' she said. 'The prize is a holiday for two in Egypt.'

I did not tell her the magazine was out of date. She needed to keep her hopes up quite as much as I. She had not noticed my new suit and in a way I was grateful.

That evening when I went to Lipp's I took a cab and found that although the restaurant was quite as full as the day before I was now fitted into a corner of one of the long tables upstairs. This did not quite satisfy me, since regular and favoured customers tended to use the ground-floor restaurant. I ate sparingly of the food, which was more German in some ways than it was French, although I developed a relish for their asparagus, so that although my bill was relatively small I could leave a generous tip. Such things impress waiters. The news is swiftly carried to their fellows. I wanted to be certain next time of getting a seat downstairs. When I left, I looked about for Kolya, but he was not there. On my second visit I would ask the head waiter. But before I could come back to Lipp's it meant going through the distasteful business of seeing Sergei Andreyovitch. My tale of the doctor and his lotion could not last me for more than two further visits before I must either succumb or run. Again I waited outside Lipp's for a while. It was midnight before I went home. Esmé was asleep and did not wake when I got in beside her. I went immediately to sleep.

Three more visits to the increasingly impatient Seryozha, three more meals at Lipp's. Seryozha had warned me he could not keep lending me money for 'treatments'; my doctor seemed to be charging me without curing me. Seryozha knew a very good doctor, his own, whom he felt would be sure to help me. On the fourth visit I was forced to tell him I was cured but, on the excuse that I was still very sore, managed to avoid the worst of his passion, though his self-control (never his strongest virtue) was severely tested. There was little else I could do. I needed the money if I was to find Kolya and if I did find my friend, then anything would have been worth while. Soon, after a week or so, my main problem became how to refuse moving in with Seryozha, who also wanted to see where I lived.

I was sitting at a downstairs table, near the door, at Lipp's one evening, considering my plight and trying to imagine a valid excuse for not going to Seryozha's when he returned from the theatre. As I lifted my first piece of asparagus to my mouth a tall, handsome man, dressed entirely in black save for his linen, came through the revolving glass. On his arm was an equally startling woman. The head waiter approached them with obvious pleasure. When the man turned his wonderful eyes towards me he frowned slightly, then grinned broadly like a schoolboy. My heart leapt. The head waiter was already pointing towards me (I had by now asked after my friend). Prince Nicholai Feodorovitch Petroff had never looked better. I was ecstatic. My body trembled. I could hardly rise to my feet. My asparagus fell to the floor. I was weeping. He was laughing. We embraced. 'Dimka! Dimka! Dimka.' He patted my shoulders. He kissed me on my cheeks. I became so excited I believe I flushed, breaking into a light sweat. 'Oh, Kolya, I have looked for you everywhere.'

We gathered ourselves, still weeping and smiling, and he introduced me to the woman. 'The Princess Anais Petroff, my wife.' I felt no jealousy. She had eyes of black plush and skin as white as Kolya's, like new ivory. His hair remained pale blond, almost the colour of milk, while hers was raven. Her tawny evening frock had a summer cloak of pale fawn thrown over it. They were impossibly attractive: a pair of storybook lovers, the Prince and Princess of Fairyland. I kissed her hand and in my confusion knocked the rest of the asparagus to the floor. Amused, Kolya waved for a waiter to pick it up. 'You're dining alone?'

'As I have dined night after night in the hope you would come.' I shrugged, embarrassed by my own revelation. 'My companion is not well.'

He was sympathetic. 'Is your companion Russian?'

'By origin, yes. But I met her in Constantinople.'

'So you've been in Turkey, eh? Lots of adventures, Dimka? Join us at our table!'

We moved to the back of the restaurant, to a more secluded area. I was brought a new plate of asparagus. Kolya ordered their hors d'oeuvres. He told Anais I was his oldest friend, his dearest companion from the days before the Revolution, that I had inspired his poetry and informed his sense of the future. Again I felt the blood rise to my cheeks. It was not wrong to love a man, particularly a man like Kolya, a sort of god put amongst mortals to make them aspire to perfection. He asked for my news. I told him briefly what had befallen me since I returned to Kiev, that I believed the Cheka was even now looking for me in Paris.

'And I thought I had suffered!' He had been in Paris for two years. A year ago he had met and married Anais, who belonged to an old French family. He still hoped to get to America, but continued to have problems obtaining his visa. He suspected this was because of his service with Kerenski – or rather his political affiliations at the time he joined the Government. 'But how do you pass your time in Paris, Dimka?'

'Chiefly in seeking a backer for my new company. And I go to the cinema a great deal.'

'That has become our passion, too. We have just seen *Otets Sergii*. Do you know it? I believe the director's in Paris now.'

'His name is Protazanov.' Anais spoke a soft French which was not Parisian. It was both melodious and humorous. Her lips were always smiling. She very evidently worshipped Kolya as much as I did. Perhaps because we had this passion in common, I liked her a great deal.

'I scarcely ever see Russian films these days,' I admitted. 'They are too painful.'

Kolya poured white wine for us. 'I understand. Have you a favourite director?'

It could only be Griffith. I spoke of *Birth of a Nation*. Where other films were concerned, I thought in terms of actors and actresses. Lillian and Dorothy Gish, Douglas Fairbanks, Charlie Chaplin, Buster Keaton, Mary Pickford. I had seen everything of theirs.

'You must love Harold Lloyd!' Anais was delighted. 'Isn't he wonderful! So frightening! So funny!'

'And Fern Andra or Pola Negri, don't you find them as attractive as all these Americans?' Kolya was sardonic. 'Really, Dimka, you're becoming an Americophile! I thought you hated the place. Is that where you plan to go?'

'I'll content myself with London. Do you remember Mrs Cornelius? She has agreed to help me when I arrive. But I'm also having visa problems. Perhaps if I were alone it would be easy, but my friend Esmé has no papers at all.' He knew of my original Esmé. I told him a little of the meeting in Makhno's camp. 'She is the image of her. Esmé repurified.'

Anais said: 'Perhaps you could have her adopted by a nice English family.'

Kolya laughed at this. 'You're being cruel, Anais. We'll put our heads together and see if we can come up with a solution. Your father has business connections in England. Could he help?' He turned to me. 'Anais's father's a Captain of Industry, a holder of the Legion of Honour and an ex-Deputy! You see what grand circles I move in now, Dimka. Yet I can't get permission to go to the United States and teach Russian. I am, instead, a leech.'

Anais was disapproving. 'When hostilities finish in Russia you'll be able to claim at least part of your fortune.'

Kolya winked at me. 'Do you think so, my dear? Russians have become everyone's penniless guests. Poor relations to the rest of the world. People will soon lose patience with us.' The waiter began to serve us our main course.

'How far advanced is your Airship Company, M'sieu Mitrofanitch?'

Anais pushed the chuckling Kolya back against his chair and bent across the table towards me. Naturally I had been introduced under the name I used in Petersburg.

'I've some interest from the financial world, but nothing concrete as yet.'

'You think it's a good business venture?'

'It would take advantage of the increase in tourism since the War. The volume of passengers between New York and Paris alone has grown considerably. My ship would be far faster than a liner, in many ways smoother and safer. My designs are advanced, of course, but I've absorbed everything about airship construction I discovered during the War. Presently the Germans lead the field. The British plan to begin a commercial service in a year or two. In a matter of months we could be ahead of both: if the ship received appropriate publicity: a maiden flight, for instance, which crossed the Atlantic in record time.'

'You're fascinating, m'sieu.' She sliced her liver. 'And convincing. What do you think of it, Kolya?'

'He's a genius,' said my friend simply. 'I believe him capable of anything.'

The conversation drifted onto more general topics. Suddenly I was completely happy and consequently at my most charming. It was a very successful evening. We were eventually the last to leave Lipp's. Both deities kissed me goodnight and Kolya took my address, swearing he would get in touch with me very soon. 'We must never be parted again.'

It was only as I walked, whistling, back along the Rue Saint-Sulpice I realized I had forgotten to tell Kolya of his dead cousin, Alexei Leonovitch, the pilot who almost killed me when he crashed his plane into the sea. Perhaps it would not be tactful, I thought, to introduce such a note at present. I could tell him soon enough.

As usual Esmé was asleep when I returned, but tonight her breathing was rapid and shallow. She had a temperature. I held her sweating little body in my arms and rocked her as she moaned: 'Don't leave me, Maxim. Don't leave me.' I brought her some water to drink, some aspirin to relieve the fever, then I lay beside her trying to tell her about my meeting with Kolya, but she fell back into delirious sleep again.

Next morning I went out to find a doctor. The nearest was in Boulevard St-Michel. Doctor Guilac stank of tobacco and rosewater. His walrus moustache was yellow with nicotine: he had a skin spotted like tortoiseshell, grey, thinning hair, over-polished boots and an old-fashioned frockcoat. After his examination of my girl, he told me firmly Esmé must have 'real rest.' He gave me a tonic. He insisted she take it three times a day. She was anaemic, he said. She was suffering from nervous exhaustion. 'But she is young,' I told the old fool. 'She is full of natural vitality. She's a child!'

Doctor Guilac offered me a disbelieving glance. 'Her ingestion of alcohol has been prodigious, I would say, and I hesitate to catalogue the drugs she has doubtless been taking. Someone should keep a responsible eye on your sister, m'sieu, if you will not.'

I could not tell him Esmé consumed no more drugs or drink than did I.

'She's suffering from a common complaint for these days,' he continued disapprovingly. 'Have you no parents she can stay with?'

'We are orphans.'

He sighed. 'I cannot judge you. But you need a wiser hand to guide you, m'sieu. I advise you to leave Paris. Visit the country for a month or two. Reconsider your way of life.'

I had asked for a doctor, not a priest. His moralising made me impatient. Nonetheless I thanked him politely, saying I would consider his suggestion, and paid him with our last money. As I sat by Esmé's bedside, holding her warm, limp hand, which was moist with sweat, I wondered if I were being selfish. Should I demand she lead the same life as I? I had always been famous for my prodigious energy; the mark, I suppose, of an active mind. Others had rarely been able to keep up with me. It was probably unfair of me to expect it in Esmé. She was young enough to have no real sense of her own capacities. This collapse into an almost completely comatose state might well be her own way of resting. I determined to nurse her until she was recovered. Then I would review the situation, sure, once we had a fresh direction in our lives, matters would arrange themselves better. She had every reason for uncertainty. Instinctively she probably knew I was worrying about the Cheka. Moreover I had told her we were going to England and we were still in Paris. Her grasp of language remained rather weak. She might easily be homesick without wanting to tell me. There is no feeling of helplessness worse than watching someone mutter and sweat their way through a fever which has no obvious medical cure. I controlled my panic, however. I considered requesting another opinion. I decided, as soon as I saw him again, to ask Kolya to recommend a doctor: someone rather more eminent than this local quack. Depressingly this would almost certainly mean more visits to Seryozha.

Had Esmé, I wondered, always been subject to such fits? Some form of epilepsy? Perhaps that was why her parents had seemed so glad to see her go with me. As soon as I could, I visited the nearest library and took out medical books. There was no suitable description of her case. She had been without her 'coco' for several days. Could she be suffering from withdrawal? I managed to get her to take a little cocaine, but it did no apparent good. My frustration with the medical profession, which to this day remains, frequently, in the Dark Ages, was never greater. I sometimes wish fate had allowed me to become a doctor. With my analytical and creative gifts I could have done much more, I think, than anything I achieved as an engineer. My abiding desire has been to help the human race; to be of use: to lift mankind out of ignorance and animalistic, reflexive behaviour, a little further towards Heaven. I shared a misconception of my time, believing social conditions were the chief cause of the world's ills. I thought a technological Utopia would solve the misery of the human condition. I now believe most people suffer from serious chemical imbalances. We should be searching for the correct mixture of substances which directly feed the brain. Even I am not always as clear-headed as normal. It is probably the food. We know the calories and vitamins, but what of the minerals, the subtler materials we ingest? Tiny pieces of metal, which never affect us physically, could be entering the cortex, reacting, say with magnetism in the streets, with random electrical impulses. These metallic atoms might be more terrifyingly crucial to our daily lives than the Hydrogen Bomb itself. One day we feel like making friends with the world and the next we want to blow it up. This could be for instance why personalities change so radically during thunderstorms. I wish someone had given me facilities to research this field. I made every effort. I applied to London University some years ago, listing my qualifications, and prepared my paper *Electrical Emissions in the Atmosphere and their Effect on Human Higher Brain Functions*, hoping they would at least allow me to address their doctors. In the end I was reduced to paying a Jewish printer to run off a few hundred copies which I distributed in surgeries and clinics in the Kensington and Chelsea area. I had one or two letters about my theory, but they were from lunatics, from hippies who wanted to tell me the electrical discharges were really messages from flying-saucer people! I disdained to reply. Whether Esmé's malaise was due to electricity or some other, as yet undiscovered, source, I do not know. At that time I could only nurse her. I got a woman in to make her soups and change the bedding until she should recover. Unknowingly, Seryozha paid for this service.

A few days later, I received a note from Kolya. He was in town again and would like to meet for lunch. He suggested Laperousse at one o'clock. I left Esmé tucked up in our bed with some water and a note telling her where I would be. In my new suit I went to meet my friend. I will not say that I stepped lightly, however, for I was still nervous of meeting Brodmann on the street and, moreover, had no great desire to bump into Seryozha. It seemed my fortune might be about to turn – but everything could be destroyed if either of those individuals found out the truth.

Kolya was wearing black as usual. He stood up to greet me as I crossed the cool, comfortable upstairs room of the restaurant. His doublebreasted jacket gave him the air of a well to do merchant banker and made him seem if anything paler. He apologised for not bringing his wife. 'I thought it would be nice to chat alone.'

I was only too glad of the opportunity. There is a special love which exists between men, a love which the Greeks knew and described, which excludes women. It is noble and it is Spartan, far removed from those sordid meetings in the public lavatories and backstreet pubs of Hampstead Heath and Leicester Square. Kolya and I were almost part of the same being. I shall not deny I worshipped him. Equally, I am certain he loved me. We formed a unity. He was happy with his wife, he said. She was delightfully intelligent and very pretty, as I had doubtless noticed. Unfortunately, doting on him as she did, she wanted to pay for everything and this was not an ideal situation for a man who had always controlled his own fate. However, she had expressed serious interest in my Airship Company and, if she could convince her father and some of his friends to back it, Kolya wondered if he might be made Chairman. Would I object to this? Of course I welcomed the notion. 'I can think of nothing better!'

In the gloom of a nearby hotel room we opened champagne to toast our coming together again. I could smell his body through his beautiful clothes. I had longed for him more than it was possible to admit, but till now my emotion had been suppressed. He said he, too, had missed me. There is nothing wrong. Christ says there is nothing wrong. It is spiritual, above all else. They accuse me of what their dirty minds in-

vent. My life is my own. I am not their creature. How can these insin-
uating dwarfs understand my agony? They put a piece of metal in me.
They move a magnet behind a card, trying to shift me in the direction
they think I should go. But I resist them. I despise their pettiness, their
unimaginative morality. It is not based on any true ethic at all. I am
above those judges and magistrates. There was no purer love. No purer
joy. I was helpless before it. Who could blame me? Their metal turns
and twists in my womb, but I shall never conceive that demon-child,
no matter what they say or do. *Ich vil geyn mayn aveyres shiteln. Ich vil
shiteln mayn zind in vasser. Ich vil gayn tashlikh makhen.* What do
they know with their accusations? Even more than his body, I loved his
mind, giving myself up to both as I now give myself to God alone. I
deny everything. I have done nothing wrong. I am my own master. My
blood is pure. I did not let them make me a Mussulman. I was strong,
accepting all blows. I did not challenge their lies, save through my actions. I kept silent and was true to myself. Let them believe what they
want. They failed to keep me in their camps. They knew it was unjust.
They called me vile names, hating me because they said I was perverted. But how could they know? The words were not there: they were
dumb and I thrilled with the heat of my salvation. I conquered through
the power of my brain, my God given gifts. Kolya knew what this
meant. He never accused. He was Christ's messenger; an angel. He was
Mercury. He was silver intelligence, the essence of true Russian nobility, yet like me a victim. They took his power. We were beaten down
like corn in the rain. But steppe-nourished corn is hardy; it grows back
even before the ashes of the fires have dissipated. Kolya said the meeting was fated. We should both find ourselves again. The wings are
beating; that white metal sings. All those cities have failed me, yet I
cannot hate them.

Within a week the Company documents were being prepared. A
dozen cultured faces with soft mouths and important eyes bent heads
and dipped pens until I emerged christened, once more, as Professor
Maxim Arturovitch Pyatnitski, Chief Designer and a leading shareholder of the Transatlantic Aerial Navigation Company of Paris, Brussels and Lucerne: Chairman, Prince Nicholai Feodorovitch Petroff;
President, M. Ferdinand de Grion. Anais's father had been immediately impressed by what I had shown him. France, he told me soberly,
would benefit from the folly and the distress of the Bolshevik beast.

Esmé and I moved to wonderful rooms across from the Luxembourg

305

Gardens. We had the clothes we desired and ate dinners in ancient halls, attending dances in tall civic buildings. My darling rose began at once to bloom. That doctor was a fool. She needed the very opposite of country air. Like me she was nourished by what the city offered. Deprived of it she began to fade. For her sake, however, I did not take her everywhere, but made sure she rested, or found some means of entertaining herself while I visited the clubs of France's leading men of business. Sometimes I took my huge scrolls of linen paper to a little hotel in Neuilly where, undisturbed, Kolya and I discussed the details of our adventure. With a regular salary I was relieved of my previous anxieties, though Brodmann and Tsipliakov still occasionally haunted me. Now I had powerful friends they would be circumspect, those two, about bothering me. Esmé encouraged me to go out alone; she said she could see it did me good. She was content to remain in our apartment and read or sew. I could now purchase the best quality cocaine. Kolya had abstained from the drug, he said, since Petersburg, but was more than willing to resume an affair with what he called his 'cold pure mistress of the Moon.' He admitted how bored he had been, how my company brought him back to himself. 'Even before the ship is built, I can feel myself flying again!' He was writing poetry, too, but, as he told me with a laugh, he still burned it almost before the ink was dry. 'Poetry is too indiscreet, expressing inappropriate sentiments for a man of affairs.' On land to the north of Paris owned by Anais's father a giant shed was going up. Mechanics and all necessary varieties of craftsmen were hired. And I became a celebrity.

The newspapers featured announcements of our enterprise and illustrated magazines printed fanciful realisations of the great aerial liner which would eventually sail the Atlantic skies; drawings of cocktail parties in the main salon, of bridal suites and billiard rooms (so stable would our craft be). Both Kolya and I were frequently interviewed. We were described as Russian engineers, geniuses who had escaped by aeroplane the horrors of Revolution. This huge file of cuttings I pasted in a special book. Esmé was fascinated by the sight of her own lovely little face in the photographs, sometimes staring at them for hours, as if she did not believe they were real. Our apartment was on two floors, with a regular maid and a cook. We could entertain people from all walks of life and Parisian society became entranced by the romance of my beautiful sister's history; her separation from me in Kiev as a child, her abduction to Roumania and finally to the Sultan's Constantinople where she was rescued by me; the daring balloon flight over the Balkans and our arrival in Italy. So frequently did these stories appear in the journals I think she came to accept them as true. Certainly our guests wanted to hear them confirmed. More importantly, so much evidence had accumulated by these means we would have little trouble with passports when we needed them. Very quickly, she was issued with temporary resident's papers giving her name as Esmé Pyatnitski, born Kiev 1907. People remarked on how alike, how devoted we were. Only Kolya knew the whole truth. These shared secrets added to our pleasure in each other and were never hinted at in any press report. It is the best way of preserving one's private life, I find. Let them write what they like. The myth protects far more than it harms.

Our huge airship hangar, built almost overnight at St-Denis, was frequently photographed, but reporters were never allowed inside. Industrial espionage is not a present-day phenomenon. Under my personal supervision construction of the aluminium hull began. Meanwhile I discussed with engineers which kind of engines would be most suitable. We had decided to use diesels but were unsure about manufacturing our own or seeking an outside tender. At that time no firm was making exactly the motors I needed. Every stage of the planning was crucially important. As soon as the aluminium struts were delivered from the foundry they were weighed to the last gram. Nothing on the ship could be heavier than was absolutely necessary. We had applied to America, the largest manufacturer of helium gas, for quotations. M. de Grion had begun by hoping we might receive additional funds from the French government, but in the end we decided to put shares on the market. Our costs, of course, were astronomical; but we knew the rewards were likely to be even greater. However, finance scarcely concerned me now. When I stood in the middle of a shed almost a thousand feet long, staring up through bars of sunshine streaming from wide glass skylights onto the slowly forming skeleton of my glittering ship I felt myself in the presence of a force both mysterious and awe-inspiring. I am sure the builders of medieval cathedrals were filled with an identical emotion. At long last one of my dearest dreams was to become, as it were, flesh and bone. The first step to the aerial ship the size of a small city, which in the next two decades must surely become reality. Soon there would be great fleets of such monsters, bearing cargo and passengers back and forth across the skies as casually as ferry boats on a lake. Someone else might understandably have felt a terrific sense of egocentric power at this achievement. I, however, experienced only incomprehensible humility.

Work was advancing so rapidly I was forced to devote more of my time to St-Denis and less to Esmé. I took her with me whenever possible, but grew guilty at being unable to give her as much attention as she needed. I begged her to make friends with the wives of our business acquaintances, to continue her visits to the cinema. But she was sometimes miserable. She complained, just occasionally, expressing her fears. 'I worry that you do not love me any more.'

'Of course that's nonsense. You're everything to me. It is because I love you I am doing all this.'

She said my airship seemed an excuse to leave her just as I had abandoned the Baroness. I denied all this passionately (including the suggestion that my jealous, scheming mistress had been abandoned by me!). She, Esmé, was my sister, my daughter, my bride. She must trust me now more than ever. Could she not imagine our reception when the vessel arrived in New York? She was already enjoying the benefits of fame. Soon she would have the chance to be a world celebrity and enjoy riches as well. But Esmé would not always allow herself to be cheered by this. 'It hasn't happened,' she would say. She lacked the imagination to visualise my finished ship. 'It takes too long,' she complained. 'There must be a faster way of making it.' I laughed spontaneously at her naïveté. We were working at almost unbelievable speed. The cost of materials rose virtually every day, so it was in our interest to complete the ship as soon as possible. Secondly, we were hearing several rumours of both British and German plans for big commercial airliners. The Germans were officially banned from making Zeppelins under their treaties with the Allies, so I dismissed those stories. The ships they had already built had been requisitioned by the British and Americans and renamed. There was, however, talk of Zeppelin engineers being invited to America to work and that could have more substance (my own guess would be that the Americans were our most dangerous rivals). The Zeppelin firm itself was making aluminium pots and pans in Germany. It would be years before they received permission to build. (When that time finally came, they made unconscionable use of every innovation I developed in France, claiming my ideas as original! I was always the first to acknowledge Count Zeppelin's tremendous influence on airship design. His successor Eckener, however, had no original ideas. Any reputation that lackey achieved was a direct result of his old association with Count Zeppelin. But there is nothing to be gained from reminding myself of his infamy, nor the unscrupulous treacheries of his Jewish masters.)

By Christmas 1920, I believed my moment come at last. Little more than a year after fleeing from the Bolshevik fury, convinced that all was lost, I stood sipping good-quality champagne side by side with my dearest friend Kolya and my reborn sister Esmé, watching visored riveters in blue overalls and huge gauntlets hang high overhead in cradles and hammer red hot bolts, joining together the main sections of my first liner. Isambard Kingdom Brunel, as he watched the *Great Eastern* taking shape, must have known the joy I felt, the warmth in the groin, the silver light in the mind, the certainty of immortality.

'What are you going to call her?' Kolya raised his glass towards the half constructed rounded framework of the nose section.

I had a dozen ideas, but one dominated all those others. I put my fur-clad arm about Esmé's yielding little shoulders and looked tenderly down at her. There were tears in my eyes, I know. I was not ashamed.

'I shall call her *La Rose de Kieff*.'

Twelve

I ATTAINED MY majority on the day snow fell heavily to smother the shed of my *Rose of Kiev* and I received at last a letter from Mrs Cornelius. She had re-occupied her old house in Sidney Street, Whitechapel. I would not believe how good it was to be in Blighty. She continued to do everything she could to help me come there. What was more Major Nye had promised to look into my case. He now had a permanent position at the War Office. Between them, she was sure, they could get me to England by spring at the latest. In the meantime 'good old London' was 'holding up nicely' and she was 'pleased as Punch' to be back. She had been to lots of shows. She herself now had a job on stage again, though it was only the chorus, with a chance of a better part later, if she played her cards right. I was delighted she had been able to resume her career and while there was no immediate need for me to visit London, I saw little point in her discontinuing her efforts. I sent her one of my clippings as proof I, too, was 'getting on' in the world. 'Soon,' I wrote, 'I shall be able to offer you an engagement entertaining passengers aboard my first aerial liner.'

The black shed, a mountainous square slab rising from the pure snow, was empty of people that day. I had ridden in my new 3½-litre Hotchkiss Tourer out to St-Denis mainly to have the driver show it off to Esmé. She thought it the most beautiful car she had ever seen. I suspected, tolerantly, she was chiefly impressed because its blue paintwork matched her eyes. Wrapped in white ermine, her breath like fine powder, she was almost invisible. As usual, I wore my bearskin overcoat, with the Cossack pistols, which I identified as my luck pieces, still in the pockets. Christmas and the New Year had been a heady progress from party to party. We had met everyone then fashionable in Paris, including the strange negress Janet Baker, whose mannish hauteur seemed so perverse to me. I was surprised when she went on to star in Opera, though I suppose a form lending itself so readily to extravagance and grandiosity readily accepts any new sensation. We became great friends with M. Delimier, one of France's leading ministers, a private shareholder in the Company and an enthusiast for a French government commercial airship line. He was interested in my origins. He said he had a number of good friends in the Russian community. At the same party I met the pseudo-intellectual Communist Jew Léon Blum, who led Frence so decisively to her doom in the 1930s. In those days it became impossible to avoid Jews in any sphere, be it business, the arts, or politics. They were busy cultivating scapegoats and dupes to blame if their schemes went wrong.

My birthday drive through the snow to St-Denis remains one of my clearest memories of that time. Everything was perfect. I had acceptance, fame, fulfilment and friends. Few young men have celebrated their twenty-first year with such achievements. Straight, bare trees, like saluting soldiers, marched on either side of the avenue; clouds of dark birds cried their applause; a few flakes of snow fell from the branches and hissed on the pulsing bonnet of my car; Esmé clung close to me as the driver operated the controls. Children sprang from doorways of cottages to wave their caps and yell their enthusiasm; church bells sang and even the sheep lifted their heads to bleat a huzzah as we went by. I raised my respectable hat to a family group in a gig drawn by a pair of prancing greys; I reached and squeezed my horn as a peasant and his family made their way across the road from field to field. I shouted with delight, pointing into the steel sky at a flight of geese rising above the great shed and climbing until they disappeared. 'An omen!' I told the driver to stop the car and made Esmé get out. The watchman on duty at the gate knew me. He let us through as we tramped across the crisp snow to the shed, entering by a small door set into the main one. The skylights were frosted and magical. Ice had formed in the chilly blue air so struts and scaffolding gleamed like silver. 'It's fairyland!' She advanced into pale light. There was rime in her furs; little stars.

'It's fairyland come true.' The smell of the frost was so good to me. As

I spoke snow stirred the echoes. 'Wait until we're flying above the clouds together, you and I, sipping cocktails, listening to an orchestra, on our way to America.'

'You must invite Douglas Fairbanks to make the maiden flight.' She was directly beneath the massive hull. 'He'd love the adventure!'

I said I would write to him that very evening.

On the way home Esmé complained the snow was blinding her. She had a dreadful headache. By the afternoon she was in bed, unable to visit the de Grion's that evening. She insisted I must remain in their good graces and go alone. I left her, sipping tea, with an ice pack on her head, a tiny, touching figure amongst the lace and linen of our bed. I felt I was failing her. Perhaps the transition from the Galata slums to Parisian high society had been too sudden? She frequently became self-conscious in the company of older, more sophisticated people who of course assumed she was from their class. She would be at a loss for words, though all praised her shy charm. As my sister she was courted by handsome young men. I did not blame them for their attentions. I was in no way upset. Esmé's childlike attachment to me was never in question. I had already made it clear I was content to let her accept their invitations to drive in the park or even to have lunch, though I warned her their intentions would not always be honourable. She should guard against those who invited her to music halls or private suppers. She trustingly accepted my advice without objection. I knew so much more of the world, she said, than did she. In such matters I was her infallible guide, a true brother to her. Sometimes it seemed she had accepted the whole deception as truth. Often she would call me 'brother' in private. When we made love, which was rare enough for a whole variety of reasons at that time, she said it gave the occasion a delicious tinge of wickedness, of incest. She remained my fresh, beautiful, unspoiled rose, beyond any real vice; in spirit my virgin girl with the world before her. I myself was at last an adult, so I knew there was plenty of time for her to grow. There was no need for haste. Her girlhood should be enjoyed while she had it. My own youth had been stolen from me by War and Revolution. I envied those who could experience the careless days of adolescence. If I had children I would ensure their absolute security, a long and well planned education. Nothing is gained by early exposure to the world. I felt as if I had a full lifetime behind me, but not one I would wish upon anyone else.

Happily I could leave the Grion's party early, with Kolya. We said we must discuss engineering problems. At *Neuilly*, after we had taken some of Kolya's new cocaine supply, he asked after Esmé. If she continued with her bouts of illness he thought I should engage the specialist he recommended. 'But possibly she simply suffers from the *malaise du papillon.*' I wondered what on earth he meant by 'the butterfly sickness'. He refused to elaborate, adding: 'You should be prepared, Dimka, to let her go her own way soon.'

This seemed to me a revelation of unexpected jealousy on Kolya's part. 'She has everything she wants! Every freedom she requires. Anything else and she would have it. You know that, Kolya. She's a child. I have a duty to protect her. Perhaps, when she, too, reaches twenty-one, I'll marry her. That's all I expect.'

Kolya was impressed, I think. He agreed there were certain comforts in marriage. He always spoke affectionately of his own wife. He loved her as thoroughly as I loved Esmé. But we were becoming too melancholy. He got up, putting on his clothes. 'Come along, young Dimka, we'll go to a decent party now.'

We drove in my Hotchkiss to a nightclub in the Rue Boissy d'Anglais, although it was already two in the morning. Here Kolya felt at ease. It was full of painters and poets. The garish green, red and purple murals were in the latest cubist styles. The music had a frenetic high-pitched neurotic, fitful quality, associated with the current Russian ballets. I was nervous of seeing Seryozha there, for the place seemed crowded with Russians from Kolya's past; exorcised ghosts lending their sociopathic talents to the general chaos. Here men two-stepped openly with other men. Many women wore tailcoats and had their lascivious arms round young girls. All kissed, squeezed, stroked and touched as they danced. Kolya boldly ordered 'C et C' from the waiter and the mixture was brought at once: a magnum of champagne and a little test tube of cocaine. We were almost immediately surrounded by acquaintances, pressing in on our table from the semi-darkness. Some I knew quite well, from our nights at *The Scarlet Tango* and *The Harlequin's Retreat.* They might have come straight from a Petersburg club to this Parisian version without even changing their eccentric clothes. They had seemed harmless enough in those old days, but politicians and gangsters hid amongst them. I assumed the same was true in Paris. Certainly some, who seemed mere clowns, would soon try to squeeze the throat of their protectress Mademoiselle Liberty.

From that unsettling den we went on to a private party where Mistinguett and half the artistes of the Casino de Paris were giving impromptu performances. I was enjoying a ridiculous song about going up in an aeroplane when soft hands fell on my arm. A well dressed man, dark-eyed and swarthy, smiled at me in uncertain recognition. To my surprise (for he seemed French) he addressed me in Russian. He was from Odessa, but was no one I had known well.

'Stavisky,' he said, shaking my hand. 'We arranged a little business some years ago. You were a boy then. You haven't changed.' I now remembered him from a single meeting. Through my cousin Shura he had been the man buying cocaine off the Dutch dentist at whose surgery I eventually met Mrs Cornelius. Stavisky's clothes had been more flamboyant in those days, the clothes of an Odessa dandy, though even then he was living in Paris.

'You're doing well for yourself, it seems.' I was pleased to see him. He grinned. 'I can't complain. And you, too. This airship racket's a winner, eh?'

Although I disliked him calling my project a racket, I had become used to Parisians' dismissive slang so was not offended. We had a vodka and grenadine together, for old time's sake. He hoped to see me around, he said. If I had any more patents, I must let him know. As he returned to his own table I asked if he knew anything of Shura. 'I can tell you exactly where he is. Running a little operation down in Nice. I saw him a week ago. Shall I give him a message?'

'Just that I'm in Paris. He can find me via the airship works at St-Denis.'

'I'll tell him.' Stavisky winked. 'You don't want to pay these prices.' He pointed at the remains of our cocaine. 'Come to me next time. I give special rates to friends.' He waved and disappeared into the jigging disturbance surrounding us. He was a good-hearted soul who would rise to eminence in the next few years, but was already marked as expendable to the conniving politicians who, Jews themselves, would brand him a Jew. They would have him shot down in a little shack in the Swiss mountains. In some ways, I suppose, I should feel grateful for the events which followed, although I did not welcome them at the time. If I had stayed in Paris longer, I, too, might have met Stavisky's fate.

The original signs did not seem particularly disturbing. On January 30th there was a strike at the airship sheds. All engineers and fitters demanded higher wages. This was a blow, simply because I believed relations with our workmen excellent. We stood shoulder to shoulder in pursuit of a common ideal. Some Socialist agitator doubtless would be at the root of it. There was an emergency meeting of the Board. M. de Grion said we must certainly refuse all demands. Already these saboteurs were insidiously poisoning the roots of French society. It would not merely be against our immediate interest to capitulate, it would be against the interests of all decent people. Understanding his principle, I was nonetheless alarmed by its implications. Our schedule was threatened. We had promised to complete in a year. Our prospectus announced a maiden voyage in November 1921, a regular service by January 1922. To stop work now would be madness. We could not afford to break the rhythm of our progress. It would be more than just losing a week or two: there must be unity between designers and engineers at all levels. De Grion was sympathetic, but his argument won the day. Only Kolya and myself voted against a resolution refusing negotiations with the workers.

From that point I became the incredulous witness to a crazy, uncheckable avalanche. Within a month half our people had deserted to other jobs. It was impossible to proceed without a full team; the hiring and training of new personnel would take ages. M. de Grion remained unmoved. I told him his obstinacy threatened to ruin us. I saw my dreams collapsing once again, at the very moment I thought them most secure. Gradually stories began to appear in the more obscure newspapers. The Transatlantic Aerial Navigation Company was in trouble and seeking funding from the government. Shareholders had begun to sell their stock. By April there were even a few who spoke of suing. At least one scandal sheet described Kolya and myself as 'a pair of Russian charlatans bamboozling the French public with a fraudulent engineering scheme.' Increasing numbers of reporters would appear at my door, night and day, to demand if there was truth in these rumours. Was the Company on the edge of bankruptcy? I was frantic. I could not answer. I explained I was a scientist, not a financier. The scheme was solidly founded because my ship was the most advanced of its kind. Given the chance to complete it, I would show the world. I blamed the strikers for their short-sightedness. This was a red rag to the Bolshevik press, of course. They ran headlines indicting half the eminent business men of France (as well as 'White Russian entrepreneurs') as deliberately perpetrating a fraud. The Airship Company's shares became worthless overnight. M. de Grion told me sadly he would have to resign from the

Board. Only Kolya stood by me, attempting to persuade people to stay, for without them the Company would surely collapse. 'Why throw away a goldmine when all that's needed is a little more digging?'

They would not listen. I was disgusted with them.

At home, Esmé scarcely understood what I meant when I described this betrayal, our difficulties. Why must we consider moving again, giving up the car, dismissing the servants I asked her to try to make sense of our household accounts. Earlier, to give her a feeling of purpose, I had put her in charge of our food and clothing purchases. She cried, saying it was beyond her. It was for me to decide what to do. I lost my temper. She should pull herself together. It was an emergency! I took my rage out on a child. I stormed from the house, walking up and down our street for half an hour until I was in control of myself. But when I returned she had gone. The servants said she had left in a car, that was all. I was not unduly worried.

Kolya and I dined together. He found the news upsetting but superficially was taking it better than I. He showed me a packet, received at the office that afternoon. He placed it in my hand. 'What is it?'

'Escape,' he said. 'If we need it. Luckily, I'd anticipated requiring these if we wanted to be on the *Rose's* maiden flight.'

Opening the envelope I found a brand new French passport in my name, stamped with an entry visa for the United States. 'It's all quite above board.' Kolya was reassuring. 'M. Dalimier helped. Don't you remember signing that form just before Christmas?'

I had signed so many. In general I was worrying about things bearing my signature, not knowing how many had made me personally responsible for the fate of our firm. I recalled nothing specific.

'Well, we were all very busy then,' he said.

'And is there a passport for Esmé?'

'She's a minor. Unlike you she had nothing to prove her Russian nationality or, indeed, her identity. But her passport will come through soon, I'm sure.'

The new documents, placed in my breast pocket, seemed to protect my heart. 'But how shall we keep the Company going, Kolya? Every other director has resigned. None any longer own stock, including your father-in-law. We're the only major shareholders.'

'Oh, indeed.' With two pale fingers he pushed his plate away. He took a sip of claret. 'It was cleverly done, eh? I wonder if they ever thought the ship would really get this far?'

I could not follow him and said so. He gave me a friendly, sardonic smile and sighed. 'Dimka, I think you and I have been set up as the front to a stock swindle. Why else did nobody warn us? No tip to unload our shares. No suggestion we resign.'

'But the whole disaster was the result of a strike,' I pointed out. Kolya touched the back of my hand with his palm. 'A strike, my darling, is easily arranged. Once arranged it can be maintained to the advantage of the management, rather than the workers.'

Still at a loss, I shrugged and shook my head. 'The strikers were bribed?'

'The Devil doesn't always carry a red flag, Dimka. Sometimes he pays a proxy. Agitators can be bought, particularly if they're professionals. Once tempers are high the working men hold their ground, Capital holds its ground, and someone makes a fortune from an airship which will never fly.'

'But who? I have bills unpaid. No salary. Rent. Various debts. Servants. I've hardly a penny in real cash.'

'Same here, little one. M. de Grion seems solid enough, doesn't he? And his friends?'

'He wouldn't let you down, surely. He has the scandal to consider. His daughter would suffer.'

'I'm quite certain if I seem seriously hurt by the Company's crash it will actually look better for him. Later my wife will receive a present. I shall no longer have capital of my own. And all will be satisfactory again. For him, the situation's ideal. He might have planned it in every detail. However, I think it was a solution. He'd hoped to get large government grants, other contracts. This is his way of writing off his losses.'

'So only ordinary shareholders suffer.'

He looked hard into my eyes, as if telepathically trying to convey his message. 'And you, dear Dimka. There are also outstanding Company bills. Wages unpaid to office staff and specialists. Engineering firms, raw materials, rent. It probably comes to at least a million.'

I was dizzy with shock. I could hardly speak. Surely, I asked, I was not personally responsible for every debt! Kolya gripped my arm. 'But the scandal of bankruptcy will attach itself primarily to you. The yellow press is already blaming "foreigners". They'll have a perfect victim in you. A foreign swindler? Possibly a Bolshevik agent. The anti-Semites will have a field day, too.'

317

'I'm not a Jew! Nor a Communist!'

'How will you prove it?' Kolya spoke persuasively. He was trying to bring the realities of my position home to me. I knew an investigation of my antecedents, traced back to Odessa if nowhere else, would provide 'proof' to anyone determined to make me out a liar and a thief. Nonetheless I resolved to fight any such insinuation. It was in my interest, ultimately, to do so. 'I know lawyers. I'll prove my innocence, Kolya!'

Prince Petroff was unenthusiastic. 'You'll need money for that. I'll help, but I have limited means now. Is there anyone who'd lend you a large sum?'

At this, suddenly I slumped. I had spent months avoiding the only person willing to give me money (and that at great cost to myself). I could think of no one else in the whole of Paris who would for a second go out of their way for me. I was once more in a weak position. In some ways weaker than ever before. The Cheka can sniff out weakness. My alarm came flooding back. I had sworn never to suffer prison again. The Bolsheviks had accused me as a swindler once, in Kiev, and now swindlers themselves threatened to send me to prison, accused as a Bolshevik! Yet my faith in the value of my airship persisted. It was a good design. A reality. That and the truth must surely save me! 'The British have been investing in commercial aeroplane services. So have the Dutch. Couldn't we appeal to them for funds?'

'It's politically impossible.' Kolya spoke very quietly. 'We need private money. And private money hates scandal.'

'Most of the frame's already built. We have firm costings for gas, fabric and engines. Quotations for the gondola are arriving now. It will work, Kolya!'

My friend's expression grew sadder. He had tears in his eyes. 'My advice, Dimka, is to abandon any hope of completing her. Design another airship. Find a new backer abroad. Use that passport as soon as you can!'

'Must I go to Constantinople?'

'To America, of course. They have real money. They're genuinely interested in new notions. Well, if it were my choice, I would head for New York.'

'It's impossible, Kolya. Esmé's papers aren't through.'

'They'll arrive any day. You can't help her if they arrest you.'

'I haven't enough money for the fare.'

318

'I could just about find you the price of a first-class passage.' He was begging me, with every part of him, to save myself and I loved him all the more, but I remained confused. My life had seemed so secure, my prospects perfect, and now it was falling to pieces by the moment. 'I must have time,' I told him. 'I can't abandon Esmé. You know what she means to me.'

'There's no suggestion you abandon her, Dimka. She'll follow almost immediately. I'll make myself responsible for her. She can live at our house.'

I knew he was right. I should go before there were charges. Then, at least, I would not seem a wanted criminal. 'Thank God I have one trustworthy friend. But suppose you, too, are indicted?'

'I shan't be. My family connections, my title, guarantees that. I'm afraid it's you alone will directly suffer, Dimka. I can't swear to it, but it looks almost as if they deliberately arranged for you to take the whole onus.'

How could ordinary people be capable of such complex perfidy? I had gone through so many dangers, risked so much, abandoned more to reach what I believed a safe, just and decently ordered world, only to be betrayed more subtly, more coldly, than ever I had been in Russia. France, the Mother of Modern Justice, was about to sacrifice me to satisfy the greed, guarantee the social standing of her great men. An idealist, a person of intellect, is helpless against the forces of the Fifth Dimension, the Dimension of Secret Power. The ungodly delight to bring down the poets and the scientists; to lay them upon the altars of Gog-Magog and with bloody knives cut out their innocent hearts. The Fifth Dimension is the Land of Zion, a place beyond the ordinary limits of geography; a dark world of dark men and women determined to infiltrate and inhabit our own, to replace every one of us with a doppelgänger whose spirit once belonged to a dead Carthaginian. This is how Carthage conquers. Through money and human folly. Gone are the elephants and the bronze gongs, the clashing of bright metal and the cries of red-lipped bearded soldiers. Their slaves no longer drag themselves in chained convoys, bowed beneath the whip and the throbbing sun; instead they move from desk to desk in hygienic offices; they crawl up to coalfaces wearing modern safety lamps, they work as bunnygirls in gambling clubs, and most never have the dimmest understanding that they are owned, body and soul, by invisible creatures, powerful rulers of the Fifth Dimension. Zion is Carthage and Carthage shall not die. She adopts a thousand guises and her victims are the honest, the sane, the innocent and the holy. This war continues, but we are few. I can hear their laughter, distant and merciless, mocking and rapacious, echoing across the disipating barrier dividing one dimension from the other. This laughter of Carthage gives me strength to resist. They cannot understand. They have beaten me with their rods. They have forced me to my knees. And yet I walk still. *Im darf men keyn finger in moyl nit araynleygen!* The armies of Turkey and Israel combine against me, but I shall continue to fight. My friends are few, but they are strong. I wish they had been with me in Paris, in those dreadful hours of my betrayal. But there will come a time for vengeance. We shall trample down death by death and upon those in the tombs bestow life.

On April 1st 1921 the city had begun to turn green and luminous. There were early blossoms appearing like blemishes upon the perfectly manicured body of the Luxembourg Gardens and citizens emerging from their winter cocoons walked with a livelier step. Pretty girls put on spring paint and glanced at my handsome car as I drove past but I barely noticed them. I was immersed in my anxieties. I had decided at last, as letters began to arrive from creditors and I was regularly abused by people on the street outside our deserted offices, that I could wait no longer. Either Brodmann and his Chekists would sense I was unprotected and strike, or the French Fraud Police would arrest me. Matters were worsening daily. There was no doubt I was to be sacrificed by de Grion and his high society friends so they could claim to have been duped by a foreign adventurer. Some of the newspaper stories in the conservative press undoubtedly had their source in de Grion. Kolya and I, together with most ordinary shareholders, were the only real dupes, but there was no way to prove it. Everything was on de Grion's side: more than he knew, in my case. I read the reports: it was suggested I was a Bolshevik agent fraudulently gathering gold for Moscow, that I represented German Zionist interests, that I was a wanted criminal in Italy and Turkey. I knew enough about such campaigns to predict the outcome of this one. I was a perfect scapegoat, as Kolya had told me. I must forget any hope of continuing my fight in France. It would only mean imprisonment. I would go abroad and there clear my name. With my French passport I would have no great trouble getting to England, but I was still too close to the source of danger. Kolya, as always, gave me the best advice. I would spend some time in America, meet

Esmé and Kolya there, then enter Britain later, when the publicity was forgotten.

As I drove home that afternoon I made up my mind to tell Esmé my intention of taking the ship from Cherbourg to New York. Kolya would keep her safe until she followed me. I had no choice. In America I would swiftly redeem my name. By the time she arrived I would be well on the way to re-establishing myself. The naïveté and optimism of Americans now looked attractive. Obviously they had money for new ideas. They had not yet realised how successful the War had been for them. They were now, for the first time in their history, a major international creditor, still with no notion of their enormous power in a world where almost every other nation faced bankruptcy. Once in the United States, my earlier press cuttings would prove my credibility. These were the interviews which chiefly mentioned my earlier successes in Kiev and Constantinople.

I arrived at the house to find it completely empty of people. A week before, the servants had left but now Esmé, too, was gone. Since the foundering of the company she had been frequently absent. She had been forced to find a social routine to relieve herself of boredom in my absence, now she used it to help her forget the terror of renewed poverty. I promised myself to make it up to her before I left. We should have a marvellous few days until I boarded the *Mauretania*, the liner I had chosen for my voyage. No longer the greatest ship afloat, she was rarely fully booked, but everyone said she had a pre-war elegance lacking in Cunard's recent vessels with their emphasis on contemporary décor and pastel colours. At my desk, I wrote a letter to Mrs Cornelius. My last, describing my successes, had not been answered. Now I must tell her of my change of fortune. I would not be visiting England for some time. I had a visa permitting me six months in America and might even renew it if necessary. I would first stay in New York, then travel to Washington. There I intended to contact government officials and show them my patents. I wished her luck with her stage career. I suggested she might find the film medium suitable to her talents. I asked to be remembered to Major Nye.

Esmé was still not home by eight. I left her a note and went to see Kolya. He insisted on visiting the nightclub in the Rue Boissy d'Anglais and eating 'hot dogs' – 'So you know what kind of food they serve in America and will not appear unsophisticated on arrival!' He seemed in high spirits but was, I am sure, merely presenting a good front, to cheer me up. Leaving him was, in a different way, as painful as leaving Esmé. He said he would probably follow in a couple of months, as soon as the scandal died. For all he knew he would bring Esmé to me himself. I had only this hope. I was in danger of falling back 'within the nightmare', scarcely able to think clearly around emotional matters. I had no wish to leave my two dearest friends or to desert Europe. The United States seemed so far away. It might have lain beyond the edge of the world. But that was also its attraction.

At our little table under an archway smeared with bright yellow and crimson grotesques, Kolya and I watched a negro dance band play for ballet girls twisting themselves in parodies of classical movements. My friend had more information for me. 'Stay at the Hotel Pennsylvania. Everyone insists it's magnificent. It's so modern an underground railway leads directly into the basements, justs for the convenience of guests. I've made reservations for you through Cook's. Your passport describes you as an engineer, so you'll have no difficulty. Engineers are national heroes in America. Next time you come to Paris, you'll be aboard your own air liner. Never fear, Dimka, you'll prove the lie to the press!'

We drank to my success, but I remained fearful. In Russia I had been swept along by profound historical forces, but in France mere financial trickery had dictated my fate. (Yet the Shadow World of Carthage, the Fifth Dimension, exists on the fringes of our own, preparing to engulf us, and its modern weapon is money, the stock exchange. It lies in the East yet at the same time is everywhere, for it intersects our own dimensions on levels conventional science cannot as yet define.) That night, too, Kolya and I made our private farewells. Having given up the little place at Neuilly, we took an hotel room in Rue Bonaparte. It was a sweet goodbye and we both wept. We were fated to be together, just as Esmé and I were fated. His delicate features in the light from the street was the moon haunted, tragic face of a nineteenth-century pierrot. We were to meet again, of course, before I left for Cherbourg, but this was the true time of our parting.

I arrived home to find Esmé still dressed. Her hair was dishevelled. In her white and silver evening gown she resembled a frantic Christmas fairy fluttering about the empty rooms. She was drunk. She had returned, she said, to find me gone. Believing herself deserted she had taken a taxi to search the streets. I showed her my unopened note where I had left it for her. She looked wildly at it, shaking her head dumbly.

For a moment her eyes had the flat glow of a puppet's, without expression or consciousness, then she lowered her lids while at the same time shrinking into a chair, as if her entire body folded in on itself; as if her mind were being sucked into some unfathomable secret place. I became alarmed that I had caused this condition. When I tried to rouse her she shivered, looking up at me only once with an expression of terrified anticipation. I stepped back from her. 'What's happened?'

She could not move. Her lips closed, then remained partly open. Eventually I picked her up and carried her to the bedroom where I undressed her. She lay with the sheets to her chin, her eyes following me as I moved, preparing for bed. She made no response to my questions. I decided I was worrying too much. Drink and the late hour were responsible for her behaviour. I went to sleep, determined to tell her my plans in the morning.

At breakfast she was herself again, unusually bright, happy as a canary. She had arranged to lunch with her friend Agnes in the Champs Elysées. I did not know Agnes. Would she object if I accompanied her? But Agnes had a secret to discuss and a man would not be welcome. 'I, too, have an important secret, Esmé. Something I wanted to say last night.'

Esmé cocked her head to one side, her blue eyes unblinking, a piece of toast halfway to her mouth. 'Are you buying a new car? Is the airship out of trouble?' Careless and light-minded, she had become a true Parisienne, taking nothing seriously save the exact effect on her looks of the latest mascara. While not begrudging her this happiness, I was a little irritated. Yet I could not sustain anger. I laughed. 'The news is bad, darling. Our Company is worse than dead. The vultures close in and I'm the only meat left for them. Everyone else has run away.' Her giggle was unexpected, like the trilling of a blackbird at a funeral. 'They can't harm you, Maxim. You're invulnerable. You'll come up with a plan.' I had hoped for sympathy or at least concern and was disturbed rather than encouraged by this statement of confidence. 'It's a desperate plan, however,' I said. 'You must listen to me, Esmé.'

She was on her feet. I think she wished to avoid the truth, escape the disturbing facts. That was why she had behaved so strangely last night. She moved rapidly, nervously, still a dressed-up little girl, towards the door. 'Then we must talk, of course, Maxim. I'll be home by this afternoon. Let's have tea somewhere at four. Shall I meet you here?'

'I want to talk now.'

'At four.' She turned back, ran forward, put her arms round my neck, kissed me on the nose and smiled. 'If it's bad news, four o'clock's the ideal time to hear it. If it's good, we can celebrate tonight.'

I looked at the pile of letters I myself was too fearful to open. All were connected to the Company's failure. I would never open them. I returned to bed, staying there until lunch time while I tried to review my situation. I was furiously incredulous that I was destitute. I lay in my huge, clean bed, looking up at the ornate ceiling while sunlight brought Parisian spring into the beautiful room. Yet my only asset, save for my Odessa luck pieces, was the Hotchkiss, which would have to be sold and the profit handed to Kolya for Esmé. Letting Esmé have her own money would be foolish. She had become habitually extravagant. She could spend anything I gave her in a day. The house would only be ours for another month and most of the furniture was gone. There was very little left to arrange. I could rely on Kolya to take care of anything else. My only fear was that my news would bring Esmé too heavily down to earth. I was afraid she would fall back into her delirium; I should not be able to leave her if she suffered another. I tried, with this in mind, rehearsing the exact tone of my revelations. But half my brain would not respond to the other. I hate to admit the truth: I was to be torn away from the girl I regarded as my own flesh. Yet I at least had become used to disappointment, disillusion, betrayal. She had known only sunshine and ease since she had met me. How much worse it might be for her, with no automatic means of anaesthetising herself.

I ate a sandwich and drank a glass of beer in the brasserie round the corner from the house, walking down St-Michel to the Seine. It was damp spring weather with a slight mist in the air and on the water. The quayside bookstalls were mostly closed up, but a few patient old men like unkempt dogs sat guarding their wares. Traffic clogging the bridge was so still, so muted, I imagined time had frozen and myself the only unaffected individual in the entire city. Sounds became increasingly muffled and faint. The people I passed took on an unreal appearance, like projections in a cinema film, though the colours were brilliant. I crossed over the bridge to Notre Dame where I stood looking up at the cathedral's massive doors. They represented a barricade against the corruption of the world outside. In all her sensual beauty, Paris surrounded me; her trees, just budding, were isolated one from the other. She was the least compassionate of cities, the most self-involved. She rewarded success grudgingly while quickly punishing failure. In her present haughtiness it was impossible to imagine how she had been during the Revolution or the Siege, with the mob in her streets, screaming and destroying. I could understand, I thought, how she had come to be attacked by her own inhabitants; by pétroleuses with crazed, wounded eyes, trying to burn her into recognition of her own mortality. They had failed, if indeed that had ever been their ambition. She remained impassive. Poverty and distress merely disgusted her. Noise offended her. She turned away from it.

By the time I walked back it had begun to rain. Beside the little round church of St Julien le Pauvre, I heard the almost mechanical click of water on her laurels, smelling the dampness of her graveyard as a curtain of drizzle moved slowly across to me. I kept to backstreets and doorways. I could not afford to be found either by Brodmann or Tsipliakov. But Paris knew I was there: she intended to purge me as if I were an alien microbe. I longed for the warm chaos of Rome, even the filth and clamouring greed of Constantinople. I could not begin to imagine New York. In other cities, in their marble and granite towers, the world's Mapmakers were still at work. The arms dealers and the grain merchants tested the pulse of a desperate planet. Greeks were betrayed to Turks; Russians to Poles; Ukrainians to Russians and Italians to 'Jugo-Slavs'. Ideas of virtue and probity were subtly discredited. Jazz music drowned all protest. Would America, providing so much of this distraction, be even worse than here I countered my fear. There were Russian colonies in Venezuela, Brazil, Peru and Argentina. If the United States failed me I could go South. From there it would be easy to find my way back to Europe. With this consolation I turned into the little cinema at L'Odéon and watched part of *Birth of a Nation* again, emerging into sunshine, my optimism restored.

I arrived back at the house by four, but Esmé did not return until six, full of pretty apologies, cursing buses and taxis and the traffic on the South Bank, kissing me all over my face, telling me about the present she had bought me. She had left it on the tram. She would get me another on Monday. It was too late to have tea, but since she seemed in such fundamentally good spirits I decided to speak.

'Esmé, I have decided to leave France.'

'What?' She looked up from where she had been sorting through her purse. 'For Rome?'

'They'll put me in prison if I don't get as far away as possible. So I'm going to America.'

She was half smiling. She thought I joked. 'But I want to go to America with you.'

'You'll join me there, as soon as Kolya has a passport for you. There's a delay, because you have no proper documents. There are so many émigrés in your situation everything takes longer. It will only be a question of weeks at most. Then we'll be together again.'

'Where shall I live?' She looked up frowning, putting the purse to one side. 'The rent here is only good for another month.'

'Kolya has offered you a room in their Paris apartment. He and Anais are not there half the time so you'd have the place to yourself a good deal. And servants. Everything you want. Possibly Kolya and Anais will be able to bring you to New York. They intend to go soon.'

She had grown pale and was biting her lower lip. Her eyes cast about as if she had lost something.

'You mustn't be afraid.' I was gently reassuring. 'You'll soon be meeting Douglas Fairbanks.'

She smiled. 'Maxim, do you love me?'

'With all my heart.' The question somehow disturbed me. 'You are my wife, my sister. My daughter. My rose.' I moved towards her.

'Why do you love me?'

'When I first saw you I felt something. An echo of recognition. I had always sought for you. I found you again. I've told you this before.'

'I love you too, Maxim.' She still seemed distracted. Perhaps she was resisting the meaning of my news.

'I'll stay, my darling, if you need me.'

She was brave, my little girl. 'No. That would be wrong. I want you to go. I'll join you soon. You must fulfil your destiny. It lies in America now.'

'You're behaving splendidly.' I had expected tears.

'It's for the best,' she said flatly.

I reached out and touched my fingers to her lips. She kissed them, glancing up at me with a strange, almost tragic, expression. Then she gasped and dropped her head. I held her shoulder. 'You won't notice I'm gone. You'll know I'm with you in spirit the whole time. I love you, Esmé.'

'I always feel you're with me.' Her voice was small, sounding oddly ashamed. Her response was mystifying and yet touching. 'You must try not to miss me,' I said.

'You're not leaving me for good, are you Maxim?'

326

'Never! We shall be married one day. When you're legally old enough.' I smiled. 'Perhaps in America where the age of consent is lower. That might be best. Would you like to be married in the Wild West? With Indian braves for guests? In a little wooden church on the plains?'

'That would be wonderfully romantic.' She stood up. Suddenly shy, she took my hand. 'Let's go to bed now.'

Our evening was beautiful in the peace and delicacy of our love-making. It had been the same with Kolya. There is a kind of release when lovers are about to separate for a while.

Oh, Esmé, my sister. My wistful spirit. My ideal. I never wanted you to be a woman. They took you and forced your face into the dirt and horror of the world. You said you were awake at last. But what is wrong with a dream? It harmed no one. It leaves no stain. Why talk of death when it is inevitable? What drives these people to spread despondent news like rats spread plague? Why should we know fear? They tore me from beauty and hope. With whips and pistols they drove me from my childhood, into this unbearable, cold, futureless wasteland. Children are trudging through the mud of the twentieth century; trudge across the wreckage of the world, homeless and without love. *Questo dev'essere un errore. Non mi dimentichi. Men ken platsn!*

It poured all the way to Cherbourg: waves of light rain drifting like smoke across meadows and woods as the bluebells of France bloomed and the trees came to furious leaf. The train was warm. It smelled of coal and garlic and old women's perfume. My brave little girl had stood with Kolya on the platform, waving a handkerchief, turning and smiling suddenly at my friend as if he had made a joke. He was frozen in black worsted, hat on head, hands in pockets, his white face expressionless as he watched the train pull out. Esmé, in red and white, leapt like a flag at a fête; she seemed still to be bouncing as the train curved and I lost sight of her. I was not at that moment much distressed. The prospect of travel as usual drove all other thoughts away. I refused to brood on that disaster which overtook my first real chance of public success. It would have produced unnecessary melancholia at best, insanity at worst. So I sat back in my seat, raised my hat to the three maiden ladies going to visit their sisters, to the dignified schoolboy sitting with Zola in his hand, and then took an interest in the countryside.

I looked on the bright side. I was, after all, Maxim Arturovitch Pyatnitski, a citizen of France, a man of affairs, on my way to catch a ship. The scandal would be forgotten. My achievements would be remembered. Presently, I was well dressed, carried my patents in my luggage, together with my Georgian pistols. There was no need to waste time on regrets. I was a free man. I was twenty-one years old. I had experienced more than most people do in a long life. And in America my diplomas, my honourable War record, would be even more impressive than in Europe. The sisters, when they spoke to me, were plainly admiring of my bearing and my appearance. When the train arrived I helped them onto the platform before attending to my own affairs. With a whole entourage of porters I marched from station to docks. It was impossible to miss my ship. She dwarfed every building, every piece of machinery in the port. I had never seen a ship so huge. I stared upwards, trying to make out the details of her decks. Little white faces peered back from far away. The *Mauretania* was a massive wall of dark metal topped by terraces of white and gold: the *monstrous nine deck'd city* as Kipling described her. Having served creditably thoughout the War she was back in private service again; still the ship for whom most travellers had the greatest affection, particularly now, since cowardly U-boats had sunk her sister, The *Lusitania*. Leading my porters, I ascended the ramp specially prepared for First Class passengers. Entering an arch as tall as any palace's I was greeted by a uniformed steward who inspected my ticket then led me towards the First Class boat deck. In the harbour intrusive tugboat horns were contentious and ill-mannered beyond the fading mist. My ship's brass, woodwork, impeccable paint and silvered metal, glowed with an inner radiance, as if she were a living beast. I never knew any security greater than I experienced on entering my stateroom.

Having tipped steward and porters and stopped to look through the porthole at Cherbourg's roofs and steeples, I lay down on a wide bed. I lit a cigarette. I did not care if my voyage took a year or more. Momentarily there came a tremendous, unexpected pang, as I realised neither Esmé nor Kolya were here to share my impressions; but a little cocaine soon helped me pull myself together. I was determined to be positive, to enjoy every moment of my stay on board the floating city. After all, I had no clear idea of what I might have to deal with when I arrived. I washed and changed my clothes.

Two hours later the bustle of the ship suddenly grew still. Anxious not to miss the experience I stepped outside my cabin just as the shorelines were let go. I went to join other passengers at the forward rails. Tugs were towing us slowly out to open water. The sun was dull, diffused, a splash of orange near the horizon. The sea was grey and white, alive with birds. The ship's horns sounded a triumph, a farewell. When the hawsers were released, humming and hissing, they curled away and sliced into the waves, to be hauled in by invisible winches. The *Mauretania* dipped her prow, then rose gracefully. A breeze-borne spray striking our faces, we cheered with delight. Already there was a sense of comradeship between us, as there must always be on such a vessel. We moved into magical twilight. Slowly battery upon battery of electric bulbs blossomed everywhere on the ship. She was magnificent. She was a fabulous, unworldly apparition. She turned, this dignified aristocrat, towards the sunset and the West. I went below. I wished to put the final touches to my costume before dinner.

I inspected myself carefully as I tied my tie. I was not dissatisfied, for I was undeniably handsome. I had an excellent figure, my high forehead spoke of brains and breeding, my strong nose of aggressive but fair-minded confidence, my dark eyes of romantic sensitivity. I could mix easily with nobleman and intellectual alike. Straightening my back, I gave a final salute to France. I was more than glad to leave that land of haughty thieves with soft hands and old names. Now I was breathing the clean air of the ocean. This was the first time since leaving Odessa that I could resume my full title without fear of jealousy, cynicism or assassination. Tonight it would not be considered in good taste to wear uniform, but I would wear one tomorrow.

At length, in crisp and well cut evening dress, I strolled wide white and brass companionways. The drums and bass fiddle of an orchestra issued from the far off dining-salon. They were playing a waltz. I almost wept with relief. Raucous jazz, dazzling cubist colours, smart nonsense, Constructivist distortions, all were abolished here. This was the world of breeding and affluence I had always prepared myself for, since a child in Kiev. Until now it had always been snatched from me by the hands of the ignorant mob or the over sophisticated bourgeois banker. I was, I will admit, in an elevated state of mind. I experienced feelings which I can only describe as holy. I felt I had attained something very close to a state of grace.

In the floating land of Mauretania I could now join my own. I had at last found a true spiritual home!

Thirteen

A SCIENTIFICALLY ORDERED City State, Mauretania embodies the best of all possible futures. Every monitored function is perfectly designed to give her inhabitants maximum benefit and comfort. Providing protection from the elements, luxury, security and mobility, the metropolis of the future will also fly. She will locate herself geographically at the convenience of her citizens. She will be heated, lit and provisioned from a central energy source maintained to perfection by a benevolent Master Engineer. Social discipline will be achieved chiefly through good will. Citizens will know that transgressing her code will mean isolation or perhaps banishment to a less hospitable environment.

Mauretania is beauty and freedom: a country where art, intellect and business success are properly honoured, where health, good looks and wit are the norm, where everyone is truly equal, having already earned the right to be here. Thus every man is a Lord and every woman a Lady. This future has conquered nature but continues to respect it, unhampered by the past's banalities, yet remains conscious of its fallible humanity. The world will have control of all its affairs. A central board will govern through selected officers, allowing liberty to all prepared to live and work for the common good. The Grand Patriarch of Constantinople shall be head of a reunited Church. The black and yellow hordes of Carthage shall wither away within a few generations, by a natural process of inbreeding. Fair-skinned, athletic young men and women shall look down through clouds and see the gentle gardens of India, the vast cornfields of China, the game reserves of the Congo; their inheritance. Human nature will not have changed, but certain temptations and threats will vanish: with the voice of Carthage stilled forever, Islam and Zion shall perish as shall everything pagan and ignorant; unnourished it shall rot under the light of truth. Krishna and Buddha will be pleasant myths of a time before the New Dawn. The Jew, the Negro and the Tatar shall be no more than those goblins of prehistoric legend. Byzantium's world of free City States shall eventually send settlements to new planets, crossing the darkness of interstellar space to spread humanity's benefits over whole solar systems, filling the universe with the love of Christ. *Velocità massima!* shall be the cry upon the lips of our clear eyed pioneers.

Not for nothing were our liners named after Roman countries, modern cities, provinces, sometimes whole nations: Places suddenly no longer tied to specific locations on the atlas. Free from the bondage of Space, we shall start to consider the bondage of Time. Nationality becomes a matter of individual application, just as the sailor selects his ship. And the choice is considerable: *Umbria, Campania* or *Lusitania; New York, Paris, Stockholm, Rome, St Louis, Glasgow, Bremen; Oregon, Minnesota, California, Bourgogne, Lancastria, Saxony* or *Normandy; Great Britain, United States, France* or *Deutschland.* Replacing old earthbound states they release us from all outmoded thinking, useless economic theories, decrepit moralistic behaviour. We are truly free because we possess complete freedom of movement. We wander in terraced parks and lush forests just as I wandered through the galleries and passages of Mauretania. We dine in comfortable surroundings where fountains arc; sweet music plays as we observe the passing world below. Elsewhere great undersea tunnels connect land masses, bear cargoes by automatic railway; orchards are tended by mechanical servants; herds of beasts live in controlled environments. Disease is conquered. We are escaped from old fears, from starvation and exposure. Perhaps even death itself is defeated. When I was young I read Jules Verne's romance, *The Floating City,* in which he visualised a world very much like Mauretania. I, in turn, visualised its successors. Here, amongst my peers, my mind was unburdened, able to examine the most stimulating problems. I was never without a fascinated audience. Fired by my visions, some people even asked for my autograph. These educated, wealthy men and women were not easily impressed. From the second night aboard, which was the night I dined as a guest of the Captain, I wore my Don Cossack uniform with its discreet ribbon and became known as Colonel Pyat by most English-speaking passengers. By some friendly, lazy-minded Americans I was called 'Max Peterson'.

They found the Russian too alien for their ears but it was also their way of accepting me as one of themselves. I had no objection to Anglicisation. My interest, as always, was to adapt as quickly as possible to the host culture. Names were never of much consequence to me. It is what people are that matters, as one English gentlewoman wisely said during the voyage. She was a viscountess, connected to the finest families in Europe.

In her carved oak and mahogany, her wrought iron elevators, her open fireplaces and leather upholstery, the *Mauretania* represented the best of English good taste. It was easy to imagine oneself part of that country's noble past. This atmosphere of security persisted even on deck in a high sea when she rolled magnificently, her bow lifting sixty feet before plunging down, burying itself in the waves, thrusting back mountains of water on either side. Crashing and creaking she roared with exultation at her own enormous strength.

As a man of science I was welcomed in the wheelhouse. Captain Hargreaves talked proudly of the ship's wartime service, her long record as fastest Atlantic liner. He spoke of the sad murder of her sister ship *Lusitania*, struck by treacherous torpedoes off the Irish coast, a signal for the whole American nation to rise in arms and rush to fight the Kaiser. I was impressed by her huge steam turbines. She had only two main condensers but these could develop a million pounds of steam an hour. Her twenty-five boilers were stoked round the clock by hard-bodied, sweating men who never seemed to tire. 'Liverpool Irish,' said Hargreaves. 'The only stokers to match them are Hungarians. Of course we have nothing but British crews since a British ship is legally a floating piece of our nation. That's why Cunard never sought foreign capital, even in bad times. Cunard and England are synonymous.' He was a proud old sea dog, not an easy man to impress. I was flattered by his interest in my ideas for larger and faster ships. Later I learned he sailed home on his last commission, so attached to his ship he died the moment she docked at Southampton.

Two particular friends (I think these originally christened me 'Peterson') were, like me, young ex-army men, Captain James Rembrandt ('as in Van Dyke') and Major Lucius Mortimer, both fashionably dressed, personable and good looking: American gentlemen to their fingertips. We originally met in the first class smoking room. They taught me gin rummy and poker. I won quite easily and they said I was evidently a natural player, suggesting I give them a chance to win their money back the next evening. I agreed, though as it happened I had to cancel our appointment when I met Mrs Geldorf, who was travelling alone and needed a dancing partner for the 'novelty ball'. Mrs Geldorf was dark, curly haired, a lady of about forty. She swore I was the handsomest boy she had ever met. She introduced me to Tom Cadwallader ('I pack meat in Mississippi, but I used to pack a six-shooter in Arizona'). He told me of his early life fighting the Apaches and was curious to hear all my Cossack experiences. He invited me to join the company of George Stonehouse, an Atlanta lawyer with business interests all over the world. Mrs Geldorf told me Stonehouse was one of the richest and most influential millionaires in the South. A neat, small, soft-voiced man with terrier eyes and a way of chewing a cigar like an old slipper, he was excellent and humorous company. We shared many views in common. In my presence he told Tom Cadwallader they could do with more like me in the South. Cadwallader himself was short and fat with the ruddy complexion of the habitual drinker, but his little blue eyes possessed a steady candour at odds with the rest of his appearance. He and Stonehouse talked of their troubles since the War. Everything had been shaken up and things were even more problematical than before. The main difficulty seemed to be with Eastern agitators sent down to disturb the working people. Much of what they said was fairly meaningless to me. 'Carpetbaggers trying to get in by the back door since we stopped them coming in the front.' My visit to the South would illuminate me.

A Bostonian, Mrs Geldorf laughed at them. The Civil War was over 'but silly old fogeys go on fighting nonetheless'; she seemed to enjoy these arguments. They called her a 'gol-darned Yankee', yet were evidently fond of her. Their rivalry, similar to that between Ukrainian and Great Russian, was meant in fun. It was well bred and never offensive and this was the tone everywhere aboard our ship, whether I spoke to Lord and Lady Cooper, of the famous beer concern, or Sir Humphrey Thin-Garbett, the well known QC. We formed what Mrs Geldorf called 'Our Clan', which also included Sir James Maggs, MP for Kerry, and his charming wife and daughter, Mr and Mrs Wilkinson of South Audley Street, London, who were couturiers, Sir Laurence Lane, the Shakespearian actor and Gloria his beautiful actress bride, William Browne, the industrialist film producer; Mr and Mrs Dewhurst, land owners from Croydon; Mrs Gladstone, widow of the famous Chancellor, Mr and Mrs Steenson, garden manicurists from Chicago, and Mr Fred T. Halpert who had made his fortune, he said, with a new type of screw. He and I had many interesting conversations, but my ideas were beyond him, as he frequently and admiringly admitted. To Mr Browne I gave the address of Mrs Cornelius, telling him she was one of the finest actresses on the London stage. He promised that as soon as he returned to London he would write and offer her an audition. He thanked me for my kindness in recommending her.

Meanwhile, missing Esmé and frustrated by the absence of feminine company, I discovered consolation in Mrs Helen Roe. This thin, red-headed lady, recently divorced from the tennis player, was on her way back to New York. She would stay with her parents before visiting California for, she said, a long rest. There was a possibility she would go to Florida instead. Since her interest in me was more than platonic, we passed several energetic nights together, though her tendency to sob loudly while at the same time calling upon me to 'push harder you foreign bastard' could be disconcerting. However, she gave me her New York address and this, together with other invitations I had received, meant I would not be completely friendless upon arrival in America.

Mauretania is a land lacking only forests and rivers, but some day her namesake shall have even these. There are shops and services to suit every need; cinemas, theatres, sports, lectures and exhibitions. There are bars, of course, and Americans patronise them with urgent gusto since the sale of alcohol at home became illegal. The days are ordered by a succession of meals; one exists in a timeless and opulent dream, with every need catered to by well mannered stewards anxious to discover one's smallest desires. Press reporters sail back and forth on her, hardly ever landing, save to deliver an article, for she is a world with a thousand brilliant stories. Discretion frequently vanishes out of sight of land. The affairs of Mauretania's citizens are of absorbing interest to the less privileged, for whom a voyage aboard a great liner shall always be an unrealised ambition. These buoyant worlds, able to distinguish the orbit of their choice, the epitome of glamour and breeding, are the ideal symbol of success. A society which refuses such symbols has neither standards nor progress. They offer the promise of a future we could all share. The finest combination of modern technology, they encourage almost every human creative talent to its greatest expression. No wonder the worth of a nation is measured by the number of great liners sailing under its colours. That is why the governments of the world bestow such considerable honour upon their leading ship-owners. Prestige is not lightly won. Prestige is both the measure of a country's power and the uses to which she puts it. The past and the future merge. The best of both worlds can, after all, be ours. The little, whispering, wicked voices of Carthage shall not touch us here. We are our own free nation. We ascend to the upper air, leaving the land to the brutalised, the ignorant and the depraved. Let them slaughter one another into non-existence. Down there the weary arms of helmeted half men rise and fall, hacking at the flesh of their fellows; a black smoke rolls into the valleys and the churches are burning. There are no trees which are not withered, no water that is not poisoned. Starving children crawl through mud which stinks of blood and urine while their dying mothers spread unwholesome legs for gangrenous soldiers, sobbing for life already lost. We, however, have escaped the Apocalypse, by virtue of our honour and our foresight. Russia shudders in suicidal agonies; Germany shrieks in chains; England stinks of untreated wounds, while France at last looks in the mirror and sees her cosmetics cracking, peeling to reveal the hideous canker beneath. But we have found the sky and populated it with civilised steel, with silver wings and golden domes. We can only weep for those below who are trapped in a terrible folly. We weep for them. To do more would be dangerous. If the mob scents weakness (and generosity is perceived as weakness) it strikes.

The mob cannot reach the ship. Here we are purified. There is no security in those flying cylinders, packed end to end with people unable to walk or feed themselves, waiting passively for malodorous trays. No wonder they complain, grow angry, panic. This is the flying the mob deserves: anything better would be unappreciated. It offers nothing for people of refinement. That is why I never travel now. What is left on the Atlantic? A single great Cunarder on which they do not even, I hear, dress for dinner? One Polish tub; two pathetic Soviet hulks built in Germany, full of rats and leaky lifeboats, grotesquely aping the glories of their overthrown masters? A Dutch tramp? A couple of South American banana boats? A single container carrier? Meanwhile the skies, which could have been glorious with my aerial cities, are littered with smelly steel tubes, worse than tourist buses. Those golden cities fade and fall like autumn leaves. Squalid winter covers the world with impure white; the blood and the filth, soaked upwards, encrust the surface like a cancer. When this snow melts everything revealed is misshapen and the colour of mud. The grey planes land to disgorge dazed and shambling cattle. Loaded up again with identical cargo, they move it as speedily as possible to another patch of mud. Some of these crea-

335

tures are 'on business', some 'on holiday'. How can they tell? By painted signs *Red tsu der vant!* Is that all that is left? Our prophets are reviled. Our children are slaves. Our cities are conquered and we are driven from them. O Carthage, thou hast triumphed by treachery alone! By thy stealth and thy cunning hast thou overwhelmed us. With poison and with calumnies. And we are without place or name. Our faces are hidden and our raiment torn. Thou hast taken our daughters in fornication and placed our gold upon thine altars. O Carthage, thou has spat upon our holy things, cast down our temples and scattered the ashes of our books upon the wind. We wept for thee, Carthage, and thou turnest our tears into weapons against us. We did not know the Greek when He spoke to us. We heeded Him not. We are banished to timeless night. We can no longer find the Greek. In the awful midden of modern Russia swine stare stupefied at huge portraits of their masters; perhaps the Greek walks there, bringing compassion to those still calling for Him. Carthage has stolen our future. Our wings have shrivelled to stumps on our shoulders. They have torn out our eyes so we raise bloody sockets to the skies, seeking only for the sounds of our lost cities. Little by little we are forgetting our future. *In shul arein!* Soon we shall remember nothing. Carthage shall be secure in all her citadels. They will not let me fly. I refuse to accept their *yiddishkeit*. They put a piece of metal in my stomach. They tried to hold me but the doctors could find nothing wrong. I looked in Springfield for the Greek but He had gone to Los Angeles and I no longer have the means to follow Him. I will not travel in their filthy cylinders. Why become wadding in a bullet aimed at your own heart? I have known true wonder, walking on the glowing balconies of an aerial city, a mile above the clouds, while an invisible orchestra plays music. There are people dancing. I hear their laughing conversation. They are elegant and courteous, these new Mauretanians, lovers of beauty and intelligence. They do not need to find the Greek. He has come to them already. There is a surge like a great, steady wave, and the city shivers, her white towers shimmering under the haze of her huge protective dome. She mounts the air, floats upon cloud masses which are rolling surf against the peaks of the Himalayas. Then, with a monstrous thrust, she turns towards the wild blaze of the sun, heading for the West, riding as a ship might ride upon the water, her hull rolling and vibrating and her steam whistle, pitched two octaves below Middle A, sounding like a lament for her lost dreams, her vanishing future. They took my children, *meine einiklach.*

The *Mauretania's* four red-and-black funnels send plumes of smoke up into the blue pallor. The sea is calm, from horizon to horizon, and here we are secure until Liberty is sighted and Babylon's terraces rise yellow, cream and orange in the setting sun. Until then I shall walk along her polished decks, nodding to acquaintances, lifting my hat, taking the air while a little light spray refreshes my face and Helen Roe seizes my arm and cries, pointing, 'Can you see the dolphins?' We are somewhere near the West Indies. Helen is certain she saw a gull yesterday. 'Or at least some sort of bird.' The decks stretch ahead of us like so many cloisters around which we stroll, talking softly, a chosen community. We give ourselves in gentle and unconscious celebration to the spirit of practical science which is represented by the vessel herself; thousands of cubic feet of man-made metal and machinery, kept alive and on the move by the sophisticated ingenuity of our engines. These alone, a hundred years ago, could not be imagined.

History does not change, because people will always prefer the false comfort of repetition. In crisis they look for the familiar, they fall back on convention, no matter how unsuited it is to their situation. Neophobia is the great destructive disease of the human race; it is spread through hysterical gesture, anxious phrases, nervous tone: a smell.

Our ship glides towards red and gold cupolas and spires: Moscow and the Kremlin. Formal salutations are offered to the Tsar, the constitutional ruler of this noble democracy. In turn his welcome is extended to us. The Great Powers are in peaceful balance. They have taken charge of the world again. The ship rocks like an old house in the wind. 'They'll put yer in an 'ome, Ivan, if yer go on like that.' Mrs Cornelius means well. Hers is a more ordinary human vision, perhaps, than mine. America should have accepted responsibility. It was no one else's fault. We have seen some good times, she says. Remember L.A., do yer? She roars as she recalls an anecdote. Her memory is better on the little details. I can still see the huge white seaplane rising over Long Beach and banking towards Catalina Island. Water pours shining from her floats. She is obscured for a moment behind a clump of tall etiolated palms. Then she appears again, her engines yelling as she makes the tight turn and finally disappears. The sound fades; the surf remains. I am not sure I was meant for such brilliant and perpetual sunshine. I never accepted their injections. Perhaps I should have stayed on the horse. White faceless heads turn towards the Cross. Christ is remembered in fire and moonlight. In Tennessee Christ is revenged in blood and steel.

Mrs Cornelius says in the long run everything usually turns out for the best. It is a tribute to her tolerance and optimism. Personally, I can no longer keep my spirits up. Too many have suffered. Too many have failed. The little girls sing their songs in the Church. Christ is Risen! We have trampled death with death and to those in the tombs we bring life! I see no evidence. All but a handful of us are left. The rest, we should face it, are all *Judenknechte* these days. On a Thursday afternoon I close my shop. I walk up towards the tranquil convents in the norther parts of Portobello Road. Here the scrap-metal merchants advertise what they will pay for lead, copper, zinc on greasy blackboards propped outside doorways hung with old coats and clean rags. There is an air of peace on Thursday afternoons, a stillness; a pause in the conflict. The sound of car engines becomes muted and distant, like bees in a summer garden. In July and August you see butterflies in the street, dancing over the walls of the monasteries. The children run up and down the kerbs and steps; they cry secret names from unwashed mouths, grimace with unwanted faces. The nuns smile without meaning. The litter of the morning waves and flaps. Nervous dogs with tucked-in tails sniff carefully from stack to stack and any prize is seized swiftly, then they run, forever guilty, anticipating attack. They snarl and huddle in the alleys and sidestreets. Buildings lean and sway under the burden of degenerate poverty; old women pick rotten fruit from the gutters, moving ponderously and bending painfully. Swaggering boys purse their lips at you, their hands in back pockets, and call like carrion to one another across the gaps in the city. Little painted girls ogle you from lascivious, contemptuous eyes. A bank of cloud rises above walls and roofs, blinding white with the sun behind it; a choir of angels and the Virgin Mary. To inhabit a city with a pulsing golden dome I should have to go back nearly fifty years. Then all this seemed capable of remedy. Mrs Cornelius's sons call me a sleazy old fascist, but they say this to everyone. I am a visionary, no more, no less. They could not understand how desperate things seemed. They have come to accept this horror as the norm. We hoped for better. In 1959 I wrote that our chances were almost all gone. What was left of the Empire? What of the Law? Does this make me a *luftmentsh*?

338

In 1964 I wrote to Harold Wilson begging him in the name of sanity to consider the real problems of this country. He must have laughed as he crumpled up my letter and put his two hands firmly on the wheel, turning our ship towards the mirage. They said we had easy money. They said we were enjoying a new age of Liberty and Hope. I saw only Licence and Damnation. They said I was a complaining old Jew. They will say anything to diminish my warnings. Today some of them surely must understand how, on every level, they deceived themselves. Little creatures scuttle amongst the ruins, tittering and grinning, creeping from fissures, retreating under broken slabs. This is the inheritance of Carthage. Is the Socialist glad of his euphoria now? Did it achieve what we hoped? *Khob'n in bod!* These champions of the working class added a new dimension to property speculation; and sold the country lock, stock and barrel to the red-lipped brokers of Carthage.

I do not expect to live much longer. I have been too outspoken, for all my warnings were useless. Mrs Cornelius says I waste my breath. It is a mistake to give your real name. We went to the cinema last night. We saw *Those Magnificent Men In Their Flying Machines.* It is all a joke to them now, our achievements. The slack mouths bellow, the empty heads are thrown back. The aeroplanes are merely props for a clown's comic disasters. Then I was a true *luftmensch.* It is raining on the roof. The electric light is flickering in the rafters. My engines need attention. I must connect them properly. All I ever asked was for a pupil to whom I could pass my ideas, but they sent no one. In the forties and fifties I used to see more intelligent people. They inhabited the wine bars and drinking clubs of Soho and Chelsea. Dylan Thomas told me I was a pure, bloody genius. He wore a suit some sizes too big for him, but responded to my words as poets always have. I hear he is making records now. A superstar. There was some talk, in *The Mandrake,* of writing a play together. The poet has ears which can listen to the voice of God. Thomas drank because he heard too much. But what he is doing on the radio now is sheer noise. He deafened himself completely. Henry Williams, the otter trainer and successful novelist, said my political ideas were the soundest he had ever encountered. He had the beard and hair of Jehovah; a great healthy face. His girlfriends dyed their hair blonde for him. By the sixties, however, I was in Springfield. It was a different age. The same people who praised me as a brilliant scientist ahead of his time now referred to chemical imbalances in my brain and made me incoherent on largactyl and tranxene. *C'a trappo rumore.* These drugs originate in Switzerland. They were developed to suppress individuality. This is the main mission of the Swiss. They devote most of their time to it. They are frightened by thought. They expelled Mussolini. They would have expelled me. Instead they sell drugs to Carthage, profiting from all Europe's misfortunes. I had plans for a city to cover the Alps but nothing came of it. Mauretania is a nation at peace. I should like to be a permanent citizen. Captain Rembrandt says he has crossed the Atlantic almost twenty times. 'But you can't beat the good old *Mauretania.*' Her speed record has never been matched. Rembrandt won his money back at cards but I chose to pass too often for his taste. He complained it made for a dull game. I apologised saying I was short of ready cash. Rather than play cards with me, he and his inseparable partner Mortimer bought me drinks and asked about my patents. They were high-spirited, enthusiastic young men, very neat and trim, typical products of Harvard or Yale, with those rather well scrubbed good looks of their type. They said my ideas would be infinitely commercial. I should have no difficulty selling them once I reached New York. Investors would be 'waiting in line'. However, if I needed help, they would be delighted to put themselves at my service. They gave me a post office box in New York where they could be reached. They tended, they said, to be on the move quite a bit.

I sauntered through arcades of Mauretanian shops with Helen Roe, inspecting glass display windows full of dresses, coats and perfume, mink, jade and gold. The best of everything was available. I bought Helen a monstrous box of French chocolate. She kissed me on the cheek. She said I was a sweetie. With the calmer sea, the ship hardly seemed to be moving, yet we were actually making the fastest time of the entire voyage. Her coal-burning turbines were a match for any oil fuelled vessel afloat. Later that year, when she caught fire, she would herself be converted to oil and continue to hold the Blue Riband for another eight years, longer than the entire lifespan of some rival liners. I recently read Cunard financed the experiments of a young man with an enthusiasm for modern airship development. I was relieved the dream was not dead, although the person selling the idea sounded something of a charlatan. Nonetheless I wrote to his company and offered my services. I received no reply. Of course I have read nothing since. Such people discredit the ideas of genuine visionaries. *Nit gefidlt.*

As the *Mauretania* slowly approached the harbour, Tom Cadwallader offered me one of his Havana cigars and said that much as he had enjoyed the voyage he would be glad to get off the ship. 'The worst part of the journey is crossing New York to the railroad station.' He hoped we would berth at a reasonable hour since he would hate to spend a night in 'Synagogue City'. I asked him if he was familiar with New York and what was his opinion of the Hotel Pennsylvania. He had heard it recommended. 'I've never spent more than eight hours at a time in the city. And most of that was in a friend's apartment. I don't know New York and never wish to. There are almost no Americans there.' He believed he had made a blunder and added, 'Not that I have anything against people from abroad. New York is bad Irish and worse Jew. When it isn't either, it's the sweepings of Naples, peasants from the poorest parts of Sicily. It's the chief breeding ground of Anarchy. And it believes itself superior to the rest of the country. New York, Colonel Pyat, is not America. You should never confuse one with the other. Come to Atlanta if you want to know the real America.' I already had his address. I thanked him. I would try to visit him after I had decided on my itinerary. My main intention was still to visit Washington. Mr Cadwallader understood I had no plans to make a permanent home in America and this made him I think all the more affable. He had already convinced me that the legislation limiting immigrants was the best new piece of Law since the War. But, as usual, the tolerant Christian is too late. The Jew is already past the gates and settling down to his business. He says he wants only to live and work and do no harm. *Ikh kikel zikh fun gelekhter!*

The great city slows to half speed. Twice she sounds her long operatic greeting. Outside is the angry crash of water displaced by tremendous screws; officers shout to their working parties; the jangle of signals from the wheelhouse makes it impossible to understand a dozen voices already distorted by speaking tubes. Her wood panelling dances on her inner bulkheads; her smoke grows dim. She is held in check now, pulsing and panting, as the captain awaits his orders. Just beyond the horizon lies New York. We move forward, hundreds of us, some with binoculars, wishing to be the first to glimpse our destination, but it is not yet possible. A steward advises us to take lunch. He assures us it will be several hours before we enter the Hudson.

A mood of impatient excitement spreads throughout the huge vessel. People are suddenly more animated as they eat. They order caviare, they drink champagne; already they are celebrating their departure. These women are so beautiful in their marvellous clothes, in silk and

341

ermine, the men so confidently elegant. With my back straight, I stand on the upper boat deck, proudly wearing my own white uniform, an uprooted Son of the Don, smoking a cigarette as I watch the crew rapidly making ropes fast, preparing our anchors and lines. I am alone for the moment. I am filled with a sense of well-being. The ozone is good in my nostrils. The cocaine works at its best to clear my head and sharpen my senses. I am completely alive and without fear. I have been accepted by the aristocracy of the Anglo-Saxon world, by great men and women whose ancestors, holding a fundamental belief in the rule of Law, spread their language, their customs and religion across half the planet and continue, even now, to spread them further still. The horizon darkens. A slender line. The whole ship murmurs. It is land. Steadily, mile by mile, we move into a wide harbour until there, directly ahead, are the unbelievable towers rising taller and taller from the ocean itself. It is unique. It is Manhattan: a city without a past. A city with only a future. A dream.

On our right, green and grey and seemingly far smaller than I imagined, stands Liberty; France's grandiose gift to the New World. She is blind. She holds a stone torch which, presently at any rate, illuminates nothing in particular. Helen Roe enjoys my pleasure in these fresh sights. 'Her head's empty,' she says. 'You can go in there some day, if you like.'

Fourteen

A BEAUTIFUL MONSTER, a machine with a generous soul, New York cheerfully tolerates the horde of fools and rogues who seek the security of her deep canyons and cliff-like tenements. What was a virtue, however, is now displayed as a vice. Since the days of her Dutch founders she refused to fear those Catholic and Jewish elements who scrambled to her warmth, to suck her lifeblood and offer nothing in return. In 1921 she was still able to confine them to the Lower East Side, Harlem, Chinatown, the Bowery and Brooklyn, yet steadfastly refused to see how Carthage grew in the womb of the city all named New Babylon. Carthage devoured the kindly parent from within. It was this which D. W. Griffith attempted to show us in his much abused parable *Intolerance*. A subtle masterpiece, it was made a financial failure by the very Jews and Catholics it warned us against! Griffith's company was ruined, his voice was effectively silenced and his own people turned a blind eye to his martyrdom. They had much, after all, to distract them: Tammany, Zion, the Vatican, Tatary were all scattering gold, erecting diversionary sideshows, setting up brothels and gambling casinos, providing every conceivable sensation designed not so much to exploit the poor as to seduce the rich: those old patrician families who had founded America's wealth. Their sons and daughters were meanwhile lured to destruction by pretty baubles, negro jazz and bathtub gin.

Griffith created the greatest work of its kind. Every line and scene, no matter how splendid, drummed home the same urgent message:

BEWARE THE SERVANTS OF ROME AND ZION!!! FOLLOW ONLY CHRIST!!! YE SHALL FIND THE ENEMY WITHIN YOUR OWN WALLS! BE WARY OF THE PRIEST

AND THE RABBI – FOR ONE HAND IS EXTENDED IN FRIENDSHIP WHILE THE OTHER HIDES A KNIFE!!! BE FOREVER ALERT! BE DEAF TO FALSE PROPHETS AND THE TEMPTATIONS OF LUST, PRIDE & GREED!!! JUDA VERRECKE!! THE DAY OF THY JUDGEMENT DRAWS NEAR! In the modern scenes we see a young man falsely accused, ruined by forces of international finance. We witness the treacherous betrayal and slaughter of the French Protestants by their Catholic Queen Catherine de Medici. We see the priests of Babylon destroying their own civilisation from within and opening their gates to the invading Persian tyrant! Also we have the spectacle of Jesus of Nazareth offering us both hope and the solution to all this terror. And they complained this was obscure! Obscure! *Er macht die Tür auf! Lassen sie ihn hereinkommen!* It is simply that they refused to see what was obvious. It did not suit them to let him in. It is the same old story. Ironically it is also Griffith's own story, just as it is mine. I have sometimes wondered at the significance of the coincidence; his life and work frequently mirrored my own. I am sure it is not difficult for anyone, realising how much of my optimism and faith had become invested in Griffith and the America he represented, to imagine my horror when, almost as soon as I had passed the last immigration barrier and a porter was loading my trunks into a motor cab, I read in the *New York Herald* that the great director's company must inevitably be declared bankrupt. This was a terrible blow, particularly since I had planned to offer my services to him as soon as my business in Washington was completed. Stunned, I climbed into my seat. I was borne off to the city's heart, through densely crowded streets flanked by enormous skyscrapers and criss-crossed by the metal bands of an intricate elevated railway. At last, as my mind began to receive this profusion of new impressions, I tossed the paper aside, certain that Mr Griffith would find a means of resolving his difficulties. I had not been prepared for New York to remind me in the least of my Mother Country, yet somehow it was as if I had come home. It was all far grander and more highly concentrated, of course, but to me the city was nearer to being a blend of St Petersburg, Kiev and Odessa than it was of any European city I had visited. I had not, for instance, expected to be impressed by so much solid, old-fashioned good taste in buildings and decoration. As the cab at last drew up outside the Hotel Pennsylvania's vast structure and the door was opened by a uniformed black man whose white glove saluted me in a most dignified manner, I almost thought to see my mother and Captain Brown waiting for me beyond the massive entrance. It made me long for them, for Esmé and for Kolya, to share this experience. Porters again took charge of my luggage. The interior of the Pennsylvania was even more impressive than the exterior. The lobby seemed more spacious than Notre Dame cathedral, with shops and restaurants around its edges. One restaurant alone boasted a full-size fountain. High overhead an elaborate balcony surrounded the lobby. Its columns and the richness of its materials gave it the appearance of a pagan Roman temple. If the staff had been wearing togas, rather than tasteful conventional suits, it would not have seemed incongruous. I was glad I had chosen my finest uniform. In it, I did not feel overwhelmed by the hotel's magnificence. I made the long walk across mosaic and deep carpet to the reception desk. My reservation was confirmed by a polite, open-faced individual who softly told me his name was Cornihan, an under-manager. I must let him know if there was anything I needed or anything which did not suit me. Then, within an elevator so festooned with gilded wrought iron and carved oak it could have carried Zeus himself to Olympus, I was borne up to the eighteenth floor and escorted to a room which, in luxury and size, was the equal to the best I had known in Europe. Again, my Kolya had not let me down. I felt immediately secure, even though I had never been situated so high above the ground before. The porter was genuinely grateful for the tip. He said he was at my service. Here was another unexpected feature of this city: the good manners and cheerful helpfulness of her citizens. From my windows I could look down at the distant street to where a tiny Gothic church stood sandwiched between much taller buildings, its steps alive with miniature figures, constantly coming and going. This, I learned, was actually St Patrick's Cathedral. I think it heartened me at the time to see this citadel of Papism so thoroughly overshadowed.

It was immediately obvious that New York was a city consciously and vigorously dedicated to the Future, impatient with anything or anyone threatening to stop her march forward, her constant experimenting, her willingness to tear down the old in order to replace it with something newer and better. That she still cherished tradition was obvious from many of her interiors, which paid wholehearted tribute to our common culture; nonetheless she was unafraid of progress, as most European cities were. As soon as I was unpacked, changed and rested, I followed my old habit and plunged straight into her streets, to explore for myself the mysteries and wonders of Manhattan. In 1921 the Empire State Building was merely a vague notion, while the Chrysler, most beautiful of all skyscrapers, was still being designed. It would be these which would completely outshine New York's great rival, Chicago, so that she finally refused further competition. Knowing nothing of any of this, I was sufficiently amazed by the strange proportions of the twenty-storey Flatiron Building, the gigantic classical majesty of the Times Tower. I had sailed on Leviathan to a city of Behemoths, and though one element in me was daunted by the sheer hugeness of the place I was primarily delighted. No photograph could prepare a European for that kind of scale or offer any understanding of what the city really is: a truly modern, unselfconscious, aggressively unashamed urban massing of steel, stone and brick, insouciantly balanced on a tiny slab of rock in the shallows of the Atlantic Ocean. As for what she had become, since the Carthaginians overwhelmed her, I shall not speak. In 1921 she radiated a convincing aesthetic, an authentic, boundless confidence in scientific and social progress. In her were quintessentially combined all the other cities of the Earth; she was a metropolis conceived as nothing more or less than herself, when millions of people might live together and work for humanity's triumph over Nature, the Past, our very origins. I lay awake on that first night and heard her heart pounding as violently as my own. I could believe, in some barely understood way, that she and I were the same entity, with an energetic, unsleeping mind, an active will to put a mark upon the world and leave it radically unchanged.

Here was the sum of six million humans beings' optimistic hopes for a better world. Here, mankind's technology could defeat those ancient demons which enslaved its forefathers for uncountable generations. Here were fortunes greater than all previous fortunes, ambitions higher than any earlier ambitions, possibilities which until now had never been conceived. It was no longer any surprise that provincial minds, rural minds, the minds of small people, might draw back from this and brand it evil because it was so dramatically unfamiliar. Many Americans refused even to stand on the far side of a New York bridge to look upon this wonder from a distance. To them not only was she the new Babylon, she was Sodom and Gomorrah, Rome and Jerusalem all rolled in together. I was not to know that my mockery of their fears would one day prove foolish, that they understood something I, in those days, did not. New York was a mighty machine. Like any machine she had no morality. Her goodness or her evil depended entirely on the motives of who controlled her.

She was a sensitive and highly complex machine. All she lacked was the capacity to move from place to place and one day, I thought, she might even have that. The astonishing geometry of fire escapes, water towers, elevated railroads, streetcar wires, baroque ironwork, telephone lines, power cables, bridges, lamp posts, illuminated signs and arches in combination with the buildings themselves formed a profoundly complex grammar of its own; the infinite variety of curves and angles made up the characters of a mysterious and scarcely decipherable alphabet. As many-levelled as the human brain itself, New York appeared to possess the same limitless potential for creativity and intricacy. Her traffic was unceasing, flowing like blood through a maze of veins and arteries, most of it motor-driven, though there were still a good many horses. Constantly moving, these trams, cabs, buses, cars and wagons possessed the boisterous momentum of logs in a torrent. The great avenues and cross streets, conduits of this vast machine, steamed and hissed from a thousand vents and grills; yet no one could claim her citizens were grey-faced automata, designed only to serve her, as Lang claimed in his film *Metropolis*. New York was then firmly under the control of her citizens, who were still primarily true born Americans or English-speaking settlers. They had made her, now they used her. For their own convenience. This was evident in the postures they struck in the streets, their easy familiarity with modern innovation. I had never seen fresh ideas treated with such amiably casual interest as in New York and I never would again. All the inventions pouring from the factories of Edison, Ford, Tesla and America's other twentieth-century wizard-heroes, all the gadgets and marvels of our machine age, were taken by New Yorkers as available to them by right. Here every family appeared to own a motor car, a phonograph, a vacuum cleaner, an electric iron, a power wringer, while telephones, refrigerators and automatic washing machines were the property of quite ordinary people. Only the degenerate immigrants, the uneducated, jealous, desperately greedy sons and daughters of European gutters, of Asiatic opium addicts and African savages did not have these things (in such quantities at least) and this of course was largely because they had neither the intelligence nor the background to understand them; indeed, many developed deep superstitious terror of, for instance, washing machines, and would not allow them into their dens, even when they were offered.

The city dazzled me with brilliant signs picked out in thousands of tiny coloured bulbs. Everywhere I heard the slamming of metal upon metal, the humming of motors, the clicking of cogs, the whirring of dials and indicators, while from the network of railroads, big and small, overground and underground, came a squealing of wheels on tracks, of warn-

347

ing horns, escaping steam and efficient airbrakes. To me this was a symphony whose themes emerged gradually, as in Wagner, forming a unity when sometimes one least expected resolution. Back and forth in the streets ran ragamuffins. They sold newspapers, soft drinks, ice creams, candy. They yelled impossibly garbled phrases; words I could not even begin to interpret. Moreover, this unceasing vitality flourished in a climate of pressing, almost tangible heat, making me sweat so badly I was soaked from top to bottom before I had walked a few hundred yards from the hotel.

On my first morning I went nowhere in particular. I merely strolled from block to block, taking stock of my surroundings as I always did. I enjoyed the bustle and the anonymity. Somewhere around East 19th Street I stepped into a little café and ordered a cup of coffee. New Yorkers, generally thought ill-mannered by other Americans, seemed elaborately polite compared, say, to Parisians. When I had finished my coffee, I made enquiries and was directed to a large pawnbroking house only a block or two away. Here I was able to change a gold ring, inscribed and given to me by M. de Grion as a Christmas present, into a moderately good-sized sum. Next I walked on a little further until I reached Sixth Avenue and soon discovered a reasonably decent gentleman's outfitters who provided me, within two hours, with a white linen suit, white spats and gloves, a Panama. I was now better equipped for the weather, if not for the dust and dirt. I had the feeling, on the question of style, however, that it would not have mattered much what I wore. Aside from Constantinople, I had never seen such a huge variety of racial types and national costumes. Some were strange, such as the Hassids or pigtailed Chinese, but others displayed their cultural origins more subtly, in Bavarian hats, Russian boots, Turin-cut trousers. What was most cheering for me was that I had been led to believe I should see swarthy aliens crowding every sidewalk but this was far from the case. There were no more of these in the ordinary parts of New York than in any cosmopolitan city. New York was in this respect little different from Odessa.

That afternoon I walked down Seventh Avenue to the secluded tree lined squares and eighteenth-century houses of Greenwich Village. These relatively low apartment blocks and ordinary shops reminded me in their general respectability of my boyhood Kiev, though at that time, because the area was pleasant and cheap, increasing numbers of artists were moving in, giving the neighbourhood something of the quality of the Left Bank. Here and there it was possible for me to imagine myself suddenly transported to the country. The abundance of flowers and foliage pleased my senses as, sitting for a while in Washington Square, I watched children playing familiar games. These quasi-rural areas are required in any real city, I think. The tranquillity one finds in them is somehow more positive than anything discovered in the country itself. Here I used to visit the roof garden of Derry and Tom's Department Store. I would go there two or three times a week in the summer, for this same sense of peace. The traffic could be heard, but it was in another world, so distant. On a fine day, listening to the fountains and seeing pink flamingoes wade from pool to pool, one could experience few greater pleasures. But presently of course Derry's is sold to a Russian Jewess who refuses the consolation of her roof garden to lonely old men and women and makes it the exclusive territory of the fashionable and wealthy. Who cares if I have nowhere to sit now; no birds to feed; nowhere to throw a penny and make a wish?

In New York, more than anywhere else, I developed an immediate sense of competency; the kind of security which comes from an instinctive understanding of one's environment. The more complex a city, the better I felt. The country dweller retreats in confusion from the city's images and noise, baffled by its millions of intersecting segments of information. To him it seems all contradictions, mystery, threat. As in Constantinople, I immediately relax. Dangers in the city are easily recognised or anticipated. In the country I am helpless. What does the crack of a twig, the angle of a leaf, the way a plant has been pressed down underfoot mean to me? If New York was, as many said, a jungle, then I was a beast naturally bred for that jungle. Within a few days of strolling aimlessly around and absorbing images, sounds, scents, I knew virtually all I needed to survive and, if necessary, conquer. Helen Roe saw me once or twice, but she was anxious to leave for Florida. She said New York was a filthy city and the people in it were scum. Our shipboard romance died immediately she reached land. Now that more familiar young men were available to her, cajoling her to speakeasies and nightclubs, she no longer had use for me. I was relieved, for I too was reluctant to continue the affair. I had written to Esmé, describing my arrival, the hotel and so on. I had written to Kolya and sent a postcard to Mrs Cornelius, mentioning William Browne, the film producer. I longed for all of them to be with me, particularly Esmé. She would have delighted in the city's variety as much as I.

For the first week, however, I will admit I gave less thought to my dear ones than usual and neither did I do much in the way of furthering my career. I lived a dream of excited discovery. I ate steaks, lobsters and hot dogs, Russian dishes as fine and as elaborate as any in Odessa. I tried Italian, French and Chinese restaurants. I visited cinemas to watch the latest films and I went to the vaudeville. I rode on streetcars, buses and trains. During that period I was content with my own company and any escort would have been a distraction. I was swimming in waters at once strange and deeply familiar, modern yet full of nostalgia. Here were soda-fountains which were fantastic extensions of cafés I had known in Kiev, smelling of syrups and candies, vast tiers of carved mahogany and oak, of brass and chrome and decorated mirrors; restaurants in which small forests appeared to be growing, picture palaces which might have been transported stone by stone from ancient Assyria, mansions grand enough to be the seats of European Emperors. Standing at the intersection of Fifth Avenue and 14th Street I watched black clouds of a thunderstorm come rolling towards me, abolishing the sun, block by block, before at last it reached me, a wild hissing of rain, roaring and flashing, driving me into a doorway. I walked almost the whole length of Broadway at night, visited the Zoo, bought sweet potatoes from a vendor in Central Park, purchased for next to nothing the favours of pretty prostitutes (some of whom spoke even less English than those in Constantinople), chatted with strangers in an easy way I found impossible in Europe. I told them how wonderful their city was. The true New Yorker believes there is no world but his; questions are rarely asked about your country of origin: he merely wishes to hear if you approve of New York. This was perfectly agreeable to me for it maintained anonymity while affording sociability. I still had plenty of good cocaine and more could easily be purchased through the girls I patronised. I cheerfully drank grape juice or Coca-Cola when no spirits were readily available to me. Alcohol, of course, was an abiding and somewhat tiresome topic everywhere. The newspapers thrived on rum-running tales. Prohibition and its consequences were the national obsession. But it meant little to me. I was a child on vacation. All I wanted was to be able to go down to the waterfront, watch the liners come and go, enjoy with fascination a sea plane exhibition provided by ex-War airmen. America (though falsely believing herself the first to fly) had taken to the aeroplane as readily as she took to her native Model T. The paradoxes of a culture able to accept technological innovation so readily while allowing the antiquated morals of religious extremists to be imposed on the entire nation had not become apparent to me. Careless of the rest of the sub-continent's opinions, New York City, in the days of her glory, functioned as an independent City State. Financiers were called Morgan and Carnegie. The power of the Orient was limited to the corner drapery shop. New York fell resoundingly to Carthage in 1929; she was their greatest conquest amongst the world's cities. As Constantinople, the centre of Christendom, was made the Ottoman capital, so New York became the capital of Carthage. Mastering her, they mastered America. Eventually, inevitably, this would lead to mastery of the world.

Innocent of future disaster, I followed the marching bands into Brooklyn and Queens and went to see George M. Cohan, that quintessential American, in his latest musical. I ate baked clams and fresh oysters at Sheepshead Bay. I sat at a lunch counter near Grand Central Station reading a *New York Times* which made all the troubles of Europe seem remote, unimportant, even mildly irritating. My own interest, indeed, was in the doings of scientists and how they were honoured in America. President Harding, I read, gave Madame Curie a radium capsule worth a hundred thousand dollars as a gift from American women. After a slump, Henry Ford's cars were selling well again. I also learned that the Edison company had given a questionnaire to all prospective employees. To my despair (for I had planned at a pinch to offer my services there) I could scarcely answer a single question. One asked 'Which American city leads in the manufacture of washing machines?' Edison was, I found from the newspaper, utterly baffled by the results of these tests. He decided university people were horribly ignorant. Perhaps it was as well I did not have to endure the frustration of working for a fool.

In a very short time the discovery of an illicit whisky-still in the heart of the Bronx became more exciting than a report on Warren Harding's adamant refusal to join the League of Nations. My only reaction to an editorial denouncing the British Trade Agreement with Soviet Russia was the vague hope I might now in a letter to my mother tell her how stimulating America was. Perhaps she would be allowed to join me here. Most of us were then led to believe that now, with the Civil War over and foreign governments resuming relations with her, Russia would become increasingly moderate. The fate of my mother and Captain Brown aside, I felt this was no longer of immediate importance (besides, I was officially a Frenchman). Neither did the defeat of the Spanish Army by Abd el Krim in Morocco seem significant. By far the best news was the American Government's willingness to fund domestic aviation development. It spurred me to take stock of my limited resources and begin arranging my affairs. My vacation in New York was coming to an end. Soon it would be time to set off for Washington.

Some three weeks after my arrival in New York I bought stocks of linen paper, all the engineer's necessary drawing paraphernalia, confined myself to my suite with a large amount of cocaine, coffee and the occasional room-service meal, and began carefully to copy out designs and specifications of my already patented inventions. These I set aside in a large folder. Next I prepared the unpatented designs. These included my transatlantic aeroplane staging platforms, hospital airships capable of being sited wherever they were immediately needed, intercontinental tunnels, a cheap method for extracting aluminium from clay, a means of producing synthetic rubber, a long-distance aerodyne and a rocket-propelled airship. All would go for registration to the U.S. Patent Office. The others I would send directly to the Secretary of the Interior, whom I understood to be in charge of scientific projects. I also included copies of various press reports, although these were mainly in French. The ship's newspaper had done a little piece in English about me and my work and this, too, was enclosed.

After several days I was totally exhausted, but the work was done. I took both envelopes to the post office, sending them by registered mail to their destinations. Afterwards I went to the German Café in Chambers Street for huge helpings of sausage, veal, sauerkraut and dumplings. With its carved marble and dark onyx, its pillars, its animal heads, its polished stone counters, the restaurant was a monument of reassurance. Afterwards, in the company of one of my young ladies, I went to see a musical and some movies at the Casino Theatre. By midnight I was back at her lodgings somewhere near 9th Avenue and 53rd Street, with a line of the elevated railway running only a few feet from her front windows and there I remained for two days, entertained by Mae and her little, bright-eyed friend Irma. When I eventually returned to the Pennsylvania there was a message for me. To my considerable delight I learned Lucius Mortimer had called. He was staying at the Hotel Astor. He wondered if I would like to join him there for dinner. The note had arrived that morning. There was still time to telephone the Astor and accept his invitation. I looked forward to enjoying the company of the personable young major. I spent the rest of the day bathing, resting and tidying up various papers. By seven I had dressed

352

and because the evening was warm decided to save a cab fare by walking the few blocks to 44th and Broadway. I was now thoroughly familiar with central New York. The grid system, like so much in America, was rational enough to make life much easier once it was understood. *Der Raster liegt fest, aber die Vielfalt der Bilder ist unendlich. New York ist eine Stadt der nah beieinanderliegenden Gegensätze.* The air smelled of sweet oil and pungent smoke, of coffee, fried ham and sour cream; the wild turmoil of the daytime traffic had eased to a moderate, almost sedate, pace and I found myself wondering at my good fortune as I made my way, whistling, towards the best hotel in New York. The Astor was both opulent and dignified, but not as impressive, in my view, as the Pennsylvania. From outside it was restrained red brick, limestone, green slate and copper and inside had a somewhat hushed quality more suitable for a church or a museum which, in its solid murals and dark wood, it closely resembled. A graceful porter showed me, at length, through the Art Nouveau splendour, the marble and gold, past Ionic pilasters, painted panels, tapestries and trophies, to what he called 'the bachelors' quarters' and a room crowded with huge hunting scenes where, at a table near the far wall, my friend awaited me. The blond-haired Mortimer like me was no longer in uniform and rose in evening dress to greet me, full of smiles and good cheer. 'I'm so glad you're still here, Colonel Peterson. I was afraid I'd have to follow you to Washington.' As we ate he told me had crossed the Atlantic 'once or twice' since he last saw me. Now he had decided to give sea travel a rest for a while. Some people on his last trip had mentioned my name and he remembered his conversations with me. That, of course, had led him to try looking me up. Cutting his meat, he said how sorry he was to hear about the French scandal. I put down my knife and fork. I asked him what he meant and he became confused. Before he could explain, the waiter arrived and we ordered the next course. Then Mortimer reached into his jacket pocket to produce a substantial press cutting. 'It's from *Le Monde*,' he said, passing it to me. It was almost a month old. 'You haven't gotten any of this over here? That must be a relief.'

As I read I become increasingly horrified. The headlines were clear enough. There were pictures of myself, M. de Grion, Kolya, in happier days. A fanciful sketch of my completed airship. The shut down hangars near St-Denis. Our Aviation Company had collapsed completely and fraud was alleged. According to police reports the Chief Engineer (myself) had fled France, taking crucial documents proving the

honesty of his partners. M. de Grion's son-in-law, Prince Nicholas Petroff, was quoted as being baffled. He had been completely duped by
me. It seemed the majority of stock was mine. I had sold it at a profit
and escaped with my fortune, perhaps back to Constantinople where it
seemed I might be wanted by the British for aiding Mustafa Kemal's
rebels. My sister, still in Paris and desolate, had never guessed what I
was planning.

'This is meaningless,' I told Mortimer. 'Prince Petroff is my best
friend. He's obviously been misquoted. But it's damned bad news for
me. I had no idea!'

'I doubt you can be extradited on the evidence they seem to have.'
Mortimer was deeply sympathetic. 'Presumably you didn't anticipate
this sort of publicity?'

'Petroff warned me there might be an attempt to make me the scapegoat for the company's collapse. That's why I came to America. But I
hadn't guessed how vicious the papers would be. What they say is nonsense. They're plainly putting words in Kolya's mouth. He's my oldest,
closest friend. M. de Grion must be giving them all that. He was never
over fond of me. Esmé's due here soon. I hope to God she doesn't suffer!'

'She'll still come?'

'No question of it. And Petroff, too.'

'They have your address? Maybe it's as well you're going to Washington.' He frowned at me almost suspiciously, as if he hardly believed
I could be so innocent.

I was offended. 'My dealings have been honest at all times, Major
Mortimer. For your information, I'm not a wanted man in Turkey,
either. I was instrumental in some arrests of nationalist rebels and spies.
I left Constantinople entirely for personal reasons.'

'By the looks of it, you've been poorly treated, colonel. If the scandal
broke over here it could have some mighty unwelcome results. You
know what the yellow press thinks of foreigners. They're all anarchists
and crooks trying to take over the country.' He bent his body away from
the table as the waiter set out fresh plates. Then Mortimer grinned suddenly. 'Doesn't it make you long for a drink?'

For the first time since I had arrived in America I desired a large
vodka. I nodded vigorously and he winked at me. 'We'll finish here
then go visit some friends of mine. They'll accommodate us. What do
you plan to do about this?' He folded and replaced the cutting.

I was at a loss for an idea. There was no easy means of clearing my name. Only Kolya could help there. Esmé would agree to be a witness. But where and when could a trial be heard? I asked Mortimer.

'In Paris. I'm damned sure of it. You're safe enough in the States. The chances of a visa extension, however, might be a shade slim. You need friends in high places, old man!' He looked critically at the cheeseboard, his knife hovering. Then, with a sigh, he impaled some Boston Blue.

'There's Mr Cadwallader in Atlanta.'

'The lawyer? But it's your word against theirs. I was thinking along slightly different lines. Who do you know in Washington?'

There was no one. Deep in thought, Major Mortimer abstractedly chewed his cheese. 'I might be able to help. I know one or two people with good political connections. Would a letter of introduction be of use?'

'You're very kind.' I doubt if I sounded enthusiastic. My future had again become uncertain. I could not go back to Europe. I might have to flee the United States. Was Esmé forever lost to me? I resisted panic. Desperately I tried to keep my mind in balance, but now things seemed blacker than ever before. I remember little of finishing the meal. At some stage Major Mortimer helped me to the sidewalk and hailed a taxi. Within a quarter of an hour we had entered the blue swing doors of one of New York's many cellar bars. Inside was noisy jazz music, wild dancing, everything I had been glad to leave behind in Paris. Just then it was the last place I wanted to be, but Mortimer steered me through the crowd to a shadowy back room. He ordered drinks. They were not very strong cocktails, but I was glad of them and drank several. The speakeasy was patronised entirely by the well to do. It was no ordinary bohemian café. Lucius Mortimer was acquainted with many of the other clients and was obviously a regular and popular visitor. To them he spoke a patois almost impossible for me to follow. I had heard him and Jimmy Rembrandt using it between themselves on board ship. I grew rapidly drunk. By about one o'clock, as I continued to babble my problems to him, Lucius put a hand on my arm, looking me directly in the eyes. 'Max,' he said, 'I think of myself as your pal and I'm going to try to help. Jimmy's turning up here soon. We'll talk to him. What if we went with you to Washington? I could introduce you to my friends. Do you have all your patents with you?'

I told him what I had done. My letters had said I should be in Washington shortly and would call to ensure the plans had arrived. I had been sensible, said Mortimer. I should relax and take another drink. Once I knew the right people my troubles would be over. 'You can rely on me, I need hardly say, not to breathe a word of the airship scandal. But sooner or later it could hit our papers, then you'll have to be completely prepared. Forewarned is forearmed. The press like nothing better than screaming for foreign blood these days. Only last week, in my hometown – in Ohio of all places – the Ku Klux Klan lynched two Italians. They were either anarchists or Catholics. People are even less fond of Russians, so you'd better make it clear you're French and go on calling yourself Max Peterson. You could be half English. That should stop suspicion. I'll cover you. We met during the War when you were flying with the Lafayette Squadron. Everybody loves the Lafayette.'

I was reluctant to involve myself in lies. However, I accepted Mortimer must have a better sense of the situation's realities, so I agreed he should decide what was to be told to people. I would back him up in anything he said. I remained impressed by the American's open-hearted generosity. What European near stranger would have done so much? I was almost tearfully grateful by the time Jimmy Rembrandt arrived, with two young women, actresses from a nearby show, and embraced me as warmly as any Russian. He slapped me on the back, announcing how much he had missed my company since the ship. A bottle of outrageously dubious champagne was ordered. This he chiefly fed to the ladies who, clucking and preening in their pink and blue feathers and silks, soon took on the appearance of confounded chickens. 'Sounds like a great adventure!' Rembrandt was in an ebulliently reassuring mood. 'We'll get the train to Washington tomorrow. Can you leave that soon, Max?'

We toasted our good fortune, our mutual destinies, the happy chance of our Mauretanian meeting. With such splendid companions I should have no difficulties when I came to confront and win over the American capital. Jokingly, they encouraged me to 'remember' my English mother, my father, the distinguished French soldier, and his father, who had fought for the South in the Civil War. We even considered an ancestor who had raised a volunteer regiment for the War of Independence. By the time we left the 'speakeasy' I was cheerful again, already half believing my new identity. They had struck exactly the right compromise, particularly in view of our destination. Their friends were Southerners to whom the only acceptable foreigners were those who had supported the Confederate cause sixty years before. Jimmy Rembrandt's own mother, he told me, was from Louisiana and his Pennsylvanian father had been in Democratic politics until a riding accident just before the War. In the small hours we took a taxi back to my hotel while they lifted imaginary glasses to 'Max Peterson, Gentleman of France' and attempted to teach me how to whistle *Dixie*. The tune was important, they told me gravely, but the ability to remember all the words would prove crucial if I was to endear myself to their friends. As to my political views, they said, these were hardly in need of improvement at all.

With friendly good humour they helped me to an elevator before continuing on to the Astor, promising to collect me in the lobby next morning. Our association was going to be of enormous mutual benefit. It would make my French aviation schemes, they said, look like a cardboard model of the real thing. I reached my room and tried to pack, but unexpectedly the melancholy returned in full force once I was alone. I lay on my bed and wept for Esmé. How long must it be before I could be reunited with her? What crime had I committed in the eyes of God, to be so severely punished while the cynical rich and ruthlessly powerful went scot-free?

I would be wise to leave New York. Those same forces were lying in wait for me there, though I hardly guessed it then. In my wanderings I had seen the dark emissaries of Carthage scurrying about their destructive work. Here and there the signs were still up, but they would not stay there for long. In those parts of Harlem occupied by decent German families, threatened on all sides by blacks and orientals, I had seen the placards in the windows: *Keine Juden, und keine Hunde.* But it would be no more than a year or two before they were removed. Then the families themselves would be driven from the city and grinning negroes would turn those comfortable houses into squalid slums. New York would try to accept them: it was a question of pride. But New York was wrong to let it go so far. It tolerated monumental heresies: these black messiahs and philosemitic quasi-prophets abounding there today. Christians are taught to tolerate everything and so we do – but we cannot and should not tolerate evil, nor should hypocrisy and theft go unpunished. Those Sephardic Jews, they claimed to be Dons of Spain, as if that were something to boast of. The Spanish Empire was financed by Carthaginian gold, advanced by Catholic ruthlessness, informed by a pagan lust for destruction. Americans had already driven them back

357

in a series of heroic wars. Now they are returning in a thousand guises. They cannot be stopped. And their *Einiklach* gloat in their massive towers, their steel and concrete fortresses, riding in Rolls Royces up and down Wall Street, controlling the destinies of all the world's nations, while the Dons of Little Italy, of Brooklyn, the Bronx and Spanish Harlem, are richer than any Morgan or Carnegie, yet leave no charities, no foundations, no libraries behind them: only ruin.

I cannot blame myself for what became of New York. The rot, if I had chosen to look, was already there. I was blinded by the fabulous potential of the city, its grandiosity, its beauty. And for me it remains the most beautiful city on Earth. When the warm morning sun shone on those grey and yellow towers, or when it set, brilliant scarlet over Brooklyn Bridge, I would gasp in wonder, no matter how many times I had seen it before. I have heard they are demolishing more and more of it, replacing the old skyscrapers with things of black glass and featureless stone, that they have torn down almost everything and what they have not torn down they have gutted and spoiled. The Pennsylvania Hotel is now a grey, uncomfortable warren, without style or taste, taken over by the Hilton firm: a machine for processing travellers when they step out of those flying cylinders. And all done in the noble cause of democracy. This is egalitarianism corrupted. The dreams of New York's great builders, of the murdered architect Stanford White, become wretched nightmares. The ghost of the old city hovers over the new. White was murdered in the roof garden of Madison Square, across the street from where my hotel stood. He built the set for his own destruction. And now that is demolished, too. He brought the best of Europe to America and he created architecture which was purely, confidently American in style and proportions. They mock all that now. Everywhere in the world the forces of Carthage are dynamiting our culture, our memories, our aesthetic monuments, replacing them with buildings indistinguishable one from the other, or from one country to another. They are wiping out our heritage; they are driving away our memories. Our very identities are therefore threatened. In 1906 White's enemies conspired to kill him. The assassin was a Jew named Thaw who alleged White had seduced his wife. It was significant, however, that Thaw was eventually found 'not guilty because insane' and so avoided the consequences of his crime. Another shot fired for Carthage which went unpunished. *Ich vil geyn mayn aveyres shiteln*, indeed!

By eight the next morning, having pulled myself together with the help of cocaine and packed my trunks, I called for a porter, following him down to the echoing lobby. As I paid the balance of my bill (which took an alarming bite from my remaining funds) Jimmy Rembrandt approached me. He was smiling and full of energy, shaking my hand and saying I looked one hundred percent. Mortimer, he said, felt ill and could hardly speak, but would be with us on the train. We began to cross from the entrance hall to the Pennsylvania Station, immediately over the street, my bags on a trolley behind us. 'Luce is afraid he has the 'flu. But we know what's caused his symptoms, don't we, Max.' Entering the Doric arcade with its rows of elegant shops and shafts of dusty sunlight, we saw Mortimer waiting for us near the Grand Stairway. He was as smartly dressed as Rembrandt, but did look pale and sorry for himself. He tried to smile at me. 'Ah, Colonel Peterson, the famous French aviator.'

Jimmy laughed. 'I hope you can learn to like the colour red, colonel.' He was amused by my confusion. 'They'll be rolling out the carpet for you in Washington very soon now.' Everywhere around us vast numbers of New Yorkers came and went about their business. The station actually lay below us and we descended steps forty feet wide (built in 'Travertine' stone after a Roman model) to the main waiting room which was also of the same mellow cream-tinted stone and was meant, apparently, to resemble a Roman bath. For many years the original New Yorkers had seen themselves as following on from the traditions of Classical Rome. Today, of course, the armies of the Vatican have created an unexpected and unwelcome comparison with a more recent Rome. 'Rely on us,' Jimmy went on, 'and within a week the whole of Washington will be eating out of our hands.' Our luggage was stowed and we went to have breakfast at one of the station's many lovely restaurants. By noon we were aboard a magnificent 'limited' train, a symphony of dignified steel pulled by a massive articulated locomotive. We slowly moved out of Pennsylvania Station. Only the old Tsarist trains could begin to match American luxury. She, like Russia, had been a country more dependent upon the railroad than any other kind of transport. Like Russia, she had lavished all her pride and creative artistry on these rolling citadels of comfort. We had reservations in the dining-car, but Major Mortimer did not feel like eating. He let Captain Rembrandt and I leave him to his misery and take our seats beside the wide window. Slowly New York's skyscrapers gave way to single-storeyed suburbs and then to New Jersey's rolling hills and forests. We crossed wide iron webs of bridges spanning rivers as broad as any I knew in Russia; we steamed along the ocean coast itself, then turned West through fields of corn which might have grown on my native Ukrainian steppe. Soon we passed the occasional factory or power station, flaring and belching against the shimmering summer sky, and I thought suddenly that all this timber, this cultivated farmland, these steel mills and generators, represented not merely enormous wealth, but tremendous optimism, too. The size of the country became apparent to me for the first time. It shared that sense of limitless space with Russia and it also shared the same richness of resources, the same will to expansion. The problems of Europe became as insignificant as their parochial ambitions. There was no need for me to fear little countries with little ideas. Here in America I should be able to grow as I had once hoped to grow in Ukraine. Eating lunch, I looked out at the plains and meadows of America, at her great, grey cities and her golden hills, and I spoke to Jimmy of the technological Utopia I envisioned. It would be fundamentally American, rejecting the old hampering traditions of Europe, concentrating on a future wholly 'Made in U.S.A.'

Jimmy was delighted and at the same time seemed almost surprised by my fervour. 'That's the stuff,' he kept saying. 'That's exactly the stuff.' He was as convinced as I that my genius had been wasted on Europe. My talent was too big for them. The United States was large enough and confident enough to welcome what I could offer and pay me what I deserved. America was about to boom bigger than ever before. So much money was being generated there were not enough things to spend it on. He told me I should think of forming a company like Edison's. I should employ staff, technicians, different experts, and I should have workshops built. 'Invest in America, Max, and you will win all the hearts and minds you'll ever need. This is the right time for it.'

The very rhythm of the train, steady, ebullient, increased my notion that Washington must provide me with the funds, prestige, resources I had always known were my due. The Parisian affair had been an unimportant diversion. It had taught me to be careful of those in whom I put my trust. I prayed Kolya would soon escape that dreadful web of greed and intrigue and, bringing Esmé with him, join me in the American capital.

'France has neither the cash nor the nerve to go for anything really big,' said Jimmy. We were crossing the Delaware. In the distance an alliance of tall pines, smokestacks, pylons, marched up both the river's steep banks. 'That was where you went wrong, Max. It doesn't matter how good the scheme is. It has to have a true grounding in the realities of time and place.'

I said I still blamed the socialist trade unions, but he disagreed. 'Unions strike one way or another because it pays them or their leaders to strike. They might have meant to get better wages. More likely someone was slipping them the dough.' He paused significantly and looked at me, but I had no idea what he wanted to hear. He went on: 'It could have been anyone. Your own directors. The Germans. The British.'

'I still find it hard to believe people could be so devious.'

'You have that in common with Americans, old man. We're shocked by it. And that's why we're determined to have no more truck with Europe. Let them knife each other in the back. They won't have a chance to get a crack at us.'

Having made sure Lucius was not seriously ill, we continued on to the deep plush chairs, the brass and mahogany fixtures, of the Club Car where we smoked cigars and drank root beer into which Jimmy had somehow introduced strong Scotch. The Limited now moved with stately, unhurried swiftness through wooded hills and valleys. It was supremely comfortable with its padded seats set in spacious carriages served by efficiently trained waiters capable of finding almost anything one desired. I wondered if, when she came to her senses, Russia could one day restore her rail service to the same standard. After all, Russia, like the U.S.A, had an almost limitless supply of suitable raw materials. Here was the model we should seek to emulate. America had learned to deal with the Bolshevik threat. Unlike New York, the rest of the country recognised the danger, pursuing its Reds with a directness Europe should have imitated. The most lazily tolerant of all nations before the War, America, as a result, quickly found out the heavy price of such decency. Now when she closed her doors no one could blame her. She was anxious to quarantine herself from the social and mental diseases rife beyond the Atlantic. She would not discover until 1929, when Carthage struck, that she had acted too late. The whole country tottered and cried desperately for help. And who should turn up with smiling lips and helping hand, as if out of the blue? An apparent Samaritan calling himself by the name of a great American Franklin D. Roosevelt, Bolshevik sympathiser and *Mishling,* stepped forward, took the helm and from then on the United States was doomed. She became the greatest single prize that ever fell to Carthage. But when I sat in the Pullman smoking Coronas with Rembrandt, the fight was still undecided. I was more than willing to join the struggle. I did my best along with so many noble Americans, but we were laughed at for our pains; we were hounded from power. And all the while the Orient was patiently biding her time. *Nito tsu vemen tsu reydn . . .*

She put a Jew in the White House just as, a half century before, she put one in 10, Downing Street. Another ruled France. A committee of them ruled Germany. Of Spain, we need say nothing. Portugal? Denmark? Who knows? They would say *Ver veyst?* And the terrible thing is they would probably be right. Oriental fatalism seizes them. They sprawl on the public street, the opium pipes still in their hands. And they call me a fool? They are zombies, drugged by secret masters, then sent in a howling mass against the President. They are not killed. The police are humane. They know what corrupts these shambling, filthy creatures, the sons and daughters of respectable citizens. What can they do?

It was not long before the train began to near Washington and Jimmy led me back to where Lucius Mortimer lay curled in sleep across three seats. He woke up suddenly, glaring at Jimmy as if we had attacked him, then as he recognised us he began to smile. Upon our enquiring after his health, he said he felt much better. We prepared to disembark.

Since our carriages had been cooled by fans, I was not ready for the heat. It struck me the moment I stepped onto the platform. I had thought, since New York had been so warm, I was suitably dressed for Washington, but the humidity here was profound. One waded in it as if eye deep in a lake, constantly struggling for breath. I was aware of nothing else until we had entered the cab taking us to our hotel. I sank back, gasping, while Jimmy and Lucius laughed at my discomfort. They had known what to expect and were used to it. I asked what kind of person would site the centre of government in the middle of what was plainly a tropical swamp. For a moment, through the windows, I saw nothing but confirming greenery, but this gave way to lawns, brick and stone buildings spaced so far apart I felt almost uneasy, for I had become used to the dense concentration of New York. Indeed, I had a desire to pull down the cab's blinds until we reached our hotel. It was close to dusk, yet the air was still hot and damp, and to me the city seemed virtually deserted; hardly a city at all. 'You'll either learn to take it easy here,' Jimmy explained sympathetically, 'or the weather'll kill you.' Now there were vague glimpses of wide, tree-lined streets, large white buildings, a few illuminated signs. The buildings came closer together and grew a little taller by the time we stopped, but I still felt uncomfortable, physically and psychically, as we entered the dim lobby of the old-fashioned hotel my friends had selected. It was called Wormley's and was apparently very respectable. We seemed the youngest guests by twenty years. In contrast to the world outside, the hotel seemed unusually cramped and everything in it crowded together. My room was small. Its wallpaper displayed a succession of golden eagles. It had a large fan on the ceiling and this cooled the air enough for me to recover, wash, and dress for dinner. Jimmy and Lucius had already arranged to meet their political friends, so I wished to look my best.

By the time we went out again, the city was dark. The streets were well lit, though unnaturally wide, and the electrics glinted off the thick foliage of oaks, chestnuts and cherries. Washington gave the impression of being half town, half forest. Again I felt extremely uneasy, as if foolishly I had allowed myself to be lured out of an environment where I could trust my judgment and into one where it would be impossible for me to make well calculated decisions. There was something at once artificial and rural about the place. It was even less of a 'natural' capital than St Petersburg. Perhaps its only industry was politics? I suggested this to my companions and they were amused. 'Its main products are hot air and niggers,' said Jimmy, 'and you can't see much of either in the dark.'

Pennsylvania Avenue was as wide and tree-lined as the other streets I had so far seen. Set back from the road was the Colonial (what the English tend to call 'Georgian') neo-Graecian structure known as the Restaurant Pocock. Inside was all the atmosphere associated with the best sort of London club. Women were not allowed there and the main rooms were filled with well-to-do, self-confident men, most of whom evidently knew one another. Again, the three of us were the youngest guests. I assumed most of the restaurant's clients were in politics. They carried themselves with the amiable assurance of men used to authority. There was a preponderance of grey hair and white whiskers, large cigars and quiet, private humour. I could not remember ever before visiting an establishment which had, down to the pattern on the carpet, such an impervious ambience. One could be certain that every single individual in the place was a true born American. I think this added to my own sense of relaxation. As our trio ('the Three Musketeers', Jimmy called us) entered we were greeted by a deferential negro who showed us to a table already occupied by two older men. The table was in an alcove made invisible from the street by lace curtains and heavy drapes. Arranged about the Restaurant Pocock's walls glass cases contained old books, ornaments, a variety of bric-à-brac. All of these, Jimmy assured me, had historical importance. This was my first real encounter with the American obsession for honouring almost any artefact older than twenty years as an antique. He apologised for arranging the meeting at Pocock's which he thought stuffy and 'dry'. It was almost impossible to get a drink in Washington unless you were at someone's private house. We should have to go through the dinner on grape juice and pop. I am still more amused than upset by this state of affairs, though wine had become commonplace to me, but it was a source of permanent anger to many Americans.

At the table I was introduced to Mr Charles Roffy and Mr Richard Gilpin who received me with exquisite and elaborate manners. They said they were glad to know me. 'Delighted to welcome such a distinguished visitor to our capital,' said Mr Roffy. I was to call them Charlie and Dick. I said I also was glad to know them and would be flattered if they would address me as Max. They smiled and laughed and patted my arm saying they were easy-going people down here and not given to a whole lot of formality. They were pleased I found their rough country ways acceptable. This self-deprecating style was, I knew, a feature of genuinely good breeding in America. Charlie Roffy was a tall man whose large, comfortable belly threatened the buttons of his waistcoat. He breathed heavily, as fat men sometimes do, and the redness of his face served to emphasise his slate-coloured eyes, a shock of fading sandy hair and greying moustache. He had heard my mother was English. His own ancestors were from Yorkshire. Did I know Yorkshire? I said I had rarely been North of the Border, save as a boy. This evidently satisfied Jimmy Rembrandt who glanced at Lucius Mortimer with the air of a teacher observing a favourite student. Dick Gilpin, older, with that stern, military face once identified with Victorian generals, a thick white walrus moustache and snow-white hair worn rather long, was the epitome of the distinguished statesman. He looked me over shrewdly even as he joked that his own forefathers had been somewhat more cautious in describing their exact origins. He believed some to have been cattle thieves in Kent. Quite possibly my ancestors had hanged some of his. This was another feature of the American aristocrat, they frequently claimed wild antecedents in a vaguely located past. I was a little confused by the statement. Later I would meet men who boasted romantically of their Indian blood while their grandfathers, who had been settlers, cheerfully described how they had almost single-handedly wiped out an entire aboriginal nation. Moreover nothing had really prepared me for the dry humour, subtlety and breeding of these two Southern diplomats. Russia had always identified Americans as rough, naïve characters wearing shaggy buckskins or vulgar checks, eating raw buffalo meat, loudly bullying waiters with demands for 'pie'. These called me 'my dear sir' and discussed with some regret the decline in the cuisine at Delmonico's.

The two charming gentlemen won me over at once. They led me into a world I had never thought to experience, a fresh dream of Southern elegance and power, so potent it almost compensated me for my temporary loss of Esmé. Charlie Roffy told me they were both from Memphis. Their money was in cotton which was presently booming. They foresaw however an ultimate decline in the cotton trade. Memphis needed new money. That meant Memphis had to have industry. The river had always done well for the cotton trade; perhaps it would continue to do well for some other enterprises, but he and his partner were thinking in terms of speed. Since the War, he was convinced the future lay in aviation. Dick Gilpin agreed enthusiastically. Both men feared that unless investment were swiftly found for an indigenous Southern aviation industry, the North would, as he put it, once again beat them to the draw where commercial plane services were concerned. A completely Southern aircraft industry was needed, with its own brand of machines, its own aerodromes, its own power structure. Hundreds of flyers returning from Europe were Southerners. In that respect, at any rate, the expertise was available. He knew a number of politicians close to the Harding administration who were of like mind and could help push through government funds. 'What we have to come up with first, Max, is a better plane, together with some solid designs for the 'drome. Then we can discuss the various services we'll provide. What's most important is that the machines be built in Tennessee. Only solid manufacturing will make us secure. We have to stop thinking of ourselves as farmers. We must put our profits into factory plants while we still have profits. Money isn't stocks and shares, it's bricks and mortar. We hope you'll be able to help us realise that dream, sir.'

I was pleased with his directness. I already had some experience running factories abroad, I said, and, of course, I had the most advanced designs available for aircraft, both of the lighter-than- and heavier-than-air varieties.

'We need to convince government departments of that, you understand,' said Dick Gilpin. 'Look good as well as do good, if you follow me. We have plenty of competitors in this town, as you can guess.'

Hoping it was not untoward, I took the liberty of showing them some of my press cuttings. They were my affidavits, after all. I also produced my diploma from the St Petersburg Academy, various letters, and all the documents I had carefully brought out of Russia. Of course, they were in foreign languages, apart from the ship's newspaper report, but the two men seemed satisfied. Only the Russian papers disturbed them. In my anxiety to impress I had made a stupid mistake. 'What language would this be, son?' asked Charlie Roffy, stroking his pepper and salt moustache.

It was Rembrandt who saved me. 'That's Greek. A whole lot of those European universities still write their diplomas in it, sir, as you know.'

Dick Gilpin was relieved. 'So long as it ain't Russian! I'd hate to discover you were a Bolshevist, boy!'

I could not avoid a serious response. 'I am dedicated to the destruction of Bolshevism in any form.'

They in turn were comforted and approving. Dick Gilpin raised a hand, nodding rapidly, his chin on his chest, his lips thrust out. 'You've been in Europe and seen what they can do to a country. Forgive our bad taste, sir.'

Jimmy Rembrandt said he would have the diplomas translated and a general list of my 'credits' typed up by tomorrow. Meanwhile, some of my plans were already before the Secretary of the Interior and at the Patent Office. This, too, enthused our hosts, though they were puzzled as to why I had sent patents to the Department of the Interior. I said I had believed it the best place for them. My inventions ranged, after all, from planes to ploughs.

'We've plenty of good friends in that department.' Dick Gilpin lit a cigar. 'If we can be of use to you please let us know.'

We agreed to meet in a day or so. Then we might discuss future plans in greater detail. The older men regretted they had business commitments and could not spend the entire evening with us. They insisted on paying the whole bill before saying goodbye. They left us with our coffee. Captain Rembrandt was delighted. 'You've made a hit,' he said. 'Those two codgers are amongst the cunningest old foxes in Washington. They know everybody and can get almost anything they want. They'll be checking on you now, Max. But don't worry, they won't look in the foreign papers.' I was a little surprised by this apparent cynicism, yet he spoke of Roffy and Gilpin most admiringly. He said it was not cynicism. 'It's realism, Max. This here's a political city. They have to be as sure of you as they can be.'

'I'm still not clear what it is they want.'

'Expertise,' said Lucius Mortimer. 'Authenticity. They need at least one genuine scientist, a real authority to develop and project their plans, if they are to get government backing. They mean to have the first licences to operate commercial flights out of Memphis. Gilpin didn't mention it, but his son was a pilot. The boy never made it back from France. He'd talk of a time when passenger planes would replace trains. That's why Gilpin wants to get in early. Look at the fortunes made in railroads. And Ford with his automobiles. The next real killing must be in the air.'

I said it was rare to encounter such vision. But I could not determine why they should want a new plane.

'Roffy believes the man who controls plane manufacturing also ultimately controls the air roads, Max.' Mortimer warmed a fresh cigar. 'J. P. Morgan didn't just own the rolling stock. He bought the factories which made the locomotives. Roffy's a man dedicated to pulling the South out of her industrial decline. You've spoke often of *Birth of a Nation*, so you know what I mean. While she remains mainly a crop economy, Dixie'll never have the power to challenge the big Northern financial interests. Roffy gets a lot of resistance from the more old-fashioned people in Memphis, but he knows exactly what he's about. His great-uncle was a steamboat owner in the days when Mississippi water could hardly be seen for river traffic all the way down to New Orleans. But Memphis has relied on the river and cotton too long. Gilpin sees it ending. Not in ten years, maybe. But twenty. In the meantime, you could say, they're buying themselves insurance.'

'You said he was cunning.' I was cautious, not completely satisfied everything was as it should be. 'I don't want Gilpin to involve me in another swindle.'

'This isn't a swindle, old man, it's a symphony,' said Lucius Mortimer.

'He means it's an idealistic venture as much as a financial one. It will bring something good to everyone associated with it.' Jimmy Rembrandt had noticed my puzzlement. I was never wholly able to master American slang, though my proficiency would, of course, increase, and when they spoke together they remained hard to follow.

Later that night we drove out of the city towards Arlington. Jimmy and Lucius said we should celebrate. Our rented car was one of the better types of Ford, though unremarkable compared to what I was used to. Steering by moonlight we eventually turned off the main road and rolled slowly up a wooded track, into the driveway of a large house. It resembled an old Southern mansion, with a stone verandah and marble pillars, though most of it was of red brick, with white shutters. Here, my two friends said, we would be able to get a decent drink.

The house turned out to be a kind of discreet club, evidently suited to the needs of the wealthy. Save for the foyer, there were no public rooms. We were ushered, by a conservatively dressed middle-aged lady, to a suite of chambers furnished in red velvet and dark pine. 'It's on the expenses,' Jimmy told me mysteriously. 'You can order whatever you like.'

Once again that evening I found myself embarrassed, having no clear idea of his meaning. The room was beautifully decorated in a style reminiscent of French Empire. There were two or three small anterooms leading off the main one, together with a marble bathroom and toilet. The windows were closed to the world outside so the whole atmosphere was hushed and still. I remained hesitant and baffled. It evidently suited my friends to keep the secret for a while, for I was sure they could tell my state of mind.

'I think we should have some champagne.' Lucius loosened his tie. 'Even if it's a little premature. What would you say to some peachy female company, Max? Only the best. We're privileged to be here, you know. Normally you have to be at least sixty and a Senator or an Admiral to get through those doors.'

It dawned on me at last that the house was actually an exclusive bordello. I had heard that they existed in America; places where men of affairs could come without fear of interference or scandal. The discretion and sophistication of modern Americans continued to astonish me. There were subtleties to the culture which could never be guessed at unless one was exposed to them.

I spent my first night in the American capital sniffing excellent 'snow' and sharing a bottle of mediocre sparkling wine with a luscious flapper. She was a strawberry blonde in a green satin shift who called me 'handsome' and said I was 'simply cute'. The girls of New York had been nothing more than ordinary harlots one found in any big city. These Washington whores were the playthings of generals and congressmen. They were on a higher level completely. *An oysnam fun der velt!* I have never enjoyed myself so thoroughly at a brothel. Next morning Jimmy Rembrandt asked me if I had been satisfied with the girls. *Sind die Russen und Polen Freunde?* I had tasted the rewards awaiting success in America. This helped relieve me of my burden of melancholy. I could scarcely bear to think of Esmé or the difficulties poor Kolya must be encountering in Paris where he must still desperately be working to clear my name. But no good could be served by brooding. The better the distraction the more effective I could be when the time came for our reuniting.

There is a price to be paid for this method of survival.

Ich habe es dreifach bezahlt.

Fifteen

THERE IS A WIND from Tatary which blows the spoors of decadence across the world. In palaces ferociously isolated from reality languid Sultans conjure wicked and fantastic abstractions affecting the concrete destinies of millions. Trained houris, forever nibbling and sucking at their masters' private parts, confirm them in their illusion of absolute authority. Many who inhale this Oriental wind are immediately drugged; its perfumed currents permeate the world's richest merchant cities, making men believe they have only to speak of fortunes to become immediately wealthy, only to invent fanciful plots to be themselves at once possessed of political power. Hundreds of others can be convinced by these fantasies; thus providing spurious confirmation of authenticity. In Washington I began to walk on air.

Jimmy Rembrandt and Lucius Mortimer were themselves some feet above the ground, so made no attempt to hold me down. Even Charlie Roffy and Dick Gilpin encouraged me to talk first in thousands, then in millions, then in billions. Bills were either 'on expenses' or 'on the house'. My money, they would tell me frequently, was no good. It was in Washington, a place so unreal as to seem hardly a city at all, I learned that the 'grand' had become a unit of currency; one always referred to so many 'grands' and 'half grands'. The grand is beyond money. It is used in the purchase of dreams and to impress others with the glory of those dreams. So common was this currency it seemed almost vulgar to think in terms of ordinary dollars and cents. As an official of the Mississippi & Tennessee Cotton Consortium I was given my own bank account, but did not have any immediate use for it: almost everything was done on someone else's credit.

Washington is more mirage than city. Her dignified monuments are so carefully preserved, her cosmetic appearance so deeply important to her that little else seems to matter. The politicians and the public they are supposed to represent set enormous store by appearances. Sometimes Washington seemed less substantial than Griffith's Babylon. Here I learned the true meaning of political hypocrisy for while federal agents hounded the makers of home-brewed wine, jailed the farmer unable to pay his taxes, laid siege to houses of ill fame, America's senators, congressmen, generals and industrialists, her financiers and entrepreneurs, drank themselves stupid on the best quality whisky and fucked a different girl twice a day. To one another they signed over innumerable grands while in public they praised thrift and hard work, common sense, a fair day's pay. They filled the palaces of government with sonorous rhetoric, giving the vaguest euphemism the ring of reasoned truth. In the evenings they boasted of friendships with madams and bootleggers and sold their votes to the highest bidder. Meanwhile Warren Harding, soon to be murdered for his dawning realisation of their corruption, smiled blindly with innocent pride at the purity and nobility of his country's institutions.

Washington is white marble and grandiose architecture whose chief function is to impress and overawe those innocents whose money went to build it. It is as much a denial of democracy as it is a testament. For all the richness of her building materials, her weight of granite and alabaster, she is insubstantial. One sometimes felt she would take to her heels, vanishing at any moment.

I was, temporarily at any rate, successfully seduced. The chorus's rounded calves kicked up in a line from tiny, tossing skirts; bobbed hair bounced above the bright, perfect smiles; the music of saxophones, syncopated, raucous, set the place; and flivvers sped from Montreal and runners cruised off Maine. Americans had learned from Europe there was money in contradiction; a killing could be made in a climate of ambiguity; where there was abstraction, there, too, was credit. Talk was cheap and paid huge dividends. The wind from Tatary had reached the New World. In Germany the mark inflated to the point of disintegration and Washington was dismissive: it was the price a country paid for its own folly. We were watching Rudolph Valentino's enlarged lips curl around a cigarette; singing *Second-Hand Rose* in tones of whining sentimentality, pretending to a sorrow and despair most of us had not earned. Nothing had been earned. Hardly aware of the fact herself, America had become a Great Power, yet refused the consequent responsibility. Her exports went abroad and her capital stayed at home, so it was Europe who paid for America's pleasures while at the same time she was dismissed as feeble and worn out. It would be almost ten years before America's bill came in. And twenty years or more before it was paid. HenoBEK CéeT, a BéTEp BéeT.

Within their enormous temples, erected in imitation of the Greeks but to Egyptian scale, those politicians played at Romans but practised the habits of Carthage. Their city is a central core of privilege surrounded by outer rings of diminishing wealth, the rings broadening the further they are from the centre, until one reaches the great mass of negroes inhabiting broken down nineteenth-century houses, shacks and shanties situated so far from the lawns and monuments they become in a strange way entirely invisible. The negroes were like an army without a purpose, laying siege to a city they had neither the courage nor the means to attack. They could not be employed, bought off or turned away. They remained entrenched, lost in drink and drugs, whining their dreadful blues, sometimes sending a few cripples or women and children into the centre to beg. Most of them, I learned, had left good employment in the South with the idea they might be better off here. Having discovered their mistake, they were too cowardly to return to the work they were happiest doing, which is manual and mechanical, such as picking cotton or building cars. Like baffled Huns, abandoned by the main horde, they lived off the charity extended by those too good-hearted or too nervous to drive them away. These lazy creatures have always mystified me as a race. They are amiable enough when not inflamed by lust or the rabble-rousing words of some cynical white using them to his own ends. If any further sign were needed of Washington's growing narcissism and blindness to reality it was in this refusal to do anything about the growing negro problem. (Eventually they were to become the advance troops of Carthaginian conquest; the cannon fodder of their Oriental commanders. The few genuine patricians left, scions of older Southern families, warned of this consequence but the mood of the times was against them and like me they were mocked, driven into obscurity, their heritage plundered, their visions denigrated and destroyed.)

I make no claims to be a great prophet. I was never certain of doom. Indeed, I was optimistic in those days; I sought confirmation of my own faith in civilisation. It was easy enough to find. I believed if people of good will banded together justice must ultimately triumph. The wave of hedonism sweeping the West would eventually subside as people forgot the War. Was there much wrong with that? How could I guess the ramifications, the complexity of a conspiracy aimed at nothing less than the total subjugation of the White Race? Some understood, of course. I read reports about growing strength amongst the Knights of the Fiery Cross. I was attracted by the romance of their costume and their gatherings, but had assumed the movement a legendary one from Reconstruction days, used by Griffith to give colour and meaning to his marvellous allegory. To find it still alive fired my imagination. In Washington there were not many who openly shared my enthusiasm, but quite a few privately wished the Klan well. Those ivory tower politicians were more than happy to let other men don the battle hoods, mount war horses and do the real fighting. Since they had just given the vote to women (who were notoriously short-sighted and tolerant) they were now unwilling to speak out. They feared losing votes and, consequently, their soft lives in the corridors of power.

Meanwhile, spurred on by my young comrades' enthusiasm, I conceived a notion involving broadcasting radio waves on directed bands to control flying machines from a central station. By beaming electrical impulses to the engines the power supply would be all but limitless. With no need to refuel, planes could fly easily from New York to Los Angeles carrying a hundred or more passengers and never having to land. It was even conceivable a plane could travel completely around the world without a single stop! After leaving my companions in the evenings, I would work in my hotel room until the small hours. Sometimes I hardly slept, constantly reviving myself with cocaine and other stimulants. I had plenty of female company to numb the terrible sense of loss which came whenever I let myself think of Esmé. There had been no word as yet from Paris. I think this drove me to work so hard. My Memphis friends were making progress, they said, in interesting Congress, as well as private financiers. Strings had to be pulled, palms greased, but they would soon have what they wanted. Moreover, if I grew bored with Washington, I was welcome in Memphis. They travelled between the two cities constantly. For the moment, however, I was content to remain in the capital. Jimmy and Lucius had found a circle of politicians who enjoyed playing cards, so had decided to stay. They were always ready to introduce me to young women from the offices and stores, bored married ladies, delicious harlots. I had a plethora of lewd partners willing to enjoy the most imaginative sexual excesses. The great truism, I learned, of a puritanical nation is that its private gratifications exist in direct proportion to its public morals. I spent Christmas, for instance, in a little hotel near Arlington, stark naked in the company of six other men and over a dozen young women, two of them quadroons. By that time my patents were confirmed and registered (but the Interior Department had sent only polite notes and I had heard nothing from the Secretary of Commerce). To finance particular needs, not covered by my backers, I sold commercial rights to one of my minor inventions, a wireless oscillator for the cure of rheumatism. This went to a Northern businessman who was later to put my machine on the market and make his fortune, but I had left America by the time his advertisements appeared. (I saw one by chance in an old magazine.)

The day after Christmas I accompanied Lucius and Jimmy to a Ziegfeld show. They were worried I might be impatient with the slowness of developments. I reassured them. I had learned how to wait. I privately saw the aviation company as the first step in my ambition to eclipse Edison as America's most famous and successful inventor. Jimmy asked if my hotel were comfortable enough and everything else to my satisfaction.

I did not wish to seem too infatuated. 'It is all perfectly satisfactory. I'm a man of simple tastes.'

'And of course you have no financial problems.'

Lucius laughed at this. 'That must be the least of Max's worries!'

While grateful for their hospitality I had decided to let them believe I had ready means of my own. Even the fairest minded businessman is easier to bargain with if you do not seem short of assets. My occasional lack of funds I explained vaguely as something to do with the problems of negotiating cheques drawn on foreign banks. From this they concluded I kept my money chiefly in Switzerland. I refused to disillusion them. This information doubtless reached their Memphis friends. When the time came to agree salary and shares I would be in a strong position. Everyone has heard the story of the steel company which decided to sell to J. P. Morgan for five million, planned to ask ten, then were told he would give them twenty before they could open their mouths. As a matter of necessity I studied the subject of business while in Washington. One wished to be accepted, and it was therefore a vocabulary one could not afford to ignore. The Pilgrim Fathers equated godliness with material wealth. To admit to a Yankee you are poor is almost as bad as admitting to a Catholic you have been excommunicated. Also a rich foreigner, in almost anyone's eyes, is very different to a poor one. Perhaps because of my understanding and my caution, and through the good offices of Messrs Roffy and Gilpin, I had no trouble extending my visa.

New Year's Eve and my birthday were celebrated in one continuous party somewhere in Maryland. My companions were a group of well known socialites and political and army people. I remember very little of it, save that I made love to one lady in a blue lace dress behind a settee and to another in yellow on the library carpet. Because of President Harding's recent broadcast from the Arlington Cemetery everyone was interested in my radio ideas. There had also been something of a passing reaction against air travel since the crash of the ZR-2 in England, when she had collapsed in flames killing, among others, sixteen Americans. People now said commercial flight was a thing of the distant future. It was currently too dangerous. I argued with them. So advanced were my designs such an accident was impossible. Radio steering would improve my plane's safety even further. In those weeks surrounding the New Year of 1922 I explained the principles of radio waves to dozens of eminent people. I became a familiar figure in Washington, being frequently asked to parties or small dinners to present my views on science and its promise. As 'Max Peterson' I was quoted in gossip columns. I was used as an authority in the proliferation of articles about the Future which always seem to appear in newspapers at the beginning of the year. Usually I was described as Professor Max Peterson, the well known French aviator and inventor. I still have the articles. They appeared in *The Jackson Examiner, The Washington World, The Delaware Despatch, The East Texas Defender* and many other leading journals. I was not always accurately quoted, my name was occasionally misspelled, but it proved to me, and others, that I had established myself firmly in America. When Charlie Roffy and Dick Gilpin arrived back from Memphis at the end of the month they were delighted by my growing fame. It would help them considerably. They, too, had suffered a setback with the loss of the ZR-2. But a monoplane flight by Stinson and Bertaud, setting the new continuous flight record of over twenty-six hours, had improved the atmosphere, as had the new altitude record. We were now 'steaming at full speed' towards completion, said Roffy. Word would arrive from the Capitol at any time. I must seriously think about packing up here and planning to base myself in Memphis.

I was more than pleased to put Washington behind me. I still had a few hundred dollars left from the sale of my patent, but Jimmy Rembrandt had found himself short earlier and I had lent him $500. Moreover a certain married woman, wife of a New England Senator, had begun to pester me at the hotel, telephoning at inconvenient hours, threatening to charge me with rape and have me deported unless I accommodated her. I resented being blackmailed into the position of a stud stallion to be used at will. If I left the city I should have no more trouble. She would cease to interfere with my work which was nearing completion. I had finished the specifications and diagrams for the directional transmitter. When Charlie Roffy next came to see me he asked if I could leave for Memphis by February 3rd. I was at his disposal, I said. He seemed extremely excited. Everything was settled apart from a little paperwork. Our aviation enterprise could be off the ground in less than a month.

It did not take me long to put my affairs in order. I registered my new invention. I wrote once more to Esmé and Kolya. It was dangerous to contact me directly, but a message could be passed through Mrs Cornelius. I wrote to my cockney friend, telling her what I needed, wishing her luck. My star was about to ascend in Tennessee; before long I should doubtless have my own mansion and plantation. She could contact me, under the name of Colonel Peterson, at the Adler Apartments, Lindon Street, Memphis, Tennessee, where Dick Gilpin had rented me rooms.

That night I dined for the last time with my two young benefactors. They themselves were returning to New York on business. They would try to see me in Memphis as soon as they could. Inevitably we should be reunited in the near future, said Jimmy. After all we were still 'the Three Musketeers'. He would send my $500 in a few days.

On February 3rd 1922 I boarded a Pullman car in the service of the Southern Railroad Company which would take me in no more than forty-five hours to the 'City of the New Nile' as Mark Twain once described it. A little light snow had begun to fall. Wrapped in my bearskin coat, feeling the security of Cossack pistols against my thighs, I sat in a private cabin. I imagined myself a nineteenth-century explorer about to examine the interior of the virgin continent. I had had my fill of Washington and her decadent delights. I was looking forward to the more austere pleasures of Memphis. A bell rang. The train gasped. Later, at dusk,

I walked back to the observation car. Behind me the great monuments and columns were falling away. The track became two thin black lines in blurred air which gradually grew more and more agitated. Soon all I could see was the driving curtain of the blizzard, wiping away one dream so that it could be replaced by another.

Sixteen

THE MISSISSIPPI RIVER, as heavily used and as vast as the Volga, as important to American history as the Dniepr to our own, wide and shallow and winding through gentle hills, brought a frisson of recognition. It was as if I had never left Russia at all. As I raised myself in my bunk, peering through the gap in the blind, I could easily believe myself on a train bound for Kiev. All my experiences since 1917 might have been no more than a prolonged hallucinatory fever. Then the billboards and signs in English appeared and we shifted course in a scintillant dawn for the outskirts of Memphis: Little rows of miserable, unpainted shacks, sudden clearings in which stood grandiose Victorian houses whose carved wood imitated Gothic churches and French châteaux, all under a threadbare covering of snow. The impression of pre-Revolutionary Ukraine continued to persist. These suburban streets were low and wide. Tram cars in smart liveries of brass and primary paint moved decorously along avenues of bare trees. The brightly painted gables and shutters seemed those of a well to do small town rather than real city, even as the higher buildings of the centre emerged from a haze of sunrise. As the train took a bend I glimpsed rows of tall sternwheel and sidewheel paddle steamers moored to wharves on which stood piles of cargo. I might have been in Nizhni Novgorod, save for sharp Baptist steeples taking the place of our Orthodox onion domes. There was also far more motor traffic than was ever found in a Russian town. Consequently there were more metalled roads.

A little dark smoke drifted in the mist. The stillness gradually gave way to sounds of a busy trading port preparing for the day. Then the illusion of familiarity was further distorted by the sight of a gang of negroes who puffed short-stemmed pipes and joked amongst themselves as they walked up towards the levee from the railroad tracks. I was by now used to black faces, but sometimes they still materialised in unexpected contexts. All servants were black in the South, from the conductor on the train to the well groomed coachman who had been sent to take me from the station to my rooms. His name, he said, was Gibson. He wore an old-fashioned brass-buttoned uniform, brown top coat and white gloves. He spoke in a low, cultured voice, a surprising contrast to the whining sing-song of the porters, paperboys and other urchins who moved everywhere with that ground-watching, half bestial lope. This was largely absent in the niggers of the North East, whom I assumed to be of different stock. The carriage took me along Main Street, through a city far more modern than I had expected, with construction going on everywhere. Although not reaching the vast heights of New York's, some of her skyscrapers were at least fourteen storeys. Her trolley cars, overhead electric lighting, illuminated signs, automobiles, department stores, as well as her plentiful restaurants, created that reassuring blend I had missed so desperately in Washington and found at its finest in New York. Relatively small, Memphis was still a real city. The carriage stopped outside the Adler Apartments on Linden Street. To one side of the entrance was a Western Union office, which I was glad to see. Here my bags were transferred to two porters while a white manager welcomed me and showed me to my suite on the second floor. Mr Baskin wore a dark gabardine suit. He carried a hat and overcoat, explaining he had an appointment to keep. He showed me the amenities, wished me a pleasant stay in Memphis and courteously told me he was at my service if I needed anything further. By noon a maid had put away my clothes and I was able to bathe, change and lock my blueprints safely in a drawer. I decided to have some lunch.

Lacking the vibrant texture of New York or the self-conscious grandeur of Washington, Memphis had an attractive atmosphere of her own which I found welcome after the unreality of my past months in the capital. Turning out of Linden Street onto Main I strolled past cinemas, a theatre, large stores and public buildings, all of which comforted me, as did the network of signs and billboards advertising everything from tobacco to paint, drugs and electrical goods. In a pleasant, middle-class restaurant with a German name I ate peculiar local dishes which were not at all European. It was my first experience of blackeyed peas and

379

cornbread, which seemed compulsory. A sweetish thick white 'gravy' was poured liberally over my chicken and potatoes. Having eaten, I felt like a ship which had taken on concrete ballast. Moving with some shortness of breath I made my way back to the Adler to be saluted by the doorman who already addressed me as 'Colonel Peterson'. The efficiency, conscientiousness and eagerness to please of these coloured servants was remarkable. The unkindest thing anyone ever did was to make them discontented (as Griffith showed in *Birth of a Nation*). The status quo worked excellently for all concerned. Moreover, I experienced no prejudice from the Memphians. I had had no trouble in the restaurant, though my accent was not readily identifiable to them. Old-fashioned Southern courtesy still existed here. In the coming weeks I would find the people quite prepared to accept my accent as regional English or French and while I received occasional badinage, being told for instance that I sounded as if I held an egg in my mouth, I experienced little of the suspicion allegedly extended to foreigners in the South. They shared with other Americans an open curiosity never offended if you reply there are some questions you would rather not answer. Mainly I was happy to answer, however, even if my replies were not always strictly to the letter of the truth. I was forced to support Jimmy and Lucius in their perhaps mistaken effort to invent a more acceptable identity for me. I did not want them embarrassed.

Back at the Adler, I stretched myself on my bed and read the local *Memphis Commercial Appeal*, most of which I found at that stage bewildering. I was interested to discover, however, that there was already talk of the city's need for a permanent aerodrome. I was not quite sure what I was doing in Memphis, but decided it would be best to wait until I heard from either Mr Roffy or Mr Gilpin. The apartment was comfortable enough, though a little old-fashioned by New York standards. I had a bedroom, a sitting-room, a bathroom and a dressing-room. It had limited services, but self-catering facilities were provided. This was the first time I had experienced the phenomenon. It suited me well enough, though I was not very experienced at making tea, coffee and the like for myself. Being above all adaptable I would learn reasonably quickly. The maid, Mr Baskin had assured me, would be willing to prepare me breakfast for 'a small consideration'.

Now that the first excitement was gone, my spirits began to decline again. Thoughts of Esmé, Kolya, my mother and Captain Brown returned. By way of consoling myself, I began to write letters describing my journey via Knoxville to Memphis, my first view of 'Huckleberry Finn's own river' and my impression of Southerners, which was good. I had written several such letters when I heard a knock on my door. I got up from the desk to answer it. Charlie Roffy stood there, full of enthusiasm and apologies, his belly rising and falling, his face red from climbing the stairs. 'I'm real sorry we couldn't meet you at the station, colonel. You must think us the worst kind of ill-mannered rogues. Dick and I were travelling in from Jackson and were held up. I do hope everything is to your liking.'

I told him I was perfectly comfortable. I thought I might have a few minor difficulties adjusting to the flat and might need a few words of advice later, but was sure I would feel like a native in a day or two.

'Of course you will, sir. We'll get a boy for you, if you like. Is there anything else you need? Cash?'

'I've adequate means at present.' I hesitated. 'I take it you'll be able to direct me to a source of female company.'

He was amused. 'We're not as backward as some people choose to think. One has to be discreet, as I'm sure you'll appreciate. The smaller the city the more eyes it has, eh? But certainly all that can be arranged. Now, tell me, have you brought your designs with you?'

'They are in this drawer.'

'Splendid!' Charlie Roffy drew his chin back into his neck, a quizzical rooster, and looked sideways at me from his sharp, grey-blue eyes. His rosebud mouth curved in a smile. 'I'm real pleased, sir, that we met when we did. It was most fortunate. It was fate. Memphis is about to boom again. She's eager to move into the future as rapidly as possible. We could not have come together at a better time. Tell me, sir, would you care to dine with Dick Gilpin and myself later?'

I told him it would be a pleasure. I found myself echoing the older man's elaborate courtesy. Again his style was frustratingly reminiscent of my own past. Southern etiquette is persuasive; often, in a strange way, aggressive. It indicates a culture and institutions carefully preserved and maintained. It challenges the outsider while seeming to do the very opposite. As I discovered, a Southerner could frequently decry his own uncouth ways in direct proportion to his genuine arrogance. It was the habit of a beleaguered culture and immediately familiar to me. Since the Southerner shared our Russian taste for racy speech and colourful sayings I was often more at ease than anywhere else in America. I rarely had to offer an opinion; they had the trick of always assuming my agreement, and this of course proved particularly convenient. (As it emerged, there was little conflict of opinion in any case.)

'I'll pick you up here at around six,' said Charlie Roffy as he left. 'Meantime you might like to see the sights. There's a hack outside now.' Again I was impressed by his Southern thoughtfulness. I would leave the rest of my correspondence until later.

Like many towns founded on river trade, Memphis's 'centre' was her quaysides. Fronting the river were warehouses, then came exchanges and offices, next shops, hotels, services, public buildings. Finally the residential areas shaded through a spectrum from black poor to white rich. I found the run-down prospect of Beale Street and its neighbours, with their pawnshops, miserable cafés and second hand clothing stores, without attraction for me. A glimpse of shambling black figures, the sound of some howling babies were more than enough to deter me. I could not (and still cannot) share in a sentimental admiration for singers of jungle chants and slave laments who lived lives of licence and immorality in disgusting streets. Even in the nineteen-forties I would meet people who wanted eagerly to know if I had met Memphis Minnie or W. C. Handy. I told them: I never spoke to, and neither had I ever listened to, these or any other caterwauling negroes. Only a generation sated on every possible sensation could make heroes and heroines of wretched drug fiends and alcoholics, most of whom died deservedly early deaths. And as for their white imitators, they were traitors to their heritage. Now I see they have put a statue of some Blind Melon in a public square and named a street after the effeminate dervish Presley. When I was in Memphis she represented the best of the South. Now, apparently, she honours the worst. Where white apes black, there Carthage has entirely conquered.

Is modern Memphis drowned now beneath a weight of Oriental *shmaltz?* Has she gone the way of the others Have they substituted false fronts of plastic and plaster in celebration of some nostalgic never-never world where once stood impressive stone and rich marble Those great brick structures spoke of dignified success and old wealth, of civic pride and social ambition. Her central arteries carried telephone wires, electrical current cross-hatching the sky wherever one looked. Her trolleys sang like the bells of Notre Dame and from the river her great steamers called out a lament to a departing past. Her cotton and her lifeblood were threatened by chemical silk. Once she had fed the dockers of Liverpool and the mill workers of Manchester and they in turn rewarded her. She had christened her greatest hotel after the English philanthropist Peabody whose name can still be seen on London's Peabody Buildings. She was no provincial settlement to be destroyed by a single shift in the economic wind. She had known one great period of prosperity and now prepared for another. She would build the first municipal airport and eventually, by a mysterious historical and geographical process, would become the medical capital of the South, the home of dozens of hospitals, nurses' colleges, clinics and research centers. A guide book might say that where her chief industry had been based on cotton now it was based on disease. My own theory concerns the curative properties of the Mississippi mud and its similarity to that found in the old Odessa limans before the Revolution. Sometimes I imagine Memphis transmogrified into a thousand featureless white skyscrapers surrounding a few acres of an idealised nigger town encased in preservative where tourists come to listen to darkies play banjoes, wailing of their miseries for a hundred dollars a day. At other times I dream nothing has changed, that I ride down Main Street just as I rode the first time. She is jammed with traffic. Horns are blaring, horses rearing, trams and omnibuses clatter and clank while frantic policemen fight to control the flow of automobiles and goods wagons.

I remember how my cabby reined in his horse with a fatalistic shrug. He said such congestion was unusual but it could never be anticipated. He suggested I walk the few blocks back to my apartment if I was in a hurry. It would soon be six. Since the cab had already been paid for, I gave him a good tip and wished him luck. I enjoyed making my way through that busy city thoroughfare. Unlike Washington, Memphis was a natural city. She had grown up spontaneously, out of the need to trade. If New York was the future, then Memphis was the familiar present. I moved amongst yelling drivers and dancing pedestrians, smiling with sheer pleasure. For too long I had known only capitals. Here at last was a city still chiefly characterised not by her ancient power, her monuments, but by her inhabitants. I did not feel overwhelmed by her. Indeed, it seemed possible to impress her. Perhaps here I could find a new starting point, as Kiev had been my first. I had been born in a city owing her existence to a river. Therefore I might easily flourish in Memphis.

I dined that evening with those generous elders, Roffy and Gilpin, at a restaurant called Jansenn's, not far from my apartment. The food was unremarkable, but it was wholesome and seemed to the taste of my hosts. They had brought a young woman with them and I thought at first, with some delight, she was to be my companion. Pandora Fairfax was a bright-eyed, dark-haired little thing with a pert, bold manner who reminded me a little of Zoyea, the gypsy girl. To my astonishment I learned she was an aviatrix. She had recently come to Memphis to give flying displays. She was now thinking of settling. She and her husband were both flyers. 'We've been barnstorming all over,' she said, 'but we think it's time to quit.'

Charlie Roffy beamed. 'Your teeth are bound to get too loose after a while.' He explained genially: 'Miss Pandora's most famous trick is to hang by her teeth from a trapeze fixed to her husband's plane. She also does wingwalking and parachute jumps.'

I was extremely impressed. Miss Fairfax was attractive and entertaining. She was eager to hear my own flying stories. Where had I flown, in what type of machines? I answered as best I could. She said she envied me the Oertz ('for all it's supposed to be a pig'). I was welcome to take up their De Havilland DH4 if I felt like it. Touched by her generosity I said I would clamber into that cockpit in a flash if the opportunity ever came. Gilpin had already told her about the new airport and aircraft I had designed. She wanted to see my plans. 'You may study them whenever you wish,' I said. She and her husband were in the process of trying to establish a private airfield, but our plans were complementary. 'The more of us the merrier at this stage,' she said. She left early. Shaking hands with me she smiled warmly. 'I hope we're able to help each other out, Colonel Peterson.'

When she had gone Dick Gilpin spoke of her admiringly. She was famous all over this part of the country. She had begun adult life as a typist but had learned to fly after only a few days of office work. 'She proved a natural. Her husband's a War ace. You might even have met him.' I said I could recall nobody named Fairfax. 'A fine man,' said Charlie Roffy, offering me a large cigar. 'And with more downright common sense than most of his breed.'

Dick Gilpin told me that, unless I objected, they had arranged for me to be interviewed for the *Commercial Appeal*. The paper was the best in Memphis. It might also wish to run a photograph of me, perhaps in uniform. I readily agreed. Charlie Roffy said it would help their case considerably. He asked if he could call on me at around nine the following morning. I was at his disposal. 'I am here as your guest,' I said. 'And I wish only to do what will best serve our mutual interests.'

384

My friends dropped me off at the Adler Apartments before going their separate ways. For the first time in many months I went directly to bed and fell into a deep sleep. I dreamed of Memphis rising above the river on a silver cloud and I was the captain, steering a course over the prairies of Kansas and Dakota. Old Shatterhand, the buffalo hunter, was at my side, dressed in deerskins, his long gun crooked in his arm. The prairies will belong to the nomad cities of America again and death shall be abandoned. I could not have seen Brodmann in Memphis and mistaken him for Hernikof. Hernikof was murdered and his body desecrated on the cobbled wharves of Batoum. Why should Brodmann follow me? He was a Jew and a Communist. They would never have allowed him through. The city dips and wheels as I direct her towards the sun. I am blinded by too many reflections. What did I find in the City of Dogs that Brodmann desired so greedily? The horizon re-emerges. *Saat kactir? Jego widzialem, ale ciebie nie widzialem.* The dream shifts always to the West, always just a little out of reach. Surely it must stop at the sea. I am a man of courage. I can pilot the ship. I am in control. But what is this pursuit? I must concentrate. We are falling. I feel sick. *Ich will nicht Soldat werden!* What could Brodmann do to me? They think a piece of metal makes me their slave? I would not become a Mussulman. I am an enemy of the Sultans. *Der Gipfel des Berges funkelt im Abendsonnenschein. Gibt es etwas Neues?* I shall not go to Berlin.

After breakfast I found myself at the newspaper's studios. The journalist who interviewed me said the story would be out next day. What did I think of Memphis? And the South? Both were beautiful, I said, and the people were very well-mannered. He asked me where I was from in England. Whitechapel, I told him (I almost believed I knew it, so often had Mrs Cornelius spoken of it). He asked if Whitechapel were anything like Memphis. I said it had quite remarkable similarities. The river, of course, and the numbers of darkies. The reporter wished me to elaborate. It was impossible to tell him much more than our darkies were decently behaved and worked chiefly in the docks and public conveniences, which proliferated everywhere in London: a fact frequently remarked upon by travellers. It was close enough to the truth, after all. My invention has often anticipated the actuality. The interview proved more exhausting than I had guessed and I was glad, that afternoon, to motor out with Pandora Fairfax to meet her husband. He was a tall, aquiline man whose good looks were unharmed by a couple of small scars on the right side of his face. Like many flying veterans he was not much of a talker and had a modest way with him which tended to add to his charm, as well as his authority. We agreed how terrible flying had been during the War. He had flown mainly English planes, as well as one or two French and American machines. He hoped I would stay for supper. That evening I said very little myself but drew Henry Fairfax out, or rather I asked him questions which frequently Pandora would answer on his behalf. He was from Minnesota and liked this part of the world better. The Memphians were very open-minded on the subject of flying. An air base had been sited nearby during the war and the local people had become familiar with all types of planes. He had been an instructor there briefly. I could do worse than to invest in Memphis. They were far more forward looking than was thought.

It would have been foolish to tell him I had nothing save my talent to invest. If Memphians thought I had come to put money into their city it would only make for improved relations. The Fairfaxes asked how long I had known Messrs Gilpin and Roffy. I mentioned that we had met in Washington the previous year. Henry Fairfax was curious about my friends. Mr Roffy had contacted them only recently. He wanted their support for the proposed airport. Some thought it could be based on Mud Island which lay out beyond the wharves. I knew nothing of this but was dubious. 'I wonder if the island will be big enough. It makes the possibility of future expansion almost impossible.' They agreed. 'But land isn't particularly cheap in Memphis,' said Pandora. 'There are plans for several big hotels and other buildings. You've probably seen some of them going up. Everyone's saying Memphis will boom. So everyone's speculating.'

'We're speculating ourselves in a way,' said her husband.

She laughed. 'I'd call that just taking a chance.'

Their little wooden house, on the outskirts of the Memphis suburbs, had an almost rural quality. They normally had electricity but the cable was down so they lit their rooms with oil lamps. It was a comfortable sensation to feel oneself back in the past, talking wonderfully about the future. After supper an acquaintance of theirs, another flyer, dropped by. His name was Major Alexander Sinclair. For all his honest, matter of fact manner, he was a little mysterious about the reasons for his visit. He had recently come from Atlanta. I asked him if he knew Tom Cadwallader. 'Only by repute,' he said. He was rather withdrawn, though evidently doing his best to be sociable. Later, after a tot of fairly good 'moonshine', he warmed to me. He was interested to learn I was a French airman. He was obviously relieved when the subject turned to the Catholic church and I expressed my view that the Pope had much to answer for. Only a very strong man, taking an anticlerical stand, could save Italy. He mentioned some of his own experiences in Europe and asked if I knew any of his surviving comrades. I told him the truth, that I had flown principally on the Eastern Front. I had been with the Allied Expeditionary force during the Russian Civil War. By now he had become deeply interested in my opinon of both Bolsheviks and Jews. I gave him my honest views at some length, apologising that he had 'woken up the bee in my bonnet'. But he was enthusiastic. 'You don't have to hold back with me, colonel. You're a man after my own heart.' Had I ever thought of addressing a public meeting on the dangers of Catholicism and Bolshevism? I told him any warning I ever gave the American people would be heartfelt and based on solid experience. 'But I am really a man of action more than a man of words, Major Sinclair.' It was very late and I could see my hosts growing tired. He insisted on driving me back into Memphis, even though he was staying with the Fairfaxes, and I rather selfishly accepted his offer. We had taken to each other in that way people sometimes do, though culturally we had almost nothing in common. We were both, however, intellectuals who believed in 'doing' rather than 'moaning', as he put it. He dropped me off outside the Adler Apartments at two in the morning, noted my address and said he looked forward to seeing me again.

This time when I prepared myself for bed I was in far better spirits. I had received an excellent impression of my new friends, particularly Major Sinclair. Here were people with whom I could most comfortably work: clear-eyed young Americans who were prepared to face the dangers of the modern world and at the same time take advantage of the great opportunities opening up to them. Thereafter I was again to find myself something of a social lion. During the coming days I would be introduced to other Memphians, young and old, who were deeply concerned for their city's future – and for the future of the whole Christian world. Any impression I had received in the North that the Delta region was old-fashioned and slow was proven wholly false. Dixielanders might set great store by their historic traditions but they had no lack of faith in modern technology or new ideas. All they had lacked until now was finance, for since the Civil War Northern industrialists had systematically milked the South. The North, with its nerve centre in New

York, had up until now totally controlled the American economy. Plantation owners, encouraged to grow enormous quantities of cotton, were then told in their best years that their price was too high. Thus New York and Chicago bought themselves artificially cheap raw materials. But I knew as well as anyone that what a defeated nation sometimes lacks in material wealth is frequently compensated for in a deeper spirituality and punctilious pride. These qualities might seem abstract to the scallawags and carpet-baggers so accurately drawn by Mr Griffith, but in the end they always prove far more valuable than any number of sweatshops and spinning jennies. They are qualities which provide men with the will to bide their time. This singular obstinacy allows them to choose their own terms, their own moment, their own form of action. I began to realise how true this was of modern Memphis. Without relinquishing the principles for which her people had fought a great war, she now prepared for a carefully engineered forward movement on all fronts. I could not help but be reminded by a similar determination I had witnessed in Italy, for so long impoverished by Papal tyranny, and now ready to move with relentless, measured step into the second quarter of the twentieth century.

Not for Memphis the hellish factory towns of the North, the urban poverty, the miserable conditions which, as in Russian cities, created a breeding ground of anarchy and unrest. Memphis was about to march from cotton and mules into engineering and services. Here small work forces could exist in ideal environments while producing something for which the whole world would willingly pay! I enjoyed the confidences of the city's most influential leaders. My opinions were sought by 'Boss' Crump, whom everyone recognised as the strongest force in the city: the charismatic possessor of enormous political energy and brilliant insight, his only mistake would be to turn his back on those who most wished to help him. But for a single mistake of judgment he might have become the South's own Mussolini. Crump's sophisticated opinions on the Negro Question were illuminating. They expanded my horizons considerably. His plans for Southern self-sufficiency were years ahead of their time. Another far-sighted individual was then a leading businessman in Memphis, the inventor of modern supermarkets in his famous Piggly Wiggly grocery chain. He was building himself a magnificent house of pig-coloured marble near Overton Park and one afternoon treated me to an individual tour of his half built palace. Jewish interests ruined him before he could occupy his own mansion; his name, of course, was Clarence Saunders. I remember him being particularly interested in my ideas for an electrically operated automatic self-service market. I believe that towards the end of his life, still battling bravely against the combined might of Carthage, which by then had all but crushed the entire country, he attempted to make my dream a reality. He was dragged down in the end, however, by the Great Depression. People seemed to think this some sort of natural force, like a drought or an earthquake. Ask any Ukrainian if Stalin was an earthquake.

But these were golden days for me, and the burden of my heartache at being separated from Esmé was considerably lifted. It was wonderful to share a vision in common with so many others. I had never experienced this before. I had always felt isolated, a lone prophet with only a few good friends who, like Kolya, offered their loyalty without fully understanding my dream. We were striving to build an enlarged, more beautiful, more efficient Memphis, epicentre of the South's cultural and financial renaissance. She would be a city where railroad and automobile were totally outmoded; a city of the electronic plane and the dirigible, with moving walkways, multi-levelled shopping arcades, art galleries in which were displayed the world's finest works. A city where crime and poverty were abolished, where the black race was no longer required. All manual work would be accomplished by machines. We were not prepared to abandon the negroes. They would have a township to themselves where they could grow at their own pace, with their own schools, churches and theatres. The Southerner feels his duty to the negro most strongly (that he is a heartless tyrant is another misconception encouraged by the North). On principle I always made it clear that while I willingly provided my services, I had no intention of settling permanently in the United States. It suited my idealism, at that time, to link my fortunes, however temporarily, with Tennessee's leading city. The Fairfaxes were by now firm friends. They, too, were 'outsiders' who had been fully accepted by the hospitable South. Though I never actually flew their DH4 I was taken up by Pandora Fairfax twice and profited both intellectually and spiritually from the experience. From the air it is a unique sight, giving one a fresh understanding of the size and nature of the vast Delta flatlands and the broad shallow river twisting into what seems the infinite distance, arriving eventually at New Orleans. I was all the more impressed by the people who had first negotiated this river, who had fought their way across such enormous distances so their children might cultivate and civilise the land; by the rivermen who sailed flatboats back and forth with furs and cotton and gold to make St Louis and New Orleans two of the richest and most vital cities of their age. Sometimes I could wish that my father, in all his revolutionary nonsense, had been one of those who emigrated to America. Then, at least, I might have had a chance to grow without fear, without the perpetual threat of being drawn back into the nightmare. As a native American I could have done so much more for my country and in turn I would have received a fair reward. *Mein Vater kam bis an die Grenze. Wohin gehen wir jetzt?* Who knows? The same forces which destroyed Clarence Saunders might equally have destroyed me. At least I remain alive to remind others of a time when there was genuine hope and optimism in the world and men and women were still able to recognise the enemy. What does it matter today? The enemy is so strong he laughs at me. Even those who listen to me in the pub think I am joking.

In Memphis I was taught to drive the new Buick Mr Gilpin put at my disposal: a simple enough matter, for all I was frequently hampered by the stupidity of other drivers possessing neither the natural instinct for automobile manipulation nor sufficient imagination to consider the wishes (or indeed the very existence) of their fellow road users. In the Buick (and later, when that was being repaired, a Ford) I motored through tree-lined suburbs of Memphis or took the great road over the bridge into Arkansas. I had very soon grown more than fond of the city and was not at all impatient when Mr Roffy explained how the government and local authorities were moving rather more slowly than he had hoped in finalising the grants necessary to begin work. Everywhere along Main Street sites were being prepared for finer and bigger buildings. New trolley cars were soon to be introduced. That complicated cat's cradle of wiring crossing and recrossing the city's streets indicated, in its own simple vocabulary, our continuing progress. On a day in February warmer and damper than most, when the city suddenly smelled of fresh tar and the coal smoke from the trains or riverboats for once was not dissipated in the colder atmosphere, I received a welcome visitor. It was Major Sinclair. He had come to Memphis by air this time. He was full of excitement for his new vessel. The small non-rigid airship was tethered in one corner of the Fairfax airfield. On its side it prominently advertised the name of a new journal, which was his other abiding obsession. He was ebullient. 'The paper will sweep the country. It's the foremost banner of the greatest crusade America has ever known! There's a fresh wind blowing through the United States, Max, and it has its origin in Atlanta!' The ship (like the newspaper it advertised) was called *The Knight Hawk*.

Sinclair and I walked out to the mooring mast the evening after he had arrived. We were both smoking cigars, in that calm, rather comfortable silence old comrades share when they are merely enjoying each other's company. The little airship's gondola almost touched the ground. It was made from light metal, rather dented and scratched, and had been sprayed white. A large red Maltese Cross was painted on either side. Although several cables secured it, the whole ship swayed in the mild south-westerly breeze. Occasionally it creaked a little, as if struts were somewhere under strain. The gondola was not enclosed. It had three open cockpits, rather like aeroplane cockpits, in one of which the steering gear was located. The ship was the last made, said Sinclair, in the British SSZ class, most of which had been sold to America. The British had nicknamed them 'blimps' after the legendary Colonel Blimp, one of their great patriots. Behind the cockpits was mounted a single Rolls Royce 75hp Hawk engine. Major Sinclair was evidently proud of his machine. 'It's only the first,' he said. 'I already have plans to build an improved type. I was hoping for some advice. But that's not the main reason for coming to Memphis. I've been entrusted with a mission. There are one or two places I must visit before I go back to Atlanta. I'm here to promote the paper. To drum up subscriptions if I can.' He had other business here, too, but was not as yet prepared to speak of it. He planned to spend at least a week here. 'Anyway, look her over. I'd like your opinion.' He helped me climb the short ladder into the main cockpit and inspect the controls. I studied the steering mechanism for achieving height and direction, the engine switches, the various gauges. Major Sinclair was not to know this was my first close view of an ordinary airship and I was fascinated with the workings of the rudder and ailerons. I told him I thought it an excellent machine of its type.

'Of course it's a bit primitive.' He was almost apologetic. 'But we have to make a start.'

I agreed with him. I was still unsure what he meant.

'There was some idea of providing canopies for the cockpits,' he said.

'But I gather they were next to useless most of the time. She's no worse than the average plane and the gasbag helps keep some rain from your head.'

Standing up in the swaying cockpit I steadied myself with one of the six hawsers which attached the gondola to the main bulk. The bag was faintly yielding silvered fabric of the usual kind. Though she was a far cry from my own planned ship, she was nonetheless a genuine and thoroughly tested aerial vehicle. I was as delighted as a schoolboy at a cockfight. Major Sinclair enjoyed my pleasure. Soon he had climbed into one of the two rear cockpits. Leaning over me while I sat at the controls he explained the special techniques involved in flying this particular craft. I worked the foot pedals (which controlled both height and angle of flight) and rapidly mastered the whole thing. It was much simpler than flying a heavier-than-air machine. I imagined myself a thousand feet above the ground, flying wherever I chose, and drew a deep breath of satisfaction. It would not be much longer before my dream was fully realised. Then I would pilot a far larger ship. I would be admiral of my own aerial armada!

Light was fading as I descended the little metal ladder to the ground. Major Sinclair followed me; then he made an odd sort of gesture which I could not interpret. He lowered his head, rubbed a gloved hand across his aristocratic mouth and frowned to himself. I was now expectant.

At length the flyer looked up. He seemed very serious, either reluctant to speak or unable to find appropriate words. Silently he took my arm. We walked back through the twilight towards the wooden shacks which presently functioned as the Fairfaxes' administrative buildings. There was a stillness about the evening. The wind had dropped and the air felt warmer, even as the sun vanished. Major Sinclair began to speak in a low, sober voice, addressing me formally where before he had used my first name, as if what he had to say needed increased objectivity.

'Colonel Peterson, sir, I know you're of French and English blood. I gather, welcome as you are, you one day intend to return to Europe.'

'That's so, major.'

'I understand you're of the Protestant religion. We can take that for granted. I hope you'll forgive me for seeming ill-mannered. I wonder if you could bear with me and tell me again your views as to the current plight of this country's native born Anglo-Saxon citizens.'

I gave him my unhesitating answer: 'I am not afraid to speak my mind on the question, major. I believe them to be in mortal danger. I have reason to know they are threatened by an increasingly unified army of Bolshevik Hebrews and Papists, plotting tirelessly to rouse the black and yellow races against them. I have witnessed at close hand the violence and lawlessness unleashed by these forces in Russia. I live in horror of the same nightmare spreading further across the world.'

He nodded slowly in profound agreement. 'You have confirmed what I already understood. What would you say if someone offered you the opportunity to play an active part in the struggle?'

'I am not a man of violence, major.'

'You have made that perfectly clear also.' He sucked in his cheeks. He stopped suddenly in the semi-darkness, just before we reached the buildings. 'I am about to ask you a great favour. You should feel no obligation to me if you decide to refuse.' He buttoned up his flying coat. 'Would you be prepared to address a group of sympathetic friends on your own direct experience of Red Revolution? You'd be doing them and America a mighty important service.'

'You wish me to make some kind of speech?'

'An informal talk, Max, to concerned individuals, all these people of substance in the community and sharing the same views.'

I had never spoken publicly in English before and was of course nervous. Secondly I had no great desire to call unnecessary attention to myself. Yet the offer had a number of attractions. Moreover, I felt as strongly as I do now that what happened in Russia should serve as a dreadful warning to the rest of the world. It was, of course, my duty to accept. I asked what was entailed.

Major Sinclair continued to speak in low, deliberate tones. 'In a few days time, a certain steamboat will leave the landing stage at Memphis and steam downriver towards Vicksburg. At a given hour she will turn back to Memphis where, before morning, her passengers will disembark. All aboard are sworn to the deepest secrecy. Decisions will be taken that night which will affect the fate of the entire nation.'

I was both intrigued and impressed. 'I am honoured, major, by your confidence.'

'Can you spare a few hours to be aboard that boat next Wednesday evening, Max?'

I assured him, come what may, I would make the time.

He reached out and firmly shook my hand, staring into my face with an intensity I had never seen before. 'Thank you.'

No sooner had we returned to the road and the Buick than he was ordinarily cordial again. It was as if he had never made his request. I told him I should one day like to see how *The Knight Hawk* handled in the air. He promised to take me aloft whenever I desired. By now, of course, it had dawned on me that Major Sinclair was rather more than he had claimed. Plainly he represented powerful political interests. I must congratulate myself on being fortunate enough to gain his friendship. Even then I had not understood the full significance of his questions and his request. It would not be the first time someone of his type would know instinctively I was trustworthy. I have never clearly understood what is in me which encourages this. Probably it has something to do with my lifelong hatred of hypocrisy and intolerance, the directness with which I am prepared to approach important issues of the day. I have always loathed compromise.

That same evening I sat at my desk and and by the light of a gas reading lamp wrote Esmé another long letter describing all my successes. America was accepting me far more readily than I could reasonably have hoped. I would make every effort to have her join me as soon as possible. In a short note to Mrs Cornelius I recommended America as being full of tremendous opportunities. If she chose, she could rise as high as she wanted. For my part, there was every chance I would soon be a household name like Marconi or Wellington. Soon she would hear of the Peterson plane, the Peterson domestic washing machine and the Peterson radio-powered automobile. Actually, it did not matter to me if my real name were used or not. My ego had no need for popular acclaim. To accomplish the work was enough, even if Pyatnitski were forgotten forever.

Memphis had taken me to her large and benevolent heart. And she was the city abused by the Northern press as 'the murder capital of the USA' because a few partial statistics had been arranged to confirm accusations of the city's high homicide rate! Memphis was in fact the friendliest city I had known since I left Odessa. The murder figures came as a direct result of her very tolerance since she admitted so many black and Catholic immigrants to her poorer suburbs. What was more, because of her hospitals' splendid reputation many victims were sent to Memphis to be saved. If they died, they increased the irony by adding another number to the statistics! Memphis was growing, as my political friends were forever telling me, and growth is never achieved without pain.

That evening I dined with Mr Roffy and a Mrs Trubbshaw. She was the thin-faced but attractive president of a local women's club. I spoke enthusiastically of Major Sinclair's airship. We should consider manufacturing several such smaller vessels as auxiliaries to our main fixed wing fleet. Charlie Roffy thought the idea very sound. Mrs Trubbshaw was greatly impressed. Evidently, she said, I was a man of enormous scientific and political vision. She envied me my adventurous life, which reminded her so much of Count Pulaski's.

That left me entirely baffled. 'Forgive me, madam, if I admit to ignorance.'

'You must read about him in the library. He came all the way from Europe.' Her style became hushed, intense, ecclesiastical. 'To fight in our War of Independence. He was a great believer in freedom, colonel. A Polish nobleman, a soldier. A true American in all but nationality. He gave his name to Pulaski, Tennessee, where my father was born, and died in the service of Washington. You could be Count Casimir reincarnated. Do you, by chance, believe in having lived before, Colonel Peterson?' Her dark curls shook with sincerity.

Since I was neither a Pole nor a Catholic, I said, but an ordinary Christian, I believed of course in redemption and rebirth. If that were the same, then I shared her faith. She was, like many women I met in those circumstances, a peculiar mixture of hard practicality and wild romanticism. We shared a motor cab when we left. Almost as soon as we were in it she kissed me passionately, then, somewhat clumsily, seizing my private parts, declared me a hero she could not resist. I, too, found resistance impractical, thus the cab was directed to the Adler Apartments where we rapidly consummated our mutual admiration. Most of my other women during that time were of Mrs Trubbshaw's class. I believe they found me attractively exotic and unlikely to remain in Memphis long enough to embarrass them. I in turn became fascinated with learning the desires and inhibitions of the American bourgeoisie. Although I periodically visited (with Mr Gilpin and others who referred to themselves as 'sporting men') the city's thriving and famous red light district, I came to prefer the more bizarre and educational adventures frequently offered by outwardly respectable matrons most of whom, oddly, were not Memphis born. The usual theory was that post-war life had abolished repressions and people were frequently making up for what they thought they had missed in a climate of 'Victorian morality'. My own view was simpler: a shortage of men made many women behave as if they were at a garment sale. They became at once more ruthlessly competitive and less discriminatory, frequently finding they had picked up material they would normally not have blessed with a second look. This state of affairs suited me perfectly, since I remained loyal in spirit to my Esmé, saved money and stood far less chance of catching a social disease. (It was at a bawdy house, however, I had my first experience of a full-blooded negress.)

Like many American cities of those days, Memphis presented a contrast of extreme public puritanism and unchecked private lechery, greater than any I had encountered in Europe. With her weighty inheritance of low-church morality, America's attempt to check her native exuberance and vitality by creating laws having nothing to do with her natural and historical expansionist character merely fostered further hypocrisy and confusion. A nation's laws must always reflect to some degree the national temperament. America's often did not. They were cold, English laws which became virtually meaningless, say, in California. In seeking to shape herself through the dreams of her founders rather than the needs of her living inhabitants she weakened herself, became schizophrenic. Of course she was a threatened nation. The settlers who had suffered and died to establish the United States did so in the name of a great Anglo-Saxon egalitarian ideal. In 1922 that ideal was being exploited and abused by immigrants demanding the benefits of struggle but unwilling to pay the price. It was too late to control this population by the methods of the Pilgrim Fathers. Most newcomers did not even recognise the Faith on which the principles were based. They had loyalties to the Chief Rabbi, the Pope, to Karl Marx and V. I. Lenin; they served an ideal above nationalism. No wonder that however many Baptist ladies tried to abolish alcohol there were as many Italians and Hebrews (not to mention the renegade Irish) to sell it. Americans sought desperately to establish order and stability in a world threatening Chaos from all sides. Those who condemn them have no proper understanding of their fears. I helped fight that last battle against America's enemies; a noble and doomed defence, like the last stand of the South against the Union. It was conducted with courage, honour, decency and common sense by ordinary people, the brave descendants of Kit Carson, Buffalo Bill and Jesse James. Their attempt to fight with the moral weapons of Protestantism was understandable, if misguided. A time comes when only political strength and fortitude will win the day; an unpalatable but courageous ruthlessness.

Christ is our champion, that gentle Greek shepherd. Yet the Lamb must be protected from wolves and jackals by other weapons than Old Testament texts or a ban upon the few comforts which lessen the burden of our journey through this Vale of Tears. I had no desire to offend worthy pastors and churchwomen who saw evidence of overwhelming Evil in the abuse of life's pleasures, but I refused to relinquish those pleasures in private moderation. I used to see drunkenness on the streets of Kiev (we had prohibition in Russia long before Volsted) for in the uneducated person the element of self-control is usually absent, so I shall not argue against the need for a firm, paternal hand, but a general ban leads only to general crime. Democracy is powerless to control the degenerate refugee, who all his life has understood only tyranny.

I saw Mrs Trubbshaw several times over the next few days and enjoyed her considerably for all it sometimes proved difficult negotiating the various items of underwear which her own version of morality insisted she somehow retain at all times on her person. It was she who at about noon brought me some sandwiches and a copy of the *Commercial Appeal* with the appalling news which was to have a far greater consequence on my life than I could guess. The *Roma* had gone down at Hampton Roads Army base. This semi-dirigible, bought from Italy only recently, had crashed when her rudder failed. Exploding on contact with the ground she killed thirty-four out of forty-five crew members. My chicken and mayonnaise was set aside half eaten. I grieved for those poor aviators. The splendid story of the airship has been written in the blood of those brave pioneers who, in a spirit of joyful discovery, flung themselves into the upper atmosphere, never quite certain what their fate would be. Mrs Trubbshaw stood fiddling with the pale blue bows of her camiknickers. 'What's wrong, dear?'

I began to weep.

With a snort of disappointment, she began awkwardly to comfort me.

So fickle are financiers than almost any minor shift in the social climate can frighten them. This what I knew as I plunged into the folds of sweet-smelling silk, cotton and flesh and sought, with some initial difficulty, the consolations of Mrs Trubbshaw's feminine charms. It was not long before we were interrupted by a loud knocking on the door and a voice calling my name. Mrs Trubbshaw recognised Mr Roffy. She gathered her outer clothes together before disappearing into the little dressing-room.

Roffy looked like a turkey who had been bought an axe for Christmas, as they said in the South. He was distraught and he held a crumpled copy of the newspaper. 'I won't keep you long, Colonel Peterson. I see you've already read the report. What do you make of it? Can it affect us?'

'Since we're proposing in aerodrome and fixed wing planes, I hardly think there's a comparison. What's more, that ship wasn't even American made.'

He calmed down a little, but remained worried. 'I still think it could seriously affect our plan. If our people in Washington lose their nerve, our Memphis business interests will also get cold feet. Where will that leave us?'

'With a sound, practical and worthwhile scheme, Mr Roffy.' I searched for the cord of my dressing-gown. 'I share your fears, of course. But I suspect it will at worst involve a very small delay.'

'You're more confident than I am, sir.' He looked vaguely, without understanding, at my rumpled bed. 'And considerably more confident than Washington's likely to be, what with everything else that's going on.'

'Then we must restore their optimism.' I was positive and rather disapproving of his nervousness.

I think my tone made him attempt to pull himself together. 'The problem, colonel, is how do we do it? They'll only keep their nerve if we're seen to be doing the same thing. We have to show that we're completely confident in our company's future.'

'Perhaps another interview in the newspaper?' I suggested.

His smile was hopeless. 'It might help. But words aren't enough. Not just now. For a while we might have to lay our money on the table.'

'I don't understand you, Mr Roffy.'

He sighed and ran his fingers through his distinguished locks. He cleared his throat. 'I'm willing to put up $150,000 in cash right now. If each of us invested the same amount in the company that would show we meant business. It would also keep our credit good. What we lose from Congress we might gain locally. That way, there would be no loss of momentum. There are a lot of smaller people in this city who depend on us, even now.'

'I realise that, Mr Roffy.' Of course I was thoroughly taken aback. Having allowed them to believe I was as wealthy as themselves I now had no way of refusing what was a perfectly reasonable suggestion. 'My money is tied up in foreign bonds and banks, as I'm sure you appreciate. There is no way in which I could rapidly raise the sum you suggest.'

He was regretful. 'It might prove our only answer, colonel, believe me.'

When he had gone I returned to bed and was joined by Mrs Trubbshaw with whom I shared a small sniff from my declining cocaine supply. She had heard only a fraction of the conversation and of course she was the last person in whom I could confide my dilemma. I felt my position not merely embarrassing but also to some degree dangerous. In Memphis the six-shooter was still regarded in many quarters as the best means of settling affairs of honour. 'Is Mr Roffy worried about the airship accident?' asked Mrs Trubbshaw later. 'Did you have a financial interest in it?'

'In a manner of speaking.' I could afford to admit to no one that I was virtually destitute. Everything depended on my blueprints gaining the reality of metal and wood. Thereafter without doubt the money would come in. Until then I would be separated from Esmé. I could not bear the thought. She trusted me to send for her. Memphis, too, had high expectations of me. My gigantic six-engined passenger aeroplane with the four stacks of wings and four separate 'carriages' was due to begin production the following year. Local factories were expecting orders. My radio-beam energy projector should be at the prototype stage within months and my radio-controlled automatic landing system was to grace the main tower of the aerodrome, now due to be sited at Park Field. Models had been made, artist's projections prepared. Every stage was planned and a great many Memphians were expecting their fees. Once we had news from Washington confirming our Federal funding, every major financial personage in Memphis was ready to invest, as was the city under the guidance of Boss Crump. Yet now it seemed all of this was in peril unless I could raise what to these people was a tiny sum. I had at least to make some attempt to raise it.

As soon as Mrs Trubbshaw had left to keep her afternoon appointments I went downstairs to the Western Union office and sent a wire to Paris, to Kolya, my only real hope. There was no time for mysteries. I wrote: MUST HAVE $150,000 FOR IMPORTANT VENTURE, MATTER OF GRAVE URGENCY. PETERSON. I took the risk and for my return address gave c/o Western Union, Memphis, Tennessee. The officer assured me he would let me know as soon as there was a reply. He gave me a copy of the wire. This would enable me to prove to Mr Roffy my serious intention of raising the capital. I telephoned my partner at the rented house in Poplar Avenue, near Overton Park, which we also used as a business address. I said I had some information for him. He suggested we meet that evening at a private club called May's in Front Street.

For the next hour or so I walked aimlessly around downtown Memphis, staring in store windows, inspecting the wrought-iron pillars of those covered sidewalks which seem to exist nowhere these days but which were so functional, buying a paper cone of chocolate candy, studying the mass of signs along Main Street, and eventually finding myself on the steps of the eight-storeyed neo-Arcadian fortress which was actually the Union Station. Once there, I picked up several time-tables, praying that I would not have to leave Memphis as hastily as I had left certain other cities in the past. I had still not allowed enough time for Kolya's reply. I took a cab to the Zoo in Overton Park and wasted another hour with the somewhat miserable representatives of American and African wildlife. At dusk, I returned to the Adler building and the Western Union office. No reply had yet been received to my telegram.

Determined to maintain morale, I dressed in my best evening clothes and took a taxi to Front Street. The club was in a private house, once used as a steamboat company's offices, a few blocks from the Post Office. There were a few lights on the iron bridges over the river and some from the cluster of steamboats by the levee but otherwise the area felt deserted. I entered May's and had my topcoat and hat taken by a pretty octoroon wearing a frock so short it resembled a Greek tunic. I began to feel more comfortable. There was a warmth about such establishments which excluded all the outer world's cares. Mr Roffy, too, had made some attempt to improve his appearance. Again he looked the dignified Southern elder he was. He smiled as he got up from the couch in the corner of what May called her 'ballroom' and came towards me. We went upstairs to a private apartment whose walls were completely covered in dark yellow and red velvet drapes and whose main furnishings consisted of a huge ornamental bed, a gilt chair and a wash stand. I showed him the copy of the message I had sent. He beamed with relief. 'That will do the trick, I'm sure. I'm so sorry to put you to this inconvenience, colonel. But confidence has to be maintained. It's crucial as I know you understand. As soon as you receive confirmation, have the funds cabled to the First National Bank. Then we'll turn them into cash.'

I was surprised. 'Surely that will invite unwelcome attention?'

'We need all the attention we can get, colonel. Mr Gilpin's in Washington right now, getting his money moved and mine's already at the bank, in a safety deposit. The moment it's all together I'll be standing by with the photographers. Believe me, colonel, there's nothing impresses people more than the sight of a pile of real dollar bills. In these parts that will provide better proof of our sincerity and dedication than a letter of unlimited credit on the Bank of England.'

'Well, Mr Roffy, I pray you're right. It's extremely tiresome and a little complicated for me to have so much money cabled all at once. You know how the French are about such things.' I did not for a moment believe Kolya could lay hands on so large an amount, but even if he sent a sixth of it I knew it would be enough to prove my financial standing. In a few days the *Roma* disaster would fade from the public eye and things would return to normal. The American newspapers required fresh sensations more than most. Doubtless some terrible fire or a collapsing building would serve to drive the airship crash from any place of importance in the public's imagination. Meanwhile I would explain how my funds were being sluggishly liquidated, on account of French government policy, and then they would no longer be needed. This rational view of the matter was coloured a little with anxiety. Next day, when no cable arrived from Kolya, I sent another: MONEY MATTER OF URGENT MOMENT. PLEASE RESPOND. This one I did not show to Mr Roffy when he called by on his way to lunch with Mr Gilpin ('Back from Washington with a carpetbag full of bills') who was staying at the Gayoso Hotel. It occurred to me I had heard nothing from Kolya because I no longer had his current address. Ironically, he might even be on his way to the United States, bringing Esmé with him.

It was frustrating to me that I could not let Kolya know more, but I neither wished to involve him in my troubles nor did I intend to reveal my whereabouts to the French police. Perhaps I had already gone too far. Kolya might believe he protected me by not responding. On the following Wednesday I had still heard nothing. I placated Mr Roffy by telling him my French bank was actually the branch of a Swiss one. The Swiss bank was claiming that there was no branch of the First National in Memphis. I next resorted to sending a cable (as 'Peterson') to my old bank, the Crédit Lyonnais in Boulevard St-Germain, giving the address of the Memphis Bank and telling them it was important they cable the 'agreed sum' at once. A copy of this satisfied Mr Roffy, although he still continued to display a certain grim nervousness. Mr Gilpin I encountered only once near Court Square, a small park in the centre of the city. The meeting was accidental and he looked at me strangely. It was as if he believed I had already betrayed his trust. I told him with mock-cheerfulness that everything was in order. He said 'pleased to hear it' and hurried on. He seemed to be taking the setback with less fortitude than his friend.

It came as a welcome relief to be collected that evening in a large limousine and driven by Major Sinclair towards the levee. The steamboat, he told me, had been hired from the ailing Lee Company (who had owned the original *Robert E. Lee* of the song). 'Not long ago there were a hundred big boats going up and down this river. Now there can't be more than ten.' Showboats and private tourist trips were mostly what maintained the little business there was. He asked if I had mentioned the meeting to anyone. I assured him that I had not. 'Tonight's a big night,' he said. He repeated this several times on our way to the landing stage. 'Important decisions are going to be made.' I thought of asking him for help with my financial problem but stopped myself. It would be the most foolish thing I could do at that stage.

The sun set over the muddy sluggish waters of the Mississippi. Filtered by cloudy moisture it gave a dull shine to the iron struts of the various massive bridges and made the wharves unreal, like a poorly focused cinema film. There were four boats moored at the landing stages, two of them fairly small and one impressively large. The sun stained their white paintwork a shifting, brownish red. A shadowy party of negroes trudging towards Front Street might have been Chickasaw Indians returning from a hunting expedition in the days when Davy Crockett drank at the *Bell Tavern*. A celebrated frontiersman and representative to Congress, a man of vision and action, like myself; and like myself abandoned by his friends. Crockett died a martyr in one of the earliest battles against the Pope's minions. A dozen black cars, similar to our own, were already drawn up on the levee. From them issued a number of men wearing heavy overcoats and wide-brimmed hats. It was impossible to see more than a glimpse of their faces. Indeed, they seemed to be taking great pains not to be recognised as they went aboard the large stern-paddler which dominated the other boats moored nearby. Her name was newly painted in gold on her high cream-coloured sides. In the tower of her wheelhouse uniformed sailors could be seen preparing for departure. Other hands stood by to cast off. The *Nathan B. Forrest* was already making steam. Every so often she would hiss and shudder and her hull would bump against the sturdy wood of the wharf. With our own coat collars turned up to protect us from the cold we made our way through bales and casks to the gangway where we joined the line of men. Unlike the seagoing vessels I had grown used to, the steamboat had three decks topped by the wheelhouse, the first deck being virtually on the waterline, since in common with all such craft she had a flat bottom making her able to negotiate the river shallows. She smelled of paint. When I put my hand on a wooden pillar to steady myself it felt sticky. She had been redecorated not more than a day or two earlier, primarily in red, white and blue. Major Sinclair led me by a series of metal staircases up to the top deck occupied by a number of small private cabins. 'We'll share this one.' He opened a louvred door and turned up an oil lamp which hung by a chain from the ceiling. 'Make yourself at home.' He spoke with all his usual courtesy, but it was plain his mind was on other matters. He pointed out the cabin's facilities, the range of soft drinks in a small locker above the single bunk. The cabin was also done up in the national colours, with blue walls, red carpet, white sheets and pillows. On the wall over the bunk were arranged the crossed flags of the Union and the Confederacy. It now seemed obvious that this secret convention, so momentous it had to take place where there was not the slightest chance an outsider might witness it, was to do with State politics. I could not imagine what they wanted from me, unless they wished to offer me an official post, perhaps as Tennessee's first Scientific Adviser. In that capacity I could oversee the development of revolutionary new aerodromes at Nashville, Memphis, Chattanooga and elsewhere. Tennessee could easily become the model for the rest of the United States. Within a matter of a few years I could see myself returning to Washington, perhaps as first Secretary of Science. I would coordinate massive scientific and engineering schemes from California to the Canadian border, building power stations, aerodromes, factories to produce my planes, cars and locomotives, modern shipyards to facilitate the new kinds of supership I dreamed of creating. I am no *ligner*, like that arrogant *shnorrer* Einstein who fooled them all so thoroughly they made him a national hero. My flying cities would rise from Kansas to hover, scintillating and roaring, over prairies where Sioux and Pawnee had once wandered.

Man would become nomadic again, yet truly civilised. But where he had once used the wigwam and the travois, now he would use electrical energy, moving to wherever the weather was good and raw materials plentiful. By 1940 the United States would be a citadel of enlightenment and scientific wonders. She would stand firm against Oriental Africa, bring salvation to Europe and offer to Russia the promise of her new Byzantium. How could I know enough then Carthage would creep through all our defences, attacking our most vigilant guardians while they slept. The gift of prophecy was granted me and I was too self-involved to make proper use of it. They put a piece of metal in my womb. It threatens to grow. All the time it threatens. But I can control it. I will not bear their monstrous child. I am not their *n'div*. I am a true son of the Dniepr and the Don. I am the light against dark. I am Science and Truth and I shall not be judged as you judge ordinary men. *Ho la febbre*. I am Prometheus come down from Mount Caucasus. I bring the words of the Greek and the lamp by which ye shall read His words and know all heretics. *I nachalnika zhizni nasheya*. Christ is risen! Christ the son and the only God has cast down the Father who betrayed Him. He has exiled the Jewish Jehovah. Their God wanders the earth with a begging-bowl and an outstretched claw. Abraham betrayed his son. Jehovah betrayed us all. Let the Greek know we follow Him. Let the Pope and all his legions fall upon their knees crying: 'Kyrios! We acknowledge thee!' And Rome shall have a new master and He shall be a lord of strength. He shall look to the future and see that it is good. And His chosen ones shall be men of knowledge, builders of miracles, and wonders; captains of the flying cities.

I must admit I was in an over-excited condition as Major Sinclair offered to show me the rest of the boat ('since there's a little time to kill'). The second deck, with tables and benches, was evidently a restaurant in the summer. Partly enclosed and partly covered by a canvas awning, it was deserted and there was plainly no intention to use it tonight. We descended to the first and largest deck, virtually one vast room, a miracle of ornament, of gilded scrolls and carved muses, of crystal and copper and silver filigree, of marbled columns and mirrors; all with the predominant theme of red, white and blue. Again the twin flags were prominently displayed everywhere in the hall, particularly on the good-sized stage at the far end. The *Nathan B. Forrest* had plainly once been a queen amongst the great showboats which in their heyday had plied the Mississippi for its entire negotiable length. Major Sinclair stood

404

with arms folded, his back against a pillar, smiling a little as I marvelled at the opulence. 'I used to come aboard as a boy,' he said, 'and watch the minstrels.' His voice had a melancholy note. 'But now the railroads and the movie theatres between 'em have almost made this kind of transport, not to mention entertainment, a thing of the past. And men like ourselves are to blame, eh, Max? We'll be putting a lot of the modern world into the past soon, I should think.'

I was sympathetic. 'It's ironic how we hurt ourselves with our own power of invention.'

My friend looked at his watch. 'We'd better get out of here.' Taking a short cut between the rows of widely spaced seats, he led me from a side door out into the open air, then up to third deck. It was dark now. I heard a muffled shout from the wheelhouse and saw sailors busying themselves with ropes and chains below. The steam whistle sounded a long, low moan. There came a rattle and a massive shudder, then the great stern paddle smashed into the water. Electric light glittered on white foam. The boat's machinery was engaged. Her boilers boomed and growled, her pistons squealed. Suddenly we were free of the wharf. We moved with slow majesty out into a dark infinity that was the Mississippi River. The lights of Memphis fell away from us as we sailed steadily into midstream. From other parts of the boat I heard the tramp of feet. At this Major Sinclair hurried me inside our cabin. The whole vessel was filled with that regular beat, positive and military. It kept time with the sublime rhythm of oiled brass, rotating steel and trembling iron. My friend picked up a small bag, asking me to bear with him for a short while. He would be back to collect me as soon as he could. I poured myself a Coca-Cola and sat on the bunk, considering the prospect of meeting the Governor and his staff. Deciding to steady my nerve with cocaine, I was just able to return the packet to my pocket as the steam whistle sounded for the second time. The marching sound died away entirely. The boat was silent again, save for the vibration of the engines, the steady splashing and groaning of the paddle. I was tempted to go out on deck, but respected Major Sinclair's wishes. A few moments later the pale-faced aviator opened our door, apparently more relaxed than before. He had something tucked under one arm and his body was covered from throat to feet by a long, blue silky robe. Upon the breast of the robe, over his heart, was embroidered a yellow Maltese cross in a blue circle. It was identical, save for the colours, to the one on his airship.

'Are you ready, colonel?' His voice was low, as serious as it had been when he first asked me those mysterious questions and issued his equally mysterious invitation. My immediate response was of relief. I was not to undergo the ordeal of meeting the Governor after all. I was to be inducted into a Society of Free Masons, in itself a useful honour. The long gown rippled in the breeze from the river and looked incongruous on the tall flyer as he stood aside to let me out onto the deck. Against the darkness he might have been a householder roused from his bed and caught accidentally wearing his wife's housecoat. At his request I followed him back down the steps to the lowest deck. The water was black and the banks invisible. We could be drifting in space as easily as on the river, save for the spray from the paddle. He opened a small metal door in the stern and we passed through into dim electric light. We were evidently in a dressing-room area, where the coons had once blacked-up before going out to entertain their audience. The place had a musty smell to it and I thought I could still detect stale greasepaint.

Then Major Sinclair had raised his arms over his head, pulling material down to obscure his face before opening a door. Light almost completely blinded me as he lead me out onto the stage.

I blinked, trying to get my bearings. Gradually I saw that the stage was illuminated by a gigantic cross consisting of hundreds of tiny bulbs. In front of me curtains had been drawn back. In the gloom of the auditorium, lit only by the great crucifix behind me, was a mass of variously coloured hoods and robes, each robe bearing the bold insignia of encircled cross, each right hand raising a clenched, gauntleted fist in salute. There were other robed and masked figures around me on the stage. It was one of the most inspiring moments of my entire life. I gasped. Like some ancient, saintly hero in the presence of the Grail I had to resist an inclination to fall immediately to my knees. I knew now I was in the presence of those legendary Knights of the Fiery Cross, the Freedom Riders who had saved their land from total chaos, who until now I had seen only in news photographs or, of course, on the screen in *Birth of a Nation*. My legs began to tremble. Sweat formed on my skin. From these satin hoods stared several hundred pairs of eyes, as if in judgment on me. *Ich war dort!* I was under the steady gaze of the warrior-priests of America, the highest officiaries of the famous Ku Klux Klan!

The sense of power emanating from the men in that room was tremendous. It was psychic energy so enormous I momentarily imagined that floating hall, unable to contain it, must burst like an exploding sun and bring sudden daylight to the shores of Mississippi and Arkansas. In the eery brilliance of the fiery cross, amidst the rustle of robes – white, green, grey, crimson, black and blue – and the growing murmur of deep, manly voices, Major Sinclair led me to a seat at the side of the stage. An impressive banner hung behind the cross, a flying dragon with the legend *Quod Semper, quod ubique, quod ab omnibus*, red and black, framed by an isosceles triangle. My senses were profoundly affected by all this and especially by the vibrant presence of the mysterious figure which now stepped forward, his shining purple outlined against the cross, a ripple of light and shadow. It dawned on me how tremendous a privilege had been granted me as it was sonorously announced that we were graced by the presence of the Imperial Wizard himself. Then the opening ritual began.

They bowed visored heads in prayer, led by the firm, musical tones of their Grand Kladd; a simple yet heartfelt plea to God to help them maintain and uphold at all times the most holy ideals of their Klan. The prayer completed, the Imperial Wizard raised flowing sleeves to bring complete and reverential silence upon the gathering.

'All Genii, Grand Dragons and Hydras, Great Titans and Furies, Giants, Exalted Cyclops and Terrors, and all other citizens of the Invisible Empire, in the name of the Valiant and Venerated dead, I affectionately greet you and welcome you to this most Special and Secret Klonverse. Ye have been summoned from every Realm of our Empire on a matter of great and terrible import, to discuss the very future of these United States of America, to which ye have all sworn undying loyalty unto death.'

I remember only hazily the rituals which followed. There were chants and counter-chants, declarations and revelations, most of which were conducted in the secret language of the Klan. It was impossible to follow the cries of 'Ayak!' and 'Akia!' or 'Kigy!' and 'San Bog!', but the chant of *The Klansman's Creed* will never leave my memory, for I was to hear it more than once in the time which followed.

I believe in God and the tenets of the Christian religion and that a godless nation cannot long prosper. I believe that a church not grounded on the principles of morality and justice is a mockery to God and to man. I believe that a church that does not have the welfare of the common people at heart is unworthy. I believe in the eternal separation of Church and State.

I hold no allegiance to any foreign government, emperor, king, pope or any other foreign, political or religious power. I hold my allegiance to the Stars and Stripes next to my allegiance to God alone. I believe in just laws and liberty. I believe in the prevention of unwarranted strikes by foreign labour agitators. I believe in the limitation of foreign immigration.

I am a native-born American citizen and I believe in my rights in this country as being superior to those of foreigners.

The sound of those heartfelt voices moved me almost to tears. It was as if I was in the Alexander cathedral in Kiev again, listening to the chanting of the priests, hearing the names of the Heroes of Kiev pronounced in holy memory, though now they spoke of the Knights Kamelia, the Knights of the Midnight Mystery, the Order of American Chivalry, the Knights of the Great Forest. *Pyered bogom klyanus klyatvoy vyernoyu: Klyatvoy tyazhkoyu, klyatvoy strashnoyu: Pyered bogom klyanus klyatvoy strashnoyu na Rusi Gosadaryu, kak pyos sluzhit Spasi, gospodi, lyudi tvoya!* O Lord, save thy people! God Save The Tsar! How we wept and kissed that sacred book. And they called out the days, weeks and months according to the Klan: Deadly, Wailing, Hideous and so on. Even the years they dated from the first year of the third reincarnation of the Klan, which was 1915, only a short while after *Birth of a Nation* itself was first released as *The Clansman*. Here was religion and morality become militant and glowing with a just anger. O, the Greek has taken up his sword. Christ has risen! Christ has risen! Those noble, valiant men stood and listened in awed silence as the Imperial Wizard began to speak. It was a statement of the Klan's ethic, a reminder to all present, of the noble ideals and true purpose of the Order. He quoted Colonel Winfield Jones who was not, he said, a Klansman, but an objective outsider who had written *The Story of the Ku Klux Klan*. The Imperial Wizard stressed the importance of winning and maintaining such friends.

'Colonel Jones, fellow Klansmen, has told us that the Anglo-Saxon is the typeman of history. To him must yield the self-centered Hebrew, the cultured Greek, the virile Roman, the mystic Oriental. The Psalmist must have had him in mind when he struck his soundless harp and sang: "O Lord, thou has made him a little lower than the angels, and hast crowned him with glory and honour. Thou hast made him to have dominion over the works of thy hands, thou hast put all things under his feet." The Ku Klux Klan desires that its ruling members shall be of this all-conquering Blood. The Ku Klux Klan stands for the noble, the true and the good, for the majesty of the Law, for the advancement of the human race. Our most mystical order, fellow Klansmen, now numbers millions. It has come to speak for the great mass of Americans of the old pioneer stock who are opposed to the intellectually mongrelised "Liberals". A blend of various peoples of the so-called Nordic race, the race which, with all its faults, has given the world almost the whole of modern civilisation, these Americans have found themselves increasingly uncomfortable and distressed. The sacredness of our Sabbath, of our homes, of chastity, and finally even of our right to teach our own children in our own schools fundamental facts and truths were torn away from us. Those who maintained the old standards did so only in the face of constant ridicule. We suffered economic distress. The assurance for the future of our children dwindled. We found our great cities and the control of much of our industry and commerce taken over by strangers, who stacked the cards of success and prosperity against us. They came to dominate our government.'

The Imperial Wizard's speech was one of the most moving, one of the most truthful I have ever heard. He went on to say how native Americans were discriminated against in business, legislation and administrative government. He pointed out how the World War revealed that millions who had been allowed to share the Nordic American heritage actually had other loyalties. At last we realised an alien usually remains an alien no matter what is done to him, what veneer of education he gets. The melting-pot was a ghastly failure. The very name was coined by a Jew; a member of the race most determinedly refusing to melt. The American could outwork the alien, but the alien could underlive the American. Aliens from Eastern and Southern Europe were accustomed to squalor. And alien ideas were as dangerous as the aliens themselves no matter how plausible such ideas sounded.

'The Klan goes back to the American racial instincts, to the common sense which is their first product. Modern research finds scientific backing for these convictions. Three of these racial instincts are vital to our Order's intention of building an America fulfilling the aspirations and justifying the heroism of the men who made the nation. These are: Loyalty to the white race, to the traditions of America, and to the spirit of Protestantism. They are condensed in the Klan slogan: *Native, white, Protestant supremacy!'*

Then, like a tidal wave, the response roared from the floor: *'Native, white, Protestant supremacy!'*

As if lifted by this wave, the Imperial Wizard swept his arms above his head. He spoke of patriotism, of keeping pioneer stock pure. 'Racial integrity means good citizenship. Races and stocks of men are as distinct as breeds of animals. One does not train a bulldog to herd sheep!'

As the applause went on, the Imperial Wizard made a gesture for silence. The cheering stopped at once. 'The Klan is not opposed to aliens, only to aliens who attempt to rule Americans!' The Western Jew had great abilities, but his separation from the Nordic race was religious even more than racial. Far worse were the Eastern Jews of recent immigration, known as Askhenazim, the Judaised Mongols called Chazars. They show a divergence from the Nordic denying any hope of assimilation. 'The white race must be supreme, not only in America but in the world!' The idea of white and coloured races living in harmony was absurd. The whole of history had been one of racial conflict. This fact disagreed with maudlin theories of cosmopolitanism, but it was a truth.

'The Klansman says whites will not become slaves! The Negro is a special duty and problem of white Americans, the Negro is here through no fault of his own. Nevertheless, we should not make promises of social equality which can never be realised. The Klan looks forward to the day when the Negro problem will be solved on a sane basis, when every State enforces laws making sex relations between white and coloured a crime!' The Wizard again dampened the applause. He spoke of Rome's attempt to rule America. 'Our first Colonies were settled for the purpose of wresting America from the control of Rome.' He explained how Protestantism and the Nordic people were the same thing. All other peoples wished to destroy it, particularly the Catholics. 'As the biggest, strongest, most cohesive of all the alien blocs they frequently form alliances with other alien groups against American interests, as with the Jews in New York today. It is a Klan duty to make as many people as possible aware of all this. It is our duty to use the democratic system to ensure Klansmen are candidates in every possible type of election and that Klansmen win! That is how we shall save America. Not through violence or mob rule, but through the purity of our ideals. To this end we are already working!'

Wie lange wir es dauern? Not long. Other Klansmen rose to speak of Klokards working in all walks of life. Kludds preached that Klan and Church were synonymous. Friends in high places, non-members supporting Klan views, were willing to help. Distinguished visitors from abroad applauded the Klan fight. 'They deny the wicked lies of those newspapers who say we are a narrow, illiterate people!'

When this clamour died away the Imperial Wizard said in even, thrilling tones. 'One such visitor is with us tonight. The Grand Dragon of the Realm of the Air will introduce our guest.' For some moments there was polite applause, dying down until again the steady pumping of engines and paddle were the only significant sounds. Then Major Sinclair stepped forward to intone: 'Brothers of the Fiery Cross, we are honoured by the presence of a great scientist and aviator visiting us from Europe. He has fought the Turk, the Bolshevist, the Catholic and the Jew, and he shares blood with our ancestors who explored and settled this land. His mother was French, his father British. He has often spoken in private of his own ideas which are, I think you'll agree, one hundred percent American. He does not come to us to criticise and confound, like many strangers to the South. He respects our traditions. It was the British, we shall always remember, who supported the Confederacy. But if I seem narrow in my loyalties to the South, I beg to be forgiven by my brothers. I seek merely to demonstrate that not all outsiders are critics, bigots or agitators.'

He told them how I was a professor of science, an engineer, a flyer and a God-fearing Protestant. 'An opponent of all we fear and hate. I have invited him to this Klonverse as a representative of those who support us objectively and freely. But also, brothers, he is one who has personally witnessed the horrors of unchecked alienism. We take to our hearts a true Knight of the Air, who has fought hand to hand with bloody Bolshevism, saved thousands from the Red Terror. I give you my friend – as I know he will be yours – Colonel Max Peterson!'

The applause I received was generous but reasonably cautious. I had not expected to speak and was nervous. Nonetheless now that I was here I determined to speak from the heart. All I had was sincerity. I was moved almost to tears as I began my address. While the *Nathan B. Forrest* continued down the muddy Mississippi on her way to Vicksburg I told them of the terrible dangers facing Europe, how I had been a prisoner of the Bolsheviks. Indeed I gave them in a sense my whole life story. Gradually I captured their interest and their sympathy. Encouraged by this my oratory began to soar to heights it had known only once before, when I made my matriculation speech in Petersburg. I described the pathetic sight of desperate women and children begging to board refugee ships, the victims of jealous and vindictive Jews. The Catholic church weakened Italy, France grew feeble by allowing Jews to control business and parliament. Even England was in danger from the same atheists, Socialists and Zionists who attacked beaten Germany. I described how Mussolini and his people resisted the Pope, and consequently building a nation which would attract back many U.S. immigrants. In Ireland the Orange Lodge and other Protestant organizations were directly attacked by Catholic republicans seeking to impose tyranny upon Ulster. (I knew many Klansmen had been recruited from such lodges and noticed a stirring of interest.) Then I spoke of the threat of Islam. I explained how Jewish money, Catholic guns and Negro bloodlust formed a united threat to all our great institutions. I went on for at least an hour, describing the virtues of Americans, their originality in all fields, particularly science and engineering. I showed how industrial centres were threatened, how aliens crept into the entertainment world at every level, many owning newspapers, some already planning radio stations. Only strong legislation could fight the lure of gin and jazz. Russia was destroyed, Europe teetered on the brink. If America were not to fall to Chaos she must set an example. They were on their feet now and stamping, waving their assent. I was elated. I concluded with my own vision of an American future. It would be strong and untainted. Clean, independent cities and towns and richly cultivated land would provide for people in plenty; they would never be afraid to walk down a street or lane at night. The alien, discouraged from procreating by heavy taxes imposed for every child he fathered, would disappear in a matter of decades. Genetic science would produce stronger, healthier Nordic Americans to impress the world.

'And finally,' I concluded, above the steady rise of applause, 'it will be an America where the word "Klansman" is synonymous with honour, nobility and good blood. Your descendants shall again lead this nation. The Klansman alone, as Mr Griffith has shown, stands for progress and decency. He is willing to fight to the death for his Christian purity, for a faith whose vitality has created the finest civilisation in the world, which mighty heroes have defended down the centuries with strength and courage, since the glorious days of Athens and Sparta!'

My idealism, my honest spontaneity, impressed every man aboard. I sat down to sustained applause. My accent, normally a matter of suspicion, was confirmation of my integrity and proof of their own Christian tolerance. I had no selfish reason for holding my opinions and this gave my words extra meaning. I felt I had found my own at last. The Grand Kladd acknowledged my stirring testament. I was so elated I hardly noticed when the Kladd began the ordinary reports of the meeting. Klan recruiting was proving enormously successful in all Realms, particularly the Western and Mid-Western heartland, where Klansmen or Klan-backed candidates held many important offices. They remained misunderstood, savagely resisted in places, but their strength grew daily. I was impressed by their trust in allowing me to be present at these secret speeches, particularly when the Grand Klokard rose to report on the various prominent men who could be relied upon. 'Elections come up all the time. And we're taking them. Next year, for instance, when Memphis holds her elections we'll win across the board. We've already picked candidates for State elections. Our momentum simply can't be stopped. Membership counts in millions while millions more will vote Klan. Republican and Democrat candidates are being prepared by us for the Presidency itself. Within five years a Klansman could be our nation's Chief.'

This last piece of news was as novel and as exciting to those on the floor as it was to me. I now realised why this particular Klonverse was so important. Both funds and morale had to be raised to embark upon an important new phase in the Klan's political programme. From the crowd stepped a Grand Cyclops who announced his rank and Realm. He was in accord with all that had been said. However he was unhappy about bad publicity which could lose the Klan key elections. Certain members had taken the white hood merely to fulfil personal vendettas. Twice in Missouri recently Klansmen had shot to death members of families with whom they had feuded for years. 'Even the niggers have rights. I know of a case where a nigger girl and her father got killed on account of her having a Klansman's child. These iniquities, however rare, are fuel for the alien-backed press. They're blown out of all proportion by our political enemies. I believe the Imperial Wizard should issue an edict banishing transgressors from the Klan. If he doesn't, we'll lose support when and where we need it most.'

Raising a purple- and gold-trimmed arm, the Imperial Wizard showed his willingness to reply. 'Wouldn't you agree that what's appropriate for Massachusetts, Brother Cyclops, isn't necessarily okay for Texas?' His accent was slow and reasonable. 'Those people have specific and serious problems out there. The same goes for California with her Jap farmers. If some of our boys brand or whip the people who step out of line – and I don't say I approve – it could be it's the only way, in that part of the country, that makes sense. I'm sure none of us here bears any man ill-will, irrespective of his race, colour or creed. But we must never forget the fundamental reasons for our Order being reborn that fateful night on Stone Mountain, Georgia, seven years ago. We have to bear in mind what attracts ordinary folks to our Order. We've shown we're prepared to take action which others are afraid to take. In defence of a decent Christian way of life, we must always be prepared to take up arms when the occasion demands. Fear has to be a weapon in our arsenal as much as conviction or faith. It's our duty to set an example.'

A grey Klansman raised his hand for the Klonvener's attention. 'I say we can't compromise Christian principles in order to win a few liberal votes.'

'Exactly so.' The Imperial Wizard approved this attitude.

A Grand Klabee from Iowa spoke next. 'If a Klansman is to become next President of the USA, we have to condemn mob violence wherever it occurs!'

There was a pause, a certain tension, before the Imperial Wizard answered with measured dignity. 'That is also true. Today it's within our power to elect half the country's Governors, maybe more. Since I've been organising this Order we've risen in three years from a membership of a few thousand to a force large enough to make Washington think twice.'

Near the back of the floating hall a voice cried: 'That's a fact!'

Graciously, the Imperial Wizard acknowledged this, adding: 'We must also acknowledge the redoubtable efforts of Mrs Mawgan in the membership drive.'

The Grand Kladd motioned from where he sat on the far side of the stage. As he got up the boat shuddered, perceptibly altering course. 'I'd be the first to agree. The Imperial Wizard and Mrs Mawgan came up with a damned near foolproof method of swelling the ranks. This puts money into our campaign chests and like it or not that's our prime consideration here. Until we can elect both Republican and Democrat presidential candidates, preferably on an open Klan ticket, we might as well be throwing shit at a dungheap.'

'We are Americans!' The Imperial Wizard's dramatic tenor cut through the general murmur. 'We have a fundamental belief in democratic processes, the cornerstone of our nation. That means winning votes. Votes cost money, particularly when it comes to nominations. We must have strong candidates. Men above reproach. True white men to speak up for our principles and our religion. The men we need do not come cheap. We need the nickels and dimes of every possible member.'

The Iowan Grand Klabee replied forcefully. 'The men you want are the very people who draw the line at nightriding and lynching. By restraining the rougher elements now we'll soon be able to have our own judges and police chiefs. They'll do that we do now as vigilantes. I say we should have no truck with the branding-iron boys. Use your power to cancel or suspend their charters. Then tell the press. Look at how many join the Klan for business reasons. Insurance salesmen, storekeepers, bankers, factory owners, all kinds of solidly respectable men. Educated men. How long will they stay with us if they believe too many wear the white hood simply because they're outside the Law?'

'The mask makes us equal,' said Grand Klaliff from the shadows. 'An insurance clerk has as much anger, as much wish to right a wrong as a fieldhand. A banker enjoys the thrill of the nightride as much as any blacksmith. You're underestimating how many approved of what our boys did in Harrison last year but would never say so right out. We smashed that strike and run that so-called Methodist out of town. Ninety-nine percent of Arkansas was behind us.'

'Washington's more important.' Another Grand Cyclops stepped from the ranks, gesturing urgently. 'Blood likes money, but money don't like blood.'

Suddenly Major Sinclair was on his feet. 'Remember why we exist, sir. If we ever forget that we are primarily the protectors of the White Race we might as well disband this minute. We must be seen to be firm, strong, right minded. I joined this brotherhood in the early days, in Atlanta, because our women were threatened on the street, leered at by niggers and aliens. I will not live to see my children seduced into a life of drudgery by marriage to a money grubbing Jew, persuaded into renouncing their religion by some Jesuitical jazz baby. Surely, gentlemen, I need say no more!' He was enthusiastically applauded and the Imperial Wizard said soberly, 'Thank you, Grand Dragon. I think you speak for all.' But even this did not completely silence the approving grunts, the occasional shout or whoop from individual Klansmen. I felt immediate comradeship with these people and their direct, honest habits of speech and action. Idealistic principle has always moved me deeply, wherever it manifests itself. Had it been appropriate, I know I would also have leapt to my feet and clapped.

The Imperial Wizard was stern. 'No man has ever cast doubt on my dedication, nor on my ability to build this Order into the power it has become. When Colonel Simmons made me responsible for running the Klan it was in full knowledge of my faith in his ideals. He will tell you so himself when he returns from his well deserved rest and stands amongst us as our Emperor. Colonel Simmons wrote the book by which we all stand or fall, our great Kloran. I swear by that book, or by the Holy Bible itself: he'll endorse all I've done and all I shall do. For now I beg you to tolerate our more exuberant brothers. And I agree we must use subtler means wherever possible.'

In clipped New England accents another Grand Dragon endorsed this. 'I don't believe anyone here doubts Colonel Simmons's faith in our Imperial Wizard.' He hoped to reduce tension, though I saw no harm in their debate. King Arthur's Court, after all, was not without its disagreements. That subject was brought to a close and the atmosphere became more relaxed. The Imperial Kladd spoke next. 'While the Imperial Klabee makes his financial report, some dignitaries must leave you for a short while to discuss certain matters raised here tonight.' At this Major Sinclair signed to me and we followed the Imperial Wizard through the side door to the little dressing-room. Here the leader let out a long sigh as he removed his conical headdress. 'These things get awful stuffy, even in winter.' He smiled for my benefit, extending a well kept hand. 'Thanks for coming, colonel. I've heard all about you. I'm Eddy Clarke. I gather you're a drinking man.'

I told him I drank moderately.

'Then let's all revive ourselves in my cabin.' He was slim and graceful. His cultured, intellectual manner gave the lie to those who depicted Klansmen as brutes with unshaven jaws. Horn-rimmed glasses and dark curly hair lent him the appearance of an academic from some dreamy campus rather than a powerful political force. His easy charm demonstrated how he had achieved much of his success. He had joined the Klan as its recruiting Kleagle in 1920. Now he was effective leader. Colonel Simmons, a romantic and noble old Southerner, lacked enough political ambition to make the Klan the genuine threat it now was, but 'that fateful night on Stone Mountain' when he had gathered a few fellow spirits together to re-form the Knights of the Fiery Cross again was still recognised as the most important moment in the movement's history.

The Imperial Wizard's stateroom was at the forward end of the boat where the vibrations were less pronounced. He crossed to the wall, pressed a secret button and revealed a small cabinet of good-quality alcohol. 'This is part of the service, apparently, when you rent the boat.' I accepted a straight vodka. The American habit of adulterating drinks so they taste like soda-pop never transmitted itself to me. Major Sinclair and Mr Clarke both had rye whiskey. We raised our glasses in a toast. 'Here's to a long and profitable association, colonel.' Clarke was openly enthusiastic. 'I was mighty taken by what you said and how you put it across. From the horse's mouth. It was well worth the risk of inviting you. This Klonverse, you probably realise, is especially significant to us. What's more it was a good chance for our top people from all over to get a good look at you. Now you, in turn, have a good understanding I'm sure of our specific ambitions and problems.'

He spoke calmly but significantly. This was not merely an amiable discussion. He was almost courting me, treating me, I sensed, with unusual respect. 'You know my admiration for the Klan, Mr Clarke. While still in Europe I was fired by the dedication and courage of your Knights. Though she surely needs it, Europe has nothing to compare with your Order.' I spoke sincerely, yet was curious to know what he wanted from me.

Clarke refilled our glasses. 'We've a large and constantly expanding membership, Colonel Peterson. In certain States it has a preponderance of what they call "poor whites." Doubtless you noticed there's pressure on me to discipline folks who go a little too far in their enthusiasm. I'm reluctant. My answer is to strive with every means at my disposal to attract the better class of citizen who presently supports us in spirit but not in deed. To go forward as a real political power we have to win over that class and its finances. Do you follow me?'

'Given the record of the Klan in handling strikes, I'm surprised you don't have more large industrialists funding you already. Your interests are surely identical. It can only be bad press which makes them hesitate.' I hoped this assessment seemed intelligent.

'In a nutshell, Colonel Peterson.' Mr Clarke clapped Major Sinclair on the shoulder. 'You were right about this man, Al. I'm beholden to you.' He turned to me again. 'That's why we want to sponsor you, colonel. To make a nationwide lecture tour. Every newspaper in every town you visited would report your words. I've read the Memphis papers. You have a fascinating reputation. You speak with authority as one daily exposed to the terror of unchecked alienism. Respectable, intelligent, well to do people would listen to you. A distinguished professor, with no axe to grind in American politics, your quiet support of the Klan could prove invaluable to us in our recruiting drive. We would propose to fund you indirectly. The fees would be generous and all travel accommodation and so forth would be first-class. The Klan can be an implacable enemy –' he paused and I wondered if this were some sort of warning to me '– but it is a loyal friend.'

Naturally I was gratified. His offer could be of substantial use in improving my status. Sadly, I thought, it conflicted with my desire to oversee our Memphis aerodrome and aircraft scheme. Yet there were many advantages to forming an association with so powerful a political group. It could mean ultimate security for Esmé and me, perhaps the important government position I so much deserved. For this reason I did not refuse point-blank. 'I'm flattered, sir. However, I have pressing business interests at present, so would be grateful for a few days to consider your proposal.'

The Imperial Wizard had already assumed I would need time. 'Major Sinclair will be in Memphis for the next few days. He'll be flying back to Atlanta in *The Knight Hawk*. You're off to Little Rock tomorrow, aren't you, Al?'

'If the weather's okay. I might make the whole trip at once. Whatever I decide I'll be in Memphis for quite a while.'

Mr Clarke beamed. 'So when you reach a decision, Colonel Peterson, simply inform Major Sinclair. He'll convey the news to me at Klankrest, our Atlanta headquarters.'

'I'll be able to let you know shortly, sir.' There was a strong, almost supernatural rapport between the three of us as we stood in that red, white and blue stateroom. Mr Clarke told Major Sinclair a story about 'some Federal snooper' who had 'met with an accident.' If the tale was for my ears it was unnecessary. I already knew how the Klan punished spies and traitors and was thoroughly approving. At length we lifted our glasses in one last toast. 'To America!' Major Sinclair, the light of idealistic patriotism shining from his eyes, reminded me in stance and expression of those brave White Russian aristocrats who pledged their lives for Tsar and Christ in the fight against Bolshevism. Again I came close to tears. 'To America,' I said.

In the small hours of a bitter Memphis morning the *Nathan B. Forrest* steamed slowly towards the landing-stage. With Major Sinclair, I stood at the rail, watching the water turn the colour of mercury under a gradual dawn. During my time aboard I had made friends with leading Klansmen from every part of the country. We were all jubilant. The Klan had grown rapidly since 1920. There had hardly been time to draw breath. Many members scarcely realised how powerful they had become. An Indianapolis Kleagle had explained to me how the Klan had been forced to secrecy. The 'Invisible Empire' was formed in direct reaction to foreign-born groups with supranational loyalties and societies: Zionist, Knights of Columbia, anarchist, Sicilian Black Hand, Mormon, Tong. Mr Clarke had amplified this. 'If they openly declared their interests and ambitions so should we. In the interests of democracy we're forced to adopt enemy methods until we have power in Washington. Then we'll force 'em into the open by Law. They'll pay the price for all those years of hypocrisy and deceit, whether they're voodoo cults in Louisiana or Catholics in Tammany Hall.' Like me, he never lost sight of his moral goals, no matter how circuitous the route sometimes seemed.

Major Sinclair was in particularly good spirits as he drove me back to the Adler Apartments. Before I went inside, we shook hands warmly, standing together in that white sunrise. He said I had made a fine impression. He sincerely hoped I would choose to help the cause, his life's work. I climbed the steps to my rooms, considering the notion of a worldwide Klan. I thought how much in common Greek Orthodoxy had with Protestantism. Both opposed Rome. Shoulder to shoulder the Knights of the Ku Klux Klan could defeat all the enemies of Christendom. In bed I dreamed of a future where the fight was won at last. Free men in a free world stripped off their masks; regalia now only to be worn on ceremonial occasions as distinguished Southerners still sometimes assumed the uniforms of the Confederacy. Then great shining cities would ascend to the heavens free forever from alien threat. I think

419

I was also a little fearful. By accepting the invitation to board the *Nathan B. Forrest* I had actually taken an irretrievable step. From somewhere in the shadows the figure of Brodmann, grinning and mocking, wagged its finger, hinting at a subtle and unguessable revenge. I looked up to see the last of the cities departing. I had been marooned.

I slept only a few hours. I was thankful, in fact, to be awakened by a loud banging on my door. Stumbling in a hastily donned dressing-gown, I answered. It was Mr Roffy. 'You're sleeping late, colonel.' His manner was disgruntled, almost impatient. He strode into the dark, curtained room and sat down in my armchair. Pulling aside drapes and shutters I was dazzled by unexpected sunshine. Meanwhile Mr Roffy smoothed his hair, adjusted his waistcoat, recovered his manners. 'Forgive the intrusion. I have some tremendously good news, sir. I had to come straight round to let you know.'

I was surprised at the contrast between his appearance and his words. 'Would you care for some coffee?' I began to hunt for the can.

'Thank you, I've already breakfasted. However, I'll smoke if you've no objection.' Lighting his large cigar he sucked like a starved baby at the breast. 'Mr Gilpin had a wire this morning. Our strategy is working perfectly. We are within an ace of everyone signing at once – the Chamber of Commerce, the State legislature, all the way up to Congress. They're calling this the "Memphis Experiment," you know. The whole country's going to be watching us. If it succeeds, Nashville's ready to begin her own scheme, using our company as overall controller.'

I still could not equate this with his distracted and harassed manner. 'When do we begin work?' I asked.

'Early June, if we get the land we want.' He sighed deeply, perhaps to control himself. 'It was our offer of $450,000 as security which turned the day for us. All we do now is put up the cash. Everything else will go ahead like clockwork. We'll get our money back immediately, of course. Our profits will be a hundredfold within the first year. You've heard from Europe?'

I sat down heavily on the edge of my bed. I had heard nothing, of course. I did all I could to stop myself shaking.

Mr Roffy stared at me through the cigar smoke. 'What's wrong?'

'I rather hoped you were the boy from Western Union. My agents tell me German inflation's creating a panic throughout the Continent. That's why things are moving so slowly.'

'This scheme stands or falls on your contribution, colonel. Maybe you've funds in New York you could liquidate?'

'Not enough.' I could think of no further excuses. Soon, unless Kolya responded, I would be forced to admit I was virtually penniless. Irrationally, perhaps, I believed there would then be a chance my life would be put in danger. At last I added: 'The reply will come today. In the meantime will my note of hand be of any help?'

'Better than nothing.' His voice sounded both suspicious and frightened.

Excusing myself I went into the bathroom for some cocaine. When I emerged the trembling was scarcely better, but I prepared a sheet of paper guaranteeing funds up to $150,000 to the Memphis Aviation Company. 'The cash will follow,' I promised.

'It's today or never, colonel.' He folded the document carefully and put it in his breast pocket. Rising slowly to his feet, he turned towards the door. 'It depends on you. Tomorrow we three will either be at the helm of a great enterprise or we'll be tarred and feathered, run out of town on a rail. Mr Gilpin and myself have made personal assurances to banks, senators, congressmen, State officials and current creditors. If your money fails to materialise, we'll all be ruined. It will be bad enough for Mr Gilpin and myself. We are men of honour. The ridicule and the disgrace would probably kill Gilpin. But it will be that much worse for you, colonel. Prison? You would certainly be extradited. Where would that be to?' His hand twitched as he lifted his cigar to his face. 'France?'

This prospect alarmed me most. I would be arrested the moment I stepped off at Le Havre. I hurried him out. Allowing myself a further liberal dosage of cocaine I bathed, dressed, drank the lukewarm coffee I had prepared. I had to risk another telegram to Kolya. What alternatives were there? Then suddenly it occurred to me. Our wild Italian friend had once offered to put me in touch with his successful cousins in America. In French I composed a wire and went downstairs to Western Union. I sent the wire to Annibale Santucci, care of the Ristorante Mendoza, Via Catalana, Rome. I explained I needed to borrow a large sum for a few days. Did he know anyone in America who could help me? He could reply to Colonel Peterson. In my panic I sent further wires to Esmé, telling her I loved her and had not forgotten her, to Mrs Cornelius, asking her to contact me as quickly as possible. I had done all I could. As I took the stairs back to my rooms, Mrs Trubbshaw, whom I had arranged to see, entered the main door and called up to me. She was the very distraction I needed. The rest of the afternoon was spent with her buttons and bows, her inventive, guilty lewdness, and my last supplies of that universal healer the locals called 'candy'. Mrs Trubbshaw remarked at one stage how neither Mr Roffy nor Mr Gilpin looked as well as usual. She was afraid they had been burning the candle at both ends. They would find themselves dead of heart attacks if they were not careful. 'Those two old rogues just won't grow up,' she said. By early evening, when Mrs Trubbshaw rushed home to prepare her husband's supper, I had received no replies to my telegrams. If I was to face my partners again I must have an especially good reason for not having the money. I toyed with the notion of a share crash, incompetent brokers who had invested in some fly-by-night scheme. But that would require confirming evidence. Once again I dressed myself carefully in my best evening clothes, then sat down to wait for the inevitable knock on the door. If they did not arrive within the hour, I had decided, I would visit the nearest bordello, if only to replenish my cocaine.

At seven-thirty I put on my top coat. As I reached for my hat and gloves, I heard a knock. Opening the door to Mr Gilpin I was shocked by his appearance. His normally healthy face was pallid. It seemed to have sagged, no longer a soldier's but a prisoner's; even his moustache had drooped. He said nothing as he shuffled in. I told him at once that I had as yet received no news.

'We figured as much, colonel.' He sighed deeply. 'We're buying what time we can. I'm a fair judge of character. I know you wouldn't welsh on us.'

'I've been sending wires all day. To France, Italy, England.'

He nodded vaguely. 'You understand the consequences will be drastic?'

'Our scheme's rock solid. Surely in reality we only face a delay. We'll weather the embarrassment.'

'It's not so simple, sir. Mr Roffy has made firm guarantees. Our $300,000 can't cover them. Your share will make the difference between life and death. Roffy's on the brink, sir. He's contemplating suicide. I hope you're not in any way suspicious of our credentials . . .'

'I have no lack of trust in you, Mr Gilpin. It's the problem in Europe. Almost every government blocks the flow of funds as a matter of course.'

'But $150,000 can't be a great deal of money to you, sir?' He passed his hand through what a day or two before had been a white leonine mane. Today it was a dead cat.

'The funds are solidly tied up, chiefly in securities. My agents are doing all they can. I hope to borrow from my bank against what they know exists. But no word so far.'

Lost in his own thoughts, Mr Gilpin let his bleary eyes wander about my room. When he next looked at me his expression was tragic. 'It's Roffy's family, you see. He's a man of honour. If he finds he cannot keep his word . . .' He sighed deeply and returned this attention to my writing desk.

I believe he was growing suspicious of me, yet was still unwilling to air his opinion. My moral position was appalling. Through my fabrications it now seemed I might drive another human creature to take his own life. 'It will not come to that, Mr Gilpin,' I said.

'I have secured a short extension.' He looked at me as if I had already personally assassinated his old friend. He did not offer his hand as he left. I went out shortly afterwards and walked up Madison Street. The trolley cars bellowed and steamed in the cold air; light from various cafés and stores failed somehow to penetrate the darkness. Turning a corner I found myself outside a very respectable speakeasy where I had been carrying on a casual affair with a young Chattanooga girl who worked there. I knocked and entered. With what was almost the last of my cash I bought several large packets of 'candy'. I was determined to do everything I could to avoid anxiety and yet save Roffy from ruin. I spent the night with my lady friend, returning to my apartment the next morning. To my delight a telegram was waiting for me. Santucci had replied. He had not bothered to condense his message. It was as voluble as if he were speaking to me in person. I had been lucky to find him in Rome. He was normally in Milan these days. All our friends were doing well and had become 'very serious about politics'. Everyone sent their best wishes to myself and Esmé. He gave me two addresses, one in Chicago, the other in San Francisco. Both people were called Potecci or 'Potter.' He was not sure which city was nearest Memphis. Where, in fact, was Memphis? Was I the prisoner of a lost Egyptian tribe?

This uneconomical reply, so full of friendly good will, so typical of Santucci's exuberance and generosity, cheered me considerably, even though I had hoped for something a little more useful. Nothing had

423

come from Kolya, Esmé or Mrs Cornelius. I found my folded map of the United States. With a piece of cotton I was trying to work out which of the two cities was, in fact, closest to Memphis, when the janitor arrived at my door. He gave me a note. To my great joy it was from Jimmy Rembrandt! He had just arrived in town and was lunching at Plunkett's Café on Monroe Street. If I was free would I please join him. He urgently wished to discuss a personal matter. My first thought was that he had news of Kolya. Then it occurred to me he merely wished to return the $500 he had borrowed. Jimmy might even help me find the money to save myself and my partners. Accordingly, my hopes coloured by desperation, I changed and hurried to the restaurant. It was an old-fashioned establishment, of oak booths, marble-topped tables and rococo brasswork. Jimmy had already started eating as I called to him down the aisle and he looked up irritably. His expression did not change when he recognised me but froze into lines of grim anger. Almost reluctantly, he stood up behind the table, wiping his lips on his napkin, avoiding my eye, as if I had caught him eating human flesh. I could make nothing of this. As he sat down I saw he had plainly been travelling all night, for his suit was crumpled. With almost mechanical deliberation he rearranged the lines on his face and smiled. He asked the waiter to delay the main course until I could order. I said he seemed very tired. He made an effort to be his usual courteous self. This gesture served to make me rather more nervous.

For a while our conversation was stilted and conventional. By the time my food arrived I was wanting to ask Jimmy what was wrong. Was he getting round to admitting he could not yet pay back my $500? When he had finished his own pork chop he put his knife and fork carefully together in the plate, drew a breath, then turned his clear, grey eyes directly on me. 'Max, I'm here as a pal to wise you up.'

He spoke in a different accent, harsher and somehow lazier, in style closer to Santucci's. He used slang normally confined to private conversations with Lucius Mortimer. I could follow him thanks chiefly to my familiarity with hookers, who used a similar patois. I understood the gist of his opening remark, therefore, but had no idea what it actually implied.

'It's Roffy.' Rembrandt paused. 'He's mad enough to bite. He thinks you're a yentzer. That's why I'm here. To try to get you to see reason.'

'Mr Gilpin said Mr Roffy was very anxious.'

'He's going crazy. He told me you're holding out on him. Your cash will save the airport scheme. What's up, Max? Are you planning to cop a sneak? D'you think they're a couple of skin-gamers or what?'

'Of course I trust them. I've done everything in my power to get the money. I feel terrible about it, Jimmy. Mr Gilpin told me Mr Roffy's considering suicide.'

'Let's just say he's a little unstable at the moment, Max. He's sure angry enough to blow the whistle.'

'On what?'

'On you. He's saying he'll turn you over to the cops. Maybe belch on you to the papers. About why you left France in a hurry. He's got the goods on you, pal. Your whole sidetrack.'

I fell back in surprise. 'How could he have found out? Jimmy, I insist –'

'Someone must have slipped the info to him. Or he saw the same stories I did.'

I felt very sick. I pushed my plate away. 'You know those charges are completely false! I explained that when we first met in New York. You believed me!'

'It's not making any difference to Roffy, the way he is now. Look at your position, Max. A bum monicker That's enough for the front office. You'd be deported to France. It'd be the hatch for sure.'

Weakly I signalled the waiter to remove my plate. I asked for a glass of water. My entire body began to shake. This time I could not stop it. 'He has my IOU, Jimmy.'

'So what?'

I put my head closer to his, speaking in an intense undertone. 'You know the charges were false!'

'So it's a hype. But it could stick. You must believe that or you wouldn't be here. They'll beef you, Max, unless you come up with your third. What's it to you? A hundred fifty measly grand? Thaw it as soon as you can. Square Roffy and Gilpin. You'll get it back fast. You can't want to see your friends go down. At least take my tip. I owe you one. Roffy's crazy enough to do anything. If this goes on the wire I wouldn't lay evens you'll leave Memphis in anything but a case of ice.'

'He'd kill me?'

'Maybe not Roffy personally. But he has friends who aren't squeamish.'

I believed him. I was already sweating. I could hardly breathe for the terror which suddenly struck me. Familiarity with the threat of death made it no easier to accept. Something seemed to press hard on my chest. 'Can't you appeal to him? Tell him I'm doing my best?'

'Max, just give Roffy his kick-back. What if he does doublecross you? It's a small enough slice of your pie. The papers said you took twenty million. They always bullshit, I know. I'd guess at ten. You can afford it.'

'Jimmy, I told you the papers lied!' I was by now soaking in my own juices.

'Five, then?'

'I stole nothing. I arrived in New York almost penniless. I've been living off Roffy and Gilpin here. In New York I sold some jewellery, but I haven't a cent now!' My whisper became almost a shriek. I tried to lower my voice again. I was hoarse. I had at least admitted the truth to someone. I felt the burden lifting from me. But a worse one was settling and I had completely lost control of my tongue. 'A patent in Washington went for a pittance. That's how I could lend you the five hundred. If I'd told them I was broke they wouldn't have trusted me. You said yourself you had to pretend to be rich for people to take you seriously, no matter how good your ideas. I listened to your advice, Jimmy!'

Rembrandt's face lost all colour. He lit a cigarette and he looked at me through careful eyes. 'Max, you're caught in a snowstorm. How can I know this is the m'coy?'

'Cocaine doesn't affect me that way.'

'You're telling me you're actually innocent? The Frogs really did set you up? You're down to the cotton?'

I nodded. 'You believed me before.'

'You can't even raise a couple hundred bucks?'

'If I pawn my clothes, maybe.'

Jimmy swore under his breath. 'But every damned paper agreed you were the big shill, Max. The gyp of the century!' He looked at me like a stricken child. 'Jesus Christ.'

I felt obscurely guilty. 'Someone benefited, I suppose. It was not I.'

In an expression of incredulity he blew smoke through pursed lips. 'So you're the friggin' yap! Set up for the gum job. Freighted out of the country before you knew what was happening. Perfect! Well it sure makes us look like boobs!' He shook his head. 'So Christmas has been cancelled,' he added, as if to the restaurant at large.

'If you're suggesting Kolya betrayed me you're wrong. I suspect de

426

Grion. My friend is a prince of the royal blood. He saved me, Jimmy. He'd save me now if he could. I don't have his latest address. However, a friend in Italy –'

'What a beautiful scam!' Jimmy was hardly listening to me. I found it odd he reacted as he did. It was as if he was admiring the criminals who betrayed me while also laughing at himself. Yet only minutes before he had warned me my life was in danger. Possibly ironic amusement was his way of disguising his own fear, but it disturbed me. A smile began to form, then he frowned. 'And what a bunch of suckers we turned out to be. Conned by a Michigan roll! All those months of planning. The outlay. We blew every dime on this. It was me got Lucius to talk those old pros into it! Oh, Christ.'

Though many of his remarks remained obscure I could tell he was genuinely upset. 'I assure you, Jimmy, I'm heart and soul behind the scheme. I never meant to deceive anyone, least of all you and Major Mortimer. I offered my services, my patents, my skills, my brains. There's nothing wrong with any of them. If I had the cash I'd give it to Mr Roffy immediately! I've as much stake as he has. I don't want our scheme to collapse.'

He was plainly bitter. He had vouched for me to his friends and I had let him down badly. I could not stop babbling. I leant across to take his arm. He was unaware of my touch. Jimmy had lost all concentration. He stared vacantly up at the gas-globes overhead, grinning to himself. Had we both gone mad? I could not then see any reason for his reaction.

It was shock, of course. I had to make notes, puzzling over that meeting many times before I realized why, quite suddenly, he began to laugh. I stared at him in amazement.

'Oh, Jesus Christ!' He was helpless. 'We've sweet-lined our own asses!'

He had no reason to take the whole blame. Part of the moral responsibility was mine.

I have never been one to deceive myself in such matters.

427

Seventeen

THE CAUSE OF other people's mirth is a subject which has frequently defeated me. Jimmy Rembrandt's reaction to my dilemma remained a baffled note in my diary for some years. Even as I parted from him outside Plunkett's Café he was still occasionally seized by an attack of snorts and grimaces. He wished me luck, 'though I guess Roffy and Gilpin need it more'. Speechless once again he gave a shaky salute and walked rapidly up Monroe Street to vanish in the electric shadows.

I saw little humour then in my situation and none at all the next day when, coming empty-handed from the Western Union office, I saw Pandora Fairfax jump from her car with an agitated shout and run towards me. She asked me if I had seen either of my partners. It emerged both had disappeared, leaving rent unpaid on their own apartments and mine. They also owed considerable sums to various printers, designers, model-builders, researchers and advertising agencies in the city. She herself had been promised cash for the hire of her plane and in expectation of an agreed consultant's fee had made a down payment on another aircraft. 'There's a rumour,' she said, 'that Boss Crump's men have orders to bring them in dead or alive.'

By that evening I was in the extraordinary position of trying to explain why my partners had left no forwarding address. I believed they were based in Washington, I said. One of Boss Crump's hard-faced lieutenants said he would check. He seemed angry and suspicious of me but his common sense must have made him realise I was telling the truth. Also he was aware of my standing with certain members of the community and it was obvious even to him that I was innocent of any fraud. Nonetheless I was taken to a little office over a dairy depot on Union Avenue and interviewed by E. H. Crump himself. He was quietly spoken and polite, taller than I had expected, and dressed in a pale blue suit. He had round, smooth features, manicured hands and wore horn-rimmed glasses. He, too, was quickly convinced that I knew nothing of my partners' whereabouts and had not been aware of the amounts of money owed in the city. Of course, he now began to deny he had placed any trust in the two men and claimed never to have heard of the $450,000 warranty demanded of us. It would have been imprudent to tell him that if the demand had not been made, the bills would have been quickly paid and Memphis would have been richer in a dozen ways before the year was out.

In fairness to Roffy and Gilpin, I did not offer my own opinion, that my partners, convinced I had deliberately betrayed them, had fled in panic. Unable to raise the extra $150,000 they had taken their own money and abandoned the project. I am not one to lay the blame for my own misfortunes on others. I had let them believe I was wealthy. They had acted in good faith. If they had wanted revenge on me they could have revealed what they knew of my past. Thus I remained convinced of their basic integrity. Some of us are stronger than others. Whereas, in their shoes, I might have stood my ground and explained my predicament, they had lost their nerve. My main regret, of course, was that another far-sighted, bold and commercially viable project had been shelved. Boss Crump's political machine had turned against anything to do with my plans. He made that clear. My association with Major Sinclair could have contributed to this, I now realise. Because of his misguided stand against the Ku Klux Klan, Crump never really succeeded in pushing Memphis to her full potential. This opposition, reflected in the prejudices expressed in the Catholic-dominated *Commercial Appeal*, was the single reason he never reached the high office for which his excellent judgment and character were suited. Perhaps he saw the Klan as a rival. An alliance would have given him national, rather than merely local, influence.

For a while I was also puzzled by the disappearance of Jimmy Rembrandt. I wondered if perhaps he feared my anger, believing he had let me, as well as Roffy and Gilpin, down in some way. Possibly he was still embarrassed over the $500 he owed me. Nervous of Roffy's anger, he might also have decided not to risk involvement if by chance I was murdered. Presumably he had returned to New York.

My moral and practical problems were not eased by having to hear my friend Major Sinclair's honest opinion that Roffy and Gilpin were 'a pair of scallawags' who had used me for their own ends. I could not see what they had gained from their association. There was no point now in explaining my own part in their predicament, but I assured him only the most terrible circumstances could have forced the two men to abandon me. I pointed out I had lost no cash in the affair. I was not responsible for the Aviation Company's debts, nor my partners' personal debts. In my wildest flights of speculation I wondered if alien interests, scheming the ruin of our great venture, had not kidnapped them or otherwise disposed of them. It has long been obvious to me that all major airship disasters of the 20s and 30s were the result of Zionist sabotage. Alternatively, my partners could easily have fallen into the clutches of Jewish or Italian moneylenders. Loan sharks were known to deal savagely with defaulting debtors unable to pay their exorbitant interest. That would also explain why Roffy and Gilpin seemed so desperately frightened towards the end, when I could not produce the money. I explained this theory to the police officers who called on me. They promised to explore the matter thoroughly. But they were Crump men through and through. Their conviction was that I and the city had been victims of 'a pair of high-class con-artists'.

Privately, of course, I blamed myself for the whole unfortunate business and continued to defend my partners even at police headquarters where I was asked to make a formal statement and was afterwards interviewed by the press. But the next day's headlines, needless to say, were not favourable to Roffy and Gilpin. I received some sympathy but ironically they were branded 'villain' just as I had been in France. I suppose Kolya defended my name as vociferously as I defended theirs, with equal lack of effect. Once the press makes a scapegoat it will not relent. The case in point was Adolf Hitler, of course. Nobody ever writes about the benefits he brought to Germany; they merely reiterate the bad things. Such injustices become all too familiar when one has lived as long and seen as much as I. They cease to be worthy of comment. The world falls into Chaos. Justice is a fantasy, soon to be forgotten, as the white race which invented it is forgotten. Anyone will tell you I am a man of feeling, of intellect, of unusual moral strength. I am prejudiced against no race or creed. But when me and mine are threatened by a blood drinking brute, what shall I do? Say nothing? Make no defence? In their moment of trial the two old men fled. If they had remained they might now be heroes, statues in Overton Park. Yet, as it was, their decision was to prove of considerable benefit to others, though they would never receive public recognition for it. They ran away from the devastated dream which had been so close to achieving enduring reality and left me with no choice but to accept at once the Imperial Wizard's commission. I would fly to Atlanta and from there would take up my banner, marching side by side with noble knights in a mighty crusade whose aim was nothing less than to rescue sanity, justice, decency and freedom for the whole world. I reached my decision within a day of my partners' disappearance. A certain element in Memphis seemed determined to cast doubt on my credentials, my sincerity, my very honour. Twice I was harassed in the street. Mr Baskin arrived to give me notice to quit my apartment. Even Mrs Trubbshaw, who I thought at first had come to offer me consolation, had some ludicrous claim that she had lent Mr Roffy $2,000 and insisted I had a 'moral duty' to pay it back to her on his behalf. Time alone would show who bore false witness and who, in fact, was the victim of deceit!

As ancient saints and heroes turned from selfish and material concerns upon receiving a sign from God, so I took all these events as a sign I should go forth into America, to spread our message across every square mile of that great and vital nation. Within a year I would become so famous the matter of one small factory and an insignificant municipal airport would seem a petty concern indeed. I had been given the opportunity to conquer the entire New World with my genius. A strong, scientifically advanced America would be the most powerful country on Earth. Once celebrated here, I would automatically come to influence the world. Then at last Russia, my old, spiritual Russia, could be rescued from the Bolshevik scavengers. The steppe would grow green and beautiful again; the wheatlands would bloom, the forests retain their tranquil profundity and new golden cities would arise, the cities of reborn Byzantium.

I am not so vain as to claim God Himself created the circumstances driving poor Gilpin and Roffy from Memphis, releasing me to fulfil His work through the medium of the Knights of the Ku Klux Klan. However there is no doubt in my mind that what originally seemed a disaster actually set me on my proper path, to use my God-given powers of prophecy in direct service of the Christian faith. As Paul the Greek was chosen to become Christ's envoy to Rome, so might it be said I, inheritor of the Greek ideal, was to be envoy to this New Rome. Having made my decision, I was at once suffused with joy. My confusion died away. I no longer waited desperately for news of Esmé, Kolya or Mrs Cornelius. I should see them again in the fullness of time. I knew, with every atom of my being, that I had at last found my true vocation.

I departed from Memphis the next day, into the sky above the old Park Field air training base. I left sad friends and scowling critics alike, amidst the noise of a great crowd which gathered to witness *The Knight Hawk* slip her moorings. We would ascend into a terrible sky, in which black clouds rolled and streamed against a ground of deep, greenish blue. A storm was coming. A storm was gathering in the South. A storm was coming to sweep the whole United States. And her prophets would stand on the decks of flying cities or the platforms of gigantic airships to cry their warnings, as if from Heaven itself: BEWARE THE HERETIC, THE INFIDEL, THE PAGAN! WAKE UP, AMERICA, TO THE PERILS WHICH FACE YE. WAKE UP TO THE VISION OF THE ALIEN SWORD WHICH CUTS YOU DOWN AS YOU SLEEP; THE ALIEN VOICE WHICH SEDUCES YOUR CHILDREN; THE ALIEN CREED WHICH ROBS YOU OF YOUR RELIGION! WAKE UP, AMERICA, IN THE NAME OF CHRIST. WAKE UP TO YOUR PERIL AND YOUR SALVATION. *The storm carries God's prophet on noisy wings; the thunder and the lightning herald his coming. Out of the South, out of Memphis, which was once in Egypt, he shall come as Moses came to lead the children of the New World towards a glorious future, their rightful scientific inheritance. From fertile Florida to frozen Alaska, where the Tsar once raised his standard, where the two-headed eagle cast his eyes upon the land and saw at last an ally with whom to build Christendom afresh, he shall be heard. Wake up, America! The ship of the prophet is seen in the sky and his sign is a fiery cross, the cross of Kyrios the Greek. Thus did the Greek give name and substance to His knights. Kuklos: a circle. Kuklos: the Circle of the Sun. The Circle and the Cross are One! Kyrie Eleison! Christ is risen! Christ is risen!*

The Knight Hawk, free of her moorings, rose steadily into the air above the field. Strong winds hurled their power against her hull. She shuddered and slewed with every blow. I gripped the side of my cockpit, watching the crowd fall away from me. The winds were so strong I feared we must crash, but Major Sinclair had handled this type of ship many times since the War; he held fast to her wheel while operating height and trim levers with graceful expertise. The Rolls Royce engine whined to full power. We began to push forward until we were directly over the great river and her anchored steamboats. Memphis, with her steel and concrete centre, her brick and wood outer zones, her bridges and her railroad tracks, gradually lost identity, meaning no more or less than a dozen other urban settlements along the riverbanks. I leaned over the lip of the cockpit, studying Major Sinclair's techniques with the controls. The wind slapped at my face, tugged my clothes, threatened to rip helmet and goggles from my head. Our gondola was vibrating so violently I thought the rivets must soon be shaken out of her. Everything aboard not absolutely rigid or completely flexible rattled vigorously, yet Major Sinclair was plainly not in the least alarmed. To him all this agitated commotion was so familiar I doubt if he was greatly conscious of it.

Later, when he had reduced the power and there was a lull in the wind, the major shouted above the engine's whine: 'These smaller blimps don't have enough power, so can't keep their course as efficiently as the big ships. In decent weather they're a lot easier to handle.' The altimeter in my cockpit showed we were now a thousand feet up while my speedometer indicated forty-five knots. At first I had felt uneasy in my stomach but the sensation was forgotten as I peered through the windscreen at wide fields and strips of trees. Immediately below were the railroad tracks which, as was normal in those days of primitive instruments, Major Sinclair followed. Soon I was enjoying the spectacle of a long freight train moving like a fire-breathing snake across the brown and yellow ground. Occasionally there would be a tiny car or, more commonly, a horse-drawn buggy on a dirt road, a small farm, a collection of shacks, a mansion, still doubtless the core of some great plantation. The sky remained lively, the sun was frequently obscured by garish, unstable cloud. Major Sinclair planned to put down in Little Rock for the night. There he could also refuel, complete his business in Arkansas, then head South East for Tuscaloosa and more benzine. From there, he said, it would almost certainly be a direct flight to Atlanta. He usually carried a rigger with him, but the man had been caught drunk by the police in Knoxville some nights ago and was in jail. (Major Sinclair no longer had any use for him. 'He can let me down and I'll give him a break. But I won't let him drag the Klan under. He knew what would happen to him.') Our job in Little Rock was chiefly to 'show the flag'. We would advertise the newspaper by taking a few turns over the city, drop some leaflets, drive home the fact that the Klan was not the mob of disaffected farmhands and backward manual labourers people claimed. Then we would land just outside the city

433

and take delivery of funds for the central treasury in Atlanta. Personally, I would be glad to be heading east again. At that moment we fought headwinds. If they remained constant they would help us when at last we turned towards Georgia. Major Sinclair constantly had to correct course while I, checking map and compass, acted as observer. Great stretches of land were virtually featureless to my unfamiliar eyes and I prayed I correctly identified the few rivers and small forests, the tracks and plantations which occasionally appeared below.

As we crossed deeper into Arkansas on the Western banks of the Mississippi I noticed less land under cultivation. There seemed to be more virgin forest. We had entered a country of smallholdings and cropsharers and consequently found still fewer features by which to steer. The wind gradually reached its former strength. Major Sinclair was forced to give his whole attention to controlling the ship while I desperately scanned the ground for landmarks even remotely resembling those on my map. Soon it began to rain and I could see little of the terrain. Eventually we were flying entirely by our compass. The rush of sleet and wind on the hull overhead, the roar of our engine, the whining suspension rigging made it impossible to hear anything else. My goggles streamed with water. It was difficult even to make out Major Sinclair's head and shoulders in the forward cockpit. This extreme discomfort and uncertainty was frequently the most familiar aspect of the 'romance of flying' in those days.

Almost at the moment I had managed to adapt myself to all this, the wind suddenly hit us like waves. It pounded us with enormous force. Our gondola began to bounce dramatically in her cables. I was certain we must either be flung out of our cockpits or be wrenched piecemeal from the battered gasbag. I saw Major Sinclair shaking his head urgently and signalling with his hand. We were going down. I was convinced we were crashing. My shaking body at once became still. Calmly, I prepared myself for death.

The machine's nose already dipped towards the ground; the gondola had begun to swing from side to side, like a crazy pendulum. As Major Sinclair valved out gas for a rapid descent, the engine's noise was lost behind us. We had hardly been in the air for five hours. I thought it ironic that, with all my dreams of magnificent flying liners, I should die in this ramshackle government surplus antique. But then the ship eased out of her descent and I knew Major Sinclair had regained control. I hoped we were close to Little Rock. It was more likely my friend

434

wished to get below the worst of the storm to check our bearings. The gusting rain continued to swing us from side to side and I was still fearful our hawsers must snap. Gradually I was recovering my nerve when without warning the engine cut out.

The ship was thrown helplessly backwards and sideways by the wind. I could understand nothing of Sinclair's gesticulating yet it was plain we had no choice but to land. I had no idea how he planned to accomplish this. Normally there had to be people on the ground to take our mooring lines. My friend was probably hoping to find a small town or large farm able to supply a party of men large enough to pull us to eath. I was experiencing at first hand the real disadvantage of the small airship over the light aeroplane. Moreover, without wireless equipment *The Knight Hawk* had no means of requesting assistance.

The rain gradually became lighter and the air much calmer by the time we had drifted low enough to make out a dismal panorama of waterlogged fields, a scattering of thin trees. In the grey light it seemed the whole world had been turned into a wasteland of yellowish excrement. For a moment I thought we were already dead, condemned to Limbo. Then Sinclair shouted and stabbed his left finger at the starboard horizon. Emerging from the mud, almost like a natural formation, were buildings little different in colour to their surroundings. Again the major concentrated on his engine, cursing to himself, forced to stop every few moments as he shook water from his arm or wiped his face. Then, shuddering in its frame, the engine spat rapidly, let out a series of unhealthy coughs, and came to life. Sinclair was yelling to me; the propeller spun, we lumbered forward. I could not hear him. Urgently he signalled for me to lift our grappling hook out of the spare cockpit to my right. With this, as he had earlier explained, he hoped to effect a temporary mooring. Once I understood, I leaned over to obey him; whereupon the gondola swayed sickeningly. I was only able to save myself from being pitched out by driving my knees into the side of my compartment. Busy with his control vanes, Major Sinclair could not help me. The rope was curled on top of my surviving suitcases. Sweating and close to panic I finally grasped an end, drawing it in towards me as the gondola resumed a relatively normal angle. For a second or two I sat back, taking enormous breaths, then I prepared the grappling hook in my right hand, ready to drop it over the side.

With a glance back to make sure I was ready, Sinclair tilted the ship even more radically, driving it down like a monstrous artillery shell at

435

the shacks ahead. The light was fading so rapidly I was afraid I would be unable to see to aim our anchor. 'Get a tree!' Sinclair shouted. 'Or a hedge. A fence is no good!'

He reduced speed, holding the ship almost stationary against the blustering wind which still caused the gondola to sway horribly. Twice, as I squinted through the gloom, I missed the chance to hook a stunted tree. By now it was twilight. Finally, in desperation, I hurled the thing at random into a field. It stuck into something but we continued to drag for yards until, to my enormous relief, the machine halted with a jerk. Major Sinclair switched off the engine, steadying the craft as best he could. We peered into the semi-darkness below. We were less than fifty feet from the swampy ground. Sinclair reached behind him and pulled back the cover from the little winch. We each took a handle and, by careful calculation, gradually got *The Knight Hawk* down.

Our good spirits recovered, we grinned like fools at each other. The winch was secured. Major Sinclair shouted to me to put my rope ladder over the side and get down to check that the anchor was firmly planted. The wind was still high; our gasbag boomed and rippled; the hawsers creaked. I was still cheerful as I climbed down the swaying ladder and, after about ten feet, felt my flying boots sink into mud. I followed the grappling line to where it had dug itself behind a rock, called up for some slack, then wound the rope around a small oak. Our machine was safe for the night.

We should now, of course, have to wait until morning before continuing our journey. This was normal practice in those days when bad weather would bring any kind of aircraft to an unexpected stop. That was why aviation experts like myself were struggling to produce machines unaffected by sudden storms, which would be able to fly at night. My own ideas were far in advance of Sinclair's ship, which was of a type first built in 1914, but design had not altered much in eight years. Airships were more costly to develop and maintain than small aeroplanes.

Although inconvenienced, neither of us was surprised by this turn of events. A flyer tended to congratulate himself if he completed a journey without coming down at least once. By the time Major Sinclair stood beside me in the field, it was very dark. He shook his head and shrugged. He had been over-optimistic, he said. He had expected the north-easter to subside. We now had no choice but to request hospitality from the nearby buildings. I asked if it was prudent to leave the ship unguarded. He laughed, taking me by the arm. 'You think some nigger'll steal her! Let's go, colonel. We'll see if we can get a bite of hot food.'

We struggled through the mud towards the dim, yellowish lights of oil lamps. Overhead, clouds moved swiftly in the sky. From time to time the moon revealed buildings ahead: rough, unpainted shacks repaired with patches of rusting metal and miscellaneous lengths of timber. As we approached, a figure appeared in the light of an entrance, staring out of its lean-to for a few seconds. Then, suddenly, the door was slammed. In another unglazed window several small black faces observed us from cover. I began to feel uncomfortable. Major Sinclair chuckled. 'They're just nigger shacks, colonel. There should be something else further on.' We made our way through this decrepit *shtetl*, hearing the clucking of chickens, strange, stealthy sounds, the creak of a shutter, until at last we reached a dirt road. A little further on we found a group of houses on either side of the road. These were in almost as bad condition as the others. However, Major Sinclair seemed confident we should do better there. Advising me to imitate him, he removed his helmet and goggles. 'Folks here are a little wary and more than a mite superstitious. We don't want some fool taking a shot at us because he thinks we're robbers or spooks.' While I waited at a broken-down gate, he selected one of the nearby houses and walked up the yard calling out, 'Hi, there! Is anybody home?' He knocked at the frame of a ragged screen door. I saw a candle flicker on the other side. Major Sinclair began to tell someone we did not need to speak to the man of the house. We were passing through and wanted a place to stay for the night. 'Thank you kindly, ma'am,' he said. He returned to me, shaking his head and smiling. 'They aren't much brighter than the niggers. None of the men are back from the fields yet and she won't open her door to strangers. There's a preacher down the road about half a mile. Let's hope he's more helpful.'

The muddy track took us between broken fences, collections of unidentifiable detritus, thin, bare trees, hen coops and pig pens. We passed the occasional silent, wide-eyed unhealthy child or ragged, thin-faced woman. Nobody spoke to us. In the moonlight the whole miserable settlement was eery and menacing, stinking of hopeless poverty. I had never expected to experience again those weeks when I had the misfortune in, 1919, to be stranded on the Ukrainian steppe. Yet here, in America were everyone was supposed to be so much richer, people of European descent plainly endured the same burden of un-spoken, habitual despair; villagers so starved of food or mental stimulus they lived out their entire lives in a helpless trance. I could not tell if their general appearance of idiocy was a result of circumstance or in-terbreeding, but I had seen the same expressions in Russia, in the slums of Constantinople. I was glad to reach the clapboard church with the preacher's shabby house beside it, a collection of youngsters, scarcely any more articulate or better fed than the rest, playing in the yard. A woman in a cheap print dress came out to the porch door. She grunted a question. She had light grey eyes, a cancerous skin and was not more than forty, though her hands had the stained, blotchy look of the very old. Returning a cautious, tired smile in answer to Sinclair's courteous question, she said her husband was over at the other church holding the Wednesday prayer meeting. He would be back around nine. Major Sinclair explained our problem. The preacher's wife said we should go back down the road a piece, to Miss Bedlow's. She rented rooms. My friend saluted and said we were much obliged. Again I was reminded of the wretched *shtetl* synagogues, the ramshackle churches of Ukrainian peasants, their priests often as ignorant as the communities they served. I said nothing of this to Sinclair, however, for in a dim way I thought I might offend him.

Eventually we made out a sign we had missed on the way to the church. Miss Bedlow's house had once been painted green. Someone had attempted to cultivate the front yard and the porch seemed in rea-sonable repair. Major Sinclair advanced up the few wooden steps. Again he knocked. This time I could clearly see the man who an-swered, for the light was brighter. He was fat. He had red, weather-beaten features, a bullet head, pale hair, almost no eyebrows. He wore a pink undershirt and overalls which he had loosened at the top. Some-thing he was chewing stained the corners of his mouth. Though he did not seem greatly suspicious he made no attempt to disguise his curios-ity, staring from me to Major Sinclair and back again. My friend ex-plained our predicament. The fat man slowly became impressed until he almost stopped chewing altogether. 'You boys flyers?' I could hardly understand him. The words had actually sounded to my ears like 'Y'baahs flahars' but with extra vowels. I am famous for my quick ear and ability to reproduce accents and vocabularies. This came close to defeating me. The man went back into the house, calling for Miss Bed-low who emerged, a well scrubbed colourless woman in an old-fash-

438

ioned woollen dress. She had one room she could rent us, she said, but we would have to share a bed. The charge was a dollar each, plus twenty-five cents apiece if we wanted breakfast. She could fix us supper now. Pork and greens would be another thirty cents. Gravely Major Sinclair told her the terms were reasonable (I think the woman was asking the most she dared) and she relaxed, inviting us in. The house smelled of mould and boiled food. The fabric of furniture, curtains and carpets was threadbare but clean and save for some differences of decoration was what one might find in the home of a Ukrainian moujik in similar circumstances. This was my first real experience of the American peasant and it depressed me. I had expected more, I suppose, of the United States. We went up the creaking staircase to our room, stripped off our flying gear, washed in the basin provided and went down again to be introduced to the other guests. Two elderly widows, the fat man, a grim farmhand and a young half-wit all showed comical astonishment at my accent. When Major Sinclair told them I was from England it created no specific change in their expressions.

The fat man spoke first. He had served in France for over a year. He had heard England was pretty. Was it anything like France? In some ways, I said. In others it was more like Maryland. He had never been to Maryland. He heard it was pretty there, too. He frowned for a while, then offered his view that France could also be mighty pretty, though it was a terrible thing what those Bo-shees had done to her. Shrugging, he added: 'But I reckon she's more cleaned up now than she was.' I said her wounds were healing.

Seeing the difficulty we were both under Major Sinclair took over the bulk of the conversations, since I could follow them scarcely any easier than they could me. He explained where we were bound, why we had come down. He also managed to say a little about the Ku Klux Klan, the problems of whites undercut by black labour. The fat man said they never had trouble with their niggers, except once some buck got drunk on moonshine and the Sheriff over in Carthage had to come out.

'Did you say Carthage?' I thought I had misheard.

'Sure did,' said the fat man, wondering at my obvious curiosity. He waited politely for me to say more.

'There's Carthages all over,' Sinclair said with a smile. 'And Londons and Parises and St Petersburgs.' He returned his attention to the fat man. 'Then we're not too far off course.' He unfolded our map.

'Here's Pine Bluff. And this here's Little Rock. Yes, now I see.' He was pleased. 'We'll be there by tomorrow noon for sure,' he said to me.

Like me, Major Sinclair ate sparingly of the abominable mess of grease and pulped vegetable served us. Then there was nothing else to do but say goodnight and return to our room where we slept uncomfortably, back to back in our clothes, until dawn. When I looked out of the narrow window at bare trees and broken rooftops, I was relieved to see the wind had dropped. The grey cloud had lifted; an early morning sun rose into a sky full of heavy cumulus promising dry weather.

After a breakfast of bacon and grits we paid Miss Bedlow. She told us who she thought would be able to help us with our ship. Two or three houses back down the dirt road, in a yard full of old tyre rims and rusting metal, we approached two wiry young men who lounged outside on a porch so rotten half the boards had fallen in completely. These were Bobby and Jackie Joe Dally. Major Sinclair quickly struck a bargain with them and the four of us set off to where we had moored the ship. By now word had evidently spread throughout the settlement. We were the centre of attention. First the white children, then the women, then the old people fell in behind us. By the time we could see *The Knight Hawk*'s swaying gasbag we had come to the negro section. Scores of blacks, keeping their distance from the whites, crept in a staring mass at the rear as our procession entered the field.

I was becoming alarmed by their numbers and by their silence, which seemed to have a sinister quality to it. Those hungry, unhealthy features might have belonged to cannibals. They made me feel sick. Black or white, there seemed little difference to me. They pressed around us in their torn, patched rags, with thin ungainly limbs, rolling, vacant eyes, red mouths, stinking of sweat. I could feel my hysteria building. I longed for some cocaine to steady my nerves but that was still in my luggage. Major Sinclair seemed unperturbed. I said nothing of my fears, yet I became convinced these people would never allow us to leave the ground, that they would jump us at any second, strip us of all we owned, tear the very flesh from our bones, and feast off it. I sensed a tremor in my legs as more and more of those ill-fed bodies touched mine. Sinclair was smiling. He was joking with them. Could he not see what I saw? This was Carthage indeed! The degenerate dregs of humanity greedy for everything I had worked for; the ignorant, hopeless, unconscious enemies of civilisation, as unable to imagine or create a better world as the wretches I had left behind in Kiev, as the Jews

440

I escaped in Alexandrovskaya villages or the subhuman tribespeople of the Anatolian hinterland. Only by a massive effort of will could I make myself move forward. My mouth grew dry, my knees weak; my heart beat at terrifying speed. Sinclair would have thought me utterly irrational; this poverty did not for a moment threaten him. But I knew if we did not reach the ship as soon as possible we could be submerged by this mob. It wanted what we carried in our ship. It hated us for what the ship represented. It was jealous because I had managed to make something of myself. It loathed all that was different. Innovation threatened change, threatened the hideous familiarity of their lives. They would protect this familiarity at all costs. The metal shifted in my stomach. I was dizzy. I could not run. *Desidero un antisettico!* They stank of disease. The mass swelled, the pressure increased. I could not breathe. They were skeletons with huge, yearning eyes, reaching out their ragged claws for something they could not even name. I refused to join them in the camps, though they said I was a brother. That is how they recruit you. I never became a Mussulman. Seductive Carthage was resisted. I fought against her with wits and courage. I know her tricks. I know her ingratiating whine, her beggar's pretence at poverty, her pleading attempts to win sympathy, her cajoling murmur. They would do anything to drag me back. They call you the same, but you are not. An accident with a knife and they say you are one of them! A misguided decision of my father and I am denied my fame. My future is stolen, together with my true place in the world. Carthage crowds in like poison gas. Brodmann leered out of the cloud. My stomach churned. I could hardly climb the ladder into the cockpit. I stared down at those awful eyes. The blacks yelled wordless exclamations and began to caper. Some of the children tittered. Others wept. Major Sinclair was speaking to me as he slid his body into the forward compartment but I could not hear him. My breathing was erratic. They could still drag us down into that yellow mud. I put my goggles over my eyes so they should not see my tears. Major Sinclair waved. He was confident and relaxed. The wretches had our ropes and were towing us across the field. The whole crowd had begun to run. They cried out: strange, bestial ululations. Major Sinclair was shouting at me. 'Winch in the mooring line, man!' I needed water. I could not reply. Still shaking, I obeyed. I could see those voracious mouths twisting to display rotting teeth, those greedy hands clutching at my very substance. I owe nothing to Carthage. I am a true Slav. I was not of their blood. I had no debt of pity or charity or brotherhood. Poverty stank on their breath. They were my enemies. It reeked in their rags, in the food they ate, in their huts and their fields. I screamed down at them to release me, to let go of the rope. They were running like a single wave escaped from a dam; a flood of human flotsam. Scarecrow boys still swung on the mooring line, refusing to relinquish it. Their shrieking voices filled my head.

I had not sought any of this. I had been ill-prepared for it. They are the wretched servants of despair, the enemies of optimism, the willing slaves of Bolshevism. Carthage rose again, not merely in Arkansas, or Missouri, or Louisiana, but in every part of the United States, like the warning signs of cancer. In Europe, too. In the East it already conquered the entire organism. Everywhere was ignorance, hunger, fatalism, corrupted blood, blind hunger. It had been dormant in the *shtetls* until the great drums began to beat and the brazen trumpets rang, when Carthage shook herself from sleep and reached with a red grin for her spear and shield. She licked her thick lips and looked with confident envy upon the fruits of our labours: our harvest of civilisation. Her hot black eyes glared and there was a deep growl in her throat as she stretched and tested her limbs, her heart filling with anger against those who had sought to destroy her, who had, through their superior morality and courage, meanwhile enriched themselves. And her swarthy hands curled in anticipation. Her hungry, stinking breath is heard in the alleys of the city, the shadows and shacks and shelters, the tents and camps of the countryside, until the sound threatens to drown all others. It drowns the hymns and prayers of true Christians. Our beautiful songs and our poetry, our pure-voiced little girls, our sacrament is extinguished by the roar. Carthage stands laughing on the ruins of our just dreams; our blood runs down her chin; our monuments are ashes beneath her sandalled feet. The beast has conquered! The mindless mob rules on Earth. Chaos becomes the sole condition of Man. This I predicted. And we who were given signs (like the sign God sent when He brought the airship to rest) took heed. It became our duty to warn anyone who will listen. The fight is not completely over, though we have lost so many battles. They never made me a Mussulman. I do not stumble. I keep my back straight. I will not be seduced by the comforts of the trance. I will survive even the most terrible mistakes. *Gehorsam nicht folgn. Ich bin baamter! Bafeln! A mol, ich bin andersh.* Can't they see? I do not know their language. Podol is nothing. One must work where one can.

They were laughing their mockery as they finally let go of the rope and our ship flew free. They had been playing with us, showing off their power. Arms, white and black, waved like sickly reeds. I fought to recover my self-control. Major Sinclair had still not realised how close I had been to losing consciousness. We were still climbing into a silvery sky. I was so glad to leave Carthage behind. Little Rock lay clear ahead. I could imagine no experience before us as terrifying as that which we had already escaped.

They put me in Springfield when the roses were in bloom. Oh, Esmé, my sister, you never came to see me. They removed me from your memory. I know now how they work. They told you I did not exist. They desired you for themselves. Carthage descended upon us and carried you away. They destroyed my mother. Mother, did they turn you into ash? Did your bones smoke in their hideous pits where starving soldiers floundered through smouldering human flesh, while machine guns chattered night and day and the voices of the damned echoed in the gorge where I and Esmé used to play? Were you with her, Esmé, or were you already dead, churned to fertiliser by the Steel Tsar's implacable machines? Or had you sought the consolation of the Mussulman in a Carthaginian prison camp? I did not see you in Springfield, but Springfield is a dozen different places. The maps change and the locations move. My flying cities will know where to go. They tell me at the police station there is nothing they can do about the blacks. They sympathise, but their hands are tied. We are all afraid to speak our minds. The great movements have been suppressed; our heroes are dying in chains or already murdered. Only grey people are allowed to survive. They are the shadows left by Carthage to deceive us into believing our world still exists. But I am not deceived. I have not been dragged down. They shall not confine me in their camps, nor to their ghettoes, their nigger towns and stateless barbed wire pens. I shall not wear their *pe'os*. I am not the same as them. I deserve better. What right have they to call me *mishling*? *Halbjuden*? I was betrayed before I was born. *Das Blutt gerinnt. Das Blutt gerinnt.*

As Major Sinclair had promised, we were in Little Rock by noon. Our printed handbills fell into the neat furrows of her streets like seeds at springtime. A small crowd cheered us when we moored in a small park on the outskirts, took aboard the money we had come for, refuelled our tank and were quickly on our way again to Tuscaloosa. The illness which had seized me in Carthage seemed to disappear not long after we left Little Rock. As we sailed above the unremarkable rooftops of Tuscaloosa I was completely free of it. I began to think I had suffered food poisoning, for pork has never much agreed with me. With the wind behind us and clear skies ahead we set course for Atlanta, Emperor City of the South, core of a world once thought crushed and defeated but now growing into a golden, avenging phoenix. Atlanta, burned to the ground by ruthless enemies, raped and robbed and left for dead, rapidly gathered back her strength. Her great silver towers were rising from the wasteland. White, curving roads would sweep through her skies. I saw her in the distance and she was impressive. At her heart was a massive crown of gold. Major Sinclair was in excellent form now that the weather was clearer. Below the countryside steadily became more varied and pleasant. The city, seen above a line of dark green pines, had a clean, modern appearance which I had not expected. Before we reached the golden dome we turned north of Stone Mountain, heading for the extensive grounds of Klankrest mansion, seat of the Imperial Wizard, hub of the Invisible Empire.

We sailed in towards evening, flying over the brow of a hill towards a wide lawn surrounding an ornamental lake in which a fountain gushed. Orderly paths ran through the lawns. Above them was a great house so beautiful it would have been the envy of the Tsar himself. It was the epitome of fine Southern taste, with marble columns and lintels, a neo-Graecian mansion, solid and serene in the warmth of the late February sun. One could imagine some Georgian cavalier strolling in these grounds in the golden days before the Civil War. As Major Sinclair brought *The Knight Hawk* to a gentle halt over the lake, negro servants impeccable in red, white and blue uniforms of the Colonial style came running from the house to catch hold of our lines, securing us to a pair of special posts erected near the house, evidently for this very purpose. Next we were gradually winched to the ground and the ship was firmly anchored, enabling us to step easily from our cockpits to the grass. Major Sinclair, with his usual pleasant good manners, thanked the negroes and instructed them to take our luggage into the house. Looking up at the blue-veined marble and polished stone, the tall windows of Klankrest, I decided the Imperial Wizard's chief residence already rivalled the White House which I had seen in Washington and found disappointing.

We began to walk round the extensive marble veranda towards the front of the building. Just before we turned Mr Clarke himself appeared. For me, it was more thrilling seeing this unassuming, intelligent looking man, than if I had actually come face to face with Mr Harding himself. In his lightweight grey suit he approached us with easy grace. He and his family might always have inhabited the mansion. Retaining the mild, academic manner I had noted before, he confirmed my opinion: he was a natural gentleman, bearing himself with quiet dignity as he warmly shook hands with us, enquiring how the journey had been, saying how pleased he was I had decided to join the service of the Klan.

With some amusement, Major Sinclair told of our enforced stay in Carthage. 'I'm not sure Colonel Peterson was too happy about the accommodations.' He chuckled. 'All niggers and poor white trash. Wasn't that so, colonel?'

'It's a side of the South nobody's greatly proud of, sir,' said Mr Clarke soberly. 'Not so bad, I suppose, as New York slums, but a living reminder of carpetbagging days. It will change in time, especially when the alien exploiters are finally driven out.' He began to lead us towards the front entrance. 'In those days, sir, as you may know, the Klan dealt harshly with thugs who took advantage of Reconstruction. More harshly than they do today.'

Birth of a Nation had shown me this graphically. I nodded in enthusiastic agreement.

'It was an economic war, whatever Yankees pretended to the contrary. They were no more interested in the lot of the slaves than Simon Legree. The welfare of the negro was treated as a duty and an enduring responsibility in the South. When we were ruined, those poor wretches were amongst the first to suffer. If we had been left in peace to found our Confederacy, this part of the world would be a paradise now, a model to the rest of America, to the whole world.'

We paused outside the glass and rococo-iron doors. Major Sinclair seemed singularly happy as he surveyed the tall hedges, the neatly raked gravel drive. 'We're too big and varied a country to be administered as a single nation. Each State knows where her best interests lie. It's the Federal Government which always causes the trouble.'

We entered a spacious hall, also predominantly of marble, hung with old canvases, its alcoves containing alabaster urns trimmed in gold. 'You'll reduce the influence of government locally as well as nationally, I understand' I wished to impress him with my sophisticated grasp of U.S. politics. I rested my hand lightly on the polished wood of

445

a full-size grand piano and raised my eyes to the sweeping staircase with its huge Klan banner, the Grand Klensign.

'The rights of the individual are of paramount concern to the Knights of the Ku Klux Klan.' Mr Clarke was about to expand on this when a tall, handsome raven-haired woman appeared on the stairs and began slowly to descend. 'My dear! Colonel Peterson, this is my colleague, Mrs Mawgan. She has done as much as I to make this organisation the force it is today.' Mrs Mawgan wore a formal black frock. Her jewellery was jet and silver. With her broad forehead and heavy jaw she had a manner more immediately striking than Mr Clarke's own. I guessed at once she must be his mistress, even, to some degree, the power behind the throne. They were a splendidly well-matched couple. As she reached the bottom of the steps she extended her gloved hand, smiling pleasantly. 'You're the foreign gentleman who'll help us drive our aliens back to where they came from.'

'Now, Bessy, that's not exactly right,' began Mr Clarke chidingly, but I laughed heartily. She was a woman of considerable irony and I appreciated her wit.

'Mrs Mawgan,' I said with a bow, kissing her hand, 'if I can stop America making the mistakes of Europe before I, myself, am driven out, I shall be more than satisfied.'

'Oh, Colonel Peterson, you're far too well-bred to overstay your welcome I'm sure. I appreciate your ideals. And it's a good salary, too, I gather.' With this she treated me to a ladylike wink to put me at my ease. In some ways she reminded me of my baroness. 'You two boys must be tired out. What d'you want first? A drink? Or would you rather clean up?'

We chose the latter.

'Wilson will show you to your rooms. We'll meet down here before dinner.' Mrs Mawgan acknowledged my subtle bow with a smile of equal delicacy and we parted.

Wilson, the butler, took us up to the second floor, along a carpeted marble tunnel, to our suites. Mine was more luxurious than any hotel's. I had never been in anything of this size or richness. The sensation of genuine opulence which swept through me reminded me exactly of the feeling I received at my Uncle Semya's house in Odessa when I realised I was actually to have a whole room to myself, that many people thought it quite natural not to sleep in the same room as the one in which they ate! It was all I could do to stop from running from place to place opening cupboards and inspecting the elaborate toilet fittings. The whole was tastefully designed in the same patriotic colours, with the addition of gold and silver where appropriate. The wallpaper at first seemed fairly plain until inspected closely. Its chief motif was of lozenge shapes containing the initials KKK. The main feature of the suite, however, was my huge four-poster bed in the Napoleonic style, its headboards painted with scenes recalling the great triumphs of America's struggle for freedom and honour. Inset over the tallest point of the headboard was a stylised Klan hood on which, in beautiful Gothic script, had been imposed the motto *Suppressio veri suggestio falsi*. This reference to the methods of our enemies could not be too frequently reiterated. The french windows of my sitting-room opened onto a balcony directly overlooking the lawns and the lake. How I wish those fools who even now insist to me that the Klan was a gang of ill-bred ruffians could have visited Klankrest in the days of its glory. They, who would not even know which fork to use for fish, would have been speechless with amazement. It was the epitome of civilised and gracious living. Nobody there questioned my *yichuss*.

Eighteen

IF I AM A MARTYR brought low by my beliefs, then I am in excellent company and should not complain. Certain contemporaries have suffered far worse than I. They were reviled, imprisoned, tortured, hanged or burned alive. No single individual betrayed me in my fight. I am history's victim, but I have had many exquisite moments, seen the world in all her beauty, made love to delightful women, enjoyed lasting friendships and the warmth of public acclaim. I am not one to whine over misfortunes, or blame others for my failures. I stand by my actions. What if I no longer receive the general respect which perhaps is my due? I have at least been true to myself. The Sultans sail from the City of Dogs. They come out of Carthage on a black and bloody tide. Their ships ride at anchor in harbours blocked with corpses. Scarecrow boys hang in the yards, grinning at the ruined cities of the West. Only the Slav remains ready to resist them and the Slav is still in chains. The Steel Tsar died, forgetting to tell where he hid the key. Those girls are so lovely with their pale hair and blue eyes, picking at my clothes, looking for silk stockings and satin drawers like the ones Esmé might have worn. I cannot help myself. I give it away.

The West is on her last legs and I shall not live forever. The Sultans strut from their gloomy men-o'-war onto a festering shore already conquered by its own degeneracy. They who ruled only a few yards of Buchenwald or Auschwitz now claim mastery of the world. But the Sultans are liars if they claim me as their subject. I am not of their *blut*. *Ich habe langen geschlafen*. *Jesus erweckte die Toten*. I refused to become a Mussulman. I lost my mother. I wrote several times but nobody knew what had happened to her. Then, after the War, in London in 1948, I met Brodmann. He was already old and probably had TB. He told me he had been in Kiev when the SS came. He had worked for them in an office and had recognised her name from the list, had seen her as she went down to the trench. All this he could have said just to wound. Why was she on a list? Why was he not in the gorge? It was in the gorge I worked, he said, I was captured, too. I have no reason to trust Brodmann. He lied even then, trying to placate me. Why did you pursue me? I asked. I did not, he said. I never got out until '46. I was sent to Czechoslovakia. It was distasteful, my mother's name on Brodmann's sickly lips. I guessed he was out of favour but still a Chekist, hoping to redeem himself by luring me back. I was too old a hand for him. Anyone might have learned my mother's name, which was doubtless in my file, together with our old address. That was not, of course, the name I use. I at least am willing to show responsibility and protect those relatives still alive in Russia. Somebody told me Brodmann had died in Spain in 1950. Doubtless he was by then claiming to be a Sephardim Don! The Catholic pseudo-Fascist Franco must have welcomed him as a brother! I wonder how he explained what happened at the Tempelhof Airfield in 1939! They are all the same. They, too, would have been Sultans, given the opportunity. Maybe Brodmann was exactly that, living by betraying the likes of my mother. The black ships are the size of towns, prows throwing up yellow mud as they invade the land. They are implacable. They fly a dozen cryptic standards, but I have always recognized the banners of Carthage. That is why they hate me so. Yet certain of us, all of whom have this gift, recognize each other, frequently without having to exchange words. So it was between myself and Major Sinclair and later with Eddy Clarke and Mrs Bessy Mawgan.

It is a form of telepathy, I think, or something spiritual revealed in the eyes; an instant rapport. We are a brotherhood secret even to our own kind! I was never, however, to be granted an opportunity as miraculous as that offered to me by the Imperial Wizard: to speak to an entire nation! Nothing like it could have happened to me in Russia. Indeed, Mr Clarke had many recent reports of worsening terror as some assassin bungled the killing of Lenin, giving Trotski and the rest an excuse to pound the Bolshevik hammer with still greater ferocity on the wretched remains of one of the world's noblest nations. I became incensed at dinner that first night, finally uttering a tirade against Russia's murderers which, to my astonishment, had my hosts and Major Sinclair on their feet and clapping. Even the negro servants were impressed.

I remained a guest at Klankrest for over a week. Major Sinclair returned to the Delta ('on unfinished business') leaving me to discuss the strategy and logistics of my proposed tour with Mr Clarke, Mrs Mawgan and several prominent Klan officials. Eddy Clarke confided he had opposition within the organisation itself. 'They resent my closeness to Colonel Simmons and believe I'm somehow feathering my own nest. Nothing could be further from reality. There'll always be a few, I suppose, who see another's altruism and believe it to be a reflection of their own greed. We shall have to teach them a lesson soon.'

I asked, by the way, where the great founder was. My ambition, naturally, was to be able to meet him one day.

'He devoted himself body and soul to the Klan, Max. He's no longer a spring chicken. He's worn himself out and will be going for a rest in Florida. When he returns he'll scotch those damn' fool rumours. He knows what we've done for him. Three years ago they were glad of nickels and dimes. Today there's a turnover in millions.'

Under these circumstances I greatly appreciated the time he allowed me. Mrs Mawgan herself assumed chief responsibility for coaching me, providing structure and detail to my proposed speeches and warning me where to be diplomatic, when I could be as forceful as I pleased. My basic text was taken directly from Griffith (whom I knew by heart) and Mrs Mawgan helped me amplify it. The first tour would begin in Portland, Oregon and encompass some fifty cities in the South and West. Mrs Mawgan thought I should be 'broken in' before I assaulted the North-Eastern citadels of Carthage's greatest power. So busy were we I saw nothing of Atlanta itself and had time only to telephone Mr Cadwallader. Perhaps he had read the Paris newspapers for he seemed distant. He said vaguely he would call me at the house to arrange a luncheon. My social life consisted finally of two large parties held by my hosts to entertain wealthier and more influential sympathisers.

This was how, in a vaulted ballroom to rival Versailles, I met at Klankrest many of America's leading citizens. Under the strictest secrecy came judges, senators, bankers, union bosses, industrialists and financiers, some of them already committed to our cause, others curious to discover what the Klan actually meant to do for them. A few, I suspect, watched the social wind, wondering how profit might be made by association with this new political force. Mr Clarke impressed them as an educated gentleman of the old tradition, while no one could fail to be charmed by Bessy Mawgan. My attendance, I was told, showed how unprejudiced in actuality the Klan was. 'We don't attack individuals. Only those who declare themselves our enemies are our enemies,' Mr Clarke explained to a puffy-featured individual called Samuel Ralston, an Indian politician, I gather (though he did not look it). Klan votes sent him as a Senator to Washington the following year. I wonder how many liberals would have voted Sitting Bull into the House of Representatives! Ralston was not in my view anything more than an opportunist. He was openly rude when I tried to interest him in my methods of raising crops under massive glass roofs in permanently controlled weather conditions. Anyone who genuinely had his people's interests at heart would have known what I meant. However, I had been overheard by a huge, shambling individual, some six foot four inches tall, bulky and wearing one of those loosely fitting dinner suits often favoured by the elephantine (who seem to believe they must wear clothes they can grow into). About thirty-five, with mild, boyish features, he beamed at me a little vaguely and, smoothing back his untidy blond hair, asked if I were an engineer.

'An experimental scientist.' I smiled back up at him. 'My business is inventions.'

He was eager to talk. 'I'm no good here.' He apologized for himself. 'These brawls give me the eagers, I'm afraid.' His huge hand enfolded mine. He was John 'Mucker' Hever, he said, living mainly on the West Coast these days. He specialised in oil technology but as we talked it quickly emerged his enthusiasm was for the cinema. 'I love everything about the movies, don't you?' For over an hour we discussed the charms of Mary Pickford and Lillian Gish, our mutual liking for Griffith's films, our fury at the people who had plotted the failure of *Intolerance*. I found his company far more enjoyable than that of the mainly pompous, self-important individuals attracted to Klankrest by 'the powerful smell of cabbage', as Mrs Mawgan put it. Hever knew nothing at all of politics, he said. His interest in the Klan seemed simply romantic and he had contributed, I suspect, in order to obtain the robes and pretend he was 'the little Colonel' of the movie. Unusually for an American he was familiar with many European directors, including Grune and Murnau. In fact his taste was rather broader than my own. At last Mrs Mawgan drew me away from 'Mucker' Hever to introduce me to Judge O'Grady of somewhere called Tarheel (possibly Tower Hill) which to this day I am unable to find on any map. It seems to me now that he was an imposter, one of many agents, private and Federal, then making it their business to spy on the Klan. Evidently he had succeeded in ingratiating himself with Eddy Clarke, for they were on very friendly terms. If Eddy Clarke had a weakness it was a tendency to trust too many people. Of a naturally agreeable disposition, he was perhaps a little over-confident, unable to accept with real conviction the meanness and cunning of some who surrounded him.

The final part of my evening was perhaps the most interesting, spent with an important newspaperman, originally born in Sacramento but presently on a North Carolina paper, who had written a book conclusively proving Abraham Lincoln was shot on the direct orders of the Pope. Thanks to Griffith I had seen John Wilkes Boothe kill the President then make his wild leap from the Ford's Theater box to the stage, hobbling to freedom on a broken leg. 'Sic semper tyrannis!' he had cried in expert Latin. That alone was proof of the enormous power over human minds wielded by Rome. The journalist spoke of the Secret Treaty of Verona, the determination of the Black Pope, General of the Jesuit Order, and the White Pope of the Vatican, to crush democracy. Five presidents assassinated, he said, and all on the orders of the two popes. The Papacy was heavily indebted to the Rothschilds. Roman Catholics were infiltrating Japan, steadily gaining power with the intention of turning a yellow tide against the United States. Already Californians were feeling the effects of a Japanese invasion. These secretive and baleful little people multiplied rapidly. They were the advance guard of the Jesuits' Oriental armada. 'The tools sometimes change,' he told me, 'but the tactics never do. Will we have our Sir Francis Drake ready when our turn comes?' His arguments, backed by his evident erudition, made sense of apparently inexplicable events, especially the large number of US presidents who met violent deaths. Many involved in the Lincoln plot were never brought to book. The instigators of course remained in Rome, continuing to send everything needed for further disruption, including guns and ammunition-belts inscribed with the Papal Arms, personal gifts to the so-called Knights of Columbus, the Knights of the Golden Cross. I was to find these facts of great use on my tour.

At dawn, March 15th 1922, Mrs Mawgan and myself took a closed car to the suburb of Smyrna, quietly boarding a royal blue Pullman and thus avoiding unwelcome publicity or revealing my connection with Klankrest. We were on our way to Portland, via Kansas City, Denver and Salt

Lake City, almost 2,700 miles from East to West and by far the longest single journey I had ever undertaken. I was excited, thoughtful, and grateful for the luxury, thoroughly enjoying the Escape of Railway Travel in the amusing company of Mrs Mawgan. With the build and general appearance of the Baroness von Ruckstühl she combined something of the disposition of Mrs Cornelius. Mrs Mawgan taught me her native Music Hall songs, also, but could not render them in the lively fashion of my Cockney thrush. In the Club Car we joined other passengers to sing *Meet Me In St Louis, Louis, Shine On Harvest Moon, Sweet Adeline* and *Hello, Central, Give Me Heaven*. I still greatly miss the comfort and good fellowship of those old American Club Cars where strangers met and chatted or entertained one another, just as in Imperial Russia, while the huge articulated 2–6–6–2 locomotives dragged us over deserts, prairies, mountains and swamps, through endless forests and down deep tunnels, steady, relentless and confident. They are all gone now. The grey forces have nationalised American passenger trains, I hear. Just as in England, they have become dirty, without character, unromantic and unreliable. They do not even have a Pullman for private rent any longer. Thousands of Indians and pioneers died, millions of labourers sweated, and scores of financiers risked their all to ensure the progress of the great Iron Horse. Now their sacrifice is meaningless. I often wonder if matters might have been different had Russia succeeded in her hopes of colonising America. San Francisco would still be St Petersburg. Instead St Petersburg is a miserable town in Florida where Jewish matrons eat blintzes and herring and sweat poison into the humid air. Why did they drain one swamp merely to create another? I still dream of America as the New Byzantium, Slavic bastion of our Orthodoxy. If Slavs had made a nation only in the West and North, with their own Tsar and their old Law, neither Hitler nor Hirohito would have dared go to war.

Mrs Mawgan was glad to be away from the 'in-fighting' as she called it. She had been working for Mr Clarke and his partners in a Georgia advertising company when Colonel Simmons had asked them to help him save the ailing Klan. Now it was gaining momentum she felt she could gladly give it up and return to a more sedate life. 'The trouble is, Eddy's grown so hopped on it. It's more than food and drink to him.' She sat in the Club Car, her legs crossed under a ravishing dark green frock. I understood her womanly desire to be free of the burden of politics but sympathised with Mr Clarke. Women rarely understand matters of principle. To Mrs Mawgan her task had been to build finances and membership. 'Now it's getting too dangerous. I'm sometimes afraid a few of them hate me so bad they'd cheerfully kill me.' She laughed at her own fancies. I said she was plainly exhausted. I hoped this trip would be something of a vacation. She agreed, but as we neared Oregon gradually became more businesslike. 'First we make you an official Kilgrapp in the Royal Riders of the Red Robe. That's an affiliate group of foreign-born One Hundred Percent Americans. It's the main reason we're going to Portland initially. They have the most influential chapter. You'll speak there, but Seattle will be your real début.' Her warmth and her perfume as we sat close together in the padded velvet of the corner made me swell with lust. I think she noticed this, but did not seem offended. It would be after Seattle, however, that we became lovers.

These were to be happy months for me. In Portland the ceremony of induction was so moving I could scarcely hold back my tears. I swore to support all things Truly American and Defend the Honour of the United States above all other considerations. The public meeting, as Mrs Mawgan had predicted, was a limited success. Two days later in Seattle, however, I had a massive audience for my oration. I was taken back to that wonderful moment in St Petersburg when the entire college applauded my diploma discourse on the ontological approach to Science. I began with a quote from *Birth of a Nation*: 'The former enemies of North and South are united together in common defence of their Aryan birthright.' I spoke of the envy other races felt for the White Protestant, of our duty to counter the enduring threat in all its guises. I closed with another quotation from the Griffith masterpiece, where Lynch the power-mad mulatto proposes marriage to Lillian Gish. It must stand as an example to us all: 'My people fill the streets. With them I shall build a Black Empire and you as Queen shall sit by my side!' Lynch's ambitions are the ambitions of those jealous of what we have won for ourselves, I said. I reminded them of the flag bearing 'the red stain of life of a Southern woman, a priceless sacrifice on the altar of civilisation', how 'the little Colonel' had raised the 'ancient symbol of an unconquered race of men, the fiery cross of old Scotland's hills' and quenched 'its flames in the sweetest blood that ever stained the sands of Time!' That flag had born a slogan, I said. A slogan we might do worse than make our own today. 'Conquer We Must For Our Cause Is Just! Victory or Death! Victory or Death!'

The audience was still cheering and stamping its feet when I left the hall on time to catch the night express to Chicago. It was later, as the great engine pounded through the North Western darkness, that Mrs Mawgan stretched her large, greedy body on mine, dragging back the blankets from my bunk. With unhesitating lechery she positioned herself upon my stiffening penis and fucked me, her gusto proving her as lustful as she was intelligent. When halfway through the night I began to flag, she produced a small box of what she called 'wings'. It was pure cocaine. She was to become my best source, a free supply. In return for this she received the use of my willing body. The tour progressed. I grew to know her well. It even occurred to me she had been 'kingmaker' of the Klan. With Eddy Clarke experiencing difficulties, trying to control rival factions, she might be preparing me to be the next. But I would not have betrayed my friend. I would betray Bessy first, if I was forced to. My honour would allow me no other action. Having given up most Klan duties, she was devoting the greater part of her time to me, occasionally disappearing on mysterious visits when we had a day or two to spare (I think she had a child somewhere). Otherwise she was concerned in what was essentially her own pleasure. Sometimes she would contact a woman friend in a certain city and all three of us would frolic until the hotel's sheets were soaked with our juices. Everywhere we went I was greeted with enthusiasm. I always made it clear I spoke from conscience, that I was paid via an agency called the South Eastern Speakers' Association and had no connection with any political group. I was first and foremost a scientist. I gave press interviews, even made a few radio speeches, something of a novelty then, and Klan recruitment improved wherever I went. I was 'doing my bit' for the cause of freedom. And naturally there were those who would have stopped me if they could.

At first I was frightened by the threatening letters in which mad people offered to kill or maim me in a hundred ways, but Mrs Mawgan laughed at them. This was, she said, 'par for the course,' a sure sign I was 'putting it across'. When a gun was fired from the back of a hall in Baltimore, the bullet chipping moulding in one of the stage's pillars, covering my suit with plaster, she assured me it was for the publicity. The gun had been fired by a Klansman, to make sure the newspapers had a good story and thus reported my speech. I was hugely relieved. We laughed about the incident a great deal. When a similar shooting took place in Wichita, Kansas, I was able to brush it off easily, with a smile and a joke, and thus impress my audience with my cool nerve, even though the plan went slightly askew and the local woman who was introducing me received a minor shoulder wound.

This unfortunate event, however, in comparison to the other fly in our otherwise idyllic ointment, was nothing. As well as malevolent fanatics, Bolsheviks and foreign born agitators who tried to disrupt certain meetings and were handled firmly by Mrs Mawgan's people, I had to contend with Brodmann. I saw him the first time at Union Station in Chicago while I was changing trains, bound for Cincinnati. His hands in the pockets of a leather coat, his broad-brimmed hat hiding his eyes, he stood in the shadows of a stone archway, next to a tobacco kiosk. He stared at me but made no attempt to follow. I suppose it had been easy enough for him to pick up my trail from Paris. The Chekist seemed to be playing his own game. I was never to determine the exact rules. Perhaps he hoped to unnerve me. I did in fact become edgy, wondering how many agents he might have on the train. Happily Bessy Mawgan was always conscious of security and only staff entered our compartment. The second time I saw Brodmann was as we waited at a St Louis intersection. Suddenly his hatless, malevolent face was glaring from the window of a passing trolley car. Thereafter he kept himself better hidden or possibly lost the pursuit. Nonetheless I continued to feel I was being spied upon. At last I accepted the fact without letting it affect me too badly. My mission was more important than Brodmann's ridiculous personal vendetta. We warned them and many heeded, but America as a whole had fallen asleep. By refusing to admit her interdependence with Europe she became euphoric. She ignored her role in international affairs; abstractions proliferated. The result was a disaster. America had taken me to herself, I shall not deny. She was generous in those days before the Zionist coup of '29. I did everything I could for her.

I spoke in towns called Athens, Cairo, Rome and Sparta. I spoke in St Petersburg, Sevastopol and Odessa while behind me came efficient Klan recruiters, signing new members wherever I passed. I still wrote regular letters and postcards to Esmé and Kolya, but only Mrs Cornelius responded to my notes. She was in a successful theatre troupe. What they called 'concert parties,' she said. She worked chiefly in the chorus, with the occasional chance to do little solos. The manager was a dear. He thought they should try America where English shows were catching on. There wasn't much chance of that, but you never knew.

She might yet be looking me up wherever I was. I wrote to say how pleased I was for her and asked if she would do what she could to trace Kolya and Esmé. I said my own 'stage career' was going well. In those months of 1922 it was easy to believe Chaos had been successfully contained. Everywhere the Klan flourished. Washington listened to us. President Harding extended the immigration restriction act. In Italy Mussolini gained prominence, standing firm against the Pope. But I suppose the signs were there to be read if I had wished to see them. Socialist Germany hobnobbed with Bolshevik Russia and Turks defeated Greeks at Smyrna, allowing Mustafa Kemal to declare himself 'President.' Rome seemed to have the upper hand in the Irish Civil War. Harding, weak from poison, tried to make railroad strikes illegal and was ignored. Carthage came seeping in, for the dam had rotten foundations. Mrs Mawgan told me miners had beaten, shot and hanged twenty-nine strikebreakers in Illinois. This at least provided fuel for my oratory proving my prophecies. Still the Klan gathered strength, ever ready, with all its courage, to stem the flood. Klan-endorsed candidates won in the Texas primaries. Thousands of hooded members pledged allegiance at mass klonvocations, under fiery crosses a hundred feet high! Labour racketeers controlled Chicago. The Klan worked tirelessly, night and day, to destroy them. It struck decisively at bootleggers and vice-tsars. All evidence showed the battle was to be ours. In Major Sinclair's airship I flew from Houston to Charleston, incognito because it was still thought unwise publicly to identify myself with the Klan. I flew in a variety of other machines, but never stopped planning for the day when my own gigantic passenger aircraft would mount the skies. Daily it seemed my opportunity drew nearer. Newspapers reported me nationwide. British Prof Predicts Great American Tomorrow, they would say, or Air Ace Warns Bolsheviks Imperil USA. With this recognition I had every reason to be optimistic. Soon I should have unlimited resources at my disposal. This great political power I would use for the common good. In New Mexico I became the target for an anarchist's bullet as I rode to an outdoor meeting. The shot went hopelessly wide, killing some youth. In Texas came the privilege of a nightride with the Klan to a secret valley. Here, beneath a flaming cross, more than two thousand Klansmen applauded me. Wearing my splendid red robes, I was introduced as 'our first and finest ambassador at large.' Then came the trial of two men. The white was accused of adultery. His sentence: KKK branded on his back, according to Klan Law. A negro who had insulted a white woman was whipped to death at the feet of the lady he had offended. (These were not the actions of cruel, mindless men. It was a display of the Klan's remorseless justice. The papers, of course, blew the incidents out of proportion. I experienced far worse in Russia. Yet the reporters who defended Trotski were the same who accused the Klan. I need say no more.)

I was glad to keep active. I was troubled at receiving no news from Esmé. A busy man does not brood. I despise this fashion for self-analysis. It goes hand in hand with narcissism. If one keeps one's mind busy it becomes impossible to harbour a grudge or hold on to pain for long. Real pain, a friend once said, never lasts more than five minutes. The rest is picked scabs. In useless speculation lies hysteria and mental illness. Ideas are useless unless they can be acted upon. But I do not ignore reality. The incident of Mr Roffy is a case in point. In Warsaw, Indiana, where I had already lectured once, I had been asked to speak again. The State was 'solid Klan' and must soon elect a governor. As usual, Mrs Mawgan and I were wined and dined handsomely by local members and we returned late to Paxton's Hotel to our own more private and lustier celebration. I was awakened next morning by a porter. Closing the door on the bedroom and the still sleeping Mrs Mawgan, I asked what he wanted. 'The gentleman says, sir, that it's mighty urgent. He's downstairs now.' He handed me a note.

Clarence Roffy had written it. He had news of immediate interest to me. Assuming this to be Charlie's brother I was only too pleased to ask him up, thinking he might have news of Roffy's wish to revive our aerodrome scheme. I told the porter to give us half an hour, then have breakfast served when the gentleman arrived. Mrs Mawgan was ill-tempered, blinking as she sat up. I explained what was happening and sent her back to her own room, suggesting she reappear at breakfast and meet Roffy's brother.

I was groomed and ready by the time Clarence Roffy knocked. When he entered my first response was to utter a good-humoured laugh. I thought myself the victim of a mild joke. It was Charlie Roffy, of course, looking rather down at heel, carrying a soft felt hat and wearing a pin-stripe suit which had seen better days. His florid features were swollen, his skin lacked its old glow of health. He took the seat I offered him and said he would be glad of a bite of breakfast. I shook him warmly by the hand, anxious to show I bore him no ill will. His hand was limp, clammy. The poor devil was ill. 'Why are you calling yourself Clarence?' I asked. 'It's not much of an alias!'

He frowned. 'I meant Charlie,' he said.

'I'm so glad to see you. I feel badly about letting you down. If you hadn't left Memphis so quickly everything would have been all right. I suppose Boss Crump's murderous thugs were too much of a threat, eh? Was it borrowing got you into the scrape? How's Mr Gilpin? And Jimmy Rembrandt? Have you heard anything of Major Mortimer?'

He had lost touch with them. His tone was strained. Nothing I could say put him at his ease. Eventually he pulled from his pocket some hand-copied papers bearing translations from the French journals which had attacked me. He also showed me my dog-eared note of hand for $150,000. 'You've seen all this stuff before, I know. I have the originals.'

'Jimmy told me that. Have you come to warn me? Am I in some kind of danger?'

His eyes widened at this. His manner grew more hysterical. 'Mr Pyatnitski, it would ruin you if the public learned you're a Russian Jew whose only familiarity with science was a highly scientific gum-game in Paris a year ago.'

'If they believed such a thing, I agree. Captain Rembrandt expressed the same fears in Memphis. It's not true, of course, so I'm not greatly worried.' I placed a sympathetic hand on his shoulder. 'What are you trying to tell me? Have my political enemies found the stories?'

Roffy cleared his throat, scarcely able to speak. He nodded emphatically. 'There's some danger of that happening, sir.' He drew a breath, squared his shoulders and looked curiously into my face. 'Because of you, sir, I'm destitute and on the fly. I can't go back to Washington where I've worked for years. Now everyone knows I'm a paper layer. You owe me something, my friend. So I'm prepared to sell you all this stuff and call it quits. What do you say?'

I was horrified a gentleman of his stock could fall so low. I spoke with compassion. 'You don't need to sell me anything, Mr Roffy. I have always respected your reputation. You have only to ask for help. I was, as you say, in part responsible. How much do you need?'

'Ten grand.' He shrugged and looked towards the window. I smiled sadly.

'You still have an exaggerated notion of my wealth. Mr Roffy, for old time's sake, I can let you have a single grand.'

He was considering this when Mrs Mawgan, fresh and blooming in red velvet, walked in. She frowned as I made the introductions. Evidently my visitor's shabby appearance offended her. She asked him sharply if she had met him somewhere before. I explained Roffy was an old business colleague in need of help.

He rose nervously, speaking swiftly and softly to me. 'Okay,' he said. 'I'll settle for the thousand.'

'You're hungry. You should stay for breakfast.' But I was embarrassing him. I wrote out the cheque. He handed me the envelope.

'You're a blackmailer, then, Mr Roffy?' Mrs Mawgan was her most devastatingly sweet. I recognized her humour, but she angered Roffy.

'That's none of your damned business.' He picked up his hat and pushed past the waiter entering with our breakfast trolley.

Mrs Mawgan frowned. 'You'd better put me in the picture.' We sat down to eat. 'And don't be afraid to spill it all. You know I won't tip you up. The Klan already has the goods on you, more than you know.'

So I retailed the whole sorry story from beginning to end, explaining how I could not condemn Roffy. The least I could do was let him have a little money. Mrs Mawgan sat over untasted bacon shaking her head and sighing. Then she got up quickly, put down her napkin and said she was going down to the lobby. She had to make a phone call. I would be okay. When the Klan said it looked after its friends, it meant just that. She was back within ten minutes. With an expression of satisfaction she bent to pat my face. 'Scandal around you is bad for everybody. I already know what it's like to suffer from the press. Cancel that cheque as soon as you like.'

'The Klan is paying Mr Roffy?'

Her smile confirmed my guess. This was generosity indeed!

That evening, as I stepped upon the stage to give a packed house Bolsheviks, Bloodshed and the Coming Battle for America, I was never more confident in the security of my future. With my debt to Mr Roffy cleared, I also forgot that pernicious *doppelgänger*. Brodmann had longed for my soul ever since he witnessed my humiliation at the hands of Grishenko.

In the American wilderness I experienced too many memories. Her plains took me back to the steppe; her great forests to the forests of the Russian heartland. In the Rockies and the Blue Ridge Mountains I could frequently be free of Brodmann, Yermeloff and Esmé. Those massive peaks brought me unexpected tranquillity whenever our crossing and recrossing of the country took us into them. In the big modern, most typically American, cities I was released from memory, from the agony of my last months in Russia. They had raped you. They stole your soul and your heart. Your very identity was taken from you. In Akron, Pittsburgh, Cleveland and Kansas City the grids could swallow me; they offered anonymity. In New Orleans and San Francisco too much was familiar; there certain warrens, configurations of wrought-iron, arrangements of brick and plaster brought my mother with them. Only a fool submits to pain. Pain has no justification, brings no benefits, whatever the Catholic tells you. For a while I found Chicago the most beautiful city in America, her massive, elegant towers glittering monuments to human skill and optimism. America in 1922 sought restlessly for new paths to the future. If her enthusiasm was sometimes excessive it remained a healthy contrast to Europe's drained cynicism, Russia's grim decline, the Orient's chaotic decadence. Emerging from small-town complacency the American citizen was realising his power. Perhaps naturally he balked in those days at his international responsibilities. I was reminded of the Falstaff story in which Henry resists his divine role, rallying only at the last possible moment to defeat the weight of French chivalry as it gallops down upon his 'happy few.' Of course he did not have the Jews to contend with.

Short skirts, wine, certain drugs and most things offensive to the majority of my audiences were not to me obvious signs of degeneration or imminent social revolt. Those who spent their lives pursuing prostitutes, bootleggers and gamblers might have served their country better by attacking the 'big wheels' exploiting and controlling their ordinary daily needs, their food, clothing, housing and transportation. By making pleasures into crimes puritans place power directly into criminal hands. The puritan cries 'It should not exist, therefore it does not exist!' They allow the vice-king to say 'It does exist therefore someone might as well make a profit.' Moderation is not achieved by Law, but my example. If supply becomes unreliable a commodity gains higher value in the marketplace. This was once true of travel, of trains, ships, aircraft, even cars. It was in Detroit, at a party given by Major Sinclair for people in the aviation business, that I met, as it happened, young Lindbergh and fired him with the notion of flying the Atlantic single-handed. A plane should be almost all fuel tank, I told him, using every possible area, even the wings. But he was still obsessed with the South American routes. He never joined the Klan, though in later years he

461

took my rôle, using his aeronautical reputation to back the fight against alienism. Many engineers, scientists, soldiers and aviators share an understanding of the world. We can break down social complexities, describing them with a clarity denied philosophers and artists. Thus we are able to solve the problems. The running of America should have been left to Henry Ford and Colonel Lindbergh. We might be looking at a very different country today.

All that year the power of the Klan grew. My tours became increasingly elaborate and well publicised. Entering town in an open car I might be accompanied by a marching band, my head and shoulders covered in streamers and confetti. Preachers gave sermons, choirs would sing before I spoke. Local politicians were photographed with me. I lent my name to advertisements and newspaper columns. While I never let them or myself forget I was primarily a scientist – it did no harm to promote my real interests in this way. I had learned to value the American art of the 'bally-hoo'. Thus, ironically, despite the temporary dashing of my technological hopes, I became a celebratory. It is hard to say exactly how much I influenced the social and scientific thinking of my own and future generations. Ideas which I threw off quite casually were later claimed by others: the nuclear power plant, the television and the rocket ship. Important magazines such as *Popular Mechanics*, *Radio World* and *Air Aces* seized on my prophecies while the imitators of Verne and Wells translated them into fiction. Sometimes whole books of factual speculation appeared between 1925 and 1940 which were borrowed from me in their entirety! I did not care, then, how my visions were disseminated. I had a profusion of them and readily shared them with the whole human race. Even today I do not regret my generosity, but I feel a little wounded when I receive no recognition. I should have been glad of a small place in history. Perhaps it was a mistake to come to England. She always looked with suspicion upon the new and strange. Lately, to her own wretched tomb, with complacency and self-congratulation as always, her Union Jack the standard of broken promises, rejected ideals, she conducts herself, as if she has something to be proud of. The tourists come from May to September, staring at the beefeaters, the old stones, the royal carriages, utterly deceived by the British illusion. But in Notting Hill and Brixton, in Mill Wall and Tottenham, the houses collapse inwards, the jerry-built towers lean and tremble in the lightest wind, the pavements crack, the alleys fill with sinister shadows: for this desolation is what

462

maintains the imperial façade. We are the victims of a wicked lie. The English have lost their pride, forgotten their honour, refused self-knowledge. In a rich nation, these would not necessarily be vices; in a poor one, they are a ludicrous disaster.

Mrs Cornelius seems to think it has always been the same. I tell her it only looks that way. England is a painted corpse; the flesh rots beneath a shell of delusion. 'Live an' let live, Ivan,' she says. But what was once decent tolerance now becomes moral turpitude. I could have saved them. When my flying cities were stolen, they cut off my means of escape. Is there any reason I should not hate them? *Jene Leute sind verarmt.*

At last I visited Los Angeles. Mrs Mawgan's friends took us on a tour of the movie studios. I shook hands with Douglas Fairbanks and was kissed on the cheek by Clara Bow! Fairbanks stood for all the American virtues, though his original name was Ullman. I have his signed photograph, dressed for *Robin Hood.* I stayed only overnight in Hollywood, for I was lecturing in Anaheim, but I was impressed. There was much in the way of civilised beauty; an ideal combination of wealth, taste, security and good weather. I spoke to several people on the technical side about my proposed innovations in filming. They said I was ahead of my time. (When I arrived in England I mentioned I had been instrumental in developing talking pictures. I offered my services to Korda, but as usual came up against the old familiar wall.) I longed to return to Los Angeles and asked Mrs Mawgan to arrange another engagement as soon as possible. She said she would do what she could, but they were not exactly desperate for entertainment.

We decided not to visit Klankrest for Christmas, since Mrs Mawgan no longer cared to see Mr Clarke. Clarke was obsessed with the ambitions of what he was calling the 'Evans gang.' This group wanted Colonel Simmons to discharge him and nominate a Texas dentist in his place. If I could have helped my friend, I would have done so gladly. Mrs Mawgan said my presence would only complicate an already difficult situation. The best we could accomplish was to stay clear of internal politics and continue to do what we could in the world at large. This made sense to me, so we broke tour in Michigan to stay at a wonderful country hotel which had been privately rented for the Season by a senator friend of Mrs Mawgan's. He called himself 'Uncle Roscoe.' I never learned his real name, though I believe he was from Illinois. The hotel was like a fantasy of Switzerland, surrounded with snow-laden

463

pines, protected by hills. This was a true American Christmas; everything a Christmas should be. In the middle of the dance floor a huge tree was hung with tinsel and coloured cellophane, with brightly wrapped gifts and glass baubles. Our senator, disguised as Santa Claus, personally distributed presents to his guests. I ate far too much turkey, mince pie and other gorgeously rich traditional foods. Dressed as angels, the little local children sang carols: O, *Little Town of Bethlehem* and *Silent Night*. All I missed was my Esmé. Mrs Mawgan sang *The White Sheet of Winter Lies Cold Upon the Land* while I offered a rendering of *Any Old Iron*. A group of young flappers, hired by the senator to bring extra femininity to what was primarily a male party, added their own particular talents to the festivities. Mrs Mawgan and I left with a girl called Janey. But of course sexual pleasure is one thing, and sentiment is quite another.

Two more talks, in Sioux City, Iowa and Springfield, Indiana, and then we took the train for Wilmington, Delaware. This delightful town, founded in the seventeenth century, was associated with some of America's greatest modern painters, such as Howard Pyle, then at the height of his realistic power. We were the guests of Mr and Mrs Van der Kleer, the mine owners, to celebrate New Year's Eve and incidentally my birthday (which I insisted be on January 1st) in typical American good-hearted ceremonial style. The next day, however, was an anti-climax. Indeed, it proved embarrassing for all concerned and revived many of the fears I had been able to forget.

I had just finished lunch in the beautiful glass domed conservatory (through which winter sunshine poured) when Mr Van der Kleer's butler announced someone to see the master. Apologising, our host left. Within five minutes, the butler returned to ask me to join Mr Van der Kleer and his visitor in the library. I entered the peaceful room and closed the double doors behind me. The stranger wore an expensive tweed top coat over an ordinary grey suit. He was short, with that paleness common only to policemen, and his head was almost completely bald. His glasses slightly magnified already large blue eyes. He looked like a Chekist but he showed me a badge declaring him to be an agent of the Federal Justice Department. Mr Van der Kleer said he would rejoin his wife and Mrs Mawgan. I must be sure to summon his help if I required it.

The Federal man was called Harris. His questions were so oblique I could scarcely follow him. It had something to do with my 'ex-partner' who had been mixed up on the fringes, Harris claimed, of a North Dakota land swindle. My answers were, it appeared, satisfactory, for Harris soon relaxed. 'One of them's dead now. Could have been suicide. They all dropped him like a hot potato when the Memphis sting collapsed. Have you any connection with the Ku Klux Klan, Mr Peterson?'

I think the question was supposed to trick an answer from me. Instead I wanted to know who was dead. 'You didn't tell me his name, Mr Harris.'

'How about Roffy?' he said.

'Of course I knew him. Has the poor fellow killed himself? Surely he wasn't mixed up in anything illegal?'

Harris answered off-handedly. 'You should wish, Mr Peterson. Anyhow, I'm satisfied with your story. I think you were goofed, too.' He shook my hand, but his parting words upset me. 'We'll talk about the Klan another time, maybe.'

This encounter left me uneasy. I felt Brodmann's presence again. The Federals could deport me if they wished. My visa had been extended 'indefinitely' but it might be revoked at any time. As soon as I returned to the rest of the party, telling them I had satisfactorily settled a minor immigration problem, I signalled to Mrs Mawgan. I wished to speak to her alone. An hour later we strolled in the grounds, our boots breaking a crust of snow. Harris's final words, she reassured me, were simply meant to faze. He wanted to see how I would react and was perhaps curious to see what I would do next. 'We carry on the same as always. Your money's going into the lecture agency and from there to our banks. The agency pays the expenses from its profits. It's all on the level. They can't throw you out for warning America about her enemies! And you have your own accounts, so you're okay there, too. Relax, Max.' She kissed my frozen cheek. 'Most people keep away from shit. Feds like to sniff until they find some. But you're clean. You're sitting tighter than a nun's ass in a monastery.' I allowed her to calm me. I could not, however, completely free myself of a suspicion that someone was waiting for me to make a mistake. Perhaps, when I was no longer under the Klan's protection, they would strike. Other than Brodmann, I had no obvious enemies but of course had spoken boldly against malevolent forces threatening the nation. Any one of a score of interests, any combination of them, might have embarked upon a vendetta. I could be attacked without ever discovering who my antagonist was or what he represented.

The following weeks proved if anything more successful than before. As a tribute to my powers of oratory, Mrs Mawgan told me, several halls had actually cancelled bookings, doubtless under pressure from what we privately called the AMOCK: African, Mediterranean, Oriental and Catholic Klonspiracy. Mrs Mawgan was undeterred. After this tour, due to end in early spring, I should consider a rest, she said. There was plenty of cabbage in the pie dish. Against her advice I already had all my money in bank accounts and refused even the most tempting investments. I realized I was still naïve in financial matters. If ever I became involved in another company it would be after considerable coaching from experts. I still intended to return to France to clear my name and if necessary discover the whereabouts of Kolya and Esmé. I now worried that they had become victims of the Cheka, that they were imprisoned, kidnapped back to Russia or possibly already dead. Once my chief mission was satisfactorily accomplished I hoped to visit Italy again. My affection for that country remained as strong as ever. I was following Mussolini's career with excitement and I was eager to see what was happening for myself, since American papers were unreliable reporters of European news.

By the time we reached Kansas City I had begun to recover my usual happy spirits. My popularity was never greater. We took the entire upper floor of a small hotel in a residential street near the river, then went out to dine at an excellent restaurant specialising in local dishes. When we returned by cab, Mrs Mawgan was told she had a telegram at the desk. It was from Eddy Clarke in Atlanta. She read it carefully, since it appeared to be partly in code. Then she squared her shoulders, drawing a deep sigh. 'Is it bad news?' I asked. She tilted her head on one side and winked at me. 'Well, it ain't the greatest, Max.' We went back upstairs to bed. In the morning, before we got up, she admitted Clarke's telegram had disturbed her. Its content was gloomy but worse was the fact he felt any need to send it. If he wanted her back as an ally he was losing his battle against the Evans faction. She feared they might turn their next attack upon her. 'It means he's jittery,' she said. 'Once his spunk goes, it's all over for him.'

I said we must return to Atlanta immediately, but she shook her head. 'Stay out of it now and you stand a chance of helping him later.

As far as Evans and company know you're hired by the organisation, not by Eddy. They might be reluctant to keep you on the payroll, but they won't think you're a real threat.'

'They must know we're travelling together.'

'If we're asked, Eddy was furious when I ran off with you. Get it?'

I understood, but I felt miserable. It was a singularly petty deception, given that Clarke, my benefactor and her ex-lover, was threatened from all sides.

'You should always remember, Max,' she insisted, 'the Klan is whoever has most power at the moment. If it's Evans, then Evans has real muscle. All he has to do is holler "traitor" and you know damn' well what would happen to us. Nobody's going to put me on the spot if I can help it. We've both got too much to lose. Eddy will take his own chances. The very least would be the papers getting the blow up. They'd love to put me on the front page in nothing but my underwear. There's a lot of laundry don't need washing in Dow-Lee's window, Max.'

If she was sure this was the only way to remain free and help Eddy Clarke should he need us, I accepted her arguments. Determinedly, we continued the tour but we were both in a nervous frame of mind. In Denver we had a mixed public reception and the local Klan people seemed awkward around us, but otherwise friendly. We cut short the rest of our Colorado tour, heading instead for the friendlier waters of Idaho and Oregon where I enjoyed my usual enormous audiences. Oregon always has a special place in my heart. No one could say she had any immediate race problem of her own, yet she remained thoroughly alert to all potential danger, boasting one of the highest Klan memberships in the country. From Eugene we were due to go on to Redding, California, but at the last moment heard the booking had been cancelled.

Mrs Mawgan became thoughtful after receiving the news. Later she made two or three telephone calls and sent a couple of wires. Eventually, in our bedroom, she was able to tell me our next engagement. 'It's in Walker, Nevada,' she said. 'The local Kleagle's agreed to cover our expenses and arrange a hall. After that we've still got a couple of big ones in Fresno and Bakersfield.' She was vaguer than usual. I asked what was wrong.

She admitted she was not sure. 'It's an instinct, Max. The smell of fish.'

467

'Are we in danger?'

'I wouldn't pitch it that strong. But we'd better be ready to lie low after Fresno and see which way the wind blows. You can come with me to New York if you like.'

'It would be pleasant to spend some time there. Thank you, Bessy.'

'Don't mention it.' She grinned suddenly and kissed me. But her eyes were alert, like a deer at the waterhole.

Matters became immediately worse next morning as we checked out. I heard Mrs Mawgan at the cash desk shout, 'What the hell do you mean, not certified? I've had my fill of this. Since when have I had to give a hotel a certified check? The room should have been paid for ahead of time. No I don't have the damned cash. Get the manager. Call what's his name, Mr Ainsfield. Here, I'll give you the number. Our checks are always guaranteed locally. It's in the contract.'

I put down my bag and went to where, red with anger, she trembled against the desk. 'What's wrong?'

'The dumb bastards who organised your talk, colonel, have forgotten to pay the hotel or give them a letter of guarantee, that's all.'

Usually the Klan was responsible, under various different names, for all our booking and travel details. This was the first time there had been a problem. I had always been impressed by the courtesy and efficiency of local chapters. Mr Ainsfield was reached at his store. He was the Kleagle responsible for organising my talk. I heard Mrs Mawgan say sweetly, as she continued to glare balefully at the embarrassed woman clerk two feet away, 'Well, perhaps you would come over right away, Mr Ainsfield, and reassure them?' She listened furiously to his reply. 'No, Mr Ainsfield, we have a train to catch. How about right now? Don't you think it would be a shame if we had to come there and found you hiding under a sheet, ha, ha.'

Her threat succeeded and Freddy Ainsfield arrived in a taxi ten minutes later. He apologised to us both and paid the clerk in cash, even tipping the porter who took our luggage to the same taxi. 'We had no instructions,' he said. 'We don't know what's going on, Mrs Mawgan. Everybody's confused. I heard Mr Clarke had his contract cancelled. Mr Evans is supposed to have accused him of immorality. Is that true? Are the Feds gunning for him? Is that a rumour, ma'am?'

'We wouldn't know, Mr Ainsfield,' she said coldly. 'We have no connection with the Klan, though of course we are frequently invited to speak by you fine people. You should get in touch with Atlanta.'

'We've been trying. All lines are busy. Someone said Colonel Simmons was shot by Roman Catholics.'

'It's news to me, Mr Ainsfield.' She ducked into the taxi and I followed, relieved to escape the embarrassment. I said I thought she handled it well. She shook her head. 'That smell of fish is getting stronger, Max.'

We just had time to buy our tickets in the marble foyer. With our porter, a running mound of baggage, ahead of us, we barely made the platform. The train was a regular coach class with no Pullmans, but we were glad to be on our way. We should have to change at Reno. Panting, I leaned out of the window to catch my breath and saw one other passenger who had given himself even less margin than we. He came running through the steam to swing aboard the caboose as we pulled away from Eugene into her featureless suburbs. I sat back down again. Mrs Mawgan was sorting through some letters of invitation. Soon craggy forested hills appeared and rivers rushed through little gorges. Walker was on the edge of the desert. The barren State of Nevada had never previously invited me to speak. I suspected it was because people lived so far apart. A Kloncave must be a rarity, I thought. As she put her papers back into their case I asked Mrs Mawgan what she thought. 'It's just luck, I guess,' she said. 'They needed someone to speak in a couple of days and we were suddenly available. Don't expect a lot from Walker, Max. We'll be lucky to cover expenses on this one. If a hundred people pay fifty cents to see you it will be a miracle.'

Adjusting his dark brown suit, the man who had caught the train via the caboose sat down with a thump in the seat across the aisle from us. His long face looked unsmilingly at me as I passed a friendly word. 'Just made it, eh?' I said. 'I saw your magnificent dash. Bravo!'

He began to fumble at an inner pocket. In a gentle brogue, he asked, 'You'd be the gentleman known as Colonel Peterson?' His badge appeared in his hand. Another 'Fed.' 'That's my name, sir.' I concealed my anxiety.

'This is going to need a damn' good explanation,' said Mrs Mawgan. 'What the hell d'you mean tailing us as if we were crooks? What do you want –' she peered at the badge '– Mr George H. Callahan?'

'Don't get this out of proportion, ma'am.' He was conciliatory. 'I tried to catch you at the hotel. They told me you were taking this train. That's the whole of it. I've been instructed to ask Colonel Peterson some questions. Routine stuff.'

The rest of the car was taking an enormous interest in the proceedings. We might as well have been actors for their free entertainment. 'Let's go back a ways, if you prefer,' said Callahan. We followed him down the length of three cars, arriving at last at the small observation platform which was draughty and noisy but free from other eyes and ears. As the day grew warmer and sun shone on the silver rails behind us, Mr Callahan raised his voice above the clattering to ask if I could say who organised my tours. He made notes of my replies. 'The South Eastern Speakers' Association,' I said.

'And what's that exactly, sir?'

Mrs Mawgan explained the nature of a speech circuit agency.

'And who runs that, sir?'

She again replied. 'I do, officer. It's my business. What's the mystery?'

He noted this, then asked to see my passport and visa. I gave him the documents, explaining Peterson was a professional name, easier on Anglo-Saxon ears. 'I'm not here to embarrass you, sir.' He spoke as if I had offended him. 'There's nothing illegal in changing your name as far as I know. Unless it's in pursuit of a fraud, of course.' He chuckled. He suspected me of nothing. He was, after all, merely making a routine check on a foreigner in the public eye. 'We had an idea the Ku Klux might be staking your tours,' he said. 'Why should we think that, do you know, sir?'

'The Klan frequently hires the halls and issues the tickets to Colonel Peterson's talks.' Mrs Mawgan never believed in telling lies which could be easily checked. 'Our agency merely handles what requests it receives. Obviously, not a few are from different Klan groups.'

'And you've no direct connection with the Ku Klux, ma'am?'

'None.'

'None now?'

'If you like. Jesus Christ, officer, it's no damn' secret me and Eddy Clarke put that show on the road, but I resigned a long time ago. They don't like me, never have.'

'Well enough to use your agency,' he said.

'My agency is completely independent. We take the work which comes in, whether it's from the Boston Ladies' Sewing Circle or the Knights of Columbus.' This, too, was noted. 'But Mr Ainsfield, for instance, is a member of an entirely different organisation.'

'He's a prominent Klansman, ma'am. Weren't you aware of that?'

'We were engaged by the Protestant Defence League, Mr Callahan. I have the contract in my bag. It's on the rack over my seat.'

'I wonder if you could give me an idea of the fees, ma'am.'

'They vary considerably between as little as fifty dollars to as much as five hundred.'

'That's a tidy sum your agency's turning over, ma'am.'

'We're a successful business. We know what we're doing.'

'I'm sure you do, ma'am. We've been checking on those two who tried to swindle you in Memphis, colonel.' He had changed tack suddenly once again. 'One has eluded us completely. The other called himself Roffy. Have you seen him, at all, sir?'

'That's not good enough, Callahan.' Mrs Mawgan was contemptuous now, as if she witnessed a bad pass at football. 'Roffy's dead. One of your own boys told us that nearly three months ago. And yes we've seen nothing of the other one.'

'Roffy was unstable,' I offered. I felt she took too much of a risk by offending him. 'A friend warned me last year he was suicidal, but I couldn't believe it.'

'Sure,' said Mr Callahan, closing his book. 'I thank you for your time, sir. Can I ask where you're bound for?'

'This is the Reno train,' snarled Mrs Mawgan. 'I thought you knew that.'

He smiled quietly.

'Walker,' I said. 'I'm speaking there in a couple of days.'

'Walker,' he repeated slowly. 'I don't know the town. And who is it has invited you this time?'

'The Bolshevik Revolutionary Party.' Mrs Mawgan began to move back down the train. 'The Society for the Assassination of the President. The Vatican City Veterans' League. The damned mick. Catholic bloodhound. Don't help him, Max. He hasn't the right.' I looked from her to Callahan and he shook his head, as if to dismiss me. I began to follow her. Callahan remained on the observation car, calmly writing in his notebook while we returned to our places. From the window we now saw a wide, tranquil lake. 'He's going after the Klan, Max, not you.' Mrs Mawgan was curious and agitated, seeming almost to relish the encounter. 'He's just hoping you're sap enough to blab something useful. We're okay. The IRS can't touch us. We're filing and paying regularly. The books are air tight. Everything's kosher. But all this is a good reason for never seeing Atlanta again.' She smiled to herself. 'We can't admit to a thing, although he knows what's going on. He'd have a hard time proving criminal intent. My hunch is he hopes to flush us somehow. I'm not sure why. We'd better duck our nuts for a while, change our names and live in New York till this blows over.'

I did not care for her solution, but it would have been pointless saying anything then. I think Mr Callahan got off at the next stop, though I suspect other agents were still aboard.

We had to wait an hour on Reno's unremarkable railroad station until the train for Walker came shunting in at twilight. Aside from a group of Indians on their way back to the reservation, we were the only ones to board. It was night by the time the train moved out. Our car was hideously new, vivid yellow and black upholstery, like the carcass of a gigantic bee. We moved slowly into a land which grew increasingly featureless. By the time we stepped off at Walker, the station was deserted. It was dark, poorly lit and there was a chill in the air. We found no porter, so dragged our luggage to the exit gate. The ticket collector had gone off duty. The street outside was empty of traffic. A few lights and a couple of small electric signs enlivened the town at the far end. It was not much of a monument to the high-living, hell-raising scout and Indian fighter Jim Walker. I guessed the place had seen better days. I became uneasy. This was not at all what we were used to. Normally we were met by elaborate bands, by the mayor and other prominent citizens, by church groups or women's guilds. Even at this time of night there were usually three or four local Klan officers to welcome us. Tonight, in the cool breeze, I felt puzzled, vaguely threatened. Brodmann could have turned everyone against us. The methods of his kind were often very subtle. The logical explanation was that all Klan chapters were temporarily disrupted because of the power struggle currently going on in Atlanta. But this would not completely ease my mind. In the bleak street outside the station I heard a car engine. Then headlamps glowed as a Ford Model T turned at an intersection and advanced towards us. The Ford drew up at the kerb. 'Colonel Peterson'? A nervous face peered through the gloom.

'I'm Peterson.'

A youth of eighteen or so climbed from his car and introduced himself as Freddy Poulson. 'Sorry I'm late, sir, ma'am. My Dad couldn't make it. A special meeting he wasn't expecting. Some of the Reno boys should have been here, too, but they can't get over till tomorrow, either.'

I relaxed at once. My reasoned guess had been accurate. 'Can you help us with our luggage?' We shook hands. I had only one suitcase, but Mrs Mawgan had several. He was eager to do whatever he could. He had red cheeks, blond hair and the wholesome looks of the better Russian steppe-born peasant. He was not in the least sinister and drove us to a building only a few minutes from the station. Brick, with a fancy false front, it bore the legend *Philadelphia Grand Hotel*. This also appeared to be locked up for the night. There were no lights. Mrs Mawgan was beginning to lose her temper even as, oil lamp in hand, dressing gown wrapped round him, an old man unbolted the doors. We entered an inhospitable lobby and, at his insistence, signed the book before going to our rooms. The place reminded me of a large private house converted to a hostelry. It was clean. The orange carpeting and yellow and white fleur-de-lys wallpaper was recent, yet the place seemed indefinably shabby; not what we had come to expect. But then neither was Walker. Freddy Poulson said he would drop by in the morning.

When I joined her in her room, Mrs Mawgan remained downcast. Her bad mood had not lifted. 'I was stupid,' she said. 'I've let myself get spooked. If Eugene was the frying pan, this dump's one hell of a fire.'

'We can cancel.' I consoled her. 'And leave in the morning.'

She considered this. 'I don't know, Max. Looked at another way Walker's not exactly in the limelight.' She sighed. 'But if that's what I was looking for I could have picked any one-horse town. I can't get over the notion it was us who were picked by Walker, or at least by Reno. See, I don't know Hiram Evans well and I couldn't tell you who owes him, who's in his pocket, what kind of troops he can call out and from where. Also, I don't know how much he has it in for Eddy or how hard he wants to hit Eddy's friends.'

'You can't be expected to know all that, Bessy.'

'It was my job. I guess I thought I could keep taking a percentage without getting my hands dirty. Well, here's the pay-off. Walker, Nevada, at two in the morning. I think they're trying to tell us something, Max.'

'Who,' I said, 'and what?'

'That's what I think.' She drew me down to her warmth and her delicious scents. 'Better make this a good one.' She tugged at my belt.

Next morning we joined Freddy Poulson in the lobby. Hard sunlight pierced the windows, creating dramatic shadows. Outside was the

473

sleepy main street of a small Western town. Its low buildings were so widely spread its texture seemed faded, its detail unclear, like a photograph blown up too large. The whole town might have been improved by reduction. We ate breakfast at the *New California Café*. Everything in Nevada was named after another State, as if nobody was really sure they wanted to be there. From boredom Mrs Mawgan arranged cutlery against the red and white oilcloth squares. A fine dust, possibly sand, covered the white enamel sugar can and cream-pitcher. 'Maybe you could put us in the picture, Mr Poulson. What's the programme for tonight?'

His attitude apologized for the town and everything in it. He knew, as Mrs Mawgan said, we were getting a 'bum deal.' 'I'm a little misty myself. They're putting you on at the Opera House. Eight o'clock, I think.'

'And what sort of publicity do we get, Mr Poulson?' she asked.

'I gather this is just for, you know, the lodge?'

She frowned. 'Have you heard what's coming down from Atlanta, Mr Poulson?'

'Only that Mr Clarke's contract was cancelled. A new man's taken over. Seems a good enough egg from what I hear.' He cleared his throat. 'I'm really not who you should ask.' He got up to pay the bill.

Looking at him dragging his wallet from his back pocket and smiling awkwardly at the woman behind the cash register, Mrs Mawgan said, 'He knows he's out of his league.' Pensively she sipped her coffee, staring through the glass at the placid street. A few horses and cars went by, sharply outlined in the harsh light. I should not have been surprised if a herd of cattle had wandered through. 'My guess is his father's one of the only Klansmen in town. They're banking on Reno for support. In which case why give them the word to set the thing up here?' She became decisive. 'You wait and go back to the hotel with Poulson. Tell him I've a few things to buy.'

'Where will you be?'

'Western Union, maybe. Or Wells Fargo. Whatever I can find.' She intended to send more telegrams.

By noon conversation between myself and Mr Poulson, as we sat in the empty hotel bar drinking Coca Cola and sarsaparilla, had dwindled to nothing. I did my best on the subject of aviation, ship building, engineering in general. All he knew was cattle and mining, and not a great deal about those. When Mrs Mawgan returned she was brisker;

her old, positive self. I felt more confident. She suggested, since we had time to kill, we meet the Press. Mr Poulson actually blushed at this. 'Bill Straker, who was going to cover the story for the *Informant*? Well, he had to go out of town on another assignment.'

We went to the movie. The theatre was the same Opera House at which I was due to speak that night. I was surprised no bills were posted, then remembered it was supposed to be a 'members-only' affair. The Opera House was an ornate mixture of brick and carved wood outside and neo-Roman plaster inside. All the mouldings had once been gilded. Now the gilt was peeling. We watched an episode of *The Purple Mask*, a newsreel, a short Fairbanks comedy, a ludicrous sex melodrama with Gloria Swanson called *Male and Female* and two Bronco Billy adventures which seemed virtually identical. I think the whole town had come to the performance; the air was virtually unbreathable. For all that, the show was better value than anything you get today. The triple features at the *Essoldo* across the road from my shop are trash. Monsters have taken over from people.

It was growing dark as we returned to the *Philadelphia Grand*. Mrs Mawgan had seemed girlish and romantic after the picture show, but became practical again once I dressed myself in my usual tuxedo. She took an intense interest in my appearance, combing my hair for me, adjusting my tie. 'The worse the crowd the better you should look,' she said. We returned downstairs to meet a nervous Mr Poulson who took us to a restaurant two blocks down the street. It was called *The Lucky Indian*. We ate hamburgers. 'Evidently the Indian ran out of luck,' said Mrs Mawgan, leaving hers unfinished. 'Listen,' she said, 'I know how to get there. You boys run along. I have something to do . . .' And she glanced towards the washroom door. This brought another blush from Poulson. She reached her hand under the table. In it was a little paper packet. I took the cocaine from her, though I had no opportunity to use it. I guessed she had a plan, perhaps something to do with the telegrams she had sent, so I assured Poulson she would be all right and we drove to the Opera House. No lights burned in the front at all. Possibly this was to be a secret meeting of the kind I had attended on the steamboat. I hoped I would learn the fate of Eddy Clarke, at very least. The stage door lamp was on in the alley as we went inside. It was gloomy and silent and smelled of rats. 'They said to go straight onto the stage.' Poulson was sweating. I remember feeling sorry for him.

There were dazzling footlights smoking on the stage itself and dim

475

electrics in the auditorium. The silvered expanse of the movie screen was still in place and my shadow spread across it, just as if I were in a German expressionist film. I was experiencing a rare attack of stage fright. My stomach was audibly gurgling and churning. When the footlights were suddenly switched off I peered, baffled, at the ranks of empty seats before me. In the middle aisle, where the stalls divided front and back, I eventually made out a dozen silent Klansmen, in hoods and gowns. With folded arms, their attitude was threatening and baleful. I was reminded of *Birth of a Nation* when the negro renegade Gus is sentenced to death. 'I'm so glad to see you,' I said. 'I was beginning to feel I was on my own!'

'We're all set now, jew-boy.' The voice had a deep, almost Russian *timbre*. 'Go ahead. Let's hear you whistle *Dixie*.'

It was only then I realised that these were not, of course, true Klansmen at all!

Nineteen

THEY TOOK ME TO the desert. Buzzards roosted in the *Totenburgen* and red dust clogged my throat, making my arguments unattractive. Brodmann was one of them, I know. I recognised his jubilant eyes as their whips shredded my expensive evening clothes. I could scarcely believe she had left me to them. Had she known? 'Your fancy woman had the right idea. You should have gone with her.' They would teach me a lesson, said the deep-voiced leader, and I had better remember it good. I was sick. They drove me to the wasteland among buttes like ruined citadels and I vomited on the sand. 'Get his pants down. Let's check him out.' Certainly that was the only evidence anyone required. My father should pay for every blow, every welt and bruise. The moon and stars were enormous and possessed a rare brightness. I was alone on a rock in the void while those spurious hoods waved over me and the white arms rose and fell. She was the Judas, not I. Women have no conscience. They will always betray you. I had been left to placate them while she escaped on the Northbound train. I held up my hand. I wanted to tell them the truth. The whip struck my knuckles. I watched the blood push its way through the dark swellings. It was all I could see, that *blut*. I know their infernal Inquisition. I understand their pacts. Even they are not always conscious of their interdependence. Had the Klan in its entirety been infiltrated by them? Was Evans the Pope's own candidate? From then on, from 1923, the Klan's power declined. It must have been a plot. The propaganda against Clarke became hideous. *Nito tsu remen tsu reydn! Yidden samen a Folk vos serstert. A narrisch Folk. Sie hat nicht geantwortet. Ich habe das Buch gelesen und jene Leute sind verarmt. Wer Jude ist, bestimme Ich!*

477

Wer Jude ist, bestimme Ich! Zol dos zayn factish. Fort tsurik. Vue iz mayn froy? In their desert my blood and tears were absorbed under clear black skies. They stared with impassive cruelty from the shadows. I held on to my agony. I would not become a Mussulman. Carthage could kill me. Carthage could not conquer me. The metal in my womb makes me vomit but the dibbuk is mastered again. I am stronger, always, than him. In the deep prehistoric dawn I crawled towards my bagazh. It was unopened, they were so arrogant, and all my things were there. My wallet, passport, some money. Everything I had left in the *Philadelphia Grand*. I found some more cocaine. It gave me the strength to change my clothes but I could not remove the blood, which had congealed everywhere on my body. I dragged my bag through the scrub to the dirt road and soon comes a truck. It stopped. The boy at the wheel scratched beneath his overalls but otherwise exhibited no surprise. He accepted I had been attacked and my car stolen. He said for a dollar he could drive me to Carson City. Some Samaritan! It was for the gas, he said. I gave him his dollar. He threw in a little water from his bottle so I could wash the worst of the blood from my extremities. He let me off at the station. From Carson City I took the first train leaving. It was going to San Francisco. I needed to find real streets where I could hide. I was careful to make sure no one followed me on board. I knew I had to discover deep anonymity. Brodmann, the Federal agents, and now the Invisible Empire itself had revealed their animosity. It was a conspiracy of which, I suspect, only I was aware. *Diesmal wollte der Jude gans sicher gehen.* For a while at least I would have to find still another name.

Having used the train's facilities and killed the worst of the pain with unusually large doses of cocaine, I was somewhat calmer by the time we neared Oakland. I had a broken rib, which I could strap up myself. Otherwise, it was merely a question of waiting for the flesh to heal. I was now prepared to try to take rational stock of my situation. I should logically assume the various factions showing me ill will were not in league, as such. I was in danger largely because I no longer had protection. This obviously made me more vulnerable than I had been to those who already threatened my life. Half-dead from my beating I was not in a good position to cope with further attacks. I knew my assailants could not be true Klansmen, yet I had no proof of that. I must assume the Order to be riddled with spies. Evans himself could be an infiltrator. The Klan had declared itself the enemy of Pope and Bolshevik, of Jew and Jap. Going to earth in San Francisco was tantamount to hiding in the lion's den, of course. This had always been the East's beachhead in America. Her huge natural harbour made her the perfect and most important Pacific port while gold and silver from inland mines had made her the richest. My own ancestors might well have settled on her steep hillsides, coming in sailing ships from Odessa and Port Arthur to trade first with the Indians and later with mountain men, trappers who brought their beaver, bear, buckskins and buffalo hides from as far as the Rockies. When San Francisco was still part of Mexican California the Russian envoy Razanov had fallen in love with the sister of Don Luis Antonio Aiguella, but the Catholic Church had played its usual destructive role and Consuella Aiguella had ended her life in a nunnery. Eventually Slav and Anglo-Saxon banded together and drove Rome back beyond San Diego, establishing the rule of law in a land first named Nova Albion by Sir Francis Drake. Pan-Slavism was never an Anglo-Saxon enemy; rather it was always a potential ally.

My train steamed slowly to a halt, almost on the very edge of the shore. I could see masts, blue ocean, a mixture of water traffic. We were at the Bay. The locomotive had stopped on a great mass of stone and concrete: the Oakland Mole. Passengers trooped down from the cars to file aboard Southern Pacific's ferry, in those days the only means of crossing to San Francisco. I was glad to smell salt again, to lean on the ferry's rail and watch gulls swarming overhead as we sailed steadily through deep turquoise waves towards the mountain and its towers which many called the finest city of the Pacific Shore, the New York of the West. With its misty greenery and sparkling stone it was reminiscent of Constantinople, yet also a contrast. On these hills had been built, since the Earthquake, a modern metropolis of offices and apartment blocks, buildings as elegant as Chicago's. From a distance she was beautiful. And was a mere century of violent history any different, finally, to a millennium? Violence and human rapacity has a repetitious quality to it, after all.

Our boat docked at last against the quay dominated by what at first seemed to be a church steeple, the Ferry Building's tower. We filed through shabby archways, then I carried my own suitcase out into a wide square full of automobiles, cabs and rumbling cable cars which began and ended their journeys here. I was still moving, kept on my feet, I suspect, solely by adrenalin, not daring to let myself stop, so I pulled my body aboard the nearest heavy red and gold cable car. It lurched forward, bell ringing, clanking and whirring, its window glass rattling, up Market

Street which was crowded as always with people and traffic and every kind of shop. In my battered and confused condition it had not been my best choice of transport, this odd development of the ore wagon. I disembarked before it made another sickening hump. I had no clear idea where to go. I had thought of Russian Hill, which I gathered was an artists' quarter, the area I usually sought out, but I was afraid now of being recognized. Intellectuals read newspapers and some of them were liberals. I took two or three streets, stumbling up and down impossible elevations which also rivalled Constantinople's (though in the main lacking her stone stairways) and depressingly found myself back in Market Street with its four rows of cable tracks, its bustle and cosmopolitan clamour. I took another street, running off at an angle, and to my horror realised the emerald, crimson and gold carved wood possessed the forceful barbarity of Chinese handiwork. Unwittingly, I had stumbled into San Francisco's notorious Chinatown, home of a score of warring Tongs. I could smell it, a mixture of spices, vinegar, old fragrances, strong food and opium. An alien nightmare.

Not knowing when I could get to my money, I was preserving my small store of cash. I resisted hailing a taxi. I put the yellow peril behind me by as many blocks as possible. By then I was utterly exhausted and running a fever. I decided I must try to find accommodation in the first low-priced hotel I came to. The district here was lively but somewhat squalid, a lower class restaurant and entertainment area, advertising cheap meals, burlesque shows, movies and dance halls. Many of the women already on the late afternoon streets were evidently harlots. I had no prejudice against them. Indeed I felt immediately comforted by their familiarity. In this district I could relax and recover myself. I climbed the dilapidated steps of a five-storey redbrick building called *Goldberg's Hotel Berlin* on Kearny Street. The desk was at the far end of a short, unlit passage. I could hardly see the swarthy individual dozing on the other side. He grunted at me. They had rooms. I registered under the name of Michael Fitzgerald, sure that my accent would easily be taken for the rich, rolling brogue of the Emerald Isle. I went so far as to let the desk clerk know I had until recently been with a Catholic mission in Harben, China and what a pleasure it was to speak English again, after so many years. For the moment I felt safe. I had gained time to think and rest. I would remain in San Francisco as long as possible. At least there were ships here to take me to any part of the Pacific world or the great harbour cities of the continental American coast, South and North. I had heard that Argentina was a progressive nation, anxious to experiment. In Buenos Aires they had a branch of Harrods! My room was decorated from floor to ceiling in dull orange paint. The furniture was the same colour. Grey sheets and chipped washing facilities stood out in almost brilliant contrast. I put my suitcase under the bed and went to the nearest grocery to buy a few necessities, things I could easily drink and eat through swollen lips. My face had begun to throb as the effects of the cocaine wore off. The rest of my body was a single rising wave of pain. I bought a newspaper at the corner stand when I saw the headlines.

The paper was delirious with delight over the 'K-K-KRACK UP!', the division in Klan ranks. A certain obscure Texas dentist, Hiram Evans, proclaimed himself, the paper said, Imperial Wizard, and announced his intention of ridding the Klan of its traitors, people of loose moral character, of doubtful loyalty. Minutes after the successful putsch Eddy Clarke had been indicted under both the Volsted and Mann acts for licentious and vicious behaviour, which they claimed had occurred some years earlier. Mrs Mawgan was described as a woman of doubtful virtue, mistress of a Jew speculator. Colonel Simmons was in open conflict with Evans. Major Sinclair was not mentioned. I wondered if he, like me, had been beaten up, or even killed. According to the reporter, Klankrest had become as sinister as Caligula's court, with plotters and assassins skulking in every corridor. The entire Klan seemed on the point of falling apart. I took with a pinch of salt much of what I read ('Knives Out For Klan Renegades', 'Death Threats For Clarke and Supporters') but it was clear I had no friends left in Atlanta.

The Justice Department's investigation of me could be part of a general attack on Klan members. Doubtless traitors within the ranks were giving information (much of it highly coloured or simply false) to the Federal men in the hope of charges being dropped. That was why Callahan was hounding me. And Brodmann, of course, posing as a White policeman, could be helping him while telling lies about me to the Klan. Things became clearer. Anyone associated with Clarke, Mawgan or even Simmons was 'fair game' for a witch hunt. The Klan itself, split by factions, could no longer help. Mrs Mawgan had been thrown to the wolves. She, in turn, had given them my hide. It would be sheer insanity to try to claim my money from where it had been deposited. If I were to cash a check, very likely Callahan would soon know and quickly trace me. If he was indeed working with Brodmann, my nemesis was bound to try to stir up further Klan hatred against me. Perhaps I should try to reach Canada, and from there head for England.

Meanwhile, as long as I was reasonably careful, San Francisco, in spite of her capacity to revive unwanted memories, was ideal for my needs. Her busy slopes were filled to extravagance with the nations of the world, with the very rich and the horribly poor, with eccentrics, madmen, cripples, beggars and every kind of criminal. Her slums lacked the worst miseries of Galata, her mansions were marginally less opulent than Stamboul's, but she was otherwise that city's equal in vulgar variety. I stayed in my room, bathing my wounds in witchhazel and antiseptic, waiting for the bruising to subside so I would be at least unremarkable, if not presentable. I decided to seek the help of Santucci's cousin, Vince Potecci, at the *Ristorante Venezia*. I checked the map I had bought and found the address was not very far away on Taylor Street. I could get there easily by streetcar. Since Major Sinclair and *The Knight Hawk* had vanished (I learned some time ago he had escaped in his ship to Mexico and ended his life giving joy rides to dagoes) Mr Potecci was my only safe contact in America. I was willing, until matters settled a little, to return to my old trade of jobbing mechanic, but I hoped to be offered a loan. I would throw myself as much as I dared upon the mercy of Santucci's cousin.

As soon as my face and hands only marginally betrayed the signs of my beating, I set off for Taylor Street, near fishing quays where the rigging of little crab boats cross-hatched the spaces between the houses. There was a mouth-watering smell of fresh seafood and cooked lobster. Clouds of gulls hung over the wharves, wheeling and shrieking, fighting for scraps. I found the restaurant, left my message with a sleepy old woman who held the envelope carefully in both hands. She yawned, assuring me it would be safely delivered. Then I strolled back. In a typical San Franciscan morning, foggy and damp, thin sunshine was breaking through. I decided to explore the city, as was my habit. I had become stiff from spending so long in bed. I needed exercise. Trudging through little streets and alleys in the general direction of my hotel I came eventually into a slum favoured by hop-heads and winos. Occasionally I was whispered at from a doorway, but was not otherwise disturbed. I turned into Clay Street, glancing at a small, sleazy theatre and found myself staring in astonishment at the smiling face of Mrs Cornelius. She was one of three girls in a photograph, part of a chorus line, advertising a show called *Beauties from Blighty. The Latest Concert Party Sensation From England*. I burst out laughing at my own surprise. So close was the threat of the engulfing nightmare I was sure I had begun to indulge in wishful hallucinations. I forced myself to go on a few feet and peered into the cluttered window of a faded delicatessen while I collected my wits. I returned slowly. Like most of the places in this area the theatre was run-down, an edifice of damp, flaking brick and peeling red and white paint, called for some reason *Stranoff's Russian Commedia*. It advertised 'movies' as well as 'live-shows.' It occurred to me, cautiously, that Mrs Cornelius's film contacts had paid off: she was not physically in San Francisco, but was appearing in a kino play. I tried the doors. The place was locked, back and front. The Matinee began at 2:30 pm. In a daze, I returned to Goldberg's hotel and sat down on my narrow bed to write another note. I would assume Mrs Cornelius to be working at the theatre. If they would not allow me through the stage door she would at least read my note and have me admitted or send word when she had finished her turn. Once again I congratulated myself on the saving instinct which led me always to large cities where such coincidences were the stuff of ordinary experience. Mrs Cornelius, my guardian angel, might again be able to save me. The hope revived that my present circumstances were merely a minor setback in a career which, with a tiny amount of good fortune, could only prosper.

As it happened, when at two o'clock I arrived at the stage door, there was no one to stop me. I was able to wander freely through a mysterious succession of musty tiled corridors until I found the dressing-rooms. There were only three. One was marked Actors, one Actresses and the third, cryptically, Others. I knocked on the ladies' door and heard familiar English giggles and shrieks. A voice shouted for me to enter. I turned the handle and was immersed suddenly in a confusion of tinsel and cheap brightly coloured fabric, the smell of sweat, paint and strong perfume. Smoking and still wearing her street clothes (a gorgeous pink frock with green trim) Mrs Cornelius stood leaning against an unplastered wall. Her blonde hair was fashionably waved. She wore bright red lipstick. With her emphatic mascara and rouge, she looked even lovelier than when I had last seen her in Constantinople.

She recognized me. At first she was expressionless, shaking her head. 'Bloody 'ell,' she said. 'Wotcher, Ivan.' She began to chuckle. 'It's abart time ya turned up. Yore lookin' the toff orl right. So yore doin' as well as yer said, eh! 'Ave yer come ter take me orf ter 'Ollywood?'

I moved forward uncertainly between the clutter and the two other young women, oblivious of them. I took her hand and kissed it. 'You remain the most beautiful creature in the world!' I was entranced, as always. I could not disguise my ecstatic emotion. Behind me the skinny little girls giggled and whispered. Mrs Cornelius leaned forward to kiss me on the cheek. Her fragrance was intoxicating. 'Come orf it, Ive. We ain't on stage fer anuvver ten minutes! Still, I carn't say I'm not pleased ter see yer, 'cause I am. Wot yer bin up ter?'

It was my turn to smile. 'Oh, all kinds of things. In the past year I've been on tour.'

'Wot? Actin'?'

'You could say so. They call it lecturing. How long have you been here?'

She had arrived in New York the previous summer. The show had been booked by an agency which led them to believe they would be appearing in major theatres. 'Instead we come on between ther bloody flickers while they're changin' the effin' reels. Ter keep ther bleedin' customers from tearin' up ther rotten seats!' She shrugged, dismissing a wealth and variety of disappointments with her usual good humour. 'But at least we're workin'. An' ther Yanks ain't bad audiences, mostly. This is ther biggest bookin' we've 'ad since Phily-bloody-delphia. We got anuvver week, then it's renewable. Dunno wot we'll do if they don't bleedin' renew. Ther bloke managin' us run off ter Brazil in February, wiv ther juvenile lead, littel effin' poof.'

As she talked she began, with unconscious grace, to change into her costume. 'Wot woz yore management like?'

'I'm in a similar predicament. A change of directors. No further bookings. I'm currently at a loose end.'

She looked back at me, cigarette in the corner of her mouth, a small frown in her eyes. 'Ya bin duffed up, ain't yer? 'Oo dun it, Ive?'

'Cowboys,' I said. 'My last appearance wasn't received too well. One of those Western towns.'

'Yeah,' she agreed, 'they let yer know when yer ain't goin' over too well. So yore art o' work, eh? Ya c'd orlways come in wiv us. Ya couldn't do worse'n ther larst bloke. Managin', I mean.' She made small, dainty adjustments to her tights and spangled bodice. The costume matched those her friends were wearing.

484

I had nothing else to do. I would dearly love to be close to the woman who had been my most reliable friend. Yet I had no general experience of theatre work. I did not know what rates to charge or how to approach owners. There again I was sure to learn quickly. I said the idea had its attractions. She seemed pleasantly surprised. 'Buy me some supper after ther show,' she said as the distorted sounds of music came from the auditorium. 'And we'll tork abart it some more.' She tripped towards the darkness.

'Oh do, please do help us!' whispered the last girl hastily, turning huge, vulnerable eyes on me. Then all three ran for the stage. The girl at the rear offered me a red grin.

That night Mrs Cornelius and I ate at Hong Kong Willy's on Grant Avenue. 'It woz yore fault, reelly,' she said. 'Writin' orl them bleedin' letters sayin' 'ow great it woz 'ere. So I jumped at ther chance, din' I? Yer orta think it over, this opportunity I'm offerin'.' She had already convinced me (as she would always convince me) that my 'gift of the gab' made me ideally suited to manage the Beauties from Blighty. 'It only needs a few 'undred dollars extra cash ter get us orf ther grahnd. An' you've got that much easy, aincha? Give it a try, Ivan, since yer've nuffink else on. We got orl the leaflets an' stuff. Ya could do it! A small stake an' you own ther Beauties.'

I was too embarrassed to tell her that my money was hard to 'liquidate.' I promised her a decision as quickly as possible. I was certain I could manage the troupe. She had explained how the important trick was to keep the attention of theatre owners long enough to convince them of the value of the act. But money would be needed for improvements, to pay travel expenses for a while, and so on. It would mean that I should have to risk a visit to my bank. It was only on this point I hesitated.

When I returned to Goldberg's a youngish man was waiting for me in the alcove beside the desk. He was tall, fashionably dressed and courteous, carrying himself with a straight-shouldered stance suggesting a military or sporting background. I was sure he was from the Justice Department and was on the point of asking how he had traced me when he introduced himself as Harry Galiano and vigorously shook my hand. With relief I realized he was an emissary from Annibale Santucci's cousin. My message had been received. 'If you ain't too busy, the boss could see you tonight.' He spoke with grave politeness. I asked for a moment to go to my room. There I used some of Mrs Mawgan's remaining 'wings' to ensure I had a few more hours of wakefulness. When I rejoined him he smiled suddenly, with the same cheerful insouciance as Santucci. He was quite as proud, when he escorted me round the corner into Broadway, of the large blue Packard parked there. 'Be my guest,' he said. With a flourish he opened the passenger door.

For some time we drove in silence through the diffused, multicoloured night of downtown San Francisco. The fog was growing thicker. Harry was content to concentrate on steering his big machine through the confused traffic of Market, past the cable car terminus, and to the wharf, visible as a series of yellow lights barely piercing the fog. We were guided up the ramp by at least half a dozen shadowy men in blue overalls and then, with a moan, the ferry staggered in the water, lurched sluggishly from the dockside, settling down to a steady speed as she ploughed out into the unseen waters of the Bay. It was only then, as we stood smoking beside the shackled Packard, that Harry became talkative. He and Vince, he said, were 'buddies from way back,' first in the hotel trade, as chefs, later as restaurant owners. These days his boss ran a select countryclub out past Berkeley. That was where we were going. I would like the club. It was very European. Very high class.

We drove off the ferry on the Oakland side. The dark water fell behind us; the steep town dwindled to isolated homes, then we were on a highway, running wide and straight between hilly woods. At last, turning into a shrub-bordered driveway, we approached a large building, three storeys high resembling a marble hacienda. It bore the illuminated legend *Gold Nugget Road House*. Clearly a fashionable restaurant, the place had at least twenty cars parked outside. Nothing could be seen through the thickly curtained windows from which music and laughter warmed the chill of the night. Harry parked the Packard at the rear, led me to a side door and knocked lightly. We were admitted by another Italian, lugubrious and thin in tight-fitting evening clothes, who said the boss was upstairs and expecting us. Two flights of concrete steps took us to the top of the building and through a fire door. Suddenly we had entered a passage expensively decorated in the latest somewhat jazzy fashion. I was reminded of Italy and her Futurists. We passed through several rooms, all in the same style. Everything was grey, blue or pink, including the glass tables and wall mirrors. Then, on the other side of a soft archway, a squat, swarthy man in middle years, also wearing a tuxedo, came forward to take my hand. 'Mr Peters? I'm Vince Potter. What can I give you to drink? It's all McCoy.' Expansively, he opened the flap of a huge cocktail cabinet resembling one of the more elaborate cinema organs. 'You do partake?'

When I told him I did, he seemed to hesitate. Then he shrugged and poured me the McCoy. It tasted like scotch.

He was solicitous in a humorous, slightly bantering way. 'So what happened to you? I get a wire from little Annibale in Rome to say to look out for you. Then nothing. We thought you was dead, you know? From where was it Minnesota? St Paul? Now you need a job or what? You got experience? What experience?'

'I'm fundamentally a scientist and engineer.' I explained a little of my career, how I had run up against both the Ku Klux Klan and the Justice Department through no fault of my own. I needed employment under a fresh identity for a while 'I can work on planes, boats, cars. Anything mechanical.' I thought it best to play down my lecturing career, seeing no point in offending an immigrant who had almost certainly been raised as a Catholic. Besides, it had no relevance to my current situation.

When I finished talking he was frowning but seemed impressed. 'Let me get this right,' he said. 'You can start an engine, for instance. Okay? Without keys?'

'Of course. That would be easy.' I could not quite follow his reasoning.

He shrugged and poured me another McCoy. 'Always a good talent. But what was your main racket? In the old country, I mean. With Annibale, you must have been selling and buying, you know. That's what he does mainly.'

'Yes, indeed.'

'So you were in Paris. What was your line there?'

'Aeroplanes, chiefly.' I did not want to raise the matter of the airship company scandal.

At this, to my surprise, he began to grin. 'Jesus Christ! How the hell do you get rid of a hot Curtiss? No, don't tell me. Over there, sure, it's all governments and revolutions and what not. Like in Mexico and down in South America generally. Okay, I should tell you, the rum-running business is small bananas in comparison, though I will admit it gets competitive. We've got a pretty large territory to protect.' He displayed mild, friendly puzzlement. 'What can I say to you? A job? You could always have a job. But I don't want to insult you. We got boats and cars need fixing, sure, but there's plenty of mechanics. Start as a driver. You're welcome. But you don't want that. Another year, we could offer better for someone like yourself. I'm expanding, going into legitimate business. Now, short of starting a war with Panama, I can't see how else I can help you out.'

I reassured him before he became even more apologetic. I could easily find work. What I really needed was a new identity, a passport, preferably as an American citizen. He brightened at this. He was a warm hearted man and felt obliged to be useful to his cousin's friend. He could not put me into a job worthy of my skills, because it would offend other employees, but he dearly wanted to show his concern in a practical way. 'That's no big deal. You got a name you want? Or do you care? A few photos and we'll give you a whole new history.'

I told him I was currently using the pseudonym Michael Fitzpatrick. He seemed surprised by my choice of an Irish name. After some consideration, he said: 'You don't think maybe that's stacking the odds just a little against yourself?' I took his meaning. I, of all people, should know the suspicion with which Tammany was viewed. 'What about Manny Pashkowitz?' he said. 'I used to know a Manny Pashkowitz who passed on recently. That would be useful in itself, since he copped a John Doe tag in the morgue.'

'I would prefer something a little less Jewish.'

'I understand.' He hummed to himself, staring off into space. 'Then how does Pallenberg sound? Matt Pallenberg, a Swede. Nobody hates the Swedes, except maybe Finns and Danes. But who cares what they think? A nice name. He lost an argument with a Customs cutter near the Santa Barbara islands a couple of months back. I know for sure he never had no ID on him when he checked out. He'd be about the same age. Born in Stockholm, I think. Came over with his folks twenty years ago. A piece of cake. What could be neater?'

'I'm very grateful, Mr Potter.'

'Don't mention it. A pleasure. Stay in touch. We're sure to have openings soon for an educated person like yourself. Some day we'll do business, I'm certain. Now, is there anything else?'

I asked if he would mind my having mail sent to me care of his restaurant in North Beach. He said it would delight him. With the joviality of the embarrassed host to the untimely guest, Vince Potecci slapped me on the back, insisting I take one of his Havana Corona Coronas before he returned me into the keeping of Harry Galiano who chatted nostalgically on growing up in Toledo as he drove rapidly to catch the last ferry back to San Francisco. It was only as we arrived outside Goldberg's I realised he had been referring to Toledo, Ohio. Harry promised to come the next evening and collect my photographs. He assured me, it would be three days at most before I was completely fixed up. I asked him how he would get back to Oakland with the ferries shut down for the night. He laughed. He looked after the North Beach businesses, he said. It was five minutes to home. His parting words were significant. 'Take care. Best to keep yourself to yourself until I get back to you. In this town you have to be careful. Never believe anyone's who they say they are until you've checked them out.' I think he knew Brodmann was looking for me. It was possible he had even heard something about Callahan, the Federal agent. Without wishing to alarm me, he was trying to warn me to be wary of them.

In my bedroom I settled down to think. I could again begin to make plans for the future. I found Mrs Cornelius's suggestion by far the best, of course, but remained uneasy about cashing a check. Shortly, it was true, I should soon be leaving San Francisco behind me and with it my old Peterson persona. Nonetheless, it was scarcely sensible to give my pursuers an idea of which coast I was on, let alone which city. Without the 'float' *Beauties from Blighty* would almost certainly collapse, leaving Mrs Cornelius and her friends destitute. With a few hundred dollars, there was a strong chance of going from strength to strength and, moreover, making my living in a reasonable way. The chief attraction was that I would earn my old friend's gratitude (after all, how many times had she saved me from death, let alone discomfort?) and be close to one of my two enduring loves. That alone, surely, was worth the risk?

The following evening Mrs Cornelius invited me to her rooming house to 'talk things over'. Having given my photographs to Harry Galiano, I felt somewhat more relaxed as I entered a building which made Goldberg's seem like the Ritz. It was disgusting that so fine a woman as she, who had been the intimate of princes and world leaders, should be reduced to this roach-infested hovel! No wonder she needed financial reinforcement! It was morally wrong. A woman of her sensitivity and breeding, talent and beauty, should not have to concern herself with keeping the bedding as far away from the floor as possible in order to reduce the number of verminous creatures running over her body at night. 'Oh,' she said courageously, 'I've known a lot worse, Ive. Still, I must say, ther wages might not be much bigger over 'ere, but the bleed-in' insects certinly are!' And she laughed, offering me some gin she had bought for the occasion. She asked if I had given any further thought to becoming 'chief share'older an' manager of our littel troupe'. I refused to burden her with my own problems. I merely said I was waiting to hear from my accountant. 'Better make up yer mind soon, Ivan,' she said, 'or I'll 'ave ter look up ther nearest nunnery an' take ther vow!'

I was horrified at the notion of her becoming enslaved by the Church. I asked if there were alternatives. 'It's gettin' darn ter 'awkin' me 'a'penny,' she said ambiguously, 'or bein' picked up on wot I gather they corl in these parts a "vag rap." Ter vamp or ter vag, thass ther question, Ive!'

There was desperation, I was sure, beneath her light-hearted words. I was the only one who could save her. She said as much to me that night as she kissed me on the cheek and waved me good night.

A little drunk, doing everything I could to disguise the fact, I made my way up steep, unfamiliar streets in the small hours of the morning. Somehow I found myself on Stockton, in the no man's land between Little Italy and Chinatown, foolishly wondering whether to go North or South when, had I considered the problem sensibly for a moment, I should have gone East. At last I got my bearings, thankfully recognising a late-night drugstore on Dupont. This part of the city was virtually de-serted. It was three o'clock. A light drizzle had begun to fill the air and the street lights shivered and grew dim. I wore no topcoat or hat, so turned up my jacket collar and pressed on until I could round the cor-ner into Kearny Street. My head was down. I did not look up until I was less than a block from Goldberg's. As I raised my eyes I recognised a fig-ure, in heavy leather coat and wide-brimmed hat, who moved abruptly from the yellow circle of gaslight and walked with unnatural speed to-wards Broadway. It was as if I had disturbed a thief. Then, as the figure pressed on, labouring through the rain until it was out of sight, I knew I had seen Brodmann! He had been watching the hotel and had not ex-pected me to surprise him from the rear!

Closing Goldberg's street door and moving carefully across the rag-ged linoleum in the gloom, I considered this new factor. If Brodmann were working on his own (or with his Chekist comrades) I might have a little time; if he was in league with the Justice Department or the Klan, I would be wise to leave the city immediately. Whichever was the case, I now had relatively little to lose by obtaining the 'float' for Mrs Cor-

nelius. I grinned carelessly to myself. I would give them the slip again.
I was to become an actor-manager. A Sir William Shakespeare. A miniature Flo Ziegfeld. A travelling player in the footsteps of Dickens and
Oscar Wilde! And the wonderful, the eternally feminine Mrs Cornelius was to be Juliet to my Romeo, Frankie to my Johnny!

The following afternoon I went round to Stranoff's to tell her of my
decision. She need no longer feel torn between Skid Row and the Little
Sisters of St Francis. A living death in the service of the Pope would
never be her lot while I could still draw breath. She was overjoyed, like
Lillian Gish saved at the last minute from the clutches of the evil mulatto, and she hugged me, telling me I was 'a brick' and 'a godsend.'
She immediately began to make plans and suggest suitable locations for
our future performances. I offered her $500, saying she could invest it
in whatever she believed was of paramount importance to the continuing existence of *Beauties from Blighty*. 'Well,' she said, almost skip-
ping with delight, 'number one's gotta be a decent motor! Don't worry,
Ive. Ya won't regret this, I promise.'

Next day my new identity had arrived, more detailed and more convincing than any previous one. Still making sure Brodmann had not returned to 'shadow' me, I hurried to the Nob Hill branch of my
California bank. There I presented a legitimate check for $750 made
out to Matt Pallenberg and signed 'Max Peterson.' At least nobody
would automatically guess we were the same man. A check to cash
would have made it immediately clear I was in San Francisco. I must
admit I was a little clammy as the clerk, learning I had been mailed the
check from Milwaukee (a further obfuscation), significantly recruited
advice from hushed nether regions, bore the check to invisible arbitra-
tion, conferred in pious murmurs with various other officiates, then
eventually returned, inspected my identification (even the address was
in Albany), found it satisfactory and at last briskly demanded my choice
of denominations as if I had handed him the check only a second or
two before. I asked for $500 in large bills. This I would hand immedi-
ately to Mrs Cornelius for our Company. The rest I had in ones, fives
and tens, for various emergencies, including the purchase from a
source in Chinatown of high quality cocaine. The money made me
substantial again and gave me the feeling of controlling my own fate. I
was no longer a foreigner with suspicious Romantic blood but a Nordic
descendant of Vikings (like, indeed, all the old families of Kiev), that
hardy, adventurous race who, discovering America long before the

Spanish Jew Columbus, had carved their runes on the sea-battered cliffs of Long Island and Nantucket, claiming the land for their wholesome, self-sufficient deities Odin, Freya and Thor; far more practical gods to rule a vital subcontinent than that repressive Jehovah of palefaced, constipated puritanism.

I put the Ku Klux Klan behind me. Those fools had missed their chance of greatness by petty internal bickering, by turning on their best friends. They would destroy, through further stupidity and quarrelling, everything they had gained. For a while Indiana might have been the first Klan state, but another scandal ended that dream. Colonel Simmons, Eddy Clarke, even Major Sinclair and myself, were martyrs, destroyed by small-minded, cautious people or by treacherous friends like Mrs Mawgan. My own gifts, so cynically abused by money-grubbing politicians of the kind who destroyed idealists like Roffy and Gilpin, could still make America the world leader of technological innovation. If they wanted me in the future, they would have to crawl and beg. I was determined to renounce the false lures of their world and devote myself to play acting and private scientific speculation. I would not let them hound me. I would choose for myself when and where I left America, when to reveal my true identity. How astonished they would be! How I would laugh at them as my efficient steam-powered airship, my own refinement of the *Avitor Hermes Jr* which had flown from San Francisco in 1869, swam through the skies above the Golden Gate, outsped the great locomotives of the Southern Pacific. When the fiery cross next burned, a thousand feet high, on Mount Shasta, it would be the signal to all that the Invisible Empire was purified and ready to ride out once more on its holy purpose, to free America from the Orient's envious chains! But this time I would be at the head.

We should ride in machines of gold and brass and blinding silver and our enemies would know the helpless thrill of absolute terror. We should take our vengeance, but we should take it honourably. Wake up, America! Your skies fill with an avenging army and only the just shall survive! The first phase of my *Kampfzeit* had drawn to a close. The second would soon begin. Meanwhile, as a simple, strolling player, I would mingle with the ordinary people, drawing my strength from the grassroots, the backbone of America. I had flown too high, too soon, through no fault of my own. Now I must restore myself, plant my boots firmly on the ground and begin again. You would not hear my voice whining *Amerika! Twoje dzielo.* Our little band would grow, but not by many, and I would continue to remain true to my ideals. For a while, however, they would have to be adapted to the requirements of the musical comedy. *Erst waren es Sieben. Sie kämpften und blutetan für Amerikas Freiheit.*

Mrs Cornelius had bought an old Cadillac ambulance for a song. Slightly refitted, with the name of our Company painted in the latest modernistic lettering on her sides, the machine was a bargain. Mrs Cornelius and the other two girls were all that remained of the original troupe, but she was confident we should swell the ranks back to seven by recruiting as we travelled. They had bought material and made new costumes, some of which would be for the new sketch I had outlined to Mrs Cornelius as my first contribution. Within a very short time we were ready to begin our northward journey along the Pacific Coast. I was excited, of course, but also more than usually nervous, uncertain of my abilities as an actor-manager. Mrs Cornelius constantly reassured me that it was 'a piece of cake' and 'far easier than it looks.' Nonetheless, I twice came close to giving the idea up and taking the first tramp to Tahiti.

Eventually I rallied. I wrote further letters to Esmé, to Kolya and one to Santucci, thanking him for his help. I told them all I could be reached in care of the *Ristorante Venezia*, Taylor Street. I had given up politics because I was disgusted with the corruption I had discovered. Eventually I planned to resume my scientific career.

I should not have delayed as long as I did. Coming out of Goldberg's on my way to meet Mrs Cornelius, who already had my suitcase packed in the back of the van, I saw Brodmann – or rather his leather coat – slip from view round the corner of the bakery across the street. I ran after him but he was already flying down the pavement to disappear below the horizon. I could not decide why he should go to such pains to avoid recognition. There was no telling what complicated game he was playing with his allies as well as his quarry. Rather than go directly to where I had told Mrs Cornelius to pick me up, I took a series of side-tracks, moving in and out of alleys, doubling back on myself, and so arrived outside the little Dupont Street drugstore rather later than I had said. Everyone else was ready in the van. The two girls sat behind while Mrs Cornelius, a little drunk, waited in the seat beside mine. The engine was started and we were, in her words, 'ready to roll'. With a great sigh of relief I let off the brake, engaged the gears and began the labouring journey towards Market Street. The van had an excellent engine for its age, but was somewhat overloaded. Mrs Cornelius was full of her old exuberance, leading the other girls and myself in the choruses of her favourite songs.

By the time we were on the road to Salinas we had sung our way through most of her repertoire and I was teaching her *My Old Kentucky Moon* which I had learned only a month earlier from the treacherous Mrs Mawgan. Occasionally I would glance back the way we had come, but saw no driver resembling Brodmann. I was childishly happy to be with her again and travelling. *Es dir oys s'harts!* I could put the past entirely from my mind and concentrate cheerfully upon the future. I kissed her cheek affectionately.

Mrs Cornelius giggled. 'You'll do, Ivan. We're on our way ter Glory, mate!' A moment later, with an astonished groan, she threw up in my lap.

Twenty

I COULD NOT GO BACK to Odessa. Even if it were possible, what would I find? A rationalised corpse; a poor reproduction? Nothing is left of my cities. All that remained was a future; now even that is denied me, for Carthage laid waste its foundations. The present is obscene. What do they expect me to make of it? Those lost cities: those stillborn marvels! I offered the solution. They rejected it. Surely the Jew in Arcadia did not betray me? I loved him. The metal was introduced out there, while I lay helpless against their synagogue. I choose who is and who is not a Jew. I choose the way to a safer, ordered world. I choose to say what is fact and what is fiction. Dissatisfied with mere victory, Carthage made war on my dreams.

Carthage came marching against Byzantium. I fought. I drove the enemy back. My dreams soared again. No little black hands clung to my anchor lines. No mocking nigger eyes traded on my guilt. What reason I should feel guilty? I have done something with myself. I am an engineer of long experience.

For all that year and the one which followed Carthage hid her masts behind the horizon. How could I know she still pursued us? I journeyed into a world of illusions. I cannot say I regret it. Indeed, I would dearly love to see the fantasy restored. Reality is not in itself valuable. But I did not know that. Those Nazis were barbarians. Like the Bolsheviks before them, they were willing recruits in the infantry of Carthage. They called Hitler their 'new Alexander.' What cities did they leave in their wake? What enduring monuments? Sachsenhausen? Buchenwald? Dachau? Twelve million slaughtered *lagervolk* (50% Jewish, 50% Slav); another

495

twenty million miscellaneous cadavers and a crude rocket? What did Speer build which lasted just fifteen years? Even Turks showed respect for Constantinople, albeit by imitation. Carthage creates only ash and mud, mixes these together, moulds the result on frames of twisted barbed wire, then hails the result, these shambling grotesques, as the *Obermenschen* of their impoverished mythology. Today I have no time for self-professed enemies of Carthage. They are too easily seduced. My Baroness von Ruckstühl was killed in Berlin. That city was never the best refuge for a philosemitic Slav, yet it was a Russian bomb which took her life. Stalin's answer to a problem was the simplest of all. If it could not be quickly solved, he destroyed it. *Nit problem.* This is fundamental to the philosophy of Carthage. I fail to understand this *Liebschaft mit der Nazi. Er verfluchte die Zukunft. Er verlachte den Amerikaner. Er lachte laut!* But *was ist Amerika und seiner Venegurung in kontrast Es ist komish! Der Nazi er eine Wille* to self-destruction has in stronger form. *Um so besser. Begreifen sie das Problem* These *daytsh broynfel lombard-tseshterniks* are no better than Bolsheviks, concerned with the same silly sport. Auschwitz? Treblinka? Babi Yar? I offered them a sky-borne Alexandria! Always in sunshine. Always warm.

I claim only novelty as the explanation for any success we achieved on the Pacific Coast. Mrs Cornelius had a real show business talent which she owed chiefly to her exuberant vitality. She herself would always admit she had no outstanding gifts. Because I was more comfortable there (having made few public appearances in the State) most of the bookings I organized were in California. We became innocent again; *Wandervögel*, moving from town to town. This had definite advantages for our theatrical troupe. If you remain only briefly in a place and then swiftly travel on, your ability is rarely questioned while your novelty frequently passes for talent. Most of our audiences were grateful for any entertainment and we were able to satisfy them reasonably well. We toured regularly from the vicinity of Crescent City on the Oregon border all the way down to the San Diego region. We were tempted to cross into Mexico, but thought it unwise, given the problems we were likely to encounter with immigration. We were rarely the only feature on the bill. Sometimes, to fill in for a late or missing act, I even resumed my old rôle, lecturing to miners on the wonders of the future, or talking to fishermen about the perils of foreign Communism. We also performed our little musical play. It was of my own concoction. Wearing Don Cossack uniform and brandishing Georgian pistols, I played a Russian prince in love with Mrs

Cornelius's Bolshevik commissar. She elects, at the end, to go with me into exile. I called it *White Knight and Red Queen*. I was rather flattered when this proved to be our most popular act, frequently drawing more applause than cinema films shown before and after the performance. We had become *Limeys in Limelight* and Mrs Cornelius had chosen the stage name of *Charlene Chaplin*. I was most frequently billed as *Barry More*. Most employers believed such names attracted custom. Privately I felt this deceptive association with the famous was likely to confuse and annoy audiences led to believe their film favourites were taking the plank stage of a tent theatre in Redondo Beach.

I became adept at securing cheap lodgings and bargaining with the proprietors of carnivals, opera houses (saloons before prohibition) and ramshackle movie theatres. Our van proved a sound investment. It often served as shelter. The gypsy life was not unhealthy and indeed we all benefited. Though frequently tired and short of money we were rarely downhearted. A good climate makes an enormous difference to one's spirits. Sunshine is an antidote to almost any ills. English people appreciate it almost as much as Russians. The other two girls were Mabel Church and Ethel Embsay. They were usually known as *Gloria de Courcey* and *Constance Buckingham-Fairbank*. Both were plain, cheerful creatures whose popularity had much to do with a fairly indiscriminate dispensation of off-stage favours. We acquired a drunken juggler-cum-comedian called Harold Hope: he drew more applause for his lack of dexterity than for any intrinsic skill with the Indian Clubs. For a while we also had a young black-face minstrel, Will Olsen. He left us outside Monterey after attempting to force himself on Mrs Cornelius. Next we employed Chief Buffalo Nose, a fire-eater from Brooklyn. His tribe was closer to the *Plattfussindianern* (as the joke went in Germany during the 30s) than it was to the *Schwarzefussindianern*. He rarely needed artificial help in lighting his breath. What always astonished me was how he kept his stomach from igniting.

These were idyllic days. I had women almost always to hand, friendship and common sense from Mrs Cornelius, little thought for the future and less for the past. The small California towns were generally welcoming. They also possessed an innocence missed by modern Americans. Here were settlements unsullied by coloured invaders; unthreatened by godless ideologies. The soda fountain, the drugstore and the barbershop were the local meeting-places and the saloon, when it existed, was as sombre and peaceful, as respectable, as any church. I have seen the Disneyland brochures. But you cannot create Main Street as a nostalgic sideshow in a funfair run by Mormons dressed as cartoon mice. *Devo tornare indietro?*

America forfeited Main Street when she turned her back on Europe, leaving us to struggle alone against Carthage. She looked inward at the moment her power and idealism reached zenith. If she had looked outward, she would still have everything she yearns for now. I was there. America was euphorically taking the path to self-defeat. She suffered the perpetual delusion of the rich: that their wealth is the reward for some inherent moral superiority. I, who shared the benefits of California's irresponsible youth, saw no better than did they the end to the privileged golden years, the gaiety and extravagance. But my time as an actor was not wasted. I learned much about ordinary people living on slender means, experiencing the daily realities of a world many Europeans still insist is wholly glamorous, naïve or spoiled. My disappointment with America was to come later when I realised she refused her proper rôle of leader merely because she would rather be liked than respected. In the twenties she still had self-respect. That was why you could safely walk down Main Street, smelling sodas, malts, coffee and syrup in towns where only a generation or two earlier men had killed for a nugget of gold, a parcel of dirt.

We travelled in the footsteps of Lola Montez, who had danced her way through the lumber camps and tent towns seventy years before. From the wooden metropolises of Lost Hill to the new, brick-built dignity of Calaveras County, through the great deserts and redwood forests, over mountain ranges and between steep hills, from gold to silver to oil, we sang our songs and declaimed our lines. In cities whose boardwalks protected our feet from mud we could turn a corner and find a full-sized oil well erected in the middle of the street. The great Mother Lode, which had brought San Francisco one of her richest and wildest periods, was played out, yet the hills remained full of prospectors. We drove through the shimmering passes of the High Sierras and the vast San Joaquin Valley when the plum blossom was at its fullest, through fields of cotton, across irrigated plains with lines of eucalyptus as far as the eye could see. We rested and breathed the almost narcotic scent of orange groves, plucked fresh peaches from the tree, feasted on trout caught from cool rivers. We performed in barns, tents and the public rooms of dilapidated hotels. We travelled as far as Flagstaff, Arizona, and one night made camp close to the rim of the Grand Canyon. That primeval vastness can only be experienced, never conveyed by word or picture. We drove our old ambulance through the Painted Desert. In Monument Valley the Indians' eyes stared upon the death of all dreams. Navajo children had the trancelike expressions I already knew from Galata and, before that, the steppe-*shtetls* of Ukraine. They had been born into a century which had no place for them. Their rituals and traditions had lost function and reason. Now, through no fault of their own, these Indians could never be anything but outcasts. They were parasites in their own land, like the conquered Armenians, the Palestinian Jews and Russian kulaks. They had become *Musselmanisch*, as they said in Buchenwald. They had, in essence, ceased to live, these exemplary citizens of Carthage.

Occasionally our tours would take us to larger cities, or at least their suburbs. It was in Auburn, a peaceful Northern Californian town, where the telegraph poles were still taller than most buildings, that I saw Brodmann again. I was crossing from a café called *Rattlesnake Dick's* to the local post office. The only moving traffic on the wide steep street was a horse-buggy and two or three bicycles. The afternoon was sleepy and sunny. Auburn seemed to be enjoying a siesta. I had in my hand a note to Esmé and a postcard to Kolya. As usual I was begging for news, praying that soon one of my letters must reach them, wherever they were. I refused to consider the possibility they had been kidnapped back to Russia. Brodmann was standing on the wooden balcony of the old Freeman Hotel, at the very top of the hill. I could make out his figure clearly. Before disappearing back into the darkness of his room he waved once. I was fairly sure the gesture was simply a mocking one, but he might have been signalling to someone. I became very wary after that and insisted on leaving Auburn, to Mrs Cornelius's annoyance since we had originally planned to spend the night there. For the next week I had difficulty playing my parts but saw no point in alarming anyone else with my knowledge. I still had no clear notion of Brodmann's intentions. I was glad, however, when we began to move back towards the South.

We played fairs and carnivals, wooden booths and magnificent theatres usually built for populations which had failed to materialise and which were slowly falling into decay. We played seaside resorts on piers and boardwalks, local fairs, fruit and flower festivals. We had become gypsies and were content enough, even if we sometimes dreamed of the moment when Florence Ziegfeld or Cecil B. DeMille would see us and put us under contract. We knew in our hearts it would never happen. The nearest we came at that time to someone of means taking us up was in San Luis Obispo when we heard one of William Randolph Hearst's lieutenants was in the audience. Apparently he had been told by his boss to find some local entertainment for a party at Hearst's ranch in the hills above the little town. I gathered we were unsuitable. No contract was offered.

In November 1923, at Huntington Beach, we were doing our Russian playlet, a couple of sketches and a song medley, filling a bill with two 'movie-dramas' and four other acts at Maddison's, a little beach-front vaudeville theatre on the fringes of the 'entertainment strip'. Like several ocean-front villages in Southern California, Huntington Beach had become part resort, with the usual small hotels, fairgrounds, boardwalk sideshows, and part oil town. Very noticeable amongst the mixture of family groups, inebriated oilriggers, bored-looking old people and other seaside regulars, an expensively dressed but untidy man sat in the front row, transfixed by Mrs Cornelius. I admit I felt some jealousy. Ethel guessed he was a theatrical agent when he sat through both that day's performances but when he appeared backstage with a bunch of flowers I found vulgar in both colour and size, I remembered him. He, however, did not know me, perhaps because of my makeup. I was able to block his way before he got into our dressing-room. He was apologetic, even humble. His huge greying bulk (he was not yet forty) trembled in its loose suit as he blubbered how he would dearly love to make the acquaintance of Mrs Cornelius and express his sincere admiration for her acting. I had met him in Atlanta, at the Klankrest party. John 'Mucker' Hever, the oil engineer, sweating a little in the heat, somewhat fatter than before, would probably not have recalled me in any event. His eyes were full of Mrs Cornelius. His mouth was full of her. He was completely smitten. I did my best to get rid of him as quickly as I could. The last thing I wanted was for my alias and whereabouts to be passed on to the Klan. I was equally frightened that the Klan's enemies might find me. Furthermore I did not think he was an appropriate suitor for Mrs Cornelius. I took his bouquet and his card and sent him away. I gave the flowers to Mrs Cornelius, but I kept the card. I told her I had no idea who they were from. Next day, however, he was back again, with roses and gardenias, more demands for an introduction. To my dismay I had to cope with him each evening for an entire week. At least I protected Mrs Cornelius from him. I was relieved when we were on the road again, moving down the coast to San Diego. The huge white-topped breakers of the Pacific, the palms and the yellow beaches soon took my mind off 'Mucker', his ludicrous passion and my dismay at encountering this unexpected reviver of my previous persona.

While we played the little mock-Spanish theatres near the border, life became increasingly easy. We even had a few dollars in our cash box. I often wondered what it would have been like for me had I chosen to remain an actor. Probably I should have soon grown restless, like John Wayne or Frank Sinatra, and returned to politics. It is fashionable these days to mock Governor Reagan's ambitions, but who can say if his natural talents would have been allowed to develop had he not taken his opportunities where he could, donning the stetson and six-gun as a champion of old virtue? He was a successful actor because he believed in his lines. Surely that is also the mark of a successful politician? The point, I would think, is not that you play a part, but that you choose which part you want.

Through the rest of 1923 and into 1924 we continually found enough work to keep body and soul together. We became polished enough to refuse the poorer bookings. Now we appeared only in permanent theatre buildings, and once or twice reached the top of the bill. Life was good. We did not overly mourn Warren Harding when he died (another victim of the Black Pope). Calvin Coolidge seemed a man of great commonsense. Our circumstances remained unchanged. For a short while the news of Lenin's death in January 1924 brought a mild hope I might see my mother again. Nothing improved. In England the Bolsheviks increased their influence when the socialists under Ramsay MacDonald seized power. Carthage was making steady gains, but I could not see it. I scarcely cared. I agreed with Mrs Cornelius who said one morning after reading the item about Hitler's Munich failure, 'we're well art of it orl, if yer arsk me, Ivan!'

Only in Italy was there any chance of political stability. In Russia, the Bolsheviks actually tightened their grip. It became clear that Lenin had been a restraining influence on the Oriental elements now apparently in power. In April 1924, at Mrs Cornelius's insistence but against my better judgment (though I looked forward to city life again) we returned to Stranoff's in San Francisco. They had offered us triple their old rate. We could not afford to refuse. The place was a little more decrepit but otherwise unchanged. Mrs Cornelius even found a piece of chewing-gum where she had stuck it on her last visit. We were doing *White Knight and Red Queen* as part of a bill including Douglas Fairbanks's *Mark of Zorro* and Rudolf Valentino's *The Four Horsemen of the Apocalypse*. On our second evening Harry Galiano arrived in my dressing-room. He was full of good cheer and with a broad grin pumped my hand. 'Hey,' he said, 'you're doin' great!' He had brought me a letter. It had arrived earlier, in care of Mr Vince Potter at the North Beach address. 'From Italy,' said Harry. I reached out for it. I trembled. This letter was to bring a significant change in my life and remind me of my duty, my *Lebensplan*, my original course. Before I could open it Harry removed his hat somewhat awkwardly and told me with controlled sadness that Vince had been treacherously murdered about a week before the letter arrived. Harry knew Vince would have wanted to be sure I got it. I asked if he knew who killed his boss. Harry assured me with quiet confidence that justice would soon be done. He apologised for his poor manners. If there had been time to find me he would have invited me to the funeral, since I was 'almost a relative.' I was surprised to hear Vince had followed my career with close interest. 'We come to see you one night when you was outside Eureka some place. But we only caught half the show on account we was heading for Weaverville. We thought you was swell. Very classy. Vince was thinking about hiring you for the club. He was one of the sweetest guys in the world. But too soft, you know, for his own good. This letter come inside one from his cousin Annibale. I kept an eye on the posters, you know, and the *Examiner*, saw the show was in town. And here we are.' The envelope was creased and crumpled, as if it had been thrown away and then recovered. I scarcely dared open it. Harry grinned. 'That reminds me. You been writing bum checks, Matt?'

'What on earth do you mean?'

'Maybe you heard of somebody called Callahan? He's looking for you. Or, anyway, Pallenberg. It's to do with a check. That's all I know.'

'You've seen Callahan?'

'No. This came down the grapevine.'

'He's from the Justice Department.'

'Bad hockey,' said Harry. 'There ain't much you can do to a Fed.'

'And you've heard nothing more?'

'You think I should put the word out? Wise you to anything that comes in?'

'It could do no harm, Harry.'

'Sure.' Harry gave my arm a friendly punch. 'Stay in touch, eh? We got plans, same as Vince, to go into the entertainment side more. We'd rather give the work to an old friend.'

I thanked him, assuring him I would contact him again, even if I heard nothing more about Callahan. Although not handsome, Harry possessed the natural poise of a Renaissance Medici gallant. He was to put rum-running behind him in later years and turn, as he had predicted, to show business and leisure activities in Las Vegas. The last I heard, he was still alive and in excellent health.

The letter, of course, was from Esmé. I still have it, but if I did not I could quote it in full. *Sie war es. Ich gebe all mein Weltstadten weg; aber ich gabe nicht alle meine Briefe.* Her childish hand, her misspellings, her unconscious drifting from one language into another, revived all those profound feelings I had shut away when I left her in Paris. I had always known a reasonable explanation would emerge. At last I was to discover why she had failed to communicate or follow me to America. *Māyñ shvester, mayn froy!* She had only, she wrote, recently received any of my letters. Almost immediately after I left Paris she had decided to live alone since Kolya's wife Anäis seemed displeased by her presence. Kolya had kindly helped her find a flat. For a while she had worked as a receptionist in the office of one of Kolya's business friends. Then something had cropped up. She was vague. 'A stupid, pointless argument,' she said. She left that job to work as a waitress in a night club. Then, unable to stand the advances of the customers, she had luckily bumped into Annibale Santucci one day. Santucci was sympathetic, offering his friendship and protection. Knowing she was my fiancée the Italian had behaved honourably and so she returned to Rome with him. There she lived with his cousin, a lady of Christian convictions, eventually finding a job as a hostess in a club. She worked and saved hard to get the fare to America. She had written me, but the letters were returned. Nobody knew my address. Unfortunately, just as she had enough money for a ticket, it had been stolen from her by the woman who shared her flat. As a consequence the police had arrested her for vagrancy (it was much harder nowadays to get along in Rome). Finally, meeting Annibale again, she had seen my last letters to him and at once wrote to this, my most recent address. She was longing to see me, was delighted I was doing well in America; she would be there with me now save for her lack of money. She had a genuine Italian passport, thanks to Annibale's government friends, but to come to

America she would need 'dollars' from me. Could I send word as soon as possible? She gave the address of an hotel near Tivoli where she was registered as Signora Sylvana Rastelli. This was also the name on her passport. She hoped I still wanted to get married. She had been a good girl. *Mayn freydik, mayn gut bubeleh!* She loved me faithfully and her heart had broken the moment we parted. *Wann kommen Sie wieder?*

I was, of course, overjoyed. I was so proud my little girl had managed to look after herself sensibly for the years we had been separated. In my elation I scarcely considered Harry's news about Callahan. *Mayn froy. Sie fährt morgen!* I showed the letter to Mrs Cornelius. She read it carefully, first with pursed lips and a frown, then with a peculiar smile. Naturally I had completely failed to realise how ordinary female jealousy can distort the most objective information. Mrs Cornelius was typical in this respect. She spoke with flat significance. 'Ya gonna send 'er ther cash, then, are yer, Ivan?'

'That's the problem. I haven't anything like the amount she needs. And I'd have trouble getting more. Of course she must have a first-class ticket.'

'Better write an' let 'er know yer carn't afford it, then, 'adn't yer?'

'I can't do that, Mrs Cornelius.' I was surprised at her. 'Esmé is my betrothed. We intend to be married. I left her behind only because she had no passport.'

'Got one easy enough nar, ain't she.'

'Italian. Not French. Can you imagine what she must have gone through? She hardly mentions it. She can't bear to. I knew Kolya wouldn't let her down. It was that bourgeoise Anaïs. I always found her a snob. The wicked bitch! Thank God, though, for Annibale's generosity. I owe him a great deal. He's been a true friend to us both.'

'I'm sure.' Her rivalry was patent. 'An' she's bin a perfec' lady, a bleedin' nun. Keepin' 'erself by the sweat of 'er brow while stayin' pure an' untouched fer 'er 'usband ter be. Makes yer weep.' She was pitying. 'Yore ther softest touch on earf, Ive, for orl yer 'orrible ways. If y've got an ounce o' sense y'll tear that bleedin' letter up an' 'ave done wiv it.'

Of course I ignored her. She meant well, as she had in Constantinople. But she had not met Esmé. Once I introduced my girl, everything would become clear. I became obsessed with the problem of raising the money. Mrs Cornelius pulled herself together. I think she realised what profound forces were at work. She offered no more negative advice. It was, she admitted, my own life. All she asked was that I spend my own, not the company's money. She should not have feared. I possessed my usual means of earning honest cash. What I had to find quickly was a backer for my patents. Happily I was in the perfect area. Los Angeles and San Francisco, not to mention the five hundred miles between, had attracted several newer fortunes, such as Hughes' and Davenport's; many big industries were based in the State. But I had no idea whom to approach, nor how best to begin. My circumstances meant I could not contact Washington or any old Klan associates and Harry Galiano's news of Callahan alarmed me. I did not dare cash a further check. I had to be more than usually circumspect about anyone whose financial assistance I sought. The patents were in my own name. I required a sympathetic ear and absolute discretion as well as an enthusiastic chequebook.

I had to offer my patents, therefore, to someone willing to keep a secret until I cleared my name and became officially resident in the USA. Harry Galiano evidently was not yet interested in industrial expansion. He might, however, have friends who were. Similarly most film people were notoriously wary of investing in anything speculative, save movies. I went on stage in a daze, my lines and gestures performed completely automatically. I considered a mental list of firms: Gilmore, Curtiss, Lockheed, Douglas, Studebaker, Martin and so on. Most were exploring some field of aviation. For the moment I had no faith in dirigibles or aeroplanes and did not particularly want to be associated with them. They had brought me too much ill-fortune. Oil was my next thought. I had detailed specifications prepared of my gas-powered car, a machine designed to make use of oil well by-products or even sewage waste. It would be cheaper to run than a conventional petrol-fuelled vehicle. The only serious technical problem lay in the storing and accurate valving of the gas. It was less stable than petroleum. To counter this I had invented a new type of cylinder (and, incidentally, the method of safety ignition still used today). Everyone knew the expense of refining Californian crude oil and realised it must eventually run out. Gas was cheaper to process. Unlike petrol it could be artificially manufactured. It seemed inevitable that my gas car, even perhaps my dynamite car, must in time replace the conventional automobile. Together with these designs I had a suction pumping method and a rapid refining process both of which would radically reduce well maintenance costs and produce a million barrels a day for every current thousand. By the time we finished that evening's performance, I was certain I should soon possess more than enough money.

I went from the theatre to the nearest Western Union office and cabled Esmé: I had received her letter, noted the contents and a ticket would shortly follow. I returned to our digs, having celebrated thoroughly in a low-priced gin joint I knew, at about three in the morning. I was staying at *Mulvaney's Apartments* on Jones Street, not very far from the theatre. It had a fancy glass door, reinforced with wire mesh; the desk was in the vestibule between this and a similar door some five feet further along. As I picked up my key from the Japanese night porter, he whispered something to me. I thought he was asking if I wanted a woman (it is a standard question from night porters at that time in the morning). I told him no. On the other side of the second glass door a slender figure was rising from where it had been sitting on the stairs. I grew alarmed at first, thinking it must be Brodmann. But this man was much taller. I went through the second door and turned up the gas in the hall. Smiling uncertainly, his hands deep in the pockets of his raincoat, Officer Callahan seemed apologetic. I did not care why. With Esmé so close, it now appeared I was to be locked away from her. I had no visa, false papers. I would spend time in a Federal jail, then be deported. It was about the best I could hope for.

'I suppose I'm speaking to Mr Pallenberg,' said Callahan.

I did not reply. I stood staring at him, almost tempted to kill him. I was desperate. I could not be separated any longer from my girl; it would be an outrage.

'Well,' Callahan looked away from me, 'where do you care to do this, sir?'

I took him up the flight of stairs and unlocked the door to my room. He waited for me to enter, then he followed me in. After I lit the globe I glanced quickly around to make sure I had left none of my cocaine in view. It was hidden, but if he decided to search my luggage he would find it easily. I wiped my moist forehead.

'You know your money's frozen, do you, sir?' The Irishman lowered his eyes towards the bed. It was unmade. He reached down and pulled the threadbare coverlet up, then seated himself, unbuttoning his raincoat and drawing out the same notebook he had used on the train. 'We noticed you haven't used the account. Besides that one check.'

'I suppose it was my only mistake,' I said.

'Maybe. You didn't do yourself much good blowing Walker without paying your hotel bill.'

I was not sure how much I should tell him. In a similar situation, with the Cheka in Russia, I had learned all information is worth hoarding. I waited to see if he would reveal anything else.

'That was a pointless, petty crime,' he said. 'Up until then you'd kept your nose clean, at least as far as we had evidence. You could be charged for it.'

When I still remained silent, he went on: 'And now you've changed your name, plainly to remain here illegally, since you've made no attempt to renew your visa.'

'Is that it?'

He sighed. 'A good lawyer could keep you in the country for a few months, maybe longer. Plainly you prefer it here. Is there something in Europe you'd maybe like to forget?' He looked up at me from ambiguous, Catholic eyes. Suddenly I realised he was very probably a failed priest.

'Can you help me?' I said. My mouth was dry. I was trembling. Deliberately I let him see how nervous I was.

'Help's what I wanted to offer last year.' I watched him grow slowly into his rôle. 'We're not ghouls. And we don't always go by the book. What happened?'

'I was frightened, Mr Callahan.' Seating myself on the other side of the bed, I did not look at him directly. I tried to imagine a confessional grille between us. 'My life was threatened.'

'Who by?' His voice grew softer. 'Can you say'

'I had no clear idea what the Ku Klux Klan was when I arrived. I love America. They offered me a speaking circuit. It seemed an ideal means of earning a living while I toured your country. I never planned to stay here forever. By the time I realised what the Klan actually was, I was deeply enmeshed. Nothing specific, but I knew it would be unwise to anger them.'

'I guessed as much.' He sighed. 'Go on.'

I had no choice but to encourage this mockery of religious ritual, to paint him a picture of my terror, of Klan threats, of my attempts to get out and finally, after I had talked to him on the train, my decision to refuse any further lecture engagements. Whereupon Mrs Mawgan had turned me over to the organisation's bully-boys. They had beaten me, left me for dead. It was the Klan, not the Justice Department, I had hidden from. Certainly I had no wish to return to Europe. I had done nothing wrong. I had fought the Bolsheviks in Russia. I had been instrumental in getting hundreds, possibly thousands, to safety through Odessa. The Chekist Commissar Brodmann had been specifically commissioned to hunt me down. I got up to open the closet containing my clothes. One of my Russian uniforms hung there. 'Those decorations were honourably won,' I told him. I explained how I had flown against the Reds, how I had crashed and almost drowned. Yet Brodmann had searched me out until I was forced to flee Odessa, returning to France, my birthplace. There I had been the victim of a Chekist conspiracy. I had come to America hoping I might eventually be forgotten. If I went back now I would probably be going to my death. I had worked for the Klan because I thought they were anti-Bolshevik. I had not realised their own revolutionary ambitions.

Now Callahan was nodding rapidly, still making his notes. His 'Go on' was automatic. He was a monument of pious sympathy. 'That's it, Mr Callahan. There's no more, save a few details. I believe the Klan and the Cheka are still hunting me. If you succeeded, then they too must soon find me. I suppose I'm as good as dead.'

He shook his head adamantly. 'Only the Justice Department could investigate your bank accounts. You should bear in mind it's our job to protect people, as well. Why didn't you come to me? I had a notion you were innocent. I gave you my card.'

'I thought you had finished your enquiry. I could not believe I had done anything criminal. But Bessy said you'd jail me.'

'Mr Whiskers wasn't interested in you. He wanted to get the dope on Bessy Mawgan, enough to send her down for a long stretch. We're pretty sure she was the Klan fronter for half a dozen side rackets.' He paused. 'Including narcotics,' he said. 'Prostitution. You name it. She and Clarke and that other woman, Tyler, moved in on a fairly small-time gyp. They turned the Klan into big bucks. But Mawgan had the weight as well as the pedigree. Her old man went to the chair for a double burn down in Toledo. We were pretty certain he was her fall guy. Did you have any idea of that?'

'None.'

'That was my hunch. You, I could get through to. You were an amateur. But she was an old campaigner. She was spreading the slush money. She was delivering the chippies and practically anything else, from gazoonies to moonshine, to darned near every official and politician in the country willing to take a squeeze. So, we need to have the goods on her if we want her to sing.' He paused. 'That's why I'm willing to do a deal with you, Mr Pallenberg.'

'You want information from me?' I had none worth the name. Mrs Mawgan had always kept her other business affairs secret. He took my hesitation for fear, or possibly loyalty.

'She put you on the spot. Why shouldn't you tip her up? If you're worried about recriminations, I'll guarantee you'll never have to take the stand. We'll cover you all ways. And you can go on doing whatever it is you're doing now. Anything you like, once you've whistled the whole tune and put your signature at the bottom.'

I saw a chance of immediately saving Esmé. 'What about the money in my banks?' I asked. 'Will you release that?'

'Can't. On account of the order we used. It's recorded as suspected criminal profits. When Mrs Mawgan takes a fall, or better still when all the crooks she was slipping the squeeze to are in the slammer, we'll be able to do something about that. Meanwhile we prefer to know where you are. As our secret witness, we don't want you leaving the country. You get an automatic "indefinite stay." All you have to do is finger the floozy who put the spot on you. If you won't, it's hello Russia.'

I was convinced. It seemed I could gain my freedom, but disappointingly still had to find money for Esmé's fare. I decided, in the interests of justice and for the sake of those I loved, to make a statement. I felt like a rat, but I had no choice. I talked into the night, dearly wishing I could get to my cocaine to keep my thoughts in order. I mentioned every name which came back to me. I made it clear that Major Sinclair was an idealist. Prompted by my Confessor I invented orgies, murders, perversion and pay-offs. Some I did not know by name, I said, but I gathered they were big wheels in Washington. I excelled myself as an inventor. George Callahan was almost crooning with joy by the time I took the fountain pen from his hand and signed myself Max Peterson on the last page. 'That's peachy,' he murmured in his strange Irish accent. 'That's peachy, Mr Peterson.' He closed the book. 'Now, so long as you haven't pattered me, we're in business. All we have to do is locate Mrs Mawgan, get her lagged and tagged on the strength of this little brief and we can start going against the politicians we're really after. I'm much obliged. You might not understand, or care, but you've performed an important public service this night.' He was virtually rubbing his hands.

'I do realise it, Mr Callahan. I've no desire to associate with criminals. Had I been a degree more *au fait* with your country I should not
be in this position.'

'For my part, Mr Peterson, I'm mighty grateful.' There was a gleeful
smirk on his thin, monkish face which he could not quite erase. As he
left, he handed me a fresh card. 'If you're in any sort of a scrape, call
that number and ask for George Callahan.'

'Will the Klan be out for blood now, Mr Callahan?' I knew I had sac-
rificed a great deal in order to be united with my Esmé. The beating
outside Walker would be nothing to the ferocious tortures for which the
Klan were famous. A *good friend, but an implacable enemy*, as Eddy
Clarke had said. At least he was in jail, though he did not deserve to be.
He would have understood my position. Indeed, if he had not been betrayed, I should not have been troubled by the Justice Department,
Brodmann or this urgent need to raise money for Esmé's ticket. Mrs
Mawgan, on the other hand, had earned whatever came to her. No one
would ever accuse me of betraying her. She had fled Walker, leaving
me to the renegade Klansmen. Even then, given a choice, I would not
have brought witness against her. But any rational person would agree
that if a woman had to be sacrificed it should rightly be Mrs Mawgan.
Esmé was in need of help. My innocent sister, my daughter, my love!
Oh, how I would pile roses on her bed. *Schönen roten rosen for meyn
freydik froy! Moja siostra rózy. Meyn gelihte!* She will save me from this
groylik gadles! She will restore the truth. With her beside me, my cities
shall take to the air again. No enemies shall I fear. *Die Freunde sink ge-
kommen und die Feinde entkommen!*

Mrs Cornelius sitzt am Steuer. She could see I had not slept.
Though she hated driving, feeling she somehow lost face by doing so,
she took over when we left town next morning, bound for Hollister.
She was an inexpert, if lordly, motorist, with her fringed green satin up
to her thighs and her powerful muscles flexing as she manipulated the
van towards the highway, cursing continuously. She paused long
enough to ask me, almost sympathetically, if I had been frightened by
something. Then I told her of my visit from the Federal officer. 'Blimey,' she said, 'we c'd orl be in jug. Me an' the free girls're illegal too,
ain't we?'

'Only until I can make a phone call. This man trusts me. I was able
to assist the State on a matter of grave national importance.'

'Wot ther fuck've ya bin up ter, nar, Ive!' She gave the wheel an exasperated wrench. 'Ya little bleedin' judas!' She laughed heartily. 'Nar, don' tell me! I didn't arsk!' I laughed with her. I could now almost always tell when she was joking.

I sent Esmé another telegram from Hollister and phoned my new friend Callahan. He was not in the office. I was given another number to call. It was long-distance to New York. He had not yet arrived. I would remember, in a day or so, to telephone again and ensure Mrs Cornelius's legality. *Der Hund verfolgte der Hase.* Already he was on the trail. We played the Berberich Theater that evening and my performance, while less abstracted than the earlier one, was again poor. The audience was noticeably restless. Mrs Cornelius kicked me twice, surreptitiously. As we came off she hissed, 'If yore gonna keep changing me name from Rosa to Esmé I don't care. But bleedin' make it one or the uvver. They were beginnin' ter fink it wos a bleedin' comedy tonight.' I apologised. I said she must understand how I was feeling. 'Too well, Ivan,' she said savagely. 'Too bloody well!'

Soon I was spending all my free time studying specialist magazines, looking for likely investors. Callahan's guarantees, when I considered them, were not watertight. It would still be foolish of me to reveal myself as Max Peterson. The Klan, I remembered, had powerful financial support from the great farming alliances of the West Coast. Doubtless industry had similar links. I made a considerable effort to play my parts with full attention, but I was growing increasingly abstracted. Every day I failed at raising the money was a betrayal of my little girl's hopes. In Fresno Mrs Cornelius suddenly refused to continue the play and sang her songs instead. She would not speak to me for a whole day afterwards. Time was running out. I did not have a single reply to my circulars. Esmé would believe I no longer loved her. From Mojave, where we did three shows of *White Knight and Red Queen* a day, I sent my rose a cable assuring her all problems were being overcome. Under the benevolent sun of Southern California, I drove our little truck along the white highway, beside the sea. I saw only her. Already I imagined how delighted my beautiful child-wife would be. She would sit beside me, holding my arm, marvelling at undreamed-of natural luxury. I would again be doing my work as a scientist. We should be respected all over America, hobnobbing with the great and the famous. But this image only served to bring me closer to panic. I could lose it all. I had to find financial support. Sooner or later, when Callahan caught up with Mrs Mawgan, I would be in danger of my life. I had to act with reasonable speed. The one thing I had not told Callahan was where I guessed Mrs Mawgan to be hiding. That information was too valuable to throw in with the rest. She would have changed her name. She might be running a fresh operation. I knew therefore it could be a few months before Callahan would run my ex-mistress to earth. In those months I planned to make some money, bring Esmé to America, marry her and then escape to Buenos Aires, where engineers were in short supply, but where wealthy people willingly invested in schemes likely to add to the Argentine's prestige. Moreover, many Russian émigrés were already there, supplying their military experience and skills to the government. Nothing of this could come true, I reminded myself, unless I quickly found what we in the theatrical profession called 'an angel.'

We stopped for a late lunch at a little mobile hot-dog stand alone on the beach. Mrs Cornelius drew me aside. 'Yore lookin' orl dizzy, Ivan. I'm gonna say it once more an' thass that. Ferget 'er!'

I smiled graciously at my old friend. 'Can you forget perfection, my dear, good Mrs Cornelius? When the girl you've longed for all your life, who you thought forever lost, is by a miracle returned to you, not once but twice, it's hardly a casual affair. I mourned my Esmé for five years. I have sworn I shall never mourn her again.'

To her eternal shame (she apologised only three weeks ago in *The Elgin*), Mrs Cornelius answered this with one of her many new American expletives. It did not touch me, then. I knew in my heart she, whose instincts were normally so good, feared she must soon be parted from me. I could have reassured her, if she had listened. I loved her, as I would always love her. But Esmé possessed me. I looked up as a motor launch, shrieking like a bleeding sow, came in close to the shore, then swerved hard against the surf to squeal out towards the horizon again. There were two men standing upright in the launch. One had the wheel. The other was studying the beach through a pair of binoculars. I wondered again how much of the truth Callahan had told me. I had forgotten to question his links with Brodmann. Certainly, he had never contradicted my contention that the Cheka remained on my trail. I was sure the man with the glasses was Brodmann. Mrs Cornelius thought I was merely exhibiting pique as I hurried her and the others, who as usual giggled like children, back to the van.

Just before sunset next day, we arrived in Santa Monica where I again cabled Esmé my whereabouts, swearing a first-class boat ticket would soon be hers. I was becoming so desperate I thought of selling the van until I remembered my promise to Mrs Cornelius. It was not in me to sink to such depths. We planned to establish ourselves at Huntington Beach for at least a week and do our usual circuit of the nearby seaside resorts. It was close enough to Los Angeles for me to plan the area as a base from which to approach potential 'angels.' By the next morning I had written another two dozen more or less identical letters and would mail them at my first opportunity. I was trying to will Esmé, six thousand miles away in Rome, to trust me and not to lose heart. I checked sailing times, discovering several ships leaving from Genoa in the coming month. My next telegram listed these ships and dates, asking her to choose which she would prefer. That, at least, would assure my child I remained sincere. I would never let her down, *mayn shvester, mayn sibe!*

That afternoon we did the first of our matinees at *Maddison's Famous Vaudeville Theater* on the noisy, carefree boardwalk. The theatre looked out towards the big concrete fishing mole and the sandy beach. This resort was so characteristically Californian I had grown to love her. In spirit at least she reminded me of old Odessa, of her more vulgar suburbs along the coast, where brass bands played and carousels turned, in Fountain and Arcadia. From her cliffs, crooked wooden stairways wound down to beaches where huge mountains of water flung up their spray and the breakers rolled all the way from the horizon. Here were parties of bathers, older people sunning themselves, picnickers under bright umbrellas, less than a stone's throw from a score of massive, full-sized oil derricks marching unchecked from cliffs to ocean. This forest flanked Huntington Beach on two sides. Here was the source of wealth and the means of squandering it rolled into one community. Amusement arcades, fun fairs, rickety nickelodeons, cotton candy stalls, magazine stands, ferris wheels, roller coasters, pleasure boats, many in primary colours made even more dazzling by the steady Pacific glare, contrasted with the twinkling blue of the ocean and an infinity of perfect sky. Sometimes an aeroplane flew over, just missing the roller coaster. The plane gave joyrides to excited grandparents, frozen-faced children, terrified oilmen and their happy girls, serious youths. Sometimes speed boats would howl and ululate on the water, reaping a watery furrow, marked by a wound of white foam. And all the while the oil pumps rose and fell, solid old beam-engines like gigantic feasting swamp fowl. Coupled with the towering lattices of the rigs, they made a scene from H. G. Wells, with Martians invading from the ocean depths, looking with baffled curiosity on the careless, festive crowd which simply characterised them as a not very interesting novelty. *Alas, unconscious of their doom, the little foxes play*, as Mrs Cornelius's swindler friend, the Bishop, would always remark as he finished his fifth pint in *The Blenheim Arms* on a Friday night (it was before he was committed to an Old Folks Home near Littlehampton). Unlike Europe, America has never been ashamed of the sources of her prosperity, unless, ironically, they lie in brewing, distilling or cereal crops. Some years ago I met a Mr Schlitz. I believe the young man was attending university over here. He confided to me he did not mind in the least that his ancestral brewmasters had made Milwaukee famous; what he objected to was that their beer on his name, as it were, embarrassed him 'all to hell'.

Greater Los Angeles, her earlier adobe and wooden Gothic now overshadowed by skyscrapers modelled on sixteenth-century haciendas, her blazing stucco flanked by enormous imported palms, from Africa and Australia, shading the parameters of implacable boulevards, now fills four thousand square miles. She is truly the *Zukunft Kaiserstadt Imperye Yishov fun tsukunft!* The Emperor City of the Future. And at her core history converges, coalesces, transmutes, reforms; not in the cool serenity of her City Hall, twenty-five storeys of splendid white Sumerian cement, not on the site of Yang-Na, *mestizo* Carthaginian outpost destroyed by internecine wars of her Catholic soldier-priests; not in her tar pits or observatories, her museums and universities; not even in her fantastic cults which have made of reality a globe filled with quicksilver. The core of Greater L.A. is where Vine Street crosses Hollywood Boulevard, that unremarkable collection of office blocks, shops and cinemas. Daily, when I was young, this intersection and the surrounding area might fill with Roman Centurions, Spanish religious processions, convoys of Indian elephants bearing great howdahs from which drifted clouds of multicoloured silk; the armies of Norman France and Anglo-Saxon England, of Catherine the Great and Bismarck and Napoleon; the mob of the Paris streets in 1793 and the fighting Cossacks of Stenka Razin; the Royal Progress of the first Ming Emperor; Cowboys, Indians, Comic Police; the very failure of 'authenticity' is a sign that here was America's true melting-pot. It was a melting-pot of Time. Of cultures. A million points of view like the infinite facets of some unstable gem. The Yellow and Red Cars come and go in their electric confidence; lines of power and communication strengthen Hollywood's already complicated aesthetic. Etiolated Tahitian palms wave in an unlikely breeze next to the cypresses of ancient Jordan, the oaks of England and the poplars of the Rhône; all washed to pastels by her misty light. This same light lends shivering magic to her hills, as if, when we step beyond a certain *umbakant* frontier, we will find ourselves elsewhere in Time, possibly Space, too, and Hollywood vanished behind us: a whisper in the distant skies, a faint scent of coffee, paint and freshly sawn wood. She, above all, is still free. She is the perfect model of my *flitshtot*, my promise of hope. To her majesty, those beach towns were boisterous tumblers, summoned for her entertainment; save for Long Beach, a resentful, hard-working *boyar*, forever predicting the capital's unrealised doom.

Mrs Cornelius, Mabel, Ethel, Mr Harry Hope and myself (our Brooklyn Indian had been lost to some nameless drunk tank) were now in direct competition with the chugging pumps and rattling rigs, the calliopes of a dozen whirling rides, with barkers' shouts and the noisy excitement of the crowd itself; but we did not care. Here were the easy landscapes of childhood interludes and we felt, as always, that we had come home. I was now determined not to let Mrs Cornelius down. I put everything I had into my part. Never had a Cossack officer spoken in such thrilling fury, with such meaningful gestures, as I cried to the unseen hordes of Bolshevism encircling me: 'Back, you cowards! Before God, the Tsar and Holy Russia I swear I shall be revenged on some of you and send you to that Last Tribunal where a greater power than I shall judge and condemn you for your crimes!' (I was then saved by Mrs Cornelius, in her khaki tunic and tights, who had been convinced by my earlier arguments that the cause she had served was evil, cruel and destructive.) She responded marvellously; acting with boldness and flare. If Cecil B. DeMille had actually been in the audience he might have offered us contracts on the spot. From habit, I looked to see if John 'Mucker' Hever was in his usual place. He had deserted us. No flowers appeared backstage.

That evening, before we went on for our final performance, Mrs Cornelius remained in high spirits. She appreciated the effort I had made. She told me I could be a wonder when I wanted to be. She hoped I would stop making a fool of myself and maybe have a try at the East Coast theatres again. We could start in Atlantic City. I reminded her I might soon be sitting behind an engineer's desk but I promised not

to leave the company without fair notice. We heard our music beginning and virtually danced out onto the stage with our opening number
(*The Devil Came To Russia And The Devil Waved A Flag* to the tune
of *The Animals Went In Two By Two*). Again we had the audience cap-
tivated. We knew we were, as they say, 'flying.' It was not until Ethel
at the piano struck up our finale *The Hammer And The Sickle Can't
Crush Or Tear Our Hearts* to *Marching Through Georgia*) that I looked
for 'Mucker' Hever and saw instead, with arms folded across their
chests, five hooded Klansmen at the back of the hall. My mouth became instantly dry. I could scarcely croak out the remaining verse. My
legs were weak; my stomach felt as if a knife had pierced it. Mrs Cornelius was alarmed. 'Wot ther bloody 'ell's ther matter?' she whispered.
Then, as the audience whistled, stamped and applauded, the five
Klansmen began to clap. They clapped regularly, at a slightly slower
beat than the rest of the crowd and they continued to clap, increasing
the beat slightly, until one of them raised a clenched gauntlet above his
head. 'Death to the Three Jays! Death to Jew, Jap and Jesuit! Death to
the Alien Creed!' I had expected them to rush the stage and attempt to
carry me off. My first thought was that Callahan had betrayed me.
Now, unless they were playing a cat-and-mouse game with me, I believed those five sincere. Klansmen of the *Alte Kämpfer* who still clung
to the original ideals of the *Umzikhtbar Imperye*. We took two curtain
calls, which we had never done before. We bowed and waved. I
grinned like a puppeteer's idiot doll. When we came to take the third
call, the Knights of the Invisible Empire had vanished and the audience was filing from the little hall. 'I 'ope them bastards don't make a
reg'lar fing o' this.' Mrs Cornelius released my hand. 'They could
bleedin' lose us 'arf the 'ouse.' I had my own reasons for wishing them
gone. In the dressing-room she made me drink a tumbler of noxious
Mexican brandy. 'Yore sweatin' like a pig! Wot scared ya this time?
Them silly buggers in their nighties? Jes' a bunch o' overgrown kids
muckin' abart.' She chuckled. 'Didn't fink they wos real ghosts, did
yer?' She poured me another dark brown slug.

Beginning in the dressing-room we both got rather drunk, as we had
on the *Rio Cruz* so long ago, singing the Cockney songs which were
her real favourites but most of which were never appreciated in America. She revealed she had been 'almost sorry' when Lenin died. 'I
wosn't surprised 'e croaked so sudden. 'E wos a maniac fer work.' She
laughed. 'Anyfink ter stop worryin' abart real people. I must admit, my

Leon's ther same, but I fink 'e'll do a better job, if they give 'im ther chance. Not likely though, is it, 'im being' a yid?' Her prediction was surprisingly accurate. Within ten years, Stalin had cleansed his ruling committee of every single Jew. A Georgian returns always to his simple roots. We cannot be seduced as easily as your Moscow intellectual. I reminded Mrs Cornelius I had no personal or sentimental attachments to Bolsheviks. They were all bloody-handed mass murderers. Drug-besotted lunatics. She nodded her acquiescence, as if this was a fact everyone took for granted. 'Yeah.' She seemed to wait for me to enlarge on my theme, but I had said all there was to say. 'Oh, they're that orl right,' she said.

She sprawled against her tiny dressing-table, still in khaki and jackboots, nostalgically remembering how she and I first met in an Odessan dentist's surgery. Because of the drink she could not recall when she had next seen me. She was with Trotski's Red Army, I said. She had saved my life in Kiev. Put me on the train which, by chance, led me to Esmé. She smiled and patted my cheek. 'Wot a funny ol' pair' of bedfellows we are, eh?'

'Never quite,' I said.

This made her laugh.

Die Rosen wachsen nicht in den Himmel. Esmé, mayn fli umgenoyen ist. Bu vest komen. Hob nisht moyre. Vifl a zeyger fort op der shif keyn Nyu-York? Vifl is der zeyger? S'iz heys. Ikh red nit keyn Yiddish! IKH RED NIT KEYN YIDDISH! *Blaybn lebn . . . Mayn snop likht in beyn-hashmoshes . . . Es tut mir leyd. Esmé! Es tut mir leyd!*

Nekhtn in ovnt . . . Next day I once again gave my best as a performer. In our own eyes at least we had become a perfect stage union, the kind of romantic duet one now saw regularly on the screen. *White Knight and Red Queen* was almost real to us. The illusion was shared by our audience (ordinary people can, whatever cynics say, appreciate serious emotional drama) and it also served to decrease my by now habitual worrying about Esmé. I became, as a result, almost addicted to the part; looking forward to our shows as I never had before. A telegram from Tivoli told me the choice of ship was unimportant. The only problem was the fare. She loved me and was eager to see me again. Was I sure I wanted her there? *Ikh farshtey nit. Firt mikh tsu, ikh bet aykh, tsu di Heim. Khazart iber, zayt azoy gut.* I don't understand. I replied by return that the fare was on its way and I counted the hours until we were reunited.

It was at that evening show I noticed with dismay John 'Mucker' Hever back in his usual seat close to the stage, all but drooling in his infatuation for Mrs Cornelius. Yet I was in a way comforted to see him. Our performance was perfect. He must have given himself blisters on his palms, he clapped so hard. Like clockwork, Mr Hever arrived at the stage door in time to be blocked by me. Ritually, I accepted his expensive red and white roses and his ivory card. He was an eager, dewy-eyed boy, keener than ever, promising anything for an introduction to my co-star. She had never acted more brilliantly. She was an English Bernhardt. She was perfection itself. 'Please understand, sir, that I have never done this sort of thing before. I'm no stagedoor johnny. I'm in love, sir.' A thought came to him (rather late, in my view) 'My God! You're not her husband?'

I ran my thumb over the card's embossed lettering. 'Mrs Cornelius is a widow.' She was a little hazy on this herself.

I remembered how we had spent most of our time together talking about the cinema. He had shown great familiarity with Continental films. He was speaking with tearful enthusiasm of how she was fated to be recognised by the world of the silver screen. I told him I would pass on the wishes and the roses. He apologised for missing our earlier shows. 'I have just acquired an interest in a movie business. If it is of any use to you, I will put everything at your disposal.' It was ironic that this was the 'angel' I had prayed for only a few weeks earlier. Now, in that City of Angels, not one engineering firm had answered my letters. It came into my mind that I should easily demand a bribe for taking him to Mrs Cornelius's dressing-room. How else, short of direct theft, was I to keep my word to Esmé? But only a fool would carry the price of a first-class boat ticket on his person. I had the impression that, no matter how besotted he was, Mr Hever possessed a profound sense of the value of money. I brightened, however, for it had been bothering me how Mrs Cornelius would survive without my management. I did not know if his interest was a share in the local flea pit or fifty percent of Fox, but I was not impolite as I turned him away. I could feel a certain sympathy for a man in the grip of an obsession. I told him to return after our matinée tomorrow, when I hoped to have an answer for him. He was disgusting in his gratitude.

This time I gave Mrs Cornelius his card. 'I think I've made you a useful contact. He could be the help you need getting a job in pictures.'

She shook her head. 'Never 'eard of 'im.' By now she had a mental list of all the important Hollywood names.

'You shouldn't discount Hever completely. He's only just come to the business. I do know he's keen. He might be prepared to underwrite a more elaborate show, at any rate. We could make some substantial money for once.'

She winked at me. 'Somefink in it for you, Ivan?' She would bear what I said in mind. 'But you know me rule: "Don't sell cheap what don't cost yer nuffink" and "Keep yer 'and on yer investments."'

I was offended. 'I'm merely suggesting you agree to see him. He's a pleasant enough fellow. I'm not asking you to prostitute yourself!'

'It's me I don't trust, prob'bly,' she said. 'Ther smell o' gelt does funny fings ter me insides.'

I had decided I must raise what I could on my Georgian flintlocks. They were all I had left of any real value and the *nouveaux riches* of Los Angeles were rumoured to pay exaggerated prices for what were now being called 'genuine' antiques. I mentioned this to Mrs Cornelius. She shrugged. 'Seems a waste. Yore fond o' them in yer fashion. Sort o' mascots, in't they? I bet they bin up a few Jew's arses over ther years. Do wot yer like, I s'pose.' She remained unhelpful. My other alternative was to go to a loan company and see if I could raise money with the show as security. There would be no need for anyone else to know about it, since, according to the scrap of paper we had signed, my $500 had bought me 'exclusive rights.' I was now in a state of mixed panic, anger, disappointment and sheer misery. I longed for my Esmé. It would be virtual suicide to let her down and lose her as a result. It would be like murdering a child. *Wie heisst dieses Lied.*

Twenty-One

MY ACTING CONTINUED to improve almost in direct proportion to my sadness and desperation. During that brief period of my life I was greater than any Barrymore. Before long we would have been snapped up. I was grateful, however, for every show we did which lacked the approving presence of the Klan! It would take only one man to recognise me and I might easily find myself invited to a night ride. I had seen what happened to traitors. They stapled your testicles to a tree, lit a fire under them and handed you a knife with the command to 'Cut or burn.' I had felt as sick only in the Ukraine, where similar brutes had passed their leisure skinning youths alive or roasting babies on sheets of corrugated iron. They were the guards in Auschwitz, moreover. There is a kind of Ukrainian the rest of us disown.

As usual, late that afternoon, I discovered Mr Hever trembling and red-faced, almost drowning in his own seat, waiting for a word. I told him Mrs Cornelius valued her privacy more than anything. 'I can understand,' he said several times. Partly from curiosity, partly because I still had some notion I could borrow part of Esmé's fare from him, I drew him out on a variety of subjects. Did he travel much? Did he live permanently in California? Where did he live in the State? Did he have views on the political situation? It was odd to witness so much awkwardness in so large a man. With his prematurely greying hair and rather thin, stammering voice, his expression of furious despair almost demanded kindness. He had renounced travelling in favour of the telephone. He lived up in 'the hills' but still took the double-decker downtown to work every day. He was 'solid Republican,' he said, as his

520

father had been. He had spent most of his adult life in the State and in his view it was best served by the Republican Party. I found this, given his interest of only a couple of years before, the most illuminating thing he had said. It seemed to me he, like me, wished to be completely free of this new, *ersatz-Klann*, which had abandoned oratory in favour of the blackjack, the boot and the bullwhip. I was sympathetic. Nonetheless I could not resist the unworthy thought that if he one day remembered me from Atlanta, he might be even more embarrassed than I. Living here so long, I said, one must automatically become interested in the movie business. He shrugged, pointing out that movies were only 'a kind of hobby'. His real job had nothing at all to do with them. He was an engineer. I knew this, of course. 'In what field?' I was curious to see if he answered truthfully. 'Oil,' he said.

'You're employed by one of the big companies?'

'I guess so.' He was impatient to change the subject, to return to that of Mrs Cornelius. From a casual angler, however, I had suddenly become a game-fisherman. Here was someone who very likely could introduce me to an important executive! If I was careful, I might help Mrs Cornelius and at the same time help myself. It was regrettable I could no longer claim Klan connections, since we both were saying nothing of them. I had noticed, however, that he had been anxious to avoid the topic of politics. I wondered why. I considered what I should do next. It was all I could do to restrain myself from opening my document case under his nose. I longed to show him my plans. I knew that a professional engineer would be impressed by what many had been kind to call my genius. How could he expect a play-actor to be a brilliant scientist? It did not make sense. Why should a scientist choose to become a strolling thespian? There again, I thought, was it usual for oil-company engineers to squander their earnings on the movies? Perhaps he would understand. For all my optimism about his response, I decided to hang on to my secret a little longer. Instead I asked if there was some message I could take (with his hideous black and red carnations) to the object of his desire.

'If she would grant me my dearest wish,' he murmured without much hope, 'it would be that she accept my invitation for dinner tonight at the Hollywood Hotel.'

I kept a straight face and said I would see what I could do.

'Assure her my intentions are honourable!' He had grown more anxious by the second.

'She would take that for granted, Mr Hever.' I carried his blooms to the great actress's chamber. She began to interest herself in the flowers rather than what I had to say. "Ow ther bloody 'ell do they git 'em that colour, Ivan?'

I insisted she listen. He was a man of means, with excellent social connections. Some kind of silent partner in a movie studio. 'I advise you strongly, for both our sakes, to accept his invitation. The Hollywood Hotel is where all the important people dine. You've read the magazines. Aren't you curious God, I wish he was in love with me. I would jump at the chance!'

She laughed at this and her dawning anger dissipated. 'Ivan, I still fink your sellin' my body like any flashy littel pimp.'

'He insisted he had honourable intentions.'

'It's not the bloody fuckin', Ivan,' she said wearily. 'It's the bleedin' boredom I can't stand. Orl right, I'll go. This ain't normal, Ivan. If I even think o' goin' art ter supper wiv a chap yore usually poutin' orl over yer bleedin' face.'

'I'm thinking of your career.'

She sighed. 'I've got a feelin' I'll on'y find art wot yore up ter by seein' wot 'e 'as ter say! Wheel 'im in, an 'urry up abart it.' She primly arranged her kimono, picking at her Marcel waves with pink fingers. She had begun, quite unconsciously, to exude sexuality with such force it was as much as I could do to pull myself from the room, close the door, straighten my shoulders and walk slowly back towards the daylight and the looming, untidy, cow-eyed creature silhouetted in the exit.

'Mrs Cornelius presents her compliments,' I said. 'She would be glad to see you for five minutes, to discuss the possibility of her dining with you tonight.'

I all but carried the poor monster into the presence of his adored madonna. Mrs Cornelius was happy to let me remain during the interview. She plainly found Hever endearing and most of her grand manner had gone by the time she dismissed him. She said, with an affectionate smile, that she would meet him at the exit after our evening performance. He lurched away, almost taking the door frame with him. 'He's sweet,' she said. 'Wot d'yer want me ter do tonight? Pick 'is pocket?'

'Of course not. Merely mention the fact that I am a qualified engineer, that I have patents on a number of practical inventions for saving money in the oil business, that I was educated in St Petersburg and have worked with important companies in France, Memphis . . .'

She raised a plump hand. "Ang on, Ive, fer Gawd's sake. I can't remember the 'ole CV. Ya fink 'e can do yer some good, right?'

'He must have connections with the important oil men. All I ask is an early introduction.'

'You sure that's it?'

'I swear!'

She raised her eyebrows. 'Okey-dokey, if yer say so. Yore schemes ain't usually that simple. What we do fer bloody love!'

Once again that night I gave her my all. She responded with magnificent acting. 'Mucker' sat doubled up in his seat, squirming with admiration, ecstatic in the knowledge that his dream would soon come true. We took three curtain calls (this time without the aid of the Klan) and came off in a mood of cheerful elation. 'Yore reely pullin' the stops art, Ivan. I got ter admit I don't mind doin' this fer ya, as it 'appens. A favour fer a favour, I orlways say.' She was dressed specially for the high-class restaurant, in one of her hats. This was primarily of green and yellow satin. Her dress was midnight blue with lighter blue beading at throat, arms and knee. Her yellow shoes were a close match to her hat. 'Wot d'yer fink, Ive?' She admired herself. 'A stunner, if it's me as sez so!' She took a deep breath, which threatened the security of her chest. "Ere goes, then. See yer later, I 'ope.' She placed her hand on her hip in parody of a modern fashion model, picked up her jet and chrome beaded bag, and waltzed off to keep her date.

I became agitated almost as soon as she had left. I kept crossing my fingers, then uncrossing them because I felt foolish. I thought I would go mad simply waiting for her report, so I went into the next room where Mabel and Ethel were pulling on their stockings and asked if they had plans. 'Nuffink spesh,' said Ethel. She nudged her friend. They had always enjoyed our 'romps' in the past. When heavily made up and in high heels, their skinny little bodies could be almost attractive. I took them, one on each arm, along the boardwalk in the fizzing light of the fairground. The sea was black and still beyond the beach. I could hear the oil pumps, steadily grinding away, and I wondered how many lovers used the noise and the darkness as cover. Huntington Beach was at its best now, coming fully alive. Huge, crudely painted heads nodded above booths which popped and clattered or tinkled with tiny bells. The barkers yelled in a language of their own, more ancient than Romany, and the harem girls, if anything even less attractive than my two, wriggled their mean protruberances to the sound of some *fart-saytik* Edison cylinder. The stink of oil came off the beaches and mingled with the stink of oil from the fairground, with the smells of hamburgers and hot dogs, toffee apples, pink cotton candy and sugarsticks. The ground, often covered by bouncing planks where it had become too muddy, was a museum of California's *glantsik* garbage, the vivid colours of bottles, boxes and paper bags already beginning to fade. My theatrical colleagues were sharing a room with Mrs Cornelius. I thought it imprudent to go there, in case she decided to leave her date prematurely. I took them back to my own room, on the other side of the fairground. It was as if we had not left. The lights flashed and winked, the music churned out with mechanical cheer the waltz tunes of a more elegant century, and Ethel moved her skeletal, almost androgynous carcass up and down on my misleadingly trimmed member while Mabel, unusually for her, lowered a not oversweet vagina towards my head, then dropped with a slight yelp, full on my lips. I did what I could before my conviction that I was suffocating got the better of me. I had not forgotten Esmé. I could see her sweet, virginal face even as Mabel ground herself next upon my shoulder. It was astonishing how like Lillian Gish Esmé was. She would have no trouble at all finding movie parts if that was what she wished. I began to hope I might be responsible for giving the world two wonderful new stars. The temptation to remain in the acting profession was considerable, but I knew I could not resist my destiny any longer. I had other gifts to offer the world. I had my *luftshif* and boats and household appliances. Ultimately they led to my dream of maximum freedom, my aerial cities. *Eybik, fargesn, ikh blaybn lebn.*

I escorted the ladies back to their own boarding house, a couple of blocks from mine. They made coffee for me and chatted about films they had seen, men they had dated, advertisements which had attracted them. By three in the morning they had crawled into bed together and fallen asleep. Mrs Cornelius, when she returned, was mildly surprised to find me there. She gave a little jump and then hiccupped. 'Beg pardon, Ivan. Wot the 'ell are you doin' up, and in my room!'

'I wanted to hear how everything went.'

'You ain't me granny.' She frowned. 'I still carn't work art yore angle.' Then she grinned, removing her hat. ''E's loverly, reelly. Soft as butter, an' orl! Didn't lay a finger on me, like 'e said.' She was impressed by this. 'An' 'e's fixin' up a screen test wiv 'is mates at Lasky's. I ain't complainin'. A bit'v a barn, that hotel, though. I expected some-fink more flash. An' no bloody booze, would yer believe it. Woman 'oo runs it's a reformed madam, I fink.'

I was genuinely pleased for her, but I needed to know what she had done on my behalf. 'Did you manage to slip in something about my inventions?'

She sat down on her narrow bed and began carefully to roll down her fine silk hose. She grew bright red. The frame shook and creaked. She was laughing silently. 'Anyone c'n read yer like a bleedin' book, Ivan. Orl right, I carn't 'ang on ter it! If yer must know yore "engineer" wiv a bit o' spare cash is John Ewart Hever – Junior. Not on'y is 'e a bleedin' millionaire wiv oil fields all over California an' Texas. 'Is bleedin' dad's a millionaire. Thass J.E.H. Senior. 'Is fuckin uncle's a millionaire. An' when they wanna go slummin' they orl get in a big Rolls Royce and piss over ter William Randolph 'Earst's gaff ter see 'ow the ovver 'arf lives.' She enjoyed the astonishment on my face. She reached over and patted my arm. 'I carn't say I ain't grateful fer the intro, Ive. Mucker reckons 'e's ther main tip as Republican nomination fer Guv'ner, next time rahnd. Fink I'd make a proper firs' lady o' the State?' And she re-leased her laughter this time, waking her room mates who asked her to put a sock in it.

'But you didn't mention my stuff?'

'We're 'avin' dinner agin tomorrer. Some place darn near Laguna Beach, I fink. Fish restaurant. Orl on ther legit, eh?' She winked again. 'I'm lookin' arter ther value o' me assets, like I said. But I'll do it to-morrer night, Ive, I promise. It jes' didn't work art this time. Off yer go, love. See yer at ther show. I've gotter get me beauty sleep, in'I?' And humming a few bars of *Knock 'Em In The Old Kent Road* she waved me towards the door. I left, but I felt she had at very least failed to un-derstand the urgency of my situation. Although glad things went well for her and grateful for the intelligence of Hever's enormous wealth, for some reason I was seized by an additional sense of panic. Perhaps I sus-pected she might betray me (I should have known better) and claim Hever entirely for herself. It would be like an Indian who, having hunted down one of the last buffalo, refused to tell his tribe. Hever be-longed to me quite as much as he did to Mrs C.

That was why, next morning, I boarded a powerful Red Car inter-ur-ban trolley rumbling the coast-road tracks to Marina del Rey. From near Venice's huge indoor Bathing Pavilion, I took a Yellow local inland. It was a remarkable public transport system and a model to most other cities. The Huntington class tram cars were St Louis-built, superbly engineered and designed to live a century. They were named after the line's owners, that old wealthy family established in California since she was ruled by Dons. I saw almost the final run of the *Descanso*, the big silver-grey Funeral Car, last of her kind. Unable to compete with the rapidly multiplying automobile, she was extinct within the year.

The Southwestern Mineral Company was easily found. They had an entire building on Wilshire Boulevard, some twenty storeys high, standing in what was virtually a small park. I gave my name to the clerk at a vast reception desk which occupied the ground floor. He was greatly impressed when I was asked straight to the top. A pretty secretary met me outside the elevator, leading me through cool, grey corridors crowded with potted palms and ferns. We came at last to a massive door which was thrown open and there was 'Mucker' himself, as untidy as ever in his pale suit, virtually embracing me. It was as if an elephant calf had risen on its hind quarters in imitation of *homo sapiens*. 'So happy to see you, Pallenberg.' He was, even in his native environment, acutely nervous and consequently expressing embarrassment with every clumsy movement. 'Nothing wrong, I hope?' He was growing whiter even as he escorted me inexpertly through mahogany opulence towards his antique desk squatting before the shaded window and a view of the sea. From here the city looked curiously incomplete, like an unfinished jigsaw, with patches of irregular green, abrupt assymetrical mud lots or exact squares of glittering concrete. It was as if this part of Los Angeles were in the almost organic process of reforming herself. Hever put his broad back to the view, offering me a chair, a cigar and a 'pop' with one brief, hesitant wave. I lowered myself into deep, Victorian leather, looking up at his worried eyes. 'You've brought a message from Mrs Cornelius, I take it'

I shrugged, smiled and shook my head. 'She said she had a delightful dinner. She's looking forward to this evening. Laguna Beach? I doubt you'll find me acting as an intermediary from now on, Mr Hever. Mrs Cornelius is her own woman.'

He turned his head in a peculiar sideways movement which suggested approving assent. 'Strong-minded.' He beamed. This was his favourite subject. 'A woman of so many wonderful aspects.' He grinned like a half-trained puppy. 'I thought you were here to tell me I'd

526

flopped the prelims. She's no goop, that gal. If you want it straight, Pallenberg, I'm pretty much of a ham with the ladies.' He sat back with a self-approving sigh, as if he had just made a courageous revelation. He continued to lounge at this uneasy angle, his expression fixed as he waited for me to speak. I have met his type since, but he was the first millionaire I had encountered. He had none of the characteristics I would have expected to find in someone who controlled the fate of thousands. I think nobody liked to tell him how much power he had: it would make him speechless, wondering in panic what so many individuals expected of him. It was hard enough for him to deal with one of us at a time. In raising the main subject I felt like an assassin; yet, for Esmé's sake, I was determined to continue.

'Actually, Mr Hever, we've met before.' I hesitated. 'We discussed the future of engineering for a little bit. But mainly we talked about our mutual enjoyment of the movies. I recall you mentioned some Germans. Pabst? Murnau?'

He glared at me in innocent panic; his fear was purely social.

'At Klankrest? In Atlanta, Mr Hever? A party given by Eddy Clarke, a couple of years ago? You told me how you'd made a big donation to the Klan.'

Suddenly his massive body rose like a wild balloon. Hand to the side of his head he glanced at me in fear. From white he quickly grew bright red. Then he inhaled enormously, slumping his unhappy bottom against the edge of the desk. 'Mrs Cornelius knows all this?'

'Why should she?'

'So she –' The words became a groan of pain. Obviously he was wondering if the love of his life had only agreed to go out with him to set him up for me. Another massive breath. He began to roam aimlessly over the carpet as if he thought he might find the elephant's graveyard. I turned my head to follow him, saying urgently, 'Mr Hever, sir, I think you have the wrong idea.'

'You're not blackmailing me, are you Pallenberg, for God's sake.' He had ascended to Heaven only to find it inhabited by the Devil. I wanted to pat his hand and assure him his happiness was not attacked. 'The friendship of Mrs Cornelius means a lot to me. You can't know what I went through . . .' Again his manner apologized for this self-reference.

I was offended. 'I won't deny my finances are currently non-existent, Mr Hever. But,' (I was enjoying my increasing familiarity with the slang,) 'it will be a cold day in Hell before I try to put the bite on a pal. Please relax.' I knew how nervous he must be. He still could not believe his good fortune. He had been born a millionaire, had known nothing but privilege, yet he expected happiness to be snatched away from him just as if he were a child in the slums of Kiev who knew from experience that nothing of value was ever his for more than a chance moment. Hever actually expected to have his dream destroyed. I went on: 'Nothing which I say in this room will ever be conveyed to Mrs Cornelius. Whatever exists between you two can't be harmed by me.'

He looked at me with that same expression of gratitude which had been on his face when I first told him he could see his idol. But he was puzzled. 'Then why are you here?' He was in the early stages of a love affair. The rest of the world and its inhabitants currently scarcely existed.

'I thought you'd better know the Justice Department has frozen my assets for an indefinite period. If anyone's being blackmailed, it's me. I'm their key witness in a Klan knockover which could expose almost every secret supporter in the country. I'm not being melodramatic.'

'You know I'm expecting to be nominated for Governor next year' He blinked vaguely into a threatened future.

'Yes. I just wanted you to rest assured. No matter how desperate I get, I shan't give the game away. But this is the ruin of my own career.'

'You're a brilliant actor, Mr Pallenberg.'

I chuckled bitterly as I picked up my hat and rose to my feet. 'That's the real irony, Mr Hever. It's all I can do at present. Actually, if you remember that conversation at Klankrest, I'm a scientist. I told you about some of my ideas. You said you were impressed.'

For a moment he again became aware of a world which had existed before he had dined with Mrs Cornelius. 'What a prune I am! Of course! You were the whiz who suggesting roofing over Iowa! You must excuse me, Mr Pallenberg. I'm completely fog-bound this morning.' Smiles came and went across his face. He lumbered after me and my hand was shaken for the second time. 'And you had some other ideas. I remember thinking you were the only intelligent person at that whole bust. How on earth did you get to be an actor? I thought you were in big with the KKK. Don't tell me. I'm deeply ashamed. They had me completely bamboozled for a few months. I wish I could have got my money back. You came to warn me, is that it?'

'We're in the same boat, I'm afraid.' I told him part of my story. He listened with deep, mindless sympathy. 'Anyway,' I concluded, 'that's how a first-rate scientist wound up becoming a third-rate actor. Whatever happens, Mr Hever, your name will never be drawn from me.'

Hever's porcine lower lip was trembling. He grew sentimental. He said I was a white man. What specific help could he offer? What experiments had I been conducting when the Klan kidnapped me? I told him of my gas car, my new oil-refining process, my suction pump. He displayed enthusiasm. I unrolled the few rough plans I had brought, explaining I had been forced to change my name. The patents were chiefly registered to 'Pyatnitski'. He studied them, exclaiming politely from time to time, asking the occasional pertinent question. I congratulated myself: we had reached an understanding.

Before I left Hever's office I heard much more about Mrs Cornelius's virtues, his own shortcomings, my genius; but he had bought a control in me. I had a draft contract with Golden State Engineering Developments (a wholly-owned subsidiary of the Hever empire) and a cashier's cheque for $2,500; my advance on a retainer of $10,000. I would draw a salary of $200 a week. My title, Chief Experimental Engineer, was in black and white on the contract. When my inventions were commercially produced I would earn 50% of the net profits. Life had begun again for me. Esmé was coming!

Ich kann ohne dich nicht leben. I did no wrong! It was to mutual benefit. *Gold blinkte. Due wirst mich ruinieren, mein Schatz, meine Geliebte.* I could not help it. *Es ist zu spät. Ich kenhe mein Schicksal. Zu spät für den Seelenfrieden! Wir kämpfen nur, um ein gewisses Gleichgewicht aufrechzuerhalten.* I had found myself, like some engineer of the Renaissance, a powerful patron, that was all.

Mrs Cornelius was soon Hever's regular consorte everywhere. Under her picture on the society pages she was described as 'an English beauty', 'daughter of the eminent banker.' Within two weeks we formally handed over *Limeys in Limelight* to Ethel, Mabel and Harold Hope, together with all props, the van, and enough money to get the girls back to England if they chose. They now had legitimate visas. Both said they thought they would stay in California. If Mrs Cornelius had made it, Mabel told me, there might be a chance for her, 'even if it's only marrying a wealthy projectionist!' Mrs Cornelius was due to take her first screen test at the Lasky Studios on Selma and Vine. She told me privately that Mucker was the tastiest millionaire she had met and a proper gent. She generously thanked me for insisting she go out with him. 'You done us all a bit o' good there, Ivan!' She had forgiven me for 'going behind her back' to Hever. (She did not realise what she owed me for that action!) She said she was surprised he had agreed to my scheme. Normally he was slow and cautious in his business dealings.

I would visit her at her new suite in the Beverly Hills Hotel. Sometimes I would take her for drives in the lovely wooded roads behind the hotel. I had a serviceable green and gold Peugeot 163. This de luxe Torpedo had been presented to me when I signed my final contract. I liked to luxuriate in the clouds of pink and pale blue which filled the rooms in that Spanish palace. Dressed in new clothes (jodhpurs, riding-boots and ascot, then acceptable motoring wear, became my favourites) I would lounge across her sofas, passing an hour or two with her before Hever called. My own pleasant little house was in the seaside suburb of Venice, close to the Grand Canal. I especially enjoyed Hollywood's extravagances. Where else might one find this translated notion of a European city, with rococo wood and brick representing the stones of the original Hollywood, even then, had begun to influence the whole of Southern California. She was the spiritual and cultural core of Los Angeles. For miles around there were growing whole townships which, were it not for the skills and imagination of movie set-designers, could never have existed. In a region where rain was rare, elaborate architectural fantasies could be created cheaply and rapidly. In Hollywood it was possible to ape the rich and succeed. Hollywood created the world's first true democracy. For different reasons, both Mrs Cornelius and I were euphoric.

On the morning I bought Esmé's ticket, I called on her in her suite to tell her the news. She had advised me not to cable Esmé cash. Cash could always be stolen again. I had sent my girl a non-returnable one-way first-class ticket on the *Icosium* which sailed from Genoa on July 21st. 'Registered and Special Delivery,' I told her. 'I paid cash. It's wonderful to have money in my pocket again!'

'Yore a jammy littel bugger,' she said affectionately. She was trying on various accessories before the wall-length mirror. 'I reckon we're birds of a fevver, you an' me, Ive. Thass why it'd orlways be a mistake ter you-know-what.' I smiled at this, not completely in agreement. 'We wouldn't be 'ere nar,' she pointed out, 'if we'd've bin up ter a bit o' the how's-yer-fahver.' She put down the long scarf she had been winding round her cami-knickered waist. The scarf was scarlet, her underwear

pale green satin. 'So thass why yore orl antsy t'day.' She kissed me on
the forehead as she reached behind me for a headdress of bright blue
ostrich feathers. 'Ah, well. Somebody's gotta 'elp yer spend it, eh?' In
the course of her love affair with Hever she had grown, as people will,
more tolerant of what she still called my infatuation.

It was true I was trembling with excitement. By the end of the following month I should be reunited, after all those painful years, with
my darling Esmé. My entire body had quickened and come to life in
anticipation of our meeting. This ecstasy transcended fleshly sensation.
I experienced it so forcefully, I think, because I was at once confident,
relaxed and unthreatened. *Wann sehe ich Sie wider? Ich habe lange
geschlafen. Die Zeit vergeht. Sie hat ihr Tat selbst zu verantworten.* It
had been three years. *Seit 1921. Wo sind wir? Drei jahre! Ich habe
geschlafen. Der Traum is eybik. Der Traum wird morgen nicht kommen. Hat sie mein Traum missdeutet? Mit Esmé Ich . . .*

Every day I visited my new domain, my little factory. At Hever's suggestion we had taken over the workshops of a bankrupt firm (it had
hoped to build a funicular railway system between the various ranges of
Los Angeles hills). In the unremarkable area of the Long Beach docks
several small engineering firms had their headquarters. During the day
the local air was a hullabaloo of saws and rivet guns, gouting furnaces
and pounding hammers, like some gnomish nether region. It looked
out directly over the harbour. Grey warships would stand there for
weeks, apparently deserted by all save a handful of men, then suddenly
weigh anchor and be gone. I watched seaplanes coming and going.
Some of the early Curtiss prototypes were taking shape. As I got to
know him, I would offer advice to Curtiss and his people. It was astonishing how many of my suggestions they accepted, how many became
standard procedural and production features. Naturally, I never received payment or acknowledgement. I did not worry about such
things. I merely delighted in the thump of floats striking water, the
shrill early notes of an approaching machine, the wheeling and climbing of the beautiful little craft.

I had only so much to do to our own adapted Buick tourer. Chiefly
my duties consisted of overseeing the mechanics. There were three of
them, all excellent, and an apprentice. Having exchanged petroleum
tanks for compressed-gas cylinders we were experimenting with means
of feeding the gas to the engine. I studied several types of steam car, including the excellent Stanley, which had ceased production in 1920.

What we learned from these, we attempted to apply to our own proto-type. I was lucky in my team of enthusiastic young men; my band of brothers, sworn to secrecy. Sometimes, when a particularly difficult problem arose, we would all work through the night. Again I had that life-giving powder to thank for her benevolent help. With such wages, I could afford it. *Es ken nisht shatn.* Thus the gas car gradually took shape. I continued to experience that thrill of anticipation, for the day when Esmé would place her dainty feet upon the soil of America.

With no photographs of my little girl, I had to make do with many of Lillian (and sometimes Dorothy) Gish. How much more wholesome they were than the likes of Clara Bow or Gloria Swanson. Somewhere in those few years we lost 'the Nation's Sweetheart' and were given in-stead 'the Hottest Jazz-Baby in Town.' I prayed my little *shvester, mayn meydl, mayn metsie,* would not have been coarsened or otherwise changed by her hardships. Her letters suggested she was the same de-lightful *Mädchen* of my dreams, my incorruptible daughter; sweet mis-tress of my *mazl.* Yet she had lived for long in the Vatican's shade. I knew the Jesuit tricks. They would introduce sin into Eden if H. G. Wells would tell them how to build his *zeygermashin.* God help us if they become engineers. Then we shall see also their *zindmashin!* Maybe she was cynical. Who would not be after saving so long only to have the money snatched away at the very moment it is needed? I know some of these feelings. Yet I had fought cynicism, maintained my ide-alism against all odds. I was sure my sister, so much my *alter ego,* had protected her innocence equally well. Soon, together, we should be able to embark again upon that *zukhn,* that holy quest for the purity we had known in Kiev, for the tranquillity that once filled our hearts, for the *zilber* of clear thought. *Iber morgn du vest kumen.* I was confident, but I was not wholly confident, as they say. That is, I yearned for con-firmation. Here were the sunshine years of my life, in California. I, who had always loved silver, learned the value of gold. There is a clar-ity in sunlight I never understood until Los Angeles. Though I know Carthage, terrified of silver, lurks in gold, I refuse to condemn the metal itself. I lusted for our union: my purity of intellect, her purity of flesh. The days began to manifest themselves as well-defined units.

When happy I always work best. What little pressure I had exerted on Mucker Hever was completely justified. We had an excellent de-sign. The engine began to prove well. It would greatly increase Hever's already monstrous fortune and by this means he would find his judgment confirmed. He and Mrs Cornelius occasionally visited the workshop, but were so involved with one another my descriptions were meaningless to them. This did not distress me. I prefer to work without supervision. Mrs Cornelius would never know I helped tip the balance in her favour, founding her assurances from Hever in something much more solid than momentary infatuation; she was to embark on her movie career very soon. I blamed myself for nothing. *Wer hat gewennen? Das Spiel war unent schieden.* Nobody was unhappy.

Und nun ist der Traum Wirklichkeit. Es ist höchste Zeit, dass ich auf main Schiff zurükhehre. Karthago wird von einem glühenden Hass auf die Weissen verzehrt, die er als Wurzel allen Übels in der Welt betrachtet – obwohl ich andereseits wieder gehört habe, dass sinige weisse Wissenschaftler in seinen Diensten stehen. Seine Mittel wachsen folglich ständig. Gelt . . . Golden cupolas rising in Atlanta, in Odessa, and in Sparta. These domes rise in Jackson and Jubilee; copper and pewter, as any in Kiev, they rise in St Petersburg Fla and Alabama's redbrick metropoli; no longer the domes of Christ Arisen, these are the domes of Civil dignity and Law, just democracy. A clock chimes where the sun's orb blazed; red, white and blue flapping on a polished staff where for my sense of congruity should be a Russian crucifix. And these sappherine skies, are they never silver? In Arcadia alligators crusted with antiquity wallow in metal tanks. Their heavy jaws clack shut on asymmetrical teeth; they haul themselves over each others' backs, refusing even the notion of death, they have existed so long. Small cousins to the mile-deep Atlantic monsters, blind representatives of a Carthaginian future, they are now bred by men to make handbags for Beverly Hills housewives, boots for singing cowboys and belts to decorate the trousers of millionaire dentists. The Jew showed me kindness in Arcadia. *Wir steigen unter leichtem Schaukeln vom Bodenauf, wobei der Motor sin kaum varnehmbares Schnurren von sich gab.* In Arcadia I came unsuspectingly upon those old reptiles. They could not know they were bred for profit. The Jew gave me warmth and his food. With his hands he fed me; with his dry sardonic lips he offered realistic prophecy. Maybe I was wrong to trust him. *Der blut, der toyt, der kamf, der blitz, der synemmen, der oyfgeheybung!*

Der oyfegebrakhtkayt! Ich haben das Opferbereit, meine Glaube, meine Schöpferdrang, meine Arbeit, mein Genie, meine Jugden, mein Kamerad, mein Kampf, meine Mission, mein Engel, mein Schicksal. I am strong in this. *Karthago nicht viel von der Art der Leute wusste. Das*

Geheimnis seiner Kraft? Der shtof! When they took that from me, I was for a while weaker. But there is such a thing as resurrection. It is what they refuse to understand. The Jew looked at me with kindness, offering security. In this other Arcadia I hear sluggish liquid churn; claws rattle on steel floors. Those alligators smell of old Carthage's enduring evil. I look over the fence and they are grinning back, their snouts dilating. He was gentle. The better kind of Jew. *Der shtof was never der Mayster. Ikh bin abn meditsin-mayster.* He said he was going to find a job on a newspaper in Odessa. He was prepared to accommodate the Bolsheviks when they arrived. Maybe he was already one of them. I took the tram along the shore. I never saw him again.

Der Engelsfestung eybik iz. Ikh bin dorshtik. Ikh bin hungerik. Vos iz dos? La Cité de. . . The City of the Angels is eternal and must become the New Byzantium. Carthage she absorbs, utilises, rejects what she does not want. The holy wood is where Parsifal discovered the Grail. Here all shall find salvation, on the final coast. We have travelled so long. Carthage cannot conquer here, though she will always threaten. So, at least, I am inclined to believe. It could be I grew euphoric and lazy under the benevolent Southern Californian sun; they say that happens to many. It could be I was seduced by her luxury, her golden charm, her aristocracy. Yet the attraction, I would swear, was positive.

So swiftly did my car assume reality I had soon some leisure time and this frequently was spent with friends, visiting the homes of their peers. For the most part these *N'divim*, these modern princes, possessed a grace and wit usually lacking in their European counterparts. Their world was vital and constantly expanding, through art, industry and intellect. They had every reason to carry themselves with dignity, to build their palaces amongst the wooded hills and feel superior. They had no use for the petty moralities with which a bourgeois rationalises his shortcomings. Yet they never denied or derided their European heritage; indeed, they imported it in such quantities it sometimes seemed there could be nothing left of the Old World; it had been entirely reassembled in the New. Renaissance tapestries, Jacobean tables and Louis Quinze chandeliers, all of them genuine, were common to the homes I visited. Yet in almost every great mansion one found acknowledgement of native America.

When, in the middle of July, 1924, I called on Mr and Mrs Tom Mix, their French furniture and suits of medieval armour, their Scottish shields and claymores shared the same rooms as Indian head-dresses, his collection of silver-studded saddles and other elaborate mementoes of the West. They were a gracious, modest couple. Mrs Mix took to me with great warmth. She said I was 'the image of Valentino.' It was true that I somewhat resembled the star, having similar eyes and colouring, but I was anxious to point out that I did not possess a single drop of Italian blood.

John Hever preferred the company of movie people (I believe he never got over his worship of the screen) and would frequently ask me to go somewhere for dinner or for a weekend. I think he had mixed motives, for he was anxious to prove even to this easy-going world that his relations with Mrs Cornelius were perfectly respectable. I was a kind of chaperone (though, naturally, I found myself prey to the usual disgusting gossip). Thus I at last entered the portals of Pickfair. That unpretentious tribute to good taste, influenced chiefly by a 'mock Tudor' style popular in England, never proclaimed itself a palace, nor advertised its wealth. There were touches of the Swiss chalet, tributes here and there to the Spanish adobe dwelling settlers, but in the main Pickfair, in its fifteen acres of landscaped grounds, resembled everything an English country estate should be; even its huge swimming-pool did not seem grandiose. At dinner I got into conversation with the charming athlete, who did not recall our earlier meeting. 'Dougy' was a perfect host. Learning of my relish for oceanliners he produced the family photograph album. His favourite trip, he said, 'because it was our honeymoon,' was on the S.S. Lapland with Mary. He was at that time completing The Thief of Baghdad, perhaps his most exotic film. The house was piled with drawings. Minarets, domes and crenellated walls reminded me of Constantinople. Here was Asia as it should have been. Fairbanks never spared expense on his sets. He made full-sized cities and towns, castles and mountains. This is what convinced the movie-goer of the reality of the stories. Mary Pickford was at that time turning her back on childhood and attempting a more fashionable 'jazz-baby' part with Dorothy Vernon of Haddon Hall. I had seen her Rosita and been deeply disappointed. On behalf of all her fans I begged her to return to her more innocent rôles. She responded sweetly and began to explain what she was attempting to do when her husband interrupted us with a display of obvious jealousy which silenced, for a moment, the whole party. There had been no question of my 'making a pass' at his wife; even had there been I saw no call for the stage-whisper, nor the reference to 'some *yiddisher* lounge-lizard,' particularly since almost half our company were of the Jewish persuasion.

This fact had originally startled me. The Jews who settled in the hills around Hollywood were not at all what I recognised from Ukraine. Samuel Goldfish, for instance, was a man of exceptional elegance and education. He told me in confidence how much he admired Shakespeare when he was a boy. His only real ambition was to translate those great plays for the silent drama. 'They are stories,' he told me soberly. 'And stories are stories, no matter how you look at it.' He and Mucker Hever had already been co-producers of two successful films, *Tess of the d'Urbervilles* and *The Tower of Lies*. Mucker Hever had told him I was the author of a successful piece, which had been touring to packed houses for over a year. When I described the plot he nodded approvingly. He had a soft spot, he said, for the subject and with the right leading actors it could work very well. He suggested I have the synopsis typed and sent to him. 'Though if Mucker's already happy, then I guess I'm happy.' Then, to break the slight chill which had descended, Mary Pickford clapped her hands and suggested we all file in to another room 'to watch a flicker.' We saw *Merton of the Movies* with Glenn Hunter and Viola Dana, both of whom were with us in the audience! It was an amusing comedy, what today would be called a 'satire,' about the industry itself. Some of its references were obscure, but the movie people found the scenes which baffled me the funniest of all. Though I was to become much more familiar with Hollywood's aristocracy, I look back on those first few weeks of heady glamour as amongst the most wonderful of my life. I will never recapture the surprise at meeting Theda Bara and finding her a sweet, well-mannered lady whose home had a comfortable, almost old-maidish atmosphere, save for one room decorated with *memento mori*, Oriental tapestries, tiger skins and mummy cases. This, she explained modestly, was where she was photographed. She had wanted to play Gish or Pickford parts, but the public insisted she remain always a vamp. I understand these pressures. We are all, to some degree, caricatures of what society demands of us.

One of the few Hollywood *Yehudi* I found vulgar was, in fact, from Kiev. I recognised this type instantly. We knew the likes of Selsnik in Podol, swaggering in loud suits, displaying rings and gold watch chains, smoking the largest cigars they could find, parading their wealth with appalling braggadocio. It was no wonder that occasionally the ordinary people of the city would round on them. Selsnik boasted to me he had sent the Tsar a telegram in 1917. He was full of his own atrocious joke, sprawling in the powerfully scented velvets and satins of Clara Bow's living-room where Mrs Cornelius and I (without Hever for a change) had been invited for tea. Miss Bow herself was a lively, solicitous hostess. 'I heard, see, the Tsar is abdicated. So I think to myself, what the hell? I'll send him a telegram. Know what I said? You and your police weren't kind to me when I was a boy in Kiev, I said, so me and my people come America. Here we did very well. Now they tell me you're out of a job. No hard feelings about your cossacks. I'm willing to offer you a position acting in pictures. Name your own salary. Reply at my expense. Regards to the family.'

The others found it funny. I did not. I made an excuse and left.

The Cornelius boy is always asking me about the Hearst place. It was not finished in 1924 and very few people saw it going up. Hearst kept changing the size of the pool, adding new wings before the first ones were completed. Later I was invited to his 'Enchanted Castle,' with a lot of dull industrialists, engineers and newspaper editors. Marion Davies was charming. Hearst was a Zeppelin, with a wren's peeping little voice, largely oblivious to the world around him, even the one he had built. At Hearst's you were never allowed to drink alcohol, but a good many of the movie people used cocaine in secret. By that time I had my own excellent suppliers, of course. In certain circles you were judged by the quality of your 'stuff' very much as a French nobleman would be judged by the quality of his cellar. *Mir ist warm. Vifl iz der zeyger?* Far more exciting to me was my meeting with the reserved old Southern gentleman, that world-genius, resembling a soldier rather than a showman, the soft-spoken First Lord of Tinsel Town, David W. Griffith. He happened to be at the Lasky studio when Hever and I accompanied Mrs Cornelius there to make her screen test.

I could hardly speak. I was in the presence of the greatest cultural figure of the twentieth century, the only one who genuinely deserved the title *Kinomeyster*. I mumbled like a peasant drawn from the fields to greet some mighty *landsman*. He was kind and courteous, cupping his ear to catch what I said. Mrs Cornelius saved the day. "'E finks yore ther cat's whiskers,' she told my hero. 'Ter 'ear 'im goin' on, y'd fink the sun shone arta yore –'

In horror I was able to bellow a complete word: 'Trousers!'

And that was all I ever said to the one human being on Earth whose

537

work truly influenced the course of my life. I believe he was at Lasky's looking for a job. You would never have guessed from his bearing and stylish tailoring he was down on his luck. A natural prince, whose grasp of human nature was as profound as his political insights, now cap in hand to the immigrants he himself had helped establish in this idyllic World of Dreams. I should not have been so foolish. I blame myself. Mrs Cornelius was very popular with the movie people. They saw her as an eccentric English aristocrat. And everyone knew true English aristocrats could seem like *paskudnick*, they had such foul mouths. So 'trousers' it was for *Birth of a Nation*. In spite of Mrs Cornelius's shining in her test, of watching her later in huge black and white close-up, I was not easily able to escape my depression. I constantly went over the meeting in my mind, rescripting it so that I impressed Griffith enough to bring, for a second, a look of startled emotion to his eyes as he realised here was someone who understood completely everything he had meant.

Valentino in his grandiose nest proved a disappointment. I think he saw me as a rival. He had the manners of a Neapolitan whore and the taste of a Milanese pimp, with his huge self portraits and ramshackle collections of rusting swords and suits of armour. I had tried to be polite to him, suggesting how he might expand his range, given his limitations. I was only too glad to get away from his house. It was depressing. It had a smell of suicide about it. The majority of Lords and Ladies in the World's Movie Capital were nothing like the sinful, crazed, night-haunted creatures frequently depicted by the press. Most had great poise, humour and kindness. Doubtless the image of Hollywood's élite giving orgies in their swimming pools or practising perversions on the palm-fringed lawns of their mansions had more to do with the wish-fulfilment of *hoi polloi* than the ordinary lives of people they envied.

Esmé was on her way! A telegram confirmed it. She was coming to me. The remorse I had felt since my meeting with Griffith quickly dissipated. I imagined holding my little mistress in my arms again. I drove along the white, twisting canyon roads of that beloved, adopted home, pushing the sprightly Peugot almost to her limit in a joyous Escape of Motoring. I explored orchards, the fruit groves of the wide valley, peaceful, self-contained settlements like Pasadena, sleepy farming towns like San Fernando. Out beyond Hollywood there were vineyards which would one day produce wine quite as good as Europe's. The first cuttings had been brought from Bourdeaux and Burgundy and had flourished in that idyllic climate, just as her settlers, from Europe, from the East and Mid-West, also grew healthy and virile. The best of her people were young and strong, like the wine. Their dream was nothing less than to build Utopia. It was a dream we shared. And I had practical plans to make it come true.

Only once did I consider leaving my new home behind and fleeing back to Europe with Esmé. It was a miserable episode. At her suggestion, I one morning agreed to motor out to Anaheim with Astrid Nilsen, the blonde actress. At that time she was said to rival Swanson in her willingness to accept modern, daring roles. She had heard of a good restaurant on our side of the little town and insisted it would be worth the drive. Happy to pass a day or two with a pretty girl (never again would I have to make do with the likes of Mabel and Ethel) I agreed. We left fairly early, driving on dusty dirt roads, through relentless rows of artificially irrigated fields, occasionally relieved by a farmhouse or general store, clean modern villages, each seemingly pressed from the same mould, with a wooden church, a stand of trees, a café. It was twilight by the time Astrid pointed off to the right. She had wonderfully soft, fleshy arms and shoulders. Her strong-boned face was almost Slavic. I saw yellow and red lights, the sign for the road house, but as I turned into the drive was struck by its strange name. 'How's that pronounced?' I asked. 'And what does it mean'

'*Lady Korohoto's Sunshine Sushi Bar*. It's Jap food. There are a lot of Japs around here. This place is designed to please foreign devils, I think. Ever eaten the stuff?'

'Don't you know Russians are the sworn enemies of Japan?' I was amused, yet felt she had deliberately manipulated me into an uncomfortable position. I could do nothing now however but park the car and escort her up the steps to the verandah of what until recently had been a large, sprawling farmhouse. Now it was painted dull red and black, it had woven silk screens where the windows had been and a few pieces of decoration hanging here and there which I assumed were intended to make you think you were back home in old Nagasaki. We were greeted by a grinning, bobbing yellow girl, dumpy in her constricting gowns, and were escorted into what seemed a fairly conventional restaurant, with ordinary tables and chairs and a long counter taking up the entire left-hand wall. Again the colours were muted, the decorated screens illuminated from behind, but there was nothing too exceptional. 'See,' said Astrid, taking my arm and moving closer to me, 'it's all pretty unscary, eh?'

I was not nervous, I said. I was in fact somewhat disapproving. If the Japanese were moving into service industries it was against the spirit of the newly amended California Alien Land Act which made it illegal for Japanese to farm anywhere they competed with Whites, and the Immigration Act denying Japs the status of a quota nation, intended to encourage them to leave. Doubtless they now owned land secretly! As we sat down in the otherwise empty restaurant, I said as much to Astrid.

'Jesus Christ, Max, they've got to live somehow,' she said. 'They're being squeezed from every side. Associated Fruitgrowers and every other vested interest in the State.'

I suppose she, like some women, found the Orient erotic and mysterious. I merely found it threatening. I knew the truth. The Slavs had been conquered by Mongols more than once; had pushed them back again and again, and had been freshly attacked as soon as the numbers grew. These people were breeding even now in California. They were arrogant and ambitious. Voraciously greedy, they worked far longer hours than Anglo-Saxons, to establish this beach-head for their Emperor. But I had hopes of staying overnight with Astrid, so was not prepared to argue with her. Our geisha bobbed, bowed and vanished, but a waitress failed to appear. After twenty minutes even Astrid became impatient. When I walked to the kitchen doors and peered inside nobody was preparing food, though meat and vegetables were there in abundance. The place seemed, like a *Mary Celeste*, unaccountably abandoned. Could it be a custom? Perhaps an insult, I thought. Astrid was growing uncertain. 'Maybe it's their religion?' she suggested. She jumped at a noise from outside. I pulled back one of the blinds to see what had caused it and became instantly terrified.

A huge cross burned in the yard. Grouped round it, with guns crooked in their folded arms, were at least fifty silently waiting Klansmen!

I sat down heavily in my chair.

'Oh, my God!' She was white with horror. 'A swell idea, huh?'

A salvo of shots came from the yard. 'They're warning us to leave,' I said. 'This place is going to burn. We're going to have to give them a good story. Come on.' We walked to the exit and emerged onto the verandah. We had our hands raised. 'What on earth's going on?' I demanded, hoping I sounded properly outraged.

One of the leaders whistled sharply. He said, almost in delight. 'Looks like we've found the Commie bastards that's been organising them, Sam.' He offered me a mocking bow. 'Welcome to the clambake, comrades. You're the clams.' They all laughed at this. Astrid raised her hand to her face, almost like a signal.

I shall never be quite sure if the actress, who claimed to be Danish, was actually a Chekist agent employed by Brodmann to frighten me away from Hollywood. The suspicion was there from the moment I heard the Klansman speak. I was appalled at my situation. To display too much knowledge of the Klan might alert them to my identity, whereupon I would almost certainly be killed. I had to prove that I was neither a Communist organiser (these rural areas became rotten with them) nor a Japanese sympathiser. Within the nightmare, I found myself moving towards them. Rapidly I explained how my wife and I were travelling to Los Angeles to board our liner which would take us home to Australia. Thus I identified our accents, making it clear we were innocent tourists. We had stopped at the roadhouse simply because we were hungry. I was relieved, listening to them discuss this amongst themselves, to learn they were all local people. Even as the debate continued, some were setting fire to the restaurant. Now of course the absence of customers was explained. I saw two of the squealing geishas being carried, wrapped in wire, to a nearby truck. I emphasised to the cold blue eyes that we of the outbacks and billabongs were equally aware of the yellow menace. We had solved our problem by banning all coloured races from our shores. This seemed to convince them. The whole time, however, even when they lowered their guns and gestured for us to get in our car, I feared that their apparent belief was a charade. I could not guess what Callahan had done (it might suit him to betray me), or what Brodmann intended. I did not know how much power Mrs Mawgan still possessed. She might only have temporarily resigned so as not be caught in the trap which ruined Clarke and the others. She rather than Brodmann could have paid or blackmailed Astrid into setting me up. It was certainly in Mrs Mawgan's interest to have me killed.

I approached the car. After several attempts the starting handle finally kicked in my sweating hand and the motor was running. Astrid climbed in. Her face was whiter than the moon, which now, huge in a clear, black sky, framed her head like the halo on the ikons of our old Kiev saints. She seemed genuinely terrified, but that might merely mean she feared my revenge, or the punishment of her employers. The waving hoods surrounded us. Flames took hold of the building. Her silk screens burned first, leaving black holes in the wooden frame. Red fire gasped, smoke poured into the sky and the moon grew dimmer. I had thought to see the last of the Klan. I swore I would remain in cities for the rest of my life. The countryside had never been my friend.

The man addressed as Sam wore flowing purple: a Grand Dragon. 'We're neither bullies nor cowards,' he said evenly, 'but honest, simple people fighting for what belongs to us. The Federal Government seeks to deliver our birth right into the hands of aliens. You go home, my friends, and tell your folks they know what they're doing. Take them and all other Anglo-Saxon peoples this message: Wherever white Protestants are threatened, the Knights of the Invisible Empire will strike and strike hard. You can sleep safely tonight, wherever you stay, and know you are protected. Have a safe journey, now, and come back soon, y'hear.'

Never, in that last phrase, had a tone so clearly contradicted the sentiments it expressed. I think he had warned me. I could not expect a third reprieve. I said little to Astrid as we drove away from the hissing blaze. She was full of indignation. She said we should contact the nearest police force. Then she subsided. 'I guess they're all part of it.' She began to speak of contacting someone in Los Angeles, perhaps a Federal agency. 'They had those girls. What were they going to do?'

'I think you should try to forget it all.' I remained distant, for this could easily be one of her best performances. 'Everyone, from locals, like those people back there, to the President, has made it clear Japs aren't welcome in America. If you report this you could be kicked out as some kind of political agitator.'

This allowed her to think before she said anything more. I was glad, after a miserable journey, to see the lights of Hollywood's hillside palaces on the horizon. I dropped her off outside her 3rd Street apartment house. She said, 'Don't you want to come in for a while?'

'No, thanks. You never know what you're going to catch these days.' I was still angry. I had been put through too much. I had been forced to draw on mental and spiritual resources properly reserved for my gas car and for Esmé. I had almost lost her, even before she arrived in New

York. I had been made to cringe and lie in front of someone who might now be delighting in my discomfort, reporting the news to an envious, revengeful Jew or amused Catholic, even to Mrs Mawgan. Possibly they were scheming a new means of destroying me. Not content with her initial betrayal she might now wish to wipe out all past associates. How could I warn those Klansmen that they were being used to exploit the petty personal ambitions of greedy, corrupt men and women It would be a blow to all they cherished. And if they already knew, one had to face the alarming implication: that America now no longer possessed any organised means of defending herself against those millions of secret enemies already scheming her destruction. Whether they were called IWW, Labour Unions, Anarchists, the Organisation of this 'minority' or that 'racial group,' whether they had any specific name at all, they were all agents of Carthage. This was thoroughly proved, of course, in 1941. Then America, by rounding up the Japanese, narrowly avoided defeat from within. *Zey veln komen.* They will surely come again.

I drove onto Sycamore until I reached Venice Boulevard. Often I was the only car on the road. Venice Boulevard passed through forests and parkland. A few lights were visible from little settlements, office blocks and private houses set wide apart: a tribute to modern ideas of what twentieth-century civilisation could be, if carefully planned. By the time I reached Venice the amusement park and pier were shutting down for the night. A Yellow Car rattled by, the last trolley bearing tired fun-makers back to the more sedate suburbs. I turned inland a few blocks until I was on San Juan, where I had my little, unpretentious house, deeply glad to be close to the ordinary human bustle, the familiarity of a town. No matter how fantastic her surface, Venice was ordinarily lively and cosmopolitan, sufficiently like old Odessa to bring a measure of tranquillity to my troubled mind. Nonetheless, I was cautious when I opened my front door, and would have been unsurprised to see Callahan, Brodmann, or a fresh assembly of pointed hoods, waiting for me. I went straight to bed, determined to be at my best for Esmé, and for the tests which we were due to run on the car we called Pallenberg's Experimental Type I.

Next day was Sunday. I would rather have spent time in Long Beach, seeing how work was progressing, but had agreed to escort Mrs Cornelius to the pictures. She still had not received a result of her screen test. Hever had said it sometimes took a week or two. The studio was particularly busy. She was sure however she would not be offered a contract by Lasky. Hever was already making a further appointment with MGM. There, he was confident, she would 'knock them all out' immediately. He had suggested Lasky first, I suspect, because he did not want his friend Goldfish to think he was merely trying to find work for some 'bimbo.' The tycoon remained very sensitive to such suggestions and could become surprisingly angry if Mrs Cornelius's talents were ever questioned. His investment in her was by no means merely financial. We saw *Orpheus of the Storm*. As I watched, my longing for Esmé became physically painful.

On 25th July 1924 we wheeled the PXI out of her shed. To all appearances she had narrowly survived a wreck, for her paint was chipped and body work battered. Underneath her hood however was my powerful experimental engine. Gas cylinders filled the spaces where the trunk and fuel tank had been; there were extra gauges on the dash. None of these were marked, but we knew they measured pressure and flow, while a bank of switches operated individual cylinders and valves. Mrs Cornelius had been persuaded to come with Mucker Hever. She seemed a trifle unhappy, as if suspecting we would all be blown up. I reassured her. The PXI was safer than a conventional car, and far more efficient. She got in, sitting on the edge of the back seat, looking around her at nothing in particular, occasionally whistling a few bars of a favourite melody, trying to remember not to smoke. Hever loomed over me, nodding as I explained the controls and instruments. Willy Ross, my young foreman, stood leaning casually with his backside against the hood, chatting to the other mechanics and enjoying the warmth of the early-morning sunshine. A mist was lifting from the sluggish waters of Long Beach harbour. Ships moaned. A few gulls strutted up and down the concrete like Pigalle hookers, as if to be admired, possibly approached with a proposition. Here and there you could catch the occasional sound of doors being opened, electric motors beginning to turn as our fellow optimists got down to working on their own future hopes: motorcycles, seaplanes, engineering machinery, boats, domestic appliances. It appeared that the whole of America, or at least her western shores, was labouring toward the technological salvation of mankind.

Under Hever's mild but curious eyes and Mrs Cornelius's agitated glare, I switched the automatic ignition to ON. I waited for the red light to blink, then engaged the engine. It was wonderful to hear it wailing into life, shaking the whole chassis, then become a growling, urgent beast. I let go the brakes and put her into gear. Willy and our mechanics cheered. With a triumphant wave, I moved forward at speed, so elated that the car was doing everything I had expected that I forgot briefly to check for other drivers. I narrowly missed a truck and a Packard, recovered control of my roaring machine, and headed North. We sped along Roosevelt Highway with the wide Pacific Ocean on our left. The constantly growing organism of Greater Los Angeles was on our right. White towers thrust themselves from thick stands of greenery, handsome houses, set back from the road in smooth lawns, had apparently come into existence overnight; hotels and apartment blocks glittered in the soft morning sunshine. All I missed was Esmé beside me to share my glory and my happiness. There could be no experience more transforming than this. The ponderous Pacific, blue and white, rolled against perfect beaches of yellow sand. In the sky a small biplane circled lazily down towards Burbank and a flock of seabirds rose over Palos Verdes, turning and banking almost as one above the dignified grandeur of her piles. The colours of the morning were more vivid than ever before. The vast, untroubled city, so confident in her riches and her cultural predominance, was the finest of all possible worlds. The PXI shouted my joy. I had succeeded at last. I was vindicated. I was, within the space of half an hour, compensated for every minute, every year of my suffering and misfortune. Beside me Mucker Hever was laughing like a boy as he clung to the leather strap. The wind brought a flush to his features. His eyes were bright with dawning understanding of the car's potential. When he glanced at me I knew he realised he had been granted one of the greatest honours known to man: that of serving Genius. We passed Venice and Santa Monica. Only as we thundered inland from Pacific Palisades, heading for the San Fernando Valley, did Hever notice, with a little less concern than usual, that Mrs Cornelius lay back across her seat, rolling her eyes. Concentrating on keeping a rein on my monster I could do nothing save smile reassuringly over my shoulder. Her skin had turned pale green. I shouted above the noise, trying to tell her it would be folly to stop the car now, so far from base. At the first opportunity, just as the blue light flashed a warning to switch to my next tank, I took the steep, twisting road which led me at last onto Sunset Boulevard. Climbing steadily between grassy hills and landscaped woods, miniature lakes and vast private lawns, we passed a dozen princely houses all in various stages of construction. I at last eased my car to a halt outside the Beverly Hills Hotel. True to form, Mrs Cornelius had thrown up on the floor. 'Sorry, Ivan,' she mumbered as Hever helped her out. 'I never knew it'd go so bleedin' farst. Shouldn't o' 'ad ther bleedin' kipper, should I?'

'Congratulations.' Hever was distracted, trying to gather Mrs Cornelius's limp body with his flailing arms, like someone with palsy carrying china. 'You've struck a spouter there, Pallenberg. I'll send someone out to clean the car. You must excuse me.' The pair moved unsteadily towards the main entrance; two tired apes attempting to perform some primitive ritual dance across the blazing limestone of the patio. The car was attended to in a few minutes. I had a little trouble starting her up again on the almost empty No. 2 tank, but I had anticipated minor problems of that kind. I was soon alone with my dream, speeding past a procession of historical and geographical styles. My PXI continued to perform admirably. She took me from Old English to German Gothic and Scandinavian Gingerbread carrying me beside ordinary-sized houses built to look like medieval castles while castles were disguised as French cottages. Here in Hollywood and her immediate provinces was a combination of every city I had ever known. At one moment I could be back in my Kievan childhood, at another in Odessa or St Petersburg. I could glance from one hill to the next, where cypresses and palms and a white cupola recalled Constantinople or drive a little further down the canyons to find Sans Souci transported in quarter scale from Montmartre. Here was Ancient Rome; there Florence or, of course, Venice, and modern Milan. Otranto, Ankara, Alexandrovskaya were equally to hand. Elsewhere I could find Peking, Moscow, London and, always, Barcelona or Madrid. Berlin and Hannover and the castles of the Rhine; Arabia, India, and, suddenly, New York. Chicago, Washington and Memphis. My entire past was represented in this single city, just as my future was apparent in her wealth, tranquillity and grandeur, beneath a sun which scarcely knew a cloud. At night, under powerful stars and an overblown moon, you could smell her sweetness, her pines and blossoming shrubs, her cedarwood closets, her spice-filled pantries. All the perfumes of the world were carried in on gentle breezes; the salt of the sea, the musk of beautiful women, the glorious odours of tropical flowers. And yet, lying in a bed first built for some ruined despot, with your window open on those comforting hills, you could still sometimes hear the howling of wolves. The coyote had skulked in the rear of the Mexican expansion, establishing himself wherever a Catholic Mission was erected to the glory of the Pope. Now he loped through the little valleys and woods, drinking from Japanese water-gardens and Dutch wishing-wells, scavenging the half-eaten pheasants or jars of caviare, imported cheeses, rare delicacies borne to Hollywood in electrically cooled holds by liners from Hong Kong, Hamburg and Capetown.

Daily Hollywood created and exported fresh wonders. In return she received all the world's riches, all her traditional marvels, all her escapes. The flow of wealth to and from this storehouse of our deepest longings was impossible to check. I luxuriated in Hollywood's supernatural radiance; I was bathed by her healing, indescribable tides. I could again look for immortality and expect to find it. In Hollywood's imaginative opulence, in an ambience of infinite pleasure, infinite possibility, I had grown whole again. All I lacked was Esmé. Esmé was the final missing fragment of my resurrected being. She was my soul, my muse, *mayn glantsik tsil*. Esmé was myself and I was she. Oh, my rose! Separated we are perpetually crippled. Together we are an angel. *Und nu du komst!*

Twenty-Two

NOW YOU COME, Esmé! Soon you shall be real again. Her engines drumming steadily, a magnificent city bears you beneath the grey Atlantic's unquiet skies. Far below her hull are mountain peaks taller than the Himalayas, in whose inky valleys prowl dark old titans, immense and eternally hungry. These beasts are bound, by virtue of their size and gravity, to exist through lightless millennia (perhaps as many as mankind has known). These are the gods to whom Carthage would make sacrifice: the melancholy totems of an undead slavery. But the floating cities are safe, sailing high above that gloomy territory: so high as to be neither heard nor scented; beyond the imaginings of Carthage's monstrosities.

Terrible denizens of an eternally sunless sphere they survive the heavy centuries experiencing neither love, nor dreams, nor fear; they are without sensation save their dull, perpetual greed. They cannot touch you, Esmé, in your powerful city, as inexorably she challenges shrieking elemental violence with tapered steel and carries your innocent courageous vitality, your beautiful, wondering vulnerability, home to where my arms can enfold you.

Our bodies shall soon know that specific ecstasy of two perfect souls, two halves of a single globe, conjoined at last and for eternity to burn with a silver, an all-illuminating flame; a flame containing the sum of the spectrum's shades, the inviolable glare of diamonds and rubies blended. We shall unite, Esmé. We shall explore an infinity of facets; an abundance of sensuality, new artefacts, fresh cities and the glories of the natural world. Oh, Esmé, I lost you. They took me to the City of Sleeping Goats, where the warning fires of synagogues alerted me at last. I came to a City of Fearful Dogs, whose holy places were smeared with heathen excrement, and there I found you, restored to virgin mind. We travelled to the City of Whispering Priests, to the City of Painted Cadavers, and there I was again banished from you. Many other cities, Esmé, have informed me, seduced me, led me from virtue. But now I have found rest, here in this City of the Golden Dream, the Emperor City I thought destroyed. You will come to me in New York and I shall bear you back to the safety of these fantasies made real, where they have discovered a means of eternally banishing the nightmare. And in time, Esmé, we shall fly again. This city shall fly. *Vifl iz der zeyger? Iber morgn? Eyernekhtn? Ikh farshtey nit. Ikh veys nit. Es tut mir leyd. Esmé! Es tut mir leyd! Es iz nakht. Morgn in der fri ikh vel kumen. Mayn Esmé. Ikh darf mayn bubeleh. Mayn muter.*

In Anaheim the restaurant turned to black ash blowing across the endless furrows; then the concrete poured like lava over the old groves and from these ruined futures grew the antiseptic quasi-fantasy of a tranquillised *kulak* class. Every year they put their pork-fed legs into Bermuda shorts and take the road to Main Street, U.S.A. Here the children and grandchildren of Klansmen earn their holiday dollars by exercising well-trained mouths and cleaned-up wholesome limbs in a ritual of pious good will which soon, the proprietor intends, shall be exuded by genuine robots. Twice a day, a marching band, in uniforms parodying those of Napoleonic Europe, blue, red, green or yellow, play the good old battle tunes and pink girls, sweating with the effort of their grins, grit teeth of perfect whiteness and fling ornamental staffs into the air, to catch them precisely as they fall, to spin them with terrifying skill, their legs pumping up and down, echoing the Teutonic rhythms and perhaps just a memory of unambiguous lust. They cannot fail. Thus, simplified, they shorten the odds against even the threat of failure. And Mickey Mouse, once the *enfant terrible* with a crooked, almost malevolent grin, now strolls through Fantasy Land in middle-aged slacks, as respectably removed from the sources of his fortune as any other exploiter of desperate slavery. There are signs, now, for Japanese visitors. And guidebooks in Japanese. And Mickey-Tees bearing ideograms in the language of that once forbidden nation. They walk on little loafer soles across the concrete to Main Street's urinals where they piss on the buried ashes of ancestral relatives. In identical grey suits they file back aboard the buses, file from the buses to the planes, from the planes to the buses and finally home to the very latest electronic styles which fill their lives and bring

549

twenty million babbling voices into their hearts. And for that they had a generation die Why should I care? They flood the whole world with their hopeless instruments; they are the source of a sickness more destructive than any other form of fallout. I take the alleyways of this dirty place, this graveyard metropolis, and duck my head, cowed by stereophonic cat-calls, the battle-cries of a consummate horde. *Mist* engulfs me. God save my *mishling* soul. *Moyredik moyz, er* has defeated me! *Vu iz dos Alp-traum? Vi heyst dos ort?* Here is again the nightmare.

In downtown Los Angeles Mexican and Chinese destitutes, having sought the shade of withered trees, lie drunk in sun-soaked parks. The villas of old Spain are shabby. The Dons long since took their swords in the service of Carthage. Now Negroes and defeated immigrants shelter in haciendas, whose brittle lawns glitter with discarded cans and rotting candy wrappers. The palms are dusty and in need of repair. Even in Par-adise the cannon-fodder of Carthage makes camp, awaiting a signal which it might not even recognise. *Ich weiss.* From their hill-top for-tresses gracious Lords and Ladies look carelessly on steeples, cupolas and high adobe, seeing only antique romance through the blue-grey haze of noon. Their vassal city appears to dream in peace. Her boyars cannot guess how fiercely their security is guarded. Her great princes refuse to venture into ghetto slums so never confront the envious, misshapen creatures who plot, however lazily, to steal the treasures of the citadels; to steal the golden dreams. One is not supposed to speak of such things. *Ich glaube es nicht.* One joins the swift galliard and turns one's head against the warning evidence. *Ich will es nicht!* Who that has tasted Hol-lywood's luxurious opiates wishes to contemplate for a moment the threat growing like a virus in the Old Plaza, where Los Angeles began? Where, once more, Mexicans are an occupying force and the nights are horrible with their stamping feet, their wails, their melancholy self-ref-erence, their awful guitars. *Nicht wahr?* Who can blame us?

Our dreams are always real. The test comes when we attempt to turn them into money, seeking power to build still greater dreams. Do not lis-ten to the envious and the insensate. The illusion of Hollywood is thor-oughly tangible. They have never learned, her citizens, that some things are impossible. The rules are formed and broken according to their own experience. Hollywood is a self-possessed city. Her vassals of the valley and the coast will claim she is a dissipation of someone else's smoke; a mirage inhabited by poppy-chewing *luftmaystern* merely the more at-tractive alternative of *muselmanisch*. She has, they say, no special character or moral condition. She is all fantasy. This need not be challenged. The worn-out illusions of Paris and Rome were certainly as glamorous in their day. They reflected the wish-dreams, the *Wünschtraumen*, of their times: an affirmation of the popular mass. I cannot understand them. What are they saying? That Hollywood does not exist? Or should not exist? Was Periclean Athens not real? Or less real than Wren's London and Speer's Berlin? Are these critics of the *Traumhauptstadt* angry because her great palaces grew from wealth earned by answering the public's needs rather than gold squeezed from fearful peasants? Do they think age alone makes the palaces of Europe attractive? What can be more vulgar and banal than Versailles? What cathedral was ever in worse taste than St Peter's? They say Hollywood is a false scent, a gilded corpse, a trap. Did they not once say the same of Florence and Venice, and Rome herself? Hollywood attracts would-be popular actors. Florence attracted would-be popular painters and sculptors. Was she responsible for the disappointment of the ones who failed to find favour? Yet every day the tabloids tell us how some wretched ex-waitress has been 'ruined' by Hollywood. In other words Hollywood somehow conspired in her downfall, first luring her with false promises, then corrupting her and finally 'destroying' her. And what are Hollywood's motives for this senseless behaviour? *Vi heyst dos?* What would the *Sun* or the *Reveille* do with every eighteenth-century doxy who dreamed of becoming a King's courtesan but actually wound up as a serving-wench in some provincial tavern? *Was heisst das?*

Hollywood is the first true city of the twentieth century. Like Rome or Byzantium she thinks herself inviolable. I have seen it all on the television. Of course there are changes, but the core is preserved. *Was muss ich zehlen?* A city founded on abstracts (and in this she is by no means the first) she next sought to make those abstracts reality. This is a common process. *Wie lange muss ich werten?*

Hollywood, though constantly threatened by her neighbours, is the strongest fortress of the modern world. She must not grow lazy. Hollywood purged herself once. It was painful, but she was successful. She purged herself as John Wayne might purify his blood after a rattlesnake bite; by drawing out the poison with his mouth, then, with a white-hot Bowie knife, cauterising the wound. Hollywood spat the poison into the sea, sending it East where it had come from. She banished writers, a few producers, some directors, a tiny percentage of her actors, and let them try to swim in the unfriendly ocean of reality. They drowned, most of them. A few eventually reclaimed themselves from Carthage. It is time for her to draw the poison from her arteries again.

Halfcaste youths in studded leather ride their motorcycles amongst her fallen monuments. Mongrel dogs defecate upon slabs engraved with the names of honourable Lords and Ladies on that crumbling Avenue of the Stars. Gangs of gaudy vandals run unchecked over the broken walls of once unassailable castles. They loot the rotting costumes, the faded scenery. It is all that is left now of Republic and RKO, of Fox and Lasky. Hollywood offered her prophecies in so many films. She warned the world of the dangers of interbreeding and loose moral standards. Griffith drummed this message home, even in *Broken Blossoms*, the most unsound of his films (though Lillian Gish was exceptional). He died in poverty, that great man. From me he got only 'trousers.' Everything he predicted came true. Pray, all of you, for the great Tsar City, the New Byzantium, the citadel of our Faith. *Vergenen Sie nicht. Die Kapelle spielt zu schnell.* Rock-and-roll magnates, champions of all that is barbaric, are the inheritors of our sunlit, melancholy ruins. Who could know *The Jazz Singer* would lead to this? Yet God is with his Emperor *Stadt*, even now. Not the yammering, drooling old God, but the new one, the Greek. The white palaces still stand guard above the valley, only apparently sleeping. Who better to accuse her than I? But I shall not. Six thousand miles from me and careless of my name, she yet retains my loyalty. Byzantium, you *blaybn lebn*. Hollywood was ever a Christian city, though many of her princes began as Jews. *Wer Jude ist, bestimme Ich.* Why not? *Auf gut Deutsch.* The Venice of the near past is still in a perpetual celebration, a carnival. Her pier swarms with happy souls. The sea is calm today. The ferris wheel turns slowly, like a useless mill. I walk beneath rococo arcades, her wooden fretwork, her brick that imitates stone. I admire the huge gondola on the Grand Canal which, itself, is smaller than the original. The gondolier sings some mock-operatic snatch as he poles his passengers towards the watery cul-de-sac's terminal. The little railways flash and rattle. The yellow trolleys roll by. And girls in pretty beads and skimpy frocks, in cloche and aigrette, skip upon the arms of blazered Midwest dandies who walk awkwardly, trying to keep their boaters from falling off their bullet heads. I shall be leaving Venice soon, to move my few goods up the boulevard to the Hollywood Hills. A small grey and white palace of my own, for Esmé's sake. I know what she prefers. At the pier I turn, still shaded by this idea of some Doge's cloister, and here stands my bulky partner, my nervous benefactor. 'Mr Hever!' I surprise myself with my exclamation. There is a pause. The day is momentarily still. *'Sara sheyn veter!'*

'Ven kumt on der shiff?'

'You'll recall I leave by plane tomorrow.'

'Of course. I was looking for you, old man.' A wave of embarrassment rocked his untidy frame. 'I didn't find you home, so . . .'

'I thought I had put all the PXI jobs in hand with Willy.'

'Of course. That's dandy. I'm very happy. I felt like a little gabfest, that's all. Do you mind?'

I proposed we walk along the seafront in the general direction of Long Beach. The promenade stretched for miles, apparently meeting beach and ocean somewhere near Catalina Island. We walked. He said nothing for a long time. Then he suggested lunch at a nearby lobster place. Again I complied. I had time to kill. I was content. The food was excellent and became the topic intermittently for an hour or so. We finished our lobsters, our custards and our coffee and set off again. Still, save for remarks about the beachfronts, the weather, the Curtiss seaplane beginning its approach to Long Beach harbour, he was substantially mute. At last he asked if I would mind taking a Red Car and continue 'our real talk' by the workshop. I cheerfully agreed and we crossed the street to wait for the massive trolley of the inter-urban line. It was a hot, easy day. Children ran in and out of the water, chased by dogs and parents. Young people grew brown on the sands. Every town along the coast had its pleasure arcades, its little fairgrounds, its share of fun. I was amiable, thinking how much Esmé would be thrilled. I intended to bring her back by train from New York, so we could travel via the Broadway Limited and then take a Pullman all the way from Chicago. I guessed she had become unused to any luxury and what I proposed must surely pleasantly overwhelm her.

In the twilight palms, tall outlines now against the deepening blue of the sky and the rich wash of the sunset, he began to speak rapidly of his motion picture ambitions. He intended to be sole financer of a movie drama to star Mrs Cornelius. 'She's agreed to change her name to Dorothy Kord. Names are supposed to be important and easy to remember and all that rot. Mrs Cornelius wasn't too happy about doing it. Well, to keep it short, what I'd like from you is the story – that's *White Knight and Red Queen* – for which of course you'll get a generous fee. Why don't you try fleshing it out to full-length. About an hour.' He made a shy smile. 'I'm no Griffith.'

'When would you need the script?'

'About a month for the first draft.'

From his manner I knew he had not yet come to his chief subject. I said lamely, 'It would be interesting to work on such a big movie.'

He offered me a large cigar. Against my normal custom, I accepted. We stood on the edge of the quay under the trees, smoking and looking into the rather dirty water.

'Good,' he said at length. Then, as usual, out came the real topic in a confused babble of which the salient concluding phrases were: 'Pallenberg, I want her to marry me. I intend to ask her tomorrow, while you're in New York. Do you think I have any kind of a chance?' His huge eyes looked pleadingly down; he had the face of a lonely cow. I took some time before replying.

'She's very independent. She evidently cares for you a great deal more than anyone I've ever seen her with.' Of course there was no point in mentioning Mrs Cornelius's affairs with half the Bolshevik hierarchy. He would have fainted at the very notion. 'She shouldn't be rushed. Maybe you can wait until I get back from New York? I'll have a female second opinion, then.'

Though seriously disappointed, he bowed to my judgment. 'Okey-dokey. I guess I also wanted to ask if maybe you could, as an old friend, get her general feelings on the matter. What do you say?' Without giving me time to reply he continued gravely: 'See, I know she's got It – whatever it takes to be a great actress. I don't want her going through any more screen-test hoops. I'm going to cut across all that. She'll get her movie career, no matter what.' He looked out to where a tethered seaplane, some Schneider contender, bumped against the wooden cladding of her moorings. 'See,' he murmured, 'it's incidental I happen to think she's the most adorable little honey who ever lived and breathed.'

'I'll do what I can, old man.'

He was grateful. He frowned, trying to pull himself together. 'How do you think we should handle publicity for the car? Should we let the papers know we've made a successful first run? The press already has rumours. A couple of journalists were in my office today. From the L.A. Times, I think. One of them knew you. What was he called? Irish name?'

'Callahan?'

'That sounds right.'

'The other wasn't Brodmann, by any chance?'

'I guess I don't remember. I thought he was Irish, too.'

I turned away from him. I was becoming over-suspicious. I was also obscurely depressed. I took control of myself. 'Well, I'll leave all that with your publicity department. They're the experts. I can brief them further when I get back.'

He shook my hand, then lumbered inland to find a taxi. I took the trolley back to Venice.

Hever was a pleasant, kind-hearted soul. He would do Mrs Cornelius no harm. Yet I had been upset when he declared his intentions. I was disgusted with myself for my obvious jealousy. Perhaps I feared she would be separated from me for good. I determined to put a decent face on it, give them both my honest help and (assuming Mrs Cornelius accepted him) my blessing. Moreover when I saw her tomorrow morning I would do exactly what Hever had asked. She was coming with me to the airfield, to drive my car back to my new home on Cahuenga Boulevard. I tried to recover what had been a perfect mood, anticipating the flight itself, then my reunion with Esmé. I could not deny that part of me still lusted for Mrs Cornelius. Perhaps I hoped she would one day fulfil my dream. These were not sensible thoughts. Returning to my little San Juan house I telephoned the detective agency I had commissioned to investigate suspected enemies. The woman who answered said I should call back in the morning. I had been a fool to leave it so late. There would be no time tomorrow. I consoled myself. There were a great many Irishmen called Callahan in the world, after all, and I had given innumerable interviews.

Next morning, throwing my little suitcase in the back seat, I drove through empty sloping streets where telephone poles and cable lines were black and sharp against the pallor of the warm Los Angeles dawn, through suburban ease. I climbed up Santa Monica, between massive earthworks already grass-grown, to the Beverly Hills Hotel. There I would collect Mrs Cornelius and continue on to the Burbank *Flitplats*. She emerged from a main door as I drew up. More glamorous than ever before in a pink silk twin-set trimmed with bands of red, two long strands of pink pearls, a powder-blue cloche and shoes to match, she was washed, perfumed and bright-eyed. She now had credit with every fashionable store. I said she was putting the accounts to good effect. She giggled with relish and pecked my cheek. 'They bloody love me rahnd 'ere, Ivan! Lady Muck, eh?' She shrieked. 'Lady Mucker, anyway. Wot a turn up. I never fort I'd be carriage trade. Not like this. 'Igh-times and an 'arf, an' no mistake!'

As she climbed in she was bursting with good cheer. Smiling, she nudged me in the ribs. 'I done yer a favour. Left me bleedin' brekker on me fuckin' plate this time! Ow's that fer sacrifice?'

'You must never feel —'

'Stuff that, Ive.' She was serious. Her chin came up. She looked straight ahead, as she often did when she controlled strong emotion. 'My silly fault, that kipper. Besides, yer gotta look arter yer own. You an' me, eh? Birds of a bleedin' fevver.' At this she softened and chuckled. Quite uncharacteristically, she reached into my lap and gave me a quick, friendly squeeze to my privates. 'Don't let yer littel yid friend git yer inter trouble.' She was aware of my dismay, my misleading circumcision, and it was a joke she had made before. I was moved almost to tears by her consideration. I promised I would do my best.

We drove through peaceful canyons on the other side of the hills. Steep cliffs rose on either side. Precariously balanced along their rims the new houses of a minor nobility could be glimpsed through fresh-planted bushes and saplings. They had followed the stars. Now some of the great princes were moving on. There was a fashion for beach houses at Santa Monica and Pacific Palisades. The roads were improving steadily, thanks to all the immigrants from other States who flooded daily in hundreds to Los Angeles. There was work for these Iowa hopefuls, but I think they were drawn chiefly by the prospect of living in the same city as Fairbanks, Chaplin and Swanson.

Descending rapidly into the Valley we entered what had lately become an unreal half-world. Replacing farms and orchards acres of land were now marked for lots and streets not yet built. The realtors awaited their customers. (The autumn herds were coming West. If you put your ear to the ground you could hear the distant rumble of their hooves.) The sleepy fruit-growing plantations of San Fernando Valley were vanishing. Identical clapboard would rise in the shadow of the snow-topped Sierras. The old names were Spanish. The new ones here were English, echoing a dream of Anglo-Saxon villages, thatched security. All over America they were at last calling a halt to their foreign romances.

Eventually we saw the rough grass of the airfield ahead. There was one hangar covered in old barnstormer posters; one unenthusiastic windsock, one fence, one gate with a large red sign reading *DO NOT ENTER UNLESS YOU ARE FLYING*. There was one DH4 biplane with a tall, skinny pilot standing leaning against its fuselage, smoking a cigarette and polishing his goggles on his moleskin riding breeches. Roy Belgrade was a veteran of the Flying Corps who seemed too young, even now, to be an airman. He yawned as he saw me, and flicked a salute, taking great interest in Mrs Cornelius as he started forward to open the gate. He had been recommended as the best by almost everyone I had spoken to in Hollywood. It was still considered daring to risk a day's flying rather than spend three days on the train. I would have to land in a field in New Jersey and hope to get a bus or cab to the city.

Roy Belgrade glanced down at the clipboard he dug from the back seat of the plane. 'Colonel Pallenberg's you, sir? Welcome to Coast-to-Coast Airservices. That's me.' He grinned. We shook hands. He bowed as he was introduced to Mrs Cornelius. At closer inspection, he looked his age. I moved past the big, heavy wings of the DH-4 to peer into the glass-covered interior of the forward passenger cabin. Some attempt had been made to give it a comfortable appearance. There was a rack with a thermos bottle, a little hamper of food, some magazines. It was almost touching, as if a child had arranged it. The seat was padded, with arm-rests and leather upholstery. 'Everything but ma's cookin',' said Roy sardonically. 'You've flown before haven't you, sir?'

I nodded. Mrs Cornelius came to embrace me. She was nervous of planes. She had been up once, she said, but it had made her sick. 'I do 'ope ya know wot yer doin', Ive.'

This made me smile. 'My dear friend, the PXI passed its tests with flying colours. I have a splendid house in Hollywood. My reputation's completely restored, my name vindicated. In two days' time my fiancée comes ashore off the *Icosium*. Meanwhile, I should tell you, Mr Hever wants to propose to you!'

She was unsurprised. 'Wot's yore foughts on that?'

'He's kind and rich.' I could not resist a wink. 'And virtually blind.'

She began to cackle. She pushed me back. 'I'll probably do it, jes' ter spite yer by bein' faithful! You wicked littel *Shnorrer*! Yore worse than I am. You be careful nar, Ivan.' She inspected me as a mother might send her boy to school for the first time. 'An' don't let anyone pull ther wool over yer eyes, eh?'

557

'My instincts rarely betray me, Mrs Cornelius. Please put your mind at rest. My future is assured. As is yours. Soon you'll be as famous as Lillian Gish.'

She was further amused by this. 'Yeah,' she said, 'in Whitechapel. Okey-dokey, Ivan. Bon bloody voyage, pal.'

I climbed into the front cockpit of the DH-4. Roy Belgrade whistled through his fingers and a lad in knickerbockers came running from behind the hangar. He was chubby and black. For one dreadful moment I thought he was accompanying us. But he merely stowed my bag between me and the pilot. I drew the safety straps across my body, settling into the soft seat with some pleasure. To one side of my legs was a locker stencilled PARACHUTE. EMERGENCY ONLY. Curiosity made me try to open it. It seemed stuck. When I did manage to pull the door back I saw that the whole compartment was crammed with Mexican liquor. As well as the mail, Roy was taking a little private cargo to New York. I was not bothered by this. The DH-4 could only be shot down, it was virtually impossible to crash. *Der shvartseh vos kumen* spins the propeller, his sleeves falling back from muscled arms, his skin alive with dancing sweat. Mrs Cornelius waves vigorously, her left hand moving from hat to skirt and back again as she attempts to hold her clothes in place. For the engine has caught. The blade ahead of me cackles and snores, whirling faster and faster until all is wailing, frustrated energy. The black boy suddenly appears on the other side of my cockpit canopy. He's laughing. *Ikh hob nisht moyre! Vemen set er? Ver is doz? Ikh vash zikh. Di kinder vos farkoyft shkheynim in Berlin . . .* He has gone. Does he still cling, like a mocking demon, somewhere upon the fuselage? The night creatures are in the pay of Carthage. Mrs Cornelius has disappeared. But I see Brodmann briefly. Does he step from the hangar and approach my car? Or is it the *shvartseh* I see? Do they all conspire? Have I never known free will? What forces took me to Byzantium and Rome? Did I make my own decision to sail for New York? The plane's note changes and we are released from the Earth. This is the great Escape of Flying. We circle the diminishing field. A pink scarf waves from my little green Peugeot. I will be back with Esmé within the week. My blood is singing. I adjust the buckles of my helmet and goggles, drawing on my gauntlets. *Wir empfangen es schlecht. Er ist zu viel Störung.* I crane my head backwards. *Der Flugzeugführer sitz im Führersitz . . .* He nods his reassuring helm then pulls his stick to send us upwards, banking towards jagged rock and distant snow, the High Sierras. Brodmann, if he was ever down there, can no longer be seen. The little black creature continues to cling to the fuselage for all I know, threatening to drag us down. Carthage will not let the individual fly.

I shall come back to the City of the Golden Dream. I can still smell California with her ocean, her gorgeous crops, her precious metals and floral boulevards. I can smell the promise of Utopia, almost realised. Esmé will think she is dreaming. *Wo sind wir jetzt? Es tut mir heir Weh. Ich weiss nicht was los ist. Es tut sehr Weh! Wir haben drei Jahre gewartet.* We shall return to the citadel. Its substance changes so frequently it can neither be attacked nor destroyed. Barbarians believe they have conquered it but it is they who dwell in illusion. *Der flitshtot vet kumen.* Even if I am in mortal danger, the city will find a means of saving me. I never became a *Mussulman.* My mother was swallowed by their red lava. How can I trust Brodmann? He has followed me too long. No one has the right to steal my future! The little black body loses its grip and is flung away, tumbling towards the foothills which now rise from the plain. *Nit shuld! Nit shuld!* They always claim that everyone shares guilt for those great crimes. But I say: We are all innocent! If one is true, then so is the other. *Ikh blaybn lebn . . .* I shall survive. Carthage shall no longer threaten me with her whips nor shall she push my face into her mud. I am too old and proud to let her grin and point and mock unchallenged.

Outside the night street is deserted; the black rain shines and hisses, mingling with grease from a dozen cheap cafés, with everything a dog or a man can pour from bowels or stomach; and the upstairs lights go off suddenly above the pub. There are sirens, of course, and distant war-cries; the occasional rising note of a curse, a condemnation, a self-advertisement. I think there is something wrong with me. I have eaten nothing, yet the pain starts in my stomach. I turn down my oil lamp (power strikes grow so frequent) and look through the curtain again. Head down, arms limp, shoulders slumped, some happy drunkard tries to piss into the doorway of the Greek take-out. He seems almost as old as me. He wears a stained tweed jacket, grubby grey flannels, a shirt without a collar. He is addressing himself in a furious undertone, accusing himself of some *fartsaytik* crime. How can I condemn any of these? At least I know the enemy and understand what is destroying me. They could not keep me for long. I was always too slippery for them. Tomorrow is early closing. I shall put this *gelekhter* and this *glitshik fantazye* behind me and go south instead of north, into the salubrious parks of their other Kensington. I was truly a *luftmayster,* a lord of the air, long ago when it was heroic. All they want now is long hair and guitars. Well, I disdain their zoot-suits. And I am the one who has to close my window against the stink of their vomit when they have all gone home. *Ikh bin a Luftmayster, N'div auf der Flitstat. Firt mikh tsu ahin, ikh bet aykh. Firt mikh tsu ahin . . .*

The DH4 gains height to fly through the wide spaces between the taller peaks. I can see the snow blowing like an eternal tide across their flanks. I am fleeing out of paradise; but it is not true you can never return. We shall cross the plains and the Rockies, Esmé and I; the deserts and the Sierras; and come into our valley again. Here they have no *Schutzhaft, ni Buchenwald,* no Gulag for me, only for the Japanese. The future can be created swiftly here; there are people who devote themselves entirely to engineering problems involved in realising vast dreams. My cities shall begin here. Hollywood shall be my flagship. The old cities of Europe and America are noble and must be honoured, perhaps preserved. The cities of Asia Minor, Africa and the Far East: these, too, have some interest. But if Constantinople cannot rule as Emperor City, then a New Byzantium must be built to resist Carthage. I can make this a fact and do not seek even to be *balebos. Eybik eyberhar? Vos is dos?*

They are monumental, these ships. Cities self-sufficient in every respect. They move with tranquil dignity through the upper air. How easily they resist the deceptive gravity of Carthage! Here are the far-flying colossal children of *Mauretania;* the logical resolution of our Western history. They are pure and they blaze like silver in the sun. They are seen in the horizon's haze, flickering, suddenly golden, then their massive engines thrust forward, upward, and they are gone.

Wailing their earthbound despair, the conquered and the conquering, victims both, look up for an instant. If it were permitted them to think at all, they would think they had glimpsed heaven. *Es war nicht meine Schuld.* They move sluggishly, like chilled reptiles, desperate for the sun. Their wasted limbs are ensnared in filthy wreckage. They are *opfal,* say the Lords of Carthage. They gave their loyalty to the past, so they must die. *Wie viele? Ich klayb pakistanish shmate. Ikh veys nit.* They turn back to their sluggish battles, these slaves of the Sultan, these *musselmanisch,* these *lagerflugen. Ikh varshtey nit.*

In the clear upper air, a mile above, the world's great nations sail. They are invisible, optimistic and vital. These cities are the ultimate expression of human imagination. If they are attacked they could launch from their towers a million silver knights, like militant angels. Let Carthage do what she wishes with her muddy conquests. We are free.

I shall dismiss the past. It is no longer of use. Its hands snare my rigging. I go now to live in the future with my destined bride, my Esmé, my sister and my rose. I shall bear her back from the East to the ultimate city of the West, to dwell in eternal harmony with our peers, within that noblest of all dreams: *der Heim*. A golden city of hope, purified and restored: my own inviolable Hollywood.

Ven vet men umkern mayn kindhayt?
Wie lange wir es dauern?

Born in Surrey, England in 1939, MICHAEL MOORCOCK has been writing and publishing since the age of eleven, when he began contributing stories to a popular boys' magazine, *Tarzan's Adventures*. In the sixties he became editor of the influential science fiction magazine *New Worlds*, and in 1967 won the Science Fiction Writers of America "Nebula Award" for his novel *Behold the Man*. Michael Moorcock has published dozens of novels and stories; written screenplays, produced films and record albums and composed for rock stars. His most recent novel, *Byzantium Endures*, was published by Random House in 1982.